SUN & MOON ACADEMY
BOOK ONE: FALL SEMESTER

KRISTIE COOK   TISH THAWER   ROSE GARCIA

BELINDA BORING   VICTORIA FLYNN   E.J. FECHENDA

AMY RICHIE   JUSTINE WINTER   VICTORIA ESCOBAR

HAVENWOOD FALLS COLLECTIVE

To You, the Reader —
Because you're the kickass heroine of your own story

and…

To our Havenwood Falls Family —
Because reality is overrated

oh, and…

To the TV producer looking for something new
*(*cough* Eric Kripke *cough*) —*
Because you are awesome and smart and such a visionary, and oh, hey,
look what we have here…

The wooden box sat innocuously on the bed. It hadn't been there moments before, but nobody had delivered it either. It just simply appeared out of thin air. No bigger than a small jewelry box, it was made of plain, dark wood with no obvious openings. Only a wooden disk adorned the top of it, in the shape of a sun and a moon.

With a twist of the disk, the seemingly solid wood began to shift and move into pieces. A puzzle box! It was an old-fashioned puzzle box. The pieces slid apart and to the side, rotating and shifting until there was an opening.

Inside lay a black crystal, shimmering and sparkling with aether—a special kind of magical energy. A substance known by some to be in the waters of the great Havenwood Falls and had, at least at one time, been within Mount Alexa.

A simple touch to the crystal—but only by the intended person—resulted in a shower of purple sparks followed by the magical, holographic-like image of a miniature Valkyrie rising into the air. With her sword in hand and her wings spread out behind her, she danced and twirled, swinging and swishing her blade, carving purple fire into the air. After a moment, the purple fire formed words that floated upward, one line at a time:

*Congratulations! You've been selected for admission to the Sun &
Moon Academy College of Supernatural Guardians, where you will be
trained to become a future protector and warrior for the supernatural
community around the globe. Do you choose to accept?*

TIMELESS PART I

HAVENWOOD FALLS COLLECTIVE

Standing at the corner of First Street and Blackstone Road in Havenwood Falls, Colorado, I looked down at my hands cradling the wooden puzzle box. The small keepsake appeared harmless enough, but had the power to change lives.

Like mine.

And two hundred other supernaturals about my age.

Well, at least, the age I appeared to be. Or they appeared to be. Whatever. Supes were weird and sometimes hard to explain.

Tucking the box into my backpack and hitching the strap over my shoulder, I crossed the street and traveled down a nearly hidden driveway. Just a little ways in were stone and metal gates, manned by guards, although the gates were currently open. Too many cars and people flowed through right now.

The full moon spilled its light over the stone driveway that climbed upward to the Sun and Moon Academy at the edge of town, near the great falls. The school had been here for over a hundred years, educating some of the local supernaturals from childhood through high school. I'd been in Havenwood Falls when it first opened, but hadn't been back much since then.

The students entering through the archway and into the courtyard beyond, however, weren't here to attend the historical K-

12 private school. *We* weren't, I mean. Not at 11:30 on a Friday night. We were here for the new college. According to my acceptance message, this was not our campus.

Our campus was in a mountain. Go figure.

I followed a stream of students through an archway that led into a courtyard, which was quickly filling up. More than half the students waiting to enter the school wore pajamas or some kind of sleepwear. Several outfits were questionably decent. I myself tended to choose comfort and function over style, currently clad in sage cargo pants, a gold tunic, and my favorite Doc Martens, because my All-Stars were easier to carry in my backpack. My blond dreads and braids were pulled up into a massive ponytail, out of my face.

Everyone here had presumably received a wooden puzzle box like mine, announcing our admission to the brand new College of Supernatural Guardians. Once we accepted, a second compartment had opened up, revealing a tightly rolled scroll with instructions and a supply list. We'd been given barely more than forty-eight hours to get our shit together and show up.

While I only had my backpack, many students carried, pushed, and pulled suitcases, carts, and wagons full of stuff. Didn't they see the note on the scroll about the wooden box being a portal for belongings? I mean, how could they miss it when the box itself grew to the size of a large trunk? I didn't have any belongings beyond what fit in my backpack, so I hadn't tried it. Apparently, neither had many of the other students. Or perhaps they ran out of time. When I woke up this morning, the box had shrunk back to its normal size, the portal closed.

I didn't know anyone here, like some of the students did, those who had grown up in Havenwood Falls or were lucky enough to come with a best friend or sibling. I knew *about* nearly all of them, though. A special gift of mine—knowing. A gift of many deities, such as myself. Not that I was omniscient. Gads, no. I didn't want to know *everything*. But when you lived as long and as many life renditions as I had, you learned to read people.

Of course, I'd also been briefed about many of the students by my recruiter, who'd invited me here on a special mission. One nobody could ever know about. One I wasn't sure I even wanted to be a part of yet, but I was so intrigued by the idea of the school, I agreed as long as I could come as a student, an experience I'd yet to have in this rendition of myself.

So yeah, I knew things.

Like about the twins, Brielle and Elliana Knight, and Charleigh Wotsit, their cousin and BFF, but also their protector. They weren't from this world, having crossed dimensions and been given special permission to attend by the Court of the Sun and the Moon, the true leaders of Havenwood Falls and founders of the college. The dark haired twins—angel hybrids—and their witch friend, with her bright orange hair sparking in the moonlight, stood off to the side. They didn't know anybody else, either, but at least they had each other.

Loud laughter rang from the far side of the fountain, where Joe Greg, a Havenwood Falls High graduate and wolf shifter, stood with his girlfriend, Infiniti Clausman, newly designated transhuman, and other members of the Kasun pack. Chatter came from a few feet farther over, where more HFH graduates gathered, but to the side stood Roxy McCabe with a crapload of stuff piled into a collapsible wagon.

Not even eighteen yet, Roxy had already had a hard life, and it was a surprise the cougar shifter made it here at all, considering her past. Between abuse by her own family, a coup that killed most of her pride, and a cross-country escape, the cougar was damn lucky to be alive. Whether she made it through college or not only time would tell.

Speaking of . . .

I pulled my phone out and glanced at the time: 11:48 p.m. The scroll had directed:

Present yourself at the Sun and Moon Academy Falls Campus courtyard fountain at precisely 11:49 p.m. on the 16th day of August or your opportunity will be forever lost.

And exactly one minute later, everything started happening.

The gathered crowd began moving toward the side of the large, gothic building ahead, so I fell into place and went with the stream. We entered a room about the size of a standard classroom, where Addie Beaumont, a powerful witch, and others were checking people's wrists, apparently for the tattoos that had appeared upon acceptance of the admissions offer. Beyond them were three arched frames that looked like mirrors, but precisely at 11:59 p.m., magic began spinning in colorful streaks within the frames, creating portals.

Excitement buzzed through the air as students started filtering through.

When I realized I was in Addie's line, I looked about, trying to see if I had a better option. *Shit.* Everyone checking the tattoos were members of the Luna Coven. They would all be a risk, but none as much as Addie. The lines moved too quickly, though, and if I tried to change now and disrupt the flow, I'd only stand out more.

When I stopped at Addie, she peered at me over her black-framed glasses with a frown and tilted her head, her sandy brown hair spilling over her shoulder and the light catching on the diamond in her nose. "I'm sorry. I, uh, I've forgotten your name."

I offered her a smile, trying to warm her up. This wasn't normal for her. As the person who registered all supes who came to Havenwood Falls, she knew everyone.

"No worries. You've registered a lot of new people in recent weeks," I said. "I'm Rhian Delaney."

I held my wrist out to her, the tattoo of the school's crest face up.

"Oh, well, I guess you're meant to be here if you have that," Addie said, and she placed her fingers on it, her brows still pinched. I knew the moment she realized the truth, her magic zinging through me. "Oh, my Goddess!" she gasped, bowing her head but looking up at me through her lashes. "Is it really you, Rhiannon?"

I held a finger to my lips.

"Please keep my secret?" I whispered conspiratorially. Witches were often drawn to me, being a goddess of the moon and all, but I didn't want to be treated differently because of it. Especially not here. I wanted an authentic experience like the rest of the students.

Looking around to see if anyone had noticed, Addie nodded. But as her fingers remained pressed against my skin, she frowned again. No doubt the hellhound within her—the part that protected the dead—sensed something it didn't like. When she looked at me now, a steely hardness had replaced the worship that had been in her eyes only moments ago. I sighed. I didn't want that experience, either.

"Your darker side—you can*not* use it here," she warned.

"I'm well aware. It's not exactly my favorite part of myself."

Her eyes narrowed. "I'll be watching you."

"As I'd expect." I gave her another smile, as sweet as I possibly could and just as genuine. I wanted nothing more than to convince her that I would not be a problem, and my wispy stature, fae-like facial features, and large blue eyes helped to convey my message.

She finally nodded and infused more magic into my tattoo.

"That little boost should help you keep your secret. You're good to go, Rhian." She said my name *Ryan*, as most Americans did, unable to exactly replicate my pronunciation. "By the way, I love your accent. Irish?"

"Aye," I replied.

"Well, welcome to Halvard. I'll see you on campus." She sounded friendly again, but I heard the slightest edge in her voice —another warning, in case I missed the first.

"I look forward to it."

And the next thing I knew, I was passing through the portal that rippled like a pond after a stone was thrown. Magical energy rushed around me, tickling over my skin, and a moment later, I stepped into a round vestibule, a twelve-foot tall Valkyrie statue in its center. She stood proudly grasping her sword's hilt in one fist, its blade pointed downward, the tip not quite touching the base of the statue. Her other hand was held out, palm up, a purple flame blazing in it, the main source of light in the dark space. There was just enough to illuminate the domed ceiling of the vestibule and the columns and archways on the far side of the statue, but not enough to see beyond. Above three of these archways was engraved the word *HALVARD*.

I smiled to myself. Halvard was a Norse name meaning rock guardian. Knowing what I did, I wasn't too surprised to see it, nor the Valkyrie statue. It did all tickle a suspicion, though, that I kept at the back of my mind.

"Hey, Vid, she looks like your mom." The comment drew my attention to the two men standing on the other side of the statue.

Tyr Skollson looked like the demigod he was, even in sweatpants and a band T-shirt stretching over his taut muscles. He played with the piercing under his lower lip as he eyed his dark-skinned friend.

Vidar Sveen studied the statue with a thin line forming between his black brows. He ran a hand through his tiny dreadlocks, shaking them out as he did so. "Actually I'm pretty sure that's Aunt Hrist."

Tyr rocked back on his heels, tossing a long, dark braid over a shoulder. "Do you think she's here?"

"Gods, I hope not." The other guy's entire body shuddered. "She's still disappointed I didn't die at Midsummer."

With students pouring out of the portals, we couldn't stop to gawk for long, so again, I followed the crowd. We exited the vestibule through archways on the far side, and everyone paused again, breaths audibly catching at the sight. The crowd had to keep moving, though, so we took it all in as we shuffled forward, some with mouths gaping at the sight and others whispering with their friends. And more than one loud "Holy shit!" that made others snicker.

The school looked like something out of a fantasy movie. We'd entered an enormous cavern—at least thirty or forty stories tall, and I had no idea how deep, but large enough to fit a small college campus, apparently. The path we followed led to a bridge that crossed a chasm, and at the other end was an archway that opened up to what appeared to be the main part of campus.

Huge stalagmites rose many stories into the air, and some had met stalactites from above, creating columns as big as city office buildings. Tall, arched windows and doorways had been beautifully carved into the structures, yellow light spilling out of them. It looked like a palace that could have belonged in Faerie, or perhaps in a kingdom of another world.

With the architecture's style combined with all the Norse references, I had a feeling I knew exactly which world—that of my recruiter. She was an old friend, really. *Extremely* old. We'd known each other for eons, over many renditions of ourselves. She'd sent me a message about the college, giving me the mission I wasn't sure I wanted, yet here I was. My suspicions about her involvement with the school were becoming more grounded, and I'd only been here five minutes.

As we crossed the bridge—its near side flanked by two more Valkyrie statues—I glanced over the short stone wall along its edge, finding a river about thirty feet below us. It was too dark to see where the river led. At the far end of the bridge, we passed through the archway and came into a wide courtyard. The largest structure loomed straight across from us, at least a hundred yards broad and rising about thirty or so feet high before the stalagmite split into three branches that stretched hundreds of feet upward. Other buildings, for lack of a better word, appeared almost attached to the main one, they were so close together. As we approached, I realized only one was actually connected, though, the one to the left. Chasms separated the others. They connected to the courtyard and to each other by bridges, some dozens, even hundreds, of feet from the ground.

Tables filled the center of the courtyard, each one with letters magically hanging over them.

"Last name, you think?" Roxy's voice carried from where she stood, studying the cavern.

The wild haired female standing next to her, Bryony Fenn, nodded. "You're probably right. Looks like we'll have to split up."

A druid of the old ways was a rare sight. She was either taught by one of the gods at one point in her life or born of them. I wondered if I knew her mentor.

"If we're not in the same dorm, I'll find you after." Roxy moved toward the table with the floating L-M.

"Not if I find you first," Bryony called with laughter in her voice.

I scanned the crowd around me. So many people and their powers all gathered in one place! The ground practically hummed with magic.

"Can I help you?" a deep male voice boomed. A man wearing a shirt that said *SECURITY*, although he looked young enough to be a student, waved invitingly to a girl with bright red hair that hung to her shoulders. Something passed between the two, something that called to me. Frowning slightly, I turned to watch the duo.

"I'm . . . uh . . . Linnie Andrews," the young vampire stammered, holding out her scroll with trembling fingers.

"Cody Stevenson," the man introduced himself. "You go right over there." He pointed behind us, at the A-B table. "They'll give you a packet with everything you need to know."

"Thanks." She smiled up at him, her eyes glowing happily. His eyes narrowed as he watched her walk away, his interest apparent. Just what kind of interest, I wasn't sure.

As I looked for the D table, my gaze landed on another couple —Joe and Infiniti again.

"You'll be great," I heard Joe murmur to Infiniti. "Everyone is new here, not just you."

The wolf shifter pecked her on the forehead before heading to his table marked with E-G, and the transhuman went to hers marked as C-D. Her awestruck expression screamed noob. Her powers were new, and in fact, she'd only recently learned of the supernatural world. I wondered how long she'd last at Halvard. According to my recruiter, this school was not for the meek.

As soon as the pair split up, a tall, long-legged Latina dressed in tight black leather pants and a low cut white top practically pounced on Joe.

"Hi, Joe. I'm Cat, Cat Vega. We met at Burger Bar a few days ago." Her Spanish accent was thick. I silently snickered. Although another transhuman, she definitely came across like a cat, practically rubbing herself up on Joe.

"Oh, yeah," Joe mumbled, barely glancing at her. "Hi."

Cat was really working it. Standing close, moving her hips, playing with her long dark hair. Joe remained oblivious, though. His gaze kept moving from the papers in his hands to Infiniti at her sign-in table.

I followed Infiniti to the C-D table, but she left before I reached it. The witch standing behind the table barely glanced at me while asking my name.

"Rhian Delaney."

Her brow puckered as she looked over her list. "I don't see you on here, Rhian. Can you spell it for me?"

I pointed at her parchment. "It's right there."

She gave me a weird look before glancing at the paper again.

"Oh, yes." She bopped the heel of her hand against her blond head. "Wow. I think I need my eyes checked."

She turned around and fumbled about in some wooden boxes stuffed full of envelopes. While magic permeated the air under the mountain—the whole campus had obviously been created by some really powerful, ancient force, likely that of a fellow deity, only confirming my suspicions of my old friend—I could smell the tinge of a fresh spell from the woman in front of me. She finally turned, holding out an envelope to me. My name was written on its front, but I had a feeling it had been blank a moment ago.

"Sorry about that. I had trouble finding yours, but here you go. Everything you need to know is in there. Well, at least, everything for now. There's a map, your tower assignment, which is your dorm, and a schedule for the rest of the week before classes start next Monday. There's a lot to do, so be sure to go over this."

Nodding, I took the envelope from her and turned away as I pulled the packet out. On top was a map, then a page with my name, the word *Tower* and the word *Room*, both followed by blank lines. I turned back to the woman.

"I'm sorry, but there's no room assignment on here."

She looked at the page and frowned. Having no idea what to do, she called over another worker.

It took five people and a lot of discussion before the first woman turned back to me.

"Well, Rhian, it looks like there was an oversight and your room wasn't assigned. The good news is that our campus can accommodate up to four hundred students, but for this first year, we've kept it to half that. So there are plenty of rooms for you to choose from. There are five towers, and the school crest on your wrist will let you into any of them. I'm sure you'll know when you've found the right one for you. Check them all out and have your pick!"

And with that, she moved her attention to the next student in line.

I wasn't surprised by this turn of events. Things like this happened to me all the time, but that's okay. It made life exciting and adventurous.

I looked out at the courtyard and all of the students milling about, studying their maps and glancing around or talking with others as they tried to figure out where to go. I eyed Infiniti and another girl who seemed to know where they were going and followed them toward the left of the main structure, which my map called Halstein Hall.

It appeared we were headed toward Jormungand Tower, one of the student residential structures. I supposed it was just as good as any to start figuring out where I would live for the next nine months.

Assuming we lasted that long.

The campus was beautiful in a surreal way, and the energy buzzing in the air was full of excitement, anticipation, and optimism from the students and faculty alike. But another kind of energy hummed under the surface. Something darker and nefarious that sent a tingle down my spine.

Something that made my mission even more disconcerting.

CHAPTER 2

The two girls I followed looked like they could be sisters from behind, with petite slender builds and long brown hair. Taylor Augustine, the witch on the right, radiated power, while Infiniti continued to emit anxiety more than anything else. I followed unnoticed as they walked toward the base of Jormungand Tower. The only visible entrance to the stone structure was three stories above us, from the bridge that connected to the library, according to my map. Exterior stairs began up there, too, built into the side of the stone wall, wrapping upward about seven stories high.

Here at ground level, Taylor placed her palm flat against the stone and said one word: *Angrboda*. The stones shifted and parted, creating an opening. The girls hesitantly stepped inside the dark entryway, and I followed. Taylor pulled her wand out, and a moment later, the cavernous basement was illuminated. Once farther inside, lit sconces lined the wall and led to a stone stairwell. Taylor put her wand away, and that's when she noticed me, jumping a little when she did.

"Oh! Like, I didn't know you were behind us. I'm Taylor, and this is my roommate Fin. Our room is on the third floor. What floor are you on?" Up close, I could see Taylor had Asian heritage, with almond shaped eyes, pronounced cheekbones, and a slightly flat nose that was accented with a tiny star-shaped silver ring.

"I'm Rhian." I lifted the packet of papers still in my hand. "There was an oversight, and I wasn't assigned a tower, so I get to pick which one I want to live in."

"Seriously? It's not like the Board of Regents to screw something up like that. Lucky you." Taylor needlessly explained to me that her grandmother served on the Court of the Sun and the Moon, the governing body for the supernatural residents of Havenwood Falls. While her grandmother wasn't a Regent, Taylor knew other members of the Court who were.

Infiniti told me she was new to Havenwood Falls and that she was from Houston, Texas, eight years in the past. What she didn't tell me was all the loss she had suffered in her life. That poor girl was messed up.

Of course, I already knew their stories. Both girls were on the list for my mission.

While we ascended the stairs, Fin and Taylor told me a little information included in their welcome packet, which I hadn't received since I was unassigned. I was familiar with the namesake, though. Jormungand, also known as the Midgard Serpent, was one of Loki's three children with the giantess Angrboda. Again with the nods to the Norse deities. Of course, that could have been the Board's idea, but I highly doubted it.

When we reached the main floor, Taylor and Fin continued on to their room, while I explored, passing the laundry room and moving deeper into the common areas.

The main room was cozy with a fireplace tall enough for me to stand up in lining one wall. A fire already crackled, and the warmth beat back the chill that seemed to emanate from every stone. On a tan plush sectional sofa with burnt orange and turquoise throw pillows sat a bear. Well, he wasn't in his bear form, but Caleb Hayes in his human form took up almost as much space. He was stretched out along one side of the sectional, letting out a frustrated growl as I approached.

"The signal down here is worse than in Havenwood Falls," he

said and tossed his phone onto the coffee table. Then he looked at me and paused, his dark eyes taking me in. "I don't believe we've met. I'd definitely remember you." He sat up, giving me his full attention. I sensed his bear perk up, too.

Down, boy, I wanted to say, but smirked instead. Caleb had definite appeal, and if all the guys in Jormungand looked like him, then I was moving in.

"Where's your room?" he asked.

"I don't exactly know." I explained my situation.

"Let me show you around," he offered enthusiastically. "I've already unpacked, so I have the time."

"I think I'm good," I said as nicely as possible, not wanting to encourage him.

I made a quick exit to the next room—a study lined with bookshelves—then made my way to the main entrance of the tower. The bridge to the library was straight ahead, but to the right was an opening that led to a balcony. I followed it around the building to where it widened. Finding a seating area along the decorative stone wall, I sat on one of the benches, observing the lit up buildings and students walking below. Glancing up, I caught a glimpse of the night sky through a massive skylight where the peak of Mount Alexa should have been. From the outside, it looked like a normal mountain, the opening magically camouflaged. I itched to take my raven form and fly into the night to soar among the stars, but not yet. There would be time for that later.

As I sat and observed, male voices carried over to me. I turned in their direction to see two guys descending the stairs.

"These things are wicked treacherous!" the one with thick brown hair said.

The guy behind him agreed. "Nothing like the agility test at the admissions trials, though. My entire body hurt for days after, and I'm a fast healer."

I detected an accent, not British or Australian, but definitely foreign. Students had been recruited from all over the world, and as the guys drew closer, I was able to see who they were. Ah, the brown haired guy was Clay Washburn, a witch, and his friend, the one with the accent . . . *huh*. Interesting . . .

I'd only encountered a few Impundulu—or lightning birds—throughout my existence. A dangerous species, they were often under the control of a mage and forced to do their master's bidding. I was surprised the Board of Regents would take such a risk, but I sensed an internal struggle within this one. He wanted the light. I was familiar with that struggle between light and dark myself.

I slipped into the shadows, and they didn't notice me when they walked by within inches of where I stood. It was a gift really. While my appearance was certainly memorable with my blond dreadlocks and braids and my unique Celtic hippy style, I was able to move through a crowd unnoticed and blend in with my surroundings almost like I was invisible.

After they passed, I yawned. It had to be close to two in the morning, and I needed to find a place to crash. The climb up the outside stairs was dark, and one clumsy move could send somebody flying over the edge. My vision was sharp, though, and I navigated the narrow stone steps easily. Familiar voices caught my attention one flight up. The voices grew louder and led me to an open doorway.

I peeked inside to see Fin sitting cross-legged on a plush rug, her head tilted back as she watched Taylor create a mural on the ceiling of their room, using her wand like a paintbrush. A depiction of the universe began to appear with a giant moon at the center. After a few moments, Taylor noticed me standing in the doorway and jumped again.

"Oh my Goddess, you are stealthy as fuck." She held a hand over her chest.

"Sorry, I was just walking by. Nice work." I pointed at the ceiling.

"Thanks. Did you pick a room on this floor, too? That would be like, really cool." Taylor slipped her wand in the back pocket of her jeans.

"I'm actually still looking for one. Do you know of any available?"

Turned out the room next door was empty. The door was unlocked, and when I went inside, the light came on right away. I looked around for a switch or motion sensor, but didn't see one. Taylor came in behind me.

"The room is voice-controlled by its residents," she explained. "Once you claim this room, the door and the lights are at your command."

A loud thud startled us, and I turned to discover a trunk had been delivered at the foot of the metal-framed bed with its thin, bare mattress. On top of the trunk was a piece of parchment paper —instructions for claiming the room. Apparently, knowing I had such few belongings, the school had taken it upon themselves to provide me with bedding and such. Or my recruiter had.

I wasn't ready to stake a claim, though. Not with four other towers to investigate. Setting the note aside, I opened the trunk.

"Here, let me help." Taylor moved forward to grab a pillow off the top, and I wasn't quick enough to pull back before her arm brushed mine. As soon as our skin touched, I caught a glimpse of one of Taylor's memories. She was in another realm, talking to a spirit. Hmm . . . Taylor had a connection to the dead. Like me, but not.

I wanted to warn her. I had met someone like her before. Someone who was drawn to the spirit realm, and in that brief glimpse, I could tell Taylor was, too. A delicate balance had to be kept between the living and the dead. I had a healthy respect for it —necessary, considering how my power over death had changed. A sense of foreboding washed over me that Taylor was going to learn about this balance the hard way, but blurting out a warning like that could backfire.

Taylor, however, didn't keep quiet. She gasped audibly, taking a step back.

"*Necromancer?*" she hissed, her tone laced with accusation.

"No!" I protested. "I'm not—"

She shook her head, not letting me finish. As she backed out of the room, her distrust went up like a wall. "I . . . I can't."

She hurried out of the room, leaving me alone. I normally didn't mind being alone. It was how I spent the majority of my life, living as a nomad, experiencing life on my own and crashing where I could. This shouldn't have been any different, but that one touch and the look in Taylor's eyes made it feel much different.

After getting ready for bed, I curled up on the thin mattress and pulled the blanket over my body. I contemplated claiming the room, just so I could tell the light to turn off, but I wouldn't, not after what happened with Taylor. Closing my eyes, I listened to the sounds outside die down as everyone else settled in for the night.

I felt like I'd just fallen asleep, when I heard a slithery sound from nearby.

"You don't belong here," a faint voice breathed, quieter than a whisper. I chalked it up to someone talking in another room, but then it came louder. "You musssst leave."

My eyes popped open. Looming over me was a huge rainbow boa, its coiled body taking up nearly the entire room, its gigantic head poised above me as if ready to strike. Its forked tongue darted out, coming only an inch from my face.

"What the fuck?" I screeched, springing up and back, my spine cracking against the wall.

"I sssssaid you don't belong here. You must leeeeaaavvvee." The enormous head swung at me, and I jumped out of the way. Its tail came at me next, trying to sweep my feet out from underneath me, but I hurdled it just in time.

"You don't have to tell me twice," I muttered. I reached for my backpack, but the snake struck at me again.

Its tail hit the door, springing it open. "Leave or elsssse . . ."

"Okay, okay! I fucking get it!" Morphing into my raven form, I flew out the door. After a lap around the tower, I passed the room, noticing the snake was gone. I shot in and grabbed my backpack with my talons, then flew away from the tower. I didn't even know if the snake had been real, but I wasn't taking any chances. I clearly wasn't wanted there.

I found a place to perch on a nearby tower and slept in my bird form. Or tried to, anyway. My mind couldn't rid itself of the boa's warning. Did it mean I didn't belong in Jormungand Tower? Or at SMA at all?

Actually, I knew the answer: *Both*. But while I'd gladly stay far away from the tower, I wasn't about to leave the school yet. Not on the first night anyway.

CHAPTER 3

The lady who'd given me my packet last night hadn't been kidding about there being plenty to do to keep us busy for the next nine days before classes started. I perused the packet of papers while eating breakfast by myself in the dining hall. Pages and pages detailed schedules for advisor meetings, selecting classes, orientations, campus tours, meet-and-greets with professors, and more—even a social event for students. I wondered if that would be our first college party. A pit grew in my stomach as I read over the last page.

It outlined a variety of team-building exercises each tower would be doing to get to know each other. There would be leadership elections at the end of the week, but more importantly, according to the powers-that-be, the residents in each tower had values and beliefs they shared. It was up to them to figure out what they were, then give their tower a mascot and a motto that best represented them as a group. This was all to be done by the end of next weekend. But what was one to do when they didn't have a tower yet? What if I didn't belong in any of them?

I shook my head at myself. I was letting that stupid snake get to me. Now in the light of day—well, sort of, a bit of sunlight streamed down from the skylight, muted as it was—I was surer than before that the snake hadn't been real. But whether it had been my imagination or something the tower itself had conjured—I mean, it was a rainbow boa, just like Jormungand itself—I was still damn sure that wasn't my tower.

Halstein Hall was the name of the main building on campus, housing the dining hall, administrative offices, tons of classrooms and lecture halls, a small theater, and the Student Union. At the entrance was a large fountain with another Valkyrie statue in the center. Across the white marble floor from the main doors, the Student Union sprawled over the first two floors, offering lots of open seating areas, a couple of fast food and grab-and-go convenience stops, and a few shops, including a bookstore and a satellite location of Howe's Herbal Shoppe, a store on the town square of Havenwood Falls. Guess a school populated with witches needed a place to get supplies for classes . . . and whatever else they may be up to.

I liked witches. Hell, why wouldn't I? I mean, many of them worshipped me and my fellow moon goddesses, after all. But that could get old, and I was glad that so far, Addie's extra magic combined with my own kept the lunar force within me suppressed. The witches hadn't picked up those vibes. No, they just seemed to notice the dark stuff. I wondered if that said more about them or about me . . .

In addition to the snake's warning, Taylor's accusation had haunted me all night. Needless to say, I didn't get much sleep. Good thing I didn't really need it. Still, I stopped at the Coffee Haven kiosk for a pumpkin spice latte—a favorite concoction during my favorite time of year.

Later, as I waited outside my advisor's office to discuss my major and emphasis, I eventually realized he'd overbooked himself for this first day. Although my appointment was at two, he didn't get to me until nearly four o'clock. They should have given students more time to settle into campus life before pushing the important stuff—I listened as students questioned him about everything *except* classes. When the short, middle-aged mage finally came out of his office after his one-thirty appointment that didn't really start until three-fifteen, he began to lock up.

"Excuse me?" I said.

Flinching, he turned on me with wild eyes. "Good gods! I didn't see you there!"

I smiled, suppressing an internal eye roll. I hadn't even been trying to blend in this time. With bloodshot eyes and his graying hair sticking up everywhere as though he'd run his hands through it many times throughout the day, he looked a bit like a mad scientist.

"Can I help you with something?" he asked, his bushy brow furrowing.

"We had a two o'clock meeting," I reminded him.

He swore under his breath. "I'm terribly sorry . . . uh . . ."

He looked down at the books in his arms, his appointment book on top—the cover closed.

"Rhian," I offered.

"Right." He nodded, his eyes sparking with recognition. "Rhian Delaney. Hmph. Your major is special forces with an emphasis in espionage?"

"It is?" I questioned back.

"That's the results the trials provided, if I remember correctly. It seems to fit, too, as stealthy as you are. Is that a problem?"

"Um . . . well, I don't know. What else is there?" It wasn't a problem really. Espionage was no doubt my strength. After all, that was the reason I was even here. I was more curious than anything.

He sighed, his shoulders slumping. "I'm so sorry, Ms. Delaney, but it's been a hell of a day. Would you mind if we rescheduled for tomorrow?"

"You know what? I'm good with the program chosen for me. Do we need to meet to go over classes?"

"Only if you need help building out your schedule. You can give it a shot yourself, if you want to. Most classes you'll take this year are the basics everyone's required to take anyway. Simply log in to the school portal and you'll see the list of what you need."

"I think I can handle that."

"Thank the gods," he muttered as he began to waddle away. "Good luck, Ms. Delaney," he called over his shoulder. "And you be sure to keep that power under control."

With that not-so-subtle warning, he scurried off and disappeared around a corner. *Huh.* We hadn't even discussed my powers. It was probably all over my rap sheet or whatever they called the results of the admissions tests and trials.

When I exited Halstein Hall, I went to the right, heading for Modi Tower. A long, narrow stone bridge connected the courtyard —aka the quad—to Modi. As I crossed it, I noticed how the cavern floor below sloped downward. By the time I reached the door, the cavern floor was a good three or more stories down, nearly even with the river bank. Windows on the tower rose up another seven or eight floors. It was possibly the tallest of the residential towers.

An archway was carved into the tower's stone, and set in it was a teal wooden door with tarnished metal scrollwork creating an intricate design across its front. There was no handle or knob, so I lifted my right hand to see if it would push open. It didn't budge on that side. Raising my left arm, I was about to give that side a shove when I felt a slight zing on my wrist and the door slid back on its own.

The entryway opened onto a wide balcony that overlooked a large great room below. The balcony ended just to the left, where three-story tall windows wrapped nearly halfway around the tower's circular wall. To the right, the balcony curved around to meet the far edge of the windows, seating areas scattered about and bookshelves lining the wall. I glanced up to find another balcony above, but down was where the action was. Several comfortable sitting areas were scattered around a huge hearth in the center of the room.

Twenty or so students gathered down there, laughing and messing around. A couple of girls—I recognized one as Charleigh Wotsit with her bright orange hair—were flicking spells, changing the room's decor. Others ooh'd and ah'd at the results. It was then I remembered that the first team-building exercise was scheduled to begin in a few minutes. I made myself scarce by crossing the walkway over the great room to the center and entering the stairwell that spiraled down and up.

On the third floor of the commons area, I found some smaller gathering rooms off of the balcony, which was narrower here than the one below. I took a seat in a plush chair and stared out the windows at the campus alit in the shadows of dusk. It was a gorgeous view, really. I could even see what appeared to be an underground lake off to the right.

Someone burst into song below, strumming a guitar. I peered down at the growing group. Aithan Lanrete. *Go figure.* I didn't know if he'd remember, but we'd met before, twice. Once at Burning Man two years ago and before that at Coachella. I'd known his family for eons. His dad was an arrogant dick, as demigods with tons of money tended to be. I couldn't fathom how Aithan had come from that background, though. The opposite of his father, he'd been fun to hang out with, and if he was any indication of the "personality" of Modi Tower, this might be home.

"He's good, isn't he?"

I looked over to see who had managed to sneak up on me. Usually that was my thing. A fae with white blond hair streaked with purple highlights stood by the balcony, her violet eyes focused on Aithan.

"Aye, he's not bad for a rich pretty boy." I said this jokingly, knowing that Aithan didn't take himself too seriously.

The fae snorted and held out her hand, introducing herself. "Hi, I'm Paisley. I don't think we've met?"

I shook her hand, amused by the human greeting. "Rhian."

Paisley tilted her head. "I detect a brogue. It's not Scottish, though. My cousin's fiancé has a thick Scottish accent. Irish, is it?"

"Aye."

"Were you recruited from Ireland? That's so freaking cool!"

I nodded. It was easier than explaining where I was really from. Paisley had good energy, and I sensed her healing touch when we shook hands. I explained my housing situation and asked if she knew of any vacant rooms.

"Oh, yeah. There's a single room available on the sixth floor, which is my floor. Come on, I'll show you."

Paisley helped me find a nice room with an arched window that looked out over the courtyard below. She was friendly without being pushy, and I took an instant liking to her. I even went down and met some of the other residents and hung out for a while. They were my kind of people—independent and adventurous, based on the tales they shared, and totally laid back. Like me. Could I be so lucky to have found home so quickly? It'd be nice after last night's weirdness.

Sleep came easily, but I awoke in the dark in a completely different place. An empty room with arched ceilings and supportive columns. I hurried over to the window that was similar but not the same as the one in my room. It looked down over the quad and the bridge—I was still in Modi, but on a higher floor. The tenth, by my guess. How the hell did I get here?

I peered through the darkness, hunting for a door. Locating it, I opened it to find a ribbon of black energy swirling through the air, as though seeking something. Peering around the bend, I realized it was trying to enter a door. Sending my senses outward, I found three souls beyond—the Knight twins and Charleigh Wotsit. What did this dark energy want with them?

As though it sensed me, the black ribbon swirled into a mass that became tornadic, spinning right for me.

"No," I whispered. My own blood rose, like the tide to the moon, reaching for it. I fought for control. If I lost it . . . Addie's warning rang in my head. Taylor's accusation of necromancy echoed, too. "No," I said again. "You can't have me."

I found the central stairwell and rushed downward, taking two steps at a time, spiraling down to the sixth floor. Once back in my room, I curled up on the bed, hugging my knees to my chest. The dark force didn't follow me. It took a long time for my heart to slow down enough to realize that. I could sense it, though, hovering up by the Knight twins' door. It seemed to be more interested in them than me. I briefly wondered why, then remembered what my old friend, my recruiter, had told me about the girls.

Shit. I couldn't stay here. Modi could not be my home, or we'd all be in grave danger.

CHAPTER 4

I took a deep breath, soaking in the cool morning air while enjoying some time outside. Behind Halstein Hall stretched a long sky bridge that led to Steivar and Ansgar, the fitness center and armory, respectively. Beyond them was an opening to Clifftop. On the opposite side of Mount Alexa from the town of Havenwood Falls, Clifftop was exactly that—the top of a cliff. Just barely below the mountain's treeline, it was a cleared-out area about the size of three football fields and surrounded by forest. To the left of the opening was a greenhouse, but the rest of the space was open, perfect for combat training. And the surrounding woods would be great for shifters to hunt and witches to forage and gather. Somebody really knew what they were doing with this place. I had a feeling I knew who that somebody was.

Today was Sunday, and the only scheduled activities were socials within the towers. Since I hadn't found my tower home yet, I considered spending my day out here instead and perusing the class catalog to pick my classes. I was still pretty disappointed by what happened in the middle of the night, but it was probably best for everyone. And maybe Modi really wasn't the right place for me, even without that Dark energy.

The next tower on my list was Hel. I laughed to myself. The

jokes here could go on and on, but I knew who the tower represented: the Goddess Hela. The Norse deity served as Judge, Jury, and Executioner, which was definitely no joking matter.

After spending the morning on Clifftop writing in my journal, I decided I might as well go to Hel.

A cobblestone pathway led over the bridge that accessed Hel. It was the shortest residential tower, only five stories total, but with its flat roof and stonework that looked like a crenelated battlement, it could serve as a great lookout over the quad and main campus below.

Easing up the steps, I came to the deep red double-doors. They made quite the statement, wrapped in black, scrolling wrought iron. The doorway came to a pointed arch high above. Pulling open the doors, I walked inside and was greeted by two witches.

"Hello. I'm Rhian." I raised my natural guards, blocking out as much of my essence as possible. Even with Addie's magical help, I felt the need to be extra-careful with these two.

"Hey, there! I'm Natalie, and this is Tempest. Are you in Hel Tower, too?" They slid closer, welcoming but unaware that their draw to me was happening on a subconscious level.

"Not exactly." Smiling, I took a step back, giving them my spiel.

"Whoa, cool," Tempest replied, flipping her dark hair over her shoulder. "Have fun exploring. There are some rooms still available on the second floor, but ours and Vanna's are the closest to the bathroom." She winked.

"Great. I'll check it out."

Natalie smiled, and the two moved past me, leaving me to investigate. The short hall opened up into the great room, which looked like an elaborate Victorian salon draped in red and black accoutrements. The walls and built-in shelves were black and scrolled with detailed coping, while the interior backing of the alcoves were a deep, vibrant red. A gothic black chandelier hung in the center, and the decorations looked like a hobby store during a Halloween sale. With silver highlights breaking up the main tones, it was moody, and sexy, and all-around impressive.

The tight spiral staircase was underlit with red lights, giving it an eerie glow. I skipped up the stairs to the fifth floor. If I chose Hel as my tower, I'd want to be on the highest level. Moving down the hall, I noticed that none of the rooms on this floor had been claimed, but as I made my way back to the staircase, I heard voices coming from above. I continued up the stairway to the roof access and found two other girls, chilling up top.

"Hey. I'm Rhian."

A statuesque blonde lifted her chin. "Vanna."

I sniffed the air…hellhound. *Great. Another one.*

"Hi, I'm Marina," offered the other in a much friendlier tone. Salt water and magic assaulted my senses. Sea witch.

"It's nice to meet you both. I was just finishing up my tour of your tower. It's quite lovely, and if I may say so, kinda fierce."

"Oh, you can say so. It definitely is, and I bet the parties we're going to throw up here will be fierce, too." Marina giggled.

"I bet." I smiled. "It was nice to meet you both. Also, I'll be snagging a room on the fifth floor for tonight, if that's okay." I felt the need to ask permission here, since Vanna seemed like she'd be harder to win over than the other girls. While the others were attracted to my lunar energy, she undoubtedly sensed my darker side.

"You're spending the night?" she asked.

"Yes."

"Awesome," Marina chimed in. "Be sure to come down to the great room later. I think that's where we're all meeting up once we have our schedules tonight."

"Great, I definitely will."

I followed the corkscrew staircase back down to the fifth level and selected a room at the end of the hall. The rounded brick walls were smooth and uncluttered, begging for a personal touch. I was immediately drawn to the open window that overlooked the campus. From this vantage point, I could see the whole quad, almost opposite from where I'd been last night at Modi.

Even though Hel had fewer floors, it rose from a slope in the cavern floor, allowing me to see almost every building, or at least pieces of them, and I liked that. Heimdall Tower loomed behind Eirhall and Asketill to the right, and the Faculty Residence was located to the immediate left. Though, now that I could see it clearly, I had no idea how it was accessed. There was no bridge or path leading from the quad, and it practically hovered over the river, so I doubted there was an underground tunnel. I looked to the main bridge and suddenly wondered if their tower could only be accessed by a portal. It made sense, providing extra privacy for the professors.

After a good hour or two of soaking in the campus and people watching, I was excited to head down to the great room and see what else this tower and its residents had to offer. I found Natalie and Tempest sitting on the elaborate brocade couch, gushing over how they had the exact same schedules. While their magic felt very different to me, it was clear they both held a talent for the Healing Arts, which wasn't where the similarities stopped. They also looked very much alike. Their long brown hair was barely a shade different, and even their mannerisms seemed to be in sync.

"Have you gotten your schedule yet?" Tempest asked as I sat in a high-back chair across from them.

"No, I've been more focused on finding my room."

"Where have you visited so far?" Natalie pulled her legs up under her and leaned forward.

"Jormungand, Modi, and here."

"Well, you can't tell me Hel doesn't outshine those other two gloomy towers," Tempest teased without any real knowledge of either place. "I mean, come on, we're like family here already." She elbowed Natalie, then pulled her up from the couch. "See . . . we've even done some trust-falls." Without warning, Tempest pitched herself backward into Natalie's barely ready arms.

"Wow. Yeah. You guys definitely seem in-tune."

Plopping back onto the couch, Tempest giggled. "We may be misfits to most, but here, we're thick as thieves."

"Speak for yourself, Bell." Vanna and Marina sauntered into the great room, joining us as they looked over their schedules. Seemed like everyone here got a jump-start on those.

"Did you get the classes you hoped for?" Tempest asked the hellhound.

"Eh. What's it matter? School's school, right?" Vanna's cool demeanor eventually shifted, and we spent the rest of the night talking, laughing, and watching the witches conjure up some seriously good food. A definite benefit to residing in Hel Tower.

But as I climbed the stairs to turn in, Vanna caught my eye again. She was checking me out, closer than I was comfortable with. Not that she posed a threat, but I just wasn't sure if living in a tower with this many witches, and a hellhound to boot, was a good idea. I was used to keeping my nature hidden, but here . . . I wasn't confident I could keep it a secret. The girls were on my mission's list, but it would be like living with four Addie Beaumonts.

I debated going up to the roof and transforming to fly off, but didn't want to spark even more curiosity. So I retired to my room, anxious for morning to come.

The girls were great, but my time in Hel was done.

The next morning, I woke up early, grabbed my backpack, and made a beeline for the roof. Besides the activities of the day, Heimdall Tower was my next stop, but just as I stepped up to the edge of the battlement, ready to fly off, I was tossed backward, bouncing off an invisible energy field and straight onto my ass.

"What the hell?"

I hadn't noticed the field last night and wondered if this was simply the tower's way of confirming I didn't belong here. At least it was better than a snake.

CHAPTER 5

I spent Monday building out my schedule, which was harder than I expected. There were too many classes to choose from, and I wished I could major in everything. Maybe I could be one of those lifetime students and stay here forever. But first, I had to find a place to live.

Standing just outside the back doors of Halstein Hall, I took in the amazing view of the back side of campus. Off the skybridge to Clifftop was another bridge to the right that led to Heimdall Tower. Making my way toward it, I heard chatter and footsteps from behind me. I moved to the right and slowed down.

"Yeah, all you can eat," Kase Kasun, the wolf shifter, was saying.

"I know!" Joe Greg, his best friend and fellow wolf shifter, responded.

I did an inward eye roll. *Boys and their food.* Especially shifters. The pair came up beside me and slowed their pace to match mine.

"Hey," Joe said. "I saw you at check-in. I'm Joe, and this is Kase. We're wolf shifters."

"Rhian," I answered, leaving out my supernatural status.

"Do you live in Heimdall?" Kase asked with stitched brows. "I don't remember seeing you before."

I was getting tired of going into the whole *I'm not assigned to a tower yet* explanation, so instead I said, "I'm supposed to stay a night in each tower, and tonight is my night to stay at Heimdall."

I shrugged, trying to add to my nonchalant attitude, like I wasn't the only student doing this.

"Oh," Joe said. "Well, if you want, I can tell you what I know about Heimdall from the pamphlet we got on move-in."

"Sure, hit me," I answered, studying the oddly shaped eight-floor tower with its wide base, narrow middle, and wide top.

"Well, the tower is named after one of the Aesir gods who's also the guardian of Asgard. There's a big common area on the first floor and a lounge on the eighth, which is at the top. In between are the rooms."

"Neat," I said, coming to the entrance of the tower and opening the double doors. We walked in, and I did a quick visual sweep of the massive great room. Chairs, couches, and coffee tables took up most of the middle of the room. All along the perimeter were shelves lined with books. From my vantage point, I could see stairs at the back of the room, the kind that split off and went to the right and to the left.

"Well," Joe said, "we're on the sixth floor if you need anything."

"Thanks, guys."

"Oh my goddess, isn't this amazing? It's like the best day ever!"

As the guys disappeared, a tiger shifter caught my attention. Her long platinum-blond hair flowed around her shoulders, and fake black glasses covered pretty blue eyes. They had to be fake. Supernaturals with poor vision weren't exactly common.

I sidled up to the girl, curious of her friend standing beside her. Though friend seemed like too bold of a statement. There wasn't much warmth emanating from the Amazon.

"Hi, I'm Rhian," I interjected, earning a beaming smile from the tiger shifter. The Amazon, however, barely glanced at me with indifference.

"I'm Tess, and this is my roommate Nadine. What floor are you on?"

Here we go again. I sighed.

"I haven't chosen a room yet. You got any recommendations? Anything I should stay away from?" I pried, trying to get Nadine talking. Like so many here, she'd led a rough life. I wasn't sure if this was the best place for her, though—not when she looked like she'd rather be anywhere else in the world.

"The rooms are all pretty much the same. Can't really go wrong with picking. The eighth floor is pretty cool, though. It's where the study lounge is. Have you been up there yet?"

"Nope."

Tess pulled me forward, leaving little room to wriggle from her grasp. "Nadine and I will show you."

I glanced at the beautiful Amazon, her curly red hair and piercings portraying the fire within her. She visibly cringed as though my presence was an annoyance to her.

"Is there a problem?" I finally blurted, frustrated by the Amazon's attitude.

"I don't have one, dude. Just not the kind to revel in small talk." She shrugged, as though that was explanation enough.

"Well, don't stay on my account."

Nadine shrugged again, her loner vibe coming off strong. How did Tess cope? They seemed like total opposites.

My eyes widened with surprise when we reached the top floor. Large circular chandeliers hung from the ceiling, highlighting a space filled with sofas and glass tables. It felt like we'd stepped into some comfy cafe-slash-suave-club.

"Isn't this cool? Tell me you don't feel like we've traveled through time? Like there should be gentlemen in suits with top hats sitting with a cigar in one hand, whiskey glass in the other, jazz music in the background." Tess bounced, full of energy. Perhaps Nadine's lack of enthusiasm was less about being rude, and more to do with Tess's inexhaustible positivity. The two of them were bound to tire each other out. I didn't want to be around when that *friendship* blew up.

Nadine sighed loudly. "Dudes, I gotta go. Laters."

She disappeared without another word, leaving me alone with her overexcited kitty.

"You'll get used to it, I hope," Tess offered. "At least, I'm trying to. I think she just needs more time to settle in. For some people it can take a while to make friends."

"Right," I agreed, though I had a more pessimistic opinion. Nadine wasn't the kind of person to rely on others, and therefore didn't *need* friends.

"So shall we go pick out a room?" Tess beamed, immediately shaking off any negativity. I admired her for that.

"Sure, just don't take it personally, but I'd rather not be too close to yours."

She laughed, charging out of the lounge, leading me down a flight and to a single room on a floor that was blissfully quiet. I stepped inside and set my backpack on the desk.

"Thanks. I think I'm going to take a nap." I hoped Tess would get the hint. She did but not before handing me a sheet of paper. "What's this?" I peered down at the checklist.

"We have game night in the common area at seven p.m. It's good for team building. Don't be late and prepare to compete." She turned with a spring to her step, and bounced out of the room.

Instead of taking a nap, I pushed the game night info to the side and pulled out my schedule to go over my classes in the catalog, taking note of which books and supplies I'd need to obtain. Sometime later, there was a knock on my door. While I was still getting up from the rather uncomfortable bed, the door flew open.

"You ready?" Tess waved at me to hurry.

"Um, for what?"

"Game night," she urged.

Crap, I had forgotten. In the common room a few minutes later with about a dozen eager game players, Tess picked me to be on her team, and we paired off against Joe and Kase. The guys grinned with confidence as Tess and I faced them.

"Okay," Makenna, a Seelie fae with long, fiery red hair, called out. "I'm going to create an illusion of another place, and you have to break free using your partner and your abilities. The first team to escape wins!"

Seconds later, Tess and I found ourselves in a small, windowless and doorless room—basically a box. The only source of light was a single sconce. The flame flickered and threatened to go out. I heard a tearing of clothing and the popping of bones. Suddenly the room was a lot smaller because I now shared it with a giant tiger. Tess chuffed at me and proceeded to sniff the perimeter. I hung back and watched her work. For being an illusion, the room seemed very real. I pressed against the walls and found them sturdy.

Tess's tail flicked in agitation as she paced the small space, looking for a way out. With a giant paw, she swiped at a wall. She didn't leave a scratch. But then the space changed, and we were suddenly in the middle of a rave, lights flashing, music blaring, and bodies moving to the beat. I couldn't help myself—I began dancing, too.

Tess glared at me through tiger eyes, snuffing with annoyance.

"What?" I yelled over the music. "It's a party! Maybe we're supposed to dance our way out." I laughed as I spun around, my arms waving in the air.

But Tess grew increasingly more agitated, running through the crowd, searching for our escape. Personally, I was enjoying the illusion.

Just as sudden as the rave had appeared, it was gone, and we returned to the black box. I heard muffled cheering and then the vision faded away completely. Back in the common room, Joe and Kase were fist bumping each other, having completed the challenge first.

Tess appeared at my side in her human form and fully clothed. I hadn't even noticed that she left. "What the hell, Rhian? You didn't even *try*. Rule number one is to always give one hundred percent."

The bubbly girl I met earlier was gone, her competitive nature bringing out a different side. The girl needed to chill. This was way too intense for me. Wasn't game night supposed to be fun?

Meandering my way down the stairs the next morning, I spotted Cat trotting toward me. She wore tight black athletic wear complete with chunky platform tennis shoes. Her hair was pulled up in a high ponytail, and her lips were painted in dark red lipstick. The girl was desperate for attention.

She stopped in front of me. "Hola," she said. "Are you lost?"

"Nope. Um, do you live here?"

"Sí, I'm on the seventh floor."

Yep, that was my cue. This tower definitely didn't need me. I was not a drama llama. Far from it, in fact, and there was too much tension here. Before she could ask me anything else, I added quickly, "Oh, cool. Well, see ya. Gotta run."

Hurrying down the steps, I felt a little bad for being so short with Cat. Maybe she wasn't as bad as she seemed. But either way, I didn't belong here. I needed to move on to the next tower. *Maybe that one will be just right*, I thought, feeling a bit like Goldilocks.

CHAPTER 6

$\mathcal{I}$ only had one option left—Muninn. I didn't want to think about what would happen if it didn't work out there, too. Maybe the whole school was trying to remind me that I didn't really belong here. But if I was right about my old friend being behind this place, why did she recruit me for her mission? It couldn't be over already—classes hadn't even started. If I knew her as well as I thought I did, this was all probably part of her plan. Surely there was a tower where I belonged, and Muninn *had* to be it.

The tower was accessed through the basement of the library. As if basements and this particular library weren't creepy enough, try combining the two and then have to go through a dark, empty tunnel that connected to the tower. From the freaky as shit library, the long, windy stone corridor was as dark and surreal as expected and led to a large wooden door, painted black with gold hinges. The door opened easily, looking heavier than it really was, and not requiring a password.

I walked down a hallway and up a short flight of stairs, which opened up to a large common area. Two guys sat next to each other at a long table, studying papers spread out before them. One with white blond hair and the other dark, they were the opposite sides of a coin in every way. I didn't sense any animosity between them, and they acted like best friends. *Interesting*, I thought to myself. Unseelie and Seelie fae weren't known to get along. In fact, there was a recent civil war in Faerie. Their dynamics piqued my curiosity.

Sinking down silently on one of the sofas, I listened to their conversation. The Unseelie was named Cole, fitting because his hair was as dark as coal. He pointed at the paper in front of him. "Look, Timber, we have Basic Combat and Ethics together."

"That is most advantageous. I can assist you with your Faerie Geography. After all, I could probably teach that course." I recognized Timber's speech as a Faerie native. He had yet to pick up any Earth slang and spoke very formally, like he was from another time. In a way, he was.

"Deal. And I'll help you assimilate to life here. We'll start with how you talk."

"Whatever do you mean? Am I speaking in a manner which is improper?"

My body shook with silent laughter as I stood up unnoticed and made my way to the stairs. It was time to see what else this tower had to offer.

"This place," a tall girl with hair white as snow pursed her painted lips and blew out a short whistle, "is amazing, Molly."

"I'm so glad you're here, Marcia," her companion said. Her dark, flawless skin shimmered in the low light of the common room. "Two bellas in one place?" She held up two fingers, giving a playful wink. "This college isn't going to know what hit them."

"Three of you," I whispered, watching Linnie Andrews shyly approach the two.

Leaving Linnie and her newfound friends, I made my way up several flights of stairs. The rooms along the first two floors were already full. I was a little late to get first pick, but there were still five more floors to choose from.

Six steps away from the stairs on the fifth floor, I came to an open bedroom door, and I stopped as though I'd hit a wall, my breath hitching.

"Oh, my gods and goddesses," I murmured.

A double-sized bed was set up in the middle of the smooth wooden floor. A canopy of paisley and mandala-print tapestries draped over the four posts, and fairy lights twinkled over them and around the walls. A shaggy purple rug was laid out in front of the bed, which was covered in colorful pillows and thick blankets. A tall window was propped open along the far wall, complete with a pillowed window seat that would be perfect for late night reading or people watching. The scene came straight out of my head, one I'd imagined my room would look like if I'd ever settled down to have one.

"This is gorgeous," I whispered. I wondered who it belonged to —she and I needed to be friends.

"Tower meeting." A wolf shifter popped his head in the door. "Down in the common room. We need to discuss leadership elections." His eyes lit up with excitement.

I followed the trickle of students making their way to the common room. People were already sitting at the table and on most of the sofas, but I managed to find an empty seat.

"All right, everyone." A young man called the meeting to order. "We're supposed to come up with ideas for mottos and a mascot. Anyone?"

"How about 'follow me, I know the way'?" Timber suggested, jabbing Cole in the side until they both snickered.

"Eh," the group booed him down.

"We need something about opportunity," Marcia declared. "That's what we're all here for, an opportunity to lead an army, right?" This statement got more than a few appreciative grins and nods.

"I never thought something like this would happen to me," Linnie whispered from her place next to me. "This is so exciting."

I felt her wonder, and a warm glow of happiness started somewhere deep inside me, too.

"What about a mascot?" the guy who led the meeting asked.

"How about a raven?" I surprised myself by blurting out the

idea. It was equally surprising that people seemed to like the idea. *Really* liked it.

As the meeting continued, I became more and more comfortable. After, I asked about a vacant room.

"Okay, so this is really weird, but there's a room on the fifth floor by the stairs, all made up and decorated, but nobody lives there," Linnie said. "We've been waiting and guessing whose it was."

"It looks totally like your style," Molly said as her gaze raked over me.

Linnie beamed at me. "Do you think . . . ?"

I nodded. I didn't *think*. I knew.

Finally. I'd found home—at least for the next few years, which was longer than I'd ever stayed in one place, by far.

I settled in at Muninn Tower surprisingly fast. By Thursday, I'd caught up on some of the things I'd missed while room-hunting. Now I was finally able to take a campus tour. Yeah, I probably already knew the campus better than most, but I wanted Addie Beaumont, the tour guide, to see that she had nothing to worry about with me. Besides, she knew where all the good stuff was.

For example, the artifact room we'd just entered. A largish room in Halstein, it housed all kinds of shelves and tables and curios of collectibles—all of the magical type. *Ha.* If my suspicions hadn't been confirmed yet, I was now ninety-nine percent sure my old friend was indeed somehow involved with the creation of this school, or at least of the campus. I wouldn't have been surprised if it'd been an old hideout of hers, to be honest. This museum-like room and its collection gave it away.

"When I say I don't recommend touching anything, I seriously mean it—don't touch," Addie said firmly. "Some of the things in here are probably more dangerous than you'll find over in that library."

Several people chuckled nervously. They'd probably already

experienced the library or at least heard rumors about it. They also moved in closer to each other, careful not to touch anything. Except for Roxy McCabe and some guys surrounding her. I looked over at the subtle commotion in time to see an hourglass artifact start to fall.

People moved in the way, and I didn't see what happened next, but I didn't need to. A gong rang so loudly, the ground tremored. The ground of a mountain. What the hell could shake that? It was the sound itself that got to me, though. I clamped my hands over my ears and squeezed my eyes shut.

I knew that sound.

I'd heard it ages ago.

It was a warning. Serious shit was about to go down.

I was going to kill that bitch, my old friend. She knew that sound, too, and I felt like she was taunting me. And I couldn't help but think that she'd sent us all to an early grave.

FIRST TIME FOR EVERYTHING

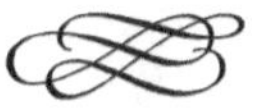

VICTORIA ESCOBAR

CHAPTER 1

A hand rubbed the top of our head and behind our ears. A purr slipped out before we could fully wake up, and we tipped our head back into the scratching fingers. The gentle touch was so far outside the norm for us, we reveled in it when anyone dared. Sadly, not many dared cuddle an almost two hundred pound cougar.

An eye slitted open to confirm Bryony crouched over us. We knew it was her by the scent, but sometimes it didn't hurt to be careful. Some of the slipperier fae and trickier witches could change their scents on a whim.

Bryony Fenn was our first friend in Havenwood Falls. She approached me and demanded my friendship in the way most extroverts adopted introverts. "My name is Bree-oh-nee" was all she said before plopping herself down at my library table and borrowing my books for herself. Since she went to the private high school part of Sun and Moon and I was homeschooled, our time together was limited, and yet I couldn't imagine not having her as my friend.

She looked ready to take on the day in her worn boots and long dress. The buttons down the front of the dress were only buttoned up to barely modest levels, revealing more of her warm golden skin

47

than perhaps was appropriate. Her long brown kinky curls were coiled in a messy bun on the top of her head. I couldn't tell if the embellished chopsticks were functional or for decoration. Small stones glowed faintly at her ears, in her hair, and around her wrists. I was comfortable enough in myself to admit Bryony was beautiful.

"It's time to get up sleepy kitty." She grinned, standing when we growled at the name. The endearment wasn't uncommon for a cougar shifter, or any cat shifter, really. No one was original anymore.

We rolled over with a big yawn. After a long stretch that included a partial tail flick, we sat on our haunches and looked up at her. Bryony crossed her arms.

A tip of our head and we caught the faint smell of bacon over her earthy scent. Our stomach rumbled. When was the last time we ate?

Friend, I reminded Missy when the cat calculated if Bryony would make a good meal. Even though we were pretty good about control now, a couple of years ago we hadn't been, and my input had become a habit we were both comfortable with.

After talking to Uncle Mike, I was pretty sure my cat was more sentient than she should be. Living in shifted form while my side healed from life threatening injuries had consequences. Almost turning feral was one of them. Since she developed her own voice, I considered my cat another form of my conscience and left it at that.

"There's a perfectly good bed in the room, you know, and if it's too hard or something, I can fix that too. Why are you sleeping on the balcony?" She nudged me with a foot but quickly retracted it when we swiped at it. "These boots are older than you, Roxy."

With a chuff, we turned from her indignation and jumped into our room through the window left open the night before. We bit back a whine as we landed wrong on our scarred leg. Despite all the healing sessions, our left side would never be as strong as the right again. I shifted forms and dug through my closet.

The bustle of the last week drained even the most energetic

people. I didn't know how Bryony had any energy left. Between tower assignments, class selections, upcoming tower officer elections, unpacking, and in my case, working at the campus's Coffee Haven kiosk, I was exhausted. What would it be like when classes actually started? I considered cutting my hours at Coffee Haven, but I liked the spending money, and one could never predict when they needed cash.

"Classes haven't started yet, Bree." I pulled on a thin long sleeved tunic, and then tugged on some leggings from the dresser in the closet.

The first thing I did upon moving in was unpack. I did not thrive in chaos. Thanks to Aunt Anne and Miss Elaine, Audrey's mother-in-law, I'd been loaded down with "necessities." Audrey, my half-sister, also added to the mess of stuff I had to have, but compared to the older women, she was conservative with her contribution.

"No underwear, Roxy, really?" Her smile held amusement when I glanced at her.

"Shifter." There was more to it than that. My body was small enough that a bra was more of a hindrance than a help and underwear was really only necessary for seven days of the month. Sometimes being compact all over sucked, but the money I saved from not buying under things was a blessing.

"Convenient, but at the same time, a bit risqué, don't you think?"

I rolled a shoulder. "Why'd you wake me up?"

"First, why were you asleep on the balcony?" She murmured something else under her breath, and the fireplace crackled to life. She called herself a druid, which to me was another term for witch, but I had to admit her magic smelled different than the traditional witches. A witch like Addie Beaumont left behind an ozone-like residue on the air, but Bryony's was more. . .natural in odor for lack of a better term. Only the most sensitive of noses would notice.

My hand waved at the flames. "That's why. I didn't feel like fighting to light it since you weren't in the room when I came in to crash. It was cold, and my cat is somewhat insulated."

She rolled her eyes. "I'll charm some stones. All you'll have to do is set them on the wood, and it'll light for you. No point in sleeping outside when you have a perfectly good bed inside. Now, I've given you some time. I've—mostly—respected your privacy, but I think we need to talk about the guys you've spent the last week avoiding. Especially considering Vidar looks to be the tower elected president." She crossed her arms and leaned against her bed.

My hands rubbed my eyes both in fatigue and annoyance. Of course Bryony would notice. "There's nothing to talk about."

"Really? You've made every excuse possible not to be in the same room with Tyr and Vidar." She pronounced it Vee-dar, which meant she actually talked to them at some point. I only knew Tyr's name, not his darker-skinned companion. Her brows rose, letting me know I wasn't going to be able to evade my way out of this conversation.

I sighed and sat in my desk chair. I liked that the bed was elevated so I had my desk and reading chair underneath it. Everything sat where it should on the desktop. "You know I met Tyr during trials—"

She held up her hand like a stop sign. "Refresh my memory. We were on different trial times."

"The wet dog that picked a fight." I scowled at the memory and fiddled with my necklace. The charm screened my scent so I didn't have to explain to every joe why I smelled feral but looked human. I still smelled like a cat, but not one about to rip out a person's throat. The distinction was important. The chain was designed to never break, and the charm would shift with my cat as well. I thought it worth the price for a little peace.

"Ooh. Your panic attack." Bryony wasn't at all sympathetic. "You branded him with a hickey though. And he called you alpha for the rest of the weekend."

Not the part that I wanted her to remember from my story but it worked. "Anyway. There's something about him—"

"I assume you're not talking about the taut, lickable muscles, and the under lip piercing. Because, yum."

"By the gods, Bree. I'm only seventeen." I rubbed my hands over my flaming face. She wasn't wrong. Tyr was gorgeous but . . .

"You're young. So what? I'm going to need you to explain." Bryony crossed her feet at the ankles, clearly getting comfortable.

"He's just—" I couldn't really pin down why he and his partner-in-crime made me so uncomfortable. I could admit, only to myself, I felt drawn to them, and I really didn't want to be.

"I need to focus on classes. I got to test out of high school to come here, and I don't want anyone to think they made a mistake." The excuse was valid, and a real fear. The Board of Regents could change their minds if I screwed up, but they could do that for anyone, not only me.

Her stare was a *don't bullshit me* face, but she shrugged a shoulder. "Fine. Let's go for a walk around campus. You need some activity since you've been asleep for the last twenty-ish hours."

"All right." There was no point in reminding her that was a solid nap for most cats. I slid on tennis shoes and caught her wrinkling her nose. "What now?"

"No socks either, Roxy?" Bryony led the way back out to the balcony and down the stairs.

I liked that our tower staircase was on the outside and that all our rooms faced outwards. Escape felt easier with this setup. There were no halls to run through or get lost in. With my past being what it was, the way out was important.

"After our walk about, you should really talk to the guys." Bryony paused on the fourth landing and took a deep breath.

My shoulder lifted and fell. "I think we're fine as is."

"We're a team, Roxy. All part of the same tower. We need to be able to trust and work together. Especially the VP, since it's pretty clear by this point that Vidar will be finalized as president and you as vice president." Bryony eyed the rest of the stairs. "Why are we on the eighth floor again?"

"Not afraid of heights." I continued down the stairs and smiled when she cursed behind me. Remy, my twin brother, and I had crazy endurance after running away from the pride. We weren't wolves, but I bet we could keep pace with them pretty well.

A wolf won't catch us again. Missy dismissed the very idea.

I entered the common room instead of following the balcony around to the bridge and glanced around. My eyes landed on Vidar and Tyr sharing a couch. The green-eyed monster rose to the forefront for a moment before I wrestled her back down. Neither of them were mine for me to feel jealous.

The way they were positioned was so . . . intimate, I almost wanted to tell them to get a room. At the same time, there was nothing vulgar about the way Tyr slept with his head in Vidar's lap while his companion read a book. Vidar's free hand ran absently through Tyr's long hair. They were definitely more than friends.

Missy whined and wanted to go join them. Rub all over them and scent mark them. I ignored her crazy. *Not today, Satan.*

I turned away from them to the whiteboard taking up more than half the wall in the commons. We decided to use it for important tower information, and so far it had come in handy.

Bryony wasn't kidding when she said Vidar and I led the votes. The numbers on the whiteboard didn't lie. I grinned when I saw she led the votes as secretary. I studied the notes on what my tower meant to me, while waiting for my bestie to catch up. Our idea of using a snake for a mascot since our tower was named for a snake seemed to take hold as well, and there were several suggestions to which type to use.

Infiniti—or Fin, as she liked to be called—came into the room with Bryony. The brunette was a sensible girl and friendly enough. I didn't make new friends easily, but I liked her. I didn't eavesdrop on their conversation, though I could.

"Proof is in the numbers." Bryony stepped up next to me as Fin walked away and studied the board.

"I'm not a leader." I ignored Missy's growl. She thought we were, which was an ongoing problem I fought to fix. Being trained to be an alpha and actually being an alpha were two different things. Uncle Mike and even Sheriff Kasun, acting as alpha for one of the wolf packs in Havenwood Falls, were true alphas. I had nowhere near their levels of authority, and living here, I never would, which I was just fine with.

"And I don't speak to All Mother. Come on, you need exercise." She flounced out, and I followed more slowly. I understood what she said, but I didn't *want* to be a leader, and that had to count for something, right?

Dim light came in through the skylight in the mountain. I studied it, and it almost reminded me of being inside a volcano, if Colorado had volcanoes. I would need to go out on the cliffs on my next day off to get some real sun since the mountaintop didn't allow for direct light anywhere but on the quad.

I didn't need a clock to tell me it was still early morning. After twenty hours of sleep, I wasn't tired, despite the hour, but it was a little early to be running around. Not for the first time in the last seven days, I wished Remy was here.

Being without my twin was still a new sensation. In my head, I knew Remy needed to live his best life just as I did, but my heart ached with his absence. Remy's road was different than mine. I prayed Ryker kept him out of dangerous trouble. When it came to SIN, the local motorcycle club, trouble was something they were comfortable with and not something I wanted my brother embroiled in, but his choices were . . . his.

Bryony grabbed my hand and brought me out of my thoughts. "We've got enough time for a run on the cliff before Addie's last campus tour. Unless you want to hit the dining hall and grab breakfast?"

"Tour?" My feet rooted to the spot. I'd avoided the large group tours for the last week. I liked people, I did, but I dealt with enough of them at Coffee Haven. I was pretty sure I practically knew everyone—and their coffee preferences—already.

Her grip tightened to steel levels. "You've been avoiding everything and everyone but necessities for the last week. This is home for the next while, Roxy. You've got to get to know it past your room and your job. Especially with classes starting in a few days. Come on. I think you need food first and coffee."

"You know I don't drink coffee." It was a quirk of mine

Willow, owner of Coffee Haven, found amusing. Coffee wired my cat, and she was already high strung.

"Make an exception." Bryony didn't let go of my arm as she dragged me into Halstein and through the dining hall doors.

Breakfast of at least five different regions filled the canteen line. There was even a waffle maker and a dark sludge they called coffee. After a sniff, it was clear why Coffee Haven had brisk business over in the Student Union.

I felt gracious enough after the full meal to go along with Bryony's plan. We descended the stairs into the quad where a bunch of other students mingled. Not all the faces were familiar, which was surprising with all the coffee I served. Then again, on a campus of almost two hundred students, knowing everyone would be a feat though, with the way Bryony acknowledged everyone, I wondered if she somehow managed it.

Tyr caught my eye and blew me a kiss. I scowled even as a small level of excitement trickled through my emotions. I needed to get my head checked.

Vidar sent me a smile that flashed his pearly whites. They must have sat in the commons waiting for the tour to start. I briefly wondered what their majors were, but told myself it didn't really matter to me.

Addie Beaumont, the witch who activated both my tattoo for town and my tattoo for school, joined our little crowd. "Welcome to Halvard. I'll be your tour guide today. The campus is a little on the large side for being inside the mountain, but I'm sure we'll all get used to it in time. Please follow me."

I listened with half an ear as Addie launched into what sounded like a prepared spiel or, considering the timing, a speech she'd given way more times than once. The group as a whole followed her around the campus like she was a pied piper. Addie looked super excited with every new piece of information she provided, despite it not being her first tour.

My brain noted the Halls important to me, though I already knew where they were from a shifted jog a few days ago. The little

Haldor building, which was partially underground, for all my tech classes. Eirhal if I got injured in the combat classes in Steiver. I wasn't planning on getting hurt, but it was always good to be prepared.

By the time we did the walkthrough of Halstein, the main hall, Tyr had wormed his way to my right side. Curiously, he didn't smell like wet dog today. Shifters should always smell the same, so if he wasn't a shifter, what was he?

I almost asked him about it several times, but then thought it would look like I was interested. And I wasn't. Just curious. Mostly curious, and we all knew what curiosity did to the cat.

We entered a room that made me think of museums. Look don't touch. There were all sorts of interesting looking artifacts on display and a table of hourglasses caught my eye. They were unlike anything I'd ever seen before. Each one was a different size, color, and shape. I didn't think there were different ways to make an hourglass, but the table display proved me wrong.

"Weird, huh? I never understood magical artifacts." The guy to my left smiled. His accent was enough to determine his origin. British, I thought. He extended his hand. "I'm Gable. Finally got around to the tour after settling in."

"Roxy. Magic artifacts tend to be weird in my experience." I controlled my flinch as a memory surfaced. The voodoo witch from Virginia came to mind. Her artifacts were . . . eccentric, to say it nicely. I changed the subject. "Where are you from?"

"A tiny place in Australia. A witch came and said I had talent. Asked me to take a test. You?" His head cocked, tipping sun-streaked hair into his jeweled eyes.

"Grew up in Virginia. Live in town now with my family." I would have said more, but I noticed Tyr's low growl. When I looked over at him, his eyes were on Gable and his face hard. There was something in Tyr's look that pleased my cat. She liked his possession.

"It's friendly conversation." I rolled my eyes at him. There was no reason for me to defend my conversation, but I still found myself standing up to him.

"His wasn't." Tyr's eyes flicked to my face and back to Gable. "She's not available."

"She's not a piece of steak, mate. A girl can have friends." Gable tucked his hands into his pockets and rocked back on his heels, studying Tyr.

"Your interest isn't friendly, is it . . . mate?" Tyr visibly bared his teeth, and to my surprise, they were very much canine. His eyes changed colors too, to an almost neon red. What the hell was he?

"Knock it off." My eyes darted around, noticing the attention the boys gathered. What was it with guys needing to prove their strengths? I never expected it to happen over me. Except, Missy didn't even react to Gable. Tyr had her undivided attention.

Tyr caught my hand in his as I turned away from the posturing. "I am only protecting my alpha."

Missy purred, pleased with his devotion. Crazy cat only liked him because he called her alpha. I would need to figure out how to settle her down before classes started or fighting with her would get exhausting.

"Tyr, we'll talk about this later." I held my tone low, mindful I wasn't the only supernatural creature with excellent hearing in the room and I didn't want to make their display any worse.

"I like holding your hand, alpha." Tyr grinned, purposely turning his back to Gable, and lifted our joined hands. He feathered his mouth across the back of my hand. Tingles spread from the touch like ants running under my skin.

"We will talk later." I spoke through clenched teeth, hating all the attention we were under.

"Hey, mate. You're making the lady uncomfortable." Gable's statement drew Tyr's focus again.

Tyr squared up, standing between Gable and me. While Tyr had more muscle, Gable was a smidgen taller. Without knowing what either of them was, a fight could go either way.

I searched the room for help, but even Vidar stood in a relaxed pose. Bryony shrugged her shoulders when I lifted a brow at her. Addie was on the far side of the room in deep conversation with another student over an artifact that looked like a chest. She'd be no help in time either if this came to blows.

With an internal sigh, I placed a hand on Tyr's tense arm, stepping closer to him. "He's not worth getting expelled over." As an afterthought I appealed to his chivalry. "You can't protect me if you're not here."

After a long breath, he relaxed under my hand. He nodded. "As you wish, alpha."

Gable snorted, rolled his eyes, and shoulder-checked Tyr as he moved past. The passive aggressive action hit Tyr hard enough to knock him back into me. I stumbled, unexpectedly off balance.

My momentum tumbled me into the table of hourglasses. The table shook, and the glass tinkled as they clinked against each other. One of the hourglasses tipped forward, toward the floor.

Everything seemed to move in slow motion. I lunged for the falling hourglass, afraid of it shattering on the stone floor. When my hand closed around the artifact, the thing lit up like a Christmas tree. Blinding blue light arced out of the hourglass like a blast wave from a bomb. A loud gonging sound rang through the room, or that could've been my ears ringing.

I gasped as fire burned into my school tattoo and let go of the hourglass. The creepy glowing artifact floated in the air, lifting itself up and back onto the table. The sand, a weird, almost electric blue, ran in a steady flow from top to bottom.

Something told me if I tried to flip it back, the thing wouldn't be moving. Still, foolish hope was still hope. The damn thing felt glued to the table when I tried to turn it back over.

"Roxy, are you okay?" Addie's brow furrowed as she pushed through the students. Her eyes landed on the hourglass, and the line between her brows deepened. "That's the second time I've heard that gong. We can't even find whatever's causing it."

When she reached for my arm, I realized I had clamped my right hand over the school tattoo. I moved my hand, surprised there was no grizzly burn on my arm. The tattoo reflected the same weird blue glow as the sand but otherwise looked intact. When it shifted into an hourglass, my stomach clenched, and I wondered what the hell I got myself into.

Addie ran a finger over my tattoo, her eyes going out of focus for a moment in concentration. I could smell the light ozone of a witch's spell. She sighed and held my gaze when she opened her eyes. "Next time, let the artifact hit the floor. There's a timer tied to you now, though it's not letting me determine for how long, or for what."

Nerves made me want to puke. A timer meant an ending and if she didn't know what it was for, how was I supposed to? Life just got infinitely more difficult.

CHAPTER 2

There was no good way to say, "I'm sorry for touching a magical device I was only supposed to look at." At the same time, it hadn't been my intent. I wasn't sure who to blame—Tyr for his posturing or Gable for goading him. Since Gable did the shoulder-check, he was the better of the options.

Addie continued to hold onto my arm and murmured something under her breath. I watched the tattoo's glow brighten and the smell of ozone thickened. She jerked back, shaking her hands as if burned. When she tried to speak, a donkey bray came out. Her hands slapped over her mouth, and I watched her face transform into horror. She stormed off before I could ask what was going on. Whatever magic was at play had to run its course if Addie's reaction was any indication.

Bryony came over, her eyes on Addie as the other witch ran from the room. She rested a hand on my shoulder, and I felt grounded. "Are you okay?"

I blew out a breath and glared at Tyr. "Yeah. Except a magic timer counting down for who knows what."

"May I?" She held up a hand.

I held my arm against my chest. "I think that's what Addie did, and it made her sound like a donkey."

"Trying to alter something not meant for you can be dangerous. It's obviously not meant for her to fix. I only want to look." Bryony continued to hold out her hand until I relented.

"Hmm." Floral odors washed the air as Bryony worked. "Well, the magic is old, whatever it is. Not as old as touching the All Mother or one of Her scions, but pretty old nonetheless. Considering some of these artifacts are older than the town, that's not really a surprise though."

"What's it for?" I pulled my sleeve down when she let go.

Bryony shook her head. "That I can't tell you, and that's likely what clapped back at Addie. By physical appearance, it's obviously a timer for something."

"Duh." I rolled my eyes.

Bryony shrugged. "You'll figure it out. You've got that big brain, and we've got a couple of big brains in our tower—"

I shook my head. "It's my mess, my problem to fix. Don't worry about it, Bree."

Her fingers squeezed. "Stubborn. Remember we're a team, Roxy. If you need us, we're here."

"Thanks, but I think I'd rather go down with the ship alone than take any of you with me. It's my problem. I'll fix it." Hopefully the timer didn't count down to my death. I didn't really want to die trying.

In the next instant, every cell phone in the room chimed with a message. Bryony lifted her brows but pulled her phone out of a pocket and swiped the screen. I waited, since my phone was back in the room, to see if it was some school wide message we should all be aware of.

"Weird." Bryony turned her phone so I could see.

WE KNOW WHAT YOU ARE.

I frowned. Catching Tyr's eye, I lifted a brow. He looked as puzzled as Bryony and turned his phone for me to see the same message.

"A prank?" I voiced, but it seemed unlikely.

The words weren't really threatening, but I felt threatened. Since we spent our lives living off the radar, anything that implied we were found out was certainly unsettling. However, the wards around Havenwood Falls kept us safe and kept us secret. A little voice reminded me we weren't technically in Havenwood Falls anymore. The wards would still apply, wouldn't they?

With the pinched faces and worried whispers around me, I didn't give sound to my thoughts. Why incite even more confusion? When I got back to the room, I'd grab my laptop and phone and head down to the tech commons. I should only need a couple of hours to backward trace the text message.

It was probably a student, playing some grotesque joke. Maybe some kind of hazing process, like at a human college. Well, when I traced the data, whoever it was, was going to get a piece of my mind.

Putting a plan together, I stretched and yawned. "I'm going to excuse myself and go take a nap. I think I've had enough excitement for one day."

"I can walk you back." Bryony moved to go with me, but I shook my head.

"I know the way. Finish your tour." Not that there was much of a tour to finish without Addie. I hurried out before she could point out the flaw in my statement.

Being organized to the extent of OCD came with some perks. One of them being knowing where everything was the first time around. My purse, where I had my phone last, hung on the desk chair, and my laptop graced the surface of the desk with its carrying case tucked under the desk. I was in and out of the room in minutes with my bags slung over a shoulder.

The tech commons weren't as empty as they had been when we toured through. A girl with a serious face sat by herself in a corner chair, working on her laptop. Two other girls shared a couch, making faces for their phones. I wrinkled my nose and made my way over to an empty chair at a study table. A sandy haired guy sat at the other end with a Coffee Haven cup and a tablet.

I thought I recognized him, but there were a lot of faces to remember. "Excuse me."

He looked up with a guarded smile. "Yes?"

I gave him my best customer service smile and pointed to the far end of the table by the wall with the outlets. "Hi, I'm Roxy. Can I sit here?"

He blinked his pretty brown eyes and glanced down at the cup. "Eryx. I don't need the whole table."

"Thanks." I moved away from him and took a seat. I set up, plugged my phone into my laptop, and got to work.

Two hours later and a million different angles, and I still couldn't find the culprit. I always lost the trail when it hit the school's servers. Following an established path shouldn't be more difficult than cracking home security systems. Sure, my skill wasn't something to be proud of, but running for your life meant doing whatever needed to survive. And that skill got me into Halvard to begin with. I shoved the computer away in disgust and nearly jumped out of my skin when I noticed the man sitting directly across from me.

His blue eyes danced with amusement, and he flashed a set of fangs when he smiled. A vampire, which explained why I didn't hear him sit down, but that didn't explain why he wore glasses. "I'm Professor Kincaid. You need to practice focused awareness. In the field, zoning out like that could get you killed."

"Oh." The name rang familiar. He taught two of the classes I signed up for this semester. "I'm Roxy McCabe. I have your Anatomy of Computer Systems and Cyber Security Basics this semester."

"Welcome to class then, Miss McCabe. You seemed to be working on something important." He didn't word it like a question, but since he was the Cyber teacher, maybe he could tell me what I was doing wrong.

"I'm trying to track the path of the weird text message we got." I gestured to the laptop. "But it's not cooperating."

"Are you a hacker, Miss McCabe?" He tipped his head, considering me.

I let out a sigh. "No. More like an unlocker. I can get around passwords or security keys, but I've only ever tried at the source. I've never tried getting into a security I wasn't hard linked into."

"You're hardly skilled then, to track a hacker that sent a message to over two hundred students in the same second."

The matter-of-fact statement wasn't meant to hurt. At least, I didn't think he was trying to put me down. However, I felt like he just bitch-slapped me. Of course my skills were lacking, but there was no need to point it out like that.

Missy's tail floofed up, and she growled. *He's not polite.*

"So are you going to do it?" I avoided his gaze by packing up my electronics.

"No. One text message with vague content isn't something the Court or the Board of Regents is concerned with."

"That's pretty neglectful."

His fingers drummed on the table, and he pulled off his glasses, tapping the end of the earpiece against his mouth for a moment. "If you want to solve the mystery of who sent the message, you're going to need more knowledge. Let me give you a list of books to look up at the library. They should help you on your path and give you a kick-start to class. Your cyber textbook would also be helpful if you picked up your books already."

I nodded but didn't admit to not stopping at the bookstore yet. "Sure. I'd like to know more."

"I'll give you some book recommendations for Anatomy too. You've probably never built a computer either, and you're going to need that skill for my class as well." He replaced his glasses and pulled a little flip notebook out of the inside pocket of his jacket along with a pen.

I struggled to wait as he wrote down what he thought I needed. My shift at Coffee Haven wasn't until much later—Willow wanted to accommodate the nocturnal among us—so I had time. With the hourglass running down on my arm, though, who knew how much time I had before meeting whatever destiny that magic had in mind.

CHAPTER 3

I dropped everything off in my room before venturing into the library. While in my room, I grabbed one of the LED flashlights Uncle Mike dropped into my belongings when he thought I wasn't looking. Originally, I thought eight flashlights and two lanterns were overkill, but after the last few hours walking around, some of the shadows were still deep enough to be uncomfortable, even during the day.

The library deserved to be on a list of magnificent locations. Even entering through the side door from the sky bridge didn't lessen the grandeur of the mezzanine and lobby. Whoever built this place knew exactly what they were doing.

Magic orbs glowed on polished wood tables and at intervals on waist high bookcases strewn about the mezzanine. No students sat around yet, but I had no doubt once the semester started next week, the library would be busier. At the moment, the almost perfect silence felt kind of holy.

A circular reference desk sat in the middle of it all, and my gaze was drawn upward as I approached the young woman behind the computer. The stacks rising above in multiple levels gave new meaning to cathedral ceiling. It was almost as if the center of the library was hollow and the stacks were the beams of support for the other floors. Bridges crisscrossed in no particular pattern, leading from one side to the other and disappeared into the darkness of the higher levels. If someone fell from a bridge, the results could be fatal depending on the level they were on.

I studied the woman texting on her phone at the desk. How the hell did she have any signal? Huge round, wire-framed glasses slipped down a freckled nose. Her lavender hair was half pulled up in moon buns while the other half curled wildly around her shoulders. If I judged by the color of her eyebrows, then her hair color was natural, but she didn't look fae, which was the only species I knew of with natural purple hair colors.

"Take a picture. It lasts longer." She didn't even glance up from the phone.

My nose wrinkled. "Sorry. I like your hair."

She did glance up then, pinning me with eyes that looked like molten pewter. After a moment she smiled. "It's a spell." She snapped her fingers, and all her hair changed to a vibrant green. "I'm happy to do one for you for twenty dollars, but if you're a shifter, that affects your animal's hair too. It'll last for six months."

No. Definitely not. Missy sulked while I contemplated a shade of brown or black. How many would mistake me as a panther with black hair? The idea pleased me.

I stepped up to the desk. "Can you do black? And not for six months, at least not to start. Maybe six days to test it out?"

"Sure." She studied me a moment then shrugged her shoulders. "I'll do the six day spell for free. If anyone asks you about it, you send them to me, yeah?"

"I can do that." I blinked when she snapped her fingers, and my skin tingled.

"All done." She grinned.

I pulled out my ponytail and played with the black strands. Since my cat didn't like the smell of the chemicals used to color hair, I never had anything other than natural. "This is all hair?"

"Yup. Six days. Twenty bucks for six months, so just let me

know if you want to continue it. We could add a touch of blue so it's a blue black too, instead of the hard flat black, if you want a smidge of color."

"I'll think about it. I need some books, too." I put my list from Professor Kincaid on the desktop before pulling my ponytail back up.

She snapped her hair back to the violet before scanning over my list. "Oh, I've read some of these. What are you in for?"

I blinked at her phrasing. "Special Ops—Tech."

"Fab. Me too. I'm Dillys. Modi Tower. You?" She handed the list back.

"Roxy. Jormungand Tower. I noticed you were texting . . ." I glanced at where she set her phone down.

"Magic infused tech. It's my specialty. Well, when it works. Most of the time it does. I've got some with me." She fished into her pocket and pulled out a headphone jack plug with a little blue stone ball on the top. "Fifty bucks, and you'll have signal no matter where you are on campus with a couple of exceptions. I'm working on those, but magic doesn't always play nice. Money back guarantee."

"Is soliciting allowed on campus?"

She rolled her eyes but tucked her device away. "I haven't been told not to yet. The books you want are up on floor five, section seven, row nine. Please, don't touch anything other than the books you're looking for. One of the profs found a less than friendly, sentient book earlier. There's rumored to be more up there. You wouldn't want to be on the receiving end of an accidental curse."

I pointedly looked at the computer she had yet to use. "You didn't even look them up."

"Sweets, I looked up all the computer books the moment I got behind this desk as a volunteer last week. The books you want are up there. Elevator is there or there." She pointed to either side of the room. I grimaced at the rickety looking iron contraption. That wasn't an elevator. That was death incarnate.

"And the stairs?"

"Behind the elevators."

"Thanks, Dillys."

"My friends call me Dils. See you in class, Roxy."

Upon closer inspection of the elevator, I decided the tower could have a bomb in it and I would never step foot in the metal monstrosity. The device suited the age-old feel of the place, but there was no way that thing was safe. I'd need a tetanus shot just from looking at it.

Magic hummed in the air when I reached the fifth floor. I almost hated to think what kind of oppressive weight it would be on the higher levels. I never asked anyone why I could feel magic in use or ambient as this was, nor have I ever questioned if it was an only me thing.

Some things were best left alone. My mother was a cougar, but I had no idea who her parents were, and some things I knew came down to blood. Purity was a big deal in the Virginia Pride. The matriarchs had a fit when Dad found his true mate, and we talked about it as little as possible. The males of the pride belonged to them, and Dad broke almost every rule to be with his mate. I was content to leave it in the grave with my parents.

Orbs on the end of the stacks turned themselves on as I approached but did nothing to light the way down the rows. A number two graced the stack nearest to me under the orb and next to it, the three. As I walked deeper into the library, I fished out the flashlight I tucked away. Stopping at the end of a row, I aimed the beam down the aisle and heard something skitter backward into the darkness.

Joy. Magic creatures of darkness in the library. Hopefully harmless since no one bothered to call an exterminator.

With a flick of my wrist, the beam moved upward, and I sighed. The bookcases were at the very least almost three times my height. Hopefully all the books I wanted were on my level or I'd have to get creative on retrieval.

Curious, I aimed the light into the blackness above a bridge, and the beam seemed to be swallowed by the dark only a few feet up. If someone did fall from the upper levels, only their screams would mark their passing until they hit the light on the mezzanine level. I shuddered and turned my attention away from mystical death, and back to my book quest.

Section seven turned out to be three aisles of computer focused books. Everything from making the components from scratch to advanced server maintenance. If I was a dragon, this would definitely be my hoard. Staring at the bookcase, I realized Dillys never gave me the call numbers for any of the books. I hoped the books were easily found or my flashlight could die, leaving me in the dark with whatever made skittering noises just outside the radius of light.

They are not a threat to us. Missy focused on the darkness beyond. *But do not linger here.*

Even without her warning, I agreed with her.

My eyes scanned the shelves I could see without tiptoeing or straining my neck. I found one of the eight books on the lower shelves, and after a second pass through the rows, I realized I would need to find a way to check the shelves soaring over my head. With a sigh, I set my found book at the end of the stacks under the orb. I hoped it didn't return to the shelves by some act of magic.

I stuck the flashlight in my mouth and tested my weight on the shelves. As a shifter, most of me was muscle weight. The frame of the stacks were stone but the actual shelf was wooden. I worried the wood would snap under my weight. The grainy slab groaned when I climbed on it but otherwise held.

Five trips up and down, and I had a stack of seven books. The last book graced the highest shelf of the last bookcase in the last row. As my hand closed over my book, another one jumped forward and slammed against my chest with the force of a ton of bricks and an electric shock powerful enough to make all my muscles spasm.

My vision spotted as the air whooshed out of my lungs. The flashlight clamped in my teeth clattered to the ground as my muscles twitched, and my hand released the shelf before I could force myself back in control. There was no time to scream.

I closed my eyes and let instincts turn us in the air. Landing on my hands and feet was going to hurt from this height, but not as bad as landing on my back. There was too much current from the jab for me to shift and no time to panic about it. Instead of striking the floor, I landed against another body, and arms wrapped around my torso. A deep inhale brought a familiar scent to my nose, and I relaxed, taking another deep breath before assessing my situation.

Huge spotted wings filled my vision when I opened my eyes. I glanced up beyond the wings that cradled us against the floor, into Vidar's worried gaze. Even though I had known it was him from the scent, a wash of dizzy relief dropped my head against his chest, and Missy audibly purred her contentment within his hold.

"Are you injured?" He ran his hands up and down, checking for damage even as he asked.

I shook my head, unable to make the purring stop. He smelled divine and felt wonderful under me. The cougar provided imagery of him under us in a much less innocent way. Damned creature must be in heat or something, which of course wasn't possible because we weren't old enough yet.

"What were you doing up there? Why didn't you put a request for pick up in?" He didn't make any move to release me, and I made no move to get up yet. In fact, I shifted just enough to press a little more of me up against his firm warmth. Gods, he felt good.

"You have wings." Perhaps not the smartest thing to come out of my mouth, but I still marveled over them. My hand reached out and touched the feathers closest. They look like they belonged to an owl of sorts with their spotting. Vidar shivered at my touch but didn't tell me to stop.

"My mother's a Valkyrie. Of course I have wings. You're avoiding the subject." He shifted a wing to fold over us so I could reach it better.

"It's a library. I didn't really think it could be dangerous. They wouldn't let us in here if it was." I ran my fingers along the offered wing. Soft, like a sherpa blanket.

"It's a school for warriors. Danger comes with the lessons. The library may be a lesson in itself."

"Never thought of it that way." I dropped my hand and lifted my head to look at him. His eyes were half closed, and I would swear he was drunk if not for the steady cadence of his words. "Thanks for the save by the way."

His eyes caught mine, and I lost my breath for the second time. Vidar was beautiful in his own exotic way. It wasn't only his appearance either. Vidar felt safe, and since that was something I struggled with on a daily basis, safe was a surprising aphrodisiac.

Missy purred louder, and I watched his lips quirk. I could kiss him in the quiet dark of the library, and no one would ever know. I licked my lips and leaned up.

"This is different." His hand moved to play in my hair. The same as he had with Tyr this morning in the common room. The realization was the perfect slap of reality, and I jerked back, jumping to my feet.

This was Tyr's boyfriend. Vidar was already taken. I wasn't interested in guys at this time. What the hell was I doing? This wasn't me. My lust-fogged brain needed a reality check. We weren't homewreckers, or boyfriend thieves or whatever it would be called.

"I'm sorry. Thanks again for the save." I snatched up my book from the floor where it fell and hurried away without looking back.

"Roxy." His voice followed me, but I didn't turn to look at him. My cheeks burned with shame and embarrassment.

What had come over me? Kissing a taken man, really? I felt hot all over, and my skin felt too tight. Maybe I really should go get a checkup.

Missy hissed and growled her displeasure.

He's not ours, I told her. *Get over it.*

Mate, she cried back.

Like hell he was. Magnetism over a gorgeous body and vibrant mind didn't make him a mate, and we weren't old enough yet. That awakening didn't happen until after our eighteenth birthday at the end of the year.

The crazy cat roared at what she considered my stubbornness. I ignored her tantrum and collected my other books, hurrying toward the stairs. Guilt and disappointment ate at me as I fled.

I needed to talk to Tyr and apologize. If he was anything like other shifters, I'd accept a beating too, and then everything would be fine again. I hoped.

CHAPTER 4

Coffee Haven cup set down next to my monitor drew my attention. Books were scattered around my laptop like casualties of war, and the device itself still hummed and clicked. I glanced up from my screen of programming to see Gable sipping from his own cup. My nose wrinkled over the bitter smell of black coffee.

He smiled. "It's a bit early to be slaving away over lessons, eh? I thought classes started on Monday?"

"Working on something else. You got me a coffee?" I picked up the cup and sniffed. The black coffee wasn't in my cup.

"I saw you at Coffee Haven last night and wanted to talk to you then, but you seemed a bit busy. I thought perhaps this was a better idea." He set his cup down. "I'm sorry for making you uncomfortable yesterday."

"Have you apologized to Tyr yet?" The words rolled off my tongue before I could think them through. He did really owe Tyr an apology more than me. I tasted the tea he must have seen me drinking last night.

Gable flinched. "No. It didn't appear you were really interested in his attention."

Missy snorted and turned her back on Gable.

"I'm not really interested in anyone's attention, but Tyr and I share a tower. Besides, rudeness is rudeness. Regardless to whom it's directed. I expect him to apologize to you as well."

"Duly noted." He looked like he swallowed a lemon.

A slammed door jolted both of us. We glanced over to find Tyr scanning the space. The table I set up last night after work was in a corner out of the way, and by the outlet. When he marched our way, dread pooled in my stomach, but I had nowhere to run to.

After fleeing the library yesterday, and Dillys coming to my rescue when I found out there was a five book checkout limit, I spent the rest of the day at work worrying over how to deal with Tyr. I still wasn't sure how to apologize for almost kissing his boyfriend, and I didn't want to have to do it in front of Gable either.

If looks could kill, Gable was certainly a dead man. Tyr pulled out my chair, and before I could protest, lifted me up to sit with me in his lap. His claim was disgustingly clear, and any kind of protest might start another fight between the men. Tyr's narrowed eyes held a serious intensity that I hadn't seen before from him. The man was always so cavalier.

"Why don't you pee on her leg, mate? Might be faster all around." Gable continued to calmly drink his coffee.

Tyr shifted so he could look down into my face. Today he reeked of earth and green. As if he went for a run on the cliffs. There was something uber pleasant about the scent, and if we were standing, I might have gone a little weak in the knees. "Roxy, can we pee on your leg?"

The ridiculousness of it stole a laugh out of me. "No, Tyr. You cannot pee on my leg."

"Worth a try." Tyr shrugged. "Vidar and I would like a proper conversation with you. Over breakfast, if it pleases you. We'll buy, of course."

Maybe he talked to Vidar, and that's why he sought me out. Well, I knew this was coming. I hoped everything was okay between them. I did my best to ignore Gable's interested stare. "I'm sorry."

Tyr glared at the other man. "We're trying to have a moment. Do you mind?"

Gable shrugged a shoulder. "I was here first. Is it customary in this country for a woman to hold a man by his balls?"

Both Tyr and I growled. Missy hadn't liked his implication one bit.

Gable held up both hands. "Right, right. I should find something else to do."

The Australian took his coffee with him as he left the tech hall. Tyr rubbed his cheek against every inch of exposed skin he could reach with me on his lap as I watched Gable leave. As soon as the door closed, I shoved him away and would have jumped out of his lap if he hadn't wrapped his arms around me.

"Scent marking is as potent as peeing on my leg." I squirmed enough to shift facing him.

"Vidar smelled like you for some time yesterday." His words froze me in place.

"He caught me from a fall. I'm sorry. It won't happen again."

"You should stay away from Gable or have Vidar or me with you." Tyr glared at the door as if he could see Gable on the other side of it.

"Jealous much?" I crossed my arms.

Tyr lifted a brow. "What do you smell from him?"

I blinked. "What?"

"Gable's scent, kitten. Your nose is probably one of the strongest on campus with the exception of the wolves, probably an old vampire or two. Maybe a jackal—"

"I get it." I cut him off before he could add to his asinine list. "Gable is—"

My brow furrowed. Nothing. Other than his coffee I hadn't smelled anything. No body sweat, no cologne, no animal. Nothing. Even a ghost had residual scent. Gable defied natural order with his lack.

"Now you understand. I can't trust something that hides their nature." Tyr wrapped his arms a little tighter. "I don't like his interest in you."

"Maybe he's some weird Australian thing, and he doesn't want to be judged for his creature." I don't know why I had to defend him. Even Missy was indifferent about Gable, but that was likely because she couldn't scent him.

"Perhaps, but why trust someone that can't be tracked? And he could have always done what you did. Your charm keeps your true scent to your personal space, but we all still know you're a cat." He had a good point.

A subject change was in order. "What did you and Vidar want to talk about?"

"You purred for Vid." He leaned forward and pressed his forehead to mine, never breaking eye contact.

"Huh?" Not the topic I expected. Missy pranced to and fro, all too eager for his direct attention. The hussy.

"In the library. Yesterday. You *purred* for Vidar." His eyes searched mine, looking for something. I had no clue what.

We can purr for him too, the damn cat offered, and I shut her out for the moment before we did something stupid. We were too intertwined for me to silence her for any length of time, but hopefully she'd take the hint.

"I didn't kiss him. I stopped. It might have been last minute, and I should have never considered it, but I didn't kiss your boyfriend."

His brows drew together. "Is there something wrong with Vidar?"

"What?" My hand rubbed over my face. I stilled when Tyr released his hold to cup my face in his hands. My eyes fell shut against my will as he rubbed a gentle line with his thumbs.

"Vidar. Is there something wrong with him?" His breath was too close. Close enough for me to kiss him as well.

I opened my eyes jerking away from his too comfortable touch. "No, of course not, obviously, or I wouldn't have momentarily lost my mind. Are we discussing the same thing? I almost kissed your boyfriend, but you don't seem angry at that part of the debacle."

His lips quirked. "I share everything with Vidar, kitten. And I do mean everything. We are battle brothers, and that's almost more powerful than blood. To love me means to love him as well. And he is the same with me. You don't get one without the other."

It took a long moment for his meaning to sink in, and yet my brain refused to acknowledge that's what he meant. "Listen, I'm sorry for almost kissing your boyfriend. It won't happen again."

"Oh it most definitely will, pussy cat. Vidar's a little shy though, so he's likely going to wait for you to be comfortable with it. I am not shy in the least, so I'll make this a little even for you." Tyr lowered his mouth, and I stiffened when his lips feathered over mine. My pulse jumped and an unfamiliar zing raced through my body.

Instinct arced my back and pressed my body into Tyr's. My hands moved to rest on his shoulders before my brain even gave the command. He murmured something I didn't catch and ran light kisses down my jaw, nipping at my neck light enough to be considered a tease. Emotions I didn't understand twisted and knotted creating confusion and a touch of fear.

Mate. Missy pressed forward while I sat foggy minded and burning with a fire I'd never felt before. Hadn't she just yesterday declared Vidar mate? What the hell was wrong with her? We can't have two mates.

The shock ran so deep, I couldn't stop Missy's very vocal purr of approval. Tyr's grin split his face when he leaned back. "There's my pussy cat. I was worried you didn't like me. Do me a favor, when you mark us, mark Vidar first. He'll try to find some excuse as to why I should keep you for myself or some shit."

My cheeks felt entirely too warm, and I shoved to my feet. I paced away then back. What the hell was happening?

Mark them? Like hell I would. That would be a disaster I didn't want on top of my already complicated mess.

We will. The confidence of the cat bothered me. Our wills were about equal, but when she enforced herself on a topic, I rarely overrode her decision. There was no way for me to have a mate yet. I wasn't mature enough. I clung to that fact like a lifeline. They couldn't be mates. I hadn't reached the age yet.

His gaze turned to the table for the first time, and I could feel tension rolling off him. "How long have you been working?"

"I want to find the ass that thought it was funny to prank the school." A huge yawn cracked my jaw as I sidled back up to the table and jiggled the mouse. If he wanted to act like he hadn't teased me into a puddle of shock and confusion, I would go along with it. I could spend some time later to figure out the tangled mess of want and emotions I didn't need.

The program stopped on the run by appearances. There were a lot more glitches to work out than I anticipated. Hacking in code wasn't as easy as password cracking.

"What could be so important that you cut hours of sleep?" Tyr stood and offered my chair back.

"Don't you have someone else to annoy?" I sighed, sitting down, and realized he had no intentions of leaving me alone.

"I've declared Vid's and my intentions so you should probably get used to our company. We'll wear you down, kitten. Everyone needs someone at the end of the day."

"I'm not interested in dating, or sex, or any other relationship activities. I'm here for learning and growth. Not you."

"No reason you can't do both."

Our phones chimed together and I reached for mine without responding to his ridiculous statement. I had no intention of dating one man let alone two of them. They interested me for sure, but I knew what a mate bond was supposed to feel like and I didn't feel anything like that toward either of them. Though that moment sitting on Tyr's lap came really close. Thank the spirits I wasn't of age yet.

I focused in on the last execution. Failed again, but I was close. I could feel it. If I could just figure out the specific lines for location . . . as far as I could tell my code worked up until the point where it hit the school servers then it lost the trail. After several dozen different methods, all provided by the textbooks no less, I should have a different result. I was missing something. What was that old saying, insanity was doing the same thing repeatedly but expecting different results?

With disgust I turned from the laptop and checked the message that came through.

WE ARE WATCHING.

With dread in my stomach and my heart in my throat, I clicked on the attachment. In the file were screenshots from what looked like the school security cameras. There was even a picture of some fae gathered in the quad without glamour, and another of a bear and a wolf wrestling. This wasn't good, but the new message provided me a fresh path to chase.

I looked up at Tyr. His jaw clenched, and his white-knuckle grip on the phone made the device groan.

"Tyr."

He took a deep breath and turned the phone for me to see. Same message. Again. So the entire school would wake up to it, if they didn't wake up to the chime.

My gut told me this wasn't a student being an ass. This was something else, something bigger. To just harass us was strange. They knew something or were reaching for something, though I couldn't put my thumb on what that would be.

"I'm trying to figure out who's sending the message. That's why I haven't really slept yet." I scrubbed my hands over my face and rested my elbows on the tabletop.

"Why?" Tyr cocked his head at me, and his frown told me he didn't like what he saw.

"Why?"

"Yes. Why does it matter who? Can't you make them stop instead?"

"That's kind of the purpose of finding out who."

He ran a hand through his hair and tugged on the ends quite hard before letting it go. "No. I mean, can't you cut them off so they can't send any more messages to begin with? Why does it matter who's sending the messages? Just force them to stop. Lock them out."

Lock them out. The thought looped. Certainly locking them out would stop the chilling messages, wouldn't it? I needed alternative books. Professor Kincaid could help with that, I was sure.

I also needed sleep—real sleep not catnaps between code tests —and a shower. I could almost smell myself, which wasn't good. Food went on the list when my stomach grumbled. When was the last time I ate?

Breakfast, yesterday, my cat groused, clearly not happy with our empty stomach.

There was no way the dining hall or Student Union was open at half past four. Tyr grabbed my books as I began stacking them up. There was nothing more I could do right now. He left me to my thoughts as I packed up the rest of my gear, and for once I didn't mind his company as he followed behind.

I decided a shower, then sleep then food would be the order of business today. As much as I wanted to chase down the new message, burning the midnight oil had consequences. The screen began to blur hours ago, and I was too stubborn to admit defeat.

The dark quad was as silent as it was still as we crossed its expanse. Even the flickering flames atop their posts didn't crackle with any kind of noise. Wicked cool, and kind of creepy at the same time. My senses were on alert but other than the flames and gently glowing hourglass, nothing moved.

"There's nothing out here that can harm you while I'm present." Tyr moved to walk at my side instead of behind me.

"I don't need your protection."

"You have it anyway."

"Tyr, seriously. I don't want to have to file a complaint. Maybe we can be friends, eventually, but I'm serious about the no relationship thing. I don't have time. We have classes, I have a part time job, and I have an hourglass curse timing down to something that could quite possibly be my death." A tiny little sliver of me wished for what he offered though.

Wouldn't it be nice to have more than family to rely on? But to have more was to admit weakness. I didn't need help or additional complications to my life. We weren't weak.

"I doubt it will kill you. Though since it's half empty already, you won't have long to find out either, I suppose." Tyr gestured to the almost holographic image of the hourglass in the center of the quad.

"What?" I glanced down at my tattoo, and sure enough, the hourglass matched the visage in the quad. "But it's only been a day."

"Maybe it's like a game of hot and cold. If you're on the right path, your time is longer; if you're on the wrong path, your time is shorter."

"You think I'm not going in the direction the hourglass wants me to? I wish the magic artifact had an instruction manual." I refused to admit it out loud but he made sense. What the hell was I supposed to be doing then?

His shoulders rose and fell. "Wouldn't be a magic artifact if it came with directions. Ruins the fun and all. You spent the night in the tech commons chasing down a ghost. Does that seem like a productive use of limited time to you?"

Of course, that made sense as well. "I hate you."

"No, you don't." Tyr handed me my books back outside of my room and while my hands were full, slipped in a kiss on my forehead that was oddly comforting even if I didn't want it. "Clean up, get some sleep. Maybe visit the hourglass and meditate. Vidar and I are both in the tower chat if you need us."

Like hell I would message them. He grinned at my scowl and walked away after ruffling my hair. I so wanted to kill him.

I did my best to enter the room as quietly as possible. I didn't want to wake Bryony, and with that thought, I reevaluated my to-do list. I would strip and shift, and worry about my shower after sleeping.

"Where the hell have you been?"

I flinched at Bryony's raised voice and blinked several times when a light came on. She had an LED lantern on her nightstand that lit up the entire room. So much for being quiet.

"I lost track of time and got accosted by Tyr and Gable." I didn't meet her gaze as I turned to my side of the room then froze. A baggie of jerky sat on the desk. I grabbed it without thought and pried it open.

"Told him he might find you there." She shrugged when I glared.

"Which him did you tell?"

"Tyr. Gable's too flirty with everyone for me to take his interest seriously. Besides, Tyr and Vidar think you're their soulmate, which means a lot more to me than some horny guy."

"Seriously, Bree?" I rubbed a hand over my eyes.

"We're a team, Roxy. I'm going to keep saying it until it sinks into that thick skull of yours."

"Alpha matriarchs don't lean on others. We don't need help. We are the pillars of the pride, not the other way around." The words popped out of my mouth before I could stop them.

"You're not a matriarch here."

My hands tightened on the jerky hard enough to crumble it. The matriarchs beat their rules into me with an iron fist, and it would take time to undo their conditioning. I took a deep breath and gathered what I needed for a shower. Since Bryony was awake anyway, there was no reason not to take a shower first. "No, I'm not, am I? What would you do, if you were me?"

"Cherish every moment. You've had a rough time, Rox, and not enough happiness. Why push it away when it comes to you?" She plopped back in bed.

"Nothing is forever."

"That's why this moment counts, Roxy. Accept what's being handed to you, hold it close, and trust me, I'm pretty sure those guys will hold you just as tight. For not having a shifter's mating instincts, they are super stuck on you. Let them love you, Rox. Nothing evil ever came from true love."

"And when love dies?"

"Then you have the memories to smile over."

hump. Whump. Whump.

The punching bag remained in place as I throttled it with full force. I couldn't decide whose face I wanted it to be more as my fist connected with the object.

Visiting the physical hourglass had been a lesson in futility. The artifact hadn't changed in any way since I knocked it over, and it was definitely half empty. The thing still wouldn't turn back over either.

At this point, it was probably best to assume the device counted down to my death. Even if it didn't, wouldn't it be better to prepare and expect the worst while hoping for the best outcome? My history didn't leave me with a lot of faith I would remain whole after this ordeal.

My meeting with Addie and two of the Regents, Saundra and Elsmed, after breakfast didn't provide much information or hope either. Despite their effort to be positive.

The hourglass artifacts came with the school. Since something backfired when Addie tried to mess with it, they were working on other methods to try to figure out what was going on. The long of the short that I got out of the meeting was they couldn't help me, and I had an hourglass counting down to the unknown on my arm.

If my time was limited, what would be the best use of it? My thoughts fell to the conversation with Tyr. I hated that he was remotely right, and my fist pounded the bag a little harder.

There had to be a way to protect the school and town before my time ran out. At the very least I should be able to manage some kind of security field before I died . . . except I didn't know how.

Therein lied the rub. I needed to get help.

The only way I knew how to create the security wall was to link directly to the servers, which would require permission from Professor Kincaid or the Regents if Professor Kincaid wasn't the administrator. I didn't remember Addie mentioning the servers on our tour.

My steady rhythm fumbled when I recalled last night's disaster. Writing the code myself was a bad idea, if last night was any indication. I didn't know anyone in my emphasis who would know how to write that kind of program either.

Should I ask Dillys? She felt more gadget-oriented than coding and hacking. She might know someone, though.

I thought I saw Aithen Lanrete at breakfast, though I hadn't known he was supernatural. If that had been Aithan, then surely he would know how to help, with his dad being the man that he was. But if I asked for help, that would mean bringing others into my problem. I was stuck.

Only if you want to be. Missy flicked her tail in annoyance.

What do you know? My left fist hit the bag harder than I wanted, and pain radiated up my arm. Cursing, I stepped back from the bag, rubbing the zinging pain in my arm.

Our tower is our pride. Ask them for help. The cat surprised me.

We didn't ask for help. Ever. Even when our throat was raw from screaming and our blood stained the floor beneath us. The matriarchs—

Are not here. Missy cut off the thought.

She wasn't wrong. They weren't present to control us, and we could do whatever we wished. Including ask for help without shame.

My chest tightened, and my heart fluttered. I didn't know how to ask for help. Remy never waited for me to ask, and neither did the McCabes or Audrey. How did one go about admitting to needing assistance?

Pain continued to zing when I tried to hit the bag again. My arm would be no good for the rest of the day. With a sigh, I continued my routine without my left arm.

Bryony first. She wouldn't judge, and she would have an idea or at least she'd know who to ask. Vidar would have an idea if I couldn't find Bryony. I'd go to him if I couldn't find her.

When I struck the bag with my left by accident, I bit my tongue instead of vocalizing the agony running up my arm. The spasm nearly brought me to the mats. I needed to go see Dr. Underwood at the infirmary and see if I ripped something or if this was normal. My arm hadn't bothered me with yoga or hunting. I couldn't afford for it to bother me now.

Satisfied with my plans for the day, I moved away from the punching bag and out of the gym portion of the building. I loved how the fitness areas were broken into several different spaces in Steivar Hall. The space I left looked like a boxing gym. I crossed into what I called the yoga room—tatami mats covered the floors from door to door.

My feet froze when I realized the yoga room wasn't empty. The Asian man didn't move from his lotus pose or open his eyes. He smelled unlike anything I ever experienced before, and I wasn't sure whether or not to introduce myself, or if it would be considered rude to interrupt his meditation. After a moment of hesitation, I continued on the way out without interrupting him.

"You need to learn control and awareness." His words, while heavily accented, were clear and articulate.

I resisted a sigh. He sounded like Professor Kincaid, and while he looked around my age, I didn't doubt he could be a professor as well. I erred on the side of caution and bowed to him in karate fashion. "So I have been told."

His eyes opened, and he smiled. "You will be formidable with control. Be emotional before or after the fight. During the fight remain steadfast. You will never be defeated as long as you retain control of yourself."

Instead of answering him, I bowed again, a little lower than the first time, before walking away.

"I look forward to your growth, Roxanne McCabe." He spoke to my back, and I gave myself a mental high five for not reacting to my name. I'd heard of teachers who learned about their students before classes started. Weird but not creepy weird. At least this professor didn't feel that way.

Bryony was MIA when I returned to the room to shower off my work out, so I didn't linger and headed out to find my tower friends. When no one sat in the commons either, I frowned. Where was everyone?

I pulled my phone out and checked the tower chat. Cell signal was still nonexistent, but Wi-Fi signal was better within our towers. Not by much but enough for the chat to load. Three hundred and seventeen unread messages. The message board was full of chatter about the last threat and a comment from Caleb caught my eye.

Caleb: Are the Regents doing anything?

Bryony: Since tower elections are final tomorrow anyway, all the leading electees for tower presidents have a meeting this morning to discuss it. Vidar will let us know the plan when he gets more information.

Taylor: We'll hold down the fort.

I continued skimming backwards, and another set of messages caught my eye.

Tyr: Vidar and I would like to declare our intentions.

Bryony: Oh?

Vidar: Tyr, way to jump the tracks. Yes, though I feel like we should discuss this with Roxy first, Tyr insisted on announcing our intended courtship.

The time on the message was last night, before Tyr accosted me, and there was no follow up message rescinding their declaration. Hadn't I made myself clear? This had to be Tyr's influence. I didn't think Vidar would be so rash, though he did go along with Tyr's madness. Maybe banging their heads together would knock some sense into them. Maybe.

CHAPTER 6

*N*oise from the laundry room drew my attention away from the messages in the chat. There was nothing else important anyway. I cocked my head and when the noise continued, crept off to investigate. My feet froze in the doorway.

Tyr and Vidar wrapped around each other in an embrace that was borderline not appropriate, again. The hug was an innocent enough action, but the way they looked at each other. . . They were very clearly dedicated to each other.

I should leave. I should let them be madly in love privately, but my feet wouldn't move. My heart ached in a way that nearly brought me to tears.

No one in my life ever looked at me the way Tyr looked at Vidar. He would burn the world for his partner and Vidar would do the same for his quirky battle brother.

I never realized until this moment that I wanted someone to look at me that way. I wanted to have the stability of love and family. Remy provided some of that, and the McCabes too, but I still felt . . . alone.

Matriarchs didn't have mates. They picked the strongest of the males and bred with them to make strong cubs. There was no dedication or familial love in the act. To love was weak. To have a mate was to have weakness. Matriarchs could not afford either situation.

Missy whined, and I understood. We were alone because that's what we always knew. In this moment, I wanted nothing more than to step up behind Tyr and sink my teeth into his neck, then turn to Vidar and do the same. In claiming them I would have achieved the unrealized desire for family, but in doing so, without discussing it first, would be a violation of their consent.

Vidar's closed his eyes and turned his head when Tyr's face lowered to the junction at his neck. A gentle kiss, perhaps? But I wasn't at an angle to tell. Their movement jolted me out of my self-created misery. *I should leave.* Their private moment didn't include me. As an afterthought, I was glad they didn't have any problems because of me.

My elbow struck the doorframe as I backed away. My face burned as Vidar's half lidded gaze locked on me. Something about the way he looked at me rooted me in place.

"We have an audience." Vidar was in no form ashamed about his situation. Instead he looked rather pleased.

"I can smell her." Tyr lifted his head and pressed his cheek to Vidar's. Now two sets of eyes witnessed my embarrassment. Tyr's familiar grin crossed his face. "See something you like, pussy cat?"

"I need help." I blurted out the words instead of admitting to finding their embrace a turn on.

"Help?" Tyr's smile widened. "We're more than happy to embrace you as well."

"Not that kind of help. Get your brain out of the gutter." I turned my full attention to Vidar since Tyr was thinking with the wrong head. "I need more books. Well, different books but since I'm still bruised from the last jaunt in the stacks—"

"You said you weren't injured." Vidar shoved Tyr away and rushed me. His hand ran over me much the same as he had in the library when he caught me. This time, however, he pushed up my sleeves. I closed my eyes when he froze, unable to witness his reaction to my scars. I forgot about them, most of the time. Others usually made a big deal about them.

"These aren't new." He lifted my hand, and my eyes flew open when I felt his mouth press to one of the thicker lines along my forearm.

"Who hurt you?" Tyr's anger ripped through the room, and yet it gave me calm.

"Wolves. Almost four years ago. It doesn't matter anymore."

"If it didn't matter, you wouldn't hide them." Tyr took my hand from Vidar with more gentleness than I thought possible in his current mood.

"My mate won't care." I fought against the urge to yank my hand away. They both stood close enough for me to feel the heat of their bodies.

"If you believed that, you wouldn't always wear long sleeves." Tyr pressed light kisses along all the exposed scarring. "So you know, we don't care."

"She's injured, Tyr." Vidar linked his fingers with my free hand.

"It's not major. Some bruising. I need to see Dr. Underwood anyway." I tugged on my hands and found them both ensnared. The guys smiled but didn't let go.

"We'll go with." Tyr's tone held a finality that sounded like he didn't want to be argued with. I was well-versed in how to get what I wanted anyway, so he could say whatever he pleased.

"What did you need from the library?" Vidar's thumb rubbed comforting circles on my hand.

"I need to return the books I have, but I needed to ask Professor Kincaid about cyber security books instead of hacking. I know some, but not enough to do what I want."

"You don't need to bother the professor for that. Between Dillys and me, we can get you set." Vidar squeezed my fingers in reassurance.

"I'll run up and get the books if you want." Tyr stepped away, relinquishing his hold.

I hesitated before nodding. "They're on my desk."

Tyr bent forward, and my spine stiffened as he placed a chaste kiss on my cheek. "You are ours, kitten."

He whistled as he walked away.

I glanced up at Vidar. "I'm sorry. I thought I made it clear I wasn't interested in a relationship."

"Our interest may seem strange to you. The Norse don't have a soulmate or fated mates tradition like some of the other civilizations in the world. Marriages were arranged, and courtship carefully pursued. My mother was a slave to a Viking family, and yet Odin chose her for a Valkyrie. From that moment, Mom embraced her role, and I know nothing about who she was before. Hell, I don't even know anything about my father. However, Tyr's mother is Celtic, and they have Anam Cara, which Tyr taught to me, and by bonding with him, I share in his Fate now." Vidar's gaze wasn't in the here and now. He was lost in a memory.

"What's Anam Cara?"

"In simplest form, a soul friend. But it's much more complex than that. Anyway, I can't speak for Tyr directly, but for me . . . As the child of a Valkyrie, I am automatically drawn to certain people with certain strengths. Your strengths are tempered with blood, and for me, that's kind of an aphrodisiac. You are beautiful because of the pain of your past. The scars are only part of it, but I won't ask."

"The path to becoming a matriarch is more a river of blood. I didn't want the future chosen for me, but what I wanted was of no importance. Resistance was met with violent discipline. Sometimes I spoke to Death after such discipline, but he never collected my soul."

"For which I am grateful." His free hand stroked my cheek. "You are beautiful beyond words. We may not feel the mate bond the way shifters do, Roxy, but do not doubt our sincerity because of it."

His eyes dropped to my mouth, and back to my eyes in silent question. My tongue flicked out to wet my lips as I considered, and I watched his eyes darken. Vidar lowered his head to rest his forehead to mine. "You're a temptation I don't want to resist."

"Then don't." The words were breathy and didn't sound like me at all. One kiss was hardly a commitment. What would it hurt?

Perhaps the act would once and for all prove to Missy the men weren't ours.

There was nothing simple or dismissible about Vidar's touch. His mouth feathered over mine in a tease of contact that sparked a fire I had no control over. In the next breath, our gentle teasing turned hungry and heavy.

Ours, Missy growled, catching me by surprise after her silence. I jerked away from Vidar before she could sink our teeth in him.

"Roxy." Vidar scanned my face. "Your eyes—"

"I know." I closed them and fought the urge to leap at him and bite. Missy almost outsmarted me. She relented with a grumble and no doubt would try again in my next moment of distraction.

"I'd like to see the full shift. When you're comfortable." Vidar wrapped me in a hug, and his embrace did more to calm the irritated cougar within than I had achieved.

After taking a deep breath, I pushed him away. It was too easy to feel safe and content in his arms. I didn't like the swirling mess of emotions he created.

"You guys ready or you need another minute?" Tyr leaned against the doorjamb with my stack of books in one arm and a pleased grin on his face.

Anger burned at myself. Things got way out of hand with Vidar. Not only that, but my reaction to him scared me. Our kiss felt like a mate bond.

"Library is on the way out, and we can stop at Eirhal for the doc before hitting the tech commons." Vidar reached out and linked his fingers with mine again before I could deny him.

"What are you planning now, kitten?" Tyr walked on my other side as we headed out.

"What you suggested. I'm going to try to lock them out."

"Time out." Vidar held up his hand. "What's going on, exactly?"

"Tyr suggested locking out the person sending the messages, so they can't do it anymore. I was trying to find them, but I always lose their trail." I tipped my head at his frown. "What's wrong?"

"Do you know what information they have? I mean, they're

sending messages to every student on campus. Do they have the student files? The town information? The coordinates?"

I blinked. "I . . . I don't know."

"Locking them out isn't going to stop anything, depending on the information they have. Maybe setting a trap instead. Something to attach to them, or notify someone when they enter the computer system. Maybe even a virus that can go in and wipe the information they have. But if they have more information than just our telephone numbers, then there's no way to prevent them from using that information if we don't know who they are. And at this point, there's no reason to assume they only have our phone numbers."

"And this is why Vidar is the brain, and I'm the brawn." Tyr scratched his nose. "So what now?"

A beat of silence passed before I sighed. "Same plan, I guess. Just different books. I don't know how to make a virus either. Maybe we can get lucky, and I can find the hacker."

"With the magic around the school and town being what it is, I don't imagine the source is outside the mountain. Hacking from the outside would be damn near impossible unless you knew the school was here." Vidar cupped his chin with a hand.

"So a mole." Tyr growled. "With all the new faces that came in for this semester, ours included, there's no way to even begin to guess who the rat is."

"That's a very anti-rat shifter sentiment." I lifted a brow at him.

He shrugged. "Rats, raccoons, squirrels. Little devils all have about the same personality. Give me the money."

"Hyenas, snakes, dark witches. We've seen our fair share of dangerous, greedy entities," Vidar added.

"Our tower mascot is a snake. Our tower name is a snake. That's an unfair stereotype." My statement was met with a brush off.

"Day's a wasting. Vidar will take you to Eirhal. I'm going to grab some food after the library. Such an undertaking requires sustenance. For a shifter, you've missed more meals than you've eaten. That worries me a little."

I didn't rise to his statement. Not that he was wrong. When the guys flanked me on the way out, I couldn't help but feeling content they were there. I wasn't alone, and they were a comforting presence.

What if Missy was right and they were ours? Did it matter, since I had a timer to death on my arm? The right thing to do was drive them away. They couldn't get hurt if they weren't attached. And if I didn't die? Well, I'd burn that bridge when I got to it.

CHAPTER 7

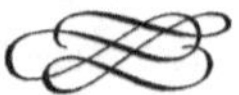

There was a saying: Give an inch and they'll take a mile. Tyr and Vidar were definitely taking advantage of my concession to their company.

Tyr wouldn't let me carry my books. Vidar wouldn't let me go with him into the stacks. Neither of them would let me give them money for the snacks. By the time we even headed in the direction of Eirhal, I wanted to drop them off one of the towers. Except Vidar could fly, so that would backfire tremendously.

"I don't need a babysitter." My statement and variations of the statement met deaf ears as it had the last hour.

"Of course you don't." Tyr patted my shoulder and kept walking. He, once again, carried my books.

"Don't you have somewhere to be?" I flicked at his hand.

"At your side?" He danced away when I punched at him.

"Is there a reason we can't hang out with you?" Vidar glanced down at me.

"The doctor is kind of private." I stopped at the doors of Eirhal and held out my hands for my books.

Tyr lifted a brow. "We'll meet you in the tech commons when you're done then."

I resisted the urge to stomp my foot like a child or wrap my hands around his throat and shake. "Seriously. Go to the gym. Make some new friends. Stop bothering me."

"We're a bother?" Vidar's face fell as if I kicked his puppy, and he stepped away.

I cursed myself twice a fool as I rubbed my hands over my face. "I'll see you in the tech commons."

"I'll have the snacks by then." Tyr jerked his head to Vidar and skipped away.

"I think I've been tricked." I frowned at his frolic.

"You get used to it. Are we truly a bother? I'll convince him to leave the books for you if we're annoying you." Vidar rubbed his thumb in circles on the palm of his left hand. I could taste his anxiety on the air.

I hated that his uncertainty wrapped knots of guilt in my stomach. "I'm not used to having constant company is all. I've only had Remy for years. Having real friends takes some getting used to."

He nodded and leaned in close enough to smooch my nose. "See you in a few then."

I watched him walk away instead of retorting. As much as we would love to get used to them, it wasn't a wise idea. I couldn't afford such distractions.

My eyes fell to my hourglass as I entered Eirhal. I frowned and tapped on the tattoo. The sand barely moved. Was I doing something right? What had I done?

"Roxanne."

All the hairs on my arms stood on end. Of all the creatures in school . . . I turned in the direction of the voice.

Owen Murray belonged to the wolf pack that killed my family and injured me. He was my half-sister's uncle, and that single fact —and the rules of Havenwood Falls—kept him safe from us. I shouldn't hate that he was here, a constant reminder of what happened, but I did.

Like Remy and me, he followed Audrey's trail to Havenwood Falls. Or rather Theo and Iris, his children did, and then they called Dad to come. Like the town needed more wolves, but I wasn't in any place to protest.

Owen had his hair up in a ponytail instead of a man bun as he usually did when he came in for coffee. The clothes weren't any different. Jeans with a button shirt he rolled to the elbow. At the moment, his mismatched eyes, one blue and one brown, studied me from a careful distance away.

I forced a smile but felt my teeth pinch my lip. There was no way we'd ever like the wolf. However, I could remain civil. "Why are you here? I was looking for Dr. Underwood."

"He's setting up his office over the weekend. Is there something I can help with?" Owen's smile held more warmth than mine.

"He's got my medical file." I shrugged and turned, ready to leave, not even bothering to wait for an answer to my question.

Owen sighed. "Roxanne, I *am* a doctor as well. If you'd be more comfortable with Madame Roth, I can call her over. I believe she's on campus, setting up her suite today."

Missy paced. She didn't like the implication we were scared of him. I didn't like it either.

"Sure. Why not? I doubt you can help, though."

"Let's find out. Follow me." Owen led the way down the hall into the infirmary and pointed to an exam room.

I hopped up onto the exam table before he could come in and ask. In a few minutes, Owen returned with a laptop and wearing a white coat. For some reason the coat, a reminder that he was a doctor, helped me calm a little as he closed the door behind him.

I struggled not to panic over the closed door. Dr. Underwood always closed it, and I was fine. This was a wolf, though. An enemy.

"So what's up?" He put a little thingy on my finger for my pulse before taking my blood pressure.

I remained silent, taking meditative breaths and searching for the right way to explain things as he did the preliminaries.

"BP's pretty good." He pulled the thingy off my finger. "Pulse is a little high. Your pheromones are also on the high side. Probably hitting early maturity."

"What?" My voice cracked.

He pointed to the closed door. "I wasn't sure out there, but with the door closed, your hormones are definitely prominent."

"I'm not old enough."

Owen chuckled. "Roxanne, age is a guideline. Not set in stone. I've seen shifters mature as early as fifteen and as late as thirty seven."

Numb shock flooded my brain. Missy's weird behavior—well, and mine, to be honest—made more sense now. Early maturity.

"Roxanne?" Owen snapped his fingers under my nose. "Did you come to see Dr. Underwood about your maturity? Has something specifically happened? Maturing females can be more aggressive than males."

More aggressive? Missy was certainly more vocal but not physically aggressive. Yet. Dear gods did I have to worry about that now, as well?

I shook my head. "No. Not for maturity. My left arm nearly dropped me to the floor this morning with pain. I couldn't use it."

Owen nodded. "Let's take a look."

With a shrug, I pulled off my tunic. Since I anticipated seeing Dr. Underwood, I wore a tank top under the tunic.

Owen frowned at the scars and ran firm but gentle fingers over them, applying pressure at intervals. "Happened during the coupe, huh?"

"Yeah."

"I hid our kids, mine and Audrey's brothers. We voted against the action but—" He continued to massage without finishing the thought.

"They got my parents first. Then my sister as we ran. I wasn't strong enough to protect her, or myself."

"Dark magic was involved with that attack, Roxanne. No one was strong enough. Two of the matriarchs died as well."

I squeezed my eyes shut. "I didn't know."

"What type of physical therapy are you doing?" Owen dropped my arm and went back to his laptop.

The change of subject was welcome. It helped hearing some of the story from him, but it was depressing. I would have to decide how I felt about it, and him, later.

"Nothing official. Dr. Underwood mentioned it, but since I do yoga on occasion, shift and run, and practice my Muay Thai, I didn't think anything formal was needed. I'm active enough."

"Not good enough. Scar tissue, especially in a shifter, needs to be worked continuously for you to regain and maintain full range. This isn't something that is going to heal itself. I'm prescribing yoga every day, and before you do any heavy activities, including shifting, do some serious stretching. I can send recommendations to your school email address. Get one of the guys I smell on you to massage your arm and shoulder, lotion or oil works, at the end of the day before bed." His brows rose, telling me I was as red as I felt.

I took a deep breath and decided it wouldn't hurt to ask him, since he was another shifter. "Can I have more than one mate?"

Owen tipped his head with a considering look. "I've not heard of it happening with cougars or mountain lions, but I wouldn't say it's not possible. I met a bear in Ohio with four mates. And in my experience, foxes are rarely monogamous in mates. It's my belief that fate gives us what we need. Number is inconsequential. I'm guessing the guys I smell triggered your maturity then?"

I shrugged. "My cat calls them both mates. I didn't take her as sane."

"Trust the cat, Roxanne. Especially yours." He patted my shoulder. "Put your shirt on. I'll send you an email of my instructions."

I hopped down and did as instructed. He wasn't so bad for a wolf. "Thanks, Dr. Murray. For all your help and information. I really appreciate it."

"I'm here if you need me."

I shuffled for a moment. "Sure, ah, my friends call me Roxy."

He smiled over his shoulder. "I'll remember that. You have a good rest of your day, and for now, don't overwork that arm."

I nodded and waved my goodbye as I left. I took my time

walking over to the tech commons. Owen's words made a lot of sense, but I was still a little skeptical.

My cell phone jingled with a text message, and I pulled it out, wondering if Tyr was getting impatient.

WE KNOW WHAT'S WORSE THAN DEATH.

My stomach dropped. There were no attachments this time, but imagination could often be worse than reality. My thoughts couldn't help but wonder: What could be worse than death? And on the heels of that thought came another—I didn't want to find out.

CHAPTER 8

With a plan in mind, I knocked on Professor Kincaid's closed office door. The raised voices told me he was in there with someone, but I really needed his help if I wanted to get into the servers. Or if he couldn't help me, he could at least tell me who I needed to talk to for permission.

When the door opened, Professor Kincaid's disheveled appearance almost had me break the sunny customer service smile I adopted for this encounter. Open and friendly usually got more things done than shouts and demands. "Morning, Professor. I wanted to ask a favor."

"Miss McCabe, I'm slightly preoccupied—"

I jumped in before he could finish his sentence. "I won't take up much of your time, I promise. I only wanted to ask your permission to access the servers so I can hard line into them directly."

His brows drew together. "Why?"

"I've been back tracing the hacking from my phone with your suggested reading, and felt like I was wasting time since they're hiding somehow in our servers. I think. I lose the thread there every time, so that's my guess. I figured since security is something I'm good at, I thought that maybe a better idea would be to update the security coding on the servers, and see if I can bug their ghosts in the system. Then by doing so, we can finally figure out who they are when they access the ghosts. Vidar is pretty sure it has to be coming from on campus."

The door pulled open further to reveal a vampire I didn't know. His neat clothes looked like they belonged in a boardroom of a fancy office and not a strand of his brown hair was out of place. He stepped forward, and it took everything in me to remain smiling and not give an inch. There was something about this new vampire that felt old and powerful, and not only his stench.

"What do you know of the messages harassing the students?" His eyes narrowed on my face, and I lifted my chin, still keeping my smile in place.

Professor Kincaid sighed. "Miss McCabe, this is Gabriel Doyle. One of the Regents."

"Pleasure to meet you, Mr. Doyle." I addressed his question. "I thought it was a prank at first, and went hunting to see if I could flush them out and give them a piece of my mind. However, they're a bit more advanced than I at this time. At least, that's the impression I get when I lose the trail. I'm not a hacker though, but I am familiar with security systems."

I took a deep breath and repeated what I had told Professor Kincaid, and since this new vampire was a Regent, I also repeated my request for access to the servers. He surely had authoritative powers.

"I've seen the trial tapes. Your skills without a teacher are already above par, Ms. McCabe. Color me impressed. But perhaps this is something you should leave for the adults." The vampire didn't look impressed. If anything, he looked bored and annoyed by my presence.

Missy bristled, and I fought not to react. Even if I wanted to rip his throat out, I held on to my polite smile. "Then what are the *adults* doing about it?"

I didn't understand the quirk of his mouth. What had I said that was funny?

The Regent's amusement didn't last long, though. "It's

interesting that you can follow a hacker, but we can't even find a trail."

My eyes moved to Professor Kincaid. "I'm not sure I understand. I've been using my phone to trace . . . but even with the suggested reading, I'm not a great hacker. Maybe after some of the classes I'll be better but right now, not so much."

Professor Kincaid pulled off his glasses to rub his eyes. "Greatness comes with time, Miss McCabe; it doesn't occur overnight."

I lifted a shoulder and let it fall. "I like results now."

"Don't we all." Mr. Doyle smiled.

Professor Kincaid shook his head. "I can't give you access—"

"I can. Only the servers here. The security servers in the second armory are off limits to everyone but the security team." The other vampire fished into his pocket and pulled out a key card. "Turn it into Asher when you're done, and Ms. McCabe, I will know if you use it anywhere else on campus."

"I understand. Thank you so much for your assistance." I accepted the key card. One step down, and probably a hundred more to go, but the first step was always the hardest.

"It's the only security door in the tech commons," Professor Kincaid offered.

"Thank you, professor. Also, I have Tyr and Vidar with me for assistance. Are they allowed entry?"

"Just you, Roxanne." Mr. Doyle leveled a stare at me. "Am I clear?"

"Translucent, sir." I closed my hand around the key card and hurried away before they could change their minds.

The tech commons was crowded when I entered. After a quick scan, I avoided Gable sitting on a couch with a laptop and some headphones and found Tyr and Vidar sitting at the same table Tyr accosted me at this morning. To my surprise, my laptop sat next to the stack of books gracing the tabletop.

Tyr's face lit up like a puppy seeing his mommy come home when he spotted me. He even stood and pulled out a chair for me as I approached.

"Busier than I've seen it." I tipped my head at the almost full room.

"One of the towers lost Wi-Fi connection altogether, I'm told." Vidar's fingers drummed the table. "I wonder if the recent message was part of that."

"Maybe. I can check the servers when I get in there." I tapped my laptop. "I didn't grab this."

Vidar had the decency to blush. "You can't write code without a computer, so I sent Tyr for it. I hope that's okay."

I couldn't really be mad with practicality but . . . "Why didn't you text me?"

I pulled my phone out of the back pocket of my jeggings and set it on the table next to the laptop.

Tyr rolled his eyes. "Because, kitten, you haven't given either of us your number."

"And the tower chat?" I crossed my arms.

"That's a little public, and as far as I've seen, you're a pretty private person. It'd be rude to put your business out there without permission." Vidar's smile wavered a fraction. "I'm sorry if we overstepped."

"So courting me wasn't a violation of my privacy?"

Both of them had the decency to look chagrined. Tyr shrugged and looked to Vidar.

"Tyr got ahead of himself, and thought by posting it, we'd eliminate some fight for your attention." Vidar stood gesturing to my chair.

"Some can't take the hint." Tyr glared across the commons, and I didn't even have to look to know he stared at Gable.

After a moment, I sat down. My fingers drummed on the tabletop. "Things worked a little differently in Virginia. I guess we should at some point have a real conversation."

"We'd like that. Whenever you're ready." Vidar sat back down.

Tyr's grin was a little maniacal as he picked up a tote bag from the floor next to his seat. "I have snacks."

The small mountain of chips, pretzels, jerky, chocolate cakes, candy, and the two liter of cola was certainly the definition of snack. The variety was unexpected.

"How many are you feeding with all this?" I snagged a bag of jerky.

"You're a shifter. You burn more fuel naturally. Tyr and I weren't certain what kind of fuel you preferred." Vidar shrugged like it was no big deal and grabbed a bag of Swedish fish.

"Meat is never wrong." I opened the laptop as I tore into the jerky.

"So meat lovers pizza for dinner? I hear the campus joint Rest in Pizza makes a great pie." Tyr sat down with a Twinkie.

"Double the meat and cheese if I can get it." I nodded my thanks at Vidar when he separated the jerky and Slim Jims from the stack and sat them next to me.

"So Vid did some reading while you were at the doctor. By the way, is everything okay?" Tyr cocked his head at me.

"Fine. I've been given instructions." I hadn't planned on elaborating until I noticed the guys sharing a look. I sighed. "My scars are bothering me. I have an order for PT and massages."

"Did you get the bruise looked at?" Vidar moved some of the books toward me.

"Dr. Underwood wasn't in. I saw Dr. Murray. Since he's a shifter, I didn't see a point."

"Would you let me look at it? I'm fairly good with bruises." Vidar touched a hand to mine.

"Later." The word seemed safer than an outright no. The guys knew too well how to play on emotions.

"Fair. So as Tyr said, I did some reading, and I've bookmarked some stuff." Vidar opened several of the books to specific sections.

"Okay. Let's get started." I arranged everything to my liking then dove into the books. With any luck, I could have a solution to the problem before dinner. Fingers crossed.

The tiny server room created tension in my shoulders, and I couldn't control my racing pulse. Missy cowered. The dark space was too alike our room in the matriarch house. We hadn't earned a room in the light in our time there.

I took a deep calming breath. Thirty minutes. No more than forty. And Tyr promised dessert afterwards.

I wished the guys could be in here. Even Tyr's jalapeno and pickle pizza breath would be a comfort. Who puts pickles on a pizza?

We should claim them when we're done. As a reward. Missy added the last part as if the claiming was better than dessert.

Claim is forever, I reminded her as I brought the servers offline.

They are ours. Missy's claim was so simple, it was hard to argue with.

The machines were state of the art. Advanced to almost the point of militaristic. Which made me question how the hell the hacker even got in and why the signal was so shitty across campus. I wondered if Dillys's signal booster tech magic would work on the servers.

While my hands moved on autopilot, my mind turned over the situation. I didn't want to get involved, and yet here they were on the other side of the locked door. Waiting to take me to get dessert, either on campus or in town. They didn't care either way.

I never asked why they insisted on being with me. Since I hadn't mentioned my crazy cat's claim, what made me special to them? Well, Vidar already told me, but what about Tyr?

"How's it going in there?" Tyr called through the door.

"Fine. Fine." I returned my attention where it belonged—on the code, not the man. No matter how delicious he looked.

I sighed. Ignoring a problem didn't make it go away. Mates, because I had to face that the cat's instincts weren't ever wrong, weren't in the game plan for a while. If I lived through the hourglass mystery, we'd need to have a serious discussion about expectations and rules. Though I doubted either of them would follow rules that didn't suit them. Even sweet-tempered Vidar had a spine of steel.

Green meant go. I took a deep breath and studied the programming one more time before hitting execute. The computer ran through the coding, and the servers whorled back to life. Nothing flashed, no fatal errors or corruption warnings. After the last execution ran, I waited with baited breath and crossed fingers that nothing would go wrong. When the machines hummed and nothing happened, I took it as a win.

My work here was done, for the moment. I tucked the flash drive with my work on it into my purse and gave the room one final glance over. Satisfied everything looked to be running, I headed for the door.

The power flickered.

Then went completely out.

My heart thundered in my chest, but the hum of the servers cut through some of the panic. Power wasn't completely out—the machines still ran. There was enough light from them that I wasn't in complete darkness.

I was okay. All I had to do was open the door and step out. Tyr and Vidar waited on the other side.

With a shaking hand, I yanked the door open. Except it didn't open. I tugged again as panic broke sweat out onto my skin.

The lock was electronic. I had the key card in my pocket to prove it. They locked us in. My fist pounded on the door.

"Tyr. Vidar. The door won't open. They locked me in. I can't get out." I could hear the fear in my voice and couldn't control it. *We can't be locked in. We can't let them hurt us again.*

"Deep breath. Stay calm, Roxy. We're here. We're going to get you out." Vidar's calm didn't break through the rising terror.

"Get me out. I'm not staying in here." My fists dented the door, and I barely registered the pain over my fear. The scent of blood hit my nose, and I still couldn't stop.

"Roxy, we're getting you out. Please stop hitting the door. We're working on getting it open." Vidar's tone sounded off to my ears, but I couldn't say why.

I threw my body against the door over and over. "I'm not staying in here. I'm not."

"Roxy, you're going to hurt yourself. Stop, right now." Tyr's voice held demand, but I barely heard him over the roaring in my ears.

Missy's screaming rage blocked out everything but the driving need to get out. *We will not be a victim. Not again. No one will touch us. We'll rip their throats out.*

The shift took over. I lost control to the cat. In her fury, we battered the unmoving door until we collapsed with broken bones for our efforts. Agony burned the edges of our vision gray, and breathing became difficult.

We couldn't give in. We had to get out. We fell when we tried to stand, no longer capable of fighting. Broken of body, we wept from our defeat. When they came, we would not be able to stop them. We slipped into unconsciousness, waiting.

Warmth cocooned me in a wondrous cradle. I snuggled down and inhaled deep. Vidar's spice and Tyr's mixed scent flooded my senses. The familiar smell made me sigh. When had I imprinted them? Did it matter anymore?

As my mind clicked on, I bolted upright. A quick glance around revealed an empty bed, other than myself, and a room that definitely wasn't mine. By smell alone, the studio apartment-sized dorm could be identified as belonging to my guys.

The space had an interior decorator feel to it and reminded me of a hunting cabin Remy and I commandeered for a long weekend during our journey. Aged wood decorated the vaulted ceiling and graced some of the walls. The fireplace roared, a fuzzy rug perfect for naps sat in front of the flames, and a comfortable looking chair with a stack of books next to it sat close enough to feel the heat.

A window looked out over a tidy harbor and a desk sat under the window. With the way our tower was designed, there was no way that window was real. Not discounting the fact we were inside a freaking mountain.

I slid out of bed to investigate further and noticed the breeze on my legs. A once over identified the lack of pants and an oversized shirt that smelled like both my guys. My thoughts froze.

Since when were they my guys?

Always. Missy snorted.

Ignoring the cat, I tried to piece together what had happened. My mind was a little fuzzy on the details after screaming for the men. Not my sanest moment, I admitted to myself. I remembered the locked door and beating my fist bloody.

I fanned my hands out in front of me. Nothing. Not even a scratch.

The door to my left opened, and Vidar stepped through, bringing the smell of soap and water with him. A towel draped over his shoulders, and only a pair of flannel pants graced his form. No, he wasn't a bodybuilder, but there wasn't an ounce of fat on him either. His smile bloomed when he caught sight of me.

"Hey, how are you feeling?" Vidar crossed the room and took my hands in his, all the while never taking his eyes off my face.

"I feel fine, though some of the finer details are fuzzy." My stomach grumbled, and he chuckled.

"Tyr went to get food. You've been out for two days." Vidar led me over to the chair by the fire, but I stopped halfway to examine the false window.

The image looked so real, as if I could open the glass and hear the water lap. Testing, I did just that, and gasped. Not only could I hear water, seals, and gulls, but I could smell the salt of the bay and feel the breeze on my face.

"It's home. Though Tyr would prefer we keep the window closed unless absolutely necessary." Vidar reached over me and shut the window.

"How? Home?" I couldn't take my eyes from the window. The place was so beautiful.

"Tyr's a decent illusionist. Not like his grandfather, but he has enough to do little things. When you open the window, it makes the illusion bigger, and he feels the pull of that, so it's best to leave it closed. And home is called Iceland nowadays."

"Iceland? I thought Valkyries were Norse. Wouldn't that be Norway?" My brows furrowed as I turned away and bumped solidly into Vidar.

His hands caught my waist. "Vikings had settlements as far west as Canada." His hand lifted and tucked my falling hair behind my ear. "Are you sure you feel okay?"

"I don't remember most of it, to be honest. That's not uncommon for one of my panic attacks. Especially considering . . ." I shrugged it off.

"You beat your hands bloody and broke three fingers. Fractured your left wrist and arm as well, and somehow managed to crack four ribs."

"Oh."

"Tyr kicked the door in. Professor Kincaid and Mr. Doyle weren't happy about it, but when we got to you . . . You were passed out on the floor. Blood everywhere. Scared the shit out of all of us."

"Thank you for getting me out." I wrapped my arms around him in a tight hug.

He tightened his hold, pulling me flush against him with no wiggle room. "I know, logically I know, there was nothing in that room that could hurt you, but the way you screamed and cried . . . You were pale, bleeding, and broken."

"Sadly by my own hand. You once called my temperance beautiful, but now you've seen the ugly side." I rubbed my nose against his chest. "I'm sorry you had to see that."

"It doesn't change who you are to me." Vidar dipped his head to kiss my temple. I turned my face to his, and our mouths met. His grip tightened, and the gentle reassuring touch turned feral.

I leaned up into him even as I told myself I should pull away. Despite the insistent cat that they were mates, I was young and didn't feel like I was ready for them. Fighting instinct was a losing battle. They would be mine whether I took them now or ten years from now. My mind was torn when I felt another body press to my back.

"I see someone is feeling better." Tyr kissed the lobe of my ear before trailing his mouth lower. One of his hands managed to wriggle between Vidar and me to hold me in a backwards hug. They felt right. Better than anything I'd ever experienced before.

"Scared us bad, kitten," Tyr murmured into my ear.

I tilted my head slightly, shifting my hair and giving him access to my neck. Tyr's hummed approval was lost in the rushing pleasure of his mouth against my newly exposed skin.

Was I really doing this? I didn't want to stop. I felt safe with Vidar, and though Tyr's antics frustrated me, he was as loyal as man's best friend.

Ours. Missy purred.

I pulled away from Vidar's mouth to nibble down his neck. As frustrating as it was, my cat was right and avoiding the inevitable was a waste of time. "I want to claim you. Both of you."

The men froze.

"Are you sure?" Tyr held himself still.

"We can wait," Vidar added.

"I don't want to." I nipped at his pulse point and felt his shudder.

"Whatever you want, kitten. We'll give it to you." Tyr licked my ear lobe.

"Vidar?" I pulled away far enough to make sure he was on board.

His lips curved. "We are yours, whether you mark us or not."

I returned his smile. "I'd rather make sure everyone knows."

"Then let's make it so." He scooped me up and carried me over to the bed. Tyr followed with a grin.

There were no certainties in life, but at least I had this one. They were mine. Nothing on this world would change that.

CHAPTER 11

$\mathcal{V}$idar's hand rubbed random designs on my bare thigh. A smile touched my lips, but I otherwise didn't move. He pressed into my back with his face resting against the top of my head. The guys switched positions several times during our mating. Not that I minded. When they focused on my pleasure it was really hard to be put out.

Tyr wrapped around me like an octopus. My claim on his neck looked red and raw but no longer bleeding. He breathed in an easy steady rhythm that spoke of deep sleep. After the last few hours, we could all use some deep sleep before classes started tomorrow.

My phone jingled, and I sighed. Probably Bryony wondering where I was. I doubted anyone else cared enough to ask where I vanished to.

With a sigh, I wriggled out from between the guys and went in search of my phone. Tyr protested with a grumble and sat up in bed. Vidar murmured and shifted enough to place his head in Tyr's lap, watching me.

"It can't be important." Tyr stretched, and his hand fell to Vidar's braids.

"You never know." I found my purse in the desk chair and fumbled through it for the phone.

The tower chat caught my attention first. A hundred-and-seventy-four unread messages. I wondered if our tower was chatty or if the other towers talked as much as we did. Skimming the messages, I was surprised to find a few asking about my whereabouts.

The text message gave me pause.

WE WILL NOT BE STOPPED.

The next message came in several hours later.

WE WILL DESTROY YOU ALL.

"What the hell?" I tossed the phone back in my purse and looked around for my clothes.

"What's wrong?" Vidar sat up, his brows drawing together.

"The hacker sent more messages." I found the shirt I wore before our antics and tugged it back on. "If my virus worked then we should know where he is now. We need to notify the Regents, and I have to pull the location. Thank the gods I connected the program to my laptop. I won't have to go back into the servers."

Tyr scratched his nose. "Why not leave it to the adults? Just give them the information?"

"Mr. Doyle said something strange the other day. He asked how I could track the hacker when they couldn't even find a thread. It got me thinking." I went looking for my shoes, though I doubted they survived the sudden shift.

"You think this is your problem to fix?" Vidar climbed out of bed and pulled on a pair of jeans from the floor. It amused me that he didn't even look to see if the pants were his or not.

"It's not rational, I know, but let's say I am the only one that can oppose the hacker, then it would be irresponsible of me to pull the covers over my head." Giving up on the shoes, I grabbed my purse and sent the guys a smile. "I'll contact you later."

"No." Tyr lunged from the bed and managed to get himself

between me and the door. "If you're going to face some crazies, even if you're only doing it virtually, you're not doing it alone."

"Tyr—" I stopped when I met his angry gaze. "Fine. What do you suggest?"

"We get a team together. Vidar and I can help with the people that you need. You'll take point but, Roxy, this isn't just about you. There's a whole school involved." Tyr caught the pants Vidar threw at him without taking his eyes from me.

"Please, Roxy." Vidar came up behind me and wrapped me in a hug. "Let us help you."

I closed my eyes and took a deep breath, letting it out slowly. The first steps were always the hardest. "Okay. Where do we start?"

"We start with you getting real clothes on." Tyr glanced down at my legs. "Because those are distracting as hell."

Vidar laughed. "I'll send some messages. We'll meet in the tech commons. Tyr will go with you. I'm going to stop at the library. Regroup in fifteen."

"Got it. Come on, kitten. Let's get you dressed so we can save the world." Tyr grabbed my hand and dragged me out before I could say anything to Vidar.

"Not the world, just our little piece of it," I corrected him on the stairs leading to my room.

I ticked off things as I hurriedly dressed while trying not to wrinkle my nose. The least they could have done was given me time to shower. Not that I completely minded smelling like my guys, but anyone with a decent nose would smell our interaction.

"Stop thinking so hard." Tyr grinned from his position next to the door. "We're here to help."

"I'm used to doing things on my own. This is new for me. I can't promise I won't try to do things on my own." I turned to him and gave him a hug.

His voice dropped to a husky vibrato. "We'll remind you as often as you need that you have us. In any way you need reminded."

I stepped back and took his hand. "Come on. Vidar is waiting. Hopefully with a crew that knows how the hell to back me up."

Vidar certainly came through. Dillys was the only face of the seven students waiting that I recognized. She popped her gum and grinned at me.

"Let's get this party started." Tyr rubbed his hands together.

"All right." I rolled my shoulders. "This is what I know."

We spent hours tracking and backtracking. My virus wasn't as stable as I thought it was, according to Aithan. Dillys found the origin point.

Our hacker was somehow in the security servers. They had control of the door locks, passwords, and the drones that were supposed to be for combat and defense practices looked to be protecting the building.

"We've got the program, Roxy." Dillys cracked her gum. "We've just got to get into the building."

"We haven't turned the keycard in." Tyr held up the item in question between two fingers.

"I doubt the hacker removed Mr. Doyle's accesses. As Gabriel Doyle is a Regent, I don't think those passcodes are easily accessible, even for our hacker." Vidar shrugged. "If it doesn't work, then we'll have to have someone force the door open."

"I can do it." John, a big ogre looking guy, rolled his shoulders. "Shouldn't be too hard to crack at the source."

"So we're agreed. Roxy goes in and resets the servers with the program we've all tweaked. I'm back up for Roxy. John is support for the door lock. Tyr and Vidar lead the ground team to distract the drones away from the security hall." Dillys stretched. "I think we got this."

We gathered at the Valkyrie statue by the portals. The secondary armory building could be seen about three hundred feet away with the drones dotting the air around it.

"Give Vid and me ten minutes before you follow. Give us a chance to pull the drones away from the hall." Tyr flexed his arms and looked to Vidar who nodded.

I chewed my lip, wondering if I should say or do something before they left. No one asked about the claims they both wore on their necks. Matters were more dire than who was sleeping with whom but still . . .

Tyr solved the problem for me when he changed directions to grab me into a tight hold while kissing me stupid. "For luck."

Vidar pressed a kiss to my cheek. "We'll see you on the other side."

Tyr took off running, and I watched in fascination as he transformed into a wolf the size of an elephant. Vidar shot into the air, his wingbeats sounding like thunder, and the ground team took that as the signal to advance. Worry ate at my stomach.

Dillys whistled. "Of all the things, a scion of Fenris I hadn't expected. They'll be okay. They're only practice drones. None of the specs list any fatal weaponry."

"Yeah." I fingered the drive in my pocket with our work on it. Hopefully there weren't any snags that would require more than a flash drive with some back up programming.

"Time," John announced standing. "Let's get this started."

"Fast and quiet." Dillys handed me a charm and tossed one at John. "You're already pretty quiet on your feet for a big guy, but let's make it even more so. It works like camouflage in a way. You're not invisible, that's beyond me, but you are harder to see."

"Let's get this done." Afterwards I'd talk my guys into a shower, together.

I dashed across the bridge, trying hard not to see parts of the distraction team lying motionless on the stones. Vidar tangled with a few drones in the air, and it took all my strength not to watch him execute his aerial dance. Tyr was the biggest damn wolf I'd ever seen. We'd have to have a talk about that later.

John hit the doors first and waved us inside. Not locked. Did the hackers not think we'd get past the drones?

Dillys led the way through the halls based on a map she procured. I didn't ask from where. After what felt like forever, we rounded a corner and immediately dove for cover when guns went off. John wasn't as fast and took the very lethal looking rounds to the chest.

He convulsed when he fell, and stilled. I swallowed hard. I knew what a death looked like, but it was never easy to face.

"What now?" I asked Dillys and peered around the corner. Four drones guarded the server door.

"I got this." Dillys reached into her pocket and pulled out some clear quartz. She chanted with the stones cupped in her hands before she threw them. Gunfire shattered the stones, and a deafening boom shook the building with a bright, blinding flash.

I went blind even as my ears went silent. After a moment, they rang with an intensity I'd never experienced before. I staggered with the disorientation.

"Go. Go." Dillys grabbed my arm and dragged me forward.

"What was that?"

"Contained lightning. Sort of. Shit fried the door." She banged her fist on the keypad.

I tried the handle, and the door opened. "We're in anyway."

"Let's get this done." Dillys rushed in and screamed, running back out.

I peered in to see something I never dreamed I'd see, and I'd prefer not to see again. Gable made up the torso, but his lower body was all scorpion. His tail lashed out, and I dipped behind the doorframe before it could strike me. The stone thundered with the blow from the stinger.

"Tyr is going to be insufferable after this." I looked at Dillys and tossed her the flash drive. "I'm going to try to draw him out, distract him or something. Can you get the lights? I don't think he sees as well as I do in the dark. You get to the computer."

She swallowed and nodded. "I hope you know what you're doing."

I stripped out of my clothes and shifted. Dillys pressed her hand to the electrical panel, and I heard light bulbs explode. The moment it went dark, I lunged into the room, taking Gable by surprise.

He roared, and I was correct in my assumption that he was strong. The side of his tail caught my bad shoulder as I avoided a pincher, and knocked me into a wall. I had seconds to move before he rushed me with a second blow. I braced myself, taking the direct hit from the side of his stinger and sunk my claws into the tail, slashing at the unprotected underside.

In that single moment I realized if Gable wanted me dead all he had to do was sting me. He wasn't trying to kill me. Which was to my advantage, because I certainly had no intentions of holding back.

Gable roared and flicked me off like a fly. My head struck the stone wall, and in my daze, I watched Dillys duck behind the servers before Gable could spot her. This wasn't going well at all.

Tyr and Vidar raced into the room, both stopping in shock when they caught sight of Gable.

Tyr attacked first. "I knew I didn't like you."

"Couldn't mind your business, could you, mate?" Gable swiped at him with a pincher, but Tyr was agile.

Vidar rolled out of the way and threw a short blade at Gable's torso. The weapon sunk into his flesh just under the collarbone. My man could throw.

Gable surged toward Tyr, his pincher knocking into him with a solid pound. With Tyr off balance, Gable used the moment to sink his stinger into Tyr's shoulder. Tyr cursed in languages I didn't know as he struggled against Gable's tail.

I pushed to my feet and shook, trying to free myself of the daze. I must have hit the wall harder than I originally thought. Still, with what strength I could gather, I jumped forward and dug my claws into as much of Gable's tail as I could.

The scorpion man roared, releasing Tyr and turning on me.

Thank the gods he wasn't a snake or some weird Australian bug. Vidar jumped toward his back but missed, his hand tangling in a necklace Gable wore. The chain snapped, dropping Vidar to the floor.

Gable screamed and not an angry-you're-in-my-way kind of scream. I recognized the sound of torture. He clutched his head with his hands and fell writhing on the floor. Tyr used the moment to kick him in the face, effectively knocking him out.

"You okay?" Vidar dropped Gable's necklace to the floor as he approached his battle brother.

Tyr shrugged, rolling his bleeding shoulder. "It's not Skadi's snake, so we're good."

"Mission accomplished." Dillys waved from the computer.

"Good." Vidar studied Gable. "We need to call the Regents."

I shifted and limped over to my guys.

Tyr opened his arms and pulled me into a tight hug. "We'll have to get checked out for injuries."

"You're okay?" I pressed a kiss to his claim mark.

"Vidar lost some feathers, but yes. We're okay."

"That was fun guys." Dillys glanced around. "I'm not sure how the higher ups are going to feel about the mess we made."

Vidar stepped out of the room and came back moments later with my tunic. He tugged it on over my head. "Let's go outside and make the calls."

"What about the bug?" Dillys nudged Gable with a toe while wrinkling her nose.

I didn't have the heart to correct her that a scorpion was not a bug. I wasn't even sure what it was but I knew that much.

"They can deal with him, too." Tyr curled his lips. "Good riddance."

Without another word, Tyr scooped me off my feet and carried me out. While I squealed in surprise, I had to say it was nice being pampered.

"I'd say we had a successful week. Mated and learned teamwork." Vidar smiled and took my hand walking along side of us.

My school tattoo burned and then cooled. I glanced down in time to see the hourglass shatter into dust. Whatever the magic wanted from me, I apparently delivered. I certainly learned a great deal more than I expected in the last week, and classes hadn't even started yet.

CHAPTER 13

We made it back to the Valkyrie statue just as Addie and several of the Regents reached it as well.

"You've got a lot of explaining to do." Elsmed scanned each of our faces.

"There's a student, Gable, in the security servers. We knocked him out. He was your hacker." Vidar gestured behind us. "You'll probably want to get to him before he wakes up."

Mr. Doyle gave some commands to the security staff with them before looking at me. "I'll be watching you, Roxanne McCabe. Keep up the good work."

I frowned at his retreating back, not really understanding whatever message he tried to give.

"We need food, a shower, and sleep." Tyr tightened his hold and stepped around the Regents. "We're happy to answer questions afterwards."

"I can answer most of your questions, now I think." Dillys winked at me while addressing the group.

They said nothing to us as Tyr carried me away with Vidar close behind.

"You should move in with us," Tyr suggested.

"Too fast," Vidar muttered but smiled.

"We have the space." Tyr glanced down at me. "Please?"

"I think that's the first time you've ever said please to me." I smiled at him and tucked a wild strand of hair behind his ear. "But, no. I'm not moving in."

"Yet. We'll work on that." Tyr grinned. "You will before the semester's over. I promise you that, kitten."

"We'll see." I leaned up against him and closed my eyes. I could trust my guys to take care of me.

The questions from the Regents never came. Two weeks into classes and other than a thank you for your hard work, we got nothing. Not even news on Gable. Despite his fighting with Tyr, I didn't wish anything bad on Gable. I hoped everything turned out okay for him.

Bryony fought good-naturedly with my guys for my attention. Dillys was an excellent lab partner. And poor Vidar couldn't fist fight to save a kitten, but I loved him anyway.

I had a tower full of teammates, my friends, and my new family. If anyone told me three years ago this was where I'd be, I'd be furious at their cruel joke. Life had a way of moving down the path least expected. The school year could only get better from here.

But then the gong reverberated through campus again, and two girls went missing by the lake.

SHADOWED BY TIME

JUSTINE WINTER

stared at the twelve-foot tall statue in the middle of the vestibule, craning my neck to take it all in. Magnificent wings spread behind her back, a winged helmet rested atop her head, and with both hands she gripped the hilt of a longsword, point facing down where it almost touched the ground. Her position was different from the night I arrived. Somehow the statue had moved. Then she'd had the sword in one hand, while the other was palm up, purple flame lighting the way.

Her stance was so strong I could feel her power emanating from her core, guarding the portals. I was overwhelmed by how potent and intense the energy pouring from the Valkyrie was. It was strange that I could almost feel a connection with the statue, a kinship of sorts.

What was this place doing to me?

"I knew I'd find you here. Two weeks in and you're still haunting this statue. Afraid she's going to wake up and get you?" Shade burst into a deep bellyful laughter. The reaper was never without his trademark tan boots and leather jacket. Did he even own any other clothes?

"The only person haunting these grounds is you, Shade. Don't let that skin suit fool you, dude. You're still bones and a black mist when a soul calls to you, old man."

Shade gasped mockingly, clutching his fake heart. "Is this why you're alone? No one else can handle your British sarcasm?"

He folded his arms over his chest, raising his brows with a seriousness about him.

I sighed. There went my fun. "You know I like my space, nearly eight years alone . . ."

"Fighting the world by yourself, I know." His features softened. "But I hoped you would've integrated with someone by now, Nadine. What about your roommate?"

I shrugged, my body shrinking a few millimeters with despair. "She's all right, I guess. Nice enough."

"But you still don't trust anyone here?" Shade filled in the blanks. For a guy who liked to crack a lot of jokes, he sure did have the knack for insight.

"Would you trust anyone so quickly knowing what I've endured?" I placed my hands on my hips, pouting my lips.

He rubbed his eyes. "Probably not. Doesn't mean I wouldn't try though. You can't spend your entire existence alone, baby cakes. Even here, you'll need to rely on others if you're going to make it through all four years."

I scoffed. "I doubt it. I survived this long on my own."

"Doesn't mean your battles couldn't have been halved with help. Don't be so quick to judge everyone by the same standards of your past. Not here—everyone's been chosen for a reason. Besides, if we were meant to remain alone in solitude, then our creator wouldn't have made more than one of us. As a species of creatures, we are designed to mingle."

I narrowed my eyes with curiosity. "Why are you here, exactly? Clearly you're not a student, and you already reap souls for a living. So what are you getting out of this?"

"Must everyone have an ulterior motive?"

Silence filled the room.

Shade slumped with exasperation. "I live here now, in

Havenwood Falls. This is the next phase of my existence. I want to make the most of it."

I raised a brow.

"By prowling on teenage girls? Or is it the boys who take your fancy?" I smirked.

"Careful, Nadine. That kind of sarcasm at the wrong adult will have you experiencing the academy's version of punishment. We may have a rapport, but I am still your senior, and there are elders in these halls who will expect you to treat me as such."

"Wait, wait, wait. Hold on." I placed my hands palms-forward in the air. "You're telling me you're a teacher here?" My mouth couldn't hang any lower if I tried.

"Not quite. More like an assistant."

"Oh, you're a gofer?" I laughed, struggling to see the reaper take orders from anyone other than Death. What did he have to lose?

"Hardly, baby cakes. Just make sure you remember to respect—"

"Oh my goddess! Did you hear? Two students have gone missing!" A group of girls walked by, distracting me momentarily, their voices too loud to ignore.

"I know! Michelle said they went down to the lake and never came back!"

"What do you think happened?"

"No one knows, but it can't be good. Makes me wonder what's down there . . ."

"Oh, shut up, Courtney! They probably left, couldn't handle the pressure here . . ."

I turned my attention back to Shade, rolling my eyes at the gossip.

A loud gong boomed throughout the mountain, reverberating around the room. My ears pierced from the sound, burning my mind with an instant headache. My left wrist scorched with a flame I couldn't see. The school's crest tattoo I had inked into my flesh as a requirement disappeared, and a new one appeared in its place.

"No," I whispered, pulling my wrist close enough to see. Shade leaned in, obviously curious by my fussing.

"Don't forget what I said about trusting others, baby cakes. Friendships are what get you through life; they make it interesting."

I nodded, walking away as I glared at my wrist, my mind racing in a million directions. The new tattoo glowed for a couple seconds and then settled.

What the hell was this?

CHAPTER 2

I walked around the campus in a daze, paying even less attention to the people around me, and more on the new hourglass tattoo on my wrist, one side full of sand. What the hell was it there for? Why had it appeared now? How did I get rid of it?

My blood coursed through my veins with a newfound energy I couldn't explain, but I could still feel the emptiness that always seemed to sing beneath my skin—a constant reminder that I was shadowed with blackness.

A curse.

"Yo, Amazon! Watch where you're going."

I stopped abruptly, forced to when my face smacked hard into some guy's chest. Thank Goddess he was wearing a shirt. Chest curlies tickling my nose would not make this day any better.

"Sorry, uh . . ." I paused, glancing the guy over. What was his name again? Daniel? No, David? Or was it Dalton? I was sure I shared a class with the guy. . .

"Dylan," he offered, grinning hard. "I'll pretend that you forgetting my name doesn't wound me, darlin'. As long as you remember that the next time you wanna kiss my pecs." He winked.

I snorted, rolling my eyes. "If I even *wanted* to squish my face

131

against your body, I would've made sure to remember your name *first*. Don't flatter yourself, dude. You're just a good boulder is all."

"Ouch. I like a girl with a smart mouth."

"Shame, because I don't like boys who get in my way. Bye." I skirted around him, leaving him tongue-tied and mouth agape.

"Hold up. You're not escaping me that easily. Not after you deliberately threw yourself at me."

I glared at the tall guy matching pace beside me. This would not end well . . . for him.

"What do you want?" I paused in the large entrance of Halstein Hall, my stomach gurgling loud enough to remind me I hadn't eaten.

"What's with all the animosity, darlin'? Are you hangry? 'Cause I know we aren't acquainted well enough for you to be so pissed off with me."

A snarky response was on the tip of my tongue when Shade's earlier warnings made me think twice. Was I being a bitch?

"You wanna grab a bite? If I don't eat soon, I'm going to collapse."

Dylan's eyes widened, taken aback by my offer. He wasn't the only one surprised. What was I thinking? It was like my mouth said one thing while my mind thought the opposite.

"Is that a medical thing?" He frowned, and for the briefest moment, he looked like he may be concerned.

"Is what a medical thing?"

"Collapsing, if you don't eat?"

I laughed. "No, I just like food. A body like mine requires a lot of calorific energy."

He took a long, slow glance up and down my body. His intense gaze made me blush, and I almost gave in to fidgeting, but I wasn't going to give him the satisfaction and reveal the effect he had on me. It was a temporary glitch anyway. I wasn't completely numb and impervious to young adult hormones, no matter how hard I tried.

I resumed my brisk walk to the canteen, needing some

distance, and a reason to move. "Did you want something from me, Dylan?"

He smirked. "Now there's an offer I can't refuse. Where do I start?"

I joined the queue with my food tray and ignored the double entendre. I took a sneak peek at my wrist, not sure whether I should expect the tattoo to still be there.

"Nadine, hello, are you even listening?" Dylan's hand waved in my face, drawing me out of my mind and back into the canteen.

"Sorry," I mumbled, taking note of the contents piled on my tray. It seemed I could handle food automatically, no thought required.

"Are you really going to eat all of that?" Dylan eyed my tray. It was full with a chicken and bacon baguette, a bowl of fries, chocolate pudding, a lemon muffin, a bag of fruit, and two drinks.

I shrugged, not ashamed by my appetite. It wasn't like I was obese either; I wasn't greedy. Clearly, Dylan never met someone of my kind before, although that wasn't necessarily a bad thing, not with how they treated me. And besides, when you lived on the street, you learned to grab food the moment you could. I'd seen plenty of days without any kind of sustenance, and with the speed of my metabolism, it took a toll on my body fast.

Killed by starvation had never been my choice of death, and yet it was the only one to have come close a few times. It wasn't pretty. There was nothing romantic about it. All these girls in the world looking up to magazines and silly programs, willing to starve themselves for so-called love were idiots. *Newsflash, dude.* No guy gave a shit whether you ate for him or not. It wasn't *his* belly growling constantly, mood worsening, or fatigue overtaking everything.

Starvation was painful and ugly. It was a slow, agonizing process while your organs eventually shut down, one by one. You didn't get thin; you became skeletal, like Shade's true form. Skin stretched so tightly over bones, your pallor became gray, almost translucent.

"Don't even think about eyeing this up. It's all mine," I warned, flashing my wrist tattoo to the cashier for payment. *Shit!* I'd forgotten the school's crest tattoo had been changed to this weird hourglass one! What was I going to do?

Wait . . . What? I flicked my wrist again and noticed the tattoo change, almost like a hologram, the cashier none the wiser to my internal meltdown. She hurried me along, and unlike Dylan, she was wise enough not to comment on my portion sizes anymore—not after that first day anyway. I certainly couldn't be the only supe here with a big appetite. I wasn't the only one growing and expelling energy at such a fast rate. Right?

"Are you always this prickly about everything?" Dylan joined me at an empty table, placing his tray on top. I rolled my eyes to myself—for all the fuss about *my* food, *his* plate wasn't much smaller.

I sighed aloud, noting how well I seemed to be doing at letting my guard down enough to make some semblance of a friend. *Not.* "I'm used to the people I normally have a conversation with trying to kill me at the same time. Sarcasm is what I know."

I didn't apologize for the way I was. It was how the world shaped me.

"You seem to have a pretty normal friendship with that reaper though. What makes him so different?"

I visibly cringed. Was he suggesting there was something between Shade and me? *Eww.* "I've known him a long time, years in fact."

He was the closest thing I'd ever come to calling a friend. How pathetic was that? I never saw him every day either. Once a month, at most, if I could find a new place to hide long enough before I offered him his next soul to escort.

"Listen, I'm not going to sit here and pour my heart out to you because you've made some brief realizations about me. And I'm not going to be your damsel either." I purposefully omitted the sense of connection I had with Shade, knowing it would be taken wrong, and the truth wouldn't be well received either. If people found out I was cursed with the shadows of black magic, they'd turn on me faster than you'd ever imagine. I'd seen it time and time again. But with Shade, it had always been different, probably because he was made of the darkness, and the shadows in me found some solace in that.

"Why are you here, Nadine? You don't seem very happy, not like most people here who worked their asses off to get in."

I shrugged, taking a mouthful of my baguette to bide my time. "I was recruited."

Dylan shook his head. "I know that, but why go through the hassle if you don't really want to belong here?"

"I didn't have any better offers at the time, so why not?"

Dylan tutted, rubbing large hands over his face. "Seems like a waste to me. Energy, time, resources. It's gonna feel like a very long four years for you."

I bristled at his insinuation. "Pipe down, dude. I heard you weren't here by choice either, so don't even think about preaching to me, hypocrite."

He smiled, licking his plate clean. "See, I knew you knew who I was before. And if you want to know my secret . . ." He leaned over the table to whisper in my ear. "I found something worth staying for." He pulled away, my skin tickling from his hot breath leaving my face. "See you around, Amazon. I'll have my bulletproof vest on next time."

He winked and disappeared, the sound of his trailing laughter reaching my ears.

"Cocky bastard," I grumbled into my plate.

"Oh my goddess! Were you really talking to Dylan Wray?"

I jumped in my seat, flinging a spoon of chocolate pudding into the air as Tess, my nice-enough roommate, came barreling at my table, her long platinum blond hair fanning around her face.

"Why did everyone want to speak to me today?" I mumbled to myself before answering Tess. "I'd call it less talking and more like oral warfare. Why?"

Her face blushed a bright pink at my turn of phrase. She chewed her bottom lip, sliding the thick, black-rimmed glasses hiding blue eyes up her nose. "You do know he's no good, right?

It's just an act. Don't ever trust a shapeshifter, Nadine. You never know which face they're showing you."

"What did he do to you?" I asked, noting her settling down into the seat he'd just vacated, dumping her bags all around her. Why did she need so many?

"What do you mean?" Her brows creased.

"What did he do to you to make you not trust him? And, subsequently, enough to want to warn me too?"

She looked down at her hands, fumbling with a hangnail. "Nothing, per se. But it's his species. You can't trust someone who can be anyone they want."

I almost felt sorry for her naiveté. "Tess, anyone can do that. All they have to do is move away from the people who know them and create a new identity someplace else. It happens all the time— don't need to be a shapeshifter, or even a supe, to be able to do so."

"Oh." She deflated, and began to mumble so rapidly I had absolutely no idea what she was saying.

I glanced at my wrist again, expecting some kind of explanation to pop out.

"Did you hear the news this morning?" Tess popped up, suddenly reinvigorated with energy.

Goddess, I was not cut out for gossip. My lack of response spurred her on.

"A student died. Someone from Hel tower apparently. His body was found down by the lake. People are freaking out about it. Even the professors are perplexed."

I couldn't believe I was letting myself get sucked in. "I thought they were just missing . . ." I began just as Tess bounced out of her seat, bags in tow, and grabbed my arm.

"They?" Her eyes bulged. "Oh my goddess, we have to go! Come on!" She dragged me out of my seat. I almost popped my arm out of my shoulder.

"Why the rush?" I whined, selfishly thinking of my own problems, like this mysterious tattoo. Did Tess have one?

"Come on, Nadine. Aren't you even a little bit curious?"

CHAPTER 3

"Damn, we're not going to make it through this crowd." Tess stopped, pissed at all the other lurkers wanting to sneak a look at the drama unfolding below the bridge. What did she expect? I saw a raven perched atop one of the twin Valkyrie statues at the end of the bridge, watching the scene below. The school was littered with the statues, some hidden in dark corners, others more on display.

I scratched my wrist, the skin becoming itchier by the second. The more I scratched, the more satisfying and itchy it became. It was a no-win situation.

"What are you do—" Tess grabbed my arm, scorning me like a child without control. "Oh my," she whispered, turning away from the crowd, forgetting the scene at the bridge and dragging me back into the main campus area. "I've seen this marking before," she mumbled. "I know I have. Where was it?" She frowned to herself, suddenly on a mission as she quickened her pace through the courtyard and found an empty bench away from passers-by.

"Do you have one?" I asked, plonking my butt on the cold wooden surface. She shook her head, eyes glazed over as though she was lost in her thoughts.

"It came earlier, just magically etched itself on my skin . . ." I babbled, wondering why I was even bothering to share. I hated to admit it, but something about her strange reaction to the ink had me more concerned by its sudden appearance. Was it an omen or something? *Like I needed more curses in my life . . .*

"Got it!" She jumped, suddenly coming alive. "Do you know Roxy from Jory Tower?"

I frowned, searching my memory for the name. Although, honestly, I wasn't sure why. It wasn't like I'd really paid attention to anyone here. "No, I don't think so."

Tess shook her head. "Honestly, Nadine. How do you get by day-to-day without being present and aware of what's happening around you?"

I bristled at her tone, though she wasn't entirely wrong. I believed I observed my surroundings well. I just did my best to not listen to it. In my experience so far, there'd been less educational talk and more rumor-mill fodder spreading like fire. I had as much interest in that as I did going to the toilet. Both were functions I had to endure as a part of this existence.

"This Roxy chick has this tattoo as well?"

"She did, but not anymore. I don't think."

"And?" I asked impatiently. "What did it do? Does it mean anything?"

Tess blinked, her expression blank as though she was trying to remember. "I was there in the room when she knocked over that hourglass. The first gong sounded and then she grabbed her wrist as if in pain. That tattoo showed up." She pointed at my wrist as though I needed clarity as to *which* tattoo she was referring.

"What happened after that?" I stood, needing to pace.

Tess shrugged. "I don't know. But she did defeat that hacker and kept us protected."

I stared at Tess. "Are the two events related?"

"I have no idea. Just telling you what I've seen. It's the upside to being a wallflower. Nobody censors what they say or do when they don't even notice you in the same room."

I contemplated her words for a second, slightly remorseful over my own attitude toward her. I imagined I hadn't been the most caring or even friendly of roommates either. Not that I had anything against her exactly. It was just my nature to distance myself from everyone.

I paused, staring above Tess. "Uh, there's another one."

I pointed to a large, glowing hourglass hovering in the air, the top half full of sand, the bottom half empty. There had been one there before, but it had vanished after the chaos with the drones and that Gable dude.

"Did that just appear?" Tess frowned.

I nodded, glancing at my wrist. They were duplicates of each other.

"They have to be connected. Let me help you with this, Nadine. We can figure this business out together. Please don't shut me out like everyone else."

I cringed at the low blow. What was I supposed to say to that? "Okay, but this is just between us."

"Yes!" She fist bumped the air as if in triumph. "What are you going to do now?"

I sighed heavily, my energy depleted already. "I've got combat class—in fact, I'm already late and Professor Shimizu is gonna kick my arse for this."

"I'll meet you back in the dorm later?"

"Whatever, dude. Laters!" I called, running out of the courtyard. I was definitely going to be in the shit for being late.

Bollocks, I was going to hurt tonight.

I crawled my way from the clifftop, sad to say goodbye to the sunshine and green forest. Shadows weighed heavily on my body as I descended the mountain. My limbs ached as though they'd been replaced by iron bars, dragging me down.

I concentrated on my feet, watching the ground like a hawk, knowing how easy it would be for me to fall over by not lifting my feet high enough. It felt as though the shadows were cloaking me, trying to push in on me and make me crumble.

I was weak, and this was when they attacked me. Forcing the darkness on me, attempting to make me pass out, allowing them the opportunity to control me.

My head pounded brutally, and I swayed on my feet. Losing my balance, I toppled down the remaining few steps.

"Yeesh, what's wrong with you, Amazon? Had a few too many drinks?" Dylan came to my side, too much cheer and energy emanating from him for my liking.

I tried pushing myself up, but my body wasn't willing to cooperate, and instead Dylan got to see his damsel after all.

"What's wrong with you, Nadine? Do you need food again?" He almost looked cute worrying about me. What the hell was I thinking?

"I always want food," I groaned. "But right now I just want to go to bed." My eyes faltered, betraying my tiredness.

"Ooh, is that an offer, darlin'? 'Cause you know I can't refuse those beautiful eyes of yours." Dylan grinned widely, showing off a set of perfectly pearly white teeth.

"Shut up and help me, will you?" I held out my hand, needing a boost off the ground. "Anytime today."

He crossed his arms over his chest. "Actually, I quite like you being vulnerable to me, makes me feel all manly. How often do you hear about an Amazon needing help with strength?"

I stared him down with as much hatred as I could muster. "Either help me or run away, because when I do get my energy back, you're going to wish you'd never met me."

He snorted, looking at me incredulously. "I don't do threats. They're just empty words made to instill fear. Please, I've lived with them my whole life." He shrugged like it was no big deal. "You don't scare me, darlin', so you can drop the act."

He yanked me up until I was steady on my feet.

Shadows hovered around me, pushing their oppression onto me.

"You need me to take you upstairs? You're in Heimdall Tower, right?"

I glared at Dylan. "Don't even think about it. I'm not *that* easy."

He grunted, moving away from me. "Just trying to be helpful. Not everyone is out to get you, darlin'."

He sauntered away, and I could see his being shimmer as it changed shape. He turned, and I was suddenly faced with an identical version of myself. The Dylan-Nadine tossed her hair and winked, blowing a kiss at me before shifting back into his usual Dylan-esque body.

I cracked a laugh. *Dammit!* He'd managed to push my shadows away ever so slightly. I couldn't let it happen again, or I'd start to rely on him, and that was a weakness I could never afford to have exploited. A warrior's weakness was always her detriment.

Shit.

CHAPTER 4

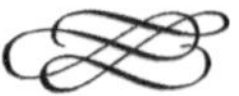

His arms were around my neck, choking the life out of me as I struggled for air. I kicked out on the wet ground, trying to wriggle out of his grasp. It was no use. His arms were locked tight.

"Die, you disgusting half-breed," he yelled in my ear, voice straining.

I refused to give in to the demand. Rain battered my body, and my skin was soaked from lying on the ground. As much as I tried resisting the chokehold he had me trapped in, the more I ended up succumbing to my fate.

I thought of the soft, sweet mother I had as a baby—of the kindness I always saw looking up into her green eyes. A face I could never look upon again.

Rage consumed me like fire, angry flames stoked my desire to live, and a newfound strength ignited within me. I felt my energy warming up throughout my body, and my attacker hesitated for a second, long enough for what I needed to do.

"Nadine."

I grabbed the more dominant arm choking me, and with this boost in strength, I felt him peel away, slowly losing his grip.

"Nadine."

He threw me to one side, and then the other, the both of us rocking on the ground. The momentum afforded me the chance to get on my feet and adjust the dynamics.

"Nadine, come on."

I shot out my arm, grabbing his neck with my hand.

"Na . . . di . . . ne."

I opened my eyes, surprised to see the face in front of me was much more feminine than the one I witnessed moments ago. Her blue eyes bulged behind her glasses, and her lips matched the color of her irises. I quickly moved my hand from her neck.

"I'm sorry," I began, realizing there wasn't much more I could really say.

"Don't worry about it," Tess's voice spluttered in a deep husky tone. "Why are you here? When you didn't come back to the dorm last night, I started worrying."

I saw the fear shining in her eyes, although that could have been from me crushing her trachea. *Oops.*

I glanced around the extra dark hallways, trying to make sense of where I was. "How did you find me?"

I noticed the area wasn't exactly heavy with traffic. In fact, the place was empty, and I was so tucked out of the way, it was surprising she found me at all.

Even in the darkness I could see her skin blush. "You were groaning. I've been searching the campus for hours, and when I came this way, I could hear you. At first I wondered if you'd stood me up because you had a much more satisfactory offer." She paused to look down at her hands. "But then you started yelling, and I knew you were in trouble. I didn't, however, expect you to be curled up in a ball, having a nightmare."

I burst into laughter, unable to control myself. "You thought I was having sex?"

Her eyes widened before she too laughed. "Honestly, I didn't think I should interrupt if you were having a good time. I don't think either one of us would've wanted to see that."

She continued to laugh, relaxing.

I dried my eyes with my sleeve. "I crashed before I could get back to the room. Professor Shimizu really laid into me for being late." I paused, thinking. I didn't remember much. "I must have found this space as a hideout to rest."

I guessed some habits were harder to shake than others—my body entered defense mode when my mind couldn't keep up.

"Come on, let's get back to Heimdall Tower. You reckon you can make it now?"

What did I do to earn such concern from her? I didn't deserve it.

"Yeah, I'm fine. Rested and rejuvenated." We stood and turned away from my hideout space, heading toward a small glowing lantern in the distance. I hated to even think what time it was.

"I'm surprised you feel rested at all after that nightmare. What was it?"

Though Tess's question was innocent enough, I knew I couldn't tell her the truth. Learning I was an abomination and must be killed was one thing. Finding out it was because I was tortured with black magic and therefore *must* be evil incarnate was something else. At least that's what I'd always been told. Any concern she once had for me would be gone.

"Oh, you know, the usual. Fighting in combat class only to get halfway through and your clothes have suddenly disappeared and everyone's staring and laughing at your naked body." I hesitated, wondering if people really did think this embarrassing enough to dream about it. I overheard a similar conversation before, many years ago, but I failed to believe in it myself. Why would we be afraid to show off our bodies? They were our temples after all.

"Oh my goddess," Tess finally reacted. "I have the same nightmare over and over. Except mine is because I've forgotten to get dressed and just strolled out of the dorm like nothing's wrong."

I stared at her dumbfounded until I remembered I was supposed to be thinking the same. "I promise I'll never let you walk out of the room like that, as long as I'm there of course."

I winked, hoping we'd moved past the extreme holes in my lie.

"I think it's because I'm afraid I'll get dementia."

I stopped. "You tiger shifters can get that? I didn't think the supernatural could succumb to such a thing."

"Well, my grandad did. I watched it riddle his brain until he couldn't remember anything. His name. His family. When he needed the toilet. I don't know how you can live and not remember how to function. And then, on the good days, he would remember my grandmother, and ask when she was coming home, only for us to have to remind him she's been dead for decades. Instantly, the wave of pain was like he was experiencing losing her for the first time all over again, and it happened so often, it broke my heart to witness it. I hate it, and this is why I'm afraid. Dementia brings you nothing but pain to yourself, and to the ones you love."

"Wow, that's deep." Disgust burned within my core. What had I done? Tess was opening up her heart to me, and I couldn't even tell her the truth of my nightmare.

"Sorry, I didn't mean to bum you out with all this seriousness."

"Don't be silly, I'm glad you shared this with me. I . . ." I paused mid-sentence, darkness clouding my vision, shadows ruthlessly pressing in on me. A sense of urgency crept up into my chest, and my heart hammered away, booming heavily as though I was supposed to march with it.

"Something's wrong," I stated vaguely, earning a quizzical look from Tess.

"What do you mean?" She glanced around as though looking for a threat.

"I'm not sure, but I can't. . ." A wave of nausea washed over me, and a sense of restlessness had me all agitated. It was as though the world around me was crushing my body, forcing me to react.

"I need to go," I decided, leading the way out of the hall. The more I walked, the more I was flooded with a sense of urgency.

"Has this happened before?" Tess caught up, matching my pace.

"Not as badly as this. I mean, I've felt like I've needed to be somewhere before, but that was more like a general sense. This makes me feel like I'm going to throw up and die if I don't hurry.

But I don't know why!" I exclaimed, feeling a whole load of overwhelm and inability to perform.

"Isn't this place amazing? It's so beautiful! Who'd have thought an academy would be deep in a mountain? It's genius!" Tess distracted me momentarily by taking note of our environment.

"It is." I couldn't deny how blown away I'd been by the landscape. Stalactites and stalagmites were everywhere, and all the buildings appeared as though they'd always been a part of the large cavern formation. Everything here seemed so authentic in its creation that it made me wonder how it all came to be. Who found it?

"Don't you just love this view? And the sound of the water gushing by?" Tess stopped on the bridge to admire the river below. "You'd never believe this was a crime scene earlier, would you? Nothing's out of place, no crowds, it's like business as usual." Her voice hollowed as though she was haunted by the idea that the world could move on so quickly. "Still, that's better than a rotting corpse on display I suppose." She tried to lighten the mood.

"You know, Tess, you have quite the unusually happy outlook on life, don't you? Although you're a bit of an anomaly—shy one minute, bubbly the next."

She smirked. "Well, it's better than being miserable. Don't you agree?"

"I think it depends on what you've already been through in life," I countered, wondering what kind of upbringing she had.

"It's still a choice. You can let life run you, or you can run your life."

I nodded slowly, seeing her point. "You know, I'm beginning to see how much of an enigma you are. Anymore hidden talents I should know about? Any more profound phrases that may make me reassess my viewpoint on things?"

Tess whacked my arm. "Are you mocking me, Nadine?"

I rubbed my arm, surprised by the strength behind her hit. "Tess, I meant it, you weirdo. Can't you tell the difference between sarcasm and sincerity?"

She frowned, looking downtrodden. "Apparently not, though it wouldn't be the first time I've been ridiculed for my beliefs."

"Damn, dude, looks like we've both got our hang-ups to deal with." I took a breath, taking a good look at my roommate. "Tess, why do you wear those glasses? I mean, you can see clearly, right? Shifters don't have eyesight issues, right?"

Tess burst into laughter, clearly enjoying how uncomfortable I was in asking what seemed like a perfectly normal question, but with further thought was quite idiotic. Did it even matter? Why was I perplexed by this?

"No, Nadine, my eyesight is perfect. But I like wearing them. They're kind of my fashion statement. Plus, it just makes me look smart." She continued to laugh, unfazed by whatever opinion I could've formed.

"You know you don't have to *look* smart to *be* smart."

She pursed her lips. "I can't decide if that's a compliment or an insult."

I shook my head, smiling. "Come on, I feel like we're getting close."

I took her arm, looping it with mine. As we reached the end of the bridge, we headed right, following the path of the river.

"Getting close to what?" Her eyes widened.

I shrugged. "I don't know yet, but it's definitely this way."

My skin sizzled with electricity, as though the air was making me come alive.

"Whoa, do you think?" Tess pulled me to a stop after veering right off the main path. We stood in front of a large wall, the smallest of holes its only entrance. I sighed loudly, already succumbing to my fate.

"Do you think I'm supposed to push through that teeny hole?" I paused. "You can bet on it, this feeling isn't going away. Hope you like the rear view." I laughed, knowing she'd have her face by my arse. I crouched down on my knees, squeezing my head and shoulders through the gap. "Man, this is tight," I grunted. The cavernous walls scraped against my skin, and the uneven surface proved difficult to navigate.

"Can you see how far it goes like this?" Tess called from behind.

I glanced ahead, seeing nothing but darkness. "I hope you're not claustrophobic."

I scooted forward, going as fast as I could. Sweat trickled from my forehead, the lack of space making the shaft a boiling tube.

"I think we're close, I can . . ." I lost my grip as the tight crawl space opened up. The base disappeared, and I fell, tumbling through air as though time ceased before I landed.

"Nadine!" Tess's voice echoed in the chamber.

My back cracked as I landed heavily, narrowly missing a cluster of stalagmites protruding out of the ground.

"Shit, shit, shit." Tess came running over, clearly saving herself from the same fate as me. "Can you move?" She hovered over me, hands moving without direction, as though she had no idea what to do, but wanted to help.

I closed my eyes, taking note of the extent of my injuries. "Guess you saw the drop?" I murmured. "Lucky I went first, huh?"

Tess tutted at my lack of humor, gasping in shock as I stood up, stretching out my limbs as though I hadn't just fallen several feet.

"Doesn't that hurt? You could have internal bleeding or something."

"Don't stress. I'm fine. I'm practically impenetrable—gifts of being an Amazon."

"You mean you can't get hurt? Ever?" Her eyes widened in shock.

"All the time. I just heal at such an accelerated rate, it looks like I haven't broken anything." I patted myself down, taking stock of this new location. Though it was dark, pockets of light beamed on the cave-like walls, like spotlights highlighting the area. The river running under the bridge flowed along the wall like a waterfall, pooling into a larger stream.

"Look at this." I followed the stream, the buzz I felt earlier returning. Tess followed, paying more attention to the ground than I did.

"It's getting wider, like another lake," she whispered in awe, as we delved deeper into the cave.

"Do you think anyone knows this is here?" I asked. "Doesn't look like there's been much, if any, footfall. It's pretty secluded from the main lake, right, the one those towers look out on?"

Tess grabbed my hands, squeaking.

"What?"

She pushed her finger to her lips, shushing me. Pointing at her eyes, she then pointed at the lake, and I saw what had her suddenly mute.

Bright orange eyes glowed in the water. "You don't belong here. LEAVE!"

"I'm not going anywhere." I stood my ground, glaring back at the bright orange eyes.

"Are you insane, Nadine? We need to go." Tess tried yanking my arm, but I didn't budge. I didn't come all this way to walk away now.

"Don't be foolish, little girl. Listen to your friend." Orange Eyes hissed at me, never revealing any more of its face. What was in there?

I put my hands on my hips, bracing myself. "No. I was made to come here, and I'm not leaving until I find out why."

Tess slinked behind me, clearly not feeling as brave, or I guess stupid, as me.

"Do you think you can kill me, girl? These waters are *mine*!"

Belatedly a thought occurred. "You killed that student!"

Tess gasped. "Why?"

"You don't intrude on my home and *not* do as you're told," the voice threatened. The water erupted, gaining height like a tsunami.

"Uh, Nadine? Maybe it's definitely time we go now?" Tess' voice was so quiet, I almost didn't hear her over the roar of the water.

I shook my head. "No, it's just a scare tactic. We can push through this," I urged, hoping she'd find her courage.

"Can you breathe under water? 'Cause I sure as hell can't, and I'm not a fan of drowning either."

I heard the fear in her voice loud and clear.

"Are you really so selfish you'd ignore your friend's worries?" The hiss penetrated the room as though the water was carrying its voice.

I wanted to prove that I could take this unknown beast on, but did I do it at the expense of Tess? I glanced at her, overcome with this need to protect her. She looked so small, eyes wide as though she'd been caught in a trap, completely out of her element. It was clear she'd gotten into the school for her brains rather than her brawn.

"Come on. Let's go," I decided, motioning for her to scramble back up to the entrance. Water swirled around us, splashing wildly as it threw us around.

"See you soon," the hiss sniggered.

CHAPTER 6

"You weren't really going to stay there, were you? I mean, you looked like leaving wasn't even an option." Tess brushed her hair, moving to sit on her bed. Tess's side of the room was ensconced in a jungle theme. Large palm leaf-print paper covered the wall her bed rested against, matching the covers. A canopy with fairy lights intertwined cascaded from the ceiling, shielding her bed, and plants of all sizes were dotted around the room, wherever they could fit.

I rubbed my eyes, tiredness kicking in again. "I don't usually run away from a fight."

"Right, but that's just in combat class."

I shook my head, moving the plain covers off my bed before I got in. Unlike Tess, I had very little to decorate my side of the room. I didn't have many possessions let alone much money to buy them. Material things weren't really my style. I liked the minimalism—everything having its precise, clean, tidy, and organized location. In fact, my piercings all along both ears, my tongue, and belly button were the most extravagant expense I'd ever indulged. That, and my trusty dagger Dave. "Tess, I've been fighting for most of my life. I know how to take care of myself."

"WHAT?" Her eyes bulged out of her head. "How? When? *Who* have you had to fight? Why?"

The questions rolled off her tongue, one after the other with barely a breath between them. I couldn't tell if she was excited or appalled. Perhaps both.

I sighed heavily. What did I tell her? "Well, I haven't exactly had a wholesome upbringing. I've been on my own for nearly eight years."

"No way!" She gasped, hand covering her mouth, hairbrush tossed on the bed, all but forgotten. "You seem so normal. Well, except for preferring to do everything by yourself, but I guess that makes sense now. You were so standoffish when we first met. I figured you just didn't like me, but I was determined to get to know you, then yesterday everything changed, and suddenly we're like besties! Why *did* you change your mind by the way? Not that I'm complaining. I prefer it this way. And oh my goddess, we can be like proper roomies now. Tell each other secrets, do make-up, talk about boys. This is just what I wanted from the beginning. I knew you were a soft center really. I just had to crack that hard shell first. And . . ."

"Dude, chill! Grab some air, please. I do *not* feel like giving you mouth-to-mouth because you forgot to breathe. Do it with me. In." I inhaled a deep breath, encouraging her to copy. "And out. And again," I urged, watching her color return to a more natural skin tone. Her bright red pallor from moments ago looked like she was going to explode.

"Let's just take things a step at a time, okay? I'm not used to being around people all the time, let alone share my sleeping space. It's taking some adjustment." I didn't let on how much of an understatement that really was. I barely slept the first week, waiting for reality to hit and an attack to be made while my guard was down. I still expected it, even now. Two weeks at the academy didn't get rid of several years' worth of habits. I'd be a fool to forget so quickly.

"What happened to your family?" Tess's voice returned to a

more sympathetic tone and less like the overexcited squawk from moments ago.

I braced myself, my heart pumping wildly as I was bashed with a slew of emotions. "I lost my mum when I was nine, and never knew my dad."

"Oh, I'm so sorry, Nadine. I can't even begin to imagine what that's like. You didn't have any other family to take you in?" I could see she was struggling with her inquisitive nature, wondering whether she should ask anything else. But, surprisingly, I was glad she did. I owed it to myself to acknowledge out loud what I'd endured, and she should know something after what she had already openly shared with me. That was how these friendship things worked, right?

"I did have a much wider family of Amazons."

"Why do I feel that's not as happy as it should be?" Tess groaned.

"They were kind, loving people. Took care of me to the best of their ability."

Tess frowned, crossing her legs on her bed as though to get more comfortable. "So what happened? Why did you leave them?"

Tess was smart. I'd give her that, picking up on things I'd not yet said.

"I didn't have much of a choice. They found out I wasn't pure Amazon, that my mother had tainted the bloodline."

"They made you leave? Like an outcast?" Tess gasped in horror. "You were just a kid!"

My limbs became stiff, and I stretched out. "I'd just had my tenth birthday. But they weren't going to let me leave." I paused, letting my words sink in. "They were going to kill me."

"WHAT!" she yelled, piercing my eardrums. "How could they do that? Why would, I mean, how can you, what! This is insane!"

"I know. I've lived it. My people, if I can even call them that"—I snorted, shaking my head—"do not abide with inter-species relationships. Clearly, my mother had done well to hide the truth but . . ."

"So how did they find out? Are you part shifter or something?"

I shook my head, choosing my next words carefully. "No, I don't recall much of what I did, but it had been obvious to the elders taking care of me that day that I shouldn't have been able to do such a thing if I were just an Amazon."

"I thought Amazons were only women anyway, so to reproduce surely you'd be tainting the bloodline regardless?"

"It's a common mistake. Our men are referred to as Gargareans —if they're referred to at all. Our females seem to get all the attention in the rest of the world."

"And that forms your bloodline? Amazons and Garg . . . Gargans?" Tess frowned.

"Gargareans. Well, at least that's what I was told."

"Okay, but what if this ability you demonstrated is just a new power because you're special? It's not like everyone in the same species can do the same thing. That would just make us carbon copies and not individuals at all." Tess exploded with passion, her sense of justice provoked. "I mean, my brother could shift years ahead of me. I didn't grow into my stripes until I was seven. I was kind of the runt of the litter, always behind on the physical aspects." She looked down, embarrassed. "That didn't mean I wasn't a tiger though."

I shrugged. "I can't say much about their thought processes. I was only ten. But when they called me in to the elders meeting to discuss my fate, one thing became very clear to me. They were afraid of what I am, and what I can do. That's why I couldn't stay. I left right away—no way was I letting them put my head on the executioner's block. I was a kid, but I wasn't stupid."

"Did they stop you?" Tess murmured, entranced by my past.

"They tried, but I fought back. Once I escaped, I ran for miles, not stopping until I knew I was far enough away for one night."

"And after that?"

"I didn't stop moving. And I was right to. They sent agents out to track me down and kill me."

"Why? Why couldn't they just leave you be? You weren't doing them any harm, right?"

I shook my head at Tess. "To them, I am an abomination.

They won't let me live because I threaten their beliefs. They won't stop until I'm six feet under."

I got out of bed, checking the window was closed one last time.

"So the people you've been fighting have been your own kin?" She still seemed appalled by my revelations.

"Yeah, it's almost become a sport to them. I'm sure there's a bounty on my head, but so far, no one's succeeded."

"Well, I'm sure grateful they haven't. Is that why you're here? A new place to disappear for a while?"

I almost snapped at her judgment before realizing how concerned she was. "Not entirely. I mean, I didn't even know this place existed. Shade recruited me in, persuaded me it was for the best interests of everyone. If anything, being in such a remote place is a perk I wasn't expecting."

"Yeah, there's no way anyone who doesn't belong is getting through here. Not when you've got to get through Havenwood Falls' town wards first, and *then* find the portal to here. Yeah, this is basically a wartime bunker for you. Seems to me Shade knew what he was doing."

I stared at her curiously. "Do you know the reaper?"

She snorted. "Nowhere near as well as you do. I just saw him around town a few times. He caused quite the stir when he first arrived. Or so I'm told."

I shook my head, smiling widely. That was the reaper I knew. Causing entertainment wherever he went.

"Are you okay? I can't imagine reliving your past is so joyful."

My smile turned melancholy. "I'm fine. I guess I've just been thinking about it more recently because it's my birthday tomorrow. It's not really a happy day for me."

Tess squirmed on her bed. "I'm sure it isn't. I'm guessing your nightmare earlier wasn't really about being naked in class?"

I grimaced, hating how calm she seemed over my lie. "Not exactly. More like re-enacting a fight I almost died in."

I failed to look in her eyes, feeling like a coward.

She shrugged it off. "If I dreamt horrors like that, I wouldn't want to share them either. Protection for me as much as them. Hopefully one day you'll trust me enough to share everything."

I smiled, my heart warming from her kindness. "I hope so too. I'm tired of feeling so alone, like the world's always against me."

"Well, I'm not going anywhere." She left her bed, putting her hairbrush on the dresser. "So I guess you really would've stayed to fight off whatever that was in the lake?"

I sighed, remembering the strange encounter that had us awake in the first place. Weren't students supposed to be sleep-deprived in college because of all the parties? I was doing this life all wrong.

"I think I would've, but you made a valid point down there. My strength is no match against an inability to breathe under water. I was too busy thinking with my fists."

"So it was a good thing I was down there with you then?" She raised a brow, pursing her lips.

I rolled my eyes, settling down on my bed, pulling the covers over me. "Did you even get to see what it was?"

She flicked off the room's main light source. "No, only those creepy orange eyes, and that weird hissy voice."

"Same. I still feel like I was supposed to be down there though. It felt right, and that feeling of urgency disappeared immediately." I paused, searching for the right words. "Do you ever feel like fate puts you where you need to be? Like there's a reason for everything?"

"As though we have a higher purpose?" she questioned.

"Perhaps. I just know deep in my gut I have some kind of duty down there to complete. It's a sensation I can't really explain."

"You think it has something to do with that student?"

"Maybe . . ." I contemplated.

"Didn't you say there were two of them missing?"

I sat up in bed, forgetting all about that. "That's what a group of girls were saying, but then you said a student died so I didn't know what to believe."

"What if both were true? That two did disappear but one resurfaced as a body?"

My mind raced in the dark room. "Oh my goddess! What if

they're still down there? Maybe that's why I feel drawn to it, like I'm supposed to save someone?"

"It's possible, Nadine, but we need to be better prepared for next time. Get some sleep. Goodnight."

"Night, Tess." I slumped back into the covers, wondering how I was supposed to sleep when someone might need my help.

Just as I began to doze off, my alarm blared, pulling me out of my bed in a fright. I looked at the stupid clock, shutting it off. "You've got to be kidding me."

"Good morning, darlin'."

I closed my eyes, wishing the pain would go away, but he kept moving toward me.

"Wow, morning doesn't look good on you. Late night, was it?"

"Not today, Dylan. I'm *really* not in the mood."

He shrugged, grinning like he knew exactly what he was doing. "How's that different to any other time I've come to talk to you? I swear I should get loyalty points for how well I annoy you. Ten points and I qualify for a kiss." He raised his eyebrows comically, clearly baiting me.

"You know how you like the sound of your own voice, Dylan? Well, kiss me, and I'll bite out your tongue. Got it?" I gave him my best saccharine smile, watching his face drop.

"Just give me time. I'll make you change your mind."

"You wish," I snorted, watching our instructor Thane Beltaine enter the room. He was somewhere around six feet, and boy did he have some muscles. In all his demonstrations, he proved lithe and nimble with all weapons. He was half fae and half elf, with long golden hair and pointed ears that proved it.

"Okay, today's weaponry class is all about archery. Before we begin, is anyone familiar with a bow and arrow?"

I glanced around at my fellow classmates, unsurprised to see the class boffin's hand shoot up. Every lesson the girl had known how to use each weapon. She was an exhausting know-it-all, someone I did my best to completely avoid.

"Okay, as most of you haven't, I will demonstrate quickly before we move on to the targets outside. Gather around so you can all see clearly."

I moved forward, joining the semi-circle forming around Professor Thane. Dylan stuck to my side like a lost puppy dog. What did I have to do to piss him off enough to leave me alone?

"When you get your bow, I want you to hold it with your least dominant hand. For me, that's my left. Then I want you to think about your stance. Your feet should be shoulder width apart, and your body should be perpendicular to the target, like so."

I watched Thane like a hawk, taking it all in, his cerulean blue eyes drawing everyone's attention.

"Now for the arrows. When you're not aiming at the target, please for the sake of my sanity and everyone's safety, keep the arrows pointed to the ground. I do *not* want to be the first instructor this semester with the most students visiting the medics. I have a bet at stake."

Everyone chuckled.

"Okay, so pointing the bow and arrow down, I want you to place the shaft of the arrow on the rest here." He pointed to a small wooden piece at the curved end of the bow. "And then I want you to click the back of the arrow into the bowstring with the nock." He pointed to a small groove located halfway down the string. He lifted up the bow for us all to see. "Like this, your bow is loaded. Now, remember your stance. Draw the bow up until your bow arm is straight. With your string hand, which in my case is my right, I want you to place your index finger on the string above the arrow, and the next two fingers below. Next, I want you to draw back the string, until your hand meets the corner of your mouth. This will be your shooting guide and anchor. Aim at the center of the target and release. Watch your form, allowing the movement to travel through you."

Excitement welled up inside me.

"Now, just two more things before we head out." Thane hung the bow up on the wall behind him. "Before you even pick up a weapon, you need these pieces of equipment first. For your bow arm, you must wear an arm guard, like so." He held out his left arm. The leather covered the inside of his wrist to his elbow. "And for your string hand, you must wear a leather tab. This protects you from friction caused by releasing the string. Do we have any questions?"

Everyone remained quiet, all eager to give it a go.

"I want you to pair up, and when you've run out of arrows, I want you to wait until I say it's clear, and you can head out to retrieve them. Let's not be brutal with these babies please." Thane waved the arrow around. "Don't be an idiot and walk head-on into the target, or you're gonna get impaled. Approach it from the side, place your thumb below the arrow and your fingers above and as far down the shaft as you can go. Use your other hand to gently ease the arrow out of the target. Once you've collected all of your colored arrows, I want you to put them by your side, point down as you walk back to the shooting line. Okay? Don't forget I'm counting on you lot to make me money this semester, not lose it. All right then, let's head out."

As I followed the crowd outside, I noticed the arm guards and leather tabs sitting by the entrance. I grabbed one of each and put them on, seeing how many before me had completely missed the baskets.

"Good eyes, Amazon. We're going to work so well together." Dylan sneaked up behind me, torturous joy evident in his tone.

"I don't remember wanting to be buddied up with you." I sighed, choosing a bow before heading to an empty target.

"Who else are you going to choose?" He laughed in my ear. "I'm the only one here who's even speaking to you, Amazon."

I grunted. "I don't need to be friendly and have conversations with someone to shoot at a target, Dylan. We're only paired up because of lack of equipment."

"A-ha! So you agree we're a pair." He winked. I'd lost all

enthusiasm to argue my point. He required so much of my energy —something I had very little of, thanks to skipping breakfast. And sleep.

"And let's not forget, if we're together, there's no way you can 'accidentally' shoot me. I can already see you've had the thought a couple of times already." Dylan crossed his arms over his chest, smiling smugly. "You know, darlin', it's easier to just give in to whatever I say. It'll save you a hell of a lot of time for what's only inevitable anyway."

I picked up an arrow and loaded my bow. "What? And completely lose my individuality to you? I don't think so."

I pulled back on the string, anchoring my hand at my mouth, and aimed the tip of the arrow at the bullseye. I breathed in and out, steadying my arms, and then released. The arrow flew through the air with such speed, I barely saw its journey.

"Are you sure you want to keep provoking me?" I questioned, letting him see my first arrow had hit the bullseye.

He shrugged it off. "Beginner's luck. It's just a fluke. I bet you can't do it again."

I reloaded the bow, desperate to wipe the cock-sure grin from his face. Again, I took another calming breath before releasing, and the arrow hit the same spot. I quickly reloaded another six rounds before Dylan brushed it off with more luck crap. Each arrow hit the bullseye, one after the other until the small black ring was covered.

"Think you can do better?" I mocked, handing him the bow. He didn't say anything, and I noticed how quiet the target range had become. I glanced around and saw all eyes staring at me and some mouths open. I'd even managed to wipe the smug grin off the class know-it-all's sour face.

"Nadine, with me," Thane ordered, breaking the silence. "Class, back to practice. Do not fail me."

As the noise resumed, I left Dylan by his lonesome and headed after Thane, expecting an earful for showing off.

"Why didn't you put your hand up earlier when I asked about

previous experience?" He placed his hands on his hips, standing beside one of the many armory cabinets.

"Sir, the last time I picked up a bow, I was just a kid. I didn't think I'd remember how to use it, let alone retain my shooting skills." I didn't add that Dylan pissed me off enough and made me *want* to do better. The annoying shapeshifter was really getting under my skin.

"Well, there's no use you training out there today. It's not advanced enough for you." He paused, his face rested in contemplation. "In fact, all your weapons training so far has been above expectation for this level."

"What are you saying, sir?" I frowned, thinking I'd messed up somehow.

"I'm moving you to a different class. I should have known basic weaponry for an Amazon is child's play." He stared me down like I'd purposefully hid my talents. I did no such thing.

"I haven't been with my people for many years," I began, but he cut me off.

"I am aware of your unique situation." His eyes shimmered, a kind smile warming his face. "This isn't a punishment, Nadine. You're too good to be stuck in this class. You need to be pushed, challenged harder. It's the only way you'll learn and become stronger. A better warrior than you already are."

My jaw hung low at the compliment from such an esteemed instructor. You didn't get to teach weaponry without first mastering them.

"So I'm leaving?" I questioned, still confused on the details.

"I'll sort the paperwork to have you transferred to advanced weaponry, and I'll see you later. Class is at midnight. You may want to get some rest before then." He winked, signaling my rough exterior this morning.

My left wrist sizzled, burning brightly.

"Aah!" I groaned, removing my sleeve for a better view at what was going on.

The hourglass glowed, and sand fell into the bottom half,

filling a quarter already. What the hell? *Why* did it move? *How* did it move? Thane glanced at me.

"You'd better go. Looks like you're needed elsewhere, but that doesn't excuse you from class tonight. Don't be late!" he called after me as I left.

CHAPTER 8

 stood outside the library's entrance, contemplating my choices. Even from out here I could hear eerie creaking sounds that were completely uninviting.

"Come on, Nadine. You've fought much scarier beasts and come out on top. What's a room going to do to you?" I psyched myself up, hating that I allowed rumors about the killer library cloud my judgment. It wasn't like some monster was going to jump out of a book, right? This place was just a fount of knowledge, right? "And it's not like the college would put me in danger," I said sarcastically, conversing with the empty space. Wasn't *anyone* brave enough to use this place?

I double checked the flashlight I'd brought with me worked, flicking it on and off a few times before pocketing it again.

"Okay, what are you waiting for?" I asked myself, bunching my fists at my side.

I stepped through the entrance, instantly chastising myself for not leaving the flashlight on in my hand. *What an idiot.* There wasn't much light at all. Some magical orbs sat on end caps of each aisle but they barely illuminated the place.

"Good thing you're not scared of the dark," I said, realizing this

165

place was making me talk to myself out loud more than usual. What could I possibly be afraid of in here?

I flicked my torch back on, moving the beam of light around. Just like the rest of this place, the library had been cut into the stalagmites and stone. A true masterpiece of work.

I found an elevator and rode toward the upper levels, stepping out into the complete darkness. The sound of crumbling stone beneath my feet made me hesitate. I pointed the flashlight beam at my feet, seeing how narrow the path was. There was only one foot's width at a time.

"Goddess, that was close." I exhaled, making it a point to highlight the path ahead rather than around the area. Up here, I was sure the fall would be great enough to even kill me, or at the very least, permanently injure me, possibly even paralyze. I didn't think even I had the ability to heal to that degree. Then again, I'd never know until I tried.

However, I didn't have a death wish for today. Maybe next time . . .

At the end of the bridge path, I was met with stacks of shelves, all filled with a plethora of books.

"So how do I know where to start looking?" I mused out loud, searching for some kind of category list for at least a general idea of location. "If I were a hidden creature in the lake, where would I be?"

I glanced along the shelves of the first stack, noting the titles were for medicine. Not what I wanted. Ahead, a dim circle of light hovered in the air.

"Hello? Is anyone there?" I called out. "I'm trying to find a specific book . . ." I walked toward the faint glow, expecting perhaps the librarian coming to help this clueless student. Where was the librarian? And wasn't there supposed to be students working here too? Where was everyone? Honestly, I could be in here for hours before finding anything remotely similar to what I was after. Didn't they have a system? Oh my goddess, had they been eaten? I'd heard the rumors about the library and its books but . . .

"Hello? Did you hear me?" I came up short, the little ball of light moving farther away the closer I came. "Please don't be afraid of me. I'm just looking for . . ." I followed the glow, wondering whether I was doing the right thing. What if it was just another student, this one more skittish?

I listened out, but besides the general shifting of stone echoing around the chamber, I didn't hear anything else. No other footsteps. No breathing besides my own. Was the light even coming from someone?

I pulled up my defenses, readying myself for any danger and double-checking my nifty dagger Dave was tucked in my boot. The small weapon had been my go-to savior on many occasions. We were practically best friends, never without each other.

I followed the cryptic light as it wound around the stacks, flicking left and turning right like a rally car driver. I quickened my pace and ended up passing through the light, its warm center pouring through me.

"That was creepy," I murmured, returning to where the light hovered, no longer moving away from me. It sat on the shelf at my eye level, its glow brightening up the book titles. "Bloody hell, I guess there is a system," I mumbled, pulling an old dusty tome off the shelf. "Water Folk." I read the title, and the book itself glowed and opened wide, flicking through all the pages quickly, giving me a glimpse of its contents. "I guess this is where I start," noting the vast amount of creatures depicted in illustration. The weird glow of light I'd been following faded out, plunging me in darkness as though its duty was done.

With the book safely tucked under one arm, I kept the flashlight in the other hand and tried to find my way out. It wasn't like there was a glow in the dark fire safety *EXIT* sign in here. Oh no. Clearly, if you weren't smart enough to find your own way out in a crisis, then you didn't deserve to be at the college. Only the elite succeeded here. Or so they kept reminding us at every opportunity.

My wrist burned, distracting me, as it glowed again. Sand fell from one half, and panic gripped my chest as a new thought occurred to me. Hourglasses referred to time, and my tattoo kept making a point to alert me when time had been used. What would it mean when it ran out?

I scanned my flashlight ahead, seeing several different bridge paths and staircases. Which one was supposed to take me out of this place?

"Great," I exhaled, wondering if the library creator enjoyed torture. "One foot forward, and a complete guess then." I headed toward a bridge path, hoping there weren't any mean surprises in store for me. "No pressure." I expelled nervous energy, glancing at the sheer drop below. Maybe I'd get to find out if I'd survive this kind of fall after all.

I buried my nose in the musty book, funneling food into my mouth automatically, never taking my eyes off the pages.

"Be still my heart, I did not take you for a book worm."

I ignored him, keeping my attention on the current illustration. If I kept my eyes down long enough, maybe he'd leave me alone.

His food tray landed on the table opposite mine, and I knew he had no intention of moving any time soon. *Dammit!*

"Dylan, aren't you bored of chasing me around yet? I can't imagine I've been *that* great at keeping company." Mostly because I made sure not to. I wasn't a fan of encouraging bad habits, at least not this one in particular.

"Darlin', I'm not chasing you, but I do want to know you. Here, at the academy, you've got to make friends with the right people to succeed. It may sound cheesy, but I see something in you that matches with me. I don't know what it is yet, but I'd like to find out. But if I'm really bothering you that much, then I'll leave. Nobody likes being where they're not wanted." He stared at me from across the table, his food going untouched.

What the hell was wrong with me? Since when did I start thinking so highly of myself in that department? It wasn't like guys came flocking to me, not unless they were trying to kill me, of course.

"Okay," I gave in. "You can stay. But you've got to stop this Southern charm crap on me. No more darlin' this and darlin' that."

"Can't make no promises, Amazon. It's in my roots, a part of me. That's like me asking you to curtail your British English nonsense. You pronounce so many words wrong, you know." He winked, trying to rile me up.

I sighed. It was worth a shot. "Maybe you can help me."

The cogs in my brain started cranking. I wondered if there was a way he could aid me with my investigation into the lake.

"Sure, but first of all, what happened to you in class today? Why'd Professor Beltaine let you go?"

Tess entered the dining hall, catching my eye. I called her over to join us. I could see the hesitation in her step when she realized Dylan was with me again. After a brief moment, she shook off whatever concerns she had and came running over, several bags hanging from her arms again.

"Dude, what's with you and the bags? Are you being made to carry them, like they're everyone else's from your classes?" I frowned, suddenly concerned. Was she being bullied?

"No, they're mine." She blushed. "I just like to be prepared for any eventuality. You think it's too much?"

I nodded slowly. "Listen, I'll help you out later. Do you two know each other?" I pointed my finger back and forth between them. They shook their heads simultaneously. "Dylan, this is Tess, my roommate. Tess, this is Dylan, my annoying classmate." I winked at him.

They shook hands like civilized people. It seemed so formal and unnecessary.

"Tess, take a seat. Nadine was just about to tell me why she left weaponry class today."

She grabbed my arm after sitting next to me. "Oh my goddess! You got kicked out of class?" Her eyes bulged, a favorite expression of hers recently. "What did you do?"

"Show off with a bow and arrows. Hit the bullseye one after

the other. You should've seen it. It was amazing." Dylan grinned widely, like I made him proud.

"First of all, why do you assume I got kicked out? And second, how about I tell the story?" I interrupted Tess, knowing she was about to let loose a whole load of new questions. "I didn't get kicked out," I said haughtily. "Thane thought the class was a waste of my time." I shrugged it off, playing it cool. I didn't let on how awesome this really was.

"So he did kick you out, but for being too good? Can he do that?" Tess pushed her glasses up her nose. I could sense her anger rising at the potential miscarriage of justice. I was determined to find out why she had such strong convictions over what was right and wrong. Something must have happened in the past for her to be so passionate about it.

"He's moving me to the advanced weaponry class instead."

Dylan whined. "What? No more pairing up?"

I shook my head. "Not unless you've suddenly stopped sucking with weapons control." I laughed out loud. "Don't think I've ever seen someone struggle with holding a sword before. The pointy end is pretty self-explanatory."

Tess burst into laughter too.

"Hey, I was just making sure I provided entertainment for everyone. I'm quite the giver, you know." He winked, his smile never faltering. It was like a permanent etching on his pretty boy face.

"Oh my goddess! Is this—?" Tess squealed in my ear, grabbing the book from under my arms. "When did you get this? Where?"

She flipped the book to its cover, reading the front. Dylan stretched from his seat, taking a look for himself.

"I took a lovely venture to the library when my services were no longer required in weapons."

Tess gasped, gripping my arm again. "You went to the library on your own? You are the craziest person I've ever met, honestly. Dylan, you should've seen her last night . . ."

I nudged her arm, giving my best *shut up* look.

"I take it you haven't been to the library?" I asked her, hoping Dylan would forget what Tess was about to let loose.

"Hell no. I order my books and pick them up from the librarian. You won't see any crazy stunts like that from me."

"Huh," I exhaled. "I didn't even know that was an option. I didn't see anyone there though. If you don't go in, how do you put in an order?" I frowned, remembering the space. "There was a circulation desk but I couldn't find anyone around to help, so I just went on up by myself."

"There's request forms on the circulation desk, and there's a pile in the great room back at Heimdall, too. I'll show you if you don't want to go there again. No one's judging you if you don't." Tess puffed out her cheeks as though just mentioning my trip there had scared her.

"Come on, I'm sure it's not that bad, right? Just a room full of books. I bet it's the killer dust you've got to watch out for, right, Nadine?"

I glanced at Dylan, noting his attempt to ease Tess. I kept the spine-tingling cliff drops to myself.

"You mean, you don't know? You haven't been?" I raised my brows at him, getting ready to lay in to him for being scared too.

"I'm not the book type." He stretched his arms, resting them on top of his head.

"Oh, I'm sorry. How silly of me to just assume you can read already."

Dylan laughed, returning to his food, the jibe forgotten.

I stared at my tray, suddenly losing my appetite. Shadows crept up on me, surrounding me as they tried to penetrate my mind.

"You hungry, Tess? I can't eat any more." I passed over my plate, ignoring the frown emanating from Dylan.

"Did your eyes finally mistake the size of your stomach?" Dylan gasped. I didn't blame him. It was only yesterday I boasted about how I liked to eat.

I clenched my fists under the table, struggling to control the negativity seeping into me. I couldn't let loose in here. I'd hurt too many people. I focused on my breathing, using each exhale to exorcise the shadows looking to expose me.

"You okay there, rock star?" Shade's voice came from behind me. I turned around and saw the concern on his face.

I brushed it off.

"Never better. What brings you down here? Don't you have some important business to deal with?" I winked, suddenly calming, my inner turmoil abating.

"I am. I came to congratulate you. Thane told me the news." He smiled widely, clearly loving his skin suit and the fact he *could* smile properly now. "Don't be late tonight though. I won't go easy on you." He winked as I gasped, becoming slack jawed.

"You're teaching advanced weaponry?"

"Baby cakes, don't be so surprised. But no, I assist. You'll see later—remember, I'm counting on you."

I flashed back to the day he brought me here, reminding me that I was here because of his faith in me. Whatever I do always came to reflect on him. I didn't quite understand it, but the thought of letting him down had always felt like a betrayal. I couldn't do that to him. Not when his presence had given me so much.

"Have I ever been late to anything?" I said out loud, wondering why everyone was reminding me about tonight's class.

"Weren't you late for combat class yesterday?" Tess mentioned.

"Yeah, you're not the punctual type, Nadine," Dylan chimed in.

"See? Even your *friends* know you already," Shade emphasized, taking note of the people around me. I bet he was beaming inside that I followed his advice.

"Looks like the darkness is abating." Shade looked at me pointedly. Tess and Dylan shared the same confused expression, checking around us. The cavern was as dark as it had always been —lanterns, a waning light from above, and magic were the only sources of light down here. Thankfully, they weren't aware of my darkness.

"Don't be so afraid of the shadows. Sometimes they give you a better view." Shade disappeared. No formal goodbyes from the reaper.

"Okay, that was weird, right? Is he always like that?" Dylan asked as I turned back in my seat, my mind calmer than before.

"Yeah, sometimes. I think it's the old age," I joked, turning my attention back to the book.

"Did you find anything useful yet?" Tess asked, moving the tome between us so we could all see.

"Yes to information, but I'm not sure if it's useful yet. We only saw orange eyes, right? A lot of these water creatures have orange eyes."

"Damn, okay. So we need a process of elimination to narrow our suspects down," Tess began.

"Uh, guys? What are you talking about?" Dylan looked so lost, bless him.

Tess glanced at me, her face bursting with wanting to reveal the secret. I nodded, letting her have the glory. As she caught him up, I thought about my next move. What did the creature want?

"Excellent, I love a quest. So, what's in the lake?" Dylan almost bounced out of his seat with excitement. *Great, there's two of them.*

"We don't know yet." I sighed.

"That's why I'm saying we need a process of elimination." Tess took over, flipping through the pages animatedly. "How far did you get?"

I shook my head, coming to a realization. "There's only one place I'm getting definitive answers. I'll have to go back down there. But first, coffee."

I stood in line at Coffee Haven, waiting for my fixer-upper. The queue was longer than my patience could withstand. Why did everyone need the java juice at the same time as me?

I took a few deep breaths, willing myself to calm down.

"Dude, you look crazed right now. Need the caffeine that bad, huh?"

I turned to see Vanna, a hellhound, grinning at me.

"Vanessa, right?"

"Yeah, but I prefer Vanna. I thought it was just me in need of a fix." She winked behind her sunglasses. "Cranky beasts are hard to rein in."

I shrugged.

"Exhaustion and stress—they don't mix well," I offered as an explanation to Vanna, finally reaching the barista to place my order.

"No kidding. I find a good stretch of the legs helps, stops from feeling cooped up down here."

I nodded in agreement, taking the cup of energizing, hot liquid with my name on it. I inhaled the bitter aroma, my mouth salivating in response. "See you around."

"Oh, thank goddess you're still here!" Tess bumped into me just as I was about to push through the double doors out of Halstein Hall.

"What?" My shoulders raised with alarm, muscles poised for impact. Was she okay?

"You haven't heard, have you? I didn't think you would, but I thought you should know . . ."

I grabbed her arm, trying to rein in her focus. "Know what? What's wrong?"

I analyzed every inch of her, checking for any kind of wound that would explain what she'd yet to tell me.

"Another group of students have disappeared."

CHAPTER 9

With absolute silence, I dangled my legs over the passageway's exit, sitting on the ledge and listening out. This time I watched out for the sudden drop, wanting to make a stealthier entrance.

I surveyed the area. The water flowing along the cavern wall and into the stream was the only sign of movement. Orange eyes were nowhere to be seen but I didn't take it for granted. The beast could be anywhere down here. For all I knew, it may not be bound to the water. It could be hiding in the stalagmites, waiting for me to come close enough. No, I couldn't take anything for granted. Not when it was willing to drown both Tess and me the last time.

I climbed down the wall, my feet touching the ground without sound. I crept around, sticking to the walls as a way to limit any surprises. With my back pressed to and sheltered by the walls, I could focus on what was in front of me.

Small pockets of light highlighted the walls again, but this time I saw flame torches sitting in holders erected out of the ground as though creating a walkway, intermittently spaced for maximum light exposure. Where did they come from? Why weren't they there the last time?

Slowly, I ventured into the area, keeping perpendicular to the flow of the water. Still no sign of anything else. My heart beat faster with anticipation. Where was it?

I reached where the stream widened to become a lake. I expected the creature to be waiting, orange eyes peeking out of the water as though I'd been watched the whole time. Nothing.

I glanced at my left wrist. The tattoo was still there and counting down, hitting halfway already. If I found and saved this missing student, did the tattoo disappear?

I skirted around the lake, noting for the first time a statue at the deepest end, overlooking the body of water. I forgot caution and inched closer, determined to get a better look.

Carved into and out of the stone was a large serpent's head, magnificent detail on every scale protruding from its skin. The head faded into the wall and then, lower down, several tentacles sprouted out, curling around one another and into the lake. Suckers of all sizes were etched into the carving. If it wasn't for its stone coloring, I'd happily mistake it for a live creature.

"Magnifisssssent, issssn't it?" A familiar voice hissed behind me, the beast having made no sound before. How did it do that? Move around so quietly, even in water? "Where'ssss your friend today? Too ssscared to return?" It mocked.

Slowly, not wanting to startle it with any sudden movements, I turned around, expecting to see orange eyes peeking out of the water. Instead, I found the monster half in and out of the lake, showing me its body.

Except, it was a woman's.

"Are you? How can?" I paused, my thoughts becoming a tumbled mess, not dissimilar to Tess and her ramblings. She was rubbing off on me already.

"What? I'm not what you imagined?" She laughed, her head tilted back, and I could see fangs for teeth. Long black hair cascaded along her back, and her chest was covered in barnacles.

"Why are you here?" I surprised us both with my question. Of all the things I could've asked . . .

"This is my home. I command these waters, and *only* I will ever do so." I heard the threat in her voice.

"Then what do you want? Attention? Revenge?"

The woman cackled, stretching further out of the water. I gasped out loud, failing to stop myself as the woman's torso ended, a serpent's tail began.

"You're a mermaid?" I frowned, wondering how she could've even made it in here. Were mermaids evil?

She hissed. "Don't insult me, little girl. I am a drakaina. My name is Keto, and I am mother of *all* sea monsters."

She rose further out of the water until I had to crane my neck up high, her tail longer than I could ever imagine. Where did it end? How *deep* was the water?

"Wow, and here I was thinking you were an average sea snake, slippery tail and forked tongue." I shrugged, unwilling to let her intimidate me.

"Do not provoke me!" she roared, voice echoing off the walls. Water splashed vigorously as though it sensed her emotions.

I shook my head. "No, no, no. We did this already."

I yawned, mocking her ability to control water. Couldn't she do anything else?

Her tail whacked my face, whipping out of the water with such speed, I failed to see it coming my way. My head snapped back from the force, and my skin smarted like I'd been struck by lightning.

"Watch your mouth, little girl, or I'll seal it for you," she threatened, slinking back into the water until we were at eye level.

"I'm sorry. I didn't think monsters have feelings. At least not any I, a child, could possibly hurt." I feinted right, then left, expecting her tail to whip out this time. I climbed onto the serpent statue's head, gaining ground as she rumbled up the water again. It built behind her, a large wave oddly shaped like the snake I was standing on.

"You know, jellied eels are a delicacy where I'm from. Maybe draikana tail is worth a fortune," I taunted, readying myself to leap at her.

"Watch out, girl. I see the large hourglass in the courtyard. Do you know what it means when the sand runs out?"

I paused, caught off guard. What did she know of it?

"Not so snappy with comebacks now, are you?" Her eyes illuminated with joy. "That hourglass has to do with the spell that keeps me down here. I'm only trapped here until the sand is gone, then there's nothing holding me back from taking everyone on this campus as mine."

The water came for me. I jumped, soaring into the air, my face sprayed with water as I landed on my feet.

"What the hell?" I questioned, frowning deeply as I looked around the dry area where students walked by nonchalantly. How was I back in the quad? The hourglass above shed some more sand, filling its way to the three quarter level. Where did the lake go?

What the bloody hell just happened?

CHAPTER 10

I stared at the pages, the pictures and words becoming a complete blur. My eyes struggled to remain open, pressure building in them, begging to be reprieved with sleep. But I didn't give in, needing to find out as much factual information about this draikana as possible. Where it came from, how many there were, its strengths, weaknesses, how I could kill it.

The being below called herself Keto, mother of all sea monsters. Did she fight for the title or was it literal? If she produced them, then where was her mate? And if she earned the title, then who had the control to give it?

My eyes closed for a brief second, and I startled awake, knowing time was of the essence. The quiet room and my comfortable bed did little to help me remain strong, the temptation to close my eyes ever prevalent. I shook my head, willing myself to be more alert, but my eyes still drooped, the pages of the book coming closer to my face as I leaned forward, sleep taking me.

My muscles relaxed, all tension from recent events faded away, and my mind emptied of stress. Exhaustion won.

The sun shined brightly on the large pond. Insects skimmed across the stagnant water while koi carp of all colors breached the surface with their pouty lips, searching for food. Bright white, orange, red, yellow, and even some black koi filled the pond, adding color to the dull water. The warmth of summertime coming to an end felt good on my skin, the seasons slowly beginning to change to autumn.

"Come, Nadine. It's time to go in," one of the elders called. Lucy, a gray-haired and wrinkled woman always wearing a kind smile on her face, held out her hand, calling me toward her.

I hesitated, not wanting to leave the warm sunshine yet. It was too beautiful to be stuck indoors.

"Now, Nadine. Don't make me ask again." Lucy stood patiently, folding her hands to rest by her stomach, calmness radiating around her.

My temper rose, my young mind frustrated by the lack of freedom. Of all days, today I deserved to enjoy the outdoors a little longer. I turned my back on her, crossing my arms over my chest, making a stand. It was my birthday. I wanted to be in the sun.

"Do not disobey me, child. You *will* come in for your next lesson whether you want to or not." Her voice raised, and her stance changed to pure anger. She strode toward me, hand raised in warning. A beating was coming my way.

I burst with rage, and pent up emotions spilled out of me. Fire appeared between us, blocking her temporarily from reaching me. Where did it come from? I paid little attention to it, grateful for another moment of beautiful sunshine before darkness returned.

I bolted awake, the room's light having burned out, ensconcing me in pure black night. My heart was pounding uncontrollably. Tears threatened to fall, but I pulled them back, determined not to show any weakness while I was here. For all I knew, Tess could spring through the bedroom door at any moment.

"Just a stupid dream," I whispered to myself. *Based on true events*, my mind finished for me. My tenth birthday, the day my life turned upside down for the second time in a year.

How much could a young kid go through before it affected

them later in life? Permanent damage bubbled below the unbalanced surface of the mind. I was probably more messed up than I'd ever know.

Suddenly claustrophobic, I left the bedroom. I needed some breathing space to think more clearly and shake away the demons of my past. As I ventured around Heimdall Tower, my mood worsened with the blaring music coming from the common room, pounding my head with its thunderous booms.

Shadows swarmed in, crawling around me and raising the hair on my arms as they threatened to overpower my mind again. Why were they more persistent lately? Usually, I only felt them once a week at the most. Why were they attacking more often now?

Why the hell couldn't they leave me alone?

"Nadine! You're finally here! Come on." Tess grabbed my arm, failing to recognize my personal space and how I needed it at this minute. I bit my tongue to keep from lashing out, even as she dragged me into the common room.

"HAPPY BIRTHDAY!" Yells came screaming at me over the obnoxious music, some from classmates, most from students I didn't even know. Who cared when there was a party involved at college, right? I mentally rolled my eyes to myself, temper peaking, shadows pushing on me harder than ever before.

"What the hell is this?" I grunted loudly, noting Dylan coming to join Tess's side, drink in hand. Her face fell.

"You don't like it? I just thought it would be nice for you to enjoy your birthday again. You know, after . . ." For once, Tess sensed when to shut up, not to reveal the secret of my past I shared with her in confidence.

"Hey, now's not the time for your prickly moments, Amazon. Tess has been worried sick about you."

I pulled a face. "Aw. Look at you two. Best friends turned lovers already. You *do* move quickly."

"WHAT!" Tess exclaimed. "No way. Not even." She shook her head.

"Wow, you really are a bitch on your birthday," Dylan snapped. His voice grew louder until he was yelling as he continued, "Do you even care that we were concerned about you and your rogue attitude? Going off after that beast on your own the moment our backs were turned?"

The music lowered as the others wanted to listen in on our argument. Nothing like drama to crank up the rumor mill.

"Why are you being so reckless, Nadine? Do you have a death wish?" Tess asked, as though my actions had wounded her.

"No, she's just got to prove she's the biggest badass all the time. Right, Amazon?" Dylan poked, sarcasm emanating from him.

"Is that jealousy I hear, Dylan?" The shadows pushed in on me, their strength growing, willing me to let them in and abuse my control. "All this nagging, and for what? Envy? Spite? What do you want from me? I'm doing what I think is right. Someone needs to find these missing students. Do you want to do it? This way you can put your lives at risk, and I'll go back to my comfy routine, sleeping soundly at night because I couldn't possibly have anything else to stress me out. Is that what you want?"

I stared them both down, my anger unhinged. My skin was so hot, I could only imagine the beetroot shade I was projecting. Neither answered me, pissing me off further.

"If you can't face the library"—I pointed to Tess—"and you have so little experience with weapons"—I looked to Dylan—"how the hell do you think you'll cope facing off with a *real* threat that *does* want you dead? And if I waited for you to *help* me down there, what could you have possibly done? You can call me reckless, but I *know* what I'm capable of. There's a reason I didn't have to do any trials to get in here."

The common room became completely silent. Music shut off, and all eyes stared at me like I was their entertainment.

"You never even gave us a chance, Nadine. Just bolstered your way through alone, because no one is ever good enough for you," Dylan roared, letting it all out. I knew I was making him feel emasculated. That wasn't my fault. I couldn't change who I was born to be.

"Don't give me that bullshit. I warned you both I needed my space. Tess, I even shared with you why. Don't you realize how big a deal that was for me?" I pushed away the hurt. I was done opening myself up. Shade was wrong. Friends didn't help you. They hindered you. I stared at them both, neither willing to say any more. "You know, I'm done. Enjoy the party."

I stormed out of the tower, down the sky bridge, through Halstein Hall, and into the quad, wanting to be with the Valkyrie statue in the entrance vestibule.

My muscles were so tight, I probably should've gone to the combat room and let out my frustrations in there, but my mind was working on a delayed reaction compared to my feet. They were busy leading the way.

I bumped into something, too busy by what was rolling in my head to use my eyes.

"Dude, watch it," I said, belatedly realizing it was another student.

"Nadine?" the girl asked, and I took a better look at my bumper.

"Oh, sorry, Vanna. Rough night," I offered as way of apology.

"You don't say. You need to let the hound out, you know, before you combust."

"What?" I stared at her dumbfounded. What was she going on about?

"Your hellhound. I can sense all the rage around you. They're like fiery shadows."

I paused, thinking she had me confused with someone else. "I'm not a hellhound, Vanna. I'm an Amazon."

She frowned, then crossed her arms over her chest. "No, there's definitely some hellhound in you. I can feel it."

I continued to shake my head, getting ready to repeat how wrong she was. It was the black magic she was really sensing.

She grabbed my arms, holding me still. She took off her shades and glared at me, and I watched her eyes become a bright red. She opened and closed them three times, keeping me steady the entire time. My body snapped into concentration, all the darkness that had been oppressing me released, and my vision changed, highlighting everything with a red hue. Fire ignited around us, drawing us into a protective circle.

"You finally did it." I heard Shade's voice, bringing me out of my mind. "Thank you, Vanessa. I was beginning to worry she'll never learn the truth." Shade blew out the ring of fire, creating a draft by shifting into his reaper black mist and back into the skin suit.

"You're welcome. Nadine, I'm sorry. I thought you knew. That's why I couldn't understand why you never brought it up in conversation before."

I thought of the few times we'd spoken, none of them particularly life changing.

I frowned at Shade. "You knew? All this time you knew what was wrong with me? It's not black magic?"

I felt as though a huge weight had been lifted from my shoulders.

"I need to bounce, but if you have any more questions about this side of you, come talk to me, okay? I won't bite. Much." She winked and disappeared, fist bumping Shade on her way out.

"Yes, I knew." Shade motioned for us to sit on a nearby bench. I obliged, wondering how long this explanation would take. "Death forbade me from telling you. I tried to help many a time, give you clues. I hoped once I had this skin suit, my next phase of existence, I'd be able to get around the order. I was wrong."

"But why would Death interfere?"

"It was a punishment for me when I stepped out of line and ruined a soul intake. He knew I had a soft spot for you. He made it so I would have to endure seeing you suffer until you became aware of your second nature yourself."

"But why me? It could have been anyone?" I mused out loud, struggling to understand.

"Because it was your mother's soul I freed. She was destined to the Infernum, but I couldn't let that happen. I knew she didn't belong there."

My mouth hung open. "You knew my mother?"

He nodded. "Briefly. And in turn I knew you, before you ever met me. Death doesn't have to reason his choices. He's only accountable to himself. He can do whatever the hell he likes. His punishment to me was to make sure you were never told who you are. I'm sorry."

I took a long breath, processing everything, pushing the confusing emotions away for now. I couldn't tell if I was angry or sad.

"Your father is a hellhound, and you inherited some of his traits."

"You know my dad, as well?" I interrupted, needing to after such a revelation.

"Most likely I will have crossed paths with him at some point in my career. But I do not know exactly who he is. I have no name or information for you, I'm afraid."

"Oh." I slouched, my enthusiasm squashed like a bug. "Why did the Amazons think it's black magic?"

"Honestly?" He sighed, his face falling. "I believe it was a scare tactic to ensure the pure bloods succeeded in giving you a death sentence. For centuries there have been warring ideas with the Amazons. The pure bloods have their ideals that tainting the bloodline will only make them weak. They've forced their agenda on the majority for so long that they can create any kind of propaganda to ensure there are no more rebels daring to think otherwise. Black magic, as you know, is frowned upon by most in the supernatural world. Claiming that you as a hybrid are manipulated by its impulses ensured that sentencing you to death would not be questioned. This kind of magic must always be eliminated, no matter the cost."

I nodded slowly, understanding. "So a young girl on her tenth birthday must be killed. For the greater good." I almost choked on those words. Manipulative and controlling; two actions favored by those who truly were afraid of what was outside their understanding. I tried to wrap my brain around it all. "All this time I've been afraid to truly be myself for fear of the pain I might cause."

"I know, but I couldn't tell you outright. You had to experience this change for yourself." Shade looked apologetic. Oddly, I didn't blame him. I knew myself well enough that I wouldn't have believed him had he told me anyway. But Vanessa was able to *show* me.

"So what were all the shadows?" I pulled my legs up beneath me, trying to make the wooden bench comfier, or to at least ease the numbness in my arse.

"Hellhounds have ties to the Infernum. They guard, but also protect the dead. Often in cemeteries and graveyards. Those shadows were the forms of the dead, looking for protection." Shade noted my shocked expression. "They're not really in your mind, baby cakes. They were projections, a means to entice the hellhound nature in you to come out fully. I had a feeling it would be today, on your eighteenth birthday. The supernatural world loves its symbolism." He tutted, and I thought I'd lost him to his own thoughts.

"Will the shadows come back? Am I going to feel that darkness closing in on me again?" I frowned, not really wanting to endure it again.

"That pressure cooker feeling should be gone now that you've emerged. As for shadows visiting you, it's hard to say. You're linked with the dead. It's how I knew what you were, how souls naturally end at your feet, ready for me. But it's not for you to be afraid of if they do return. These projections, if you will, are more like your friends. They could be warning you of danger to come. Or seeking protection from you, as I mentioned earlier. Hellhounds are highly protective of those they deem in need. What you feel as shadows could really be your hellhound instincts kicking in." Shade took a breather, checking his watch. "You should take up Vanessa's offer some time. She knows a hell of a lot more about being a hellhound than I do." He stood, stretching out his arms and back. I followed suit, enjoying the ripples of satisfaction through my body.

"Go enjoy what's left of your birthday. You spend far too much time with this old creature as it is." He smiled, beginning to walk away.

"Wait, Shade, one more thing. Did I do the fire earlier?" It had felt awfully familiar.

"Oh, yeah. That's one thing you *are* going to have to learn to control. Incinerating your classmates won't go down well on your college record. Or mine." He winked, before disappearing altogether.

CHAPTER 11

I lost myself staring in the Valkyrie statue's eyes, contemplating the lies I'd been living my life by. I never once questioned if my second nature could be anything else. I believed the elders and their black magic lie. I couldn't even comprehend that they would make it up, not when I *felt* it in me all the time. How stupid I'd been, even after knowing they despised me enough to continue trying to assassinate me when I fled. I didn't think twice. Because even *I* had been sucked in to believe in their twisted pure blood system as the sole reason for why I shouldn't exist. *Dammit*, it made me so mad, even at myself for being foolish and blind.

I owed an apology to Tess and Dylan, but was I too late for their forgiveness? Had I finally pushed too far? I sprinted back to Heimdall Tower, bolstering my way into the room of my party.

I paused.

It was quiet.

Empty.

Where did everyone go?

My wrist burned, glowing brightly, disturbing me from my inner chastising monologue. Sand fell rapidly into the lower half, and I was bombarded with a sense of urgency.

"Hey, you! Wait up! Where's the party gone?" I called to a random girl as she tried to dash out, appearing as though she'd been hiding somewhere in the room.

"Uh, uh, I, uh . . ."

I fisted my hands at my side, restraining myself from shaking the answer out of her faster. Why did she seem so scared? I wasn't that much of a monster, was I?

"They left, I mean, some did. Others, well, they just kind of disappeared."

"Disappeared how?" I frowned, not liking where this was going.

"I don't really know. I hid, but it was like something was calling to them. The way they behaved was so robotic. The next time I chanced to look out of my spot, you'd come in."

"Was Tess and Dylan with them?" Panic rose inside me.

"Who?" The girl's brows creased, I could tell I was wasting my time.

I bolted out of Heimdall Tower and dashed through the courtyard until I came up against the lake's secret entrance, my heart pounding. With time almost up, I knew I couldn't waste precious minutes crawling through the tight space of the hidden shaft.

I thought of the lies I'd wasted my life on, the fear and stress it had caused me. I thought of my arguments with the only two people who were willing to get to know me—to be my friends—and how my hang-ups once again ruined it. Issues that were born from the lies I'd believed in. Anger burst inside me. I pulled my arm back, clenching my hand into a fist, and punched the stone wall with the full force of my might, calling on both my Amazon strength and hellhound nature.

The wall cracked up the center, but didn't budge. I hit it again and again, until my knuckles bled and the stone crumbled to a dusty pile. I brushed the remnants from my hand, noting the lack of damage—my body already healed itself.

The now large entrance opened directly to the view of the waterfall, and I rushed in, bolstering my way through to the lake.

"Oh look, the mighty ssssavior, she comessss," Keto hissed, but it wasn't her presence that made me pause. "Oh, don't be afraid, come and say hello to my children." Her orange eyes glowed brightly, lip curled in a sneer.

All around the lake, some suspended from the stalagmites, others in the water, were all the missing students, arms limp at their sides, eyes glazed over as though their minds weren't present in the room. Some seemed beaten badly, from the sight of bruised faces and broken bones to the copper scent of blood hanging in the air. There was no mistaking that smell.

"What did you do to them?"

She sprang towards me.

"Nothing they don't deserve," she hissed, venom lacing her tone.

I glanced around the space again, this time noting the two beings suspended from the serpent statue. I couldn't tell if they were even alive—eyes closed, bodies limp. They were just dangling there like bait.

My protective instincts flared wildly, only I knew it was more than just my hellhound nature. That I deemed them my charge. No. I knew it was more than that. They were *important* to me, not just my *purpose*.

"You know, I read about you, Keto." I spat out her name, trying to draw a reaction out of her. "For a mother of all sea monsters, where's your doting children? Left you all alone like ungrateful bastards." I stepped closer to the water, knowing it must end tonight. One way or another.

She whipped her tail in retaliation. I grabbed what I could, expecting the move, and swung her out of the water, throwing her on the ground.

"I have my children back again now, can't you see?" Keto swished out her arms in a magnificent gesture, pointing to all my peers and friends. She was delusional. She didn't think I'd let her get away with this, did she?

"You know, I kept wondering why such a bad bitch on paper

would be stuck in here, in waters she can never escape. And then it dawned on me—"

She threw a fist, aiming for my face, but I blocked it in time. She came at me again, each hit faster than the last. Her tail swished my legs out from under me, and I landed on my back. She pounced on top of me, her heavy, slippery snakeskin pinning my legs.

"I don't care for your thoughts," she spat in my face. Her horrible forked tongue darted at me, stabbing my eye. I wrestled her arms, looking to overpower her enough to squirm out of her hold.

"I guess," I panted heavily, rolling her over with every ounce of my strength, "you must be lonely spending all this time down here on your own." I looked down on her, knowing my weight wouldn't hold her still. "You get bitter and twisted with only your own thoughts to keep you company. I should know. I recently came to the same conclusion about myself. It was quite the revelation. I thought the loneliness was what I wanted." She tried to move, but I kept her pinned. "It turns out I was just settling for what I believed I deserved, and not for what I actually do."

She hit me with her tail, and I careened forward, my face scraping against the rough ground with full momentum for what seemed like miles.

I got on my feet and charged toward her. A red hue clouded my vision as I called on my inner hellhound. "But I guess you're too far gone for redemption. You need to go."

Flames erupted around her, blocking her in as I leaped into the fire with her. She screeched and yelled as they licked her body, unable to escape. I pulled my trusty dagger Dave from my boot and plunged it into her chest at an angle, making sure to get the heart beneath the armor of barnacles.

Her screams faded out, life drained from her eyes while the flames continued to cremate the body.

I took a step back, watching the inferno. A large black mist swirled around the lake, its figure twisting and turning as it moved.

It came closer, hovering around me until it settled, and Shade appeared.

"Nice work, baby cakes. I was almost afraid your soul-gifting days were over."

I rolled my eyes, though I was grateful to see a friendly face.

"What happens now?" I pointed to the fire and its contents burning away.

"Her soul will go to the Infernum, where she belongs."

I nodded. "Good. She won't be lonely there. Maybe she'll find her lost children, too." I sighed, rubbing my arms, muscles becoming stiff already. "Come on. Let's do this." I moved forward, anxious to transport my first soul to the Infernum as a hellhound, but he stopped me.

"Not this time, Nadine. You have somewhere more important to be." He directed his attention ahead, pointing out the other students, including my friends. "Get them back to their dorms safely. There will always be more souls and monsters for me to teach you the ways of the Infernum. But friends are *never* guaranteed. You need them, and they *really* need you now." Shade transformed into a black swirl, zapped toward the fire for his luggage and disappeared.

I watched my peers traipsing out of the water and climbing down from the walls, confused mutters echoing all around me. Tess and Dylan moved toward me. I held back a little, afraid of the consequences of my actions.

"Please, just get us out of here." Tess broke down, exhaustion and fear leaving her with tear-stained cheeks. Dylan barely looked at me.

"I'm so sorry," I began, but they both held up their hands to stop me. Neither one happy.

"Not now. Just go," Dylan huffed, downtrodden.

I nodded once, leading the way out of the space for everyone to follow. Now that I'd brought down its dividing wall, exiting the lake had been more efficient than ever before. Everyone dispersed quickly, moving with pace the moment they recognized their location. As did Tess and Dylan. Neither one giving me a second look.

I was deflated. After wanting to be alone for so long, I finally got my wish. Except, it made me utterly miserable. I didn't want to live that way anymore. I didn't want to end up like Keto.

I slowly made my way back to Heimdall Tower, needing to sleep. As I walked into the courtyard, the large hourglass hovering in the air smashed into tiny pieces, raining down on top of me. My wrist itched, and I watched the hourglass tattoo disappear, too, the school's crest and tower tattoos returning in its place.

I closed my eyes, savoring the moment, taking a breath.

It was finally over.

CHAPTER 12

"**H**ow long is this punishment going to last?" I asked, sitting perfectly still while Tess stabbed at my face.

"Listen, I've already forgiven you. And learned that surprise birthdays are not a good idea for you."

I grimaced, guilt flooding me for the hundredth time that I ruined her gesture of kindness.

"And anyway, you saved my life so I guess you managed to balance yourself out on the justice scale." She laughed, prodding my eyes with what felt like a scalpel.

"So why am I doing this again?" I snuck an eye open, glancing at the garish array of colored products splayed out on the bed.

"Because it's what *friends* and roomies do," she said pointedly, playing on the guilt trip again. "Okay, I'm done. My masterpiece is finished."

I opened my eyes with apprehension, afraid of the clown-like markings I was about to see.

She handed me a mirror, and the reaction I'd been working on in my head for the last hour fell flat.

"Well? What do you think?" Tess could barely contain herself. Words failed me. Instead, unintelligible sounds escaped my mouth. "Oh my goddess, you actually hate it, don't you?" She slumped on her bed, sitting on all the make-up paraphernalia, looking dejected.

I raised my brows. "Are you kidding? I love it! I just . . . I never expected to look so . . ." I struggled for the right word.

"Drop dead gorgeous?" Tess offered, and I laughed, taking the compliment.

"You wanna grab a bite to eat? All this sitting around has made me utterly ravenous."

Tess laughed, grabbing her purse. "At least some things haven't changed."

"Are you really going to eat all of that?"

I turned to the voice coming from behind me, one I'd barely heard recently.

"I like to eat," I replied, smiling the biggest, soppiest, cheesiest smile to ever grace the world. "You've never seen a girl with a healthy appetite before?"

Dylan smiled in response, the grin reaching his eyes. "Once, and man can she eat. I think you'd like her."

He winked, pulling the full force of his charm out, just like the first day I bumped into him in here.

My face faltered. "Dylan, I'm sorry . . ."

His finger stopped my lips from moving. "I'll get over it." He shrugged, leading the way to the cashier. "I wanted to get to know you, remember? And I found out you were juggling more than just classes and defeating that monster."

We headed over to Tess, where she was already diving into a burger. It was a late dinner, most of the dining hall empty as we were one of the last to eat.

"Besides, I've decided how you can make it up to me."

I froze, waiting for his punch line. Did I dare even ask?

"Go out on a date with me, and it must end with a sexy kiss." He raised his brows, and I struggled to tell if he was joking or not.

I glanced at Tess, mouth hanging wide.

"Okay," I agreed, knowing I had nothing to lose and possibly everything to gain. "Just make it something mellow. I've had enough action lately."

"You've got it. One mundane, somber date coming up." He chuckled. Tess did, too.

I picked up my burger, unable to stay away from the delicious aroma any more. Possibly for the first time ever, I enjoyed the companionship as we ate and bantered through our meal. Even though it was late by the time we finished—the dining hall was closing up—we took our time. As we stood and gathered our dishes, a loud gong clanged around us. I dropped my tray back on the table, instinctively checking my wrist.

There was no hourglass there. I exhaled with relief, belatedly realizing my time was over.

"You okay?" Tess frowned with concern as we crossed through the Student Union.

"Never better," I said, glancing around the busy space with a single thought on my mind. If the gong wasn't for me then . . .

Who was next?

TIME TO LIVE

E.J. FECHENDA

CHAPTER 1

The sand was warm beneath me as I leaned back on my elbows to watch the lone surfer catch a wave and ride it to shore. Sunlight reflected on the ocean and on the horizon, storm clouds gathered; lightning flickered against a dark, turbulent sky. It was like that every time I came here. Cillian said that's where the angry spirits gathered, but they were far away and couldn't reach me here. This tropical oasis belonged to him. It was by some fluke I was able to visit him at all.

"Taylor!" the surfer called to me when he emerged from the ocean. Board shorts hung on his hips, his lean, muscular body on full display and sparkling from drops of water that clung to his tan skin. "When did you get here?" he asked, propping his surfboard in the sand.

He stood over me, his shadow blocking the sunlight. Cillian smiled at me, a mischievous grin that caused his blue eyes to sparkle, right before he shook his head and showered me with salt water. I shrieked and sat up, giving him the bird. This made him laugh, and he plopped down next to me.

"You're a jerk," I said but didn't really mean it. Secretly, I liked the attention, and the goosebumps that rose on my skin didn't come from the cold water, but from the thrill of Cillian making me wet.

"I've missed you," he said. He turned to face the ocean but not before I saw the sadness in his eyes.

While this secluded stretch of beach seemed like paradise, it was all Cillian knew. He was alone here, and I was the only person able to visit him. Since I started my first semester at SMA, my visits had become further apart. A light breeze blew his blond curls that were beginning to dry, and I ached to run my fingers through them.

"I'm sorry. Life's been kind of crazy." I cringed at my poor choice of words. Cillian would have given anything to be going to school; to be burdened with essays and typical school drama . . . he'd give anything for a life.

Cillian was dead, and for about six months now, I'd been able travel to the spirit realm. For some unknown reason, I was drawn to Cillian and his private beach. We didn't know each other before he died. He was from Laguna Beach, California, and I was born and raised in Havenwood Falls, Colorado.

"Hey, I get it. Don't feel bad." He lay down so he was on his side facing me, his head propped in his hand. "Tell me what magical things you have learned since the last time you were here. I still can't believe you're a witch, and vampires, faeries, and werewolves are real."

One of the reasons I enjoyed visiting Cillian, besides his gorgeous body and beautiful smile, was that I could talk to him about Havenwood Falls and the Academy. Usually, a spell prevented me from talking about our town when I was outside its wards, and there were consequences for telling outsiders, but the spell didn't work here, and Cillian couldn't tell anyone anyway.

"I failed miserably in potions class today. My vial exploded, and glass flew everywhere. I'm an Augustine witch, and this subject should be a breeze." I groaned and lay back on my towel, stretching my legs out and wiggling my toes into the warm sand. "Professor Parker is in the Luna Coven and good friends with my grandmother, too. What if I can't pass the class? I'll be an embarrassment to my family and my coven."

"From what I remember, college is all about self-discovery, and you'll find what you're good at. Besides, you worry too much about what other people think."

I turned my head to meet Cillian's steady gaze. "I know. It's hard to break free of something I've been doing my whole life."

"You'll get there," he assured me.

I had been under a lot of pressure, but admittedly, a lot of it was my own doing. When your grandmother was one of the high priestesses of the coven, sat on the Court of the Sun and the Moon in Havenwood Falls, and was monitoring your progress as a member of the inaugural class at the new college for supernatural guardians, it was easy to get stressed out. "Besides, crazy shit has been happening on campus. I don't know if the place is cursed or if we're being tested, but it's been bizarre."

"Like what?" Cillian leaned over and brushed a hair off my cheek, his fingers cool against my skin. I wondered if his lips would be just as cool, and I found my gaze had wandered to his mouth. He had nice, full lips. "Taylor?" he nudged me, and I felt myself blush.

"Just last week there was a monster in the lake."

"Like the Loch Ness Monster?"

"No, oh hell no! More like the Kraken." I shivered at the memory of some of the wounds. "One of the students in Hel Tower died, despite there being several healers on campus."

Cillian's mouth dropped open, and he shook his head in disbelief. "That's wild, man. Fucking wild," he said before his expression grew serious. "Wait, how long have you been here?"

Glancing at the sky, I noticed the sun was beginning to set. It was almost directly above me when I arrived.

"Shit!" I quickly stood up and brushed sand off my calves. "I have to go."

Before I left, Cillian grabbed my hand. His grip was cold and sent shivers up my arm.

"You'll be back soon?" he asked, and I detected desperation in his tone. His blue eyes pleaded with me.

"Of course." I squeezed his hand and stepped away. Closing my eyes I focused on my dorm room in Jormungand Tower. The now familiar tugging sensation started, pulling at my body, and then all sound was gone, only to suddenly return with a jarring vengeance.

"Taylor, wake up. Taylor!" a familiar voice screamed close to my ear. Then I realized I was being shaken, and my eyes popped open with the shock. I was back in my room, lying in bed, and my friend, Paisley Underwood, was hovering over me, her violet eyes wide with panic. "Holy faeries, I thought you were in a coma. What the hell, Taylor? What was that? Are you okay?" Paisley sat down hard on the edge of my bed.

"Paisley? What are you doing here?" I asked, sitting up and hugging a pillow to my chest. Paisley didn't live in my tower, but in Modi.

"Fin called me in a panic. She thought you were dead."

Infiniti Clausman, who went by Fin, was my roommate, and I looked over to where she was leaning against her boyfriend, Joe. He had a muscular arm wrapped protectively around her. I noticed she was shaking, and all of the color had drained from her face, like she was the one who just saw a ghost. It was only a matter of time before she discovered my secret. Since the semester started three weeks ago, I had been careful to plan my visits to see Cillian when Fin had class or was out with Joe. Only, this last visit lasted longer than planned. After the craptacular day I had, escaping the real world for a while was just what I had needed. Cillian was a great listener, and since he had no connection to my world, it was freeing to be able to talk to him.

"I'm sorry. I should have told you about my ability to astral project into the spirit realm."

Fin shot me a confused look

"What do you mean?" Joe asked.

I continued my explanation. "It's something I've recently

discovered. Usually the spirits come to me, but now I can go to them." I didn't think it was possible for Fin's brown eyes to grow any wider, but they did. She was listening to me, though, and had calmed down. "It's very peaceful there," I said wistfully, thinking of Cillian.

"Uh huh," Paisley said with a grin. "Visiting ghost boy again, huh?"

"Nope," I said, unable to suppress my own smile. Paisley was one of the few people who knew about by ability . . . and about Cillian. We'd been good friends for a few years. She was a fae who was a healer, like her dad, so it made sense that Fin called her.

"Liar!" She grabbed one of my purple throw pillows and tossed it at me. I laughed and caught it mid-air, tossing it back. "Poor Clay is going to be devastated, knowing you've been seeing ghost boy," Paisley teased.

Clay Washburn was a witch who lived in our tower. He was recruited from Maine and like me, came from a long line of witches. My friends, especially Fin, swore Clay liked me, but I didn't see it. I think they just liked to mess with me.

"Anyway, I'm sorry I scared you. I didn't know my body is like that when I travel," I said to Fin. I set my pillow to the side and slid to the edge of the bed. The rug was cool on the bottom of my feet. Despite having a plush rug, the cold from the stone floor still seeped through. I crossed the room and pulled my roommate into a hug. Joe reluctantly let her go, and I understood why. Fin's mom had died, and Fin had her own brush with death, something I could sense even more now that she was hugging me back. "I'll give you a little warning next time. I promise, okay?"

Fin nodded and smiled, letting me know she understood, before wiping away tears with the back of her hand. When I stepped away from her, I caught a whiff of smoke. My hair still smelled from the mishap in Potions.

"Okay then. I'm going to shower." I gathered up the tote that contained my toiletries and tossed my bathrobe over my shoulder.

"We're not done talking about this," Paisley said and followed me out the door, which led directly to the bathroom. "You should have told Fin. That poor girl was close to having a full blown panic attack."

"I know." I looked sideways at Paisley. Her white-blond pixie cut was streaked with lavender highlights, a change from the green streaks she had last week. Paisley was able to change her hair color with a simple thought, so it wasn't a surprise. "It's not like I don't trust her, it's just . . . I like having a place to disappear. To get away from things, you know?" I did trust Fin and had won the roommate lottery. We were on our way to being fast friends, maybe even best friends, which made the guilt about her finding out about this ability the way she did even worse.

"And a hot surfer ghost has nothing to do with it. Sure," Paisley teased before she grew serious and turned to face me. "Look, just be careful. You're still learning about the spirit realm. What if you stay too long and can't come back?"

I thought about Paisley's parting words, which sent a shiver down my spine. One of my abilities as an Itako, medium abilities inherited from my Japanese ancestors, was that I could see death and when death clung to a person. I could also communicate with spirits, and most recently, I had discovered the ability to astrally project into the spirit realm. Paisley was right. There was still a lot I didn't know about that realm. I made a mental note to ask Cillian some questions the next time I paid him a visit.

It was after nine at night, and the bathroom was busy with other students. A shower at the end was available, and I walked through swirling wisps of warm steam to claim it.

I was rinsing conditioner out of my hair when it happened. The gong that had precipitated the two recent disasters on campus tolled, reverberating off the stone walls and traveling in waves from somewhere deep within the mountain. The sound was so loud, it made my bones rattle, and I actually placed a hand against the tile wall in the shower to steady myself. As soon as the gong faded, an intense burning flared on my wrist, like I was holding it over a candle flame. Right before my eyes, the magically enhanced tattoo on the inside of my right wrist, the one that enabled me to travel through the portal to and from campus, began to shimmer. I watched as the tattoo transformed and the shape of an hourglass appeared over the original design. The monster in the lake I'd told Cillian about earlier was the most recent tragedy to happen on campus. Now this. What did it mean?

The room was empty when I returned. Fin had left a note on my pillow letting me know she and Joe were downstairs in the study. I sat down on the edge of my bed still wearing my bathrobe, my wet hair soaking into the fabric as I stared numbly down at my tattoo. The burning had stopped, and I traced a finger over the hourglass. My skin was smooth to the touch and didn't feel any different. The tattoo was infused with magic to begin with, so this wasn't some accident. There had to be a reason for the sudden change. Perhaps it would be revealed in time or one of my professors knew.

My stomach growled, and I realized I skipped dinner. Potions class ended at five-thirty, and I had slipped into the spirit realm to visit Cillian right after. I crossed the room to my dresser, one of the two that came with the room. I pulled on a pair of shorts and a T-shirt, hanging my robe up in my closet. I ran a comb through my hair. Picking up my wand from the dresser, I gave a flick of my wrist, starting a fire in the fireplace, which quickly warmed the room. I made a cup of jasmine tea in my favorite mug that had a cartoon unicorn posing dramatically with a caption that said *I'm magical AF* and snagged a handful of almonds from Fin's stash, which was right next to her precious hot Cheetos on top of our mini fridge. I settled back down on my bed with every intention of studying for my Critical Thinking class.

Suddenly Cillian was in my face, yelling at me. "Taylor, wake up!"

I jerked awake and sat up, my pulse pounding. At first I was disoriented. The room was dark with the exception of flickering light being cast by flames in the fireplace. I glanced around, noticing Fin's bed was empty, the covers thrown back and in a messy pile like they usually were. Where I made my bed every morning, Fin did not. Then screams broke through the disorientation. They were followed by a roar that shook the door in the doorframe. A thud against the wall outside my room made me jump. *What the fuck is going on?*

Tossing my comforter to the side, I scrambled out of bed and flung open the door to chaos. A bear loomed on the balcony that ran the length of the building, like a motel, and he was standing on his hind legs with his back to me, his head brushing the bottom of the balcony above us. A body lay on the floor behind him. *Oh my Goddess!* I ducked back inside, quietly shut the door and pressed my back against it as I thought about what to do. There was only one bear shifter in our tower—Caleb Hayes—and he was one of the nicest guys. Not the berserker beast standing a few feet away from my room. *What the hell happened to him?*

The floor vibrated as the bear in question started to move. He was getting closer. *Shit! What do I do?* I was strong and could fight, but Caleb in bear form outsized and outweighed me. I was still pressed against the door, which would be just as effective as a piece of paper at keeping the bear out. He was right outside—I could hear him sniffing around the frame—and I closed my eyes. *Think, Augustine!* I concentrated on controlling my panic one breath at a time and then let everything else fall away. Despite the fire, the temperature in the room dropped, and the door at my back became bone achingly cold. Caleb lumbered on, and I opened my eyes and exhaled. That's when I realized I could see my breath. Slowly, I opened the door and peered out through the crack at Caleb's retreating back. Before, I didn't notice the dark cloud hovering around him, but this time I did, and that's when I knew what we were dealing with. Caleb wasn't acting like himself because he was possessed.

By now the screams had quieted, and I assumed my tower mates who weren't lying injured on the floor were either hiding or regrouping and coming up with a solution. I raced over to my bed and pulled the emergency kit my mom had packed for me. It contained salt, bundles of sage for smudging, an assortment of crystals, and other reinforcements. I had to somehow create a salt circle around Caleb and keep him confined to that circle so when I released the spirit possessing him, that spirit would be contained. Too bad my sister wasn't here. She could freeze people and time. That would be, like, so convenient right about now.

Bracing myself, I slipped outside but came to a stop when I saw Fin lying on the balcony, blood seeping from a gash on her forehead. She wasn't moving. I squatted down next to her, relieved to see the rise and fall of her chest. I moved her long, brown hair away from her neck to check her pulse. It was slightly erratic, but at least she had one. When I pulled my hand away, I noticed my tattoo. The sands in the hourglass had started to move. *What the . . . ?* I didn't have time to worry about this new development. First, I had to deal with a seven foot possessed bear shifter. No big deal, right? *Bahahaha!* Maniacal laughter echoed in my head. Who was I kidding? This was going to be a disaster.

My first instinct was to call for help, but I also knew that with my abilities, I had to try to fix this on my own. Knowing Caleb, he'd hate himself for hurting anyone. I needed to evict the ghost that hijacked his body before he hurt anybody else. I'd never actually handled a possession before, but I had dealt with something similar last spring. That time, my mom and I worked together to draw the negative energy out.

I stood up and looked around for Caleb, but he was gone. *Shit!* Focusing on my surroundings, I felt a subtle vibration through the stone beneath my feet. Only something of great size could generate those tremors, so I started moving in the same direction. As I rounded the curve of the tower, I spotted the hulking shape of a bear descending the stairs to the first floor—the floor we referred to as the commons because that's where we all hung out. There was a media room, laundry room, and study. Fin must have been returning from there when she crossed paths with Caleb.

A large medieval-style wooden door made up the main entrance for the commons. Caleb reduced it to splinters when he barged through. I carefully picked my way through the debris, staying as stealthy as possible, like Rhian. That girl had mastered stealth and snuck up on me more than once. He passed the door for the laundry room, turning his head as he went, sniffing the air. Then he paused. I froze mid-step and literally stopped breathing to not make any noise. I'd been undetected thus far and didn't want to lose that advantage.

When he spun around to face me, I gasped and almost dropped my emergency kit. The bear roared, and he opened his mouth, revealing sharp canines that were probably longer than my finger. I didn't want to find out. I started to back up, slowly. Caleb advanced faster than I retreated, and then I tripped over something and fell backward. The stone floor was unforgiving and knocked the breath out of my lungs when I landed on my back, leaving nothing to scream with as Caleb loomed above me.

One moment I thought for sure things were going to end very badly and the next moment, Caleb was gone—flung backward by a powerful force. Rolling over onto my side, I looked behind me to see Clay Washburn. He held his hands out before him, and his dark eyes were narrowed as he concentrated on directing his element. Clay, a powerful elemental witch, had the ability to control air, and he was keeping Caleb from advancing by creating a wall of wind.

Standing next to Clay was Dingane, or D for short. Lightning danced along D's arms, bright white against dark skin. Both men were wearing boxer shorts and nothing else. I couldn't help but appreciate the view. A roar from behind reminded me that I didn't have time to gawk at rippling abs. There was a possessed bear shifter to deal with. I stood up and dusted off my backside. Caleb was still being held in place by the wind. His roars were of frustration, and his black eyes were wild with rage. Inspiration struck seeing him immobilized and pinned against the far wall. I wouldn't be able to draw a salt circle around him, but at least he'd be stuck in one spot. I'd have to improvise.

When I turned back to ask Clay a question, I noticed others had joined us. Roxy stood behind Clay. Roxy's mates, Vidar and Tyr, flanked her on either side.

"Clay, how long can you keep him pinned there?" I asked.

Clay, without breaking his concentration, replied, "As long as you need me to."

I looked at Roxy. "I'll deal with Caleb if you can retrieve Fin and the others who are injured. They're on the second floor."

In addition to my roommate, there were two other students on the floor. I hadn't checked to see if they were alive. For Caleb's sake, I hoped they were. Roxy and her mates nodded in agreement, so I focused on my part.

I knelt down and opened my kit, first pulling out a bracelet made of black tourmaline, onyx, and apache tears obsidian. The black stones began to immediately warm against my skin. Next, I pressed a hand against my chest and felt the comforting weight of my tiger's eye pendant. All of these stones absorbed negative energy and had strong protective properties. Finally, I took a smudge stick from my kit and lit it so it started to smoke, filling the area with an earthy pungent smell. Avoiding the direct path of Clay's wind, I kept to the far left wall and made my way past the media room, stopping less than two feet away from Caleb. Setting the smoldering smudge stick on the stone floor, I faced the angry bear. Caleb was well over seven feet tall in his bear form, and he was pinned so his back was pressed against the wall, his four limbs spread wide like an X. His head thrashed back and forth as he repeatedly roared. He was so enraged that his eyes rolled in his head.

Up close, the darkness of his aura looked like fog encompassing his body. *Here goes nothing*, I thought to myself and wrapped my arms around Caleb's leg that was closest to me. I burrowed my fingers through the fur until I reached skin and held on. A tremor coursed through Caleb's body, and the screams of the spirit possessing the bear echoed in my head. I focused on these screams and establishing a connection—a way to anchor myself to the spirit and force it out. It was a mental battle of wills, and the spirit fought hard. An ache formed at my temples, and it grew until it felt like my skull would split apart. I grit my teeth and held on.

You are not welcome here. You don't belong in this body, I repeated over and over in my head, directing these thoughts at the spirit, which I could see through our psychic connection. Nothing human remained—just a shadow driven by the desire for chaos and destruction. As I probed deeper, I sensed something else. Caleb. He was fighting back, too. This gave me a surge of energy, and I directed every ounce toward exorcising the spirit, which was beginning to lose its hold. I envisioned myself actually entering Caleb's body, and instead of holding his arm in my hand, I had a hold of the spirit, and when I left Caleb's body, I brought the spirit with me.

When I opened my eyes, I was shocked to see that I was in fact holding the spirit, which struggled against my grip. It writhed, howling and screeching as if it was in pain. My hand glowed, like I was wearing an iridescent glove. I turned away from Caleb, who was still being held in place by Clay's wind, and started walking back to my kit. Now I could create a salt circle. Clay briefly looked at me.

"Are you okay?" he asked, as sweat dripped down the sides of his face.

"Yeah, I just need to contain this bastard. Are you okay?"

"I'm good. Do what you need to do."

Roxy paced nearby, her honey gold eyes regarding me warily.

"Can you hand me the salt?" I asked her, nodding with my head at the canister inside my kit.

She leapt into action, and once I had the salt in my hand, I started to form a circle, walking clockwise three times, chanting:

"Goddess, Guardian Angels, and Spiritual Guides, please bless this

*circle and keep me protected. Contain this negative entity and keep
it from leaving this blessed space. The circle is cast. So mote it be."*

All the while, I envisioned pulling pure energy from the atmosphere, drawing it in through the crown of my head and letting it travel down my arm and into the salt that scattered on the stones. By the time I was done, the circle had a faint glow and I felt the protection of its barrier. I released my hold on the spirit, and it tried to flee, but the circle held. It bounced off the invisible barrier, which infuriated it even more and it tried again and again. Each thump against the barrier was followed by an ear-piercing screech. Relieved that it couldn't harm anyone else, I sunk down to the floor, the cold from the stones seeping into my bones. Sitting cross-legged, I closed my eyes and focused on the spirit realm. It was time to return this thing.

Just as I was getting ready to astrally project into the spirit realm, I reached up and grabbed hold of the spirit, which wailed in protest. We emerged into a space void of color—only inky blackness and it was cold, oh so cold. All sound was muted. There was no color, no noise, no warmth; everything was bleak, desolate, and depressing. I released the spirit, and it moved away, glaring at me with its glowing eyes. With my mission accomplished, I quickly left that place and rejoined my body.

While I had been gone, more people arrived, having been alerted to the attack. Elsmed Fairchild, who sat on the Court of the Sun and the Moon with my grandmother, stood in front of me, his shoes an inch away from the salt circle. Mr. Fairchild was also on the school's Board of Regents. Around Havenwood Falls, the centuries old fae wore a glamour so he looked like an elderly man with white hair, liver spots, and a cane. He didn't have to disguise his true self on campus, so I was greeted with frost blue eyes that stared down at me over a long flat nose. His silvery white hair cascaded down past his shoulders, and the pointy tips of his ears stuck through the fine strands. "Welcome back, Miss Augustine. I trust you are well?"

I rose to my feet and at the same time did a quick assessment to make sure the spirit hadn't followed me back. "I am well, Mr. Fairchild. And the others—is Fin okay and Caleb? It wasn't Caleb's fault, sir."

I opened my mind up to the elder. Mr. Fairchild was telepathic and used that to ferret out whether someone was being truthful or not. I wanted him to know Caleb was blameless.

"Please don't kick him out!" I blurted and immediately slapped a hand over my mouth.

"Relax, Miss Augustine. Caleb won't be punished for this. The injured students have been taken to the infirmary. Your roommate, Miss Clausman, will be staying there a few days. I'm assured that she and the other students will make a full recovery."

"Oh, thank the Goddess!" I breathed a deep sigh of relief.

About an hour later, after providing a full statement of what went down, I finally crawled into bed. My eyes were burning, and exhaustion weighed on me like a lead blanket. Thank the Goddess my first class wasn't until one in the afternoon, because I needed sleep. Little did I know, that would be the last good sleep I'd be getting for a while.

CHAPTER 3

Instead of falling asleep, I found myself on the beach, the almost full moon casting the ocean in a silvery glow. The distant storm didn't seem as severe as earlier. I thought for sure the flashes of lightning would be more visible at night. I didn't see Cillian at first, so I walked down to the water's edge and stood ankle deep in the sea, enjoying the gentle pull as waves receded and then washed over my feet. This was my first time visiting at night. It always seemed safer, less intimate during the daylight. Now it felt like a secret liaison. I imagined we were two lovers, meeting under the cover of darkness, away from prying eyes. A thrill ran through me at the prospect of Cillian coming up behind me and wrapping his arms around my waist, holding me close against his muscular body.

"Taylor?" I turned at the sound of his voice. As if I summoned him with my thoughts, the golden god emerged from the shadowy fringes that were just out of the moonlight's reach. "Is everything okay?" he asked as he drew closer.

"Yes. I didn't plan on visiting, but here I am. Surprise?" I let out a nervous laugh and reached for the tiger's eye pendant, closing a hand around the gemstone and exhaling. My shoulders relaxed slightly when the stone warmed against my palm. The necklace, a gift from my dad for my thirteenth birthday, had become an anchor. I felt safe with Cillian, and he wasn't making me nervous, but the change of pattern was. The fact that I just showed up here, without intentionally projecting myself, had me off kilter.

He tilted his head and looked at me with his eyes slightly narrowed. There was a soft breeze, a warm caress on my skin that caused my hair to blow across my face. Cillian reached out and brushed the hair aside, his fingertips grazing my cheek, a cool touch that caused me to shiver. I bit my lip and looked up at him. His gaze was intense, and I stood still as he trailed his fingers down my neck. I felt goosebumps rise in their wake, and my nipples tightened in response. My cheeks heated at this reaction. A sharp intake of my breath caused him to stop, his hand resting at the junction of my neck and shoulder.

"You're so beautiful in the moonlight. Do you know that?" he asked, his voice barely a whisper. The sad expression I was all too familiar with returned.

"What's wrong?" I placed my hand over his, and the cold penetrated my bones, but I held on.

"If only we met when I was alive." He dropped his hand and took a step back. He might as well have put a mile between us.

"I know." I swallowed hard and turned back to look at the ocean before he could see the tears beginning to form. "I dreamed about you tonight. Earlier. You shouted at me to wake up, and that warning probably saved my life. Are you sure you're not my guardian angel?" I forced a playful grin and looked over my shoulder at him.

"What do you mean saved your life? What the hell happened?" His concern wiped the grin off my face, and I rushed to reassure him I was fine, recounting my adventure with Caleb, the possessed bear shifter.

"A fucking bear shifter was possessed by a spirit and you went up against it? That's crazy, Tay." He shook his head, his blond curls glinting in the moonlight. "Your world is just so beyond my imagination. I'm glad you're okay." He reached for me, but thought twice about it, and with a pained look, he dropped his arm to his side. "You brought the spirit back here to the realm?"

"I did."

"Huh." Cillian stared off at the horizon, focused on the distant storm.

"What's wrong?" I asked, stepping closer to him.

"I don't know. Something just feels off." He shrugged and smiled down at me. "Maybe it's you being here at night. An unexpected surprise when I'm used to being alone."

"Maybe." I slid the tiger's eye pendant side to side on the silver chain and peered up at Cillian through my eyelashes. We moved closer, as if pushed together by the breeze, and just as we were about to kiss, the tugging sensation became too strong to resist, and I pulled back to reality.

I woke to knocking on my door. Groaning, I rolled over to look at my alarm clock. It was after ten o'clock, not an unreasonable hour.

"Hold on!" I yelled, and the knocking stopped.

I lay on my bed for a few seconds, staring at the mural on the ceiling I had magically painted for Fin, transforming it to a glimpse of the universe, with a swollen moon in the forefront. The moon reminded me of the kiss I was just robbed of, and I let out a growl before sitting up. I stepped into the flip-flops on the floor by my bed, grabbing the hoodie that was draped on the corner.

Before opening the door, I snagged my wand from the table next to my bed, waved it over the door, and whispered, *"Allow me to see through thee but not unto me."*

The wood on the top half rippled and then faded away, allowing me to see who stood on the other side, but they couldn't see me. This was one of the few witchy spells I had mastered. Clay stood on the other side, and he held two cups from Coffee Haven in his hands. If there was a magic password, coffee would be it. I quickly ran my fingers through my hair before opening the door.

"Hi," I said, stepping to the side to let Clay in.

"Hey. So I have a witch's brew latte with an extra energy tincture for you," he said and handed me a cup. The warmth seeped into my hand. "Roxy told me that's what you usually order."

"Thanks." I took a sip and then another. We stood awkwardly in the middle of my room. We had a couple classes together and hung out on campus with friends, but I'd never been alone with Clay before. I was about ready to offer to sit on my bed but that seemed too intimate, especially after my moment with Cillian.

"Um, have a seat." I gestured to the chair in front of my desk instead and sat down in Fin's.

Clay set his cup on my desk and leaned forward, elbows on his thighs. He wore a green and navy plaid flannel shirt, and the sleeves were rolled up, revealing muscular forearms. I knew that he had a physically demanding job for a lumber company in Maine, where he was from. He was definitely in shape. I took in his broad shoulders and thick neck. Then he started talking, and I quickly glanced down at my coffee, so I didn't get caught checking him out.

"I just wanted to see how you were doing after last night—which was wicked crazy! You were amazing, by the way." He flashed a smile before looking away. I noticed the tops of his ears had turned bright red. This made me relax a little bit. At least I wasn't the only one feeling awkward.

"Thanks for your help. If you hadn't been able to keep Caleb immobilized, so many more people might have been hurt." I shuddered at the thought. Flashes of Fin lying on the floor bleeding surfaced in my mind. "I need to check on Fin before class," I said, standing up and cutting the visit short.

"Yeah, sure. I understand. See you around?" Clay hesitated in the doorway, and his eyes met mine. They were a lovely deep brown, and he had gorgeous thick, dark lashes. He ran a hand over his scruff and cleared his throat. "Um, you know I'm here for you, right? You ever need help with anything, call me, and I'll be there." Once again his ears turned red, and I bit my lip to stop from giggling. The way he blushed really was adorable.

Once Clay was gone, I popped into the shared bathroom, and I still had to check to make sure I was going into the women's side.

It was only the third week of the semester, and I was still orienting myself and didn't want a repeat of the first week where I accidentally walked into the men's side of the bathroom. Thank the Goddess nobody was in there.

Our dorm rooms were set up so that each room had a front door leading to the balcony that wrapped around the tower. Then there was a door at the back of each room that led directly to the bathroom. It was like if the tower was a tootsie pop, the bathroom was the tootsie and the rooms were the lollipop part. It was a weird layout, but it was convenient having the bathroom so accessible.

After brushing my teeth and washing my face, I returned to my room and finished getting dressed, putting on jeans and brown leather ankle boots. I wore my new back-to-school purchase—a thin brown leather jacket—over a green T-shirt. Grabbing my coffee and slinging my messenger bag over my shoulder, I left to go check on Fin.

When I stepped out onto the balcony, I expected to see some sign of last night's events, but it looked as innocuous as ever. I took the stairs, precarious stone steps that were built into the side of the tower and wrapped around the structure for all ten stories. Thank the Goddess my room was on the second floor—less risk of me tripping and breaking my ass.

Instead of following the bridge that connected Jory Tower to the library, I took the only set of inside stairs that went from the common room to the bottom level of the tower. This was a windowless space, and the only lighting came from flickering wall sconces. The light reflected on the damp stone, adding to the whole medieval dungeon vibe.

I went this way because there was a secret entrance, for Jory residents only, which led directly outside near the courtyard. Two wood beams, about six feet apart, were built into the stone wall. They stood like sentries, guarding the entrance. To those unfamiliar, the wall looked like any other castle wall—dark gray rounded stones with crumbling grout and moss growing in some sections. I placed my palm flat against the wall in between these two beams and whispered one word: *Angrboda*. There was a low rumble and the ground beneath my feet vibrated as bits of grout and dust began to fall on the dirt floor. The stones separated, and an arched doorway appeared. I stepped outside and blinked so my eyes could adjust even though it wasn't much brighter outside. Living inside a mountain took some getting used to, especially the lack of natural light.

I cut across the courtyard, peering up at the hole at the top of the mountain. Weak sunlight filtered in, bathing the tops of each tower in a hazy glow. I grew up in Havenwood Falls and spent my life exploring the mountains surrounding our town without knowing Mount Alexa's peak was just an illusion—a strong glamour that escaped the most powerful supernatural citizens' notice for almost two centuries.

As I crossed the courtyard, I passed one of the gnomes who helped maintain the campus grounds. Garangulaird, whom we dubbed Gary, was standing still and staring. Several students milled about, whispering and also staring at something. A break in the crowd revealed a giant hourglass in the center of the quad. It hovered above the ground and emitted a blue glow. My steps slowed, and I stretched my arm out so my jacket sleeve rode up to expose my tattoo. I had completely forgotten about it. The sands were still moving on my tattoo, and as I moved closer to the giant hourglass, I realized the sands were in sync with my tattoo. *Fuck!*

I scanned the area, looking for anything out of the ordinary, but everyone seemed normal. Well, except Cat Vega, the bitch who had been hitting on Joe behind Fin's back. She was looking trashier than usual. Her skirt was so tight and short; she was a wardrobe malfunction waiting to happen.

My friends from Havenwood Falls, Paisley and Makenna, emerged from Halstein Hall, which housed the Student Union. Coffee Haven was located in there as well as the bookstore, cafeteria, and other restaurants. They ran over at super speed when they saw me and both started talking at once. Apparently word had spread about Caleb.

"You're a legend now, Tay," Paisley said. "You're not just a ghost whisperer, but a wrangler. Roxy was telling me how you held a spirit with your bare hand while nonchalantly making a circle with the other. That is so badass!"

"Honestly, it was terrifying," I admitted. "Something weird is still going on." I held out my wrist to show them the tattoo. Their eyes were wide when they looked up at me.

"What does it mean?" Makenna asked.

"I have no clue. I forgot to ask Elsmed Fairchild about my tattoo. Maybe I should talk to one of the professors. Maybe your dad?" I asked Paisley. Her father, Dr. Underwood, taught one of the healing courses this semester. My stomach was in knots as I thought about what was going to be thrown at me next. *Please don't let it involve clowns.*

"Of course you can talk to him, but I don't know how much he knows about magical tattoos and huge ass hourglasses. I'll ask him, okay?" Paisley said, giving me a reassuring smile. "Where are you off to? Mak and I just grabbed some lunch. We're going to sit by the lake and get some nature time in before class. Come with us!"

Communing with nature was something I needed, and it would help me recharge, but Fin came first. I had to make sure she was going to be okay. I told the girls this, and they understood. Paisley and I had Critical Thinking class together, and I asked her to save me a seat. They continued on, and I headed toward Eirhal Tower, which was where my potions class was held and located to the right of Halstein.

I entered the tower, which was quiet and cool inside. The lighting was dim and shadows long as I made my way to the infirmary. I used to work at Havenwood Falls Medical Center and thought it was small until I saw this clinic. It was a single room, with white panels separating the two beds for patients, which were both occupied. I saw Joe first, hovering over a sleeping Infiniti. Lying there so still with her dark hair and fair skin, she reminded me of Snow White.

"How is she?" I whispered.

Joe looked up at me with bloodshot eyes, and his blond hair looked like a tornado had blown through it. "She's going to be okay, but they need to keep her here for observation. He cracked her skull!"

Joe ran a hand through his hair, and a growl rumbled deep from within his chest.

"Hey." I placed my hand on his shoulder, feeling the emotions vibrating under the surface. He was barely holding it together. "Caleb didn't do this. He was powerless against the spirit that possessed him."

"Powerless. That's how I feel. I should have been there protecting her!"

"You can't be with her all the time."

"I know." Joe's shoulders slumped, and he reached for Fin's hand, which was dwarfed by his. "I can't lose her. Not again."

Fin had told me about their relationship. How she had time traveled from Houston and met Joe in the future, in Havenwood Falls, but she had to return to her time. They had fallen in love hard and fast. Joe had started deteriorating without her, fighting against the wasting disease that happened when a wolf shifter was deprived of his mate. While Joe and I didn't go to the same schools growing up, I knew of him and saw him around town. I remembered thinking he was sick at one point because he had lost so much weight. When Fin told me about their connection, it triggered a memory of when I overheard my grandmother talking about the "time-traveling girl" and how the Court had given Joe permission to time travel to find her. It was a tragic yet beautiful tale that deserved a happy ending. Fin may have been tiny, but she was fierce and a fighter.

"You won't lose her. She'll heal and will be begging you to bring her hot Cheetos from the Student Union before you know it." This comment actually made him grin. Fin loved her Hot Cheetos, and she left red dust fingerprints everywhere.

I stayed with Joe for a while and left after Madame Roth came around and shooed us out so she could examine Fin in private. Joe stayed out in the hallway, planning to return to his bedside vigil. I had a couple of hours to kill before class, so I stopped into the Student Union to grab a burger at Blaze's. Taking my lunch outside, I sat on one of the stone benches in the courtyard, also known as the quad.

This bench faced the giant hourglass. Sand trickled through the narrow funnel, one grain at a time, counting down the minutes to some yet to be determined disaster. What if someone else more dangerous became possessed? Could vampires be hijacked like that? Looking down at the pink meat of my burger made me think of blood and a vampire attack. My stomach turned at the thought, and with a sigh, I wrapped up my lunch. What if more than one person became possessed? I could only handle one spirit at a time, and it took a lot of energy. Perhaps I was getting worked up over nothing, but my grandmother always told me to be prepared. *"Expect the unexpected and you won't be caught off guard."* I heard her voice in my head like she was standing right next to me. She had a million sayings like that one, and I'd heard them my entire life.

I made a mental note to recharge the bracelet I wore last night since transporting that spirit back to the spirit realm most likely depleted its protective properties. If another possession was coming, I needed to be ready. I should restock on salt and replace my smudge stick. Having a purpose made me feel less lost. Just as I was standing up, someone screamed, and I jumped, immediately turning to the source and expecting the worst. It was just two students teasing each other as the screams quickly turned to laughter. My heart was still racing as I crossed the quad and walked back to Jory. I had a class to get ready for and hopefully that would take my mind off of everything.

Surprisingly, the rest of the day was uneventful. Well, except for when I threw an elbow in basic combat class and caught Kase Kasun in the nose. Who knew he was a bleeder? After class, I showered and went to check on Fin in the infirmary. Joe was still there and looked worse than when I left him. He was still wearing the same clothes as the day before.

"Have you left at all?" I asked.

"I'll leave when she leaves."

I wrinkled my nose at his response. "You might be pretty rank by then. At least shower and maybe grab a bite to eat. I'll stay with her until you get back."

He stared at Fin, who remained unconscious. "Joe," I said. "Fin wouldn't want you doing this. It's like you're punishing yourself or something."

He sighed and ran a hand through his messy hair. "Fine." He stood up and turned to face me. "I'll be right back, but call me if she wakes up. Promise?"

"I promise." After placing a kiss on Fin's forehead, Joe left, brushing past a surprised Madame Roth.

"I didn't think that boy would ever leave." She shook her head and stuck the stethoscope in her ears. She bent over Fin and listened to her chest, grunting in approval at whatever she heard. She gently lifted Fin's eyelids, shining a flashlight in each eye, and nodded with satisfaction. "Your friend is healing just fine. Nasty injury it was. Most likely would have killed a human or left them a vegetable."

"Oh my Goddess!"

"Yes, but she won't suffer that fate. Give me a few days, and she'll be good as new."

"Thank you."

Madame Roth waved me off and left the infirmary. The door whispered shut behind her, and it was just Fin and me. I sat down in the chair Joe had vacated and observed my roommate. She seemed to be resting comfortably. At the medical center, I had seen patients who were asleep but still moaned in pain or thrashed against invisible threats. To fill the silence, I updated her in on what happened with Caleb and how Clay had stopped by with coffee that morning.

"I think you might be right about him liking me. He knows what my favorite coffee is now." I told her about causing Kase to bleed in class and that my tattoo had changed. "I don't know what's going on. I guess I have to wait and see. At least you'll be safe here."

"I'll keep her safe this time."

I jumped at the voice and twisted around to see Joe. He was

back and had taken my advice. His hair was wet and glistening from a shower, and he was wearing clean clothes. In his left hand he held a paper bag from Blaze's Burgers. The smell of fresh French fries filled the room, and my stomach growled. I updated him on what Madame Roth had said, and the strain around his eyes seemed to fade a bit. I left him to go eat dinner at the cafeteria.

They were having one of my favorite meals—mac and cheese with bacon—and I piled a bunch on my plate. Several of my tower mates were eating at a circular table in the corner and waved me over.

"Hey," I said, sitting next to Roxy. "Have you seen Caleb?"

She shook her head and pursed her lips. "According to Vidar, Caleb feels like shit about what happened and isn't ready to be around anyone just yet."

Vidar was our tower president, and it made sense that he would have sought Caleb out.

"But it wasn't his fault. He knows that, right?"

Roxy sighed. "I know that. You know that. Hell, everyone knows that, and I think Caleb does, too. Honestly, I think he is scared. I think not being in control like that scared the bejeezus out of him. It would me." Roxy was a cougar shifter, and one of her fears was going feral. "He probably just needs some time. How's Fin?"

Roxy and Fin had become friends, too. We hung out together, and the little time Roxy wasn't with her two mates, she was in our room with her roommate, Bryony.

"Madame Roth says she'll make a full recovery. She's still unconscious, though. You should go see her."

Roxy shook her head and laughed when I mentioned having to force Joe to leave to shower and put on clean clothes.

"He like blames himself for not keeping Fin safe. Isn't that ridiculous?"

"And Caleb is blaming himself. Men." Roxy rolled her honey colored eyes dramatically, and I almost choked on a forkful of mac and cheese.

"I'm actually glad you're here," I said, lowering my voice and sliding my chair closer to her so no one would overhear. "I need to talk to you about this." I pulled up my jacket sleeve, revealing the hourglass tattoo. This time it was Roxy's turn to almost choke, and her eyebrows rose with surprise.

"Oh. Shit." She bent over my wrist to take a closer look. "The gong last night . . . the tattoo appeared after, right?"

"Yes. Isn't that what happened to you the first week of school? And I heard the same about Nadine right before the lake monster attack."

"That's exactly what happened. Wait!" Roxy tucked a strand of black hair behind her ear and sat up straight. I still wasn't used to Roxy having such dark hair. She had recently dyed it from her natural sandy blond. "Caleb's possession—is that connected?"

"I think so, but nothing else has happened. Not that I want anything else to happen. Last night was enough, thank you very much."

"Well, when the hacking happened, things started out slow and then got real crazy, real fast."

"What do you think it means?"

Roxy frowned and shook her head. "I have no idea." She stood up and grabbed her bag. Her mates, who had been sitting on the other side of her, jumped up at the same time. "If anything else happens and you need help, let me know." She gave my shoulder a squeeze before leaving with her mates.

As I finished eating dinner, people began to filter out, and then it was just Clay and me at the table. He was sitting across from me, and when we made eye contact, he smiled.

"So, what are your plans for tonight?" he asked.

I shrugged and yawned, patting my carb-loaded belly. "Sleep, but I have to study first. You?"

"I was wondering . . ." He paused to move over, taking the seat Roxy had been sitting in. He sat so close that his arm brushed against mine. He smelled good, clean and earthy. I detected a hint of cedar. "I couldn't help but notice you struggled a bit in potions class yesterday."

"A bit? I was a hot mess."

Clay laughed and turned the chair slightly so he could face me, and I noticed how his jeans stretched tight across his muscular thighs. "Let me help you. We can practice tonight so you're better prepared for class tomorrow." Then he lowered his voice, leaned toward me, and said, "I can be a very good teacher."

He winked, and the tips of his ears turned red. *Is he flirting with me?* I decided to play along.

"What if I'm a very bad student?" I tilted my head to the side and twirled a strand of hair around my finger while batting my eyelashes. His mouth dropped open, and he stared at me before he licked his lips and smirked.

"I think we'll get along just fine. So shall we work on some magic together?"

"You're still talking about potions, right?" I stood and slipped the strap of my bag over my shoulder before picking up what was left of my dinner. Clay chuckled before taking the tray out of my hands and carrying it over to the trash can. Passing by the water fountain that featured a six-foot tall statue of a Valkyrie at the entrance, we exited Halstein Hall and went down the steps into the courtyard. I immediately looked up, reassured at seeing the night sky through the top of the mountain. I was still adjusting to life underground. The sky seemed so far away, the moon a distant orb, but it was there.

We started walking, and as much as I tried to ignore the giant hourglass, it was unavoidable, especially since it was glowing. I lifted my jacket sleeve to check my tattoo. The two hourglasses were still in sync.

Clay noticed right away. "What is going on with your tattoo?"

He held his arm out, and his school issued tattoo was completely normal.

I sighed, tugging on my jacket sleeve to cover the tattoo. "It seems to be connected to the giant gong."

"So does that mean it's going to get crazy around here again? I swear this is the weirdest place." He chuckled and shook his head.

"I have no idea what's going on. All I know is the tattoo

appeared on my wrist last night and later on, Caleb was possessed. Will it get worse than that? I don't know."

"Well, then, since we all might be in imminent danger soon," Clay said and faced me, placing his hands on my hips. At first I thought he was going to try to kiss me, and before I had a chance to react, a gale of wind wrapped around us, his grip tightened, and suddenly we were in the air rushing toward the bridge that connected Jory Tower to the library. We landed on the bridge, and I exhaled sharply when the wind released me. If Clay didn't have his hands on me still, I probably would have stumbled like I was drunk. It felt that way.

"Whoa, you can fly?" I stared up at him in amazement.

"Sort of. Now, let's go work on potions." He released my hips and stepped away to open one of the main doors to the commons floor, which had been magically replaced. And, sounding like my grandmother, he said, "You need to be prepared for whatever is coming."

CHAPTER 4

"**I** think of this as a special Chemistry class, like in high school," Clay said when he started his "lesson," and I snorted because I went to Sun and Moon Academy in Havenwood Falls for high school, and we had a different curriculum, one that included potions. I barely passed that class.

"Science isn't my thing," I said

"Okay, how about cooking? Each potion is a recipe."

"Recipe for disaster." Clay actually rolled his eyes at me when I said that, making me laugh. "I'm kidding. That actually does help. Equate anything with food, and you have my attention."

He shook his head and laughed then walked me through constructing a potion intended to make a person invisible, and it worked!

The next day Clay held the door open for me, and I walked into potions class with confidence. The room was set up like a science lab. There were plain metal tables in rows. Each table had two cauldrons that were suspended over Bunsen burners and an assortment of glass vials in various sizes, some of the larger ones looking more like vases. Each class we were partnered with someone new, so we would get comfortable working with different witches of varying abilities. Fortunately, this time I was paired with

Clay, who I learned the night before, was very patient and had a calming effect on me. I could actually relax and focus on the potion.

Professor Parker was impressed that I made it through class without anything exploding or turning into a slime volcano. Yes, that happened my first week of the semester.

"Taylor, you have shown great improvement today," she said I was leaving the classroom.

"Thanks, I had a good partner." I glanced across the room at Clay, who was talking to Natalie Putnam and Tempest Bell. He caught me looking at him and winked before turning his attention back to the conversation.

"I see." Professor Parker smiled and gave me a knowing look. "Keep practicing, Taylor. You have potential. Always have."

I was halfway down the hallway, planning on visiting Fin before dinner, when Clay caught up to me.

"Hey, so Natalie and Tempest just told me there's a party tonight at Hel Tower. Want to go?"

"I don't know." I chewed on my lower lip. It didn't seem right having fun when Fin was in the infirmary.

"If you're worried about your little problem, there's strength in numbers," Clay said. To be honest, the day had been uneventful and my classes provided enough distraction that I had forgotten about *my little problem*, as he'd put it. Clay did have a point. Plus, the prospect of being alone in my room or in the commons didn't appeal to me. Most likely everyone else was going to be at the party.

"Yeah, I'll go for a bit."

"Wicked! I'll swing by your room around nine, and we'll go together." He walked away, leaving me speechless and confused. Was this like a date?

Back in my room after seeing Fin, who was still unconscious, I made a bowl of udon and called Harlow while it was cooling.

"Hey, Tay, how's college life?"

"It's a little crazy." I filled her in on Caleb and what happened to Fin.

"What the hell? Are you in danger? Do I need to come kick some ass?" Harlow and I were close, and she had always been protective of me. She would drop everything and come running. She did that for those she loved.

"No, but I do need some advice."

"What's that?"

"I think I have a date tonight and have no idea what to wear."

"What? I need fucking details."

This made me laugh. I told her about Clay, how he was from northern Maine, where his family settled after they fled Salem during the witch trials. A number of witch families had similar stories, including Professor Parker. I didn't tell her about Cillian, though. I wanted to keep him to myself. Plus, I knew she would warn me against developing feelings for a ghost. *Too late. That ship has sailed.*

By the time I hung up, my noodles were cold, but I touched my wand to the bowl and whispered a spell to warm them up. Following Harlow's advice, I put on a pair of black leggings and a deep red, long sleeved T-shirt. My tiger's eye pendant was on display, the stone resting just above my breasts. I wore my hair down and put on a touch of mascara and lip gloss. I debated about changing my nose ring, but left the simple star shaped stud. I slipped on a pair of black boots that stopped right below my knees.

While I was getting ready, Paisley confirmed that she and Mak would be at the party. Roxy wasn't sure if she would be there or not, which didn't surprise me. She wasn't that social to begin with, and she had her hands full, literally, with her two mates. I pleaded with them to be there as my wing bitches. It was kind of embarrassing, but I didn't have a lot of experience with guys. Havenwood Falls was a small town, and there was limited selection. Also, among the supernatural community, the fact that my grandmother was on the Court made the guys treat me differently—like they were intimidated.

I was ready well before nine o'clock, and nerves set in. I remade my bed, making sure the pillows were evenly placed and the comforter smooth. I even made Fin's bed. Then I started pacing the floor, and the longer I paced, the more I began to doubt my decision. I was here at SMA to study and learn. I wasn't here to date. What if it turned into a relationship? What about Cillian? Goddess, these kinds of complications were precisely what I wanted to avoid. I was about ready to text Clay and cancel the whole thing when he knocked on the door and brought my nervous pacing to a halt.

"Blessed be," I blurted out when I opened the door and saw Clay. He had shaved, and his brown hair was styled, trimmed on the sides and longer on the top. His wore a black T-shirt that hugged his broad chest. His ears turned red at my reaction.

"You look great, too," he said and grinned. "Ready to go?"

"Yes, sure." I tucked my wand into the inside pocket of my denim jacket and shut the door behind me.

"We'll take the express route," Clay said and stepped closer to hold onto my hips. Now that I knew what to expect, I wrapped my arms around his neck, which placed my body flush with his. I instantly became aware of his warmth, his cedar scent, and how solid his body was. Heat flooded my cheeks, and I ducked my head, not wanting Clay to see how I was reacting to him.

His grip on my hips tightened, and he whispered in my ear, his breath tickling my neck, "Hold on."

I closed my eyes and took a deep breath as the wind whipped up and wrapped around us, enveloping us in our own private cocoon.

Controlling an element, like the wind, required extraordinary power. It made me realize Clay was recruited from the woods of northern Maine for a reason. Pressed against him, I felt the power humming through him.

We didn't see or hear the party when we were approaching, but we passed through some sort of barrier on our descent and once we landed on the roof of Hel Tower, the party exploded to life around us. Someone had conjured a cloaking spell, and it was very effective to disguise thumping bass music and a magical strobe light display.

"Yay, you're here!" Paisley yelled and rushed forward with

Makenna by her side. "Let's dance." I smelled cinnamon on her breath and wondered how many shots of Fireball whiskey she had consumed already. Paisley grabbed my hand and dragged me toward the section of the roof that had become the dance floor. I glanced over my shoulder at Clay who looked just as surprised as I was at the sudden separation, but then the crowd closed in behind me, and I lost sight of him.

"What was that all about?" I asked once we stopped. Paisley danced around me. For once, she didn't have any highlights in her white blond hair, but it still picked up the colors of the flashing lights.

"We're your wing bitches, and we need to know what our objective is. I mean, you all looked cozy when you arrived. We can run interference or leave you alone. You tell us."

"I don't know. I like him and wouldn't object to kissing him, but I'm not ready to go off and have like wild monkey sex with him or anything." Of course, I had been shouting to be heard over the music and at the moment I said wild monkey sex, the music stopped for a song change. This caused everyone around us to laugh and cheer. Paisley and Mak bent over in hysterics while I wanted to sink into the roof and disappear, which technically I could do with the right spell or the invisibility potion I made earlier.

"Okay, but if he gets inappropriate with you in anyway, he has to deal with us," Mak said, tossing her mane of fire red curls behind her shoulder. "Although you shouldn't pass up hot monkey sex. He looks like he has stamina!" She wiggled her eyebrows at me, and my entire body heated at the suggestion.

"I need a drink!" I declared and left my snickering friends on the dance floor to go in search of the bar. Instead I ran into Natalie who was carrying a tray of drinks in paper cups.

"Oh, Taylor, try this. Tempest and I have been using some potions knowledge, and we're experimenting on making a supernatural brew. What do you think?" She handed me one of the cups, and a dark green liquid sloshed over the side. Before I took a sip, the smell hit my nose, and I cringed. It smelled like mildewy wet towels. Realizing Natalie was waiting for my opinion, I braved a sip and couldn't hide my reaction when my body immediately rejected it. I spit the foul drink onto the ground. Natalie's face fell.

"That bad, huh?"

"I'm sorry, but it's terrible."

"Well, thanks for your honesty." Natalie left, taking her toxic brew with her. I knew I wasn't the only one struggling with potions, but that was awful, I thought as I wiped my mouth. The crowd parted, and I spotted the bar. Amaruq was behind it, and he smiled when I approached.

"Tay! What can I get you?"

"Anything that is not an experiment."

He laughed. "You must have run into Natalie or Tempest."

"Yup!" He handed me a drink that had red liquid on the bottom and black on top, calling it a Black Widow. I took a sip, grateful to replace the taste of mildewy towels with the tang of cranberry.

When I turned away from the bar, I almost ran into Clay.

"Sorry about leaving you like that," I said.

"It's cool," he said with a shrug. "Your friends were on a mission. Having fun?"

"I am, actually. Thanks for dragging me out."

"No problem."

Once Clay got his beer, we walked around the party. There were benches upholstered in red fabric set up in a square around a black, wrought iron fire pit. Flames reached toward the sky outside of the mountain, and in the firelight, I spotted Paisley's ex-boyfriend from high school sitting on one of the benches next to his friend, Timber Greenwood.

The way Timber sat with perfect posture and moved to a slightly different rhythm set him apart from those who grew up on Earth. He grew up in Faerie and had a strange air of formality about him. He reminded me of an ice prince from a fairy tale with his pale skin, white blond hair, and green eyes that shone like gemstones. I looked around for Paisley. It had been a shock for her to see Cole on move-in night. The last Paisley had heard, Cole was living in Faerie. She seemed to have adjusted to the fact that he was here, but I still worried about my friend.

More and more students had joined the dance floor as the mysterious DJ Dragonclaw started dropping some serious beats. He was one of the students here, but nobody knew his true identity. He wore a mask and a hoodie to conceal his face. I found myself walking with the music, swinging my hips and enjoying the vibration of the bass. The drink had loosened up my body, and I set my empty glass down on the wall that ran along the perimeter of the rooftop.

"Come on, let's dance!" Like Paisley did to me before, I grabbed Clay's hand and pulled him into the crowd. He tried to resist, but I wasn't having it. Soon he was moving with me, and we danced closer and closer together until we were standing still, our bodies pressed together. We were both breathing heavy, our eyes locked on each other. I licked my lips and watched as his gaze lowered to follow the movement of my tongue. Then he was kissing me.

The hand he had pressed against the small of my back slid down to grab my ass while his other hand tangled in my hair. My arms wrapped around his neck, and I stood on my tiptoes to deepen the kiss since he was much taller than me. He tasted like beer with a hint of mint, and his lips were surprisingly soft. I melted against him, and he tightened his hold on my ass.

"Taylor!" Cillian's voice was suddenly in my ear, and I gasped, breaking the kiss.

"What's wrong?" Clay asked as I stepped away. Cillian was standing next to him, and I blinked, thinking maybe I was seeing things, but no, he was really there. I touched my lips, suddenly feeling guilty for having been caught kissing Clay, not that I had any reason to feel ashamed.

"What are you doing here?" I asked Cillian, who had moved to stand in front of me. He radiated a chill that cooled my flushed skin right down.

"I came to warn you. There's a shit storm of trouble coming."

"What?"

"Taylor, you have to go! I'll explain on the way." Cillian grabbed my hand. His touch was ice cold, but he felt surprisingly human. The laser lights went dark the same time he grew brighter, more solid.

A chorus of shocked gasps and exclamations erupted from the students dancing near us. Apparently they could see Cillian. I didn't have time to explain why the spirit of a gorgeous blond surfer, wearing nothing but board shorts, was holding my hand. Cillian's urgency and panicked expression was freaking me the fuck out. I let him lead me away, the lights flickering back on in our wake.

"Are you doing that to the lights?"

"Yeah, energy," Cillian explained, panting with effort.

"Taylor, where are you going?" Clay yelled and started to follow.

"What he said. Where are we going? What the fuck is going on, Cillian?" I broke free of his grip and stopped. Standing with hands on my hips, I refused to take another step without answers.

"Remember that storm that always hovers on the horizon when you visit me?"

"Yeah, sure. You said that's a collection of violent spirits consumed by anger and rage."

"Right, exactly. Well, last night I noticed it wasn't as strong as it usually is."

"I noticed that too, but I've never visited you at night, so thought it was normal."

"Well, it's not. I went to catch some curls at dawn and noticed the horizon was clear. The storm was completely gone." Cillian glanced nervously around the rooftop. "I was curious, so I left my beach and entered the Void."

"You did?" I stared at him with amazement. I had been visiting Cillian frequently over the summer, and he had told me a lot about how the spirit realm worked. The realm itself was like one big waiting room. The Entrypoint was where most spirits arrived at first. He described it as like walking through the thickest fog. All sound was distorted or muffled, and everything was gray. Some spirits would decide they were ready to move on completely to the other side, and they were whisked away. Other spirits, like Cillian, weren't ready. They had either suffered an unexpected, traumatic death or had unfinished business. They stayed and were able to make their own reality to help them with the transition. Cillian's beach was his reality. Then there were the spirits who came from evil, like murderers, rapists, and sadists. They were not fit to be recycled and were forced into a separate area, called the Void, which was connected to the Infernum. It was basically a general population section of prison, but for spirits. With all of these dangerous spirits housed together, their negative energy created the storm. "What did you see?"

"Nothing. The Void is empty. There's a breach in the realm."

"Oh my Goddess!"

"Taylor, what's going on?" Clay asked. "Who's this guy?"

"Shhhh." I shushed him and looked at Cillian so he would continue.

"I followed the breach, and it leads right to here. The entire campus is in danger."

The drink from earlier threatened to come back up, and my knees felt like they were made of marshmallows. Suddenly Makenna ran toward me, screaming. She was holding a hand over the side of her neck, and blood was leaking from underneath, dripping down her chest and staining her blue shirt. She was a spooked animal, running blindly, her eyes wide with fright.

"Run!" she screamed again, and I looked to see what she was running from and saw Molly Shaw, one of the belladonna vampires on campus, wiping the back of her hand across her mouth and smearing blood on her face. She grinned, and blood filled in the spaces between her teeth. Then Molly started to pursue Mak, her speed turning her into a blur of motion. Just as she was about to reach Mak, Molly dropped to the floor, hard. Vines wrapped around her legs, caused her to fall. I looked up to see Timber standing near, his eyes glittering as he caused the vines to continue to grow and wrap around Molly's entire body, keeping her secured. He created the vines with his fae magic out of the patches of moss that grew in cracks on the rooftop. Paisley ran over to where Mak had fallen and immediately started to heal her.

Then students began screaming, and chaos broke out by the bar when Amaruq shifted into a giant gray wolf and bit Fig, an elf who lived in Modi Tower. Another student, it was too dark to see who, was tossed over the side of the roof. A glimpse of orange hair caught my attention, and I saw Charleigh Wotsit, a witch I met on the first day of the trials for SMA, running toward her friend, Elliana Knight.

Elliana was a terrifying sight to behold. Her purple and black wings were spread out wide. With a pivot of her body, she was able to knock aside anyone who approached from behind. With her arms raised in the air, I stared in horror as Elliana seemed to control the spirits. She was like a mad puppet master, laughing with delight as she directed spirits to their host bodies. Then she was gone. She dropped off the edge of the roof, disappearing from sight, a swarm of spirits following her.

Everywhere I looked, students were becoming shrouded in black mists as their bodies were taken over. My biggest fear, a mass possession event, was unfolding before my eyes, and I froze, seized with panic. I didn't know where to begin.

CHAPTER 5

Cold wrapped around my arm, and I looked down to see Cillian's hand as he started pulling at me.

"You need to get out of here!" he yelled.

"No. I need to stay and fix this." I shrugged my arm free of his grip and walked around Molly as she struggled against her restraints. The vines were holding strong. I would start with the spirit possessing her, and if I had to tackle them one by one, so be it. I didn't have my kit with me and didn't have time to retrieve it from my tower, but Natalie and Tempest were both witches, and they lived here. "Clay, go find Natalie and Tempest. I pray to the Goddess they're not possessed. I need salt and elemental candles. Also, black tourmaline or onyx for all of us, if they have it."

Clay was gone in a rush of wind, and I turned to Timber, who was watching me with his glowing gemstone eyes.

"What you did with the vines—can you do this to all of the aggressors? They're possessed, and I need them contained in order to exorcise the spirits," I explained.

"At your service, fair maiden." He dipped in a bow.

Under different circumstances, I probably would have laughed, but there was nothing funny about this situation. Before he left, I removed the tiger's eye pendant and held the stone in my fist.

"Protect the wearer of this charm. Keep them free of harm. I mote it be."

There was a faint glow, and the stone warmed in my hand. I handed this to Timber. "Keep this on you. It should ward off any spirits from possessing you."

He sped off into the melee, and I prayed to the Goddess that my spell worked.

Cillian hovered off the side, watching the chaos unfold with an expression that was both terrified and amazed. He never knew supernatural species were real, and now he was seeing them in action. Clay approached with Tempest and Natalie in tow. They each carried cloth bags stuffed to overflowing.

"You're creating a circle?" Natalie asked, pulling out jars of salt and setting them on the rooftop.

"Yes, and I'm going to need your help. This circle is going to be big, and I need to somehow bring everyone who is possessed inside."

"You want to bring the dark energy inside the circle? That's not how circles are supposed to work." Tempest challenged me, and I gave her the side eye. This wasn't my first rodeo.

"It will contain the dark energy and keep everyone on the outside of the circle safe. Trust me, this worked the last time with Caleb."

"But what about you?" Natalie asked. "How are you going to stay safe?"

I stood up, holding four candles in my arms against my chest. They represented the elements: fire, earth, air, and water. "Because spirits can't enter my body, for some reason. They're repulsed by my Itako blood."

I let them know Timber was securing the possessed and directed Clay to round them up and set them next to Molly.

Tempest, Natalie, and I started to set up the circle. The candles were placed like they were the four compass points, and they would serve as an extra protective barrier. Clay arrived with a student flung over his shoulder. Cole was behind him, carrying someone else. One by one, the possessed were placed in the area marked by the burning candles. They all struggled against their vines. When one snapped, Timber was there to reinforce the restraints. The possessed shouted vile threats, like wanting to feed on our organs or violate us until we bled. I had to constantly remind myself that my classmates weren't saying these things but the spirits who possessed them.

Apparently Natalie had heard enough. She held out her hand, directing it at the possessed and shouted, "Silence!"

They immediately shut up. Their mouths still moved, but we couldn't hear a damn thing.

"Blessed be," I said and smiled at the dark-haired witch.

She smiled back and picked up a jar of salt. Clay, Tempest, and I followed suit. We started walking clockwise, and I began the chant I used before. Their voices joined mine, and I felt the strength of our combined power, like an electric current connected us. The salt began to glow before it even left our jars, and by the time we finished three rotations, the circle illuminated the entire rooftop. I ushered Natalie, Tempest, and Clay out of the circle so I could close it. Clay was the last to leave, and he turned around to face me. He reached for my hand and entwined his fingers with mine.

"Be safe, okay? We'll be right outside if you need us." He lowered his head and kissed me, just a brief touch of his lips to mine. He squeezed my hand once before letting go and stepping back, so he was completely outside the circle.

I took a deep breath and closed the circle, which flared brighter briefly, letting me know it was closed. Energy hummed in the air, and the possessed were writhing with more intensity. Following the same process as I did with Caleb, I squatted next to Molly and grabbed her hand that was exposed. I focused on the spirit inside her and locked on, dragging it out with me where it wailed and screeched, carrying on with a paranormal temper tantrum. Just like before, I focused on the spirit realm and projected myself there, depositing the spirit and making a quick retreat. Molly had grown still, and her eyes were closed, but her eyelids were moving. I imagined being possessed had exhausted her.

I moved onto the next person, the bartender, still in wolf form. His growls were silent but the snap of his jaws as he tried to bite me was audible. Holding onto one of his hind paws and staying away from his sharp teeth, I began the exorcism.

By the time I was done with the twenty-three students within the circle, I was wrecked. I wanted to collapse right there and sleep for days. I had been so absorbed with my task, I had drowned out everything going on around me. Now that I was done, awareness crept back in, and so did the echo of screams. Only they weren't coming from the rooftop. They were coming from below.

"They're everywhere, Taylor," Cillian said from beside me.

"How many spirits came through the breach?"

He shrugged and shook his head. "I don't know. Hundreds?"

My heart dropped into my stomach. Hundreds? Between students and faculty, there were over two hundred of us. There was no way I could handle that. I was already exhausted. I deactivated the circle and rushed to the edge of the roof, where everyone else had followed the screams. Hel Tower was only five stories high, so it was easy to see what was going on below. More possessed supes were terrorizing the campus. Fuck. I sunk down to the floor, with my back against the wall, and buried my head in my hands, hiding a yawn. I needed another plan.

"Taylor, I hate to tell you this," Cillian said. He sat down next to me, and his cold presence actually helped wake me up a bit.

"Tell me what?"

"All of the spirits you brought back to the realm won't stay there. You have to seal the breach first."

Oh my Goddess! I groaned and leaned my head back against the stone wall. Of course they wouldn't. It was like scooping water out of a boat that still had a leak.

"I'm an idiot. Any ideas on how to close the breach?" I asked him since he was my resident expert on all things spirit realm.

"I don't know." He shrugged and gave me a look. "You're a witch. I thought you'd know."

That wasn't the answer I was looking for. I closed my eyes and took a few deep breaths. Sealing the breach was my top priority. *Just how the hell was I going to do that?*

I stood outside the portal that led to the faculty residential tower, which was luckily located right next to Hel. Clay had used his wind power to transport us here at my request. There was one professor who might be able to help me with the breach. I held my tattoo up in front of the portal, which moved in a hypnotic, iridescent swirl. Nothing happened.

"Shit. It's not working. Maybe because my tattoo has been altered? Try yours."

Clay held his tattoo up and still nothing happened.

"Wait. I remember something about this portal was off limits to students so the faculty will have privacy," Clay said.

"Ugh!" I growled out in frustration and tried again. This time I yelled, "It's an emergency!"

Whatever guardian magic was in place must have sensed the urgency because the swirl opened up and allowed us entrance.

It took a few minutes to find Dr. Sam Fraser's apartment. He was my professor for Interdimensional Exploration and Time Travel. The druid had been around for centuries, and I hoped he had the answer I was seeking. I knocked on his door, and a few seconds later, it swung open, revealing a whole lot of Dr. Fraser I hadn't seen before. He wore his customary kilt, but didn't have a shirt on, and he must have been working out or something because his broad, muscular chest gleamed with the sheen of sweat. Good Goddess that was a distracting sight. I'd never be able to sit in class and *not* see that. His eyebrows rose in surprise when he saw me.

"Miss Augustine! What are you doing here?" He peered over my shoulder at Clay. "And you are?"

"Clay Washburn, Dr. Fraser, and we need your help."

Just then an alarm sounded, and a voice echoed down the hallway. "Attention! Lockdown commencing in two minutes. All portals will close in two minutes."

The message repeated, counting down the time.

"Dr. Fraser. There's a breach in the spirit realm, and it leads right to Halvard. I need to know how to close it. Can you help?"

"Why do you have to close it, Miss Augustine?"

"Because it's my fault, that's why!" I screamed, hysteria threatening to bubble up and take over. "I've been going there. I caused it." It made sense. Caleb's possession happened the same night I last visited the spirit realm and had spent longer than usual there. It had to be my fault. I had somehow opened a breach between that realm and mine. "Now, can you help me?"

"Attention! Lockdown commencing in one minute. All portals will close in one minute."

Nausea boiled in my stomach, and my palms started to sweat as Dr. Fraser regarded me with stormy blue eyes.

"Aye, all I can say is the answer you seek is in the library. There's a book titled *A Comprehensive Guide to the Multiverse, Realms and Timeline Best Practices*. Now go, lass, I wish you well on your quest." He shut the door, and I stood there stunned.

That was it? He wasn't going to come to the rescue of the students in danger? Come to think of it, I hadn't seen any faculty on campus.

"Taylor, we have to go!"

The thirty-second warning echoed down the hall and spurred me into action. We ran toward the portal, the swirling colors beckoning us. I held up my tattoo, and the portal opened.

Lightning crackled in the air, and I looked up to see a giant black bird with white markings soaring above. Arcs of lightning shot out from its wings and struck a stalactite. This broke off and came crashing down on the bridge that connected Jory to the library.

"Holy shit, is that D?" I asked Clay. D was Clay's roommate and the only Impundulu or "lightning bird" on campus. I hadn't seen him in his bird form before.

"Yes, and I think he's possessed."

Great, now the threat was airborne. Shit kept getting worse.

"Why are they locking down the campus? That hasn't happened before," Clay said.

"Because the tattoos we all have allow us to pass through the portals. If we're possessed, we can still pass through them. At least this will be contained to campus." The idea of this chaos spilling over into my hometown made me feel ill, and I was relieved that the portals were closing even if it meant being sealed inside.

Cillian suddenly appeared in front of me.

"Where did you go?" he asked.

"To find help. We're going to the library." I pointed to a giant stalagmite located behind Halstein Hall before stepping into Clay's embrace. This time the intimate closeness of our bodies didn't feel as awkward, but I was hyper-aware of Cillian watching us. Clay wrapped his arms around my waist and tugged me closer, the pressure of his hands on the small of my back reassuring. He dipped his head and kissed me, creating a warm flutter in my stomach that replaced the nervous tension.

"Ready?" he asked, and I nodded, tightening my hold around his neck.

Wind gathered around us, and my hair billowed out with the force as we shot up into the air. We flew over the courtyard, and a raven, one I had seen around campus before, flew alongside us before veering off. I looked down, drawn to the glowing hourglass. It was less than half full now. Time was running out.

Our landing was soft, and I was getting used to this kind of travel as I didn't sway like a drunk sailor on sea legs. We were on the library side of the bridge. The stalactite that D had knocked loose was lying on its side. A giant fissure almost ran the length of the bridge. Clay went ahead to make sure the library was safe. While I waited outside, Cillian caught up to me. He stared in amazement at the fractured bridge and then up at the ring of stalactites that surrounded the campus. Then he looked at the stalagmite we were about to enter.

"The library is literally inside there? That's fucking crazy!"

"We don't have time for sightseeing. Are you coming?" I started to jog toward the library, and Cillian fell in step beside me. Well, his feet didn't touch the floor; he just kind of glided along. As soon as we entered the library, the lights dimmed and flickered and Cillian became more dimensional until he looked like a real person. We caught up to Clay at the reference desk, and his eyebrows rose in surprise when he saw Cillian.

"Going to introduce me to your friend, Taylor?" he asked as he took in Cillian's surfer dude appearance.

I introduced the guys to each other, and they proceeded to enter a staring contest.

"Oh, for fuck's sake, we need to find the book!"

The librarian was nowhere to be found. Her desk was located in the middle of the first floor and from there, when you looked straight up, you saw floor upon floor of bookshelves, carved from the stone of the stalagmite with bridges crisscrossing the opening. I don't know how many floors there were because I swear they changed in number, and they ascended into shadows. This wasn't a quaint Victorian house converted into a library, like the one in Havenwood Falls. No, this place was dangerous and not for the faint of heart.

Reaching into my jacket pocket, I pulled out my wand. *"Goddess, hear my plea, help me locate what I seek."*

A gentle tugging on my wand pulled me toward the spiral stairs, not the elevator. With a sigh, I followed the lead and started climbing. Clay was behind me, and Cillian appeared next to me. We climbed and climbed, the tugging growing stronger with each step. My legs began to quiver, and the darkness closed in around us. A few minutes later, Cillian was gone. He no longer had energy to pull from. Clay used his wand to create light, and we pressed on. The stone groaned around us, and there was a subtle vibration, like the stalagmite was on its own axis making a slow rotation. I had to stop to catch my breath. Sweat dripped down my back, and my legs were wet noodles but I didn't dare sit down because I knew I wouldn't be able to stand again.

"Is Cillian the reason why you went to the spirit realm?" Clay asked. He was panting too, and the dim light from my wand reflected off the beads of sweat that dotted his forehead.

"Not at first. I was seeking a peaceful place and accidentally projected myself to this gorgeous beach with soft, white sand and the bluest, warm water. Cillian was there because it's a beach he created," I explained. "He's easy to talk to, and he's lonely. So I give him the companionship he wants, and he listens to me."

"I can see why that would be a draw. A private place to go to when you're feeling overwhelmed. I have a place like that in Maine. A cave that no one knows exists."

"Yeah. I could totally escape to the beach now, but I have to fix this." With a groan, I started climbing again, following my wand like it was a divining rod. Finally, after I didn't know how many steps, we were led onto a floor. At orientation, we were warned to not touch any books unless it was specifically the book you needed. I planned to heed that warning.

We passed row after row of books until my wand pointed to one at least six inches thick and bound in cracked black leather. The words written on the spine were faint and hard to read in the dim lighting. Clay held his wand closer, and I saw the title: *A Comprehensive Guide to the Multiverse, Realms and Timeline Best Practices.* Finally!

I pulled the book off the shelf and almost dropped it since it weighed like fifty pounds. Dust drifted off the pages when I opened it, turning to the table of contents. The book contained over five thousand pages. How was I going to find what I needed? Suddenly the pages started turning on their own, so fast they created a breeze that blew my hair away from my face. Just as suddenly, they stopped on page 3,047, Chapter 213, Inter-realm Travel and Responsibilities.

Three pages into the chapter, a bold subtitle jumped out at me: BREACHES. With Clay holding his wand over the pages for light, I read through certain scenarios until I found one that related to my specific situation. This wasn't a tear or a leak. This was a full-blown breach. The instructions seemed straightforward. Energy needed to be used to repair the breach, and also a personal sacrifice by the entity making the repair was required.

"Okay, let's go." We ran between the stacks and across one of the bridges to the elevator, which looked like some steampunk creation. I didn't care that it groaned and squeaked when we stepped inside. I was grateful for not having to take the stairs. The elevator whirred and hummed as it descended. The single bulb swayed with the clunky movement, casting more shadows than light in the cramped space. The elevator came to a stop with a shudder when I yanked on the lever that controlled the brake. Clay tugged the grate that served as the door open, and I spotted Cillian waiting for us by the reference desk. Good, I needed him to show me the breach. Since the bridge was blocked by the stalagmite, we went out through Halstein Hall, which was filled with smoke. I didn't have time to stop and worry about a possible fire.

We ran out into the courtyard, following Cillian as he was leading us to the breach. Out of habit, I glanced up, and based on the angle of the light coming in from the top of the mountain, I estimated it to be late afternoon. I had heard it was possible to lose time in the library, but we had lost over half a day. It would be dusk soon, on the night of a full moon. While I would be able to draw on the power of the moon, so could other supes, and that was only going to exacerbate everything. *Can't a witch get a break?* As we were running past Jory Tower, Roxy, Tyr and Vidar appeared on the main balcony.

"Taylor, what's going on?" Roxy yelled. I didn't have time to answer and kept running. Seconds later, I heard footsteps behind us and turned to see Roxy, Tyr, and Vidar catching up. They must have jumped off the balcony, sticking the landing after a three-story drop with supernatural grace. In between breaths, I explained to them where we were going and why.

"You should be somewhere safe!" I told Roxy. The last thing I wanted was another friend getting hurt.

"No. We're coming with you. I hacked the emergency system and locked down the portals when I realized what was happening."

"Besides, since Vidar and I are demigods, we can't be possessed, and now that we all share a mating bond, our immunity passed to Rox," Tyr said. His long brown hair was pulled up into a man bun that bounced as he ran.

"Wait, how? Immunity can be shared?" An idea was forming for the second part of my problem, preventing people from being possessed and expelling the spirits from those who were already.

"We exchanged blood," Vidar answered.

Was it really as simple as that? My genetic makeup repelled spirits. Could I use blood magick and make a potion with the same effect? *Potions, again. UGH!* I had to try though. Cillian led us away from the buildings and away from the threat of D's lighting strikes. There were a series of caves near a steep trail that led down to the lake. He ducked into one, but not before I saw the still form of Gary the gnome. His twisted body lay by the cave entrance, and his lifeless eyes were starting to cloud over, forever fixed on some distant point.

The idea that people might die versus actually seeing someone I knew dead changed the game entirely. I couldn't afford to lose any more time.

We had reached the breach, a gaping black hole in the side of the cave. Freezing cold air blew out from the hole, and I shivered. Looking at Cillian, I asked, "Are you ready?"

And he nodded. I turned to face the others.

"Okay, I'm going to fix the breach. Clay, I have an idea, and since you're such a great potions tutor, maybe you can work on this while I'm gone?"

"Absolutely. Whatever you need, but I'm not leaving this spot until you're back safe." He crossed his arms over his chest as if expecting me to protest, which I wasn't. At least here in the cave, Clay, Roxy, and Tyr would be away from the chaos.

"That's fine. So my idea involves blood magick—a potion using the properties in my blood that repel the spirits. We need a lot of it, and it needs to be fast acting. Do you think there's a way to make a potion like that?"

"Yeah, I think so."

"Good. Roxy?" My friend's honey colored eyes settled on me. "Can you go tell Natalie and Tempest what my plan is? Clay and I are going to need their help with the potion. Have them meet us at our potions classroom. Also, we're going to need as many healers as possible."

"I can do that," she answered.

"And Tyr and Vidar?" I turned to the mated deities who, if they didn't have different skin color, would pass as twins with their similar style and mannerisms.

"Yeah?" they answered in unison. It was kind of creepy, and maybe it was another mating bond thing.

"Are all deities immune like you guys?"

"They should be, yeah," Vidar said. He scratched the top of his head, working a long finger between two rows of dreadlocks.

"Okay, I need you to recruit as many immune people as possible to have on hand to administer the potion."

"The potion that doesn't exist yet. Got it," Tyr said with a smirk.

I rolled my eyes. "It will exist, and it will work. It has to. I'm not going to accept any other outcome."

"Yes, ma'am." Tyr gave me a cocky smile and salute before he, Vidar, and Roxy left.

I turned to face the breach. Cillian was already there on the edge, waiting for me. Looking over my shoulder, I smiled at Clay.

"See you soon," I said before taking a deep breath and stepping forward into the dark abyss.

CHAPTER 7

The spirit realm was eerily quiet. Cold, dark, and quiet. My breath came out in white puffs, and I rubbed my hands together for warmth. I could see Clay on the other side of the hole, but he seemed much farther away, like I had walked half a mile and if I didn't have such great vision, I wouldn't have been able to see him at all.

"Right, let's do this." I pulled my wand out of my jacket and closed my eyes, focusing on gathering all of the energy around me. Nothing happened. The spirit realm was quite literally a dead zone. "Shit."

I lowered my wand in defeat. *Now what was I supposed to do?*

"What's wrong?" Cillian asked. He moved closer and touched his hand to mine, making it even colder. I shivered at his touch. His blue eyes peered at my face, and I looked up at him.

"I'm out of ideas. There isn't enough energy here for me to harness. I don't know what else to do." I lowered my head so he didn't see the tears that threatened to spill. Goddess, I was tired and going on twenty-four hours without sleep. It was so quiet here and peaceful. I could just close my eyes and rest a bit.

"Taylor, wake up!" Cillian placed a cold hand against my

251

cheek, and my eyes flew open with the shock. His touch was just as effective as a slap. "Don't you succumb to it. I have an idea."

I licked my lips and shook my arms to get the circulation going.

"What's that?" I asked and yawned.

"Use me for energy."

"What? No!"

"Please," he pleaded with me and cradled my face with his hands. He touched his forehead to mine, and the stud in my nostril became so cold, it made my nose ache. "It's okay. I'm ready to go."

I jerked away and met his eyes, which were rimmed with tears, like mine.

"No." I dug in, hands on my hips. "I can't lose you. I won't do it. "

"Tay," he said with a sigh and cupped my cheek.

"There has to be another way," I choked out and leaned into his icy touch. "What if I stayed here and blocked the breach from this side?"

He shook his head and caressed my cheek before dropping his hand. "I've had my chance, and while I wish I could change how I lived my life, I know now that I can't, but I can make a difference now—for you. This is your time, Tay. This is your time to live. I'll always be looking over you, though. If anyone messes with you, I'll haunt their asses." He winked, and while I knew he was teasing, sadness clouded his eyes. "Please, let me help you. Use me."

Outside the breach, Clay had begun to pace, and he glanced anxiously at the hole.

"Taylor, if you can hear me, you need to hurry!" His voice was muffled but the urgency was clear. Clay flinched as something fell on the ground near his feet. I knew Cillian was right, as much as I hated the idea of losing him. Unable to form the words, I nodded and let the tears fall.

"Shhh, I'll be fine, and you're going to have a great life." Cillian pulled me into his arms, and his body was suddenly warm. I ran my hands along the smooth skin on his back. He smelled like the ocean and sunshine with a faint trace of coconut oil. This was his parting gift to me. I'd remember him this way. He released me and stepped back. "Let's do this, yeah?"

I nodded again and lifted my wand. Closing my eyes, I swallowed hard, and one last tear spilled down my cheek. I focused on the energy and saw it in my mind, as bright and warm as the sun. Cillian. I absorbed the energy and directed it into my wand and then I opened my eyes to see a beam of light connecting with one side of the hole. Like a spider builds a web, I drew lines of light, connecting the outer edges of the hole until the light filled it completely. Then the light faded, and the hole was gone.

And so was Cillian.

The space was cold and empty before, and it was even more so without Cillian's presence. I hesitated, waiting to see, hoping that he'd reappear, but he didn't. Choking back a sob, I focused on returning to Halvard. Since I was physically in the spirit realm and not an astral projection, I had to rely on the few weeks of lessons from Dr. Fraser's class. Using my wand again, I opened a portal. The realm vibrated around me when I created a tear in the air, using Clay as my destination. I kept a visual of him pacing the cave in my mind as I stepped into the portal. Moments later, I was in his arms, and the portal closed behind me with a sucking sound.

"Oh thank the Goddess, I was getting worried," he said against my neck as he hugged me. A giant vibration shook the cave, causing pebbles and dust to rain down on us.

"I'm fine, but we need to go!" Hand in hand, we raced through the cave, back the way we came, only to find the entrance blocked by a pile of rocks.

"Stand back!" Clay warned and threw a blast of wind against the stone. He used so much force, he blew the pile back at least twenty feet, sending rocks bouncing and rolling in all directions like marbles on a tile floor.

Once outside the cave, Clay scooped me up in his arms and manipulated the air again to fly us directly to the entrance of Eirhal. He set me down, and we were immediately surrounded by a pack of wolf shifters. They circled us, low on their haunches and growling.

"Here, puppies!" Vidar called from behind them and whistled. The wolves turned to face him, snarling and gnashing their teeth together. Then Vidar was off running, and he was almost as fast as a vampire. The wolves took the bait and gave chase, leaving us alone. We quickly entered Eirhal Hall and ran up the stairs to our potion lab, where I was relieved to see Natalie and Tempest setting everything up. Roxy had delivered the message.

"Okay, Taylor, I was thinking about your potion and think I came up with something." Clay walked over to the built-in cabinet that ran the length of one wall. It was set up like an old apothecary with tiny drawers and multiple cabinets, which he started opening and pulling various herbs out and setting them on the nearest desk. These were Professor Parker's supplies and meant for classroom use only. Usually us witches bought our own at Howe's, but we didn't have time for shopping. Considering the dire circumstances, I imagined Professor Parker would understand. "Peppermint, lemon balm, lime-tree blossoms, and apple for the base. These are purifying, but we also need dandelion and burdock root. Stinging nettle leaves help with detoxification and to draw out the properties in your blood, to make it as pure and potent as possible, red clover flower will do the trick."

We all pitched in, brewing several cauldrons at a time. Borrowing one of the classroom bolines, which was about the size of a paring knife, I gripped the handle made of bone and took a deep breath before slicing the palm of my hand. Deep red blood welled in the gash. Forming a fist, I squeezed several drops of my blood into each cauldron. The metallic smell of rich iron mixed with the herbs, and Clay handed me the spell he had thought of for me to recite. Since it was my blood, I had to perform the spell.

"Dearest Goddess, Mother Gaia and the blessed spirit, I call upon thee. May those who drink this be free of possession. Extend to power of my blood to protect them from entities who intend harm. I mote it be."

Each time I recited this over a cauldron, I added another drop of blood. The liquid surged to a boil and turned bright red.

In total, we had sixteen cauldrons full of potion. We didn't have time to test it. I had to have faith in our magic. My gut was telling me this would work. Tempest found wooden crates that served as carriers for test tubes. They were similar to what Hel Tower used at their parties to hand out shots. We filled test tube after test tube with potion and quickly left. But first, Clay, Tempest, and Natalie raised tubes in the air and made a toast before drinking the potion down. None of them fell over or puked, so that was good.

Each of us carried two crates full of test tubes, and I had a bag on my shoulder that contained supplies for a circle. We were met in the courtyard by Roxy, Vidar, Tyr, Paisley, Makenna, Cole, and Timber. With them stood Charleigh. I did a double take and realized that it wasn't Elliana standing next to Charleigh, but the other Knight twin, Brielle. Her face was pinched with worry. Aithan Lanrete stood by her side, his curly hair reminding me of Cillian's. He was a deity and therefore would be immune to possession and perfect for the task of administering the potion.

Scattered around the courtyard were several vine-wrapped students.

"Okay, those of you who are able to be possessed, come up and grab a shot. This potion will protect you. We need to get those who are possessed to drink this, too. It will expel the spirits from their bodies," I said, raising my voice so it could be heard over the obscenities being shouted by those possessed. The four fae stepped forward and sniffed the potion.

"Is there any lemon in here?" Paisley asked.

"Yes, there's lemon balm," Clay answered.

They quickly put the vials back.

"We're allergic to lemon. All fae are," Paisley explained.

"This charm has protected me this whole time. Perhaps you can make something like this?" Timber pulled the tiger's eye obsidian pendant from where it was tucked beneath his shirt.

That I could do and quickly went to work while the rest

handed out test tubes. More students began to appear, and I was pleased to see Caleb among them. Everyone drank the potion without complaint. Only a few people twisted up their mouths at the bitter aftertaste.

Teams of two spread out among the restrained students. One person would hold the possessed student down while the other forced the potion down their throat. Some were easier than others, especially when shifter and vampire teeth were in the way, but they succeeded and to my surprise, the potion worked! Black and gray clouds rose up out of bodies, and the spirits flew around looking for another host. Not finding any, they shrieked and howled. As soon as one student was free of possession, Natalie, Tempest, Paisley, or Linnet Andrews would jump in to treat injuries, which were surprisingly minor. Gary the gnome was the only casualty. What also surprised me was that Linnet was a healer. Being that she was a vampire, having to be around blood all the time had to be torture and the biggest challenge she would face with her career choice.

I couldn't contain all of the spirits in a circle, so I was forced to improvise. I opened a portal into the spirit realm and, using my wand, created a lasso that latched onto the nearest spirit. I flung the unwilling thing through the portal. One by one, I did this. The process took hours, and the sky overhead was dark by the time I finished. In total, 189 spirits were removed from Halvard.

Once the last spirit had been exorcised, it took all of my energy to close the portal. When it sealed, I collapsed onto the ground. As I lay there, I turned my head to look at the hourglass. It was no longer glowing. The sands had stopped. Seconds later, the hourglass dropped to the ground with a loud thunk and shattered. The pieces immediately turned to dust, and a mysterious wind kicked up from out of nowhere, carrying the particles away. I looked at my tattoo and saw it had returned to normal. I breathed out a sigh of relief.

Clay stood over me, looking down at me.

"You plan on staying there?" he asked.

"Thinking about it," I said and yawned. I had no idea what

time it was or even what day it was, and I didn't care. I just wanted to sleep. My eyes started to close when suddenly I was being scooped up off the ground. Strong arms cradled my body.

"Clay, I can take care of myself!" I protested.

"I know you can, but you just basically saved the campus. Let me take care of you this time." Too tired to protest further, I closed my eyes again and relaxed into his arms.

When I woke up, one of those strong arms was draped over me, but I was in my bed. Clay was asleep, tucked up close behind me. His soft snores moved my hair, tickling my neck. I did a quick assessment. My head no longer ached, and my eyes no longer burned. I actually had the energy to move, and I slipped out from underneath Clay's arm so I could sit up. I was still wearing the clothes I wore to the party, and they were disgusting. I needed to shower and then wash my bedding immediately. Then I noticed a pile of dirty clothes on the floor by Fin's bed. They hadn't been there earlier. A note on purple notepaper propped on my bedside table caught my eye, and I recognized my roommate's slanted handwriting. She was awake! I immediately grabbed the note.

Hey roomie,

Yes, I'm awake and feel great! I didn't want to wake you since you're basically a superhero badass witch and deserve some sleep.

When you and lover boy are awake, Joe and I are in the caf having breakfast. Join us!

XO,

Fin

The next week passed without incident, and life on campus seemed to revert back to normal. Well, it was a little different. First, I had Clay holding the door to Halstein Hall open for me and then a pleasant surprise was behind the counter at Coffee Haven—my sister.

"Harlow! What are you doing here?" I ran around the side of the counter and into my sister's arms. We squealed and hugged each other tight. The floral scent of her shampoo reminded me of home, and I didn't realize how homesick I was until that moment. I had been at school almost a month, but it might as well have been an eternity.

"I'm covering a shift. Now, let me get a look at you." Harlow stepped back and held me at arm's length as she looked me over from head to toe.

"Oh my Goddess, that is such a grandma move!" I swatted at her hands, and she laughed, releasing her hold. Then she looked over my shoulder, and her eyes lit up.

"You must be Clay. My sister has told me a lot about you." Harlow stepped around me and made a beeline for Clay while I prayed for the earth to swallow me whole.

"Clay, ignore her," I said and pulled my wand out from the

inside pocket of my leather jacket. With a flick, Harlow was spun around and facing me instead. I couldn't suppress the triumphant grin. "I've been learning some things."

"I can see that." Harlow smiled at me. "Now, are you going to introduce me to your man, or what?"

Undeterred, she turned right back around to talk to Clay. I shook my head and walked over to introduce them.

A few minutes later, fresh coffee in hand, Clay and I made our way to an empty table. "So, that's my sister and just wait until this weekend. You'll be meeting more of my family. Are you ready for that?"

I bit my lip and looked across the table to gauge his reaction. We weren't officially dating. At least, I didn't think we were. Sure, we had shared a few kisses and he had spent the night, but we hadn't done anything since we had been basically unconscious from sheer exhaustion. He had yet to visit Havenwood Falls, and I invited him to come home with me for Founders Day weekend. While I looked forward to spending time with him, and showing him around my hometown, my heart still ached over Cillian's sacrifice.

Clay reached across the table and gently squeezed my hand. "I look forward to meeting your family. I want to know everything about you."

When he said things like that, with his deep brown eyes locked on mine, my stomach flipped. His thumb brushed across the side of my hand, and I looked down to where we were joined, imagining another way we could be connected and licked my lips. Just like that, the atmosphere shifted, and I looked up to meet his heated gaze. He had felt the shift, too. I remembered the feel of his body pressed against mine when we soared through the air.

"It's your time to live." It was like Cillian was right there, whispering this reminder in my ear. I swallowed hard before standing up and walking around to sit down on Clay's lap. He immediately wrapped his arms around my waist, and it felt natural, like we'd been sitting like this for years.

Leaning forward, I whispered in his ear. "I want to know everything about you, too."

Then I kissed him. His arms tightened around me, and I leaned further into the kiss. The buzz from the noisy hall faded, and I just focused on the increasing beat of my pulse and the taste of Clay's mouth, rich with traces of the mochaccino he had been drinking. His hands were warm, the heat radiating through my jeans when he cupped my ass.

A loud "whoop" broke through whatever spell we had been weaving between us, and I pulled away, breathless. Dylan Wray, who also lived in Jory, smirked at us as he walked by, on his way to Coffee Haven.

"OMG," I gasped and blinked as if emerging from a dream. I never thought I'd be a PDA kind of girl, but Clay's lips were addictive.

"Let's go somewhere more private, yeah?"

"Yeah." I scrambled off his lap, and he stood. Holding hands, we left Halstein Hall and started to walk across the busy courtyard. My hourglass was no longer there. It had disappeared as soon as I sent all the spirits back to the spirit realm.

Linnie Andrews was sitting at a stone table with the other two belladonna vampires, Marcia Lawson and Molly Shaw. I flashed to that night at the Hel Tower party when Molly attacked Makenna. It would be a while, if ever, before I'd be able to see Molly as anything but a predator. Linnie glanced up, noticing me, and we smiled at each other. I had first met her at trials, and we had basic combat together. Since she helped to heal students who'd been injured by possessed students, we had become friendlier.

Clay and I kept walking, in a hurry to find a place where we could be alone, either his room or mine, as long as our roommates weren't there. Along the way, I overheard conversations of students making plans for Founders Day weekend while a few others worried about finishing an assignment in time.

See what I mean? Normal. It was like the campus hadn't just been overrun with spirits and possessed supes.

As the secret entrance to Jory Tower closed behind us, the gong echoed across campus again, filling my chest with equal parts anxiety and dread.

Oh my Goddess, what now?

THE TIME OF THE RAVEN

AMY RICHIE

CHAPTER 1

"Linnie, are you . . . ?"

I held up my hand to stave off the question I knew was coming. "No, I'm not going to town for Founders Day."

I scrunched my face at my best friend to show how irritated I was at having to answer that question over and over again.

All anyone had talked about for the past two days was Founders Day. I was already so over it. After all the crap with the possessions that had gone on last week, I couldn't blame anyone for wanting a good time. But could they leave me out of it?

"I was going to say," Molly finished forcefully, "are you done with your history homework? I need to copy it." She wriggled her eyebrows at me.

"Oh." My face flushed over my outburst. I shouldn't have gone off like that. "I finished it last night." Fishing through my bag, I dug out the right paper and handed it over.

"Perfect." She snapped her fingers with a bright smile that was impossible not to respond to. "You are a life saver. Professor Gomez already gave me a warning for not turning in an assignment last week."

"You two are going to get in trouble," Marcia commented

lazily, turning a page in her book. "I don't think they let you cheat here."

The three of us were sitting on my favorite stone table in the quad. It was the perfect place to watch everyone as they made their way around campus. After years of being hidden away like a dirty little secret, my life was finally starting. Coming to SMA was, without a doubt, the best thing that had ever happened to me.

My whole family were vampire hunters. I had always been raised to believe "bloodsuckers were evil creatures who didn't deserve to live." Considering I was born a vampire, things were awkward at home. On a hunt one night, my mom was attacked by a female vamp. Although my family had killed the creature, she left them a gift to remember her by. The doctor had previously told my mom that she would never have any more kids, so she didn't even know she was pregnant at the time, but the vamp's venom had infected her baby—me. I was a belladonna vampire.

Marcia Lawson and Molly Shaw were my best friends at Sun & Moon Academy. We had quickly realized that the three of us were all bellas, the only three in the school. There was something special about being born a vampire, and we decided that it was fate for us to be friends. I, who had never had a friend before, was okay with their decision to include me.

"We won't get in trouble if we don't get caught," Molly trilled. She swept her long brown hair off her bare bronze shoulders.

It was already the end of September, and we were in a mountain, but somehow it was warm enough that a jacket was unnecessary, at least for us. But Molly liked to show off her shoulders. Actually, she liked to show off as much skin as she could. To anyone who would look. So far, it hadn't helped her pass Vampire History.

I didn't blame her. Being a vampire made us pale, but Molly's skin was still a rich brown while mine was chalky white. With Marcia and me by her side, Molly's skin appeared all the richer.

"Can I give this back later?" She widened her eyes dramatically, clutching my borrowed homework in one hand. "Just because you refuse to be sociable, doesn't mean the rest of us want to be losers." She winked playfully.

"Sure." I grinned. "I take it you two are heading to town?"

"That hottie from Modi Tower asked me to go with him."

"The one with the scar by his eye?"

"Yep." Her lips popped delicately. "Lucky for him, I got some smudge-proof lip gloss I want to test out."

We both laughed at the instant blush on Marcia's face.

"Such a hoe," she teased. "I'm going to grab a quick shower before we go," she sang, gathering her books in one graceful movement. "You coming, Molly?"

A group of girls passed in front of us, all giggling together— undoubtedly excited over their plans for Founders Day. Behind them, a girl walked alone. Her dark hair hung slightly over her left eye. She didn't bother to move it.

Destiny Nelson.

I sucked in a quick breath at the sight of her. I couldn't explain, even to myself, why my pulse decided to race every time I saw her. Maybe there was something dangerous about her that I could sense —that had to be it. She was a vampire, but not everyone at school were vampires.

Mom had been wrong about that. When she had first heard about SMA, she thought it was a school for only vampires. She was excited for me to bring back information I would discover here. But it wasn't like that.

"Maybe we should invite Destiny with us." Molly snorted.

"Don't even think about it," Marcia growled.

"Like I was serious."

Destiny's head flicked our way slightly, obviously hearing every word they said. For the briefest of moments, her eyes locked with mine. My breath caught.

"Hey," Molly tapped my arm, "are you going back to the rooms with us?"

"No. I . . . um . . . I'm going to sit out here for a while."

"Suit yourself." She shrugged, trotting away with Marcia—and still talking about the guy with the scar.

I watched Destiny as she moved farther away from me. She didn't look back. Was she upset that my friends had practically made fun of her right to her face? Maybe I should go apologize. I didn't want her to think I thought the way they did.

Not giving myself a chance to rethink, I jumped up from the table and swung my bag over one shoulder. I couldn't just run up to her—that would be weird. I could casually catch up to her and then mention it. Nothing had to be awkward . . . right?

But why did I want to say sorry? I didn't actually do anything. My feet hesitated. It was probably best to leave it alone. *Yeah.*

Next to where I had stopped, on the back of a bench, a raven sat watching students as they passed by. I stared back. The bird didn't move. As I watched it, confused, the raven moved his head to look directly at me. I jerked my head backwards. *How bizarre.*

Suddenly, all around me, the sound of a gong rang out. It filled the space all around me, vibrating back through my head until I couldn't stand upright any longer.

I knelt to the ground, covering my ears, my books flying everywhere. Then just as suddenly as the gong had started, it stopped again.

"What the hell?" I gasped, clutching my throat. Around me, students stared at each other with worry and looked around wildly, as though searching for a new danger. I couldn't blame them. It was becoming more and more apparent that the sound was some kind of warning that something terrible was going to happen. At least, that was the rumor.

"You okay?" a soft voice grunted above me. Destiny Nelson was standing there, staring down at me. "Why are you sitting on the ground?"

"I . . . fell." I scrambled up to my knees. "Did you hear that?"

"Of course." She squatted down to scoop up my fallen books. "I'm going back to the quad to see if a new hourglass has appeared. It seems to happen after the gong rings. You want to walk with me?"

"Umm . . ." I pushed my short red strands behind my ears. "I don't know." Why couldn't I think straight? "We should probably

—" My words were cut off by a searing pain in my wrist—my tattoo. It felt like my whole arm was on fire. I clutched at the offending mark, my eyes going wide.

Destiny dropped my books back on the ground. "Is it burning?"

"No," I lied quickly, pulling my arm away when she reached for it.

"It is," she breathed. "I think this means something. I heard this happened to Taylor right before all those spirits started possessing people—spirits only she was able to contain. And before that was when the girls went missing by the lake, and Nadine—"

"Shh," I hissed, dropping my burning wrist so I could cover her mouth.

"You have to tell someone," she mumbled through my fingers.

"Who would I tell?" Who could help me? We didn't even know what it meant or what I needed help with. We both looked down to see that the tattoo had changed into an hourglass. "Please don't tell anyone. It might mean nothing, and I don't want to be an even bigger freak."

"You're in a school full of freaks," Destiny tsked, but settled down to the ground with me.

Around us, the whole school seemed to be running to the quad to check on the hourglasses. But Destiny and I already knew one had tipped. A suffocating fear gripped me. What was going to happen to me? I wasn't brave enough or smart enough to figure anything out. If it was left to me, we were all going to die. I didn't know why they ever accepted me into this school. I didn't belong here.

Pressing my hand to my mouth, I tried to stand up.

"I'm . . . going to my room," I stammered. Before anyone found out about my tattoo.

"What?" Destiny stood up with me, holding my arm at my elbow to prevent me from falling again. "Why would you do that?"

"I don't want . . ." I gestured helplessly at my wrist. "I need to go to my room for a minute. I need to . . . think."

"Alone?"

"Yeah," I gasped, clutching my arm again. The fire had started again. Or maybe it was my own fear that burned my skin. "I have my own room," I mumbled. I had been longing to talk to Destiny for weeks and now that we were finally talking—it was about this?

"I'll come with you," she offered, handing my books back to me. "You shouldn't be alone right now."

"I want to be alone." Panic was disguising itself as anger, making Destiny flinch away. "I . . ." There was nothing left to say though. As I practically ran back to Muninn Tower, my only thought was a wild hope that she wouldn't tell anyone what had happened.

CHAPTER 2

"Focus, Linnie," I whispered. My legs were curled underneath me on the single size bed in the box-shaped room I had been assigned to. "So what if your tattoo burned? That doesn't mean anything." The tear treads down my face said otherwise though.

A knock sounded on the door, a knock that I promptly ignored.

"Linnie are you in there?" a muffled voice called through the crack. "Everyone is freaking out about the gong," Molly continued, not caring that I didn't answer. She must have been able to hear me breathing inside the room; it's not like it was quiet. "We're still going to town though. We're meeting up with that girl, Cat, from Heimdall Tower."

The material of her dress rustled with the movement of her shrug.

"It's not like we can do much by hanging out here. Nothing even seems to be happening."

"Thank goodness." Marcia snorted beside her.

"You sure you don't want to come with us?"

Two tears slid down my face, dripping off my chin to land on my wrist that was cradled in my lap.

"We'll see you later then, love." The sounds of their steps faded away, leaving me alone again.

I had been alone plenty of times before—alone and scared. There were nights in my cabin back home, when my hearing was starting to become more pronounced, that I stayed up all night trying to figure out what a new sound was. It once took me almost two hours to realize I was hearing a rabbit twitching in his sleep somewhere outside.

It didn't make any sense then, why the four walls here felt like they were closing in on me. Pretty soon, the whole room would burst into flames—I was sure of it.

"Hey."

My head snapped up at the sound of a voice inside my room. Destiny stood inside the doorway, watching me with a furrowed brow.

"I knocked," she explained awkwardly, "but you must not have heard it."

"I didn't," I replied briskly. "You didn't go to town?"

"I wanted to come check on you."

"Why?"

"You were upset."

My vision blurred with the arrival of more unwanted tears.

"Understandably upset." Closing the door, she hurried to perch on the bed next to me.

"I don't know what to do." I sniffed.

"Well," she took a deep breath and let it out on a small cough, "if you don't want to tell anyone . . ."

"I don't."

"Then we'll have to figure out what chaos this hourglass has created."

"You think the hourglasses are creating the chaos?"

She shrugged. "They're magical artifacts, aren't they? And every time one turns—right after the gong sounds, mind you—there's trouble. And as far as I know, each time there's one, and only one, student whose tattoo changes, matching the tipped hourglass. When the trouble is over, the hourglass breaks and their tattoo goes back to normal. So yeah, the hourglasses are doing it. That's my theory, anyway."

"I guess that makes sense. But why wouldn't the Regents destroy them then?"

"Oh, I think they've tried, but it seems like every time one of them attempts to interfere, something happens to them."

I nodded. "That's right. Rhian Delaney was in the room when it all started and said Addie Beaumont was braying like a donkey after trying to help Roxy."

"I've heard other stories too. I'm sure they're doing what they can, but in the meantime, I guess it's up to us right now."

"Us?"

"I'm going to help you."

"Why?" She didn't even know me. Why would she want to help?

"Because you're cute." She explained playfully. "And because I can't walk away knowing you're up here all by yourself crying."

"I didn't mean to cry." My voice broke.

"Besides," she insisted, "if it's like the other times, whatever's going to happen will affect everyone—including me."

"Yeah," I breathed. She was right; if I failed to stop whatever was coming, everyone would be in danger. Of course, she would want to help. Of course. "I guess so."

"So." She smiled wide, and even if it was fake, it made me feel braver. It made me want to return the gesture. "What should we do?"

My giggle broke free from my tense lips. "I have no idea."

"Right." She nodded slowly. "Me either."

I hadn't asked for her help—I didn't even know if I wanted it —but having Destiny there in my room made breathing a little bit easier. "All we know for sure is that something bad is going to happen."

"Or is happening already," she pointed out.

CHAPTER 3

"**A**re you seriously trying to tell me that you've never been hunting?" Across the stone table, Destiny's eyes widened. "I don't believe you." A small group of students hurried past us, their heads bent over a shared textbook.

"It's true." I held up one hand to show her how serious I was.

"How is that possible? How old are you?"

"Eighteen."

Destiny had stayed with me for most of the previous day. While the entire school seemed to be going crazy, she had kept her silence about my burning tattoo. We hadn't made any groundbreaking discoveries, but it was nice to be able to talk and laugh with someone who wasn't constantly touching up her lip gloss.

It was too early for most of the student body to be up and about, especially after a long night of Founders Day drinking. Destiny and I had agreed to meet before sunrise though, so here I was—fully dressed and grinning at her.

"Eighteen-year-old vamp?" One eyebrow cocked on her forehead as her lips pouted out. My heart thumped wildly. "No way have you never had blood." She took a sip from a huge white mug she was clutching in her hands.

"I've had blood," I corrected her. "I never had to hunt for it."

"Then how did you get it?" She let both her eyes widen in my direction.

My eyes darted away from her. No matter how nice she was, I didn't think her kindness would stretch to cover the repulsion she would feel if she found out that my sister had snuck me bags of blood from the hospital. I could never tell her that. I had never been around other vampires before I came to school. I didn't know what was considered normal, and I didn't want her to think I was a freak. There were some secrets that were best left secret.

"My . . . mother, she . . ."

"You're a bella, right?"

"A what?" I stammered, unsure what to say. A few months into school, and it was still hard to get used to the casual way they threw terms like that around.

"A belladonna?"

"Yeah."

"That explains it." She nodded knowingly. "Your mom must have hunted for you. Was she super protective of you? I can't believe she even let you come here." Clicking her tongue against the roof of her mouth, she gazed down at the table where our hands rested a mere few inches apart.

"My mom hates me." The truth exploded from me, like verbal diarrhea. "She was happy to see me go." *Why?* Why did I keep telling her the truth?

Her face contorted with disbelief. "Is that even possible for a bella? I've heard of a few of you. There was a female in my old nest who wanted a baby, so she found a pregnant woman and changed her baby. Did your mom keep you pretty sheltered?"

"I was raised by my human mother." Silence followed my confession. "She was attacked but . . ." My explanation faded awkwardly. "We should talk about something else."

"What should we talk about?" She grinned.

"You."

"What do you want to know?"

"What was your mom like? Did she protect you or keep you hidden?"

"I'm not a bella."

"Then what are you?"

"I'm a Goth vamp. I was changed eight years ago."

"How old are you?"

"I was eighteen when I was changed," she said. "And you're eighteen, too."

"Yep."

"So how does that work? Are you eighteen forever?"

"I'm not sure," I replied, embarrassed by my own lack of knowledge about myself. "I guess I have a lot to learn." I had already learned a lot from watching Molly and Marcia, who were insanely comfortable with what they were, but I wasn't there yet. It was awkward to ask them things I should have already known—at least to me, it felt like I should already know. They sure did.

"Have you ever had fresh blood?"

"Nope." I shook my head hard enough for my red strands to bounce on my shoulders. "They keep some stocked in the clinic, so I get it from there," I admitted. "Just until I get the hang of hunting since I've never . . ." But hunting didn't feel right to me and asking someone to teach me was out of the question. I was eighteen; by all rights, I should have already known how. Someone didn't live for eighteen years as a vampire and not know how to get their own blood.

"I'll teach you," she suggested calmly, as if she had just agreed to tutor me in math.

"You will?"

"Sure. But first there's something else we need to do."

I was hanging on her every word, watching her lips curve up into a suggestive smile so intently that I didn't realize why she had stopped talking at first. Then it dawned on me—someone was screaming.

"What the hell is that?" I whispered, my wide eyes searching all around for whoever was dying. Was this it? I glanced down at the tattoo on my wrist. The hourglass still looked full, but there was some sand in the bottom half now that wasn't there yesterday. Although I knew this happened to Taylor's tattoo, it was still a shock.

"Let's go find out." Leaving her mug of mystery brew on the table, Destiny jumped up and led the way to a group that had gathered a short way up the path. "What's going on?" she asked a pretty blond girl in the back of the crowd.

"There was an attack," the girl explained, her eyes wide. "I think someone is dead."

"Dead?" The word echoed all around us until it seemed to sink itself into the ink on my newly formed tattoo.

"What's going on over here?" a deep voice boomed out. The noise created a wave of movement until there was a clear path to the girl laying on the rocky floor.

Blood was smeared on her neck and along the top of her shirt. Underneath the blood were two holes—bite marks. She was clearly bitten by a vampire.

"Oh my god," Destiny whispered.

As the crowd parted enough to let someone with a stretcher through, I noticed a girl with long dark hair moving away from the crowd.

"Isn't she in Modi Tower?" I asked Destiny, trying to remember the girl.

"It might be Brielle," she replied, squinting at her. "I can't tell. Let's get out of here."

CHAPTER 4

Madame Roth from the infirmary was a kind-faced woman in her early fifties. She kept her silver hair in a thick braid that hung down her back. Her tongue contrasted sharply with her face though; her words weren't always nice.

"All these unnatural creatures in one place." She shook her head. "It's not surprising that someone got attacked."

I moved my head subtly, trying to see the girl they had brought in earlier. How serious was that bite? "If you don't like supernaturals," I murmured, "why did you come here?"

"Did I say I don't like them?"

I realized a second too late I shouldn't have asked her that.

"I am one of them," she spat. "I got myself into a bit of trouble when I was younger. What? Do you think I should have crawled into a hole and died?"

"No."

"No," she practically shouted. "No matter what life throws at you, you get up and keep on going. My life might have been different, but here I am, helping people who might have found themselves in similar situations." She paused to take a breath.

I had already heard this story, several times, but I knew better than to interrupt her. I didn't want to be stuck here all day. "Of course."

"How's your hunting coming along?" She shoved a plastic bottle into my hands.

"Um . . . it's going okay."

"You haven't tried yet, have you?"

"Not . . . not really."

"Linnie," she tsked, her voice going back to normal with her concerned frown. "Find a friend to teach you."

"I think I might have." My thoughts drifted to Destiny, who was outside waiting for me. "Just—"

"You're upset over the attack?"

I nodded at her assumption. This might be the best way to broach the subject I had come here for.

"That's understandable." She patted my hand affectionately. "But you know what you are. You need to learn to hunt."

"Do they know what happened to that girl?" I asked, trying to sound nonchalant as I sipped on my bottled blood.

"Not officially." She rolled her eyes. "But it's pretty obvious she was bitten by a vampire."

"Why would a vampire attack her here at school?"

"No idea." She shrugged. "Hopefully the Sky Boys will be able to figure it out before they can strike again." I had heard of the Sky Boys, the security team here on campus led by General Sky.

In the cot across the room, behind the heavy curtain, I could hear the labored breathing of the girl who had been attacked. She must have been having a nightmare; I didn't need to be able to read her mind to know who was starring as the monster behind her closed lids. A vampire.

They had plagued my dreams as a child too.

"Destiny?" I tried to whisper but my call came out louder than I intended, excitement making me clumsy.

"Hey." She popped around the side of the building and hurried to meet me halfway to the path. "Did you find anything out?"

"It was a vampire attack," I panted.

"No shit?"

"No shit."

"What does that mean?"

"Isn't it obvious?" I had been trained to hunt vampires since I was old enough to talk. I knew they were unpredictable. I guess it wasn't much of a surprise to me that one had attacked a student.

"An attack on campus though." Destiny let her eyes go wide, clearly hoping I would catch on to something important.

An attack was an attack though. Regardless of where it happened.

"You think they'll tell the police?"

"I doubt it," she scoffed. "It's a different world here."

"Madame Roth said the Sky Boys would catch whoever did this."

"And she was right," a deep voice rang out. Destiny and I both spun around to see a tall man with crazy big muscles coming toward us, a small smile playing around his lips. "I'm Cody from the security team," he introduced himself when he reached us.

"You're one of the Sky Boys." My eyebrows puckered as my eyes traveled the length of his body. "You don't look like a boy to me." I remembered him from the night we moved in to our dorms.

Cody blushed a deep red and glanced down to the ground. "I can't believe that name stuck." He laughed. "General Sky should get a kick out of that."

General Sky. Sky Boys. That made sense.

"Are you here to see that girl?" Destiny gestured toward the infirmary. I had just been in there, and I hadn't seen him.

"She's not really up for answering any questions," Cody replied with a frown.

"Guess not." Destiny sucked in her cheeks as she stared at him.

"How are you two holding up? An attack like this, one month into school . . ."

A lot had happened at SMA so far though; a vampire attack was tame compared to some of it.

"We're fine," I told him, tucking my arm safely away from his view. Even if the weather didn't affect me as much as other people, maybe it was time to pull out a sweater to hide the hourglass on my wrist.

"They're questioning all the vampires on campus," he informed us, his eyes narrowing sympathetically. "Over in Steivar."

"What do you mean? Why?"

"Looks like we're all suspects," Destiny answered before Cody could.

"You two were at the scene of the attack," the man behind the desk accused angrily.

General Sky was a formidable man; one who could change into a bear at will. Looking at him glaring at us, it wasn't hard to imagine. His skin matched his dark brown hair that fuzzed on the top of his large head. He was practically a bear on two legs now.

"We heard the screams and went to see what was going on," Destiny carefully explained.

"What were you doing up?"

"It was morning. We met to grab some coffee."

She had coffee. I mostly stared.

"That early in the morning?" If his eyes narrowed any more, he wouldn't be able to see at all.

"We didn't go into town for Founders Day."

"What did you meet for?"

"What do people usually meet for?" Destiny curled her fingers around mine pointedly.

"I assume you heard the gong yesterday?"

"Yep."

"That, along with this attack . . ." He shook his head. "Just make sure you watch yourselves. Don't go out walking alone."

"Is that all you called us here for? To ask us why we were outside this morning?" Destiny's irritation oozed from the hard lines on her face.

"We're questioning all the vampires on campus. We want to know where everyone was in the early hours this morning when that girl was attacked."

"Hmm."

"Can you two wait outside for a minute? I might have a few more questions before you leave."

"Whatever." Destiny stood up, dragging me with her by our still-entwined hands.

Finding a spot on the ground outside the building, we plopped down together. Our hands finally fell apart in her irritation.

"I'm sure he won't make us stay here long," I assured her.

"I don't like being accused of something I didn't do."

"You heard him. He's calling all the vamps in."

"I wonder if he questioned his boy Cody."

"You mean the Sky Boy who brought us here?"

"Yeah, he's a vampire. He better have asked him where he was."

"How do you know he's a vampire?"

"How do you not know?" She scowled.

I wasn't good at being a vampire, and I had never seen another vampire up close before. I knew the logistics of how to kill them, but that was it. Things that came naturally to me had gotten me into the school. Speed, strength, hearing, and . . . other things that I was learning about myself now that I was allowed to *be* myself.

My gaze fell on Destiny's hand on the stone path. There was no reason for me to start thinking about her hand in mine. It was unnatural for it to make my heart thump so hard and my face to flame. What was wrong with me?

"Are you all right?"

"What?" I glanced up, embarrassed. "Nothing. I'm fine."

"Why are you in Muninn anyways?" she teased, pushing my

knee with one finger. "You don't belong in there with those stuck-up bitches."

"I'm a vampire," I lowered my voice to hiss the confession out. It was still really weird to admit it out loud. Even though everyone knew.

"So?" She cocked her head to one side, letting the black strands flop into her eyes.

"I —" I inhaled awkwardly— "I thought all vampires were in that tower at first. Molly said they must have put us all together for a reason."

"Psht," she scoffed through full lips. "I'm not sticking with them. Especially not now."

"You don't know that it was one of us that did it."

"Yeah—" her top lip curled up— "we kind of do. And so does he—Sky Man."

"He said—"

"Why do you think he's keeping us here?"

"It's for our own safety," I explained lamely. Maybe Destiny was right though. Maybe it wasn't our safety they were concerned with.

"If you get tired of hanging out with those losers," she winked, "you know where to find me." Before I could say anything, she got up and strolled away. It didn't take long to find out why.

"Why were you talking to that freak?" Marcia asked, plopping onto the recently vacated spot next to me.

Emptiness vibrated through me. Destiny and I had been spending so much time together since yesterday, I had almost forgotten that my friends didn't like her. I watched as she disappeared inside the building.

"They made us come here," I told Marcia, clearing my throat. "Where's Molly?"

"No idea." She rolled her eyes. "They woke us up and told us to report here before going to class."

"She must still be getting ready." I half chuckled.

"Why are we here? Do you know?"

Before I could explain anything to her, my ears picked up a faint moan coming from somewhere. "Do you hear that?"

"Hear what?" She glanced around, bored and angry to be out of bed so early.

"It sounds like moaning."

"Linnie," she tsked, "you really shouldn't be listening to things like that."

"It wasn't *that*." My nose scrunched up at her words. I had accidentally heard plenty of private moments at SMA by now. I knew what not to listen to. This was different.

"I don't hear anything weird," she snarled, leaning her head back to soak in the early morning air.

This early, the air was crisp and slightly burnt my nose. It was clearly not affecting Marcia the same way. Her milky white skin seemed to radiate in it. The older I got, the more I didn't like the early mornings. At least here, under the mountain, I didn't have to worry about the sun.

"I think it's over here," I continued, despite her doubt. Heart hammering so hard I could barely hear the faint moans, I jumped up and tried to follow the sound.

"Where are you going?" Marcia called. "What is wrong with you?"

"I think someone is hurt." I had exceptional hearing. Sometimes I could hear a person's words before they actually spoke. I had learned to trust that, even if no one else did.

"What's going on?" Destiny asked, coming back outside with a deep frown etched across her pale face. "Are you leaving? Because General Sky said—"

"I hear something," I hissed without looking back.

"What is it?"

"She hears moaning." Marcia scowled. I knew her face was twisting up without looking at her. She always made that face when she didn't agree with someone.

Even if she didn't believe me, I knew what I heard. Someone was hurt. I knew it. I had to at least try to find them. Moving quickly, I made my way toward the library. The girls followed behind me.

"It's here." I stopped at a flat piece of dirt path and dropped to my hands and knees. "Someone is under here. They're hurt."

"Under the ground?" Marcia's nose scrunched up. "You've lost your damn mind."

Destiny knelt down beside me. "Isn't Muninn Tower passage under here?" My wide eyes met hers.

The only way to get into Muninn Tower was through an underground passage that was accessed through the library. I could hear the cold air under our feet, echoing through the hollow passage. Destiny was right.

"I don't hear anyone though," she said, confusion chasing worry across her face. "Are you sure someone is down there?"

Holding my breath, I listened hard. The moans I had heard earlier were gone but I could still make out faint breathing. It was labored but still there.

"Yes," I declared firmly. "I hear someone."

"We better hurry then."

"You don't actually believe her?" Marcia clearly didn't.

"Yep."

With Destiny leading, our trio quickly made our way to the library, past the Valkyrie statue that stood against the wall, and hurried down to the basement and to the entry of our passage.

I had used this passage every single day, usually several times a day, for the past month. It didn't make any sense then, why I was so nervous.

"I hear someone now, too," Destiny whispered, moving closer to me in the semi darkness. Was it always so dark down here?

"Aren't there usually more torches down here?" Marcia wondered my own thoughts out loud.

"Over here."

Something in Destiny's voice made my breath catch. "What is it?"

"I found someone."

Still not breathing normally, I followed Marcia to a dark place where the hump of a body could be seen. I recognized her dark hair before I saw her face. Her usual rich brown hues were alarmingly pale.

"Oh my god, it's Molly."

"Is she dead?"

My eyes stayed focused on the clasped hands of Destiny, squeezed tightly together in her lap. She sat next to me on the ground in the hall just outside the infirmary. Inside, the healers were checking out the wounds on Molly.

There had been a lot of blood on her head and caked into her dark hair. It wasn't difficult to get her here; waiting was harder by far.

Marcia ran her hands compulsively through her long hair; over and over again her fingers pulled on the long strands. The sound was hypnotic, but I wasn't looking across the row of seats at her. There were too many questions in her eyes. I had been the one to hear Molly down there when she was barely conscious, but that didn't mean I knew what had happened to her.

"Girls?" Madame Roth called out gently. My gaze shifted abruptly to the woman I had grown to genuinely like. "You three came in with Molly Shaw, right?"

"Yes." We jumped up at practically the same time and rushed to her. "Is she . . ."

"She's still unconscious."

"Will she be all right?" I whispered over the sounds of Marcia sniffing.

"I think so," Madame Roth replied gently, her smile not unkind. "She got a nasty bump on her head, but your kind heal fast."

Molly was only eighteen though. All belladonnas matured differently so it was impossible to know if she was fully mature yet. There was still enough human in her to land her in the infirmary, so really, we didn't know how long it would take her to wake up.

"Can I go see her?" Marcia gulped, staring down Madame Roth until the woman couldn't say no.

"Only one at a time may go back." She held up one finger.

"You go." I waved at Marcia as if she were asking our permission. "We'll wait out here for you."

"It was another attack, wasn't it?" Destiny turned on me as soon as Marcia was out of sight. "That makes two attacks in one day."

"In one morning," I corrected. The first one was from a vampire, but who had gotten Molly in the passage? She had exceptional vision in dark places, so it was unlikely someone could sneak up on her.

"Do you think the same person attacked both of them?" she asked.

"I don't know. What are the odds that there are two crazies running around though?" My forehead puckered as I tried to link the two girls.

"Well, I mean . . ." She shrugged.

"We need to see if Molly was bitten." If a vampire got them both, we could assume it was the same person.

"Linnie." She lowered her voice and leaned her head closer to me as if she had a secret. "Do you think it has anything to do with the hourglass?"

My hand automatically covered the tattoo on my wrist. "Why would it have anything to do with that?"

A violent vampire? Why would my tattoo have changed because of that?

I knew what vampires were supposed to be like; my mom had made sure I knew. I couldn't help but wonder as I felt the low vibrations that seemed to hum inside my tattoo if the magic that had changed my ink had known what would happen here. With all these vampires in one place with other students that were magical in their own rights, trouble was bound to follow.

"Hey," Marcia called from the hallway. I was so into my own thoughts, I hadn't heard Marcia come back. "Molly's awake."

"Can we see her?" I asked, jumping up from my chair. "Is she okay? Who attacked her?"

"Madame Roth said we can go back there. I haven't asked her anything about that yet. She just woke up."

"I hope she remembers something," I whispered, filing into the small space behind Marcia. If she saw who attacked her, this would all be over quickly. It was getting harder to still that voice inside of me that was scared I was the one attacking people.

I was a vampire, and I had done it before—even if it hadn't been on purpose. I shuddered at the memory.

Molly was sitting up on the side of the bed when we reached her. The blood had been cleaned up, but it still stained the collar of her shirt. I was relieved to see the color back in her cheeks.

"Hey," she greeted faintly, her lips shaking.

"Did you see who attacked you?" I blurted out, unable to wait. I flinched away from Marcia's glare, but I needed to know.

"I already told that nurse that I didn't," she whimpered. "Whoever it was moved too fast. I barely saw anything, and I have really good vision."

Molly's was the second attack this morning. What the hell was happening?

My tongue felt like it had swollen up inside my mouth, making it hard to breathe. Vampires were fast. One could have easily taken Molly by surprise in the dark passage. They would have known it was the only way in or out of Muninn Tower. That could only mean that he or she had purposely waited for someone to come along by themselves.

"I'm going to help Molly back to our dorm," Marcia announced, her arms crossed angrily over her ample chest. "Madame Roth says she needs to rest."

"I'll come too." I nodded blindly.

"Not if you're going to keep twenty-questioning her."

"Mmm," I agreed with a small grunt. Molly didn't remember anything anyways. The four of us made our way out of the clinic, each wrapped in our own dark thoughts.

The cool morning air felt good on my flushed face. I was already late for class—late enough that it was probably not worth going. I would have to see Professor Glover and find out what I missed.

I slowed down, trying to wait for Destiny, who had gotten held up just outside the med infirmary doors.

Goosebumps popped out on my arms, making me shiver. Behind me, sitting high on a windowsill, I spotted the raven again. Was the bird following me? Maybe it was a sign.

"What are you staring at?" Destiny asked, catching up to me.

"A raven."

"It's just a bird." She scowled. "Let's go."

My eyes snapped to take in her profile. She was staring up at the raven. "You can see it too, right?"

"I can." She looked at me, her eyes questioning.

"How do you suppose it got here, under the mountain?"

"It could be a student," she suggested. "There are shifters here. There's a cougar who naps all around the campus."

"Still, that's . . . that's good that you can see it."

My relief surprised me; I was half afraid that I was going crazy. My tattoo had changed, and now I was being chased around campus by a raven. I had lived in the shadow of my sister Raven my entire life, so it seemed fitting that this raven was bent on tormenting me.

"If you're coming back to the room with us, hurry up, Linnie," Marcia called angrily. "I already told you that Molly needs to lay down."

"Coming," I automatically fired back.

"I have to get to class," Destiny said awkwardly, hesitating to turn away. "Will you be all right on your own?"

"I won't be on my own," I reminded her, jerking my thumb toward the two waiting for me.

"Right."

"I'll see you later, right?" There was no need for me to feel anxious, and yet here I was—frowning deep enough to make my forehead crease.

"I'll come find you after class." She reached forward and took my hand briefly in hers, squeezing it gently before letting it go again.

Clutching my missed assignment page in my hand, I stomped out of the library. I hated missing class, especially Professor Glover's class. There was so much to learn about Emergency Care, I couldn't afford to miss anything. And now I had a paper due.

"Wonderful," I snarled, irritated that I would have to spend even more time in the huge library that confused me more than it helped.

"Well, hey there, Red." Cody grinned widely at me.

"Hey." I grinned back, eager for a reason not to worry about the paper. Cody was nice, and I hadn't known many nice guys in my lifetime. "How's the manhunt going?" I asked awkwardly, still smiling despite the words that had fallen out of my mouth.

"It's . . . you know," he stammered. "Where you heading?"

"I was at the library for a little bit." I held up the paper unenthusiastically. "What about you?"

"I was heading out to Clifftop. How do you like it out there?" he asked, swallowing hard. "It's pretty nice, huh?"

"It's all right. I've only ever been out there for class."

"Combat training?"

"Yep." Not something I had ever even dreamed of doing, but I didn't hate it.

"What about hunting?"

"I've never . . ." My tongue slid across my bottom lip, nervous about throwing that truth out there. It was embarrassing for me to keep having to tell people this. "I've never been hunting before."

"Never? Aren't you a bella?" His eyes went wide briefly, but he smoothed his features back out quickly.

"My parents didn't like for me to go outside." My dad thought my skin would burn off, and mom was afraid someone would see me. Thank goodness I hadn't listened to them and someone *had* seen me. Otherwise I wouldn't be at SMA.

"You want to go out there with me?" he suggested, dipping his head shyly. "I could show you a few things."

My heart sped up at his suggestion. Was I ready to hunt? I mean, I already knew it was past due, but I didn't want to look like an idiot in front of Cody. "Destiny said she would . . . teach me to hunt."

"I didn't say anything about hunting. We can just go out to Clifftop. Together."

"All right," I finally agreed. As long as we didn't actually hunt, I didn't mind spending more time with Cody.

"Do you need to drop that off in your room first?" He gestured toward the paper in my hand.

"No, it's fine." I folded the page up into a small square and shoved it into my front pocket. "I'm ready."

If I didn't have to be there for class, I avoided Clifftop and the luscious forest surrounding it. A lifetime of hiding inside had conditioned me to shy away from the woods.

There was a lot of light up there, but I didn't need it. My ears were my biggest asset. I could hear anything,

"Close your eyes," Cody ordered gently, reminding me that he was there beside me.

"What?" My body jerked back slightly, away from him. Why would I close my eyes? I didn't really like to be vulnerable like that.

"Just do it."

Clearing my throat lightly, I let my eyes close. My breath was still coming in and out of my lungs in short little bursts. "Now what?"

"Tell me what you hear."

I took a deep breath and held it inside my lungs. Only by not having my own breath in my ears would I be able to hear the small sounds of the forest.

"I hear the breeze rustling the leaves," I began softly. The breeze was loud. It drowned out everything else.

"What else? Listen to what's behind the breeze."

"There's a bird in the tree to my left, rustling its feathers. Some kind of creature is inside that tree." I pointed close to where the bird was perched. "It's asleep for now, but it's twitching a lot."

"Wow." He whistled low, making my eyes pop back open.

"Did I do okay?"

"Okay?" His eyes widened. "You're amazing."

"Yeah?" That wasn't something I heard very often.

"I've heard that you have impressive senses. Looks like they were right."

I wasn't sure who it was that had said I was good, but I was grateful for the compliment. Finally, I was being allowed to show my true abilities. And it looked like they were acceptable to at least someone.

"Thanks." I could barely contain my laughter that was threatening to bubble over.

"Should we sit?" He gestured to a small clearing not far off the path we were standing on. There were several tree stumps and a fallen log that created the perfect natural sitting place.

"This is kind of cozy." I tucked several strands of hair behind my ears as I sat close to Cody on the fallen log.

"Do you miss your family?"

"Not really."

"Tell me how you really feel." He chuckled sarcastically.

"They're different than anyone here." That was putting it mildly. Talking about my family made me uncomfortable; being this alone with Cody also made me uncomfortable. "What's your family like?"

"Uh . . . teethy." He winked.

Teethy?

"Are they vampires?" Molly and Marcia lived with a family of vampires. Maybe Cody did too.

"Yep."

"Your mom and dad too?"

He looked away from me, his eyes fixed on a tall tree. "I have a sister."

"What is she like?"

"She's pretty and smart."

"I have two sisters," I admitted when an awkward silence fell between us. "They're both way prettier than me. Wren and Raven," I rambled.

"That can't possibly be true."

"I really do have two sisters. We're all named after birds."

"I mean, they can't be prettier than you."

"Oh." I dropped my eyes quickly. There was something written plainly on his face that even I could understand.

"I was thinking . . ."

"About?" I made the mistake of looking up.

"I was thinking about . . ." *Kissing you.*

"Kissing me?"

"Well . . ." *I need you to trust me.*

My eyebrows furrowed at his unspoken thoughts. I didn't have any experience with this sort of thing, but what did trust have to do with kissing?

His face moved quickly until his lips were against mine. I tried to pull away, but his hand reached around to cup the back of my head. Without my permission, Cody deepened the kiss, pushing his hot tongue into my mouth. Unsure what to do, I stopped moving until he finally pulled away.

Across from us, the black raven called loudly, making me jump.

"We should go back," I half pleaded.

CHAPTER 8

Scanning the almost empty cafeteria, I spotted Molly and Marcia sitting at one of the round tables. The three of us usually met up for dinner after their evening class, but I never expected Destiny to be sitting with them.

Rhian sat alone at a table. She looked up as I passed, but, as usual, she didn't say anything. She was in Muninn Tower, and we'd spoken some, but I didn't really know much about her. Her eyes narrowed in on me, when I returned the stare, she smiled and waved.

Hurrying forward, I made my way to my friends.

"Where have you been?" Marcia snapped as soon as I sat down with my small bowl of fruit.

"I was out at Clifftop with Cody."

"That cute Sky Boy?" She wriggled her eyebrows suggestively.

"He's okay." I twisted my face at the recent memory of the kiss we had shared. My first kiss and it was awful. Destiny watched me, very obviously not eating her food.

"Just okay?" Molly jabbed Marcia in the side. "What happened out there?"

"We kissed," I admitted, knowing they would find out anyway.

"What was kissing him like?" she demanded, her nose scrunching up at the thought.

My eyes darted briefly to Destiny. She was still watching me.

"It was weird." My nose wrinkled. "He tried to shove his tongue down my throat."

"Ew," Destiny fired off immediately.

"It's not ew," Molly snapped, rolling her eyes. "That's how people kiss. Normal people anyways."

"It was . . . wet. His spit was on my face."

"Seriously, Linnie." Molly glared at me. "How old are you?"

"Eighteen."

"How old were you when you lost your v-card?" Marcia piped in.

"My v-card?"

"Your virginity," Molly snarled, snapping her fingers in my face.

"I . . . I still . . . I'm a virgin. Aren't you guys?"

"No," Molly and Marcia chorused. Destiny shook her head.

"There weren't really many boys to date back home," I tried to explain.

"I was fifteen," Molly spoke again. She seemed to be personally insulted by my innocence.

"I'm sure it will happen for me someday." I glanced at Destiny and then away again quickly.

"Yeah, well, it seems like Cody is ready and willing."

My face flamed hot. "It was just a kiss."

"It doesn't have to be just a kiss though." Marcia flung her long wavy hair over one shoulder. "It would be pretty easy to find a dark corner somewhere and make it more."

"Hell, you have your own room," Molly threw out. "Do the deed in there."

"With Cody?"

"Was there anyone else's spit on your face tonight?" She popped a grape into her heavily painted lips. It was hard to believe that just that morning, she had been attacked by a fellow vampire.

"I don't think I like him all that much."

"What does that have to do with anything," she scoffed.

"You guys are absolutely ridiculous." Destiny suddenly joined the conversation. Her angry glare turned on me. "You have more important things to worry about than some stupid boy." With that, she flung herself away from the table and stormed out.

"What is her problem?" Molly swung her body more fully in her chair.

"Maybe she has the hots for mister Sky Boy." Marcia continued to eat daintily. She didn't like human food as much as Molly and I did, but she still ate.

"I doubt it. She's a weirdo."

I watched Destiny moving farther away from us, a strange feeling washing over me. For some reason, I felt guilty. She was upset because of me.

"I'm going to find out what's wrong with her," I mumbled.

"Why?"

I didn't turn back to answer Marcia's question. I hurried to catch up with Destiny before she got too far away.

"Wait up," I called out. She hesitated but didn't stop. "Destiny, please wait."

"Why?" She turned back so abruptly, it made me stumble backward.

"Why are you so pissed at me?"

"Why are you running off with Cody into the woods when you have that thing on your arm?"

I covered my tattoo guiltily. "He was teaching me how to hunt."

"I told you that I would teach you."

"I know . . ."

"But if you'd rather be with him . . ."

My mouth suddenly felt really dry. "I wanted to be with you, but you were busy."

"I had class."

"I know."

"So you dumped me for Cody?"

"No." That wasn't what had happened, but why was she so upset? And why did seeing her upset make my heart react so strongly?

"I don't trust Cody." Her nostrils flared.

"He's harmless."

"Pfft." She crossed her arms.

"He wants me to trust him."

"Did he say that?"

"Almost."

"What does that mean?" Her eyes narrowed into thin slits.

It was too hard to explain things to Destiny that I didn't really understand myself. Besides, was this really the time to be thinking about kissing and how I felt about Cody?

"My v-card is safe from Cody."

In her surprise, she dropped her arms. "You say really weird things sometimes."

"Something is about to happen," I reminded her, tapping my wrist where the sand was still draining. "We need to focus on that, don't you think?"

Destiny rubbed her hand roughly down her face. "I have to get to the library before class tonight. I'll catch you later."

"But . . ."

Taylor, from my combat class, walked by at that moment. She watched us until Destiny hurried away towards the library.

"Hi, Linnie," she greeted, a tiny crease between her eyebrows.

"Hi." I waved and shoved my hand into my front pocket.

"I couldn't help but notice . . ."

I'm sure she could have helped it if she wanted to.

". . . your tattoo."

"My what?"

"On your wrist." Her hand shot out and pulled my arm toward her, revealing the hourglass that had formed there. "Oh no."

"Yeah."

Taylor would get it. She had the hourglass last week. Maybe she could help me get rid of mine.

"Something big is going to happen."

"Not *going* to," she corrected. "Something big is already happening."

A low groan escaped my throat as I came slowly awake. It had been a long night of very little sleep and way too much worrying about Destiny. She was mad at me for kissing Cody.

I didn't like it. I needed to figure out how to make up to her. Despite tossing and turning most of the night, I came up empty.

Rolling over, I came face to face with the small hourglass etched into my skin. Taylor said it was already starting. The two attacks the day before had to be the beginning.

Vampire attacks. I was being forced to turn into a vampire hunter—just like my parents.

I smoothed out the lines on my forehead and continued my search for the small clock on my stand. Seeing the numbers made my breath catch in the back of my throat.

"Shit," I shouted into the empty room.

I was supposed to meet Molly and Marcia for breakfast in four minutes. In all the time we had been at SMA, I had never been late to our dates. I really didn't want to start now. I would never hear the end of it.

I had lived most of my life in a cabin in the middle of Nowhere, Maine, so it didn't take me long to get ready in the mornings. Even if I wanted to, I didn't have much make-up to cake on my face.

Molly was always shocked by my ability to roll out of bed and out the door in ten minutes when it took her the better part of an hour. After a quick glance in the mirror and a brush pulled through my hair a few times, I made record time getting out the door.

I ran down a narrow staircase and found myself in the heavily shadowed underground passage that led out of Muninn Tower and into the bottom level of the library. I had been awake less than ten minutes, but my senses were all on high alert.

Most of the torches that lined the wall had been extinguished, leaving heavy shadows that were impossible to see through. I knew from Taylor that things would get a lot worse before the hourglass was done with me.

Since my vision wasn't nearly as strong as my hearing, I closed my eyes and listened as far out as possible. On the other side of the passage and up the steps, pages were being flipped in the library. A pencil scratched furiously on a sheet of paper.

But closer than that.

Just beyond the bend in the passage—someone was standing there, breathing in small quick breaths. They weren't walking toward the library or the tower. They were standing there. Waiting.

Were they waiting for me? Or were they waiting for anyone that was down here alone?

Fear flooded me. In that moment, I had two choices. I could run back to the relative safety of Muninn Tower with its good lighting and semi-full common room. Or I could move forward and confront whoever was attacking the students here at school.

Before I could fully decide what to do, the mouth-breather moved. My heart galloped as the footsteps came closer to where I was frozen in place. I tensed, mentally preparing for a fight.

"Linnie?" a familiar voice called out of the darkness.

"Destiny?"

A light suddenly flared to life. I flinched away from the flare of light from her flashlight. "Molly said she was meeting you and Marcia this morning."

Relief flooded me, making me weak.

"You scared me," I gasped.

"Why are you late?"

"Overslept."

"Did you see Marcia?"

"You're the first person I've seen." Besides the people in the common room that I darted past.

"I was worried about you." She moved slowly, putting her hand against my face.

"I thought you were mad at me," I breathed, feeling safe in the shadows of the passage.

"I am mad at you."

"But you came here to make sure I was okay." It wasn't a question. I felt it in the fire that her touch had blazed on my skin.

"I had to . . ." *Make sure you weren't the one attacked.*

"Attacked?" I pulled away from her so I could see her face. "Someone was attacked?"

Destiny's eyes narrowed. "Can you read my mind?"

Would I need to ask what happened if I could read her mind? "Who was it?"

"Marcia Lawson."

"Is she all right?"

"She didn't get attacked."

"But you said . . ."

"She's the one who's been attacking people."

CHAPTER 10

y tongue worked furiously against the inside of my bottom lip. General Sky held his expression tight, not letting us past him into the small office where a cell was located. Inside that cell, Marcia stood holding onto the bars.

Her already pale skin looked even more washed out under the bright lights.

"I need to speak to her," I tried again, pushing my body against General Sky's immovable form.

"Why?"

"She's my friend."

"Your friend has committed a terrible crime," he boomed out. "The Board of Regents will decide what will be done to her."

"Are you kidding me, you big ugly brute?" Marcia screeched, not helping her case in the slightest. "I already told you I didn't do anything!"

"We have witnesses that say otherwise."

"They're lying!" She shook her hands on the bars. "Obviously, they're jealous of me."

I wasn't sure about that assessment, but someone was trying to set her up. Marcia couldn't be the one attacking people. She would

305

never hurt Molly. They were best friends. Besides, why would she want to hurt anyone? It didn't make any sense.

"You need to stay quiet in there." General Sky pointed a large, beefy finger at her. "We won't be putting up with any more funny business."

"Funny?" Marcia tilted her head back and barked a sound of laughter at the ceiling. "Please explain to me which part of this is funny?"

"Just sit tight and wait until they figure out what to do with you."

"I demand that you call my mother."

"You get no demands here," he growled in response.

"Just because we live in a freaking mountain doesn't mean we've left the United States. I get a phone call."

"You haven't been arrested."

"Then let me out."

"Yet."

Marcia wasn't going to stop screeching though. General Sky, irritated, left the office for the calm of the outside. With one final look to my caged friend, I hurried to follow him with Destiny.

"How are you so sure she did it?" I turned on General Sky as soon as the door swung shut behind us. "Were you there? Who was attacked?"

He held up his hand, staving off any more questions. "There was another vampire attack this morning. That makes three in two days."

"Marcia didn't do it."

"She was caught."

"By who?"

"Another student saw her. He was in the quad, looking at the hourglass and noticed a fight. Your girl in there ran off and left someone for dead."

"I don't believe it."

"There's a lot of things in this school that are hard to believe. I'm here to try to keep people safe."

"I think you don't like vamps," I accused. "You singled all of us out to question, and now you believe the first person who says it was one of us."

"A vampire did this. There was a clear vampire bite." He ran a hand across his wide forehead. "I can't change the truth, no matter how I feel."

Next to me, Destiny kept her eyes averted. She didn't offer any help, probably because she didn't believe Marcia either. It was no secret there was no love lost between them. Even though she was also a vampire, she was as blinded as General Sky.

"This has to be some kind of misunderstanding," I continued stubbornly. "Marcia did not do this. You have to let her go."

"I can't let her go when we have a witness that—" *Admitted he didn't see her clearly.* "—saw her at the scene of the crime."

"You have your doubts though." I stared up at him, daring him to deny it.

"Like I said," he sighed deeply, "what I think doesn't change the facts. Get me some proof that it wasn't her and I'll gladly let your friend go."

"Proof?"

"Proof." He nodded once. "Until then, she stays where she is." He whirled away from us and hurried off.

"How can you leave me in here?" Marcia screamed from inside her small, magically strengthened cell. "I want my phone call. When my mom hears what you did, she'll rip you apart."

That was probably true.

"What do we do now?" I asked Destiny. The lines etched on my forehead were starting to feel permanent.

"We have history soon."

"I mean about Marcia."

"I know what you meant. There's a lot of vamps in that class."

"It's Vampire History." Of course, there were a lot of vamps in the class.

"Well, General Sky was right."

"No, he wasn't!"

"I mean," she cut me off forcefully, "he was right about it being a vampire who is behind these attacks."

"Maybe it's someone in our class," I finished her half-spoken thought out loud.

"Let's go check these people out." She winked.

Even if Destiny didn't believe in Marcia's innocence, her plan wasn't bad. We had to go to class anyway, might as well use that time wisely and find a new suspect before they sent Marcia somewhere else. What would even happen to her?

"Do not even think about leaving me here," Marcia growled from inside. Clearly, she had heard everything we said.

"We need to get proof for General Sky," Destiny said before I could. "We'll be back if we can find it."

Not if. When.

"Wait a second." Destiny pulled on my arm, stopping me from going into our Vampire History lesson.

"Wait for what?" I was determined to find out if anybody in that room had done what Marcia was being held for.

"Linnie."

"What?" If she had something to say, she needed to hurry up and say it. We were wasting time out here. Professor Gomez would be here soon, and then we wouldn't have time to question anyone.

"I know you believe Marcia . . ."

"Don't you?"

"I don't know what I believe. I want you to be careful in there. If you go around accusing these people, they might not take it lightly."

I pulled away from her and went into the classroom without replying. Why couldn't Destiny be on my side? I trusted Marcia, and I was going to prove her innocence to everyone.

A boy from Modi Tower sauntered in and sank down next to Destiny. I knew the two were friends, but I didn't know his real name. Destiny called him Tank.

"You hear about that pretty little blonde?" he whispered loudly to whomever was listening.

"You mean Marcia?" Destiny didn't bother to whisper. In a room full of vamps, what was the point?

"I heard she killed someone."

"No one is dead, Tank."

"Not for lack of trying."

What did that giant meathead know?

"If she was really trying to kill someone," I snapped, unable to hold it in any longer, "why would she do it in front of a witness?"

"When the blood lust takes over, some people can't help themselves." He turned his big gray eyes on me. "Besides, she's a bella."

"Wh—what does that have to do with anything?" I sputtered. I was a belladonna, too, and I had no desire to suck blood out of anyone. If anything, being a belladonna made us more able to control ourselves. We had plenty of time to master that skill.

Whoever had attacked the three people so far on campus was a goth vampire—I was sure of it. Looking at Tank's cocky snarl, my guess was on him.

"You girls have your mommies to hunt for you," he sneered, showing off a mouth full of teeth. "Spoiled rotten, don't know how to control your impulses."

My mom hunted all right, but not in the way he was insinuating.

"Hmm," I grunted with a humorless smile.

"I'm not surprised it was her," he continued obliviously. "She's hot, and the hot ones are always crazy."

"You're an idiot," Destiny mumbled as Professor Gomez came in. I didn't miss the grin splayed across my supposed friend's face.

My back teeth ground together as I spun around to the front of the class. *Whatever.* I didn't need either one of them to help me. If she would rather play around with Tank . . . whatever.

Only . . .

I kind of thought Destiny and I were in this together. Why was she teaming up with Tank the Terror to make fun of me?

"All right, guys," Professor Gomez called happily with her usual smile plastered on her pale brown face. "As promised, today we're talking about the Carrigans, a powerful nest from Scotland. Does anyone remember when they first formed?"

There was a collective groan as students shuffled books and papers in preparation for the lecture. Of all my teachers at SMA, Professor Gomez was the most confusing. She spent the hour telling us about violent wars and nests that tried to tear each other apart. And yet . . . her pride of our species was blatantly clear.

Out of the corner of my eye, I watched Destiny make funny faces at Tank. White-hot anger seared through my stomach and up my spine. Professor Gomez could be proud all she wanted, but the one thing I knew for sure—someone in this room was violently attacking students.

General Sky and Destiny were wrong—it wasn't Marcia.

Despite Destiny's lack of help, I scanned the room for the real attacker. Everyone was there except an Asian guy who usually sat right in front of me. Instead, I got a clear view of the girl in the next seat. Her bag had a smear of blood on it. Was it Molly's? Or one of the others? How could I know for sure?

As the lecture droned on, I doodled along the edge of my paper that I was supposed to be taking notes on. Having been home-schooled my whole life, I tended to love the classes at college, but today I had more important things on my mind. Sighing enough to make my shoulders slump, I moved my eyes around the room.

Destiny and I were supposed to come in here and question our classmates. We hadn't asked a single question. Instead, she and Tank had snickered through the whole hour.

"Okay, everyone, thanks for listening today," Professor Gomez called loudly. I jerked guiltily in my chair. I didn't even realize class was over already. I hadn't heard much of her lecture.

Still deep in thought, I closed my empty notes and stacked them on top of my books. I was no detective. I didn't even like mysteries. If I couldn't find a suspect within this class, I needed to go back to the scene of the crime. Someone had seen Marcia that morning. I needed to talk to that person and find out what they actually saw.

"You ready?" Destiny asked, stopping next to my desk.

I glanced her way but didn't reply.

"What's wrong?"

Like she didn't know.

"Linnie," Professor Gomez called over the din of everyone leaving. "Can I see you for a minute?"

"Of course."

"I'll wait for you outside," Destiny promised.

"No need," I told her through pursed lips.

"I know you're probably feeling betrayed by someone you thought was your friend," Professor Gomez stated once we were alone in the room.

"Not really."

She smiled. "Have you ever belonged to a nest?"

The unexpected question wiped the snarl from my face. "I've always lived with my parents."

It was a half-truth. We all lived in the same small town in Maine, but I was hidden away in a cabin while they had an apartment in town. It was practically the same thing though.

"If you ever find yourself alone, I belong to the Lilith Nest in Havenwood Falls, and I'd be happy to introduce you."

"Thanks, Professor."

"Any time you're ready."

I wasn't sure about a nest, but it was nice to have that option. I walked back out into the hall still thinking about the offer.

"What did she want?" Destiny pounced as soon as I cleared the doorway. She had waited after all.

"What are you doing out here?"

"I told you I would wait for you."

"And I told you that I didn't need you to."

"Why are you pissed?"

"I have to go change for combat." I didn't have class for a while, but I had no intention of standing here with her.

"Linnie."

"Don't even worry about it," I called back over my shoulder. "Go and play with your friend Tank."

Flexing my back muscles forward, I rotated my shoulder as far back as it would go. Combat class always wore me out. Not being a natural fighter, I had to work extra hard to master the skills that others seemed to have.

"Good class, everyone," Professor Shimizu boomed out over the din of groans and hyped up boys flexing their muscles.

Other students filed past me. Taylor and Roxy had their heads together, rolling their eyes at Kase as he flexed his impressive muscles. My feet were sore, and my legs felt like I was trying to walk through quicksand.

"You okay, Andrews?" Professor asked, concern wrinkling his smooth brow.

"Yeah," I squeaked, waving him off.

"Rest for a minute." He laughed. "This is a tough class, but you'll be okay."

My head dropped into my cupped hands as soon as he left. I had no idea how I wasn't kicked out already. We were being trained as guardians, and I barely survived combat class every day.

"I brought you something." My head popped up at the sound of Destiny's voice. She stood in the clearing with two bottles of deep red blood in her hands.

My jaw clenched at the sight of her.

"I'm tired," I panted, wiping the sweat from my top lip. "I'm going to head back to my room and grab a shower."

Her lips pressed tightly together. "You're seriously still mad at me?"

"Yes." I bit the inside of my lip. "No." I glared at her. "I don't know."

"Stay out here for a minute and have a drink with me." She wiggled the bottle invitingly.

"Fine." I sighed, plopping down on the grass where I stood and waiting for her to come join me. "Why did you come out here? Was Tank busy?"

"I came here because I wanted to see you." She handed me a bottle of blood. "And I don't know what Tank is doing." She shot me a cute grin.

Just the day before, Cody had brought me to Clifftop. Even though he had uncomfortably kissed me, I had been more relaxed with him. I didn't like being mad at Destiny. She was quickly becoming someone important to me.

"Are you thinking about Tank still?"

"No." I wasn't going to admit that Cody was on my mind. "Clearly I don't think of him as much as you do."

"Tank's a good guy."

"Mmm." I took a sip to stop myself from blurting out any more sarcastic compliments for her new best friend.

"He's an orphan like us."

"I'm not an orphan," I snapped without looking at her. "I have parents."

"You don't have a nest."

"So what," I sneered unattractively, "is Tank going to start a nest and have you and me be his wives?"

"I wouldn't be his wife."

"Neither would I." I snorted. "I was being sarcastic, in case you couldn't tell."

"He wouldn't have me as his wife," she continued gently despite my anger, "because I don't like guys like that."

"You're not ready to get married?"

"I'm into girls."

I was quiet for the length of several heartbeats. "Are you gay?"

"I am." She laughed.

Did that change anything?

No.

"I'm mad at you because you don't believe Marcia. I thought we were on the same side." If Destiny and I were together in this like she'd said, didn't that mean we had to agree on this?

"We're not always going to agree," she contradicted.

The hourglass was still losing sand. I ran my fingers over the magical ink as if I could somehow stop the sand from escaping. As fast as it was going now, something big was going to happen. I really didn't want another attack to prove Marcia's innocence.

"Will you tell me something?" Destiny suddenly burst out. "Do you like Cody or not?"

Cody? Where did that come from? We weren't even talking about Cody.

"He seems nice," I replied tightly, unsure why she was asking.

"You kissed him," she accused.

"I did."

"And?"

"I think I was . . . confused." It was hard to explain why I had kissed Cody. It sort of just happened. "It's not really a big deal. It was one kiss."

"Confused about what?"

I couldn't pinpoint why her simple question made my face so hot.

"I don't know." I made the mistake of looking at her, and my heart thudded wildly.

"Really?"

"I just . . ."

"Just what?"

"Boys are supposed to kiss girls. That's how it works."

"Who told you that?"

"It's a rule." Right? What did I really know about those kinds of rules?

"I think you should make it a rule to only kiss people who make your heart do that funny little thing in your chest." She grinned. "The thing it's doing now."

I slapped my hand over my chest, embarrassed at the way my heart was galloping. "I forgot that you have good hearing."

Her laugh came out husky. "You're so cute when you're embarrassed."

To avoid meeting her intensity, I took another drink. Flames kissed along my cheekbones, but I was smiling. I knew full well that it wasn't the time to be getting all giddy with Destiny in the woods, but I couldn't help it.

"I know General Sky wouldn't be holding Marcia if she wasn't guilty." Destiny suddenly changed the subject as if she could read my mind.

"I think he's making a mistake." I dug my heels in stubbornly.

"We'll figure it out," she vowed, squeezing my hand.

CHAPTER 13

Sinking heavily onto my favorite bench, I let the air whoosh out of my partially opened mouth. So much had happened in a few days—three people attacked by a vampire, Marcia accused and imprisoned, and then . . . Destiny.

I wasn't entirely sure what was going on with Destiny. I wanted to be with her all the time. I was even waiting for her to get out of class. She made my heart react in ways I didn't understand.

I liked her. And not in the same way I liked Molly and Marcia.

My head tilted backward until I was staring up at the rocky ceiling of the cavern. College life was so much more complicated than I thought it would be.

As I sat there on my favorite stone table near the quad, contemplating seeing Destiny again, the sound of rapidly moving footsteps thudded inside my ears. Curious, I tore my gaze away from the rocks above me and craned my head to see what was obviously moving closer.

The lanterns did very little to penetrate the dark, so it came as a shock when someone emerged right in front of my eyes.

"What the hell?" I whispered, jerking my head back.

A boy I recognized from my vampire history class, Min Lee, stood there for a moment, obviously as surprised to see me as I was to see him. His eyebrows furrowed darkly, then he turned back to whatever he was running from before hurrying on his way again.

I was no professional on suspicious behavior, but I knew that guy was guilty of something. Considering everything going on, it had to be the attacks. Blood pumped through me at the thought, making my heart beat faster. I needed to catch him and find out what he had done.

Rising from my seat, I listened hard to his retreating steps. No doors opened, so he must have headed to the quad. Or off the path completely.

Just as I was gathering my courage to go after him, a loud thud from the opposite direction caught my attention.

"Is anyone there?" I called nervously. Craning my neck, I stood up and took a few steps that way.

In the distance, half hidden by the deep black shadows, was the lump of something. My mouth went dry. It was a body—a body with no breath in the lungs and no heartbeat.

I recognized the woman's face. I had seen her at the clinic almost every day for the past month. She worked there with Madame Roth. It was obvious from the wound on her neck that this was another vampire attack.

Nostrils flaring, I backed up several panicked steps. Help. I needed to go get help. There was a dead body on our campus and a twitchy vampire running around.

I was alone though. No one would be able to hear me if I called. Even if they did hear, it would take a while to get here, and by that time, Min could disappear.

There was nothing I could do to help the woman. She was already dead. The only thing that mattered now was finding her killer.

Breathing hard, I turned on the spot and darted back past my bench, the same way Min had run. Only a few minutes had passed, but hopefully that wasn't too long.

Considering that the guilty Min was a vampire, it didn't surprise me that I couldn't find him. By being distracted, I had given him too much of a head start. This was the closest I had come to discovering the attacker. I wasn't ready to give up yet.

I stood in the middle of a stone pathway, darkness weighing heavily all around.

My hands rested on my hips as I searched all around me for Min, even though I knew he was long gone. Disappointment was starting to weigh down my shoulders. I was alone.

"Damn it," I whispered.

A raven flew close by me and perched itself on a statue. Its head cocked slightly, almost friendly in the way I was coming to associate with the black bird.

The hourglass on my wrist was moving again, the sand emptying. I was running out of time. I had to find the attacker before he killed anyone else and before . . .

A sudden gasp cut my thoughts off abruptly.

A breath that wasn't mine whooshed in and out of lungs that weren't mine. Someone was out there with me, and they were hiding from me. My vision widened out, trying desperately to take in as much of the limited light as possible. Unfortunately for me, there wasn't enough to see clearly.

When I first decided to give chase, I hadn't really thought much about what would happen if I actually found the killer. What was I thinking to run off blindly by myself?

I was going to be the next victim, I realized with a sinking heart. Fear swooped in and stole my breath. I did the only thing I could—I ran.

My footsteps pounded hard against the familiar ground. I took pride in how well I could see in the dark, which allowed me to move quickly. The problem was that whoever was chasing me was fast, too. They were gaining on me.

This was it. I was going to be killed like the lady from the infirmary. I had been chasing down the attacker all this time, and now the tables had taken a dark turn. I took the chance to try to get a peek behind me, failing miserably. Everything was a dark blur.

In the distance, way too far away, I spotted a small spark of hope. There was a group of students singing loudly and laughing at each other.

Pure terror pushed me forward fast enough to reach the crowd before the attacker reached me.

"Hey," I panted, clutching the nearest person.

"Hello there, pretty," a boy jeered, strong scents of alcohol rolling off of him. "You looking for a good time tonight?"

It was a better option than dying.

"Yeah," I gasped.

"That's what I like to hear." He winked stupidly and roughly patted my back.

Over the din of the party, I listened hard for that other set of footsteps. They were retreating.

"He's leaving," I whispered out loud.

"What's that?" The boy hugged me tighter, making me nauseous with the stench of his breath.

"There's someone I need to talk to."

One thought burned bright inside of me, a thought that went above the terror of the night. The attacker wasn't Marcia.

CHAPTER 14

My legs felt heavy as I stood outside General Sky's office. I realized after I had parted ways with the drunken group out by the quad that I should have waited for Molly or Destiny before I came to see Sky. Truthfully, it was getting undeniably dangerous to be out alone after dark.

But I didn't want to wait.

As soon as I told Sky what had happened to me, he would be forced to admit that Marcia was innocent and let her go. It was the memory of leaving her there by herself earlier that made me shove my fear aside and come here alone.

Inside the office, I could hear the even breaths of Marcia as she slept. Despite being held for crimes she didn't commit, she couldn't be bothered enough to affect her sleep. To be so unconcerned about her fate said a lot to how pampered she had lived her life.

In an attempt to stop shaking, I took a deep breath and held it until it puffed out both my cheeks. When I let it out again, it came out stuttered. Fear was a crazy thing, a thing that I had never properly felt. Maybe I was as sheltered as Marcia and Molly had been.

"Linnie?"

I jumped at the sound of my name.

"Who's there?" I demanded, whirling around.

Cody stood there, watching me with a furrowed brow. "What are you doing here?"

"Cody." My relief almost knocked me to my knees.

"Whoa," he cooed, coming quickly to help me stay upright. "What happened? Are you all right?"

"Marcia is innocent," I blurted out the single thought that had brought me here.

His brow smoothed back out as pity replaced his concern. "I know that you think. "

"No," I harshly cut him off. "I don't just think anything. I know."

"Okay." The single word stretched out into several syllables. "What exactly happened to you tonight that makes you know?" He had turned from my friend into one of the Sky Boys— suspicious and questioning.

"I saw the real killer."

"Killer?"

Oh. In the thrill of being chased, I had almost forgotten the dead woman I had found.

"I found a dead body," I hurried to tell him, "and I saw who did it."

"If you really found a body, we need to tell Sky."

"That's why I'm here," I practically shouted. "Where is he?"

"He must be in his room." He pursed his lips thoughtfully. "I'm on night duty with Reynolds."

"What do we do? Can you go get him?"

"You said you saw who did it?"

"It was a guy from my Vampire History class—Min Lee."

"I know who you're talking about." He nodded slowly. "But I never would have guessed he would do something like this. He seems too soft."

"It doesn't matter what you think, Cody. I know what I saw. And," I held up one finger, "he chased me."

"You actually saw him biting her?"

"Well," I grunted, "not exactly biting but . . ."

"Let's find Min and ask him about it," he suggested, much calmer than any of my suggestions had been.

"What about . . ."

"The body," he finished when my words trailed away awkwardly.

"We can't leave her there."

"Right. I'll get Reynolds on it. Where did you find it?"

It didn't take long to find Reynolds. It took longer to convince him that I wasn't crazy. Luckily, I had Cody to vouch for me.

Soon, Cody and I were walking alone in the quieter campus. It had less activity at night, but there were still things to be heard. Destiny had a combat class out on Clifftop, the drunken party was still going full force, a couple somewhere in Muninn Tower was having a make-out session that I was trying to ignore.

"I saw some vamps out on Clifftop earlier when I was doing my rounds," Cody informed me. "Let's go see if he's there."

He wouldn't be there. Now that he knew I had seen him, he'd be in hiding. There was no way he was out on Clifftop with the others. It was the best lead we had though. Besides, maybe someone had seen him.

"All right," I agreed easily enough. Being with Cody made me feel so much braver than when I was on my own. I felt safe with him by my side.

He was a Sky Boy; he was trained to stop the bad guys.

The first thing I noticed when we reached Clifftop was the absence of noise. There was supposed to be a combat class and a group of vampires that I didn't hear either. Had they canceled class? Where was everyone?

"Over here," Cody called out softly, guiding me into the deeper shadows of the woods.

It was shocking to see at least half a dozen vampires sitting there in a circle of sorts.

"What are they doing here?" I whispered to Cody, abruptly forgetting why we had come here in the first place.

"Sitting?" He shrugged.

But they were doing more than just sitting. They were

touching each other, as if trying to share the burden of their confusion. We all knew a vampire at the school was attacking people. The heaviness of that sadness hit me with the weight of a freight train.

Choking back a sob, I sank down to join the circle of energy exchange. There was something inside of me that pulled me to them. I couldn't deny it even if I wanted to.

There was a soft nudge against my shoulder when someone else sat next to me. I assumed it was Cody until Destiny pulled my hand into hers. I would recognize her touch anywhere.

Across from the circle, my eyes met the hard gaze of Min. His intense emotion told me that I had been mistaken in what I thought I saw in there in the quad. Min wasn't the killer any more than Marcia was.

So who had chased me? Who was the killer?

The grass was cold underneath me, but I wasn't in any hurry to leave Clifftop. Everyone except Destiny and me had already gone back to the dorm rooms. Cody had taken Min back to the office for questioning.

"You actually thought that Min Lee had killed someone?" Destiny scoffed.

"He was acting really suspicious," I told her again, keeping my eyes on our joined fingers.

"He's probably the most genuinely nicest person I've ever met in my life."

"And he was meeting his boyfriend," I recited tonelessly.

"The one his parents don't know about."

"Yeah. It would have been nice to know that before."

"You should really listen to people more."

"People lie."

"Most people are trying their best to be decent."

"Even vampires?"

"Yes."

I turned my face to look at her profile. She certainly looked like she was being serious.

"There's a vampire killing people here," I reminded her.

"Humans kill each other all the time."

"But we're at a college to learn how to be guardians of our kind."

"Is that why you came here?" she asked me suddenly.

"I never really knew what my future would look like. I wasn't even sure I had one."

"Why?"

I didn't want to talk about my past. There were too many things to be ashamed of.

"Why did you come here?" I rolled to my side so I could see her better. "What's your story, Destiny?"

"I was changed against my will." Her pale face glowed in the darkness. "It was horrible, but I was taken in by a pretty amazing vampire family."

"Are they the ones who told you about SMA?"

"They were killed by hunters shortly after I joined them."

My stomach turned. I really, really hoped my family didn't have anything to do with that.

"I couldn't fight the hunters, so I hid for a long time. But I'm done hiding now. I came here to learn how to protect the people I love."

"You are so much braver than me."

Destiny's laugh made me smile. "We all have our stories."

I couldn't help but wonder if Destiny would still be sitting so comfortably close to me if she actually knew my story. Her family was destroyed by hunters; my family were hunters. Under normal rules, Destiny and I would be enemies.

The world SMA had opened up for me didn't play by normal rules though—not what I knew as normal, anyway. And I was grateful for that.

"What are you thinking about?" She nudged my shoulder lightly.

"Destiny," I blurted without thinking.

"Do you believe in destiny?"

"I think so," I half whispered.

"Hmm . . ." she pursed her lips thoughtfully.

"You might be mine."

"Your what?"

"My . . . destiny." I squeezed my eyes shut tight so I wouldn't see her look of horror. It surprised me when I felt her lips press lightly against my forehead.

"Maybe you're mine, too," she whispered.

Feeling safe, I let my eyelids flutter back open. "Do you believe in destiny?"

"I never used to." She raised her hand and swiped her hair from her forehead. "But that was before I met you."

"Oh . . . oh," I stammered while butterflies erupted in my stomach.

"I can't believe I said something so corny." She laughed into her closed fist. "Seriously, I'm not usually like this."

"I don't . . . I don't mind." I had never met anyone like Destiny before. She made me feel like laughing and throwing up at the same time. It made me nervous to sit next to her and yet . . . there was no other place I wanted to be.

What was wrong with me? Was this part of being a belladonna?

"Would it be all right if I kissed you?"

"I don't know," I breathed, eyes going wide.

"Oh, okay."

I made up my mind when her face fell. Not giving me any time to second-guess myself, I turned my face enough to press my lips to hers.

All my awkwardness fell away almost immediately. The kiss deepened slowly. She moved her hand to the back of my head while I traced her arm with my fingertips.

Tiny lights seemed to explode all around us, enveloping the two of us in a world far away from what was going on at campus. It was the most thrilling and real moment I had ever had, and I never wanted it to end.

When she finally pulled away from me, her lips were curled

upward into a gentle smile.

"That was so much better than kissing Cody," I whispered fervently.

"I'm not sure how I feel to be compared to that mouth-breather." She sighed as she lay back on the grass. "But I'll take it."

I lay down beside her. The stars here seemed so much closer than the stars at home. It was almost like I could reach out and grab one. What would my mother think if I brought Destiny to meet her? I shuddered at the thought.

"Tonight in Combat, we were talking about what made us strong. You know, the digging deep stuff," Destiny commented lazily.

"What did you say?"

"Nothing." She rolled her eyes. "But the more I think about it, the thing that makes all of us strong are the people we're fighting for. Don't you think?"

"I'm not really that strong." My biggest fear was that the Regents would realize I wasn't strong enough and kick me out.

"You're strong at some stuff."

"I can hear pretty well."

"All vampires can hear well."

"Sometimes I can even hear what people are going to say before they say them."

"You mean you can hear people's thoughts?"

"Sort of. I can hear what they're about to say or what they decide not to say."

"Can you hear what I'm thinking right now?"

"No."

She wiggled her eyebrows suggestively.

"But I have a pretty good guess." My face grew hot.

"You'd be right." She winked.

Our laughter joined together and swirled above our heads. The sound created a false sense of calm inside of me, and I was able to forget the hourglass on my wrist and the raven that seemed to be chasing me around campus for the past several days.

Even if it was just for a little bit.

CHAPTER 15

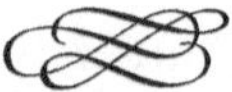

I was practically bouncing in my seat as Professor Glover brought the class to a close. I piled my books neatly on my desk, ready to drop them into my bag the second the professor was done talking. It had been a long ninety minutes, knowing that Destiny was meeting up with me after class let out.

Destiny was all I had been able to think about since we parted ways in the early hours of the morning. After a few hours of sleep, Molly was pounding on my door to tell me the good news: General Sky had released Marcia.

"It's all thanks to you," Marcia whispered before following her best friend from the room.

Now, though, I was tired and only wanted to see Destiny and tell her that we had succeeded in getting Marcia out. She wouldn't be nearly as pleased as I was; the thought had me grinning like an idiot.

"Next week," Glover called out, "we'll be doing wound care. Vampires, make sure you don't come to class thirsty." His eyes rested briefly on me.

I never came to Emergency Care thirsty. Professor Glover warned me of that on the very first day. I didn't forget.

"All right, guys." He clapped his hands together. "We'll see you next week."

I jumped up from my seat first, shoving my notebook into my bag as quickly as possible. Even with my hearing, the hall was too crowded for me to be able to pick out Destiny's voice, but I was sure she was out there. She told me she would be. A thrill of excitement made goosebumps erupt on my arms.

Or maybe it was the tattoo on my arm that was making my skin tingle. The ink was starting to shift again. My forehead wrinkled as I watched it. The sand was almost empty now. What did that mean? Someone had already died. What more could happen?

Shaking my head to dispel my doomsday thoughts, I made my way out to the hall. Students loitered against the walls in small groups, giggling and flirting with each other.

There was a killer among them. Had everyone forgotten?

"Tough class?" a familiar voice purred next to my ear.

"No." I whirled around breathlessly, coming face to face with Destiny.

"Then what has you looking so upset?"

In my pleasure at finally knowing someone who got me with a single look, I momentarily forgot my troubles. It was suddenly understandable how so many students were still laughing.

"I was thinking of this." I shoved my wrist out so she could see for herself how little time we had left.

"Let's go out and check the hourglass in the quad," she suggested. "It might give us a better idea of how much time we have."

"Yeah, but time for what? What's going to happen?"

"I don't know."

That wasn't very comforting. Still, I followed her outside without too much hassle. At least I wasn't alone, and I was starting to think I could handle whatever came along. I had proven Marcia's innocence after all.

"Linnie!" I looked up to see a short man striding toward us. His hair was cut very close to his pale head. He wasn't smiling.

"Reynolds," I greeted the Sky Boy I had met the night before. He was the one who had to go look for a dead body. I didn't blame him for looking so serious.

"Cody is looking for you."

"Cody is?"

"He's waiting on Clifftop. He said you would know where."

Yeah, I knew where. The same place we had kissed.

"Shit," I hissed after Reynolds left. "I bet I know what he wants to talk about."

He must have heard about Destiny and me. For all I knew, he had heard the entire exchange last night. He had really good hearing too, and if he came back to make sure I was okay . . .

"I'll go with you," Destiny offered. "It might not be as weird with him if you're not alone."

"Telling him that I'm dumping him for a girl is going to be weird no matter what," I spat out. "Having that girl with me might not be the greatest plan."

She crossed her arms over her chest and jutted out one hip. "I'm okay with it if you are."

The part of me that liked Destiny a lot more than I liked anyone else was okay with her tagging along to Clifftop. That part of me was even amused by the thought of it.

My compassion for Cody's feelings easily won out though. He deserved an explanation from me. If I was being completely honest, I liked him too. Just not as much as I liked Destiny.

"I'll go." I grinned. "I'll meet up with you later?"

"I need to go to the library." She crinkled her nose in distaste. "Want to have a study date?"

"Not really."

"Come on. It'll be fun." She looped her fingers in the waistband of my jeans and pulled me close to her. "We can make out in the aisles."

"When you put it that way . . ." I barely had to move to kiss her smiling lips. "Later then."

"Later."

I watched her walk away for a moment, until I realized people around me were staring. Embarrassed by my lack of discretion, I turned toward the direction of Muninn Tower. If I was going to meet Cody for this serious conversation, I needed to gather my courage. In other words: stall.

"I need to drop my books off in my room," I muttered to myself as I walked. "Totally normal thing to do."

I got back to my room quickly and deposited my bag on the single-sized bed with way more pillows than anyone would ever need. Molly and Marcia had helped me decorate. Destiny and I had spent time together in this very room not too many days ago.

That was the day my tattoo had first changed. I didn't know it then, but my whole world was changing. I grinned stupidly at my girlish thoughts.

"What's so funny?" Marcia stood at the open doorway, staring in at me. She was more grateful to me than I wanted her to be.

"I was thinking."

"About Destiny?"

A blush spread across my cheeks and burned my ears.

"No," I denied through closed teeth.

"She's weird," her smile went lopsided, "but I guess she's cute, if you're into that sort of thing."

Not that I had asked for it or that I needed it, but Marcia had just given me her blessing to date Destiny. I appreciated the gesture.

Walking at a normal human pace, I made my way slowly past the armory and toward Clifftop. Before this week I hadn't spent any time out there except in class, and now it seemed like a lot of important things were happening out on Clifftop.

My first kiss. My first girlfriend moment.

And now here I was, about to break some guy's heart. Funny enough, it wasn't as satisfying as I had once thought it would be.

I didn't see Cody when I first walked out into the forest, but I felt him. The hairs on my arm and along the back of my neck stood up, warning me that something was wrong. Very wrong.

Pausing there on the trail, I listened as hard as I could. Two people were close by, one of them with a very slow heartbeat while the other's was going way too fast.

"Hello?" I called out, unsure if that was a good idea or not. "Cody?"

"Over here."

He was farther back into the trees than I expected, and his voice sounded breathy; from fear or excitement, I wasn't sure yet. I made my way back to him with every one of my senses on high alert.

It was darker back where the trees were denser, but light enough to easily make out Cody standing there, and someone else laying near his feet. "What's going on?"

"I found her back here," he told me, his eyes shining.

"Found who?" My mouth felt dry, as if it already knew before he made his big reveal.

"Destiny."

Her name echoed inside my chest, bouncing off the walls of my heart. "Is that . . . ?"

As if on their own accord, my eyes shifted to the mass on the ground. That couldn't possibly be Destiny; she was in the library studying.

"She was here when I got here," he explained again. "I came here to meet you and she was . . . bleeding."

"Bleeding?" I choked on my disbelief. "Is it another attack?"

Cody shrugged helplessly. "Must be."

My legs finally unfroze enough to carry me to her side. She was still breathing, I desperately reminded myself. *She's going to be fine.* I knelt down beside her so I could see where she was hurt.

Cody was right. There was a lot of blood. Underneath the scratches on her chin and across her neck were two small puncture holes.

"It . . . it was a vampire," I stuttered. "But she's alive."

Thank goodness!

I was training for emergency care, and I had spent enough time in the infirmary to know that her wounds would heal fairly quickly. She was a vampire, after all. A few hours of rest and she'd be back on her feet.

"Maybe she saw who did it," I finished my thoughts out loud. "She can tell us when she wakes up."

"That's . . . great."

"We need to get her to the infirmary." I was strong enough to carry her on my own, if only I could get my hands to stop shaking. What if I dropped her? My face paled at the thought. "Will you help me?"

"I found her like this."

"I know, you already said that." A feeling of unease suddenly draped over me. The air became thick with an unspoken truth. Everything seemed to be moving in slow motion.

Up high in a nearby tree, a familiar raven landed on a branch. The bird watched us with wise eyes, knowing the things that I had just now figured out. The killer had been close by me the whole time.

Cody glanced up at the raven and then back to me and Destiny.

"I don't want you to think anything crazy." He wiped his hand across his forehead.

"Why would I think anything crazy?" I asked, my voice light and feathery.

"Your friend is . . . laying on the ground. It's only natural to wonder what happened to her."

"You didn't find her like this, did you?"

"This wasn't my fault," he suddenly gushed out. "I had to stop her."

Stop her by biting her? "Stop her from doing what?"

My teeth were clenched so tight, I was surprised he understood.

"Isn't it obvious?" He laughed wildly. "She's the one who's been attacking people."

Everything went very quiet. I willfully slowed my heart so I could hear better. "I was coming out here tonight to tell you that me and Destiny—"

"I know about your little kiss," he cut me off. "She manipulated you into thinking you're some kind of lesbian."

"She really didn't."

"You're lucky that I figured out what she was before you really fell for her."

He was wrong on so many levels, but I needed to tread carefully. "We should take her to Sky."

"He's not here."

Obviously. "Then you should go and get him."

"Yeah, probably." *But I'm not going to be able to let you walk out of here. You already know too much.*

"I'll wait here with Destiny."

"And make sure she doesn't get away?" *Do I really look that stupid?* A tiny grin played around his lips. The facade was starting to slip away.

"What are you going to do to us?"

"I'm not going to do anything to you, Linnie. I'm here to help." The raven took flight then, flying straight at him. His arms swung wildly. "What the hell?!"

Understanding that the raven was giving me a chance to escape, I stood up and faced Cody. The tremble that had started in my fingers and worked rapidly through my arms was all but gone. "I know you're the one who attacked all those people."

His short laughter came out like a bark.

"You got me," he taunted, holding his hands out wide.

"How could you do something like that?" I demanded, anger making my voice rise.

"You might have to clarify. I've done a lot of shit." He winked.

"You attacked all those people!"

"I did. Do you really need me to give you the details?" His head cocked to one side. "I mean, which one of us is the crazy one?"

"Are you jealous because I'm with Destiny? Is that why?"

His face immediately twisted up in disgust. "Are you really that delusional? This is why I hate college girls. Everything is about you."

"Then why?"

Destiny stirred from her place on the ground. Although she wasn't fully awake, a huge burst of relief washed over me at the sound of her low groans. She was going to be okay. As long as Cody didn't kill us now.

"Looks like your love bird is waking up just in time to see you die."

"How original." I rolled my eyes, despite the seriousness of the situation. "Are you going to at least tell me why you're going around killing people? Or are you seriously just crazy?"

"I only killed one person," he snarled. "She happened to have more fight in her than I thought."

"You mean she didn't lay down and die?"

"I have a sister," he abruptly spouted off as if that were supposed to explain anything.

"I have two sisters. Still not a murderer."

"She was beyond excited when she applied for SMA."

"Your sister goes to school here?" That was a little bit of a shock.

"They didn't accept her."

"They turned away a lot of people."

"She's better than all of you idiots."

Cody had come here to seek revenge for a sister who didn't make the cut? That seemed a bit extreme. And lame. "And yet, she didn't get into SMA."

"It's like you're begging me to kill you." His top lip rose off his teeth, sending a ripple of fear down my spine.

"I wouldn't call it begging," I muttered. I needed to be running for help; I knew that.

Cody had been smart to lure me out here where there would be less chance for the rest of the school to hear us. I could start screaming and hope someone came, but that would make him act faster, and I still wasn't sure how I was going to be able to get both Destiny and me out of this safely.

I couldn't run from him either. There was no way in hell I was leaving Destiny out here with Cody when she wasn't even able to stand up. It was looking more and more like I was going to have to fight him.

Truthfully, I didn't think I could overpower him.

While I was still trying to figure out my next move, Cody suddenly lunged forward and pushed me hard enough to knock me to the ground. I was up again instantly.

What had I been taught? *Lower my center of gravity.* I crouched low to the ground and faced him again.

Teeth bared, he slammed into me again. I managed to stay upright this time, with only a small cut on my arm from his sharp nails. He moved so fast it was a blur. There was no way to keep him in my vision like I had been taught.

Before I knew what was happening, he made another swipe at me. This time, he clipped my chin and forced me backward several more steps until I was backed against a tall tree.

This was it, and I knew it. No wonder no one else had seen who attacked them. Cody was so fast, even for a vampire. And he was so strong. It was a shame that he was fighting on the wrong side.

I heard a rustle of leaves to my right. Turning my head, I closed my eyes tightly, preparing for the worst.

It didn't come.

Destiny was right in front of me, between me and Cody.

"What are you doing?" I screamed. "You're hurt."

"It's kind of rude to be pointing that out now," she gasped lightly. "Leave. Her. Alone," she told Cody, her voice much stronger than it should have been.

"Destiny, run," I begged. "Go find help."

"Not going to happen."

"Aww," Cody simpered unkindly. "How sweet. I never stood a chance, did I?"

"No, you didn't," a new voice entered the trees.

I recognized his voice before Tank actually came into view. It was more than him running toward us. It was a beautiful sight to see the trees separate and half a dozen bodies appear.

"An infestation," Cody growled, his eyes wide.

Tank and Min were on him in a second, not giving him a chance to get away.

"You're a vampire," Tank pointed out. "What do you have against us?"

"He wanted one of us to get blamed," Marcia concluded, surprising me with her sharpness.

"If they thought you were unstable," he shrugged with an insane grin, "they would kick you all out."

"And what? You thought we'd lay back and just let you?" Min demanded, twisting his arm tighter behind his back.

"What do we do with this scum?" Molly asked for all of us.

Destiny was the one who answered. "We take him to Sky."

"The jail cell here is super comfy," Marcia said, whirling around and leading the way out.

We all walked together in a group, dragging Cody along with us, to General Sky's office. We were united, having defeated the villain in our own story. Although we weren't cheering out loud, there was an excitement that filtered through us.

Worry was also there, for Destiny. She was walking on her own two legs, but her steps were faltered and her breathing labored.

"You need to go to the infirmary," I hissed, walking behind everyone else with her. Judging by the whooshing sound her breaths were making, she probably had a few broken ribs. Even if they had healed right away, she was obviously still sore.

"I'll be fine," she replied quickly. "It's not like I've never been in a fight before."

"Why did you go out to Clifftop?" How did he get her?

"I was checking on you," she admitted with a grimace. "I thought you were already out there with him."

I had gotten distracted. Talking to Marcia had given Cody time to attack Destiny alone. "I'm sorry I wasn't out there."

"I always knew I didn't like Cody." She had to stop walking and press her hand into her side.

"You should go." Why did she always have to be such a hero?

"I'm waiting for you."

"Just wait here then." She clearly wanted to argue but then changed her mind and nodded instead. "I'll be right back," I promised, kissing her briefly.

Destiny grimaced, making me hesitate to rejoin the others who had drifted ahead of me. Did they really need me to get Cody to

General Sky? Wouldn't it be better to make sure Destiny got to the infirmary?

"Hurry up and go so you can get back," she muttered as if she could read the indecision in my head.

Clicking my tongue against the roof of my mouth, I turned away and darted off toward the others. There was some commotion from the group, commotion that didn't sound like a celebration.

"What's going on?"

But I saw what was wrong before anyone needed to tell me. Tank was on the ground, a circle of blood growing around him and a metal rod jutting from his chest. Several feet away, Min and another guy were struggling to keep a hold of Cody. Molly and Marcia clung to each other, staring open mouthed at the blood around Tank.

I knew from my classes that vampire blood wasn't as strong as human blood for vampires, but I knew the sight was hard for them to see. I also knew that if I didn't get that rod out of Tank, he was going to die.

And then there was Cody. No way was he getting free.

I acted without much thought. In one fluid movement, I yanked the rod out of Tank and slammed it into Cody instead. I knew exactly where to stab it into him so that it would go clean through his heart—stopping it for good.

"Holy shit," someone whispered.

"What is going on out here?" General Sky roared, storming out of his office. It seemed that the commotion had, at long last, caught his attention.

Finally, it was over.

"Will you tell me again that I did the right thing?" I sniffed.

"You did the right thing," Destiny obliged. "It had to be done. If he got away, he would have hurt more people."

She was right. Of course, she was right, but taking someone's life wasn't easy. "Have you ever killed anyone?"

"Yes."

Her arm that was wrapped around my body squeezed slightly, giving me permission to bury my face into her shoulder again. I didn't cry though. There were no tears left. We were both laying on the same bed at the infirmary, much to the displeasure of Madame Roth.

"Let me see your arm again," she grunted, pulling my wrist around so she could see it.

The hourglass tattoo was gone, replaced again by the school tattoo. "Do you think I passed? Did I fix what I was supposed to?"

Surely I did, since the hourglass was broken now.

"Yeah," Destiny nodded. "I think it's over now."

"I'm sorry I put you in danger, Destiny."

"How did you put me in danger?"

"You went out to Clifftop for me, and Cody was there waiting for you."

"I don't see how any of that was your fault," she scoffed. Her finger rubbed against the skin on my wrist, causing goosebumps to rise up.

"There's something I haven't been honest about."

"What is it?"

"My family are all hunters," I admitted with a thick throat, making my words come out all warped.

"Everyone already knows that, Linnie."

"They do?"

"Of course." She chuckled.

"How?" I hadn't told anyone.

"There's a bunch of supes around here. They have ways of knowing things and word travels fast."

"So you've known all this time?"

"Yep."

"Why didn't you tell me?" I had been tortured with the thought of what she would think after she found out, and here she already knew.

"I figured you would tell me when you were ready."

Still irritated, I settled back down beside her. I couldn't really argue with her logic. "You're not mad?"

"Nope."

"I've never met anyone like you before."

Her eyes were closed when I peeked up at her. Madame Roth said she needed rest and she'd be back to normal. Still, it was hard for me not to worry about her.

"Why are you staring at me?" she grumbled without opening her eyes.

"I have a question."

"Hmm?"

"Will you be my girlfriend?"

She grinned widely, eyes still closed. "Sure."

Biting down on my lower lip, I squirmed up the few inches I needed to put our faces closer together. She moved first, raising up to press her lips to mine. Kissing Destiny was as natural as breathing.

"Are you two going to be *that* couple?" Molly asked loudly, pulling the curtain that separated our beds back. "It's not like you're alone in here."

"I absolutely love caramel," I squealed, inhaling over the large cup of coffee in front of me.

Professor Gomez had set up a coffee date for Destiny and me to meet a woman called Alina, who apparently could get us a good word with the Lilith Nest in Havenwood Falls. Even if we decided not to go with the nest, Coffee Haven was worth the trip to town. The satellite shop on campus was good, but it didn't offer the same view—or variety.

The door opened softly, and a girl I recognized from school came in with her head down, focused on something other than the coffee shop.

"Isn't that Tempest Bell?" I whispered to Destiny.

"Yeah," she replied with a grin.

"She's pretty, huh?"

"I guess so." She shrugged.

"Prettier than me?"

Destiny quietly sipped her tea.

"I hate frilly coffee." She smirked, not begrudging me my excitement over the frills.

"Whatever." I giggled.

Clicking her tongue lightly, she swung her gaze back to me. "You're prettier."

"But she is pretty," I mumbled, leaning low to blow on my coffee.

"I don't understand why we're not meeting Gabriel," she said, yet again. "He's the nest leader."

"Professor Gomez said Alina's nicer," I told her, unconcerned. "You know what I don't understand?"

"Hmm?"

"Do you think the hourglass broke because I killed someone?" We hadn't talked much about it since we left the infirmary but out here, away from the campus, it seemed safe to talk about it again.

"I don't think you had to kill someone," she began slowly. "I think it was more about you learning that you're different than your parents."

Different than my parents? They were hunters. I had never killed anyone until Cody.

But it went deeper than that.

I had lived in the shadow of my sister Raven for as long as I could remember. She was perfect and exactly the kind of daughter my parents wanted. I always thought that made me inferior to her, but I wasn't. I was doing something worthwhile here at SMA, something I could be proud of.

My family killed vampires simply because of what they were. I had been taught my whole life that vamps were evil and would turn on me. The vampires I had met at SMA had put themselves in danger for me, though. They were willing to take on a killer.

Some were my best friends.

Destiny was more than my friend.

I had never been loved like they loved me. I had never been accepted like they accepted me. Did it really take an hourglass and all the chaos it created for me to realize that? *Maybe.*

"What are you thinking about?"

"If I should go get a scone." I giggled, not willing to go down any more dark roads just yet.

"Molly said you have to." She raised both eyebrows dramatically.

"You really should have one," a gorgeous young woman with long black hair said, holding out a scone. "You must be Linnie and Destiny?"

"Yeah," I smiled wide.

"I'm Alina. It's nice to meet you." Her warm smile alleviated some of my worries. "I'm glad you two came to talk to me."

"Us too," Destiny grinned back. "What can you tell us about your nest?"

As I listened to Alina, I realized SMA was going to change my life more than I ever thought it could. I would finally get to be exactly what I was—a vampire—and I was good at it.

Our conversation wound down, and I began to gather my stuff when I glanced outside the window, watching as a raven fluttered down to rest on the back of a car. My breathing hitched at the sight. I knew that bird.

"What do you think that means?" I hissed.

Alina twisted to see what had alarmed me. "It's just a bird."

"No, it isn't," I assured her. "That bird always knows when something is wrong at the school."

"You don't think . . ." Destiny's eyes widened.

I didn't need her to finish to know what she was thinking, and to agree with her. It was happening again—another hourglass, another gong, more trouble for the school.

BORROWED TIME

BELINDA BORING

CHAPTER 1

$\mathcal{M}$r. Westbrook stood outside the Potions lab, a concerned expression on his face. "Are we going to talk about why you missed our Friday night meeting?"

"Well," I drawled as I took one of the earbuds out, so I could hear him better. The sound of Queen singing "Bohemian Rhapsody" provided interesting background music to the discussion. "I was kind of hoping that we wouldn't." I tried giving him the type of smile that said 'go easy on me. I'm a fragile butterfly', but he didn't buy it.

"I'm not here to check up on you like your old coven did, Tempest. I'm genuinely interested in seeing how you're doing and making sure you're okay." Micah leveled me with a penetrating stare that felt like he could see clear down to my soul.

I still wasn't used to people giving a shit about how I felt. "So, I'm not in trouble?"

If something was too good to be true, it usually meant that it was.

His own brows arched in surprise. "Do you want to be in trouble?"

A voice in my head screamed for me to shut up and take the win. It wasn't every day that I was given the benefit of the doubt.

"Nooo . . ." I replied, still somewhat hesitant. Behind me I could hear our teacher clearing her throat, the sound a warning that all chatter needed come to an end. I really loved this class with Patty Parker. She was a pretty decent professor who made her lessons hands-on and fun. "But if I don't get inside, I'm going to upset Ms. Parker." I flashed him a smile. "I'm good. Promise."

Peering around me to look into the lab, Micah nodded. Damn him for always being so earnest. "Okay, then. I know we didn't meet under the best of circumstances, but you can trust me."

He wasn't wrong, either. After almost burning down my house, the fire being the final straw that broke the proverbial camel's back, my parents had the police put me into a mental health facility under a seventy-two-hour watch. It was nothing more than a ruse to give them and our coven's leader a chance to plan my punishment. They didn't care that it was an accident. They refused to listen when I begged them to understand.

The consequence was having my magic completely stripped away, leaving me to live the rest of my life as a mortal.

Micah Westbrook had become nothing short of my knight-in-shining-armor—going before the coven and convincing them to release me into his guardianship. He'd seen something in me that first night we'd met at the mental health facility—perhaps taking pity on how pathetic I was, because next thing I knew, I was to be trained and given an education. If I hadn't known he was an angel beforehand, I'd have bet my last dollar that he was a witch because that meeting had been nothing short of magical.

And here I was, at the Sun & Moon Academy, away from my family where I was free to live my life.

It was a goddess-given miracle.

"Yeppers. I'll be there shortly after class with Professor Shimizu." Now there was a class that kicked my ass . . . literally. Knowing that combat wasn't my forte, Micah always made sure there was a hot cup of healing tea waiting for me. The first few weeks had me walking about like I was a hundred and twenty with bad knees and a wonky hip.

"Don't be late this coming Friday. I won't always be this forgiving." With a chuckle, he waved at Ms. Parker and left.

I quickly entered the lab. Class was already underway. Any hope I had of reaching my table unnoticed flew out the window. Everyone watched as I did the walk of educational shame to where Natalie was sitting, an empty stool beside her.

"I trust everything's okay, Tempest?" Ms. Parker asked, peering at me from over her glasses. Which reminded me—I'd left my own on the bedside table back in my room. Damn.

"Sorry," I offered, sliding quickly onto my seat. With nimble fingers, I removed my notebook and pen, then sat up straight, eyes forward.

The teacher didn't continue, however. Instead, she tapped the side of her head, her finger by her ear.

Shit. I was still listening to my iPod.

"What's with you today?" Natalie whispered softly, not once turning to look at me. "Are you having a mid-semester crisis or something? Do you need an intervention?" The corner of her mouth quivered as she desperately tried not to crack a smile.

"Maybe," I replied. "I guess this is what happens when I don't have my Wheaties for breakfast. I've been off all day." That wasn't an understatement either. By lunchtime I'd almost ditched studying so I could go back to Hel and take a nap.

"Well . . ." Whenever my roomie started a sentence with that drawn out word, I knew it only spelled trouble.

"Shush, I'm trying to learn here," I barked, my voice a little louder than I planned. "You're being a bad influence, Natalie Putnam."

She rolled her eyes as she began jotting down the information on the board up front. The girl was a whiz at multitasking. "Need I remind you who was the mastermind behind last night's Toblerone raid?"

I groaned. We'd come so close to breaking into Vanna's room and stealing her chocolate stash. I'd just needed a few more minutes to work on the booby-trap she'd set her room up with, and we would've been victorious.

"Seems you've forgotten the most important part, bestie." I risked Ms. Parker's wrath and elbowed Natalie. "You could've bypassed her magic as easily as breathing, so why was it left up to me?"

Disguising her sudden squeak with a cough into her hand, the truth was finally revealed. "I knew what would happen if we'd triggered it. There was no way I was going to take the brunt of it."

My eyes grew wide in mock horror. "You rat."

Shrugging, Natalie returned to writing. "You took one for the team, and for that, I am eternally grateful."

She had the audacity to place her hand over her chest as though her sentiments were heartfelt.

Letting out a soft *hmph*, I opened my own notebook and grabbed my pen. Just because my thoughts were scattered didn't mean I couldn't pretend to pay attention.

"Besides, be honest, you're just flustered because he was waiting for you just now." By him, she meant Mr. Westbrook.

"He's my teacher and advisor, dork."

There was no holding back a burst of laughter as she let out a girly sigh worthy of Scarlett O'Hara.

"You know what they say about people who protest too much." She followed that up with a nonchalant shrug. "Just saying."

"He's dating someone, Natalie. I'm not like that. Besides, I don't have time for love this semester. Guys are nothing but trouble." And to prove my point, I gestured to the guy who sat two tables in front of us over to the left. "If looks could kill, we'd all be in mourning right now."

"You mean the hottie that keeps staring at you like you're on the menu?" Natalie was incorrigible.

"What restaurants have you been eating at?" I glared right back at the blond-haired guy, challenging him to keep staring now that our eyes had met. "I wonder how long it'll take before he comes over here and tells us to shut up?"

"Lie to yourself all you want, but Eryx Strathos isn't someone to ignore. Admit it, you're intrigued." We were both staring at him now, and his cheeks reddened from the attention. There were women out there who would kill for the head of curls he had, or at the very least, pay a fortune at the salon.

The guy was attractive, but was I intrigued? Not really. I'd dated plenty of guys like Eryx, and he wasn't part of my "good girl" plan.

Before I could fire back with some snarky reply, I noticed something had dramatically changed . . . the room was so quiet you could hear a pin drop.

"Could you give us a demonstration, Miss Bell?" One glimpse at the teacher, and I could tell she knew full well I had zero idea what she was talking about. "Come up to the front of the class, if you will." Ms. Parker gestured to the spot right beside her.

"Sorry," Natalie uttered beneath her breath.

"See. Bad influence," I answered, taking my time getting up from my seat.

It's funny how much a room can change depending on the situation. For the most part, I loved coming in here because the walls were covered with all kinds of magical posters, shelves lined with an assortment of bottles filled with ingredients. Some serious potion-brewing could be accomplished in here because the academy had spared no expense in making sure we had everything we needed to succeed.

Yet, now? The walls felt like they could suffocate the very breath out of me. This could only end in embarrassment.

Scrambling to figure out what I was going to do, I studied the writing on the board, hoping to glean something from the notes. My relief was almost palpable when I recognized what today's lesson involved. Ironically, it was an elixir to help with anxiety. When I'd proven that I wasn't a complete flake and impressed Ms. Parker, I would need a freaking vat of the stuff.

Once I reached the front, she pointed to the ingredients that had already been mixed in the ceramic bowl. "What's next, Tempest? How do we finish the potion?"

I knew this spell work like the back of my hand. You didn't survive my family without a few tricks up your sleeve.

I started adding new herbs to the mixture.

"Explain as you go for the class, please." She took a few steps off to the side as though giving me the spotlight.

With all the confidence I could muster, I began reciting the instructions I'd learned so many years ago. Then, with a flourish of my hand, I activated the elixir with the appropriate incantation.

Two things happened, almost simultaneously.

Natalie yelled for me to duck.

The teacher lunged for me.

All I could see was a sharp flash of light, followed by a plume of nasty smelling smoke that rose up from the mixture as it popped like bacon cooking on a stove.

Whatever I had made had exploded.

Panic set in as memories from the horrible night back home came rushing back, and I reacted without thinking. Words came flying out of my mouth—the exact same incantation that burst my room into hot, flickering flames—and that was when everything went into slow motion.

Jets of red, hot fire shot from the tips of my fingers, scorching everything in its path. The magic sizzled across my skin, and despite Ms. Parker screaming for me to say the counter-spell, I foolishly waved my hands about. Students began to yell, some already rushing toward the exit as our teacher tackled me to the ground, smothering me with her body.

My magic instantly extinguished and left me aching with pain.

This was bad. This was so very, very bad.

"Are you okay?" Ms. Parker asked, her voice loud in my ear. "Tempest, I need you to answer me."

Somehow, I found enough sense to nod and mumble a quick yes. Tears were already streaming down my cheeks, the wetness no doubt leaving sooty streaks as it mixed with the ashes flying about in the air.

With a wave of her own hands, magic flowing off her tongue in rapid succession, Ms. Parker quickly contained the damage, abruptly stopping the smoke from spreading throughout the lab.

I tried to apologize, to give some kind of excuse that would show I'd done it by mistake, but all I could see was the now-contained destruction I'd caused. Burned counters and stools littered the front of the lab as my classmates who'd been sitting in the back stood there with wide eyes. Thankfully no one was hurt other than smoke-induced coughs. Those who'd managed to escape out of the room slowly filed back in.

All eyes were on me, including Natalie, who looked as though she wanted to rush forward and throw her arms around me. I'd shared a little about my past and how I'd come to attend the Academy, so she knew exactly what was at stake here.

I wanted a hole to open up beneath me to crawl into.

"Can anyone tell Miss Bell where she went wrong?" Shit, she was making this a teaching moment.

A number of hands shot up. Poor Natalie looked on helplessly from the back. She mouthed sorry to me, but if I was going to be honest, I deserved this. I should've swallowed my pride and told the teacher that I hadn't been paying attention. *Old habits die hard.*

I knew exactly whom she'd choose to answer. Sure enough, everyone lowered their arms as Eryx stepped forward, carefully avoiding the mess.

"It's important to ensure the elixir maintains balance while creating it. A little too much of one ingredient can have the reverse effect. Instead of calming the person, it can become volatile. Literally explosive." And with a smug look dedicated solely to me, Eryx sat back down.

"I'm so sorry," I said, addressing Ms. Parker. "I wasn't paying attention."

Her stern expression was void of empathy. "I think that was more than just being a little distracted, Tempest. We're going to need to discuss this with your advisor." It was at that moment I saw the hem of her shirt was a little scorched. Seems she hadn't been standing back far enough. "As for the rest of you, you're excused. Make sure you see the infirmary if you start feeling sick from inhaling all the smoke, and I'll see you next class."

That was the down side of going to a magical school—there'd be no extended time off due to rebuilding. By this time tomorrow, the lab would be back to fully functioning, all evidence of the fire gone.

I kept my gaze trained to the floor in front of me. When Natalie passed by, she squeezed my hand in support. I tried to smile as though it didn't matter. The problem was, it did. I would need to work harder.

"I'll see you back in our room, okay?" Even she didn't sound too confident in that.

As Ms. Parker and I walked out of the classroom and toward the administration offices in Halstein, it was hard not to miss the way Eryx shook his head with disapproval.

Yep, cute or not, there was no way I'd ever date that guy. I wasn't into jerks.

Not that it mattered anyway.

I was in too much trouble, and I had a feeling my social life was about to take a huge hit.

CHAPTER 2

"This is becoming a habit."

I wasn't about to disagree with Micah. That's exactly how this looked.

The meeting between the Regent members, Ms. Parker, and Mr. Westbrook had felt like it would never end. The sight of seeing Saundra Beaumont and Elsmed Fairchild studying me with a formidable intensity had all but reduced me to a quivering mess. As tempting as it had been for me to press my ear up against the heavy wooden doors and try to hear what my fate would be, I'd chosen instead to sit on the bench and stare at my hands.

Shit, how had this happened again?

I'd been hiding this secret of mine for so long, out of fear that should anyone know that I could perform magic other than water I'd be in big trouble. My coven feared change—expecting everyone to keep with the status quo and play their part. The truth, however, was something I'd never uttered out loud. What they feared was someone usurping their authority by having powers greater than their own. The high priestess prided herself in being the witch who channeled the most energy and could wield it with the most potency. She saw me as a threat—someone to silence—and had it not been for Micah's intervention, she would've gotten her wish. I couldn't threaten her ruling over the coven if I didn't hold any magic.

I expected Mr. Westbrook to tell me the Regents had made their decision and that they required me to come inside the room to receive my punishment. A feeling of dread and absolute failure sat heavy on my chest, making it almost impossible to hold back my tears. I didn't want to leave Sun & Moon and lose all the wonderful things that had come into my life.

But the truth was finally out. After standing before everyone and answering all their questions, I'd confessed the one secret I'd never shared. You could almost hear a pin drop with how still and silent the group became. It didn't bode well for me.

And now Micah was waiting for my response.

"Any regrets?" I slowly replied, not wanting this conversation to start because if there was one thing I knew—what had a beginning always had an ending. "How long do I have before I pack my bags?"

Micah sat down beside me, and for a second, I didn't think he was going to say anything. He quietly studied the students that passed by, unaware that my future was hanging in the balance. I heard him start to speak, but when nothing followed, I dared to sneak a peek.

He was measuring his words with careful deliberation. "I managed to convince them not to expel you."

I couldn't help it. My breath exploded outwardly. "How many times are you going to save my life?" I cried, staring at the man with amazement. Shifting in my seat, I turned so I could look at him directly. "I don't know how I can ever . . ."

That's when the other shoe dropped. Shaking his head, Micah interrupted my excited apologies. "You'll continue to be a student here, but they've placed you on academic probation. From now on, you'll be meeting with Dr. Lavinia each Friday afternoon instead of with me, and based on her assessment by the end of the semester, the Regents will convene again and determine whether your probationary status needs to be extended."

I let that sink in. This was a gift—one I hadn't expected or felt I deserved.

From what I'd heard, the doctor was the therapist on campus and had already earned a reputation for someone who knew her shit. If I was to have Dr. Lavinia on my side, too, maybe I'd survive being on probation. I just hoped she really did have the patience of a saint because she'd need it.

"Done," I gushed, eager to prove that I could be trusted. "Whatever they want, I'll do it perfectly. Thank you, Micah! Thank you so much."

I was so caught up in my own exhilaration and sense of relief that I hadn't noticed Micah's lack of celebrating with me. He still wore a somber look that told me he had much more on his mind.

"They know, Tempest. While they believed your statement that it was an accident, they exercised due diligence and reached out to your parents." His admission knocked the wind out of me—ripping the good news from my grasp just when I thought I'd escaped. "They spoke with Ms. Chambers."

Sweet Goddess, they knew everything.

"And next they wanted to know why I recommended you to take the trials, knowing your history. That's what took so long—my having to explain that despite all the evidence to the contrary, you deserved a chance to be here."

If the next words out of his mouth were that he was fired, I was ready to storm back into the room and make them listen.

"This wasn't your fault, though. I'm the one that wasn't one hundred percent truthful. I didn't disclose my under-developed magic or ask for help. They can't pin the blame on you, Mr. Westbrook. They can't." Suddenly I was crying again—not for me, but for the only person to ever take a chance on me. "Let me talk to them again." I quickly stood, whirling about to head to the door.

He grabbed my hand, stopping me. "They've already left. The Regents are extremely busy, and there's a good chance you'll make it worse by going in there ready to battle." Micah patted the seat beside him. "Listen to me, Tempest. You're going to graciously accept your consequence and become the exemplary student I know you're capable of being. Next, you'll meet with Dr. Lavinia and tell her everything. Big, small, whatever . . . you will be an open book for her. No more lies. No more secrets."

I brushed away the tears that still fell. "Whatever you want. I won't let you down."

A spark of frustration infiltrated his tone. "This isn't about me, Tempest. I will always be in your corner, but this is your life. Take responsibility and decide right now not to disappoint yourself. The Regents have made it crystal clear that this will be the last time I can intervene on your behalf. See this for what it is—a clean slate."

I let out a self-deprecating snort. "Another one you mean." Who was I kidding? Part of me wondered if I'd been a cat in a past life because I was burning through these second-chances like they were lives. "I'm a magnet for trouble."

"Then figure it out. Talk with the therapist. Be your own best advocate." Rising from the bench, Micah offered me his hand and pulled me up. "You can only live so long on borrowed time. Choose."

I thanked him for his help, even though my words felt woefully weak. I resisted the urge to make him promises because I knew they would fall short. The only way I could make this right was by doing what he said—choosing to be better—by taking the feelings in my heart and turning them into actions.

My phone vibrated in my jeans pocket for the hundredth time. I'd pretty much ignored it, not wanting to reply to Natalie until I knew my fate.

Headed to the room.

Her response was almost instant. **Everything okay?**

Despite how shitty I felt and the guilt that gnawed away in my gut, I had to acknowledge that I would get through this. Mistakes happened—even big ones—but they could be survived.

Tell you when I get there.

Then as an afterthought, I added: **Make sure there's chocolate.**

CHAPTER 3

I was in love with the library.

I understood how ironic that sentiment was because until coming to SMA, I'd rarely stepped foot inside one. Not even when I had an assignment due. That was the beauty of everything being available on the Internet. This, however, was incredible enough to convert me.

It wasn't just the smell of books that appealed, but the calming ambience magic had created with the glowing orbs that were spread throughout. Whoever had thought to use them was a genius.

Natalie and I liked to joke about getting lost in the stacks—that for all we knew there was a monster deep in the center of the library that liked to feast on wayward students.

Rumors said there were mystical creatures that dwelled in the shadows, scurrying between the aisles, searching for who knew what.

I couldn't believe the variety of subjects the library had. From the simple theory texts on magic to complicated studies on the supernatural creatures we shared the world with. Some made my brain hurt when I took a peek inside—pages covered with math equations, archaic languages I was pretty sure didn't exist anymore, and frantic scribbles about the biology and neurological similarities between a griffon and a minotaur.

None of the shelves had a speck of dust on them. I wondered if it was up to Vidar Sveen, one of the students who volunteered between classes and his own course load. We'd spoken only a few times, but he seemed cool enough.

The sound of a muted conversation caught my attention, and because I lacked any kind of impulse control, I strayed from my exploration and headed toward the sound. I crossed my fingers that whatever I found wouldn't have a craving for witch flesh.

The closer I got, the more I could hear that my imagination had once again gotten it wrong. The voices were definitely male, and with a few more steps, I saw the telltale short black dreads of Vidar. He was obviously trying to give the other guy directions. Walking as quietly as I could, I froze mid-step when I saw who it was.

Eryx Freaking Strathos.

I was surprised I hadn't felt the waves of disdain ebbing off him whenever I saw him. I didn't know what I'd done to upset him, or whether he'd judged me too harshly, but half way through the semester and I still hadn't seen him smile at me.

Which was a pity because the guy was undeniably hot.

Suddenly Eryx laughed, and damn if the sound didn't make butterflies flutter in my traitorous stomach. He had a great laugh —a deep laugh that resonated from within his chest.

Goddess help me.

I did the only thing a self-respecting witch who had vowed to remain celibate this semester could do.

I turned around and fled in the opposite direction. I didn't even bother trying to disguise my hurried retreat. Perhaps a new rumor would begin about a ghostly herd of elephants thundering through the bookshelves.

All I knew was that I couldn't be caught there eavesdropping.

My footsteps slowed down, and I went back to my original intention.

Natalie and I had been asked by Fin and Taylor, fellow

students, to come up with a cup that supplied never-ending beer—a request that had excited us because exploring the fun side of magic was becoming our thing—a way for us to channel our mischief. We'd already started mixing drinks to find the perfect recipes, and so far, we'd failed in an epic way. I was still a little wary of accepting the challenge now that I was on probation, but Natalie had somehow managed to convince me that my promise to the Regents that I'd walk the straight and narrow path didn't mean I should avoid fun all together. We'd do the research and enchantment together. Easy.

"Okay, where would I be if I was a fun spell book?" I murmured softly, going back to reading the spines as I passed by. "Perhaps a book that shouldn't be in the hands of a freshman witch but easily located through sheer persistence."

Just as I slipped another book back in its place, a loud clatter rang out in the darkened parts where I was, and an illuminated orb went skittering off, extinguishing what little light I had.

I wasn't necessarily afraid of the dark, but I couldn't shake the sudden eeriness that swamped me.

Don't freak out.

Don't freak out.

Don't freak out . . . *Holy shit, what just touched me?*

Twisting about so my back was to the shelf, I desperately tried to make sense of what was happening. Something brushed my leg, followed by a tittering noise that sounded uncannily like laughter.

There was no way I would be able to stifle the shriek now rising up my throat. I was done being brave or needing to look cool. I didn't care if I was jumping at shadows or my imagination was running wild again. Bravery didn't matter much when you became some creature's dinner.

Edging my way back to where I thought I'd last seen light, I didn't get far until I felt something—a hand.

A big hand.

"Ahh . . ." I started, but before it could begin echoing through the library and alerting others, that same large hand clamped over my mouth, followed by me being tugged hard into the owner of said hand.

My mind raced to remember the different self-defense spells I'd learned throughout the years as I fought against my attacker. It didn't matter that I couldn't physically utter the words. I knew if I tried hard enough, they could manifest from my thoughts.

"Damn it," came the angry curse, and my heart dropped like an anvil. I knew that voice, who it belonged to, and frankly, I would've rather been eaten by the shadows. "Would you stop trying to spell me?"

I lashed out with my elbow, gratified when I heard an *umph* of pain. His hand dropped, and I could finally give him a piece of my mind.

"Eryx Strathos," I said through clenched teeth. "Get off me!"

I waited for him to step completely back, but instead he pressed his body even harder against mine. "Trust me, this isn't my idea of fun either."

His breath was warm against my skin, sending goosebumps up and down my body. I hated knowing I reacted that way.

"Is this how you get girls to date you?" I retorted, my voice as icy as I could make it. "Seems a little despera—"

He cut me off again, this time placing just two fingers across my lips.

"For the love of Zeus, would you please shut up?" he whispered, and despite the fact I was painfully aware of his body, there was no mistaking the edge of fear that filled his demand.

I did what I was told. My eyes widened as I looked up and met his gaze. For a jerk, he sure did have pretty brown eyes.

An energy surge pulsed around us, and the sound of little claws retreated back into the darkness. A second later, the light orbs returned as if nothing had happened.

"It took me a few days to realize whenever one of the globes goes out, magic will correct itself so not to panic. While I've never seen the creatures that lurk in the library—"

It was my turn to interrupt. "We've heard the rumors."

Eryx nodded, and the blond curls that framed his face gently bounced. "And no one wants to be a statistic, right?"

He still felt so unbelievably close—enough that my breathing started to match his.

He didn't move. Neither did I.

His finger slowly traced the side of my cheek as he searched my gaze. Every cell in my body screamed to look away—to break the connection we were held by. That would've been the smart thing, but instead I licked my lips, gingerly biting the bottom as I contemplated how it would feel to kiss him.

I knew the second he realized we were still pressed up against each other because his own lips parted, his head dipping ever-so-slightly.

"Eryx," I whispered.

His features softened at the sound of his name. "Tempest."

I loved how his mouth was shaped whenever he spoke. He had a perfectly kissable mouth—lips that promised to rob you of thought and breath should you ever feel them against your own. Why hadn't I ever noticed that?

I rose up on my tiptoes, reaching for him—my body betraying me. All that mattered was him and this moment. I could beat myself up later for breaking my number one rule this semester. For right now, I simply wanted to see what it would feel like.

We were so close.

"Tempest," he murmured again. He moved to cradle the side of my face. Anticipation was all but killing me because he was right there.

And then it was over.

Before I could register the disappointment that swirled inside my chest, his next words felt like a much-needed dowsing of frigid water.

"You're welcome. Try not to get lost in the stacks. I won't always be around to rescue you, Princess." Eryx finally took a few steps back, and the tenderness he'd just shown was gone. He was back to looking at me as though he wanted to escape the conversation.

Squashing the hurt that bubbled in my gut, I decided that two could play that game. I knew how to play the role of bitch well.

"I was fine without you, jerk." Shoving past him, I threw him the haughtiest look I could muster. "Perhaps you should keep your hands to yourself instead of assaulting people." With an extra flounce and head toss, I all but ran to where I'd last left Natalie.

I met my roomie half way. Throwing my arms around her neck, I didn't bother hiding my relief at seeing her.

"You okay?" she asked, patting my back. "You were gone for a while, so I figured you might've been lost."

It was on the tip of my tongue to tell her what happened, but that would be a conversation for the privacy of our dorm room. "Yeah, I got turned about and kind of roamed around a bit." Emerging to where our books were, I quickly shoved everything into my large messenger bag. "And now I'm starving, so dinner?"

Natalie looked over my shoulder to where we'd just been. The girl was more perceptive than I realized.

She threaded her arm through mine. "Here's hoping it's something delicious."

I fought the urge to turn around and kept my gaze forward.

"Me too, Natalie. Me too."

CHAPTER 4

This was not how I wanted to spend my evening while everyone else on campus was enjoying the start to their weekend.

Staring down at the textbook in my lap, I tried not to think about the frustration swirling about inside me. Campus life was always busy during the weekend, and I didn't want to miss a thing. I had this philosophy that if you worked hard, you had to play just as hard—balance. Unfortunately, my grades didn't agree, and if I wanted to prove that I'd changed and could make better choices, it started by making certain sacrifices.

My roomie had offered to stay in and check out the latest releases on Netflix, and as good as that sounded, I didn't want to be the reason she, Vanna, and Marina were cooped up. Even the offer of eating from Rest In Pizza wasn't enough for me to say yes, even if their pizza was to die for—pun intended.

Instead, once I got bored of playing casino slot games on my phone, I scooped up our kitty and carried her down to Hel Tower's great room along with my homework. Perhaps a change in scenery was what I needed.

The cat had shown up a few weeks after classes had started and instantly claimed Natalie and me. I'd never heard of a familiar choosing two witches, but the young kitty was the perfect blending of two cats—half black and half ginger. The uniqueness didn't stop there either. She also had two different colored eyes—blue and green.

We'd both said her name out loud. Mystic. We quickly made her a little bed to sleep on, which she promptly ignored, instead choosing to curl up wherever she wanted.

"Looks like it's you and me tonight, sweetie," I cooed into her soft fur. "Time to try to focus again." Mystic started to purr in response. "I know. It isn't particularly glamorous, but that's what you get when you claim a witch who procrastinates her homework." She nudged at my fingertips as I gently scratched behind her ear.

The large room was empty as I slipped inside and looked around. Whoever had decorated the space had a real flair and passion for all things gothic. A black crystal chandelier hung from the ceiling, the lights sparkling off the black wallpaper and grey embroidered curtains. What I liked the most was the red that lined the insides of the bookshelves, giving the room a dramatic pop of color.

I flopped down onto the chaise seat. "Looks like we have the room to ourselves."

All at once the silence settled. I wouldn't be surprised if I would start hearing my own heartbeat. The sensation was all kinds of eerie.

I huffed, bored already.

Mystic seemed oblivious to my heavy sighs. She'd found something to entertain her as she stalked and pounced something only she could see. The kitty was definitely tenacious. I expected to hear a tearing sound when her claws connected with the wall—the result of her leaping through the air. When she landed on her paws, Mystic turned her blue-green eyes to me and meowed.

"I have no idea what you're hunting." I laughed. Yet something had me sit forward on the edge of the seat, squinting for a better look. "Is it a bug?"

Fear rumbled deep inside me. I hated creepy-crawlies. My

philosophy was to get the hell out of the way, burning the place down while I escaped.

Only, that hit a little too close to home. While I wouldn't strike a match, I'd already started conjuring fire without thinking. If my coven truly knew how much my magic was growing, they would never have allowed Micah to bring me here. They hated anything that was different or didn't match their expectations. I was meant to be a witch with water abilities. One element only.

Mystic wiggled her cute little butt, her tail swishing back and forth in preparation for leaping again. Thankfully, she missed the wallpaper and had actually landed up on the second from the top shelf.

"Ahh, I get it. You're trying to find a comfy spot to sleep." Sure enough, she turned about in a small circle before curling up in a ball of black and ginger fur. Her contented purrs soon replaced the silence of the room.

I stared up at the chandelier as I relaxed back in the chair. This was impossible. I knew I could be high maintenance, but since when did I need to be entertained constantly and kept from boredom. Did I really need to be surrounded by people to feel comfortable? I tried to slow my thoughts.

Take a deep breath, Tempest. Enjoy some solitude. It's good for the soul.

I was pathetic. Trying to relax simply made me feel more uptight. Perhaps my chakras were out of alignment.

Leaning over, I grabbed my schoolwork again, giving another glance over to Mystic who was sound asleep. I couldn't help but envy the small creature. Life must be blissful being a cat.

For the next hour, I gave it my best effort, often re-reading the same paragraph over and over. When the words started to blur together, I knew I was done sitting here by myself, so I walked over to the bookshelf to see if something there might interest me.

A break for my brain instead of relentlessly trying to cram information into it.

The books that were neatly lined up in a row were titles I hadn't ever thought to read before. There were the usual classics:

Moby Dick, War & Peace, The Grapes of Wrath, as well as stories I'd read countless times—*Pride & Prejudice, Wuthering Heights*, and *The Picture of Dorian Gray*. Seeing that there weren't any recently published stories displayed, I made a mental note to order some through Sedona's Shelf Indulgence. Maybe then sitting in this room wouldn't bore me to tears.

"Come on, sweetie," I said, and I carefully tried lifting Mystic up without disturbing her too much. Her body was floppy for all of a second, and then, as her eyes popped open, she twisted to get away from me.

"I know, I know. I'm mean. I should let you sleep, but I can't just leave you down here."

Well, I could. Familiars had free range of the tower, and in regards to Mystic that was especially true because, frankly as a cat, she did whatever the heck she wanted anyway. The thing was, asleep or not, I enjoyed her company.

So I lied some more. "I'll give you some catnip when we get back upstairs."

My fingers brushed lightly over her body, and despite her not wanting to move, Mystic stretched out as long as she could beneath my touch.

The movement made a few books topple to the side and crash into the black granite Valkyrie bust that acted as a book end.

"Shit!" I exclaimed. My hands shook as I desperately tried to keep the bust from toppling over or worse, falling to the floor. The room was carpeted, but knowing my luck, the carved stone would shatter into a million pieces and prove unfixable.

Crisis averted. Pushing the bust back into its previous position, I was too busy congratulating myself to see if anything happened.

I wasn't too distracted to hear a rather loud click, though.

"Was that you, Mystic?" I asked as I tried to listen for it again.

Nothing.

I touched the bust again, waiting.

Nothing.

I tried moving over and was rewarded by a dull throb in my

foot because I'd stepped wrong. Using the shelving unit to regain my balance, I did notice that it wasn't as sturdy as I assumed.

I rattled the shelf a little. It was definitely loose, yet when I pushed forward, something clicked. There was no budging the unit now.

"Hmm," I murmured. "Looks like we have a mystery here, Mystic. What do you think?" I stared at my familiar, expecting her to answer me. The only message I saw reflected in her unique eyes was that she thought I was certifiable. Cats couldn't talk. At least this one didn't.

I spent the next few minutes trying to make that sound again. I pushed. I prodded. I searched to no avail. Finally, I had to admit that I'd probably imagined it. Maybe what I needed most was a nap.

"Okay, girl. I guess it's time to head upstairs." Before I could pick her up for real this time, Mystic had different plans. Stretching as she stood up, it almost seemed as though she stared at me before . . . she lifted her paw and pressed it against the Valkyrie bust.

The click was louder this time.

And I saw exactly what happened.

There was some kind of trigger mechanism attached to the bookshelf that separated it from the wall. Instead of pressing against the shelf, I decided to pull on it and see what would happen.

Like a door, it swung away from its previous position, revealing a secret passageway.

"Holy shit," I uttered, my eyes widening in surprise. I stood at the top of what looked like stone stairs that went downward. "Does the tower have some kind of sex dungeon or something?"

Sticking my head through the hole in the wall, I tried to see where the stairs would lead. Magic flared the second it sensed me there, and light illuminated the way down.

There was no way I wasn't going to explore.

"Mystic, you're going to have to come with me now and forget your nap. We're about to have an adventure." She dropped to the floor, brushing up against my legs before disappearing through the doorway. There was no fear in that kitty at all.

I thought about calling Natalie and Vanna and telling them what happened. Maybe I should've seen if anyone else was in the tower.

Common sense should have prevailed, but I sucked at impulse control. All I needed to do was check it out first, and if—and only if—it led to something cool, then I'd call my roommate. There was no way I'd ruin her fun with the others if it was simply a dusty old storage room filled with discarded furniture.

With a deep breath, I took the plunge and began the descent down the stairs. They weren't too steep and thankfully, there was a side railing attached to the wall. Once I reached the bottom, I gazed to the ground and saw my kitty there, waiting.

"This is it, Mystic. Any guess at what's in there?"

She meowed and placed her paw on the stone doorframe.

Never in my wildest dreams would I have guessed what I found. This changed everything, and would make Hel Tower go down in legend as the best freaking tower to live in.

Stepping completely inside and turning about as magical lighted orbs flared into existence, I grinned like the Cheshire Cat in Alice in Wonderland.

Wine. Bottles and bottles of wine.

Barrels and barrels of what I could only assume were magical moonshine or something.

Hel Tower had a secret basement.

Scratch that.

Hel Tower had a freaking secret alcohol cellar, and I'd just uncovered the holy grail of college treasures.

I needed to call the girls and break the news that we were about to become legends.

Mental note: don't trust your memory if you've been drinking wine.

Ten minutes later and my room looked like a tornado had landed in the center of it and sent everything flying. No matter how hard I looked, or cursed, I couldn't find my phone, and I was beyond impatient.

"Come on think, Tempest. Where was the last place you remember seeing it?" I closed my eyes and tried to retrace where I'd been today. It wasn't really a hard list to imagine. I'd gone to the dining hall twice, been in my room, and . . . down in the cellar. I'd bet money that I'd find my phone down there.

"Wish me luck, Mystic," I called out over my shoulder as I closed the door and made my way to the great room. The halls were quiet, with only the stony Valkyrie that stood at the base of the staircase I trekked up and down each day there to bear witness to my movement.

"Don't mind me, Gladys." I waved before coming to a sudden halt. "Actually, while I have a few seconds, I have a bone to pick with you." Stepping up closer and rising up onto my tiptoes, I did my best to look the silent Valkyrie in the eyes. "Here I thought we had some kind of connection, yet you totally failed to mention there was a hidden wine cellar." As if I could hear her trying to respond, I shook my head. "No need to apologize, I get it. You probably wanted to keep it a secret so you and all the other statues could have something to drink in between the semesters. Just stings a little. Guess I need to earn your trust a little more."

Waving over my shoulder, I snorted out loud at how crazy I must've looked and was grateful that I was alone. Natalie loved to tease me about my naming the formidable statue—choosing to ignore the fact that there were more appropriate and respectful titles to pick from and instead, giving her something random instead.

All I could answer was that it was just my thing and it was part of why she loved me so much—quirks and all.

Entering the great room, I found it still empty, which made it easy because I didn't have time to explain why there was a secret doorway in the bookshelves. I took the steps two at a time, and sure enough, there on one of the barrels sat my phone.

As a second thought, I grabbed another bottle of wine to replace the one I'd already emptied and didn't waste any more time. I pushed the shelf closed and shifted the bust back so it didn't look like it'd been moved. One of the books fell over and the title caught my eye.

This book wasn't here earlier. There was no way I would've missed it. I tucked the volume under my arm and headed back to the room—plans cancelled because I had a new mission.

The contents of the book would help the research we needed for the special cup. The quick glance I'd given the table of contents told me that this was the magic we'd need.

I was about to get my witch on.

I guess the saying was true that alcohol was liquid courage. Had I been completely sober, I wouldn't have made the mistake of trying a new spell while drinking from the bottle I'd brought upstairs from the cellar. Don't ask me how I went from a frantic search for my phone to sitting on the floor, inside the pentacle shape I'd formed with consecrated candles.

"There's no harm in trying right?" I whispered to no one in particular. Mystic was still sleeping on my bed, so it was just me, the book I'd found, and a half-empty bottle of wine. The more I drank, the more confident I felt that I could handle whatever magic the incantation generated.

Once I'd read through the notes about the laws of replacement and movement, I studied next the different spells the book's author had included. They seemed easy enough, and I didn't know whether it was the wine doing the thinking for me, rationalizing away any concerns, or my own sense of confidence, but the magic involved looked relatively basic.

Padding across the room, I opened up the small wooden wardrobe Natalie and I had assigned to store our witchy things. Inside, there were candles of all colors, bottles with a variety of herbs, and a small collection of favorite manuals. While it was nothing in comparison to the academy's libraries, they were items we wanted close to hand.

Removing a bunch of candles, I cleared away a spot on the floor, so I could begin setting up for the ritual. Candles were placed at each point of the pentacle, and crystals placed in spots to help amplify and balance the energy I would need to manifest and mold. I loved this aspect of being a witch—the methodical arrangement as I began setting my intentions.

Once I was confident everything was correct, I knelt beside one of the candles, and pulled the book down from the bed. I hadn't memorized the spell, so I still needed to reference it.

"Okay, ready." I eyed the bottle and took one last sip. "One never-ending cup spell coming up!" I clapped my hands together and took a deep breath.

Calling the four elements, I opened up my circle, dedicating the magic I was asking to create to the Goddess. I could be flippant in my daily life, but I knew better than to not show her the respect she deserved.

One by one, I lit the candles, smiling softly as they flickered to life. Adding the flowers and herbs I'd crushed with a pestle and mortar, I then poured the ingredients into the bowl at the center of my pentacle. I knew the exact moment when the Goddess accepted my offering. There was a bright flash followed by the comforting scent of sunshine, rain in the air, and my favorite, the salty ocean.

I worked quietly, following the instructions to the letter. The spell required concentration, so it was hard not to shriek in surprise when Mystic suddenly leapt from the bed and knocked over one of the candles. Before I could stop her, her tail swished hard and struck some crystals and the bowl that held my offering and a piece of parchment I was getting ready to add flame to.

"Mystic!" I exclaimed, breaking my focus. Frantically, I reached to pick her up, but she slipped my attempt, and in the process knocked over the wine bottle. The floor was now an absolute mess. There would be no magic tonight.

"What am I going to do with you, kitty?" I asked as I looked to make sure none of her fur was singed from bumping the candle.

"We could've been in real trouble there, sweet girl." Familiar or not, I was hopelessly attached to the cat. I would never forgive myself had something gone wrong and she got hurt.

I sat there, legs crossed, cradling Mystic against my chest. I slowly stroked her soft fur, and beneath my touch, I could feel her little body thrumming.

"That scared you didn't it?" I let out a pent-up breath. "That scared me as well. How about I clean this up and keep the spell between you and me, okay?" I had a feeling Natalie wouldn't be too impressed that I hadn't waited for her.

It didn't take me long to replace everything in the wardrobe and wipe up the spilled wax. I knew it would've been easier to just say a few words of magic to take care of the mess, but I felt this was the least I could do.

Tired, my head pounding, I finally crawled into bed and under the covers, making sure Mystic was by my side.

Had I been at home, there would've been hell to pay for doing an unknown spell alone. I would be on the receiving end of a lengthy lecture by my mother, and then have to endure the exact same thing from my coven leader. Independent practice was frowned on. Sun & Moon encouraged curiosity, but within reason. I'd gotten cocky—buzzed. Nothing went wrong.

I was on the verge of sleep, my body heavy with exhaustion and wine. Mystic's purr grew deeper, and for a moment, I imagined my wrist burning right where my tattoo was.

The last thought I had was of Eryx. He would've judged me the entire night, glaring at me with those sexy ass eyes of his. That, and I was in for one hell of a hangover if the loud gonging sound in my head was any indication.

CHAPTER 5

"Tempest, wake up!"

Buried beneath my comforter, I barely managed to mumble before Natalie ripped back my blanket, exposing me to the brightness of our room. My hangover was in full effect, but that wasn't the reason why I was hiding away from the world.

"Leave me be," I complained as I feebly attempted to snatch my bedding from her tight grasp. "I feel like death today, so I made the executive decision not to leave my bed." When she wouldn't relent, I buried my head beneath my pillows.

"The entire campus is in chaos this morning, and you're missing it all because you drank too much last night." Plonking herself down hard beside me, Natalie started poking me with her finger. "So much for doing your homework, right?"

Cracking my eyes open and peeking out from beneath a pillow, I resisted the urge to gag. My mouth felt like something had died inside it, and no amount of swallowing got rid of the taste.

"Okay, you've got my attention." While I didn't move a muscle, I widened my peephole so I could see her. "Just please, for the love of all that is sacred, whisper."

She rolled her eyes. "Guess what showed up over night?"

I blinked at her in response.

"Fine, I'll give you a clue. It's huge. It's in the courtyard. It measures time and means something crazy is about to happen." My roommate's enthusiasm felt like a drill straight to my brain.

Another hourglass.

Shit. Rumors had quickly spread around campus that something mystical was happening—students being called to conquer challenges that often resulted in mayhem. People had already died, and whenever the hourglass disappeared, it was often with a sigh of relief. After each occurrence, the administration would act as if all was well, and things would briefly go back to normal. But this would make the fifth time it had surfaced.

That wasn't what put the fear of the Goddess in my heart, though.

There was another story that circulated about how those students involved all shared one similar trait—their tattoos burned hot and a smaller version of the hourglass branded their wrist, over the Academy and tower logo.

My skin still felt as though someone had pressed lava-hot steel over it. That was the only benefit of being somewhat drunk still when I'd awoken earlier to go pee. The wine had acted as a pain reducer of sorts, but as the sun rose, and I sobered up, the flesh over my pulse point throbbed with invisible blisters.

I had the hourglass.

The gong I had heard before passing out wasn't my impending hangover. It was the sound of a new threat being released.

I was beyond screwed.

"Why aren't you saying anything?" Natalie asked impatiently. She finally tugged away the pillow and threw it over onto her bed. "Aren't you even the slightest bit curious what this means? Hel Tower is already a buzz with theories over who is affected, and Vanna and Marina just left to go see the huge hourglass for themselves."

Slowly sitting up, I reached for the lavender balm that I kept by my bed. The moment I caught the familiar scent, I let out a soft breath and inhaled even deeper. That's when I saw my tattoo, and panic set in all over again.

I couldn't let Natalie see it. Not until I knew exactly what it meant.

Tugging my sleeves down so they covered my wrists, I faked a smile. "Have the Regents implemented a curfew or anything?"

It wasn't hard to remember the way it crimped everyone's style last time, and how campus late at night had become like a ghost town. We mostly stuck to our own towers whenever the Regents issued the order, enabling us to still party on the weekends.

Natalie shrugged. "Not that I've heard of, but you need to get the hell up so we can join the others. Drinking by yourself doesn't mean you get to hide out in here all day. Take some Tylenol and get dressed."

That was one thing about Natalie that made me laugh. The witch could be bossy as hell when she wanted to.

"Okay, give me thirty minutes to quickly shower and feel human again, then I'll meet you down at the quad." Ever so gingerly, I swung my legs over the side of the bed, pushing Natalie off in the process. "If you truly love me, you'll be waiting with a huge cup of hot coffee." The room spun, and I winced. "Make that two cups. Please."

"I didn't know you could be this pitiful when you're this hungover, Tempest." She bent over and picked up one of the empty wine bottles. "I can't believe you didn't leave me any, you lush."

That's when I remembered. "I found a hidden cellar last night." Stumbling over to my dresser, I began pulling out the clothes I'd be wearing today. "I meant to tell you last night, but I got distracted, and everything's a blur after that."

Natalie wasn't too careful as she grabbed me by the shoulders and twirled me around, her voice unbearably loud in my ear. "You found what?"

I waved her away. "Shower first. Coffee next. New discovery then."

There was a rumble in my stomach before the most unladylike sour belch erupted from my mouth.

She didn't bother hiding the shudder that pulsed through her body. "Holy shit, Tempest. Can I suggest you brush your teeth first? Please . . . you could kill someone with that breath."

She wafted her hand frantically as if she could somehow keep the nasty stench from melting her face off.

I didn't utter another word, instead grabbing my toiletries and clothes before heading to the bathroom. All I could think of was standing beneath the hot stream of water for the next few hours, but deep down I knew there'd be no hiding.

I'd been marked.

What the hell had I done last night?

I remembered.

Standing in the shower, willing the water to wash away the fog that clouded my mind, bits and pieces slowly came back. It wasn't enough that I'd finished off almost two bottles of wine. I'd also performed magic—new spells from the book I'd found in the great room. I didn't need to be told how idiotic that decision had been, and somehow, I didn't think using the excuse I'd been intoxicated would appease anyone.

I forced myself to overlook my wrist. It wasn't that I was delusional and somehow thought by ignoring the obvious, I could somehow pretend nothing had changed. The fact was that I could tell in my gut that from here on out, if I didn't act promptly and figure this shit out, my future here at Sun & Moon was undoubtedly in jeopardy.

The problem was I needed more information. How could I face whatever challenge I'd conjured if I didn't know the first place to begin looking? How did the others handle the arrival of the hourglass? Did they have to simply wait for the threat to reveal itself or were they proactive and went out searching?

For the hundredth time in as many minutes, I contemplated telling Natalie. Going to talk with Mr. Westbrook also seemed like the smartest choice, but his disappointed expression still haunted me from the other day. How many times would I have to prove that I wasn't a risk before the man gave up and washed his hands of me entirely?

And Natalie? We joked about how we were sisters from another mister, that our friendship went beyond mere roommates, but could it really withstand dragging her into this mess with me? People always said they'd have your back in times of trouble. My gut said Natalie would stand by my side, despite the cost.

Thing was, if this situation spiraled out of control, did I really want her sharing the brunt of the damage with me just so I wouldn't have to face it alone? Sometimes protecting the ones who matter most to you meant keeping them in the dark.

"You've got this, Tempest," I whispered to myself. Wiping away the condensation covering the mirror, I leaned forward and looked at my reflection. "You've been in trouble before and gotten through it. This is no different. No one needs to know until it's absolutely necessary."

I could almost see the imaginary angel and devil perched on each shoulder warring with themselves as they yelled for me to listen to them. It wasn't that I couldn't see both sides of the story—the pros and cons. There was just too much at stake.

"Better to ask forgiveness than permission." My voice was firmer now, my mind made up. No need to overthink and worry. All I needed to do was undo the magic I'd cast last night, and everything would go back to normal.

A clattering sound disturbed my solitude, and I twirled about, my hand gripping the front of my towel. I hadn't heard anyone come in, but that didn't mean anything because the bathroom had been enchanted to provide a calming ambience for those using it. Even with all the stone and bare floors, there was hardly ever an echo or din.

"Who's there?" I called out. When no one replied, I dismissed the noise and continued getting dressed. I was almost ready to slip into my flip-flops and head back to my room when a series of crashes drew my attention.

Glass. That's what the noise was. Like thousands of crystal orbs had shattered over the stone floor.

My heart pounded hard in my chest. Was this how the challenge started? I raced toward the crunching sound of heavy footsteps, and almost screamed when I came face to face with the largest creature I'd ever seen.

Whatever the beast was, all I could focus on were the massive claws that scraped against the ground, the tufts of fur that sprouted out from between its paws. There was no telling the species due to the way bones jutted out haphazardly—as though it was a mutation of a mutation—sinews taut and muscles twisting to reveal throbbing red veins. Just looking at the creature was horrifying, and when I caught the first whiff of its heated breath, the only word I could use to describe it was rancid. The more I inhaled the tainted air, the stronger the urge to vomit became.

The most pitiful wailing came out from somewhere deep within the being.

Stepping backward until my back hit the wall, I was trapped and unable to escape. Each time I tried to carefully creep my way toward the exit, the beast countered my move, effectively blocking me.

If I didn't know better, it was engaging me in a game of cat and mouse where I was its prey.

Goddess help me, was this thing going to eat me?

I avoided looking at the creature directly in the face, terrified over what I'd find. If this was the state of its deformed body, I couldn't fathom its head.

"Be brave." I steeled myself and lifted my gaze. My astonished gasp said it all.

This poor thing was hideous.

The mystery beast stared back at me with familiar eyes.

One green.

One blue.

Mystic.

CHAPTER 6

*H*oly shit, holy shit, holy shit.

Before I could react, my once sweet familiar turned tail and fled from the bathroom, leaving me standing there with my mouth gaping wide open. What I'd just seen looked nothing like the tiny ball of fur that had claimed both Natalie and me—bonding with us as we learned to hone our craft. Whatever magic I'd performed last night had drastically backfired and had twisted Mystic into some kind of monster. She was the reason there was an hourglass displayed in the quad for all to see. That's when the next revelation hit me—this meant she was the threat I had to destroy.

I couldn't let that happen. Mystic was an innocent in all this, and I refused to see her not only suffer, but be punished for my mistakes. This was becoming a frequent freaking theme in my life, and I was done standing around, feeling sorry for myself.

Racing back to my room, I threw on some shoes and grabbed my cell phone. Natalie would understand my not showing up. Shooting off a quick text explaining why I was standing her up, I promised to treat her to whatever she wanted from Coffee Haven.

Once I was outside and free from the confinement of Hel, I

turned about in a circle, frantically searching for some kind of clue as to where Mystic had gone. It didn't take long before I heard the screams of people—someone shouting for help—and I tore off in that direction.

That was the problem with mutated kitty-monsters: they didn't always stay in one place. No sooner had I reached the small group of shaken students that stood huddled together, their arms wrapped around each other in support, than I heard a new shriek of terror.

"Wait for me, Mystic," I whispered, not caring how I appeared. Others were quick to join the growing crowd of sympathizers, and so far, I was the only one who didn't stop long enough to add my two cents' worth and see if anyone was seriously hurt.

Any thoughts that my quiet pleas would somehow cause my familiar to stop, I was wrong. If anything, she was escaping to higher ground—the long bridge that led to the outside clifftop to be specific.

Outside. She was trying to break free from the inside of campus and the mountain. I couldn't let that happen because once she breached the Academy's boundaries, the next stop could be an unsuspecting Havenwood Falls. Maybe the protection wards would prevent her from leaving. I had no idea how the mechanics of the spells worked, but this one thing I did know with growing clarity:

Should Mystic leave campus, there would be no way of containing her—at least not by myself.

The more I ran, the more I regretted every choice that led me to this point.

I should've told Natalie immediately.

I should've gone to Mr. Westbrook and Dr. Lavinia and begged for their help.

I should never have meddled with magic while drunk.

Over and over my list of guilt grew.

The only thing working in my favor was the closer we got to the bridge, the less people I passed. It seemed as though those initial cries for help had become a beacon, calling those brave enough to venture out toward the sound. Safety in numbers.

My chest burned with a lack of oxygen as I pushed myself even harder, my breathing coming out in spurts of ragged gasps. Hell, I could already feel my legs turning to jelly. How I made it to the opening of Clifftop was anyone's guess, but sure enough, I all but collapsed once I hit the cool fresh air.

"Goddess. Give. Me. Strength," I spluttered, and with my hands on my knees, I bent over to catch my breath. I was ridiculously out of shape.

"Okay, are you stalking me?"

There was no biting my tongue when I peered up and found Eryx standing there, staring over at me. For whatever reason, he was here, sitting on one of the rocks that was shaped as a bench, reading. "You've got to be kidding me, Strathos. The world doesn't revolve around you."

Snarky, I knew, but I was in no condition for niceties. I hadn't spotted Mystic yet, and the last thing I needed was for this guy to figure out my secret.

He chuckled to himself and stood up to join me. "What can I say? You seem to be everywhere I am lately, and a guy can never be too careful." It wasn't until he got closer that his teasing stopped. "Hey, are you okay?"

There was something different about him. Cocking my head to the side while I tried to slow my racing heart, I studied him to see if I could pinpoint it. The only thing I could see was that he looked the most relaxed I'd ever seen him.

"Okay, stop. Whatever this is." I waved my hand in his general direction, gesturing to him. "Your concern is freaking me out, so how about you pretend you didn't see me, and we can go our separate ways." I hadn't meant for my words to come out as harsh as they did, but every second Mystic remained at large, the more chance people were in danger.

Even this infuriating guy who always seemed to show up like a bad penny.

I scanned the immediate area, hoping to find clues to where my familiar was. There was a nagging feeling deep inside that I was struggling to ignore—a persistent voice that said I wasn't powerful enough to reverse whatever magic mutated her.

Eryx began talking, but I was too busy trying to come up with a counter spell to acknowledge him. Tears formed in my eyes, my heart still beating hard enough that I was surprised it didn't explode from my chest. All I could do was frantically look about, hastily wiping my eyes with the end of my sweater sleeve.

"Hey," he said, breaking through my thoughts. His hand rested lightly on my forearm, tilting his head slightly so he could hold my gaze. "I'm serious. What's going on? You don't seem yourself, Tempest." The sincerity in his eyes killed me because there was no way I'd confide in him.

I could ask him a question, though. "Hypothetically, how much trouble would someone be in if they performed a spell that backfired?" I dropped my eyes, hoping that he wouldn't see the truth. My hands trembled from nerves, and I knew that the way I was acting didn't instill much confidence that I was fine.

Eryx grabbed my other arm, holding me still as he tried to understand. "Is that what's bothering you?" His grip didn't loosen when I tried to break free. For some reason I didn't trust myself to not confess everything. "Believe me, or not, but I don't like seeing you this upset."

I didn't know how to process that—his admission that he cared about me reverberating in my head. Part of me wanted to bury myself against his chest and beg him to hold me. An even louder part demanded that I shoot down his kindness as the lies I believed they were.

"I can't have this conversation with you, Eryx. Not now." I wiggled hard, trying to leave. "Let go of me, please. I need to go."

"Don't do that. Don't push me away just because you don't like what you're hearing. It doesn't take a genius to see that you're struggling with something. Let me help. Please." He refused to break eye contact with me, and I felt myself drowning in his gaze, my resistance crumbling down around me. "Or do you usually run around campus as though you're being tormented by demons?"

My response bordered on pathetic. "It's the latest fitness trend, Eryx. I'm surprised you haven't heard about it."

He uttered one word that killed me. "Liar."

I couldn't bear the compassion that filled his eyes and pierced my conscience. It didn't matter, though. I wasn't the clingy type or the girl who needed a guy to swoop in and save her. As tempting as it was, I couldn't bring another person into the mess I'd made.

Instead, I responded in the way I knew best—with annoyance. "And you calling me that is meant to somehow generate this overwhelming need to confide in you?" I retorted, determined not to let him break me down. "Give me one good reason why I should let you help me, Eryx? Just one." Before he could do exactly that, I shook my head at him. "I'm still not even sure whether you like me. So, while I appreciate the offer, go find someone else to rescue."

"You know, you're right. When you act like this, I'm not sure I like you either. You have an uncanny way of making me regret being a nice guy." Eryx returned to where he'd been sitting and waved his hand, dismissing me. "Good luck with life, Tempest. You don't need anyone getting in your way."

He licked his finger before turning the page of his book, his entire focus turned away from me.

Why did his anger hurt? I'd basically bitten his head off, and he'd taken the hint that he wasn't welcome to prying about in my business.

So why did I feel the sudden need to apologize?

Backing away, I left Clifftop and raced down the long bridge that led there. It was only when I was out of his sight that my tears finally broke through the dam I'd built to keep my emotions in check.

I was more confused than ever now and no closer to finding my familiar.

I'd let him completely distract me. I was halfway home when I remembered my sole reason for being up on that clifftop. Mystic had been somewhere up there hiding, and by now, she'd probably moved on.

The problem now was that there was no way I could pinpoint her exact location unless she revealed herself. Judging from the lack of new screams, Mystic wasn't running amok through campus either.

That's when the answer slapped me hard in the face. She was my familiar, and as such, she was connected to my magic. That was the main reason why we were in this mess to begin with. She'd obviously tried to siphon off whatever energy I'd wrongly manipulated, and instead of it releasing like it should have, the spell had horribly disfigured her.

Our connection was what I focused on now. I didn't need to always be a step behind in finding her—I could use our bond and draw her to me. The solution was so blatantly simple that it was embarrassing that I'd overlooked it.

All I had to do was find a secluded spot where I wouldn't be disturbed and summon her to me. A newfound sense of confidence pulsed through my veins. This would work, and once it did, I could say goodbye to the hourglass.

Problem solved.

There were many different paths that led away from the heart of campus—places that others talked about as prime make-out spots. I'd always scoffed at them because how could you possibly relax enough to enjoy yourself if you never knew what lurked in the shadows. For all intents and purposes, the Academy was a safe place to reside, but I had a hard time trusting the dark. I threw that caution aside and made my way toward one of the trails I knew about.

All the while, I sent out my thoughts, calling Mystic to follow.

My efforts were rewarded when ten minutes after picking a spot on a crop of rocks to wait, a bulky form emerged from the gloom. Resisting the urge to shrink back, I extended my hand out to my familiar, leaving my arm out so she could see I meant no harm.

For the rest of my life I would never forget that odd sensation of seeing a nightmarish creature's head bump my hand, its throaty purr sounding more like a rusty old truck's engine than the content hum I'd grown to love.

"I'm so sorry, sweetheart," I whispered, stepping closer until I could finally place both of my hands on the side of Mystic's large head, and gently stroke my fingers through her fur. "You were only trying to do your job as my familiar, and instead, you end up like this." I feathered light kisses against her gaunt cheekbone.

Gone was every ounce of fear I'd felt. The doubt in my abilities disappeared as well. All I knew was that the magic inside me could make this right.

With my eyes closed and my hands still on her, I opened myself up to the Goddess, inviting her to hear my most earnest prayer. It wasn't so much the words that entered my mind that I focused on—it was the overwhelming abundance of love and gratitude I felt for my gift and Mystic. I'd barely started before I felt my hands heat up and a bright, white light began emanating from my touch. I pictured it flowing outward, into Mystic as it swept through her ravaged body and healed the damage I'd inflicted.

At first, it was a slight thrum that tickled beneath my fingers, but with each steadying breath, that vibration grew and built until finally it reached its apex. A strong burst of electricity shot out from inside me, and then, the spell was over.

"Meow."

A sob escaped, and I dropped to my knees, scooping my kitty up in my arms. Any thought that Mystic would reject me evaporated as she returned my affection with her rubbing against me.

"Thank you, Goddess," I murmured, relieved beyond words. "Thank you for blessing me with your grace."

I don't know how long Mystic and I sat there quietly snuggling. I wasn't even worried that my tattoo remained the same.

Perhaps these things took time to change back—like waiting for the dust to settle.

None of it mattered.

I'd faced my challenge and won.

And as the air finally cleared of the burnt smoke smell from broken magic, I once again thanked my lucky stars.

CHAPTER 7

"*D*uuuude," I started, feeling more than a little buzzed. "I wonder if whoever owns all this alcohol will be pissed if they knew we'd found it?" It took a second to steady myself because the room had started a slow spin, but that didn't stop me in the slightest.

I was in the mood to celebrate.

Vanna shrugged her shoulders. She'd already drained her cup and was pouring some more. The look of sheer concentration on her face sent Natalie into another round of giggles.

"Whoever it is, they have stellar taste in wine," Vanna slurred. Giving up on her cup, she then drank directly from the bottle, wiping her mouth before passing it on.

Natalie took possession of the wine again. "So where's Marina tonight? It's not like her to miss out on a celebration between friends."

"More wine for us!" I quipped and raised my drink in salute.

"She's working on her goals of sleeping her way through each tower." Vanna's response was delivered perfectly deadpan, which made it beyond hilarious.

Natalie picked up the notebook and flung it across the room at

389

Vanna while I laughed uncontrollably, narrowly missing the table where we'd set up our shared altar. That was the last thing we needed—to piss off the Goddess and get stuck with bad karma because of it.

A loud meow rang out, and a grumpy looking Mystic appeared right next to the discarded book.

"Sorry, sweet girl!" Natalie called out, and climbing down from the bed, she rushed over to scoop our familiar up into her arms, placing wine-laced kisses on her head. "We didn't mean to scare you."

Mystic was indignant long enough to be passed around and doted on. Once she'd had her fill and forgiven us, she went and curled up by my moon shaped pillow. She gave one last glare of warning before closing her eyes.

"Maybe it's time to go see if there's a get-together happening?" Vanna suggested. She grabbed her phone and scrolled through some of her messages. "Yep, there's one over at Heimdall Tower. Should be fun to check out, right?"

We all answered with a resounding hell yes.

Vanna quickly excused herself to go back and change, and Natalie was already searching through her closet.

"What are you going to wear, Tempest?" She held one of her favorite dresses up against her, swaying back and forth so the bottom swished. "Fancy, or sexy lumberjack?" She tugged one of her flannel shirts off a hangar and modeled it—duckface and all.

"I don't know," I drawled and cocked an eyebrow. "Sexy lumberjack definitely has its appeal. You know how cold it gets out there in the courtyard at night. If you want to wear the dress, prepare to cut glass with your nipples."

There was dead silence as I clapped my hand over my mouth and Natalie stood still—stunned that I'd actually said that out loud.

"It was the wine." I laughed, defending myself from the clothes my roomie now threw at me. "I promise!"

Natalie collapsed in a heap, tears streaming down her cheeks from laughing so hard. "What the hell was in that wine then, because I can't remember the last time I'd felt like this!"

I tried to nod and did a sort of head bob instead. "I was thinking the same thing, but I'm not complaining. It feels amazing to just let loose and laugh."

Sliding off my bed, I headed for my own closet, ready to wear the first thing I pulled out. "Lumberjack sexy for the win!" I exclaimed and waved my own flannel shirt victoriously. "Damn, all this plaid and maybe we could be the Winchester Brothers but girls. I'll be Dean, and you can be Sam."

Natalie had finally gotten back up and was halfway dressed when she whipped around and pointed at me. "Jerk."

I didn't hesitate for a second. "Bitch."

Don't ask me how we managed to finish getting ready, but thirty minutes later, we were headed toward Vanna's room, eager to leave Hel for a while. Vanna swung her door open mid knock, and it set us into another round of chuckles. The wine was starting to wear off, and that tipsy sensation was replaced by a much happier, and in control, feeling.

"Ready?" Vanna asked, looking at us both.

"Let's go!" Natalie's response came out louder and perkier than anticipated. Vanna looked over at me, and I grinned.

"I think she's hoping a certain sexy Grayson will be there." Clutching my chest, I pretended to swoon. "Oh, Bale. How are you?"

"Shut up, Tempest!" Natalie retorted, and I caught the spark of snark in her eye. "Don't pretend you're not anxious to see your new crush."

Vanna's mouth dropped open. "Wait, what? Who?"

"Oh, Eryx, your broody stare makes want to throw my panties at you. Please, kiss me now!" She laughed so hard she snorted. Maybe the effect of the wine hadn't completely lessened.

I rolled my eyes and bumped shoulders with her. "You could have at least picked one of the many other options here on campus. Hell, guy or girl, that ass would be the last person I'd hook up with."

"Suuuure," Natalie replied. "You're curious. You can't hide it from me." She threw her arms around me, and I hugged her back.

Snark and sarcasm aside, Natalie had a heart of gold and would never have made fun of me. That's what I loved about her. I didn't have to worry about her intentions. Vanna was also someone I considered part of my inner circle. I was actually surprised she didn't know about Eryx and how much he irked me.

"Well," I started, standing in the middle of them and threading my arms through theirs. "Good thing we have a bestie that's a hellhound then. Vanna can totally sniff the air before we reach Heimdall Tower and let us know if they're there. Right?" I scrunched my nose, pretending to sniff. "Male testosterone and crankiness. How will we ever resist?"

"You're such a bitch." Vanna laughed. "Just for that, I'm not going to warn you. Even if I could!"

Just at that moment, something dark swooped down from the nearby roof, causing me to duck slightly—the movement completely involuntary. There was no chance the bird, a raven, was attacking. I was just a little jumpy still, even though there was nothing really to worry about. Mystic had returned to her normal self, I was out with my friends, and we were talking about hot guys.

"He's probably working tonight at the hotline or camped out at the library. Eryx doesn't look like the type to party and have fun." That declaration did little to disguise my disappointment. There's nothing I wanted more than a chance to flirt and dance the night away with him. I was dying to see whether he'd live up to the fantasies I'd indulged in.

"That's why he needs his Tempest. You can help him smile!" It was Natalie's turn to pretend she was swooning.

"Enough!" I exclaimed, my cheeks heating with embarrassment. It was one thing to dish out the teasing and another to be on the receiving end. "How about we make it to the party first and take it from there?" My stomach felt like I'd eaten a hundred butterflies.

Natalie and Vanna exchanged a knowing look but dropped the

subject. While I tried to convince them that there was nothing going on between the two of us, I was failing miserably with myself.

I wanted him to prove me wrong—needed him to be there when we arrived.

Before the night was over, I would solve the only mystery left in my life.

What it felt like to kiss Eryx Strathos.

I wish I'd never set eyes on Eryx Strathos.

True, it was my wounded pride talking, but if I never saw the jerk again, I'd be happy. In fact, the longer I stewed on it, the more convinced I was that guys were evil, and I'd been a fool to think love was worth taking a risk for.

He'd been at the party. Leaning against the wall, Eryx had been the first person I saw when we'd arrived, and the only one I was interested in. He'd surprised me by being there, drink in hand, his blond curls bouncing slightly to the beat of the music.

Goddess, he looked sexy as hell—all broody and mysterious. The moment our gaze met, a thrill blazed through me. I took it as a sign that tonight truly was the night, and that with some heavy flirting, we'd end up in each other's arms. I knew what it felt like when a guy was interested, and like Natalie had pointed out in extreme details on the way here, Eryx was just waiting for me to make my move.

So I made it.

He rejected me.

Again.

Hot tears of frustration burned my eyes as I made my goodbyes and stormed out of the party. How could I have been so painfully wrong? We'd spent the past two hours laughing, standing closer and closer together, even swaying back and forth to the music. His stare had been blistering—his tongue darting out to lick his lips— his hands always finding some reason to reach out and touch me.

He wanted to kiss me, too. I was positive of that. I hadn't misread his body language. Yet, just as we were finally going to seal the deal, so to speak, he jerked back at the last possible second.

It would've hurt less had he slapped my face.

Now I was walking aimlessly through campus—exhausted and still slightly buzzed.

"Tempest, wait up!" His voice rang out, and I ignored it, walking a little faster. "Please, let me explain."

"What's there to explain?" I fired back over my shoulder. I couldn't bear to turn around and face him—not without giving him a piece of my mind and embarrassing myself further. "Go back to the party, Eryx. Or don't. Just stay the hell away from me."

I heard his footsteps speed up, and before I could do the same, he grabbed hold of my arm and stopped me. "For one, it's not safe to be out this late by yourself."

No matter how hard I tried to look everywhere but at him, I couldn't help it. Damn him for looking so freaking hot. "I'm a big girl, Eryx. I don't need you."

It was as if I hadn't spoken. "And second, I went to the party to see you."

I almost choked on my retort. "Well, you saw me. Good night."

I yanked my arm away from him and started walking again. He didn't move.

"Why are you so angry?" He genuinely sounded bewildered.

Something inside me snapped. "Seriously? We almost kiss and you don't understand why I'm hurt that you pushed me away? Again?" Now that the words were flowing, I couldn't hold back. "Do you like sending mixed signals, Eryx? Is it some male ego thing to string me along like this? Like I said, I'm a big girl and can deal with you not liking me, but if that's the case, stop acting like kissing me is the worst thing to ever happen." Standing before him, I poked his chest. Hard. "Am I really that disgusting?"

I waited for him to answer—to apologize—to say anything to

break this awkwardness, but instead his attention was on something behind me.

"Tempest?" His voice rattled with nervous energy.

"You know what, I'm done. I'm a good person, Eryx Strathos, and if you can't see that, your loss." It was only when I turned to leave that I finally saw what he was staring at.

We weren't alone. Hovering just above the ground was a huge dark smoky shadow—a specter-like creature whose eyes glowed with a red intensity. Snarls emanated from within the mass, and I could feel its hostility radiating from it.

"Get behind me, Tempest," Eryx ordered, already trying to shove me back. "When I tell you to run, go, and don't stop until you get somewhere safe."

I couldn't take my eyes off the creature. "As long as you do the same." There wasn't an ounce of frustration toward him left in my body. "Neither of us need to be a hero. I'm going to distract him with a spell, and then we'll go." I could already feel my magic activating inside me, and the tips of my fingers crackled with electricity. "On my count. Ready?"

I quietly counted to three and then let my powers fly.

The creature absorbed every last bit of the energy ball I'd thrown.

"Run!" Eryx yelled, and before I could grab his hand to drag him with me, the specter lashed out with a deafening roar. I expected the shadow to pass through Eryx, but the second it touched him, a bloodied gash appeared, slicing through his shirt to the skin below.

I unleashed everything inside me—firing spell after spell. Nothing. My magic barely stunned the creature, and what terrified me more was the undeniable feeling that I was somehow responsible for this beast. My tattoo burned again, or maybe it was just my imagination, and it moved even closer to us.

Was this the task? Was Mystic merely a by-product of my drunken spell, and this was the monster I'd actually created? Was this why my tattoo hadn't faded away and the hourglass remained in the courtyard?

Shit.

How the hell was this happening?

There was no more time to waste, however, as the entity grew bigger and I felt its energy pulling on mine. My magic was definitely feeding it.

I took hold of Eryx and ran.

CHAPTER 8

We found temporary refuge in a secluded cave. We probably should've run toward people, but all I could think about was the amount of blood Eryx was losing. I needed somewhere safe now, not later.

Thankfully we'd fled in the right direction and found a place to hide. A nagging thought reminded me, however, that the creature was drawn to my magic. Any spell I did would simply feed its strength.

"Take off your shirt," I ordered, my hands still shaking from the adrenaline. "I need to see how bad the cut is so I can stop you from dying." I wasn't exactly gentle when he didn't respond as quickly as I needed. Pushing him back so he could lie down, I tore his shirt into strips.

"I always figured you'd be overly dramatic." He laughed, wincing half way with pain. "I promise you I'm not going to die over a mere scratch." The paleness of his skin said otherwise.

"Natalie tells me the same thing as well. That if I didn't make it as a supernatural healer, I could always audition for Broadway." The fact that he could still make jokes was promising. The attack had terrified me.

"Is that what you'd rather do?" Eryx played with a strand of my hair that fell from behind my ear. The strange thing was the gesture was the only thing keeping me from losing my shit.

I snorted and using a piece of the fabric, began wiping as much of the blood away as I could before it dried. He'd been right. While it would leave a nasty scar, there was little chance he'd bleed out in my arms. With the right pressure and clean bandages, he would live to see another day, and that knowledge forced a pent-up breath out of me.

"That's right, Tempest. Breathe." His finger traced a soft trail over my cheek before he dropped his hand to his side. "We're going to be okay."

"As long as I don't use my magic, we should be." That still rattled me to the core. I'd been so blind with relief that I hadn't questioned whether the threat was over. Even with the hourglass still on my wrist, I'd assumed there was simply a lag in the magic.

"Well, the beast won't disturb us in here anyway. I cast a simple protection ward at the entrance. Until I lower it, nothing gets in or out." Before I could question how he had that kind of magic, he winked. The guy was practically lying in my lap, and now he was flirting. "I've made it my goal to always be prepared."

With his wound somewhat clean, I folded another strip from his shirt into a makeshift gauze and pressed it over the gash. I didn't know who flinched more when his fingers wrapped around my wrist in support. I stammered over my next words, shaken. "Kind of like a supernatural boy scout, huh? Do you think I could earn one of the badges for saving your life?"

All that was left was securing the gauze in place, and once I was satisfied with how it looked, I gently helped him sit up. Some of the color was returning to his skin—another sign that he was starting to slowly heal.

"After this, I'm tempted to give you whatever you want."

I didn't meet his gaze. "Don't. I get that we're stuck in here, but let's not pretend."

I'd been half way through my rant over his asshole behavior when we'd been attacked. While I hadn't really changed my opinion on the subject, I didn't have enough energy to battle with him again.

I was going to accept that Eryx and I would only ever be friends and be grateful I'd escaped with only a partially broken heart.

Eryx sat peacefully with his eyes closed, his breathing becoming steadier with each inhale. Why was life always putting us together only to keep throwing obstacles in our way? How was I supposed to keep my distance when every time he looked my way or smiled, I lost my train of thought? It wasn't just because he was sexy as hell, either. While my type leaned more toward someone tall, dark, and broody, there was something in the way he captured my attention so completely that no other guy existed when he was around.

"I can feel you staring at me." His lips curled into a slow grin. "Are you checking me out?"

I didn't hesitate. "No. I'm trying to figure out whether my odds of getting out of here increase if you stay wounded. You know . . . survival of the fittest." I managed to keep myself from laughing until the last possible second. "Damn, that was cold, even for me."

"But totally understandable." He cracked an eye open. "I hurt you tonight, and I'm sorry. I don't always think things through. We were having a great time, and I got caught up in the moment."

He was still looking at me, so I knew he saw the massive eye roll I did in response. "If the next words out of your mouth are it's not you, it's me, I'll summon that damn creature so he can finish you off." I leaned back against the wall beside him, confident that he'd be okay. The bleeding had slowed. "Just accept that you acted like a dick, and let's move on. I'm not particularly fond of beating a dead horse."

As much as I tried to keep my tone light, I couldn't quite keep the slight hint of hurt I felt from surfacing.

"It's the truth, though."

"And it's also true that despite what you might think, my self-esteem isn't that bruised that I'll keep chasing after you. You made yourself perfectly clear, so let's talk about something else."

He shifted to get more comfortable. "Okay. You never answered my earlier question . . . about whether you were interested in performing on Broadway."

I responded the only way I knew how—by singing something from one of my favorite musicals, Les Misérables, like I was alone in my room wearing headphones. "Does that answer it?"

I thought he'd be polite, but instead he laughed so hard, I was worried he'd ruin my triage handiwork. "I don't want to hurt your feelings, but shit, that was awful."

My impromptu performance also served as an icebreaker between us. We shared stories from our pasts, our favorites adventures, and as the night progressed, it didn't take long before my head was resting on his shoulder. My eyes felt so heavy, and I didn't know how long I could fight against falling asleep. Eryx hadn't said anything for at least five minutes so it was safe to assume that he'd already succumbed.

That's why I didn't hold myself back as everything came bubbling out of me. Keeping everything a secret was slowly twisting me up in knots, and I was desperate to tell someone. Now that he was asleep, I could purge to my heart's content, and he'd be none the wiser.

I probably should've double-checked that he wasn't simply resting his eyes, but once I started, there was no stopping me.

I told him about my past—about being classified the delinquent child for most of my life, but more importantly the thrill I'd felt when I discovered I was different from my family. I hadn't shrunken away from my magic. I'd embraced it, but without the proper training, my gift had controlled me.

Next was about meeting Micah and coming to the Academy— how nervous I'd been being alone for the first time. I couldn't stop smiling as I recounted befriending Natalie, and how quickly we'd become close. She was the family I'd chosen. Our relationship was living proof that we didn't have to settle for the ones we were born into.

If this was truly my only chance to be completely honest with someone, I wasn't going to waste this opportunity. When I finally came to the end, and had completely exhausted myself, I allowed myself a moment of peace.

"So there you have it. My life in a nutshell. Maybe you're smart for not wanting to get involved. I'm basically a magical train wreck."

I spent the rest of the night caught up in my own thoughts—torn between watching him sleep and reveling in the fact that I'd spoken the truth out aloud.

There was no sign of the creature that had driven us to hide in the cave once the morning arrived, either.

I'd escaped—for now.

CHAPTER 9

"So, bestie," Natalie started as she found me rushing toward Hel Tower the next day.

Despite trying to skip classes again so I could head to the library for some extra intense research, I'd spent an agonizing few hours barely able to concentrate while I counted down the seconds until I was free. The second class was over, I was out the door, not bothering to wait and see if Natalie was keeping up.

I'd only just caught glimpse of the golden Valkyrie that stood as a sentinel on the roof, the beautiful statue overlooking the hustle and bustle down below. Here I'd thought I'd managed the impossible and avoided being stopped by anyone, but apparently that hadn't included my persistent bestie.

Damn she could move fast when she wanted to.

"Tell me I'm mistaken. That I'm just being paranoid."

I cast a sideways glance and found her looking at me with a perturbed expression. "Pardon?" I answered, not sure what she was talking about. "You okay?"

"Did something happen between us? Maybe I offended you somehow?"

I immediately knew what was going on. In my stubborn

determination to take care of Mystic by myself, I hadn't realized how that might have looked to my best friend.

She had no clue the trouble I faced, other than being placed on probation, and even when I woke up this morning and my tattoo was still in the shape of that damned hourglass, I'd remained silent. Natalie's imagination was no doubt running wild.

I sucked as a friend and roommate right now.

The thing was, I didn't know whether confiding in her now would make the situation better or worse. I'd kept her completely in the dark, and the revelation was going to hurt. A lot.

All I could do was respond with a shrug. "I know I've been distant and like the worst person to live with lately."

"Well," Natalie drawled out, "I didn't want to be that specific but . . ." She didn't finish as she playfully bumped into me.

"I just have a lot on my mind." It wasn't necessarily a lie. Sure, it wasn't the whole truth, but something told me the conversation I needed to have with her needed to be done in the privacy of our room. There would definitely be a lot of groveling involved.

Her face screwed up in faux annoyance. "I'm not even worried why you've been in your head so much, Tempest. What I do want to know is why it took me hearing through the grapevine that you not only did the walk of shame earlier this morning, but you were also spotted with Eryx Strathos!" She tugged on my arm to make me stop. "Is that why you're in such a rush to get back to the room so you can go on a secret hot date with him?"

It was hard not to bust out laughing. "I'm going to the library, dork. Academic probation, remember?"

There was that twinge of guilt that had set up residence in my stomach. I'd been using my punishment as an excuse a lot lately. It seemed more convenient than the truth.

I'd seen that look in Natalie's eyes before—she'd be relentless in getting all the juicy details. I wasn't a kiss-and-tell kind of girl, but perhaps giving in would soften the blow and make it easier for her to forgive me.

"Fine. I'll answer all your questions . . . in depth . . . once we get upstairs." My night with Eryx had been replaying over and over in my mind all morning, and my stomach was already doing flip-flops at the thought of talking about him.

Ugh, it was official. I'd fallen for him.

"I hope reality doesn't disappoint your rampant imagination, Natalie." I chuckled, knowing full well that she'd been secretly Team Eryx for a while now. "But nothing's ever going to happen between us. I heard it from him, himself. All we can ever be is friends."

"So why has he been asking around about you?"

I almost tripped over my own feet. "Says who?"

"I have it on the very best of authority." When I didn't try to guess who she meant, Natalie revealed her source. "Marina!"

Our conversation was interrupted as we began climbing the steps up into Hel Tower. Mr. Westbrook, General Sky, the head of campus security, and a very pissed off Vanna emerged from inside.

"You have no right accusing me of this! This is discrimination, and you know it. Just because I'm a hellhound doesn't mean I terrorize the campus in my spare time. Actually, ask Natalie and Tempest. They'll tell you how absurd this is."

Her loud, indignant answer explained why Mr. Westbrook looked so serious and official. The only other time I'd seen him look this grim was when he waited to stand before my old coven.

"We can vouch for her," Natalie and I said in unison. There was no way we were going to let Vanna be accused of something based on her nature.

"Right now, we just want you to come in and talk with the administration." General Sky's tone brokered no nonsense.

It was as if he hadn't spoken. Vanna yanked her arm out of his grip and stood defiantly. "Apparently the creature everyone is panicked about was seen entering Hel Tower, so naturally that means it was me."

She rolled her eyes so hard, I was surprised they didn't hit the back of her skull.

"Resisting is only going to make things worse. Please, come with us," Micah added in a softer yet firm voice.

Nothing we could say made a difference. Natalie's gaze didn't once leave Vanna as she was led away. "I'm going to follow them and make sure she's okay. Coming?"

I hated lying to her, but there were more pressing matters to take care of. She had the decency not to question me about it.

"Once I'm done, I'll come find you. Promise."

"Damn right you will. She needs our help, and I still need details about last night."

We parted ways with a hug. As soon as I saw her disappear, I changed directions, forgetting my plans to go unload my bag and quickly change clothes. I had no more time to waste.

If I was going down with this sinking ship, the least I could do was make sure my friends didn't drown with me.

I didn't make it to the library.

My phone buzzed, and I saw Natalie was calling. Call it intuition, or whatever, but I knew it was going to be bad news the second her name flashed on my screen.

"Hello?"

The voice from the other end of the call was not my roommate. "Hello, Tempest. This is Madame Roth from the med center. Natalie Putnam was brought in about twenty minutes ago and is asking for you."

The rest of the conversation was a blur as I dropped everything and ran as fast as I could to the infirmary. Over and over, I silently begged the Goddess to watch over my best friend, and that it had nothing to do with the beast still terrorizing campus.

I was suddenly thrust into my worst nightmare, however, as I entered the small room where she lay and saw the freshly forming bruises and cuts that covered her. She'd been attacked. There was no mistaking the claw-like gash that bloodied her arm.

My gasp felt deafening. All the way here, my imagination ran wild with scenes that I'd find her beaten and bloodied, and while it wasn't as brutal as I'd worried, she'd still been hurt.

The relieved part of me tried to remind me that things could've been much worse, but that just amplified my failure until all I could see was my betrayal.

I should've told her.

"Shit, Tempest." She laughed, her voice croaky. "Talk about making an entrance." Her mouth curled into a soft smile, her way of hiding the fear she felt. I was getting good at reading my roommate and recognizing her attempts to act like things were normal.

"What the hell happened?" I thundered, rushing to her. When I went to hug her, I stopped in my tracks, terrified I would hurt her. "Are you okay? Please tell me you weren't hurt."

Shaking her head, Natalie began talking, giving me a step-by-step account of the attack.

"You know what's weird, Tempest? The creature felt like you." She took a sip of water through a bendy straw. "I think that's why I didn't scream. I just held still and waited for it to leave."

God, without even knowing it, Natalie had recognized my involvement on a subconscious level. She was lucky she hadn't been mauled worse.

"So you felt a connection with it?"

"I can't explain it, Tempest. All I know is that I'm grateful I'm in one piece." She winced as she tried to get comfortable, inching her body to the left. "Don't get me wrong. I feel like I was hit by a freight train, but I can manage aches and bruises. There's nothing a little magic can't fix, right?"

I forced myself to nod, clenching my hands into a fist so tight that I felt my nails break skin. This was my fault and I wouldn't sleep until I made it right.

"I'm so sorry, Natalie." Tears rolled freely down my cheeks. There was no stopping the emotions bubbling out. I wanted to tell her everything, beg for her forgiveness, apologize a thousand times more, but I kept it all inside. I wasn't ready for her to be mad at me. I couldn't bear knowing she might hate me once this all came out because sooner or later, everyone would know what I'd done, and also what had led me to Sun & Moon Academy in the first place.

"I need to tell you something," I whispered as I sat down beside her on the chair provided. "And you're not going to like it. Just promise me you won't interrupt until the end." There was still a loud voice in my head screaming to shut up, but this time I pushed it aside. I was done being at war with myself. This confession was a long time coming.

It was hard to read Natalie's face as I told her everything. She'd make a killer poker player because there was no hint of emotion or reaction. I'd expected her to be angry or in the very least hurt, but all she did was sit up on the bed and watch me.

Finally, the silence broke me. "Please, Natalie, say something. I'm so sorry." I was crying again, hot tears trailing over my cheeks to my jaw, before dropping to my shirt. "Tell me how much I suck. Anything."

There was a cough at the door, and I noticed her gaze darting toward the sound.

Turning around, I was expecting to see a doctor or nurse, but instead there stood Eryx and Micah. It didn't take a rocket scientist to realize they'd been listening for a while.

"How much did you hear?" Ignoring Eryx, my question was aimed at Mr. Westbrook. Hopefully they were here to check up on Natalie and didn't just get a front row seat to my confession.

I hated how hollow and hard his voice sounded. "Long enough to confirm the story Eryx just told me. All this time and you knew, yet you said nothing."

I wanted to tell him my reasoning, to explain how I wanted to solve the problem myself, but the vein throbbing in Micah's temple told me he wouldn't accept any more excuses.

That's when I realized that he'd implicated Eryx in their sudden appearance.

"How did you know?" I croaked, a large lump stuck in my throat. "I thought you were asleep, otherwise I never would have said anything." Already my mind was scrambling to remember all the details from that night. The guy's breathing had been slow and steady. How had I been wrong?

"I wasn't asleep." His admission was crushing. "And despite

how I know, this is bigger than you or me, Tempest. You might be too afraid to ask for help, but I'm not. You can't keep something like this a secret."

I shook my head in denial. "It wasn't your secret to tell, Eryx. I had a plan and was going to come clean. It just took longer than I anticipated and got a lot more out of control." I turned to Micah. "I swear I'm telling the truth."

"Then why weren't you waiting at my office this morning? Why did I need to learn about it from someone else?" The kindness Micah usually outwardly reflected was gone. He held up his hand, and I could almost taste the authority that dripped from his tone. "Tempest, I'm here to take you before the Regents immediately. I'll remain with you while they deliberate, and I'm certain they'll instruct me to escort you from campus."

Natalie finally spoke up. "For one mistake? I know she's on probation, but surely she's not the first student to get in over her head here. Hell, we've all heard the rumors circulating about magic gone wrong and people getting hurt. Last time I checked, none of those stories ended in expulsion."

Mr. Westbrook approached the bed, his face softening. "While I applaud you for defending your roommate, this is a much more complicated situation. There is a level of trust the Academy places in each student that goes beyond this situation with the hourglass."

I watched Eryx with the hope that he'd also say something—maybe share how much this had plagued me. I hadn't lied to him in the cave when I said that it was tearing me apart. He said nothing, however.

"Please," I interjected. "I know I lost any right to ask you to show me leniency, but at least let me fix this. Give me the next twenty-four hours to take care of it and then I'll go and confess myself."

He shook his head. "That ship has sailed, Tempest. I have a responsibility to every student here on campus. You've left me no choice."

Eryx picked this moment to finally add his two cents. "I'll help her, sir. While I'm not a witch, I do have a few tricks up my sleeve."

Micah seemed to weigh the offer carefully. "It's too dangerous. I can't risk anyone else getting hurt."

When he stared down at Natalie again, I knew he was thinking of just how bad it could've been. The thought was already swirling around in my head.

"Then give me an hour. Sixty minutes to give it my best shot." For some reason, it wasn't enough to have others step in to clean up my mess. This was my problem, and I needed to know that no matter what, I could see it through to the end.

He let out a frustrated groan as he looked between me, Natalie, and Eryx. We made a weird kind of group, but I wasn't alone. "You've broken trust, Tempest."

"So, let me start repairing it."

I thought he was never going to answer.

"One hour. That's it. Don't make me regret this."

Throwing my arms around his neck, I didn't care that he was my elder and that hugging him might be seen as inappropriate. All I could think was there was still a chance, and this time I wouldn't blow it.

I sprang into action the second Micah left the room. "Thanks for the offer, Eryx, but I don't need you to babysit me." When he tried to argue with me, I instantly raised my hand to stop him. "I've got this."

It was Natalie that surprised me the most. "Isn't that how you got into this mess? I thought you understood that I was your family . . . that we're in this together?"

This was a side to her I'd never had directed at me—anger.

"I know you don't understand, but I know how this is going to end, and I refuse to see them try to blame this on you as well." That was one of my greatest fears—that after ruining my own future, I would also screw up hers. "I need you to be okay."

"I need you too, you idiot. We just can't let our pasts define who we are now or the witches we'll become. There's a reason why fate brought us together. Our friendship and bond make us stronger, so quit being stubborn and let me help already."

Words failed me.

"I'm guessing that's a yes?" Eryx ventured, eyeing me closely. I think he was hoping I'd change my mind about letting him help. While the idea of spending more time with him was appealing, I still couldn't shake the feeling that this didn't need to involve him.

"Don't give me puppy dog eyes, either," I warned him sternly, all but pointing my finger in his face. Then my heart did this weird thing I wasn't expecting—it softened, and I felt myself crumbling beneath the weight of his hopeful stare. "Fine. How about if I need you, I'll text you. Deal?" That was as good a compromise as I could give.

That's when my bestie cleared her throat with a not-so-subtle cough.

"It means she knows better than to argue with me." Natalie was already removing the blood pressure cuff from around her arm and reaching for her clothes. "Just give me a second to dress, and we can go. One hour isn't a lot of time, and the clock is ticking." She gave me a quick hug before whispering in my ear. "Sisters forever."

"Forever."

CHAPTER 10

I sat on my bed, staring down at the magic book from downstairs.

How could something inanimate cause so much trouble and upheaval? As I randomly flipped through the pages, the excitement I'd once felt had long evaporated. I hated this book and the havoc it had unleashed.

Even that wasn't fully true, and standing up with the volume tucked under my arm, I couldn't hide from the truth. I had wielded magic with little responsibility and blatantly shown disrespect. I wasn't immune from making mistakes, but deep down I knew better than to mix magic with alcohol.

I glanced around my room as if to memorize every item that Natalie and I had used to reflect our style. The clear crystal chandelier that hung over my four-poster bed was almost identical to the black one downstairs in the great room. I had never gone looking for Sun & Moon Academy, but now that I'd had a taste of it, I was heartbroken over the thought of leaving. I'd miss Natalie and how we would talk to all hours of the night—baring our hopes and dreams. I'd miss the friends I'd made and the small piece of belonging I'd managed to carve out for myself that was one hundred percent mine.

I just wish I hadn't blown it after only a month and a half.

There was a part of me who'd tried to believe I could ask for help, no matter how scary it was, and someone would answer. But I also knew that leaving that meeting with Micah, and turning my back on my old coven, I had foolishly vowed to be perfect. I would prove everyone wrong, and in the process, encased myself with a thick wall of my pride.

What I was beginning to learn, however, was that some things were worth fighting for, that even if I stood trembling in my boots, there was something just beyond my fear.

Honor.

Integrity.

Acceptance.

I just couldn't seem to let go of the thought in my mind that all I would ever amount to was this—a failure.

That's when I caught a glimpse at the silver lining—the space just beyond the challenge. Life sucked, but like nature, there would always be balance.

It wouldn't matter in a year, five years, hell, six months what others thought about me. What was important in this precise instant was how I viewed myself. I was almost certain that the end result to this fiasco was my no longer being a witch and having to leave the Academy. Even though I'd already begun to waiver, the more I realized what I stood to lose and how fiercely protective I was over my new life, I knew I had to accept that I couldn't control everything.

Taking in a deep breath, I stepped over to the pentacle Natalie had just finished making on the floor. We hadn't spoken much since coming back to the room, and I knew that once this was over, I had a lot of damage control to do.

For right now, however, our focus was on recreating the spell I'd performed. The idea was that by tapping into that same energy and magic, we could then banish the creature I'd inadvertently released back into the ether.

Twenty minutes later, we stood ready to start. That's when a thought hit me.

"Wait, I remember now!" I rushed over to where I'd hidden the wine bottle in shame and brought it back over to Natalie. "This is what I was drinking. I know it probably won't make a difference, but if we're having to repeat each step I did that night, we need to take a sip."

I handed the wine to her after taking a mouthful.

"I've been thinking, Tempest." She tilted the bottle back so she could study the contents. "This packs a stronger punch than what we're used to. That, and the fact you found it in a hidden cellar, makes me wonder if there isn't an extra ingredient we didn't account for."

It was on the tip of my tongue to ask her what she meant when it hit me. "Magic."

Natalie nodded. "That we have no clue about or where it originated from. Something tells me this mystery factor, paired with your wonky powers, made your spell volatile. When Mystic couldn't absorb it all, the remaining energy took on a life of its own."

Shit, it all made sense now.

My heart started thumping hard in my chest as adrenaline took over. "So you can fix this?"

She nodded and grabbed my hand. "We can fix this. Together."

"I should've confided in you the second I woke up, Natalie."

She at least chuckled. "Damn right you should've, but what's done is done. We need to get started so you can let Mr. Westbrook know. Maybe he could speak on your behalf again."

I didn't have the heart to correct her.

A weight lifted off my shoulders as we performed the ritual and summoned the beast. The only problem was when the creature appeared within the pentacle, no amount of magic undid it.

"What's happening?" I yelled over the growing growls and snarls. "All we're doing is pissing it off!"

Sweat began beading across her forehead from the strain of keeping the darkness contained. "We're missing something. Think, Tempest. What else did you do?"

"I don't know," I spluttered, frantically trying to recall the memories from that night. I'd gone over everything with a fine-tooth comb, but no matter how hard I concentrated, I couldn't figure it out. "This should work. Maybe—" My own voice cracked under pressure, and I gritted my teeth hard, digging even deeper for the magic I knew was there. "Maybe it's grown too strong. Maybe we need more help."

We both knew what that meant—by admitting to Micah that this was beyond my abilities, I pretty much guaranteed the possibility of expulsion. The thing was . . . I didn't care anymore. This was bigger than what I wanted now. As much as it would hurt, I would face the consequences if it meant that everyone would be safe.

With the words already forming in my mouth, I began the chant to close the circle and temporarily bind the creature. I didn't get to finish, however, as Mystic came hurtling toward us out of nowhere.

Despite our cries for her to stop, our sweet familiar crashed into the pentacle, toppling over the candle.

She was the missing piece of the puzzle. I suddenly knew what to do.

As a new spell built inside of me, I rechanneled every ounce of power I held, and released it on the pulsing beast. When it pushed back trying to resist my efforts, I yelled for Natalie to join in. Clasping our hands together, wind whirling about us and whipping at our clothes, I uttered the final syllable and banished the beast for good.

When the candles blew out to signal the ritual had worked, I let out a loud sigh of relief mixed with an exhausted chuckle.

Collapsing into an exhausted heap on the floor, I didn't dare to hope. "Is that it? Is everything back to normal?"

Natalie lay beside me, breathing heavily. "I don't know. You tell me."

I reached out carefully, trying to sense if there was any lingering disturbance. "I can't tell."

That's when a voice filled my head.

"It is done."

I sat up straight, searching about the room. "Did you hear that?"

We were still alone—except for Mystic, who sat cleaning her paws beside us.

Natalie wore her own look of bewilderment. "The words, *it is done*? Yep, but where did it come from?" That's all we needed. A new threat. Pulling up my sleeve, I glanced at my tattoo.

The hourglass was gone.

"Holy shit," I uttered as I rubbed at my wrist in disbelief. "I have no freaking clue, but the voice was right. Look." Lifting my arm, I showed her my newly restored school tattoo. "It's back to normal."

We'd solved one mystery only to be given another.

"Maybe it was the Goddess?" Natalie pondered, thinking out loud.

"Or maybe . . ." I uttered, and I scooped up Mystic into my hands. "It's not possible."

Natalie took our familiar next and this time, peered into the small kitty's eyes. "Was that you?"

She scratched Mystic behind her ears, but the voice didn't return.

Leaving Natalie to clean up after the ritual, I went out to talk with Mr. Westbrook and let him know that the threat was over. The campus was safe again and could return back to normal where our only concerns were making sure we kept up with our homework and didn't fail our finals.

I'd grown to love being here at Sun & Moon Academy—finally feeling like I truly belonged somewhere—that I mattered.

One thing became crystal clear. It was time to stop letting others advocate on my behalf. As much as I appreciated everything Micah had done for me, it wasn't his responsibility any more.

It was mine.

I was ready to face the Regents and beg to stay.

CHAPTER 11

"*Y*ou won't be able to avoid her forever, you know?"

Dragging myself away from the door, I leaned back against the wall and closed my eyes. Just like I'd suspected, life had returned to normal, and although I'd been made to sweat it out, the Regents had returned with the verdict that I could remain at Sun & Moon Academy. I would still be on academic probation and continue seeing the therapist, doing whatever Dr. Lavinia required to prove I'd learned my lesson. There would be very little time left over to socialize, but it was more than I deserved.

What twisted me up in knots was the fact that Natalie could've been hurt, and that Vanna had been falsely accused. Forgiveness in my family was a long, drawn-out affair where you couldn't guarantee that a grudge didn't linger. Delight was taken in punishing those who dared hurt my siblings. So when Natalie hugged me and told me that our friendship was still intact, it blew my mind.

Vanna was another story. I was currently hiding in my room because I knew she was moving about the floor getting ready to go to class. She'd listened to my apologies, nodded, then turned around to walk away. We hadn't spoken since.

I missed her.

"Do you think things will ever be the same between us?" I asked, knowing that earning Vanna's trust again might not be as easy as it was with Natalie. "Maybe I should send her a peace offering?" That thought had crossed my mind countless times today. What says, 'I'm sorry that I almost got you thrown in jail'?

"Just give her time, Tempest. Be patient. She'll come around, and you guys will talk again." Natalie was busy painting her nails on her bed, her focus split. "She hasn't talked much about what happened with the Regents, but I think deep down she knows you didn't do it on purpose."

"She won't even look at me," I admitted. "I walked past her earlier on my way to tell Fiona to turn her music down, and it was as if I was invisible. I even tried to joke about Fiona's loud and obnoxious singing . . . to act as an icebreaker, but Vanna didn't even blink."

"Again, give her time. Once this has all died down and it doesn't feel so fresh, you can try to tell her again that you never wanted to hurt her." Blowing carefully on her nails, Natalie threw me a smile, careful not to ruin her handiwork. "Be patient."

I slid down the wall and rested my arms on my bended knees. "I swear I'm cursed or something. Maybe it's my shitty adolescent behavior coming back to bite me in the ass."

She looked up from her feet and rolled her eyes. "I love it when you're dramatic."

Natalie gave me one of those looks that bordered on challenging me to prove her wrong.

I nodded. I was done hiding behind my pride. "I just want a magical wand that I can wave about and everything goes back to the way it was. Kind of like Cinderella's fairy godmother." I pulled out the crystal hairpin that kept my bun up fairly tight and waved it about in the air. "How does it go . . . bippity boppity boo?"

I snorted over how stupid I sounded.

"Afraid it doesn't work that way. You're just going to have to do it the old-fashioned way. Tough it out." Screwing her polish bottle closed, Natalie dropped it beside the rest of her pedicure kit. "Have you heard anything from Mr. Westbrook yet?"

"Nope. Not yet."

She looked surprised. When I didn't answer, Natalie pointed at me. "You're avoiding him! Tempest, you need to go see him so you can make peace with him. I'm sure he's not holding a grudge."

That was my fear—that I'd disappointed him so completely that I'd destroyed the relationship we had.

I didn't have the heart to tell her I'd come close to leaving myself.

"He's probably busy." As far as excuses go, that one was pretty weak.

Carefully trying to keep from messing up her nails, Natalie walked over to where my crystals were. "Fine, if you want to be a coward, I'll go talk to him myself." With a mischievous twinkle in her eye, she pretended he was there. "Hi, Mr. Westbrook. Tempest is being an idiot. She didn't mean to make shitty choices that set a magical dark beast on the loose. She wants to say sorry." Then as an afterthought, she smiled. "This is Natalie, her long-suffering roommate and best friend. Thanks."

I let out a loud groan as I rested my head back on my knees, hiding my face. "I'm not that bad. I'll talk to him eventually. I just need time to figure out what I want to say."

"Fine. While you wait, you should go and find Eryx. I don't know what it is with the ignoring people, but he's someone else you can't keep avoiding."

Damn, she was relentless.

"Fine, I'll be back." I dragged my feet in protest as I picked up my messenger bag containing my schoolwork. "I'll kill two birds with one stone by getting a start on our Potions term paper at the library and then go find Mr. Westbrook so I can grovel for his forgiveness. Happy?" I glared at her, refusing to let her happy smile make me laugh. "Damn you for making me act like an adult."

What I didn't add was that I was grateful for the push. I missed my conversations with Micah—the way he always made me feel like I mattered. Our relationship went both ways, however, and it was time for me to swallow my pride and show him the respect he deserved. The only way I would truly burn my bridge with him was if I didn't cross this temporary obstacle and make amends.

There was a proud twinkle in my roommate's eyes when I turned back from the door.

"Well, as long as you don't do any drunk spells while you're there, you should be fine. Who knows what kind of demons and monsters you'll unleash next?" When I gasped out loud, Natalie laughed. "Too soon?"

"Too soon." Waving over my shoulder, I left the room to her telling me she loved me and headed outside. Vanna had already left, so our awkward conversation would wait a little longer.

Strolling through the courtyard as I headed toward Halstein Hall, I rounded a corner and bumped into Eryx. He had his nose buried in a book, and if we hadn't collided, he probably wouldn't have seen me.

But he had.

I couldn't bring myself to look at him.

"Hey," he said, closing his book. "I was hoping to see you. You've had a rough few days, Tempest, and I'd understand if you were ready to run for the hills after it all . Just remember that what truly matters isn't how much you feel you've failed, but how you rise from each challenge and recover from it."

I wasn't expecting him to be so understanding.

"Do you mean that?" I blurted out, studying his face to see if he was making light of the situation. "Or do you pity me even more now? The foolish witch who makes things explode in Potions class and turns her familiar into a mutated beast. Oh yeah, and also creates a shadowy creature with her twisted magic. Good times."

Eryx scratched his head, tilting it slightly. "Wow, I haven't done a great job of being a friend, have I?"

I couldn't keep quiet. "Is that what you want us to be? Friends?" I swore this guy was going to give me a severe case of whiplash. "Just tell me once and for all what I should expect so there's no more confusion."

I searched his eyes.

He reached out gently and brushed his finger across my cheek. I didn't move a muscle, determined to wait until he made the first move.

"Just tell me, Eryx," I whispered. "What do you want?"

He licked his lips, his gaze dropping to mine. "Something I can never have."

I wasn't sure I'd heard him right. "What?" It was my turn to hold onto him, my hands grasping his shirt tightly. "Is this really all just a joke to you? Have I really done such a shitty job showing you that I like you?"

Cupping my face now, Eryx's mouth curled into a crooked smile that flashed the smallest of dimples. "I'm beginning to learn that I'm always sticking my foot in it when you're around."

His answer simply doubled my questions. The guy was a walking freaking puzzle, and I felt absolutely clueless.

"You drive me crazy, Eryx. I tried hard to ignore you, but . . ."

His thumb began a slow seductive stroke across my cheek. "It seems fate has other plans for us."

We were leaning into each other, and if I rose up on my tiptoes, I could kiss him. I wanted to taste him so badly, but we'd been in this position too many times before, and I wouldn't survive another rejection.

"Eryx?" I murmured, desperately wanting him to make the next move. Just a few more inches and we'd discover just how explosive our chemistry could be. I still couldn't believe how strong my feelings for him were, especially after being so adamant that I wanted nothing romantically from him. Seems my education involved more than just magic classes.

"I shouldn't." His breath felt warm against my skin. We were so unbelievably close now. "I can't risk you, Tempest. No matter how much I want you . . . need you. I could never forgive myself for hurting you." His words trailed off, leaving us staring into each other's eyes.

I didn't bother asking him to explain his last comment. "Take a leap of faith. Why are you fighting so hard against this . . . against us? How will you know if you keep telling yourself not to act on your feelings?" The thought of kissing him all but consumed me. "Please. Kiss me."

And there it was. I'd finally laid my heart out on the table and begged Eryx for what I needed. I didn't care if he was right, and that this was one giant mistake just waiting to happen. If we both walked away without giving in to this moment, I knew we'd regret it.

"Please."

I saw it the second he decided. Closing my eyes, I titled my head back, shivering from the feather-like caress of his touch, and waited.

He didn't disappoint.

Cliché or not, the tender brush of his lips against mine, the slight hesitation he showed before committing to the kiss, was almost my undoing. No one had ever shown such care—such reverence—before, but that didn't prepare me from the onslaught of sensations that swept me away the instant he deepened the kiss, our tongues finally touching. I groaned into his mouth, surrendering to the way my body seemed to melt into him. Wave after wave of pure bliss crashed over us—each new dip of his tongue leaving me wanting more. My goddess, he could kiss, and standing there with my arms wrapped around his neck, weakened by how intense things felt between us, I knew that this would change everything.

No one could kiss like this and walk away from it.

I knew I couldn't, and judging by the way Eryx seemed reluctant to end our embrace, he had done the same as me—taken that leap of faith where we were free-falling together.

So when he broke away, breath ragged, his fingers digging into my arms, I wasn't prepared to see the horror in his eyes.

"Oh my god, Tempest. I'm so sorry. Please, please forgive me." His gaze jumped from my face to my body to my feet as he searched for some hidden injury. "I shouldn't have lost control."

Earlier this week, I would've lost my temper and accused him of being a player, but all I could do was laugh. "Are you seriously apologizing for giving me the best kiss I've ever had?"

I pressed my fingers against my lips, still feeling the warmth from his mouth. His shocked expression made me chuckle even harder.

"You're not hurt?" he asked quickly. "How do you feel?"

It was my turn to cup the side of his face, running my thumb over his strong jawline. "Like I've been devoured within an inch of my life."

I thought that would convince him, but my response did the exact opposite. "I need you to be serious, Tempest. I've been in love with you from almost the first time I saw you but had to keep you at arm's length."

"Why?"

He let out an exasperated sigh and dragged his fingers carelessly through his hair.

"Because bad things happen when I kiss people," he blurted out. "The last person I kissed ended up in a coma and never woke up. That's a fate I didn't want for you, no matter how desperately I wanted you."

My mind was reeling over his sudden revelation. "Wait, hold up. A coma?"

Eryx began pacing back and forth with agitation, refusing to look at me. "I made a vow that I would never surrender to my heart. That the only relationship I could have was one of friendship, but damn it, Tempest. I didn't see you coming."

I waited silently for him to finish when he abruptly stopped. His eyes widened like saucers as he stared at me like he couldn't believe what he was seeing. "How are you still standing?" He took me back into his arms. "Tempest, how are you even breathing?" Eryx stunned me further. Crashing his mouth over mine, he kissed me harder. "Are you honestly saying you feel nothing?"

How could I explain that I felt like I was simultaneously floating on air as my insides burned red hot? "Oh, I feel everything," I somehow managed to reply. "As well as confused because you're talking a lot of nonsense right now."

"Who are you?" It was like I hadn't uttered a word. "What are you?"

That last part was completely unexpected. "Who are you?" I fired back. "Why are you acting like you're crazy?"

Eryx simply stared at me as though I was some kind of miracle before he let out a chuckle. "You're right. I'm nuts. Whenever I imagined kissing you, I didn't think I'd feel so . . ." He searched for the right word.

"Dazzled?" I volunteered. "Smitten?"

The cawing sound of the raven that had just landed nearby filled the air, and for a brief second, it was almost like the black bird was laughing at my comment.

His brows crinkled into an adorable frown. "That's not quite the sentiment I was going for, but I'm sure we can figure it out together." Leaning in again, his lips hovered lightly above mine. "Starting right now."

After all the back and forth between us, there wasn't a hint of hesitation or rush.

He kissed me, and that's when the perfect word floated into my mind.

Miraculous.

I probably should've gone to see Micah first, but like the true glutton for punishment I was, I'd chosen the lesser of two evils—homework in the library. My endeavor to prove that I deserved to be removed from academic probation next semester.

Now as I stared down at the notes I'd scribbled in haste over the past few weeks, it was difficult to recognize whether I'd actually tapped into some weird, 'gift of tongues' kind of language, or that my handwriting sucked hard.

I was leaning toward the latter.

"Why didn't I just take Natalie's when she offered," I muttered beneath my breath, and with one swift movement, I tugged out my crystal hair stick so my hair could fall from the messy bun and down over my shoulders. I could feel a monster headache coming on—one that didn't involve the stress of hourglasses and danger, and merely the lack of a good night's sleep. If the throbbing didn't let up, I'd be making up a double dose of lavender tea tonight before bed.

Something had to give, and it couldn't be my sanity. Especially now that I was confident I wasn't losing it.

I checked my phone for the time. If I hurried, I would make it in time to talk with Micah before he left for Havenwood Falls for the night. Yet, I didn't budge from where I was, half slouched in my chair in the library. Coward. That's what I was.

"Treat it like a Band-aid and rip that sucker off. No thinking. Just do it." As though Natalie could somehow tap into my thoughts and sense my dramatic, angst-filled self-talk, a text from her rang through.

Stop procrastinating. She added a goofy faced emoji to soften the blow.

It was the kick in the pants I needed, I guess, because next thing I knew, I was packing up my gear, slinging my bag over my shoulder, and pushing my chair back into the desk.

Fine, I answered, and sent my own emoji back. The face with two crosses for eyes because the emoticon was dead. As an afterthought, I sent a few ghosts as well.

I'd almost managed to make it to the information desk when the most terrifying sound reverberated throughout the library— one that felt like a jolt of pure electricity.

A gong.

Another freaking gong.

I yanked up my cardigan sleeve, and my breath of relief was loud and explosive. It wasn't me—my school tattoo remained the same without being altered by that damn hourglass.

My gaze whipped around as I searched to see if anyone nearby was reacting, but all I saw were students like me who thought the library would be somewhat safe. As long as we followed the rules in here to the letter, nothing could go wrong.

Right?

I saw Vanna emerge from the stacks, followed closely by someone I'd seen around campus, but didn't really know personally. Whoever he was, the guy was hot. Like H. O. T. Hot. Something was going on between them, but that was instantly overshadowed by screams.

Blood curdling screams.

The campus had been once again thrown into danger and chaos.

Offering a prayer up to the Goddess, I asked for strength and wisdom on the student's behalf because as time slowly trickled through the hourglass that had no doubt appeared in the quad, they would need all the help they could get.

They'll be smarter than me. They won't foolishly go it alone.

And that's when I heard it—someone had been attacked right here in the library.

HEL OF A TIME

VICTORIA FLYNN

CHAPTER 1

What had made me ever consider the vampire's offer?

Rubbing my temples, I squinted at my computer screen and wanted to send a thousand curses to the sadistic asshole who invented the notion of research papers. Turns out I was a procrastinator, and now I was facing a forty-eight-hour rush to finish a five-page mid-term paper on Will-o-the-wisps. I just couldn't force myself to muster enough interest to care about the subject, which made the whole process a lot like pulling teeth—slow and painful.

Taylor Swift's new single blared through the walls of my dorm room from Fiona, the wood nymph who lived on the other side of the wall. Grabbing Venus from where she rested on my desk beside my computer, the cool metal twirled in my fingers as if by instinct. Venus was my knife, and the only one of my rather extensive collection my brother would allow me to bring with me to college.

I was still salty about it, but I refused to part with Venus. The black steel of the butterfly blade shone pristinely in the low light of my dorm room. The music ratcheted up a notch and then another until it was so loud I could hardly hear myself think.

"Oh, for fuck's sake! I'm never going to get this damn paper done at this rate," I groaned, flopping back in my chair and letting my ponytail spill over the edge.

Marina Del Mar, my roommate and fairly recent best friend, didn't even look up from her computer screen as she typed furiously.

"You missed the first concert this afternoon," she quipped, shaking her head just as I heard Fiona start singing right along with the song, off-key and a little pitchy. "She's not going to give it up for at least another hour. Go to the library, trust me. This time of night, there won't be anyone in there to bother you. Probably. Anyone you might run into will probably be doing the exact same thing you are. Plus, wasn't Professor Jameson offering extra credit if you used a physical source, not just electronic ones?"

Her dainty hand waved through the air animatedly as she spoke. It was amusing to watch Marina speak because she usually looked like she was conducting the Vienna Philharmonic, especially when she was passionate about her topic. This didn't rise to that occasion, but nevertheless, she was right. I'd toured the library when I'd first arrived, but nothing beyond that. Gathering my belongings, I resolved myself to exploring the library after the paper was finished. I hoped it would only be an hour, tops. Stuffing everything into my backpack, I headed for the door, cringing as Fiona hit a particularly shrill note. Swinging the door open, I nearly ran smack into Tempest Bell, who had the same irritated expression I'm sure I was sporting.

"Shit! Oh, um, hey," I murmured, backing up a little and adjusting my sunglasses to cover my eyes.

Her dark hair was piled high on her head, and her wide-eyed and strained face was indicative of the current standing between us —awkward and always by accident. Things had been quiet since my name had been cleared of the attacks.

"Do you think she's going to keep this up long? I've got a quiz I was trying to study for, and now I can't hear anything but that damn song!" she hollered, stepping across me to pound on the door beside ours.

"No clue, but I don't intend on finding out. So good luck with that. If you don't get anywhere with her, there's always the library," I mentioned back over my shoulder as I squeezed by her.

"I'm not sure which is worse," I heard her murmur right as Fiona's door swung open and Wren, Fiona's roommate, greeted her.

I didn't stop to voice my complaints, as much as I really fucking wanted to. Gods, some people just didn't have any consideration for their neighbors and weren't cut out for dorm life. A roommate didn't bother me in the least. Marina was great when we weren't both vying for the soaking tub she'd installed in the closet. She tended to take her sweet ass time in that department and to hell with anyone else who might want to use it. After the first few weeks, we'd sort of figured out each other's schedules, and it hadn't been a problem since.

Since making it through the trials and coming to Hel Tower, I'd thought the Sun & Moon Academy would be my fresh start. The reality was that when people looked at me, they still saw my tattoos, white blond hair, and sunglasses and saw me for the outlaws my family were. My father, the late and great Trigger Shaw, had been a member of the SIN MC Charlotte, North Carolina charter before being torn apart in a rival MC feud. My older brother, Colton, who was also patched in, moved us out to Havenwood Falls shortly after that. It was just the two of us. Thankfully, the Havenwood Falls charter of SIN had welcomed us with open arms. I wasn't a member, but that didn't mean shit to anyone else. Not even most of my friends apparently. Being accused of being a beast attacking students had stung more than a little bit, and while I didn't hate Tempest for it happening in the first place, I wasn't her biggest fan either. Her silence had been deafening. Now, I just wanted to get through the year without any more excitement.

That wasn't too much to ask for, was it?

CHAPTER 2

$\mathcal{S}$triding through the large wooden doors, I froze nearly mid-step when my eyes fell on the cavernous library. The stone structure rose from the ground toward the skylight, and windows and a grand arched entrance greeted me as I shuffled into the atrium. The library was designed like a hive, spiraling toward the skylight above with at least a dozen levels. I'd even heard whispers of students getting lost in the stacks, but that notion seemed a little ridiculous. How hard could it be to find a book and check out?

"You here to pick up? Or are you looking for something in particular?" a deep voice queried from behind the librarian's desk.

Rising from his chair, Vidar strode around the desk, grabbing a stack of books as he went. He didn't stop as he walked past me and continued onto the far wall.

"Sort of. I'm looking for what you might have on Will-o-the-wisps and a quiet place to finish my paper."

"Well, internet in here is spotty at best, but you shouldn't have any trouble if you're just typing," he answered.

With a flip of his head, the hair moved aside, and he looked me over.

"Wisps should be on level nine, section four, aisle twelve. If you hit Wisteria or Wolpertinger, you've gone too far," he answered, pointing to the rickety elevators ahead.

I followed his stare to the lift. "Thanks, Vidar."

He went about his business, loading books onto a cart and heading for the other elevator. When I had almost reached the iron-caged contraption, the librarian's assistant called after me.

"Oh, there was something else you should know. Be careful in the stacks. Things in here have the tendency to have a mind all their own, and there's been reports of some strange sightings in the higher levels," Vidar added, pointing toward the peak of the library. "That brings me to my second point: do not under any circumstances touch any books you aren't looking for. Just like everything else here, some of them are sentient and have dark secrets all their own."

Then, like nothing had happened at all, he turned and went back about his business. The muscles at the corners of my mouth twitched and turned down in a frown. Even for a college filled with the paranormal, some folks were just weirder than others.

"Great. Nine, four, twelve." I sighed, tugging open the metal grate that was the elevator door.

Searching for a button to push, the low light gleamed off a copper-colored lever in the corner of the cage. My fingers wrapped around the handle, pulling up the trigger and pushing the bar forward. The elevator jolted to life, carrying me upward slowly. Mentally, I repeated the numbers over and over again. Every level had platforms, and the floor number was crudely carved into the stone. A single light hung from overhead, and it swayed with the movement of the elevator.

"Nine, twelve, four. Nine, twelve, four," I repeated every few seconds, to make sure I didn't forget the numbers.

As soon as the ninth platform came into view, I jerked the lever back into place and released the trigger and secured the brakes. Tugging the folding grate aside, I stepped out of the elevator and let the grate extend back shut. On the stone edifice of the ninth level wall were directions pointing to the left for section four and the right for section five. I needed twelve. Stepping carefully, I followed close to the wall, searching for the twelfth section. I hadn't made it more than twenty feet before I felt a presence with me. I couldn't hear a damn thing, but I could feel it. Something was there. I took a few more steps, before the sound of someone walking behind me had me rounding on them, ready to attack.

"Whoa, there. Take it easy, killer," a deep voice mocked from the shadows, stepping forward into the torchlight.

A man a few inches taller than myself held his hands up, but his amused lips betrayed the mocking undertone.

"Are you following me?" I accused, ready to shift if I had to. This was one of the few instances where I was absolutely sure I was the baddest bitch in the shadows. His scent hit my nose, and the mystery was solved.

A little pale. No pulse. And the unnatural urge to protect him . . . dead, but not. This guy was definitely a vampire. With a really great smile . . . while he was laughing at me. Dropping my hands, I stepped back and adjusted my sunglasses. Trying not to notice the way he filled out his red plaid flannel button up shirt like it had been made for him.

"Were you following me? You practically just jumped me for no reason," he countered, crossing his arms over his chest and staring smugly down at me. "It's your first time in the stacks, isn't it?" he added after a second, dropping his voice to a conspiratorial whisper.

His eyes were twinkling like he was a child on Christmas morning. This whole fucking thing was a joke to him; he was toying with me. Irritation began to saw away at my last nerve, and I refused to be baited further.

"So what if it is? I'm sure there's a whole lot of folks who don't have the balls to venture up here in the first place. I'm counting myself lucky I'm not one of them," I answered with a shrug.

"I'd say you'd be right, but then I'd have to point out you seem pretty jumpy and probably shouldn't be discussing one's balls unless you're familiar with them," he answered, burying his hands in his pockets.

My kind, hellhounds, were drawn to the dead. We were their

guardians by nature. In this instance, I was starting to think I might make an exception. Holding up my empty wrist like I was searching for the time, I started walking away from him, hoping he'd get the hint and go back to being a shadow creeper.

"Thank you for pointing out my instincts were on point; maybe don't follow random women around the stacks. The next one might not be as forgiving as me. Wouldn't want to ruin that pretty face," I replied, casting one last annoyed glance toward the offending man.

A deep, full-bellied laugh erupted from his luscious mouth. I didn't stick around to stroke his ego more than I already had.

"The name's Asher," he called after me, but I waved him off.

"You know, *Asher*, you shouldn't be so free with your name. A name has power and giving that to the wrong person only invites trouble." My voice was barely above a whisper, but I knew he could hear me perfectly, even separated by a wall of stone shelving and dusty tomes.

I lifted my face to the bookshelf and scanned over the titles. The wrongness of what I was looking at struck me almost instantly.

Gigantes. Girtablilu.

Definitely not the Ws, then. It had been level nine, section twelve, aisle four, right?

"Shit," I hissed, turning to glance at the shelves behind me.

They were still Gs, beginning to turn over to the H section of texts. Asher's smooth voice piped up from the other side of the bookcase.

"Sometimes, a name is just a name. So, what about you, Snow White? A woman like you probably has a name with some character. Agnes? Mildred? No, I've got it. Dorcas?"

I couldn't help the chuckle his stupid joke drew from me. If only he knew how close he was the first time. No. Not Snow White. But Vanna White. At least, that's what my brother and the rest of SIN called me. My name was Vanessa, but ever since I could remember, my hair had always been the same near white blond color it still was. That's where I got the nickname from. It was just Vanna for short. Asher didn't know that though.

I shook my head and hissed, "That's it. You've got me."

On the other side of the bookcase, I could hear the sounds of books and pages shuffling around. I was half expected the man to pop his head through the shelf, but he didn't.

"I guess I could always go through the registrar. Shouldn't be too hard to find out what your name is. Not too many hellhounds in attendance, I wouldn't think," he quipped. The humor was evident, but so was his seriousness.

He would do it.

"Pretty sure they frown on things like that. They don't like the privacy of their students to be compromised," I answered, trying to get a feel for him. "Things like that could get you expelled."

His laugh was smooth, like the creamiest caramel and almost lyrical. Damn it, I wanted to kick myself for even thinking it, but that was the sexiest laugh I'd heard in a while. In a nerdy, frat boy kind of way.

"I don't think they'll expel me. I have it on fairly good authority I'm in this for the long haul."

There was a teasing tone in his voice that had me side-eyeing him through the bookcase.

"You sound pretty damn certain about that. Cocky even. Wait, I know. You're a trust-fund brat. Did Daddy write a big check to get you in here?" I volleyed back.

An amused grunt answered. "Something like that. Less trust fund, more connections to the right type of people with deep pockets. Although, I'd like to think I'm here on my own merits."

At that, it was my turn to laugh.

"So, what do you say, Snow White? Can I have a name? Maybe discuss it over a pizza at Napoli's? Or a coffee at Coffee Haven?"

I had to admit, he had balls, and he was persistent, even if it was a little annoying.

"You know you want to say yes," he challenged when I didn't answer right away.

I could hear the smile in his voice as he said it, and I found myself torn. The more reasonable side of me wanted to tell Mr. Smug and Handsome to go fuck himself. The other part of me wanted to live on the edge and throw all caution to the wind, accept his answer and the consequences be damned. He was probably one of those assholes who would be great in bed for one night only and exit just as quickly as he came. I shouldn't want that. Normal girls would want happily ever after. I wasn't normal though. Happily ever after was a myth for a hellhound, at least as a woman.

Biting my lip, I cracked a smile and knew I'd just made a deal with the Devil.

"The name is Vanessa, and I'd love both," I answered, reaching for my bag to grab paper for my phone number.

As soon as my fingertips brushed the metal pull-tab of my backpack, the tiny hairs on the back of my neck stood on end. I abandoned the task and moved to exit the aisle when I heard the sound of something heavy slide against the metal shelf, and I froze mid-step.

"Vanessa?" Asher asked, brow furrowed in confusion and concern. "Did I say something?"

I shook my head and brought my index finger to my lips, begging for a moment of his indulgence.

Turning slowly, I scanned the aisle for any sign that we weren't alone. Nothing stood out, yet when I went to turn, something caught my eye.

On the shelf just over my head, the spine of a worn, brown leather book protruded over the ledge of the bookcase. I stepped back from the wall of books and stared hard at the seemingly innocuous text. It hadn't been there before, at least not so visible. There was no writing along the binding and nothing on the cover that would give me any hint as to the book's contents. Vidar's warning was still fresh in my mind, and I knew better than to toss aside warnings as merely an overly cautious suggestion. Danger lurked at every turn in the Sun & Moon Academy, even within the confines of pages. A deep resounding gong rang loudly, vibrating every surface within Mount Alexa.

Oh shit!

Not again, not another one. My blood turned to ice in my

veins, a sensation I wasn't used to feeling, being a fire manipulator. The ominous ringing of the gong ignited a chain of whispers sweeping across campus. Another hourglass had turned; something was coming. A knot twisted tightly in my belly at the thought of the previous hourglass. That fucking beast had gotten me arrested. I wasn't sure I could withstand another run-in like the one I'd had before. I might survive, and that was a shoddy maybe at best, but the odds of getting through without being kicked out of the university were much slimmer.

I heard another thud behind me and glanced over my shoulder for the briefest second possible, seeing nothing, before the tattoo of the Sun & Moon Academy crest began to burn, an hourglass appearing where my Hel Tower sigil and the SMA crest had been inked.

Another thud sounded right in front of me, but this time, the text was no longer on the shelf above my head, but levitating in mid-air, no more than a foot in front of me. My forearm was on fire, or at least it felt like it. I hissed, grabbing at the magically inked skin like I could tear it off my body and get away from it. In a moment of complete desperation, I grabbed for the book and shoved the cover open, scanning over the pages in the hope there would be a spell, or something—anything—that would make the burning stop.

Just as soon as the scorching pain tore through my academy crest, it vanished.

"Vanessa?" Asher asked, stepping around the bookshelf at the opposite end of the aisle.

I looked down at the tome I'd opened, expecting to see elegant script scribbled across the pages, detailing some sort of magic. However, what I found was a little more alarming. The pages, every single one, were blank. I flipped the pages furiously as I tried to find something, Vidar's warning ringing loud and clear in my head.

"Asher?" I whispered, feeling the temperature in the aisle plunge.

"Don't panic. Just put the book down and walk to me." He waved, his tone urging me to act quickly.

I tried to place the book back on the shelf, but it refused to budge from where it hovered. Then, with my eyes raptly glued to the open pages of the book, they began to flip. Each page was turned by an unseen force. My breaths came in short pants, turning to puffs of clouds in the frigid air. Wind picked up and swirled around the book, driving me backward. My eyes locked with Asher's and a gust of wind that could rival a hurricane tore from the book. It drove straight through me, knocking me aside into the bookcase like it was a freight train.

I heard the thud of the double doors at the library's entrance as they were thrown forcefully open. Asher was to me in a flash, tugging me to my feet and checking me over for any sign of injury.

"Are you all right? Are you hurt anywhere? I don't smell blood . . . wait, yes, I do. Not yours, though," he added, lifted his nose in the air.

Scrambling to get up, I could smell it too, the coppery tang of fresh blood. There was a rich spiciness to it that tipped off the presence of magic in the owner's essence. A scream tore through the atrium, echoing through the cavern, and a chill shot down my spine. It was only warmed by Asher's supporting, comforting touch as he steadied me and made sure I wasn't more injured. His blue eyes locked with mine, and then we both turned to the book.

The brown leather tome was shut up tightly like nothing had happened and lay innocently on the floor of aisle four.

"What the actual fuck was that?" I gasped, staring at the blank binding with horrified realization.

"No fucking clue, but I suggest not sticking around to find out if it comes back. Let's go," he answered, urging me out of the aisle and back toward the elevator, snatching the book from the ground before he followed behind.

"What the hell are you doing? Put that down!" I hissed, trying to bat the book from his grasp.

I wanted absolutely nothing more to do with whatever the fuck had been living within those pages. My fingers wrapped protectively around my wrist, cradling the flesh bearing the Halvard crest tattoo. The burning had subsided, but I could still feel it just as vividly, like the ink was as alive as I was but separate, letting me know it was awake and in charge.

It was the same thing that had happened to Tempest. There was no doubt what it meant, and the responsibility fell on my shoulders. The anxious knot in the pit of my belly grew larger. Asher jerked open the grate of the elevator, and we both stepped on, before beginning our descent.

"You . . . you know what this means, right?" I stammered, my brow furrowed as my mind raced with possibilities.

Asher's chin dipped in the affirmative, and my fingers brushed over the lines of the crest absently. The vision of the book floating, its pages whipping wildly about, replayed in my mind like it was on a loop. What the hell had been inside those pages?

My handsome new acquaintance was scanning over the binding of the text, searching for any clues that might give us some answers. As we descended to the main lobby, we discovered the source of all the commotion. Peering through the open iron-rimmed doors of the elevator, I watched as the crowd below grew. The elevator's brakes squealed as we came to a stop in the lobby. Everyone was huddled around a table at the front of the study hall, wide-eyed, shocked whispers filling the air. Asher and I spilled out of the gated contraption and made a beeline for the crowd, desperate to know what had everyone's attention.

"Asher? What was in the book?" I asked as we approached the throng of bodies. My eyes were practically boring holes through them as I shuffled toward the source of the scent of blood.

Hushed whispers swirled around me as the few souls in the library caught wind of what had happened. We got closer, and I began to hear pained groans. Asher stopped, eyeing something on the book that had snagged his attention, yet I continued, pushing one of the Jormungand residents aside to see the man on the ground.

My brows nearly kissed my hairline as I stared at the shredded T-shirt of a Modi student—Shirley Velisk, a basilisk I knew from

Energies. He was panting and wincing every time he moved his arm as he tried to assess the damage to his ribs. Blood soaked through the fabric of his shirt, but thankfully, the lacerations didn't look like they were too deep. I tugged my phone from my back pocket and quickly snapped a photo of the carnage to examine closer later.

"Did you see what did it?" The words flew out of my mouth before I could think or stop them.

Asher was moving the few concerned students back to give the man some room. My eyes went to the bloodied flesh on his ribcage. There was something strange about the wound; it had a pattern. Whatever had made those marks had done it with its mouth—that was definitely a bite. The bleeding was slowing down as the man's healing abilities began to kick in. Yet, the wound didn't shrink in size like it should've. It was the oddest thing. As Shirley moved to get up from his chair, he wobbled, unsteady.

Stepping back, I gave the guy some room, but he went down like a ton of bricks just as soon as he stood upright and let go of his stabilizing hold on the chair. Someone on his other side caught him before he completely wrecked himself on the table, but Shirley was a big guy. The person catching him was not, and only served to soften the victim's landing. People surged forth, everyone rushing to help the guy while I just tried to get the hell out of the way. I felt sick with wondering whether his injury was related to the strange occurrence with the book in the stacks. Had anyone else seen what had happened? The cawing of a bird caught my attention, and I glanced up to see a black raven taking flight. Its wings beat quickly and carried it out through the library doors. What the hell was it even doing in here?

With the gong and my tattoo lighting up like the Fourth of July fireworks display, I seriously questioned the chance of it simply being a coincidence. Such things didn't seem to exist at Halvard. My hand absently fished my phone from my pocket, opening the screen and pulling up the photo of Shirley's wound.

The pattern was distinct, teeth marks were clear. How could no one have seen anything?

Looking up from the picture on my phone, my eyes locked with Asher's blue gaze. He slipped the book, no larger than a supermarket romance, into the interior pocket of his jacket. There was something in the tightness around his eyes that had me worried; whatever he had found left him tense. He was very clearly unsettled.

"Professor Kincaid! Let him through! Shirley was attacked!" some faceless female voice called out from the throng of bodies.

A bright, heart-shaped face popped up next to Asher, her hands wrapping securely around his arm as the woman dragged him forward. Her hold was both possessive and intimate in a way that made me pretty damn certain I was spying on something I shouldn't. Normally, I wasn't the type of girl who liked to jump to conclusions without having all the facts. However, the next words out of her mouth just had to test that notion.

"Move! Professor Kincaid needs to get through," the woman on his arm announced, shoving him through the crowd with more force than should've been capable in her small form.

Wait . . . did she say *professor?*

sher knelt down next to Shirley, asking him questions too low for me to hear over the whispers and anxious chatter. I eyed everything with disbelief from the plaid flannel shirt right down to his Converse, all while wondering how I'd been duped. The woman, or should I say student, who towed Asher away before I could say more to him, observed me with obvious disdain. Like a shepherd dog, she maneuvered her body until she stood between him and me, cutting off my view.

The bits and pieces of the puzzle that was Asher began clicking neatly into place. About roughly three quarters of the student body knew of Professor Kincaid, the cyber technology teacher. The female half gushed over him and the male half generally respected him, but I'd never seen the man in question before . . . that is, until today. The woman, a raven-haired mage if I trusted my nose, stood over him like a guard dog, warding off anyone who ventured too close to the man.

I didn't care. I was too busy trying to wrap my head around the doozy that had just been hurled at my already preoccupied brain. Nervous and paranoid, I glanced around the library, wondering if anyone had seen what happened. Hell, did it have anything to do with what happened with the book?

Shit.

The gnawing guilt in my gut and the hourglass dropping magical sand told me the answer wasn't one I'd like. This time it really was my fault. I spied Vidar from where he stood two floors up, watching the scene from the balcony. His accusing stare met mine, extinguishing any doubt about his ignorance. Panic bubbled under my semi-composed surface, and I wanted more than anything to run back to the safety of my dorm room, where there were no dangerous books, bitey things, or knee-weakening professors to worry about.

Asher caught my attention just as he was helping a rather pale looking Shirley to his feet. It looked like he wanted to say something to me, but I didn't need to hear more. Shirley's arm was thrown over Professor Kincaid's shoulder as he helped the injured man through the library.

"All right, everyone, show's over. Back to class, studies, or whatever the hell you're supposed to be doing now. Marisol? Can you see to it that Mr. Velisk makes it to the infirmary?"

The woman opened her mouth to protest, clearly unhappy with his dismissal of her. His eyes never left mine as he spoke, a fact that only served to infuriate Marisol further. He started for me, pushing his way through the crowd of bodies.

He was a professor, and I was a student. I didn't have to be a rocket scientist to know the odds didn't work out in our favor. Not to mention, the Sun & Moon Academy was beginning to grow on me a little; getting kicked out for an inappropriate relation with a professor wasn't too high on my priority list. Colton, my older brother, would be broken by that kind of scandal, especially as the sort of guy who had scared off every guy I'd liked since before our father had been killed. In a panic, I slipped into the crowd of dispersing students like he wouldn't be able to find me as I snuck out of the library.

Asher—no, that was too personal. I needed to remember he was Professor Kincaid and nothing more. Either way, he still had the book and whatever had escaped from it was loose on campus. The tattoo had been a sign; I was on my own in finding whatever escaped, and if I failed, well, I was pretty scared of what might happen to everyone under and outside of Mount Alexa. No one knew specifics, but the implication was clear: it wouldn't be good. My thoughts strayed to Tempest and the ache in my chest panged with sympathy. I fucking hated admitting that I could've handled things with her differently after the arrest, and I wasn't about to tell her she was right for what she did, but I was beginning to understand the weight of what she'd dealt with.

Professor Kincaid moved with purpose, and before I even had time to think about what I was doing, I was retreating. My feet carried me to the center of the thickest group of students, not bothering to pay any attention to the weird looks or protests of my intrusion into their personal space. Bursting through the library's large double doors, I moved quickly as I tore into the hallway of Halstein Hall. I couldn't face him, not yet. Avoidance would be difficult given the relatively small size of the campus, yet there was no doubt it was the best course of action in this situation.

"It's not every day you see a hound of Hell running like a scared little kitty," Asher mused, a cocky grin dancing on his lips.

Are you freaking kidding me?

The vampire stepped in front of me, emerging from the side hall without seeming to even have a hair out of place. I stopped just before I barreled right into him, still too close for comfort. Heaven help me, his mouth was right there for the claiming too. It would be so easy, but it was a move that could cost me everything.

Stepping back, I couldn't look at him, not directly.

"I'm not sure what kind of game you're playing here, and frankly I don't care, but I need that book."

I squared my shoulders to him and crossed my arms over my chest, putting anything I could between us. Asher's eyes flashed amusedly. Reaching into his jacket, he pulled the book from his pocket.

"This book?" he quipped, holding the binding between his fingers. "Jealousy smells beautiful on you, by the way." His voice dropped conspiratorially low, and he took a step closer.

Who the hell could I possibly be jealous of? There wasn't even anything to be jealous of . . . certainly not Asher, AKA the poster child for why vitamin D is essential, or Marisol, the teacher's pet.

"Not jealous. That would imply you mean something to me, and you don't. What I am is stressed the fuck out because all I was trying to do was write this damn paper. Instead of getting that accomplished, I've got an hourglass ticking down the minutes until its doom-and-gloom time and a professor who's being a little friendlier than the Regents would probably care to hear about. You might not face expulsion, but I could. This is . . . oh, never mind. It isn't important."

He didn't need to know that I was here as a last chance before Sheriff Kasun would haul my ass in front of the Court of the Sun and the Moon. I wasn't proud of my checkered past, no matter how recent. Colton needed me here, even if his own thick head didn't know it.

At the mention of an hourglass, Asher's brows nearly hit his hairline. He moved so quickly, I didn't have time to react before he grabbed my arm and scrutinized my tattoo for himself.

"Hey! What the hell?"

"Your tattoo had a reaction when you heard the gong?"

His eyes were intense, razor-focused on me and the next words out of my mouth. Surely, he was just concerned as a professor would be for a student in a difficult spot, right? I wasn't prepared to venture down the rabbit hole to explore any other reason he might be interested in my wellbeing.

"Yeah, hurt like a bitch too, then the gong. Or maybe the gong was first? Hell, I don't remember. Then, you saw everything after that with the book and the attack."

Thankfully, he was so preoccupied with my admission, the other topics were all but forgotten. He nodded once but made no attempt to reply or share what he was thinking. I had no time for that sort of bullshit, though. I had shit to do.

"So, about that book. You know, finish this paper, find the big baddie, and save the day? Hero shit. Supernatural Guardian worthy, even," I urged, unable to keep a straight face. "Let's call this on-the-job training."

Asher recovered his sarcastic charm in record fashion.

"After you unleashed who the hell knows what from its pages? Yeah, let me hand that right over after it went so well the last time. No. I'll hold onto it for now until we know what we're dealing with and that there's no nasty surprises waiting for us within the pages."

I could've smacked him, but I was trying to turn over a new leaf—make a brighter future for myself and all that jazz. He had a way of getting under my skin, though, and that was dangerous.

"Until we find out what we're dealing with, I think it's best I hold onto the book. I might have a few ideas about what we could be dealing with, and I'd like the chance to look into those before anything else, starting with a closer inspection of Mr. Velisk's injury. Can I trust you to stay out of trouble? Maybe we can discuss our findings over that dinner I mentioned?"

There it was again, the glaring reminder of how off limits this whole situation was.

"Pass."

I moved to step around him, resolved to finish my paper with Fiona's serenade, but he blocked my attempt.

"What's changed? Why rescind your acceptance? Couldn't be because of Marisol, could it?"

"I'm just going to pretend to know who that is and say sure. It's absolutely about Marisol. She can have you, and until you get it through your thick skull, I don't need to screw around with professors to get better grades or special treatment. There won't be any dinners, coffees, or shenanigans. I just want to do my work and move on with my life."

He started laughing, full-on deep belly laughs like it was the funniest damn thing he'd ever heard. My fists were balled so tightly at my sides, my knuckles cracked under the pressure.

Just walk away, Vanna. Don't engage.

My teeth were clenched so hard, my jaw began to ache with the strain. It was a freaking miracle that I forced my feet around him as I pushed by. Heat was building under my skin, and if Asher wasn't careful, he was going to get burned.

"I'm sorry, how rude of me. It's just that you're acting like the Board of Regents or anyone else here gives a damn who's involved with whom. They don't, for the most part," Asher answered with a chuckle and a shake of his head.

"I don't get it. Don't they usually frown on faculty-student relationships?"

He shrugged, indifferent.

"I'm not your professor, and I'm not leveraging my position to make you do something you don't want to, am I? We're both consenting adults, and what happens behind the privacy of a closed bedroom door is nobody's business but ours. Until we have an actual conflict of interest, you're borrowing trouble."

The just cause which had been inflating my anger was popped in an instant, leaving me without the foggiest clue what my next move should be. Could I trust what he was saying? He would probably know better than me what the Board of Regents and the President of the college would do if any lines were crossed. In a way, I kind of agreed with Asher on his points, but there was exactly zero percent chance of me admitting he was right to his face. The knowing leer he was giving me told me he didn't have to be told; he already knew he was right. Just like that, it came full circle, leaving me royally pissed.

I couldn't stand there for another minute, embarrassed and frazzled by every single sentence that spilled from those lush lips. He was hot as sin, there was no denying that, but whatever was going on between us needed to stop. Asher wasn't going to give up easily, though, and he didn't seem like the type to understand anything other than the clearly drawn and labeled obvious.

Thankfully, Asher was a smart man, and he knew he was playing with fire and when I was about to build into a downright inferno. Although, a well-seasoned vampire kebab didn't sound entirely unappealing. Perhaps that's even what scared me about Professor Kincaid. He burrowed right under my walls like a mole and popped up too close for comfort. He knew exactly what buttons to push, and he pressed away like I was one of his keyboards. And I was loving every second of it.

I wanted him; I would allow myself that admission. However, having my cake and eating it too wasn't possible. My mood hadn't improved by the time I returned to my dorm either.

"What's wrong with you?" Marina asked.

"Nothing!" I exclaimed a little too abruptly, not to mention loud for the small space. "What makes you think something's wrong?" I asked, busying myself with my computer to avoid Marina's prying eyes.

"Is that a for real question, right now? Just look at yourself. You're practically coming out of your skin. What the fuck happened at the library?" she replied, moving to stand beside me.

When I didn't answer right away, she slid her fingers over the lip of my laptop and guided the machine closed. I tugged my hands back out of the way, lest they be squashed by my roommate's inquiring mind. When something caught Marina's attention, she became more like a harpy than anything else and she wouldn't give up until she got what she wanted.

In that split second, I decided to only tell her what she absolutely needed to know. Asher, well, he wasn't a need-to-know. There was nothing going on between the two of us and there never would be; I'd make sure of it. For reasons I didn't really want to examine very closely, he was just mine for the time being. As long as I didn't share him, or tell anyone about him, I could hold on to whatever was there between us for just a while longer. Asher felt dangerous, everything about me wanting him was wrong, but maybe that was part of the thrill?

Marina shifted around, making her irritation known.

"Don't freak out and whatever you do, do not scream when I tell you what happened at the library, okay?" I said, looking directly at her.

CHAPTER 4

hat's how she knew I was serious. I kept my sunglasses on, so I didn't hurt her, you know, just in case. Looking in the eyes of a hellhound three times meant death for a mortal and even some supernaturals. Her perfectly arched dark brows rose at my candidness, but her arms dropped to her sides, and she moved to grab her chair. Pulling it over, Marina sat down, resting her elbows on her knees as I relayed everything as I'd remembered it, leaving out only the bits about Asher and his involvement.

"Holy stars! So that was the bell I heard. You're okay though, right? Nobody died. That's a good thing. So . . ." Marina paused, scrunching her face up like she did when she was thinking really hard. "Where's the book?"

And just like that, my whole cover story is shot to hell.

I hadn't thought that far ahead. Asher had the book. I'd been so desperate to get away from him and clear my head that I'd let him take the damn thing with him. We had no real plans to see each other again, either.

I shrugged, glancing at the floor.

"I don't know, you know . . . everything happened so fast and then the guy, Shirley was his name, I think, well, he got attacked, and I just wanted to get the hell out of there," I stammered.

450

"You know what this means, right?" Marina squealed far too giddily to be my best friend.

I said nothing but raised my brows with a questioning look.

"This is your chance to clear your name, show everyone here that you're not the troublemaker they want to believe you are. This is your moment to shine, Vanna."

Shit. I hadn't thought of that either. My luck was shit, too. The more likely outcome would be that I fail miserably, and everyone dies. Or just someone I really care about.

"I don't know, Mar. Whatever came out of that book, no one ever saw a damn thing. We don't even know what we're dealing with. For all we know, it could be something nasty," I groaned, knowing deep down that she was right, even if it meant a hell of a time for me.

"You're a hellhound, boo. Ain't no better beastie around to track down something unseen than you. We both know it. Tracking is your specialty."

Groaning, I turned my mouth down in a dramatic frown. But . . . what about my paper? Professor Jameson would never excuse my midterm paper, not for any reason short of ultimate death. Even then, I wouldn't be surprised if she asked for the document from beyond the grave.

"And what am I supposed to do about my midterm? I simply don't have time to track down this thing and finish my paper. I'm not *Superwoman*."

"You're right. You're a supernatural guardian, and you were the one who let it out. Sorry to be the bearer of bad news, but you made this mess, and it's sort of on you to fix it. Don't get me wrong. I wouldn't miss this for the world, but you don't get a pass just because your schedule gets a little busy. Buckle up, buttercup, it's time to hunt the big bad . . . again. You know, I really hope this isn't going to be a trend on campus. It's like they want us to fail," Marina quipped, her mind changing course as freely as water flowed.

Pinching the bridge of my nose, I made my peace with the notion I was probably going to fail Introduction to Energies. Odds were, I was going to be the only one without a paper to submit in Thursday's class. I had to wonder about the string of challenges SMA students had already had to face.

"Maybe it's not the Board of Regents behind what's going on? Something about it feels wrong. I can't think what they could stand to gain from this venture going sideways," I murmured, my thoughts running wild with the possibilities.

Marina shrugged, not caring one fig about the Board or what could be roaming around Halvard. Instead, she was diving into her closet and sending outfits flying from their hangers toward her bed. She had a slight obsession with clothes and had an outfit for every occasion.

"Would you say leggings or jeans?" she called into the muffling fabric hanging in front of her as she pushed things around the rack and out of her way.

"Does hunting something like invisible book phantoms have a dress code?" I replied, crossing to my desk where I flipped up the lid of my laptop.

It was evident she wasn't listening to what I was saying. When it came to deciding on something to wear, Marina would take her sweet ass time, and since time was at a premium, I would make my minutes count. As I reached for a bottle of water, the edge of the hourglass that had hijacked my SMA tattoo peeked out from under the edge of my jacket sleeve. Tugging back the fabric, I saw that the sand was already passing through the narrowed middle, almost a quarter gone.

My stomach sank. Time was running out and fast.

My roommate mumbled something unintelligible before throwing me a glare and shaking her head like she wouldn't claim me for my insolence. I let the sleeve fall back into place and tried not to let it bother me, but I was fighting a losing battle.

"Of course, it has a certain fashion requirement depending on the task. It's like you haven't been listening to a thing I've taught you for the last couple months." Marina sighed, returning her attention back to her wardrobe and temporarily distracting me from the impending destruction of my new home.

As the machine warmed up and restored every tab to my browser, there was still the task of finishing my research paper. I stared at the screen like I was half expecting it to write itself. That would've been immensely easier than the actual assignment. Absently, I began tapping away on the keys as I covered the general idea of will-o-the-wisps and began to compile the full extent of what they were. Before I even realized it, I'd cleared a page of boring information and was well onto a second when the pinging of my email inbox caught my attention.

I clicked on the email icon and froze as soon as I saw the name. Peeking over my shoulder, I saw that Marina had chosen her pants and was busy trying to find the perfect top, a process which refused to be rushed. For once, I was grateful she was too wrapped up in her fashion to notice the rigid posture I'd adopted when I saw Professor Kincaid's name. Asher was the last person I was expecting to hear from, especially this soon. Not that I was so naïve to think he would leave me alone. Asher Kincaid wasn't the type of man to give up that easily.

The muscles in my cheeks twitched, threatening to force a smile for that man, and my hands immediately went to my cheeks to cover the traitorous grin. Scrolling over his name, my eyes quickly darted over the subject.

Important.

Just a single word on the subject line, but that one word held so much meaning. I didn't have to guess to know exactly what this was about, and it had nothing to do with Asher's flirting or my growing attraction to him. I clicked on the email and read through his words carefully, sure not to miss anything.

Vanessa,

There's been another attack. Need to see you ASAP. Please meet me at my office in Haldor Hall, #28, at 7 o'clock.

Best,

Asher

PS, if you're late, I'll come to you.

. . .

Instinctively, I knew there wasn't any threat in his email, only promises. The thrill that snaked its way down my spine caught me off guard. He had me twisted into knots, and nothing had even happened between us. That damnable sense of humor, those crisp blue eyes, and gods . . . those dimples were sending me right back to my middle school years when I pined away for the Charlotte chapter SIN MC president's son, Rex.

"Earth to Vanna . . . what do you think of this?" Marina said louder, snapping me out of my daze.

How long had she been trying to talk to me? I didn't have time to think about it too hard, judging by the way she was leering at me.

"That's great. I didn't know it was possible to be runway ready and utilitarian at the same time," I quipped, assessing her

"Jokes. That's just great. Well, if you think you could do a better job?"

I threw my hands up in defeat. "You're right. I have no idea what I'm doing. You look great. Sorry, I've just got a lot on my mind right now. If we're going to look for the creature tonight, we need to get a move on."

"This thing really has you on edge, doesn't it?" she said, crossing the space and plopping down onto the edge of my bed, a couple feet from me.

I nodded, still not ready to divulge the full extent of what I was dealing with. Marina was the closest thing I'd ever had to a best friend, and she'd picked up on a lot about me since we'd begun cohabitating. That didn't mean I trusted her with my deepest darkest secrets, though. She hadn't earned that kind of trust yet.

No one had. Except Colton, but he didn't count.

"Well, I don't know about you, but I'll feel a lot better when we at least know what we're dealing with. It's the in-between, not knowing that's getting to me right now and... never mind, it's stupid." I leaned back, letting my hair spill over my shoulder, nearly touching the bed, and I stared hard at the ceiling.

"Don't be that chick who starts to tell me something big and then bails. That's like Xavier pulling out right before I come apart. Shit's just cruel. I can't say I won't be judgey when it comes to whatever shit you're holding onto, but I can promise you I'll tell you the truth and help with what I can. Deal?" Marina's dark brow arched in question as she thrust her hand forward in a formal handshake.

I had to give it to her. Marina could be odd in her mannerisms at times and she totally lacked tact, but she was a straight shooter, and I could appreciate that. This wasn't Asher-big, but it was uncomfortable and something that had been weighing on me since the tattoo had begun to burn.

Reaching forward, I grabbed her hand and shook. "What happens if I fail? No one else has . . . Shit, even Tempest sent her beast back. But . . . what if I can't do this? If it's anything like what's already happened, people die, Marina! That's what happens if I can't take care of this."

Her face softened then, and she leaned forward, grabbing ahold of my hand to keep me from panicking more than I already was. The more I said, the more the dam around my self-doubt began to crumble and send everything bubbling to the surface.

"Then I guess it's a good thing you don't have to handle this by yourself. I got you, girl. Whatever this thing is, you're a hellhound, and this bruja got your back." Marina's dark brown eyes lightened to sea green in the middle, but there was nothing other than honesty in those pools. "Now, let's go hunting."

With a quick strong jerk, Marina tugged me up from the bed and hauled me out the door before I could protest. I didn't even have time to close my computer before the door was slamming shut, cutting me off from my sanctuary.

"What if I wanted to finish my paper right now instead of hiking through the underbelly of a mountain?"

"Well? Do you? Are you telling me you'd rather be writing that boring ass report right now instead of getting some real action? Because I'm calling bullshit on all that crazy talk."

I didn't answer. There was no point. Marina was right, and she knew it. With a quiet hum of acknowledgement, we moved swiftly down the darkened hall of Hel Tower, our steps quieted by the red carpet rug that ran the length of the short corridor.

Voices spoken in low hushed tones met my sensitive ears, and I could hear them before I saw them. A small gathering of Hel Tower residents had congregated in the common area. In the swirling confusion of mixed conversations, I picked up bits and pieces here and there about an attack. Word had traveled fast about the events at the library; it would only be a matter of time before the entire campus knew about the attack and that I'd let it out.

As soon as I stepped into the room, eyes began to shift toward me, and the bodies parted as quiet fell over those gathered.

"Damn, do you feel that?" Marina quipped, moving ahead of me and taking point while I stayed a step or two behind her. "Got real icy in here. You'd think no one had ever seen—" Marina fell silent as the small group parted the rest of the way to reveal the woman Asher had referred to as Marisol, sitting on the red sofa while everyone gathered around her like she'd been telling them a story.

"That's her," Marisol accused just as Marina stepped aside to give me some room. "She attacked Shirley and bit him like some rabid freak."

CHAPTER 5

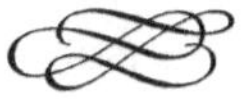

$\mathcal{A}$s soon as my friend moved, I saw Marisol's pointed finger directing everyone's attention right to me. The whispers began as soon as the accusation flew out of her mouth, swirling around me and assessing my guilt just like when I'd been arrested.

"That's bullshit, and you know it. If it was me, he'd already be dead, and you watched me arrive at the same time you did, the same time Professor Kincaid did . . . so maybe you were the one to attack Shirley? You had the opportunity to attack him before we arrived. What do you think, Marina? She sounds a little deranged to me," I pointed out, my bitch switch flipped, and anger bubbling in the pit of my belly.

Marisol's mouth popped open like she couldn't believe I'd said what I had, but I had no time, nor the patience to put up with this petty crap. The way her lips flapped around, Marisol resembled a gasping fish more than the witch she was.

"You know, seafoam never makes false accusations. Maybe I'd like her better if she was seafoam," Marina noted, stepping closer to the wide-eyed blonde as she sized her up and gave her a threatening wink. "I can make that happen."

Marisol's brows rose, and she smoothed her hands over her shirt like it would smooth over the wrinkles in her story. I felt the energy of the crowd shift as they took in the scene before us. The blonde stepped up to me, and Marina made to cut her off, but a wave of my hand stayed her motion.

Apparently, Marisol felt the change in the room too because she looked down her nose at me with disgust. "You might think I don't know what you're trying to do here, but I do. I see you for exactly what you are."

Without another word, Marisol spun on her heel and rigidly stormed back toward the bridge to the courtyard. The tense silence shattered as questions were hurled from every direction.

"Everyone! Shut the hell up for a minute," Marina hollered, quieting the crowd once again. "We all heard the gong. We know something's coming. It was only a matter of time. Now, here's what we know: a Modi was attacked in the library. He's in the infirmary getting checked out as we speak. No one got a good look at what did it, so be on the lookout for anything—"

"Supernatural?" Fiona asked, her voice dripping with sarcasm. "You've got to be kidding me. Someone had to have seen something."

I bit my tongue. There was no damn way I was giving them another reason to suspect me of anything. Only . . . this time it really was my fault. And it was up to me to fix this mess, and that started with finding out what it was. That meant I had to see Asher . . . shit, Professor Kincaid. That was going to be hard to get used to. He just seemed like a peer; someone I could talk to and relate to. Sure, he was kind of nerdy compared to the guys I typically liked. Was I admitting I liked him? Begrudgingly, yes. I didn't like that I liked him, and he annoyed me in equal measure.

"Crap," I whispered, realizing he'd distracted me again, and this time he wasn't even around to do it himself.

All eyes turned to me, even a concerned and suspicious Marina. "What? You okay?"

"Oh, uh, yeah. I just forgot that I have a meeting with one of my professors across campus," I answered, glancing at my phone. There was still forty minutes before my meeting with Professor

Kincaid, and it wouldn't hurt to be early if it meant I didn't have to deal with an angry mob.

Marina nodded, not skipping a beat even though I knew she knew it was bullshit. "I'll go with you. It's not a bad idea to use the buddy system right now if you go out and about. Until we know more, better safe than sorry, right?"

With a nudge, she urged me toward the door, not caring if anyone was in my way as we went. Any questions our fellow Helions might've had would have to wait. Thank the gods for small mercies. I kept my pace brisk, so we wouldn't be stopped again, and I didn't slow down until we'd passed over the stone bridge spanning the cavernous gap to the courtyard.

"You want to tell me what's going on?" Marina finally asked, her slender fingers closing around my arm and spinning me around to face her. "You want to tell me where you know Miss Prissy-pants from? That seemed awfully personal."

The corners of my mouth turned down with a frown as I realized she was right. Every blinking neon sign pointed to how the woman had practically hung all over Asher and he'd dismissed her like she was nothing more than the scenery.

"I have no idea what her issue was. I haven't even really met her, just saw her at the scene when shit went down in the library. So if the inquisition can wait until . . . " The words died in my throat as movement caught my eye, and I saw a few people push their way out of Halstein Hall and then a few more, until there was a steady stream of bodies pouring from its entrance.

"What the hell?" Marina exclaimed, noticing the scene at the same time I did.

An icy wind cut through the cavern, blowing open the doors just as they'd fallen shut. Marina started running first, but I was right on her heels. Unlike the rest who were running away from the building, we headed right toward it.

Just as Marina's shoes hit the bottom step of the stairs leading to the doors, I was hit by something with the force of a speeding car, and it laid me flat against the ground. I couldn't see what hit me but I could feel it . . . inside me. It moved like energy, darting around me like my body was the confines of a pinball machine. And whatever *it* was, it was very angry. I could feel it just as vividly as if it were my own emotions, but there was no rhyme or reason for me to feel the level of rage I was feeling. It wasn't of my own creation, and my stomach churned with the invasion. My gag reflex was triggered, and as my stomach contracted, the chill slid from my body. The malice left with it, like it had never been there.

Dozens of students poured from the entrance, scattering in every direction. I could hear the pounding of steps around me as I stared up at the skylight overhead. The sky was pitch black with the spattering of starlight peeking through the occasional cloud. Then Marina's face came into view, her hand extended toward me. I grabbed it, sitting up and scanning the quad around me for any sign of the thing that had invaded my body. However, just like in the library, there was nothing to see.

"What the hell was that?" I gasped, trying to catch my breath and level out.

I'd never experienced anything like it before. My innards felt like they'd been sent through a blender and left me feeling sick. Even the darkest departed souls had a glimmer of humanity left. Whatever had just crossed my path was not that at all—quite the opposite, actually. It felt rotten to the core, and there was the fact I hadn't seen a damn thing. It was puzzling.

An earsplitting scream tore through the air, and I clasped my hands over my ears to protect my sensitive hearing, tearing me from any thoughts of the mysterious entity.

"Sounds like a damsel in distress. Isn't that your territory?" Marina quipped as she pulled me after her into the massive stalagmite that was Halstein Hall.

The stone archways found throughout Halvard were beautifully crafted, so perfect they could've been sculpted by the gods themselves. Just inside the entryway we found the source of the scream. Like Shirley, a Modi tower woman was holding her forearm just below her elbow, examining it closely. There was a gathering of bodies around her with another man holding his hand up as though he'd been attacked as well. I wasn't ruling anything out as of yet.

Numbly, I strode toward the group, my eyes solely focused on the wounds. However, unlike Shirley's attack, these were much less gruesome with the woman's forearm being the only injury where the skin appeared to be broken. The second man who'd been holding his hand appeared to have something different altogether. On his hand was a bluish ring that had begun to form. The bruising was consistent between both victims though. And the marks were distinct, following a pattern.

My phone buzzed in my pocket, but I ignored the alert, busy with piecing threads of information together as I understood them. The pattern of the wound was distinct and was burned into the forefront of my brain. What would leave a mark like that? The jagged, torn marks weren't ones I'd seen before, and I hated to think what the thing could look like. An image of gnashing teeth, razor-sharp and crooked as they jutted out in a few different directions. It made a mess of whatever it tore into, shredding the flesh and making the lacerations almost unrecognizable.

"Let's go. Whatever attacked them isn't here anymore. We need to find out where it went," Marina's eyes scanned over the Student Union as though she had momentary doubts about her initial assessment regarding the mysterious being's absence.

She strode away from the crowd, no longer interested in the victims or their injuries. Instead, my best friend moved onto the chase part of the plan . . . but what were we chasing precisely?

"Did that look like anything specific to you?" I asked, right on her heels and keeping my voice low enough so others couldn't eavesdrop.

Marina frowned slightly, casting a questioning glance back over her shoulder.

"Maybe a pinch or something on the second one, I don't know. The two didn't even look like they could've been made by the same creature. She doesn't look as bad as you said this Shirley fellow did. Maybe that means this thing is going away on its own?" she offered with an uncertain shrug.

She was grasping at straws with that theory, and she knew it.

"Marina, I know what I saw! I'm not making this shit up. Those were teeth marks. That was a bite if I ever saw one . . . and no one saw a thing. Nothing."

Her expression was the epitome of confusion and disbelief until it morphed into dawning realization. Marina understood the implications as soon as she realized the gravity of my words.

"The wind—that has to be it, right? We're underground. This far down, to have a breeze like that, well, it wouldn't bode well for us. So that was it then, right?" she pieced together, her eyes flying wide as we both finally understood what this meant.

"It means we can track it, even if we can't see it," I said.

"But . . . perhaps, there's something in one of my abuela's scrolls about a spell that could render the unseen, seen," she replied, her eyes darting to something over my shoulder.

Immediately, her posture and entire demeanor changed. Pheromones flooded my nostrils like it was a damn sea witch mating season, and that's when I caught his scent, just as I heard him come to a stop behind me.

"There you are. I've been looking all over for you. Didn't you get any of my emails?" Professor Kincaid admonished. I could hear the mocking smile in his voice without needing to look at him.

I also knew those damning dimples would be on full display. Gods help any female with working ovaries within viewing distance of those suckers. They could practically be labeled weapons of mass destruction all on their own.

Marina's brows rose as her gaze shifted back and forth between Professor Kincaid and me like she'd found a new interesting riddle to solve. She stepped forward, her sultry full lips curling into her seductive smile I'd seen her use so many times before. It was a man-eating smile, one which rarely left survivors.

"Marina Del Mar, and you are?" she purred, extending her hand like some southern debutante.

His gaze slid over her, observing far more than I was comfortable with. It was damn nauseating to behold. Extending a hand forward, Professor Kincaid moved closer to her and took her hand in his.

"Asher Kincaid, Professor of Cyber Studies. The pleasure is all mine, I assure you," he answered, smiling smoothly.

Marina opened her mouth to speak, and I briefly wanted to shut it for her, but before I could stuff the urge back down, Asher shut it down for me. He turned his whole body to face me, Marina clearly dismissed as nothing more than the scenery as his blue eyes met mine. There was no denying the interest in those pools or the way he completely changed his posture.

"We have some new developments regarding our book bug," Professor Kincaid continued, his voice dropping lower so those around us couldn't overhear our conversation.

"I know. We found a new lead that we were just following up on," I replied, catching a glimpse of Marina's shocked and intrigued face.

"Yeah, we were just about to catch the little troublemaker right before you showed up," Marina mused, though I'm almost certain I saw her arch her back slightly to make her breasts more prominent.

Asher gave zero response, or at least he never let on that he noticed her move. A sense of relief and jealousy washed through me, and I knew in that instant I was well and truly screwed when it came to that man. He stripped me bare with his frankness and humor, and don't get me wrong, Asher was a little bit of a nerd. However, that sexy weirdo was starting to grow on me, whether I liked it or not. When he looked at me, I witnessed his shock to the news firsthand.

"That's not your new development, then? You didn't know about those attacks?" I asked, throwing a thumb over my shoulder toward the crowd.

The throng of people had begun to disperse as soon as some of the medics arrived on scene for triage and an escort to the infirmary. With a shake of his head, Asher flushed my whole theory down the drain.

"I came to find you to say Shirley Velisk has some interesting and unfortunate changes to his health status since the attack occurred, and I'm afraid that its worse than we initially feared." His gaze shifted to Marina with renewed interest. "How much of this are you aware of?"

She shrugged, toying with him.

Tit for tat, it was a move I could respect, but my patience was running on empty, and I wasn't the sort of woman who was willing to share. Call it daddy issues or mother-linked abandonment, the hound within and I were feeling like he was ours.

"Everything, didn't hold anything back," I answered for her, and just like before, his attention snapped back to me, intent. "What's the deal with Shirley?"

"That's sort of the problem. We don't know what's happening, but he's definitely getting worse. I've looked over what resources I have here, but I can't find anything like this in anything here. There's one more place I want to check before I reach out to a few contacts for information. Vanessa, I was hoping you could accompany me on that errand, maybe get that coffee?" Professor Kincaid offered, letting it be known to any within earshot that things were more than professional between him and me.

Inwardly, I cringed at the thought of all the rumors which would likely soon be circulating.

"Right. Well, I'm going to leave you two to do your thing, and I'll see if I can find out where the damn thing went and maybe find a way to track it, make it seen . . . something," Marina interjected, spinning on her heel as she made to leave me hanging, without an opportunity to explain what was going on.

"Marina, wait!" I said, shooting Asher a pissy glare I knew he could see despite my sunglasses.

"Look, it's cool. I know when I'm the third wheel, and it's not really a good look on me. So what's going on between you and Professor Hot Pants? Is that new? How long were you planning on keeping me in the dark on that one? Just wondering because last I checked, friends didn't lie to each other, but what do I know?"

With each sentence, her emotions bubbled to the surface more.

The scent of salty sea air hung in the cavern, a manifestation of the fact we'd struck a nerve in Marina.

"There's nothing there to tell. I met him in the library right before the insanity with the book. He's cute, but there's nothing going on," I reiterated, hoping she wouldn't hear the lie in my voice because even I wasn't buying the story, not fully.

"Keep telling yourself that and you might just miss out on the opportunity of a lifetime. Girl, he is scrumptious, and if you're not going there, then tell him that because that man's got his sights set on you and there's plenty who'd like that chance," Marina answered, smirking as she bit her lip, eyes raking over every available inch of the man.

A growl emanated from low in my throat, and I choked it down before it was too obvious, but Marina had heard me. Her bright sea green eyes twinkled with humor as she shook her head.

"I'll want all the juicy details, just telling you now. I have ways of making you talk if you want to be skimpy too. It's not every day your best friend starts sleeping with the hottest professor on campus. I'm damn well going to live vicariously," Marina said with a sassy flip of her hand.

The woman had all sorts of dark, twisted magics at her disposal, and I didn't dare to doubt the truth behind her threat. But nothing was going to happen. There wouldn't be anything to tell . . . not that I didn't want to, but we couldn't. Boundaries—I'd been smacked with a ton of them in the last year, and I had no desire to test them anymore.

"But—"

"This is college . . . This is the time to live free, love hard, and fuck up without too many horrible side effects, right? Just chill." Marina winked, before sauntering away from me in the direction the wind had traveled.

The bitch left me alone with him just like that. For a moment, I thought about the ridiculous notion that I was afraid of being alone with a professor. We could keep it professional; we had to. I'd hold my feelings down like a fort under siege . . . like the Alamo.

Shit. Didn't the Alamo fall?

"Sorry if I ran your friend off. That wasn't my intention, I swear, but I won't complain either," Professor Kincaid apologized, approaching me from behind.

I shrugged, not knowing what to even say to him. It felt awkward to address whatever was going on between the two of us. We could both feel the energy between us—it was practically magnetic—but neither of us had acted on it. Asher had asked me to coffee, and I'd almost been able to convince myself that it was an innocent offer from a new acquaintance.

"Are you angry with me?" he asked, his cool fingers curling around my shoulder empathetically, and I wanted nothing more than to melt into his touch, but I was hyper-aware of every set of eyes that was on us in the moment.

"No, just got a lot going on," I answered, the corners of my lips turning down with a slight frown. "Lead the way. We should see Shirley before anything else."

Professor Kincaid's hand came to rest on the small of my back as he ushered me forward. It was such a small gesture, but it was kind of sweet . . . if you liked that sort of thing. I'd never thought myself the sort of woman who would want anything sweet or gentle like that, and I was beginning to think maybe that had been a mistake, after all. This man was going to woo his way into my good graces, and there wasn't a thing I could do to stop it from happening.

As the pair of us headed quickly to the infirmary where Shirley was still being held, I explained what had happened with the second attack and feeling the wind. How the pattern of the bite had dramatically changed, assuming we didn't have a second creature hunting the Halvard students. Or worse—a fleet of them. Asher listened intently as I told him every last detail, but his expression gave nothing away.

"Well? What do you make of it?" I asked, pushing for an answer.

Stepping through the carved stone archway of the infirmary, Professor Kincaid stopped abruptly and spun to face me. I nearly ran right into him but stopped in time, leaving our bodies tantalizingly close.

"I don't know. It sounds like it could be something, maybe . . . But I want your take on Mr. Velisk before we jump to any firm conclusions. These things can be tricky, come down to the most seemingly insignificant of details even. As much as I want to take this bull by the horns and wrestle it into submission, this task was chosen for you."

"Chosen? By who?" I replied, suddenly enraptured by Asher's words.

It was imperative I knew exactly what he meant. Who chose this for me? And why?

"Well, there's been some suspicion you might've been chosen. Nothing conclusive, though," Professor Kincaid explained, looking much more like the professional he was.

It was just the reminder I needed. The whole notion was fascinating, but it wasn't my top priority. I had to hope there would be a time and a chance at the end of this to look back and ponder the why's of it all.

We approached the ward of the infirmary where Shirley was being kept. White sheets draped around his bed gave both the patient and the doctors a modicum of privacy while they worked on getting him better. I could hear the quiet buzzing of machines running, and the pungent scent of herbs hung in the air.

"Wait here for a moment, all right?" Professor Kincaid asked, stepping to the barely gaping opening of the sheet-walls.

I nodded and watched as he slipped into the partitioned room silently. The sound of muffled greetings and questions about the patient's condition filtered out to where I stood, waiting. I tried to listen, but when I tried to make out what was being said, a flurry of activity from behind me caught my attention. Madame Roth was bustling around, tending to a girl who was emptying her stomach onto the floor.

A Heimdall girl came into the infirmary holding her shoulder, a similar blueish mark evident through the gaps in her fingers, but this one was larger than either of the bites I'd observed earlier. This one looked angry, with red puckering around the wound, and a nearly perfect black ring surrounded the immediate bite. Lifting my face into the air a little, I tried to scent the air only to be met with the sickly stench of decay and something I was altogether too familiar with—brimstone. It was faint, but barely there. I'd know that odor anywhere, any of my kind would. Before I could get a good enough read on the scent, it vanished like it had never been there to begin with.

Just as I took a step to investigate, Professor Kincaid stuck his head through the sheet-wall.

"Vanessa? You can come in now," he called out, pulling my attention back to the task at hand: Mr. Velisk.

Abandoning the urge to inspect the woman closer, I stepped through the opening and had to hold back the need to vomit on sight. I couldn't believe the pitiful creature before me was the same man who'd been strong and able the previous day. The patient was sleeping, though I don't think it was necessarily voluntary, judging by the severity of the wound.

"What the hell? It wasn't nearly this bad earlier," I whispered, half to myself and half to Asher.

What the hell was I dealing with? As my scrutinizing gaze raked over his supine form, I noted every change since I'd first seen it. The strong and able man appeared to have lost at least ten percent of his body weight overnight. His ribs, which had taken the brunt of the attack, were swollen and weeping a black sludge. The raw, shredded edges of the wound were black with apparent necrosis. Nothing I had ever heard of worked that quickly, and without needing further explanation, I understood the predicament Asher spoke about. A faint undertone of brimstone wafted up from Shirley's unconscious form.

Interesting . . . So whatever was causing all of this had hailed from the nastier parts of Hell. It was the only way such a memorable scent would cling to a victim like this. This wasn't the work of a demon; that would be the obvious choice. This was different though, and nothing like I'd ever encountered before. Growing up, I'd listened to Dad reminisce about the insane times they had down in Hell and in the Infernum, and of the strange creatures who lived there. An invisible parasite with a toxic bite wasn't ever in those stories.

"Exactly. They've had a parade of doctors familiar with supernatural ailments through here, and we have yet to come up with any guesses as to what we're dealing with. The best we guess is it's something like a parasite."

"His case? The others are different . . ."

Professor Kincaid moved around to the far side of Shirley's bed.

"That's right." Asher nodded, sweeping his arm wide to pull aside the curtain. As soon as he pulled the fabric back, I saw the urgency of the situation. "There's a new case every few hours, it seems. Mr. Velisk seems to be our Patient Zero. He's the worst of those affected, and he's running out of time."

"How long does he have?"

As I asked my question, I tried to feel his energy like Professor Jameson had described in class. We hadn't gotten far enough to attempt it ourselves yet, but it couldn't hurt right? Just as she'd said, I could feel the thread within Shirley, that spark that made him who he was . . . his life force, soul, whatever you wanted to call it, but his was weak.

"The healers guess that he's got three days before whatever this is reaches his heart, and we all know what will happen then," Asher answered, gazing sympathetically down at the shifter laying on the bed. "Within a week, if this keeps up at the same rate it's been going, we'll have to declare a state of emergency and shut the campus down until there's no longer a substantial threat to the students. We've got an epidemic on our hands, it would seem."

Wow. No pressure there at all, I thought sarcastically. However, like everything else the man had said to me since I first met him, Asher's words stuck with me, playing over and over again while I tried to decipher what I could for the rest of the night.

When I returned to my dorm room, Marina was nowhere to be found, but that wasn't necessarily uncommon either. Staring at the closed face of my laptop, I groaned as I remembered I still had my paper to complete. It was due the next morning, and I had yet to reach the halfway point. There were a million other things I needed to be focusing on, and thinking of Shirley and the others who were dealing with a disaster of my own making only made it harder to concentrate. Whether or not they needed me, my classes wouldn't wait for the world to cut me some slack. One way or another, I had to suck it up and deal with it. Crossing to the desk, I sat down and flipped up the screen as I set out to finish the will-o-the-wisp midterm paper.

I would finish it or die trying.

CHAPTER 6

*H*ours later, although I wasn't sure exactly how long, I awoke to an icy bath of water being poured over my unconscious form where I was reclined in my computer chair. A screech that probably could've rivaled a banshee tore from my throat as I shot to my feet and prepared to shift, ready to tear the throat out of whatever had disturbed me.

"What the fuck, Marina?" I yelled as I cleared the droplets from my eyes and inspected my soggy attire.

"Good! I had a feeling the dousing would do the trick. Did you know you sleep like the dead?" she asked, far perkier than any person had the right to be so early in the morning.

"How appropriate," I snapped, reaching for the towel hanging from the hook on the wall as I shot her an irritated glare.

She was so anxious she was practically bouncing as she waited for me to finish mopping the water from my face. It was very out of character for my best friend, who typically was rather high-strung and only a little shallow if I was being brutally honest. However, she had an edge that made me wake up a little faster.

"What the hell is wrong with you? Did something happen?"

"Goddess! I thought you were never going to ask. You have no idea what I've had to deal with to get the information I'm about to

471

tell you," Marina began. Her animated expression spoke volumes. This was going to be a long winding story with probably at least two tangents if it was really important information, more if it was only mildly interesting.

"Out with it. I've got some rather disturbing information of my own to share." I glanced at the time and realized I had less than forty minutes before I had to be in Energies class; Marina would have to give me the Cliff's notes version.

"After I left you and Professor I-can-cut-the-sexual-tension-with-a-knife, which by the way, I've got a ton of questions about, questions I expect answers to," she said, raising her perfectly arched brow to make sure I knew she was being serious. "Anyway, after I left you guys, I tracked the wind along with a few more attacks down by the beach, but that's where the trail went cold, or so I thought. It hit the cave wall face and was just gone, but then I got to thinking about it. Wind doesn't go through stone. Spirits can, but whatever this was is a little more physical than that. There had to be an opening or something for it to slip through, even the smallest crack would work. Then I found the entrance. There's a cave with a winding tunnel that goes on for about a hundred feet before the space narrows. It's hard to squeeze through the gap in the rocks, but if you're small enough or agile enough, you can get through. On the other side though, there aren't words to describe it. It's a massive amethyst geode with a thermal pool bubbling up from a spring somewhere toward the bottom. It's like the Cave of Wonders."

"We're not talking about your vagina here. So what did you find? Was there anything else in the cave? Did you see it?"

Marina shook her head. "I could hear someone coming so I hunkered down in a tiny crevice in the wall so they wouldn't see me. It was just some students coming down to party, have a good time, and use the thermal pool like it was their own personal hot tub. Two freaking hours, but one thing, those bear shifters," she gestured with her hands almost a foot apart with that haughty smirk.

I rolled my eyes, but there was one part of what she'd said that stood out for me. My thoughts must've been evident just from looking at me because Marina was nodding excitedly.

"This means we need to go on an adventure and find out what's in that cave," she squealed like a small child on Christmas morning.

"But it's going to have to wait until after class, and I promised Asher I'd go with him after Intro to Energies to look for answers about what we were dealing with. Can we meet back here later this afternoon?"

Crossing her arms over her chest, she pursed her lips, and that single questioning brow rose. I knew that look. She was going to demand something in return, something probably valuable.

"On one condition. When this is all said and done, I want every detail of what's going on with you and Professor Hot Pants." Marina extended a hand and waited for me to take it. I didn't have to. I didn't need her permission. Yet if I wanted to continue the peaceful coexistence she and I had found, I'd have to give her this.

Even the most platonic of relationships took work; that was one lesson I'd begun to truly understand the meaning of since coming to the Sun & Moon Academy. I took her hand and gave it a firm shake.

"I can't wait to bore the shit out of you with all the details about what's not happening."

Marina waved me off, and I grabbed my bag and headed out the door. Without waiting any longer than I could afford to, I raced over to Haldor Hall and printed my paper before hightailing it over to Eirhal just in time for Introduction to Energies to begin. I snagged an empty seat after depositing my paper in the growing pile on the lecture stand.

Professor Jameson stood at the front of the room, eyeing every student like she could see right through them, stripping away all the bullshit they projected into the world. She could be really unnerving that way, which stood in stark contrast to the welcoming, if only a little stale as a lecturer, educator she had proven herself to be. However, the frown on her face stood out as I realized what she was noticing.

Around the room, my eyes scanned over the whispering, gossiping faces of my fellow students, too few considering the gravity of the assignment we were turning in. Empty seats dotted the room, many more than only two days earlier. Guilt and that uneasy, nauseating sensation of doom flooded my body, and I tried like hell to keep it at bay but was failing miserably. Every single one of those people were in deep shit because I couldn't follow a simple command and keep my damn hands to myself.

"Going once . . . twice . . . and no more papers please," Professor Jameson called out, quieting the class in an instant.

"As I'm sure many of you have noticed by now, we have an illness sweeping the campus and causing a significant number of absences. Because of this, I will be sending an email out later today with the notes from today's lecture to help those affected."

Hearing that the notes would be provided anyway, I checked right out mentally. My gaze kept falling to those empty seats and back over everything I'd seen. There had to be something there, some sort of clue. Throughout the rest of class, I analyzed every detail of the attacks, everything I'd witnessed firsthand, and what we'd learned the night before in the infirmary. In what seemed like only moments, the class was over, and people were gathering their belongings and stuffing them into their bags before I was driven from my thoughtful stupor. Scrambling, I collected my things and strode from the classroom, keeping my head down.

This epidemic was spreading like wildfire, and if I didn't contain this soon, there was no telling if there would even be a student body left by the winter break.

"Vanna." I heard him before I saw Asher approaching.

I tried to ignore the way my pulse leapt at the sight of him, but the smile that curled the corners of his mouth were a dead giveaway that he already knew.

Shit.

"I was just going to come find you," I answered, adjusting the straps of my backpack as I strode for him.

Professor Kincaid stopped and waited for me to reach him, then he fell in step beside me.

"Well, I beat you to the punch. Did you need to make any stops? Or are we good to go now?" he asked.

My brain blanked as I scrambled to come up with any reason to avoid being alone with him, to do this on my own, but I came up empty-handed and speechless.

"I'll take that as a no, we're good to go," he replied as he watched me falter.

He'd made his intentions well known; he had right from the start. It was me I didn't quite trust. Asher was the sort of man who catapulted himself right over my walls and into an uncomfortably close place. If he really tempted me, I'd give in and love every second of it, consequences be damned. It was a path I'd taken more than once before, and people got hurt. That was the last thing I wanted for him, and it would just kill Colton to see me screw up again.

However, as Professor Kincaid ushered me past the Valkyrie statue and to the exit portals, I made no move to protest or resist. Truthfully, I wanted to know more about him and see what sort of crowd he kept. I'd heard the Lilith Nest was a dangerous place once upon a time, but did that reputation still stand?

I wouldn't have to wonder long. Fifteen minutes after we passed through the portal under the Valkyrie's watchful eye, we pulled up to the ornate home that housed the Lilith Vampire Nest. The imposing gray stone structure loomed in front of us, and I had to take a deep steadying breath before I reached for the door handle to exit the vehicle.

"You're not going to get cold feet on me, are you?" he asked, stopping to turn around when he was already halfway out of the vehicle.

"After you, princess," I answered, swinging the door open and climbing out before he could reply.

Show no weakness.

My father's words echoed through me like he was with me, helping me with tiny nudges here and there to keep me from screwing up too badly. I mounted the steps quickly, so I didn't have time to turn around and think better of what I was about to do.

Going to the Lilith Nest without any kind of outside back up was a rookie mistake. I was walking into a potential viper pit, and I knew it; then I went anyway.

"Always the brave face, huh? Don't worry. You're not in any danger here. It's not as bad as you've probably built it up to be in your head." He winked, opening the door for me and tipping his head to the side to silently invite me in.

Steeling my resolve, I straightened a little, reminding myself who and what I was. If anything, they should be afraid of me, dead or not. One wrong move on their part and I could have crispy vampire tenders for lunch and burn the mansion to the ground. My hound wasn't a beast to be tested. She was hellfire incarnate.

The house was quiet, but I could hear a flurry of motion coming from somewhere upstairs. When I listened closer, I wished I hadn't. A smile stretched my face, and my cheeks heated.

"Sorry about those two. They're still newly engaged and can't get enough of each other," Asher said, looking years younger as he strode by me, giving the door a shove shut.

I didn't know who the couple upstairs was, and Asher gave nothing away. Instead, he went on like he owned the place, and in a way, I guess he sort of did. The dynamics of these types of cohabitating groups were usually complex, and the home was available to everyone as they needed with a few boundaries. The Lilith Nest home was exquisite, a work of art in its own right, but I didn't have time to stand around admiring it.

"The library is just this way," my host urged, trying to move me along quickly.

"What's the rush? Worried someone might see me here?" I teased, sauntering past him into the library.

I could hear his laugh as I stepped past him, but he said nothing and shut the door almost silently. Venturing deeper into the space, my eyes adjusted to the low light easily and scanned over the shelves, which were filled with aged tomes of all subject matter. Approaching a table at the center of the room, I turned to look at Asher.

He was watching me intently, his face unreadable, and right

then, I would've given anything to hear exactly what he was thinking.

"There's no shame in attraction. It's as natural as breathing. Please don't think I'm trying to hide anything. It was simply that you seem uncomfortable, and I was trying to ease any anxiety you may have about being here," Asher said after a moment.

Fighting the urge to tense up at the mention of the elephant in the room, I looked him right in the eyes and strode forward until we were separated by a few measly inches. He'd been throwing me off kilter since I'd met him, and I was done being the one off-balance around him. It was high time I gave the man a taste of his own medicine.

"Who said I'm ashamed?"

His blue eyes were locked on mine, and I knew he could see them clearly through the lenses of my sunglasses. The man didn't even flinch when in a bold moment I reached out and ran the tip of my finger over the buttons of his shirt.

"Maybe I just don't know if you're worth the potential risk, yet," I continued, peeking up at him as my shades slid down my nose, letting him see the fire that burned in my eyes.

His body was cool under my heated touch, making every sensation feel heightened all the more. The desire in Asher's icy blue eyes rivaled my own. I don't even know why I was considering it; I was playing with fire. Before I could think better of it, he made the choice for me as Asher's resolve snapped and he closed the distance, crushing his mouth against mine. I was hot and cold everywhere all at once, my resolve crumbling like stale bread, and I moved against him like I couldn't get close enough to satisfy my need. His tongue danced sensually with mine as we lost ourselves in the moment.

I was so caught up in Asher and how good it felt to be with him, I didn't hear company approaching the library until the door swung open and the Lilith Nest leader himself strode into the room. We broke apart at the intrusion, and I kept a tight rein on the hound when the urge to shift peaked.

"That is quite the search you're conducting, Asher. I'm

wondering, do hellhounds typically keep rare texts at the back of their throats?" Mr. Doyle teased, a wicked smile playing on his lips.

Before I could think better of it, words poured from my mouth. The Vanna thought vomit struck once again.

"You weren't upstairs very long. If you need any pointers, I'd be happy to show you how it's done," I challenged with a wink.

Mr. Doyle barked an amused laugh. "Feisty. I like her, Asher. Be sure you bring her around here more often."

He crossed to the bar cart in the corner of the room and poured himself a drink. Scotch, if my nose was discerning, and it was. My father had been a scotch man, and I got real good at figuring out a good cask from shit. Mr. Doyle's was definitely high-end, but that wasn't at all surprising, judging from the rest of the house.

Mr. Doyle was a member of the Board of Regents, too, which made his notice of our compromising embrace even more damning. I was going to be expelled for sure, probably banished from the town.

"Don't be absurd, my dear. We're all adults here, and I trust you both to act as such. As long as Asher isn't your professor and there's no misuse of his position of authority, there is no conflict. Honestly, you should try to be more optimistic. Your mind is a dark place for one as young as you," the vampire answered, his brows drawing together like he was truly concerned by his own statement.

Shock coursed through me as I realized what he was saying. Every thought, no matter how intimate, he had access to.

"Don't be ridiculous. I don't want to hear that any more than I'm sure you wanted to hear my lover in the throes of passion. I do try to make a point to not invade the privacy of those around me, but I would be foolish not to use it to my own advantage. People in my position have long lives and an eternity to make any number of enemies. One can never be too careful," he answered my thoughts without ever missing a beat like it was the most natural thing in the world.

Asher had been unusually quiet during the entire exchange,

and when I looked to him, I could see why. He'd taken the opportunity to begin his search of the bookshelves for any book that might be able to point us in a helpful direction. Mr. Doyle seemed to notice at the same time I did.

"Now, I'll save you both a considerable amount of time searching this library for something you won't find. Seventy years ago, I had a conversation with a man I considered a friend. Jonas Pederson's family was old Scandinavian. They'd kept the old tales alive, and he passed them on to me. However, there was one tale that stands out to me, as it was particularly nasty. It was a creature who couldn't be seen by the naked eye; one whose malevolence has warped it into an unrecognizable monstrosity. A blue bite would form, seemingly innocuous at first, but over time, the bite turns necrotic, and you begin to rot until your body can't sustain the being's toxin anymore. Does this sound familiar?"

"Are you seriously fucking telling me you've known what this thing was the past few days and you still didn't say anything?" Asher asked, rounding on Mr. Doyle with an anger I didn't know he was capable of.

"Choose your next words carefully, Kincaid. You know as well as I do nothing good comes when we interfere or try to fix these messes ourselves. Ms. Shaw came here on her own, therefore I am free to share what I know. Perhaps do not be so quick to anger, young one; it will not serve you to jump to conclusions," Mr. Doyle warned.

There was a lethality to him that put me on edge. He was well put together, professional even, but there was something animalistic underneath it all, and I'd just witnessed a rare slip of that mask.

A dozen questions raced through my mind, but one bothered me a little more than the rest. Mr. Doyle plucked that question straight from my thoughts before I could bring them to voice. I was getting really fucking tired of this prick eavesdropping, and that made me think of all the fun things I could do with the pointy ends of my collection of blades.

"If you want to know how to see the unseen, you must become

the unseen. You are a Hellhound, are you not, Ms. Shaw? Like those souls your kind guard in the Infernum, the Gjenganger is a nasty dead thing. It wants the same thing they all want—to become alive again. Its unfinished business is to cause as much pain and suffering as possible; a dead thing that just couldn't settle for being dead, so it tries to eat its way back to life."

The chirp of a cellphone cut through the heavy silence, yet no one moved to check their device, not after what we'd just heard.

"The Gjenganger will fight to keep its hold in the land of the living and to keep itself from being banished. It's smart, calculating even," Mr. Doyle continued.

There was something in the way he talked about the Gjen-whatever wanting to keep from being banished that nagged at me. This whole time I'd been so busy trying to find what could tie all the victims together, but maybe it wasn't something the victims had in common, but a place they had in common. Marina had mentioned the wind ending in the amethyst thermal pools. Ironically, it was the same place she mentioned running into some students who were going to party down there.

"Very good, Ms. Shaw. Smart and deadly. Yes, I do think you'll fit in swimmingly around here," Mr. Doyle added, his white teeth flashing as he quickly smiled and exchanged an unreadable look with Asher.

There was something in that look. I couldn't put my finger on it, but I didn't like it. I put a pin in that thought as the library door swung in and Gabriel's face darkened in an instant. A woman clad in nothing more than a short kimono that barely covered the essential bits and the scent of pheromones, sweat, and sex were so thick they nearly clogged my nose. It was immediately clear this was Mr. Doyle's mate. Their eyes instantly sought out the other like magnets as soon as they were in a shared space. I peeked at Asher, convinced he would be eyeing the half-naked woman. Instead, he was watching me intently, like he was gauging my own reaction to the scene before us.

"I'm so sorry to intrude on your meeting, but the college called. There's been an unfortunate turn of events," the woman said, tucking her long black hair behind her ear and tugging the hem of her robe down slightly lower.

"What is it?" Asher said, concern lacing through every word.

"Shit!" the vampire hissed, throwing back the remainder of his drink. "I want the Board on a conference call along with our attorney in five minutes. Losing students is always bad business."

The woman—Alina, if I remembered correctly—looked to Mr. Doyle for permission before she divulged the news we'd all dreaded hearing. With a single nod from the head of the Lilith Nest, his mate looked at both Asher and me with a small frown.

"There's been a student death on campus."

As soon as the words left her mouth, questions were hurled from both myself and the man beside me.

"Who was it?"

"Just one? Was it another attack?"

"Silence!" Mr. Doyle snapped. "She doesn't know any more than she's already shared with you. Now, if you'll excuse me, I have a few calls to make, and you have a Gjenganger to trap."

Asher looked like he was about to open his mouth to protest, but he thought better of it and stayed quiet. He might've owed the ancient vampire something, but I swore no such oath. Sure, the Sun & Moon Academy was an opportunity, thanks to him and the sheriff, but this felt like need-to-know information, and if I was going to take this nasty bastard on, I was doing it on my terms and with all of the information.

"Who was it?"

Mr. Doyle seemed surprised by my challenge, amused even. Seconds ticked by, and I expected anger to come at my defiance, but it never did. Instead, he tipped his head to the side.

"Alina, my love, what was the name they gave when the call came in? I believe our guest has an interest in this particular morsel."

She shook her head like she was over his games, the same as me.

"Sorry about him. He gets cranky when things don't go his way," she answered with a frown, eyeing the vampire in question from the corner of her eye. "Shirley Velisk was the name, poor thing. College is supposed to be fun."

Shock rocked through me at hearing his name, yet, in my bones, I'd felt this coming. Everything fell numb as I realized the man was dead because of me. For what all my efforts were worth, I might as well have bitten him myself. My stomach turned to lead, and I half expected it to drop straight to the expensive carpet.

"We've got to go," Asher said urgently, striding for the door without saying another word, shaking me from my stupor.

Was I supposed to go after him? He was my ride, but I had more questions.

"Go on, go with him. I'm sure we'll be seeing plenty of each other," Mr. Doyle answered with a knowing wink, like Asher and I were a sure thing.

My numb feet began moving before my mouth got the better of me. I didn't need to burn any more bridges than I already had. As soon as I emerged through the front doors, I saw Asher pacing by the car. He looked frantic, just as chaotic as I was feeling inside.

"His whole life ahead of him and within two months at college, he met his maker. There's something very wrong with that," Asher said, almost to himself, but I knew he was aware of my presence.

"That's true enough. I'm not going to lie, the only infections I thought I'd have to worry about in college were the latex preventable kind. I'm sure the Velisk guy could've agreed with that. If anyone here is to blame, that's me. So let me fix this."

Asher stopped dead in his tracks and turned to face me, his mouth popped open like he was going to say something, but no words would come.

"How do you plan to catch this thing? We don't know much about it," he answered after a tense moment.

"We know enough. It's a spirit; at the end of the day, it's just a spirit. Those are my specialty. Marina will be there too, and she can handle the situation if things get out of hand. We can do this, Asher. I know we can. We have to."

I blinked as he closed the distance between us in the span of milliseconds, his body pressed firmly against mine, and I squirmed to get closer. His mouth was so close, but neither of us made a move to close the gap and seal the kiss. Instead, the tension just ramped higher and left me feeling like my head was spinning. My fingers roamed over the planes of his frame, searching for what they desired most at the moment.

"Confidence is a beautiful look on you." He didn't get the chance to say more.

As soon as the words left his lips, I threw caution to the wind and took what I knew with a certainty I wanted. His mouth reacted just like I hoped, parting and bracing for my attack. It was quick, just like my decision to go with whatever was happening between us, but that was okay too.

The vampire was good and distracted, right where I wanted him. I smiled as my fingers closed around their destination, the owner none the wiser.

"Thank you," I answered, for . . . so many things.

Straightening, I stepped back and sauntered to the car, the keys clutched tightly in my palm. Success. Asher caught on quickly enough; his laugh barking as I strode around the hood of the *BMW i8* and climbed in. From behind the steering wheel, I winked, and he headed for the passenger seat, shaking his head the whole way.

I'd always wanted to drive one of these, so maybe dating Asher wouldn't be so bad after all. Hell, I'd decided to give the guy a chance when he called bullshit on me in the library before the fiasco began. Knowing there wouldn't be any official blowback from the administrative department eased most of my reservations. Before I could give it the proper amount of attention, I had a Gjenganger to track down and teach a lesson in manners and consent. No one appreciated his hickeys, invited or not.

CHAPTER 8

As soon as I stepped through the portal, I could feel a shift in the energy surrounding campus. It was like even the air was ill, and it made me want to scrub its filth from my skin. Where there was typically a fair amount of hustle and bustle around the small campus, it seemed deserted as I crossed through the courtyard. My eyes went to the hourglass suspended high above the ground I was walking on. The sand was slipping through it as though there weren't countless lives depending on each precious grain that fell so carelessly.

There was more sand gone than left, and my anger flamed anew. My blood was boiling as the inferno inside warred to escape. I heard the scampering of the cave gnomes as they moved about campus, trying to stay out of sight. Knowing there was more than them out there watching me when I couldn't see it bothered me more than I wanted to admit.

Asher had left me at the portal entrance while I went to Hel to find Marina; he'd been saying something about how he needed to get the book. The whole situation became a lot clearer on the ride back to the falls. The book had contained it before and it could once again, but Shirley's death had been a game changer. It meant the Gjenganger had siphoned the life from one victim and was well on its way to having a physical body all its own.

The text Asher had received had been from Madame Roth to update him on Shirley's death and also let him know the Infirmary was officially surpassing capacity. They would have to begin turning people away or transferring to the medical center in town. If they went that route, the Board of Regents would have to alert the town to the problem. As far as they were concerned, that was the absolute last resort.

By the time I reached Hel Tower, I was already busy planning ten steps ahead. The golden Valkyrie sitting atop the Hel Tower was gleaming in the low-lit cave, heralding a successful mission . . . I hoped. I sent up a silent prayer that it was going to be enough. Between Marina's sea magic and my hellfire, I figured we could use the water as a mirror to trap it; but first I had to get Marina. The Gjenganger was protecting the amethyst cave and punishing any who went there. That was probably because amethyst was perfect to contain some of the strongest of entities. If what Marina said was true, there was an entire cave chocked full of potential weapons to contain it. It only made sense to target the enemy before they could target you. Mr. Doyle wasn't kidding; the creature was clever.

As I strode through the massive red double doors of the Hel tower, I noticed the common room didn't have nearly as many hang arounds as most nights. Things were getting bad. I climbed the tight spiral staircase to the second floor, my floor, and came to an abrupt stop when I saw Marina talking to Tempest and Natalie in front of our respective doors.

By the deep frowns, I gathered this wasn't just a friendly chat between neighbors. Something was very wrong. I approached the group slowly and then my eyes fell to the tightly wrapped bandage on Tempest's wrist.

"You've been bitten," I whispered, stating the obvious, however I didn't know how much they'd been filled in on.

Tempest's mouth pressed into a grim line, and she gave a single nod. Natalie looked just as sick as Tempest did, likely with worry for her friend. The pair of them were practically attached at the hip.

"It's still early for her, but we heard a rumor that Shirley didn't make it. Do you know? Have you heard anything?" Marina asked, slipping a bag of sea salt into her denim jacket pocket.

I looked at the trio, and decided there would be no holding back, not now.

"Dead."

Natalie's eyebrows rose, but Tempest just nodded as she digested the information.

"Just because Shirley didn't make it, doesn't mean he has to have died in vain. We can turn this around. If we banish the Gjenganger and put it back into the book, the link to those infected is severed, no more infection."

"So you did find out more than just what Professor Hot Pants tastes like? Good job, *chica*." Marina gave a nod, chuckling at her own inside joke.

"The rumors are true?" Natalie voiced from where she was sandwiched between the two other witches.

I deflected; there was no way I was talking about my complicated and very newly discovered love life with these two, not with our history. Putting that history behind me though, that was something I could do, or try to do at the very least.

"Tempest, look I'm so sorry you got caught up in all of this. It's truly my fault this time; I released the Gjenganger. You and me are cool as far as I'm concerned; no hard feelings. What do you say?" I extended my hand to the witch and waited for her to take it.

Her eyes went from my hand to my face and then, just as I did, she decided to set our bullshit aside. Instead of taking my hand, Tempest launched herself at me and wrapped me into a hug so tight, I was helpless but to return it.

"The what?" she chuckled, stepping back and releasing her hold.

"It's like a supernatural spirit parasite. It bites its victims and sucks the life from them to create a physical body. With Shirley dead, it's started, but I don't think it's gotten too far yet if there's only been one death. There's still time to fix this," I answered.

Marina held up her index finger and spun on her heel, opening the door to our dorm room and slipping inside. She emerged a moment later with a bag filled to the brim with her favorite talismans, salts, and crystals.

"Temp, do you want to tell Vanna what you told me about how your bite showed up?" Marina tipped her head toward her expectantly.

"If you think it'll help . . . one of the guys in my Potions class was talking about thermal pools down by the lake. We got to talking, and he showed me where it was. Eryx and I went back later, and things got a little steamy. Then the next morning on my way to class, it felt like someone turned on a fan, and when I looked to see what caused it, my wrist started to hurt like someone had pinched it. When it started to get a little worse, I stopped by the infirmary, but there were too many people there to be checked out. All had the same problem as me," she explained, flipping her dark hair back over her shoulder.

Marina was grinning like a maniac the whole time like it was the best thing she'd ever heard. I really had to have a chat with her about appropriate reactions to distressing news. As if the sea witch's ego wasn't already over-inflated and borderline problematic, this was certainly going to put her over the edge.

"I was right about the amethyst pools. Marina was right. Can you say it? I know you want to," she teased.

My eyes rolled so hard, I was fairly certain I pulled a muscle behind my eye in the process.

"Whatever, fine! You were right about the amethyst pools, give yourself a cookie. Now, about those pools, do you think you can draw a quick map to the location? Ash—I mean, Professor Kincaid is going to meet us there with the book, and he should be on his way there now," I urged, checking my phone screen for the time and missed texts.

There were none, but given the time, I gathered he'd be at the beach in no more than ten minutes. Tempest and Natalie nodded to each other like they'd had a private conversation we weren't privy to. However, the pair looked back and forth between Marina and me and gave me the gift I hadn't realized I needed.

"How can we help?"

CHAPTER 9

The Gjenganger would only get stronger with time, which we didn't have. Lives were on the line. The knot of guilt twisted almost painfully in my gut over Shirley's death. I'd really fucked up this time.

"Here it is!" Marina squealed, holding up a seaweed bound book from the case she sat in front of.

Tempest and Natalie were thumbing through their collection of grimoires as they sought out a binding spell for a powerful spirit. Magic like that wasn't my strong suit, and I felt that as I watched them in their research while I could do nothing.

Marina scooted herself around to face us and ran her thumb over the delicate clasp holding it shut. Carefully, she peeled back the front cover and began turning the pages as she searched for the perfect spell.

"Are you sure it's this one? You said that about the other three," Tempest snarked, earning an elbow jab from Natalie. "Ow! What? I was just saying what we were all thinking."

Marina didn't pay her much attention, though. Her brows were pinched together, and her mouth had that focused set to it I'd come to recognize. About two thirds of the way through the book, she stopped on one particular page, and I could see her posture shift as she took in the page's contents.

"This is it. This is the spell my abuela used," Marina said quietly.

Crossing the space, I lowered myself to the floor beside her and glanced down at the page. It was handwritten in a language I could hardly hope to identify, but if I had to guess it was likely one of the ancient Mayan tongues, the language of Marina's people—the *brujas marinas*.

Natalie leaned forward, her porcelain skin marred only by her frown. Shaking her head, she took one long last look at the page and then Marina.

"Mar, this is dark stuff. It's unpredictable and dangerous. This could go wrong a thousand different ways."

Marina snapped the book shut and looked Natalie dead in the eyes.

"It can go right, too. Have a little faith," Marina urged with a reassuring grin.

Tempest didn't look completely sold on the idea, and truth be told, neither was I. But what other choice did we have?

"What do you need?" I asked.

Without risk, there would be no reward or just surviving in this case. Given the alternative, I was willing to take that chance. Marina was much more streamlined when it came to picking out her spell ingredients. However, the spell required black tar to bind to something from the beast. In our case, it was a swab of Tempest's wound and the process took all night. Once we'd found a solution, I texted Asher to let him know, but when I checked my phone an hour later, there was still no response from him. I fell asleep that night with my phone resting on my pillow, hoping he'd found something more that could help us.

The next morning, we roused ourselves early, hoping we could try to lure the beast out before the rest of campus woke up. There was still nothing from Asher, but I tried not to let it bother me. Technology and wi-fi was spotty at best under Mount Alexa, and I didn't even know if he'd received the message, but I typed out an email and sent it off right before we left our dorm for the thermal pools.

Halvard was dark, and the small gnomes were running around cleaning up and snuffing out the lamps as the sky began to lighten overhead at the skylight. It wasn't a long walk to the cave opening, but it was hidden in plain sight.

"It's down here," Marina ushered, leading the way as she held her lamp in front of her.

In a single file, we passed through the glamour and ventured down the lost tunnel. My sight was impeccable in the dark. The witches weren't so lucky in that regard, but they had magic to call on. After only a few minutes of walking, we reached the part Marina had mentioned would be hard to pass through and she wasn't kidding. The walls narrowed to almost a point, however there was maybe a ten-inch gap at the bottom of the opening. The upper opening was barely four inches wide and nothing larger than a well-fed rat would be able to squeeze through.

Marina went first, crouching and contorting herself to fit easily through the space. Tempest and Natalie followed while I brought up the rear. I could feel the air growing humid and warm as I pushed past the narrow opening and climbed to my feet. Several yards ahead of me, the trio of witches had stopped, staring ahead. Moving closer, I peeked over Marina's shoulder toward what had to be the thermal pools. There was almost no light in the space other than what we brought with us, but even what we did have gave us a breathtaking display. The low light hit the prisms of amethyst, jutting out in every angle and of every size, glistening a majestic purple, green, and blue. Water bubbled up from a volcanic vent somewhere deep under the water to create a natural hot tub in the deeper part of the geode.

"Let's get to work. We won't have long," I said, stepping forward and placing my lamp on the ground near a crystal cluster, which amplified the glow.

Tracking the Gjenganger wouldn't do us any good, not when we couldn't see it. So, we had to make it come to us. Asher was coming with the book, but in the meantime, we'd have to lay a trap. It was too risky to try a summoning; we didn't know how volatile it could be, given this wasn't the normal run of the mill errant spirit. The witches could form a circle the Gjenanger wouldn't be able to break out of though. If we made it that far, binding it within the book with an amethyst kicker would be a breeze.

We each had a task to complete. Marina handled the salt and circle-making. Tempest and Natalie covered the candles and crystals. Mine was much less exciting. It was my job to watch and listen for the Gjenganger. As Marina so eloquently dubbed me, I was also "the bait who bites." Grabbing the one blade Colton had allowed me to bring, Venus, I ran the steel edge over my palm, pressing slightly. I felt my skin part immediately, and the blood welled in my palm. Then I did the one thing I'd had no problem doing since arriving at the Sun & Moon Academy—I made a mess.

Smearing blood over the entrance rocks and the occasional crystal, I tried to cover as much area as possible and hoped it was enough to bring it running. Marina had provided us with a crudely sketched map of campus and the directions to finding the cave entrance so we could send it to Asher. He'd never replied to the message, and we'd been waiting not so patiently for his arrival for nearly twenty minutes. The directions were fairly straightforward. It shouldn't have been a problem for him to find. That's also probably why the plague-like disease had exploded like it had. It was easy to find and hidden in plain sight. News travelled fast, especially somewhere beautiful and secluded on a college campus full of hormone-fueled adults who would look for any excuse to get busy, and I didn't count myself as immune to that analysis.

"He was coming, right? We've been down here twenty minutes already, and the only thing I've seen are questionable spiders and more crystals than I could find a use for," Natalie whined.

When I turned, I found her running her fingers over the wall of crystals.

"There's a limit to crystals?" Tempest quipped, friendly sarcasm dripping from every word.

Natalie grinned conspiratorially and peeked over her shoulder to her sister witch. "I said there were more than I knew what to do with, not that I wouldn't find uses for them."

A howl in the distance, so faint I almost missed it, echoed through the tunnel, catching my attention. I froze, straining to hear it better. No one else seemed to hear it though, because they kept talking.

"Shhhh," I hushed, holding out a hand to keep still.

Once again, I listened, yet this time I could hear the faint sound of wind over stone, the only indication we wouldn't be alone for long.

"Marina? Are you in position with the salt? We've got company coming," I hissed over my shoulder.

Mr. Doyle had said if I wanted to see the unseen, I had to become it. Well, I could do that. Tugging off my jacket, I tossed it aside and got ready for the Gjenganger to get closer. When I could physically hear the wind round the last bend in the tunnel, I squeezed back through the gap in the rocks. It was an ambush predator, working with the assumption no one would know what to look for, but it wasn't stupid. I could play ignorant of its presence, but the gooseflesh it conjured as it shared the space with me was as good as a compass. Popping the button on my pants, I slid them down my legs and kicked out of my shoes, sending the pants with them.

Come on, you son of a bitch. Try to take a bite.

As the uneasy sensation intensified, I knew the creature to be getting closer as he prepared to launch its attack. It just had to get a little closer . . . When a chill ran the length of my spine, I let the beast within tear forth from me. My body broke and reformed in the glorious form of a hellhound.

My black beast was a beauty to behold, but she was pure lethality. In that form, I could see the thinly-veiled creature that had been stalking Halvard. It was nearly the size of a horse and easily the most grotesque being I'd ever had the displeasure to meet face to face. Razor sharp teeth jutted out of a too-large mouth in every direction. Its eyes were just empty sockets on a horned head. The flesh hung on the being like it threatened to fall off if it even slightly moved. Its front feet were cloven hooves, while the rear had claws.

Sensing a much fairer match, the Gjenganger took a step back like it was trying to make out what I was. I took a step and then another, trying to move around the outside of it and herd the creature into the thermal pool. However, it didn't really get the memo.

The Gjenganger turned and tried to go back the way it came, but I wasn't going to have that. I wasn't done with our chat. Taking off after it, I outpaced the cumbersome beast easily, but when I reached it and leapt, it had a surprise waiting for me. Its face snapped in my direction and its jaws opened, unleashing a toothed tentacle from its mouth. The bite hit my flank, digging deep into the muscle. It stunned me for a second, catching me off guard.

As soon as I recovered, I was on the Gjenganger, biting and tearing at what I could. My mouth felt like it was filled with ashes and sludge all at once. The beast bucked, sending me sailing. I collided with the cave wall, crumpling in a heap. That was the moment Asher showed up, book in hand and the strangest contraption on his head I'd ever seen. However, he seemed to be looking right at the Gjenganger.

The creature recoiled from him as he held the book that had contained it forward. Asher shuffled forward a few feet, and the beast backed up, keeping the distance between them constant. The pair were quickly running out of room though.

Blood soaked my fur around where I'd been bitten. I could feel the Gjenganger's toxin working its way into my bloodstream, infecting the surrounding tissue. It took me a moment, but I got back on my feet and stayed even with Asher, giving the creature no other option but to back through the opening into the amethyst pools and our trap.

Asher leapt forward, and the beast snapped at him but slid through the opening just as we were hoping. I went after it, beating the vampire to the opening, twisting and squeezing my form through the narrow gap. I bared my teeth, the threat of a howl imminent. Asher was behind me, contorting to make it through the space.

The Gjenganger realized the trap as soon as we were all inside the thermal pools and the amethyst surrounded the creature, but it had yet to cross into the salt circle. Lashing out, the beast flipped around and kicked at me with its rear claws, and I dodged, barely missing a direct hit. My teeth latched onto the meaty thigh of the Gjenganger and dragged it toward the circle. We were going one way or another. It tensed, right before it tried another attack, and with a powerful thrust, I tossed it into the circle. Marina didn't wait, sealing the circle in an instant, and the salt burst into flames. Asher handed her the book the plague-maker had been sealed in and stepped out of their way. The candlewicks burst to life as the witches' magic began to weave through the space.

Smoke billowed from the flames and gave the Gjenganger a corporeal form for the witches to see firsthand. I slumped as the hellhound withdrew and gave my body back. Something definitely felt like it was broken and would have to be reset later. Thankfully, Asher took the chance to zip out and grab my clothes. Covering quickly, I gave Marina a nod to seal the deal.

Marina's hands rose high above her head, and the waters from the thermal pool rose around the Gjenganger, fortifying its temporary prison. Tempest and Natalie took that as their signal to begin the chant that would seal the beast back in the book. Marina joined in, and the three witches linked hands, their voices carrying higher until that was all we could hear. The Gjenganger growled and wailed an unholy sound, but still, the creature remained.

"It's not working. It's too strong," Asher noted.

The amethyst was supposed to amplify the spell, but it wasn't working. I grabbed onto the nearest crystal shard and tried to hit it in such a way that sheared it off, but the gem was too strong. It wasn't impervious to heat, though.

Calling on my hellfire, flames licked my palms and bent to my will. Fire encircled the shard, tightening around it until the scent of molten stone reached my nose. The heat was so great, the violet gem was cut through like a hot knife through butter.

"Need to hurry! This won't hold too much longer," Tempest called.

I pushed it, and the red-hot stone fell into my awaiting palms with a sharp crack. The stone fit in the palm of one hand. Pulling the hellfire back into my body, I swayed a little, and Asher's arm went around my middle. He fished the amethyst from my hand and handed it off. The toxin was working through me, making me feel like I'd just been hit by a super flu. Chills rocked through me, and I shivered, trying to curl into Asher's comforting embrace, but he pulled back.

"I'm sorry." He frowned. "Cold-blooded."

Instead, he handed me my sunglasses. As I was sliding them on, I caught a glimpse of Marina's obsidian eyes with a ring of gold glowing as she held the gem high. Marina's eyes were usually green when she was casting.

Well, that's a new development.

The chant filled the air, and the magic prickled over my skin. A flash erupted from the center of the circle and the Gjenganger exploded into a shower of ash and soot. It swirled through the air, coating the book and the crystal, but it wouldn't be enough. The book and its pages were magically protected, they wouldn't burn, but now the plague-maker was split. It couldn't stay that way.

"Thank you, all of you," I said, limping forward. They let the circle fall and stepped back, seemingly satisfied with the job they'd done. "I've got this part."

As I held out my hand, Marina seemed dazed, but placed the amethyst crystal back in my palm. The light was low, but I could barely make out the black rutilated lines staining throughout the amethyst. Carrying the gem forward, I slammed it down on top of the book and let the hellfire melt the purple stone into the cover. The black marks on each half of what was left of the Gjenganger clumped together, creating a brindled appearance along the amethyst book cover. The fire licked up my arms and over the tome, encasing it in with the hottest flame. The smoke rising from the sealed Gjenganger was acrid, cloying; it made me want to gag, but I stuck it out until the job was done.

Blood was still flowing from where I'd been bitten but the achy heaviness began to slowly recede.

"That was—" Natalie began.

"Fucking awesome!" Tempest finished, practically electric in her elation at our success.

Marina was quiet, though, and she wouldn't meet my eyes when she looked in my direction. Something was very wrong with her. I could feel the shift in energy as soon as the casting was complete. I didn't know what it meant, but I knew it didn't bode well for my best friend. Tempest and Natalie were whispering back and forth to each other; their eyes darting to Marina and then to each other made it abundantly obvious they had noticed too.

I wanted to go to her, comfort her in any way I could. It's what she did for me when Mystic went off the rails and I was the campus pariah. When I went to take a step toward her, my knee buckled under my weight. Asher's arms were the only thing keeping me from needing to be peeled off the cave floor. He lifted me up and cradled my body against his cool solid form.

"Keep it kosher, Kincaid. Wouldn't want anyone to get the wrong idea," I whispered, leaning into him and relishing the feel of safety he brought.

"No, we wouldn't want that now, would we?" he teased, leaning in close enough I could've kissed him if I would've puckered my lips.

The air between us was practically crackling with anticipation, and I could've sworn pterodactyls had taken flight in my ribcage. Asher's nostrils flared, and his eyes narrowed on the red-tinged tear in my side.

"Come on, *Cujo*. Let's get you checked out," Asher joked as he started for the gapped opening to the cave, stopping only to scoop up the book from where it lay.

He handed it to me to carry, but I was reluctant to take it from him.

"I can ask Ms. Bell if you don't think you can handle it?" the vampire teased, his eyes dancing with challenging humor.

Deadpanned, I snatched the book from his hands and cradled

it against my middle, sure to keep it from opening. Glancing down at the tome, I wondered where it would go now. It couldn't go back to the library; that was a disaster. The Infernum wasn't the right place either.

Bye, Felicia.

But I still wondered . . .

"Hey, Asher? What will happen to the book now?"

He shrugged.

"I'll turn it over to the Board of Regents. They'll stash it somewhere it won't cause problems again."

It wasn't the perfect solution, but nothing was. It was the best middle ground answer I could hope for; the Board of Regents wouldn't do anything to put us at risk. I had to believe that. The girls followed closely behind us as we made our way out of the amethyst caves and toward the infirmary. So much had changed in such a short period of time, and I was so grateful to have Tempest Bell and Natalie Putnam back. I owed the pair more than a few high-potency home brews, and I would make sure I paid up.

Samhain was about to begin, my favorite holiday. Having this mess cleaned up was a good omen and for a split second, I did the one thing I shouldn't; I wondered what could possibly go wrong after everything had just worked out so right.

The loud metallic clang of the gong echoed through the cavern and across Halvard. Mr. Doyle had been too right: the games were only just beginning.

A LEGACY TIME FORGOT

TISH THAWER

"To dare is to do."
— Hel Tower Motto

CHAPTER 1

Red and silver sparks burst against the tall wood-beam ceiling of our private great room. "Happy Samhain!" my tower mates cried out—some bubbly and giddy for the holiday break kicking off today, and others fake and totally annoyed. The magically-induced fireworks sizzled brightly in our Hel Tower colors before evaporating high above our heads. They popped and faded into an imaginary oblivion I'd created in my mind's eye, where they'd lead a life of fiery glory, keeping the night sky alive with warmth and cheer forever and ever. I laughed to myself, firmly set on the bubbly and giddy side of things—I had to be, after what we'd just been through. Helping Vanna dispatch the Gjenganger was an experience I'd never forget. Tempest, Marina, Vanna, myself, and even Professor "Hot Pants" had all worked together to contain the beast once more. Unfortunately, not all of us escaped unscathed.

"Hey, Nat, have you changed your mind? Are you heading home for break after all?" A sweet voice called me back to earth.

I turned to face Tempest—my best friend—and snagged the

cup of steaming caramel-apple cider she held out in my direction. My long dark hair fell forward as I closed my eyes and inhaled the delicious aroma of sweet apples and cinnamon. I gave a silent beat of thanks to the Goddess for the delicious beverage *and* for the woman who'd delivered it.

Tempest and I had become fast friends when a lot of our entry trials ended up being the same. It made sense, of course, the two of us being witches and all. We'd even been assigned to the same fields of study: Healing Arts with a major in Field Medicine—but it was really during orientation week that we'd grown especially close. Through late-night conversations and a few dreaded trust-falls, we'd all gotten to know each other while figuring out how we were connected to the Goddess Hela, the namesake of our tower. While our greeting of *'Welcome to Hel'* may have sounded a little scary to some, we liked it that way . . . because just like Hela, we were all misunderstood, while carrying one or more characteristics of the Goddess: courage, freedom, and justice. Personally, I thought Tempest carried every single one. She kicked ass last night helping Vanna, and I was proud to have her as a sister witch. And even better, she thankfully never judged me based solely on my last name—something I wasn't used to, especially among other witches. Usually dirty looks and even pure hatred followed me wherever I went.

"Yeah, you know me better than that. Since they erased Mom's memory of this place, it'd just be too hard to spend my break with her. Constantly lying about *'how's school going?'* wouldn't make for a very relaxing Sabbath, know what I mean?" I raised a brow.

"Oh, yeah, I feel ya." Tempest grinned and bobbed her head, driving home the fact that she, too, definitely wouldn't be leaving campus to visit her parents—they were real pieces of work, those two. Both had been supportive when their coven wanted to strip Tempest of her powers, and to this day, they remained completely untrustworthy. Thankfully, her power stripping hadn't happened, but due to her circumstances, Tempest had been given special allowance to stay at the Academy year-round under the watchful eye of Mr. Westbrook and Dr. Lavinia.

"Hey," inspiration struck, "why don't we see if Micah will let us crash at his place during break so we can enjoy the Sabbath and maybe watch the Haunting on Main Street parade?" I peered over the rim of the steaming cup, hoping she'd fall prey to my pleading doe-eyes. The traditional Halloween costume parade and candy-fest would be a welcome alternative to staying cooped-up in our room.

Tempest laughed, linking her arm through mine as I steadied the cup in my other hand. "Done and done. I already asked, and the answer is yes. We leave in a couple of hours and get to stay through the weekend."

"Nice! I'm ready to get my witchy New Year started. Are we doing costumes, or simply going as our usual stunning selves?" I downed the rest of my cider and set the cup aside.

Tempest laughed and pulled me into the stairwell, sprinting passed the Valkyrie statue as its base, and then up the tight spiral corridor. "I was thinking we could just goth out our make-up a bit and go as sister witches."

Even with the magical glow of red lights flooding the space from underneath the stairs, I couldn't see her face clearly. I could, however, perfectly envision the huge smile that had spread across it as she continued to lead us higher around the curve.

"So basically, you just want to add more eye-liner and pretend it's a normal day?"

Everyone already called us sisters, saying we looked so much alike. I couldn't see it, though. I wore jeans, T-shirts, combat boots, and usually had a flannel wrapped around my waist, while Tempest preferred a more couture look, even down to her high-heeled boots.

With dramatic flair, she flipped the curtain of her own dark hair over her shoulder and winked back at me. "Pretty much."

Giggling like idiots, we crested the top of the stairs and made our way down the second-story hall. The childish exuberance being displayed as we entered our personal dorm room was far too young for our actual age, but I didn't care—the idea of dressing up and participating in tonight's Haunting on Main Street in town sounded like the type of good ol' fashion fun we could both definitely use. School had been tough lately, with midterms and training, but especially due to all the crazy stuff happening around campus—e.g., last night!

I kicked off my UGGs—a comfy alternative to my usual lace-up boots—and shuffled across the black circular rug, leaving its fluffy edge and shivering as the cold of the stone floor hit my bare feet. Climbing into my favorite spot, I pulled my knees to my chest and sat perched on the open window seat. The natural stone pathways, caverns, and the courtyard below were speckled with dappled sunlight raining down from the skylight above. I loved this campus, but I was ready for some full-on sunshine and moonlit magic of an open sky. I turned back to Tempest who was, as usual, fully engaged with our shared familiar, Mystic.

"Hey, do you know if Vanna will be staying on campus over the break? With the injuries she sustained last night, I wasn't sure if she'd be allowed to leave yet," I asked.

Tempest paused mid-pet, earning her a light tap and meow from Mystic. "I'm not sure. I haven't seen Marina or Professor Kincaid since last night but know they took her straight to the infirmary. She should heal fast but will probably have to remain under observation for a few more days." Tempest shuddered. "An infected hellhound on campus is no joke." She glanced down at the bite on her left wrist, her mood and voice shifting as she continued. "Speaking of, I have to stop by the infirmary myself to get this bandage changed before we go."

I bobbed my head and turned back to the open window. An infected hellhound, a killer beast, vampire attacks, spirit possessions, and some magical techno-hack had all been no joke lately. Not to mention the recent deaths. Oh, and let's not forget the newest hourglass hovering over the campus.

The gong had rung out last night while we were still in the amethyst cave, and while the sands had begun to fall, no one had a clue what to expect next—that alone freaked me out. Tempest's tattoo had transformed into an hourglass, then she accidentally changed our shared familiar into a killer beast. Vanna's had done the same thing right before this nightmare with the Gjenganger had started, and while no real connection had been made to the latest hourglass yet, for some reason, I had a feeling I was next. To say I was nervous was this side south of an understatement.

The great room was empty by the time Tempest and I descended the stairs again to exit our tower. Stepping beyond the thick wooden door, shadows surrounded us, creeping in from behind the enormous stalagmites that made up our dorm and all the other ancient stone structures surrounding the quad. I minded my steps—as I'd done since day one—only walking on the specific stones I deemed a safe zone while crossing the path that connected our tower to the main courtyard. I may be brave, but I wasn't stupid. The drop off either side was seriously no joke.

A group of shifters were play-sparring in the open area straight ahead, but for the most part, the campus had already cleared out. So much so, I could actually hear the bubbling river running in the chasm far below. Tempest and I veered right, crossing back over the connecting bridge to Eirhal Hall. It wouldn't take long to get her bandage changed out, but I was bummed about having to come here on my day off. Most of our classes took place here, and after spending some time in the infirmary recently myself, I'd hoped to avoid it during the break. Dragging my feet, I shuffled behind Tempest and planted myself against the wall as she talked with the nurse.

"This looks good," Madame Roth stated flatly as she

unwrapped Tempest's wrist. "So do you have any big plans for Samhain break?" Her annoyed tone made it obvious she was trying to make small talk while she worked.

"Actually, yes, we're headed to town for the weekend. Tonight's the Haunting on Main parade," Tempest replied cheerfully.

A light huff and a flicker of movement caught my eye to the right. Leaning back, I peered into the next room and saw Vanna shifting uncomfortably on her bed as Professor Kincaid helped smooth out her blankets. I moved to go say hello, but stopped as Tempest grabbed my arm.

"All set. Come on. We need to get to the portals before Micah changes his mind."

I shrugged and waved at Vanna, then followed Tempest back out of the tower and across the quad. This time we turned left and hurried across the main bridge. Looking back at the massive arched gateway, I eyed the twin Valkyrie statues flanking the entrance to our Halvard campus and tried to ignore the chill slithering up my spine.

Tempest grabbed my hand and pulled me forward. Trudging up the sloping pathway, we entered the vestibule that housed the school's transportation portals. They were the only way to and from campus, and only those with a school tattoo could access them. I looked down, pleased to find my crest tattoo glowing purple and active.

"Let's go." Tempest smiled and yanked me through the center arch. Energy swirled around us, and I wondered if any of the other species could physically feel the magic snapping against their skin, or if it was just a witch thing.

Stepping through the other side, we were immediately greeted by Micah, Tempest's guardian angel—literally. The dude was an angel but looked more like a model, sporting some seriously sexy muscles, a chiseled jaw-line, and even a couple tattoos. I licked my lips. He hugged my best friend and gave me a similar, yet reserved squeeze. *Crap . . .* I hope he couldn't read my mind.

"You're headed to the parade then straight home, yes?" He

dipped his head toward Tempest's freshly-wrapped wrist, obviously expecting her agreeing response.

"You betcha!" I linked arms with her, answering with a nervous energy instead.

"Actually," she slid out of our buddy-hold and started toward the chamber room exit, "I'm fine and was hoping after the parade we could chill at Coffee Haven for a bit. I know they stay open late for most of the festivals in town."

"Let me think about it." Micah gestured to the door. "Let's go on out." He silently followed us from the chamber room and out of the school, then stood with his arms crossed on the manicured front lawn of the Falls Campus of the Sun and Moon Academy. Surveying the area, he took note of the crowd making their way toward town. Cars, bikes, and even people hoofing it on foot were all headed down First Street toward Main to claim their spots for the parade. "All right. But you know the drill—if anything seems out of sorts, use your crystal to contact me immediately." Micah gave Tempest a final nod then disappeared.

"Wow, he could have at least given us a ride," I joked.

Tempest snickered and pulled down the sleeves of her black wool sweater as we began our trek across the parking lot. The sun had begun to dip behind Miles Mountain, but luckily Main Street was only a few blocks away. Slipping my gray flannel-lined hoodie off my waist, I snuggled into its warmth and shoved my hands into the pockets. The mountain peaks were already snow-capped, and here in town, the crisp autumn air nipped at my nose as we strolled down the street. We walked in silence for a few blocks, just enjoying the freedom and vastness of truly being outside. The magic of this town flowed beneath my feet. It had a familiar trace, and I wondered if the Howes' influence here is what pulled at me the most.

I thought back to all the times Mother had mentioned the Howe witches to me, and how they connected to our family. It was by the sheer grace of the Goddess that a Howe High Priestess took pity on a Putnam witch during the burning times, even though at the time our family had practically declared war on them.

Obviously, I didn't have all the details, but Mom made it a point to stress how intertwined our fates were from that day on, hinting that the tie wasn't always a positive one. And now here—where their magic literally flowed from the falls—I was feeling that connection even stronger.

The closer we got to the center of town, more people emerged, spilling from their homes or shops in full costume. Family units of some sort—a mom and dad with their kid, or siblings holding hands with their younger brothers or sisters—all filed down the street, ready for tonight's festivities. For being a true witch's holiday, Samhain was one of the most kid-friendly Sabbaths celebrated.

Twinkle lights hung from storefronts, while the last rays of the dying sun glinted off monster masks and princess tiaras. The innocence of youth reflected back at me in a shimmering display. *Damn, I wished I could have lived here as a kid.* Growing up, I knew my grandmother Rose Mary for a short time before she passed, but other than that, it had always just been me and my mom. My father was never in the picture, which was explained away as a 'normal Putnam thing.' I didn't get it, of course, but after getting shut down so many times for asking, it was just another part of our legacy I grew to accept over time.

"Hey, come on." Tempest grabbed my hand, pulling me toward the first open spot we saw along the curb.

We folded ourselves onto a blanket that had been spread out to share. I nodded at the generous woman with the outdated bouffant hairdo seated next to us. "Thank you."

"You're welcome." The woman's lips pulled tight. "Are you new to town, dear? I haven't seen you around."

I opened my mouth to respond but paused . . . the Sun & Moon Academy College wasn't exactly common knowledge, and I for one, wouldn't be spilling the beans. "I'm just visiting my friend."

"Ah, so you live in town, then?" The woman redirected her interrogation toward Tempest.

"Not exactly. I'm just visiting too," Tempest replied.

The women huffed, looking down her nose at the blanket then back up into our heavily charcoal-lined eyes. "Well, it's a little unusual for our town to get so many new visitors all at once, especially before the ski slopes open. Do you mind if I ask your names?"

Tempest stuck her nose in the air and turned away, making it obvious she did, in fact, mind— leaving it up to me to answer the nosy woman's question. "My name is Natalie . . . Natalie Putnam."

The women recoiled ever so slightly, making it clear the legacy of my given name had indeed made it all the way to Havenwood Falls.

CHAPTER 3

"Forget about her," Tempest said under her breath as we walked away. The words were simple and straightforward, but following her suggestion was easier said than done. We'd quickly removed ourselves from the woman's personal property and scathing looks, opting instead to stroll through the park and along the sidewalks, keeping time with the parade as it meandered down the street.

"It's hard to 'forget about her' when those same looks are exactly what I've dealt with my entire life." I kicked a rock from the sidewalk and watched it bounce into the gutter. "Putnam equals evil, it's as simple as that, or at least that's what everyone thinks." My mind immediately drifted to a particularly stinging incident that had happened just before I'd received my invitation to come here.

"Natalie Putnam, what do you think you're doing?" The sneer on Mrs. Elwell's face was one of pure disgust.

"I'm just here to pick up some supplies for my mother." I nodded toward the basket of sugar, flour, coffee, and the fresh herbs I'd gathered from the small General Store on the outskirts of town. It was my chosen place to shop since venturing to one of the major chains put me in contact with far too many people.

"Well, in case you've forgotten, we don't sell your kind of herbs here." Her lip curled up as she eyed my selections.

"And exactly what do you mean by that?" I'd dealt with this kind of stupidity my whole life, and often wondered why Mom never considered moving the hell away from here. Oh, that's right—we were supposed to be better than them and needed to 'rise above it.' A Putnam witch would never leave their family home.

"Don't play coy with me, you little devil-witch. You know exactly what I mean."

With that, I dropped the basket at her feet and walked out the door, stomping home angry and upset. Mom may have chosen to suffer here, but I was sick of being punished because of her decision—family legacy or not.

"Yeah, well, everyone is wrong. It's as simple as that." Tempest's sharp tone snapped me back into focus. It was clear she was serious, but when she nudged my shoulder, grinning from ear to ear, her mood suddenly shifted.

"What are you smiling at?"

She jerked her chin up, gesturing straight ahead of us. I followed her line of sight and sighed.

There he was—Bale Grayson . . . *Yum!* Loose dark curls hung past his broad shoulders, framing his brooding eyes. Jeans, a charcoal-gray T-shirt, and his signature long coat played straight into the misunderstood bad-boy type I always seemed to fall for.

"Hey, Bale," Tempest called out, earning her an elbow to the ribs.

He lifted his hand, though his eyes stayed downcast. He wasn't much for sharing or engaging, so I'd take his small acknowledgement as a win.

"Go talk to him." Tempest nudged me in his direction, but as usual, the second I got up the nerve to move, Scarlet Howe popped up next to him like magic. Maybe it was.

"Hi, guys," she greeted, friendly as always.

"Hey," I replied lamely.

"Are you enjoying the parade?" She stepped closer to Bale.

"We were," Tempest snapped, her snark putting me back in a good mood.

"Enjoy your night." I smiled, laughing as we walked away. "Tempest, you're so bad."

"Yeah, well, it really does seem oddly suspicious that you never get a chance to actually talk to the guy without Scarlet showing up." Tempest slowed her determined stride, carefully placing her seasonally-inappropriate wedge-heels between the checkered pattern of blankets and people as we crisscrossed our way through the town square.

Rounding the gazebo, we hopped up its stairs and claimed the first open space we saw. Leaning against the railing, I let the variety of costumes and youthful smiles continue to lift my mood; little girls in pointy black witch hats, boys in elaborate warrior garb, and even the occasional teenager sporting a white sheet, holding out a bag for candy brought a smile to my face. I took a deep breath, grateful again to be under an open sky, and quickly moved passed the annoyances of the night.

The noise of the crowd dropped to a low hum as the last of the parade dispersed. Light from the waxing crescent sliced across the sky; the tiny sliver of the Goddess's power bolstering my mood even further.

"You ready for another cup of cider?" Tempest nodded across Main toward Coffee Haven.

"Absolutely!" I rubbed my hands together and followed Tempest down the gazebo stairs, making a beeline across the grass. "Ouch!" I stopped just before the curb, grabbing my wrist.

Tempest turned back to see what was wrong as I slid up my sleeve. We locked eyes. *Fuck.* My school tattoo glowed and shifted from its normal crest into the shape of an hourglass. I swallowed a scream as it sizzled hot against my skin.

I knew it.

I stared at the warning, my heart racing and my breath

bordering on the verge of panic. I raised my head, meeting Tempest's worried gaze. "What am I supposed to do now?"

A voice sounded in my head before Tempest could even open her mouth. *"Natalie Putnam. Return to campus immediately."*

"Shit. We need to go. I just got called back to campus." I yanked down my sleeve and tapped a finger to my temple.

Tempest ushered me behind the nearest tree, side-eyeing the last of the dispersing crowd. Reaching into her pocket, she pulled out her angelic crystal and closed her eyes. A moment later, Micah appeared.

"What's wrong?" he snapped, moving protectively toward Tempest.

"We need immediate transport back to Sun and Moon Academy. Natalie's been called in."

Micah looked down at my wrist as if he could see through the fabric to the pulsing magic below.

"Come here." He opened his arms.

Stepping into his embrace felt like walking through the portals, but instead of the snapping energy of magic against my skin, this was gentler—like a flowing current running through my veins. I closed my eyes and let myself fall into his warmth.

"Okay, you both know the drill; you have to walk through yourself."

I opened my eyes, back in the chamber room of the Falls Campus. Micah nodded to the portal, giving Tempest a reassuring squeeze.

"Call me if you need anything else." His words were kind, and I opened my mouth to thank him—even if he wasn't talking to me —but stopped short when the voice sounded in my head again.

"Natalie Putnam. Return to campus IMMEDIATELY!"

The added emphasis rattling inside my head pulled me forward on shaking knees.

CHAPTER 4

Tempest exited the portal and plowed directly into me as I stood frozen in the vestibule. There, standing before me, were three Board of Regents members sporting varying degrees of disappointment on their faces. I didn't recognize two of them, but the third had me cringing as he stepped in my direction.

Gabriel Doyle, a representative from the Lilith Nest of goth vampires, practically sliced me open with his piercing blue eyes and knowing smirk. I'd heard rumors he could read minds, so I quickly muttered a spell to block the fear and anxiety driving every single thought in my head.

"Ms. Putnam, please come with us. We have some questions for you."

"What kind of questions?" Tempest blurted out in my defense.

"The kind that don't concern you." After a slow blink in Tempest's direction, he turned back to me and extended his arm—a silent insistence I go with them.

I looked to Tempest, wide-eyed and scared, then shuffled behind two of the board members as Mr. Doyle closed in behind me. My footsteps faltered as soon as we crossed the bridge. I expected to be led to Halstein Hall and the Administration Office, but instead we veered right and headed straight for Eirhal.

"What's going on? Where are we going?"

Mr. Doyle cleared his throat behind me. "I thought it would be clear since most of your classes are held here, are they not?"

"Yes, they are, but that doesn't answer my question." I tried to keep the panic out of my voice.

"Your question, and hopefully ours, will be answered soon enough."

I followed in silence as we continued through the main door and down the corridor, but my breath hitched when we turned toward the labs. The sound of our footsteps had somehow synced, producing a monotonous cadence that we marched to until nearing the room at the end of the hall. The air here was thick—almost sticky—and seemed to be getting worse the closer we got.

"Can you tell us anything about this room?" Mr. Doyle asked, standing just this side of the doorframe.

I looked back and forth between the empty room and the vampire. "Not really. It's just one of the labs we use for class."

"And which class is that?"

"Field Medicine with Dr. Underwood."

"What was the last experiment you performed here before break?" the second Regent asked.

I thought back, not liking where this was headed, but answered honestly as soon as I remembered. "Extractions."

"Extractions?" Mr. Doyle questioned.

"Yes. Extractions," I repeated slowly.

"And what exactly did that lesson entail?" he demanded.

"Spells to surround the area, potions to treat the wound, and another spell to transport us to a safety zone. Why? What does this have to do with anything?"

Mr. Doyle nodded to the third Regent who then stepped to the front of our group. Waving his hand, he muttered a spell under his breath then stood back as a glamour that had been placed over the door wavered and disappeared.

My hand flew to my mouth.

Four bodies were lying on the lab floor—three students and

one adult—and from where I stood, I couldn't tell if they were dead or alive.

I moved to step closer, but Mr. Doyle stuck out his arm, halting my progress, which forced me to bear witness from where I stood. The bodies had fallen in somewhat of a straight line, like they all walked in one after another and simultaneously dropped to the floor. *So strange.*

"What happened to them?"

"We don't know, but it's now become clear that anyone who enters is immediately rendered unconscious," Mr. Doyle supplied matter-of-factly.

"Just unconscious, not dead?" I looked back at the adult who'd fallen last and noticed the faint rise and fall of his chest. Beyond that, I didn't recognize him, but figured he was another Regent who'd gone in to investigate.

"No. Not dead . . . at least not yet." Mr. Doyle nodded to his fellow Regent who quickly recast the glamour, making the room appear normal to anyone viewing it from the outside.

I stepped away from the door and took a deep breath, building up the courage to ask the burning question. "So what exactly does this have to do with me?"

"We were hoping you could tell us. Care to explain?" Mr. Doyle extended his arm again, gesturing back down the hall, but this time . . . I didn't move.

"Well, I can't tell you anything, because I have no idea." I pushed my sleeve up, revealing my tattoo. "But I assume it has to do with this."

Mr. Doyle started down at the hourglass tattoo on my forearm and sighed. "Ah, that helps explain things a bit."

"Really?" I tossed my arms in the air. "Because it sure doesn't help explain jack to me!" I purposely softened my four-letter word, solely for the fact that Regent members held the authority of who got to attend the Sun & Moon Academy, and that required respect in all situations. Even one as fucked-up as this.

Mr. Doyle's expression hardened. "We heard the gong ring last night, but with so many students gone for break, we had no idea who was connected to this situation. We cast a locator spell of our own. Whoever heard our call to return to campus would be the responsible party for our current situation. So, like I said, it looks like you have some explaining to do, Miss Putnam."

The way he said my last name grated . . . bad. My shoulders slumped, and I dropped my head. "Well, I can't explain. Despite your implication, I'm not responsible for this. I didn't do anything."

"Then prove us wrong."

⬥

"Oh my Goddess, what happened, Nat? I've been freaking out up here!" Tempest threw herself into my arms the moment I stepped into our room.

"I'm in trouble." I shrugged.

She reeled back and tossed her hair over her shoulder. "Yeah, no shit! But what is it? What's happened?"

I climbed into my hanging chair in the corner, pulled my feet beneath me, and let it rock as I explained. "A lab in Eirhal Hall has been cursed or something, and they think it has to do with me, or a spell I cast, or whatever . . . Either way, it's all on me to figure out what's wrong."

"Hmmm . . ." She flopped down onto her elaborate goth-inspired bed. "Compared to the rest of the stuff that's been happening around here lately, that doesn't sound too bad."

"Wow. Really?" I huffed. "Well, so far it's knocked four people unconscious, leaving them on the brink of death. But yeah, you're right, not too bad." I didn't bother hiding the sarcasm in my voice.

"Damn. Yeah, okay. That does suck." She wiggled her fingers in the air, producing two steaming drinks on a table that appeared between us. "Anything I can do to help?"

Her magic had been getting stronger lately, and I was thrilled for this newest level of skill.

"I don't know yet, but trust me, if you can help in any way, I'll let you know." I snagged the cup from the table, inhaling its caramel goodness, and began contemplating how the hell I was going to get myself out of this mess.

CHAPTER 5

I opened my eyes, excited to be on break, but that lasted for about two-point-five seconds before I remembered the bullshit that had cut things short last night. I sat up and reached for the sky, stretching my back and whispering my morning chant.

"May the God and Goddess of the moon, stars, and sun, shine their bright blessings upon me as this new day has begun."

Cozy in my flannel PJs, I tiptoed to our altar and lit my smudge stick—I refused to start this day differently than any other. I cleared my energy, rubbing a finger over the obsidian tower sitting proudly in the middle of all my other crystals atop my carved wooden pentacle, and sealed my morning blessing.

"Morning." Tempest's blankets shifted as she rolled to face me.

"Morning. Sorry I woke you." I snuffed out my sage and grabbed my gray cotton robe from the end of my bed, along with my make-up bag from the dresser. "Go back to sleep, I'll be back after a bit." I smiled at my groggy best friend and headed for our community bathroom next door.

Stepping inside, I inhaled the never-ending lavender and

eucalyptus scent that permeated the room then followed the spiral path that led to the private showers. I twisted the knobs, relaxing as the hot water rebounded off the stones and splashed onto my skin. Leaning back against the rounded wall, I closed my eyes and let my thoughts drift to wherever the Goddess led them.

A rolling gray backdrop appeared behind my lids like an endless sea of stormy waves, followed by an image of black wispy ribbons floating toward me through the air. Together, they churned and roiled, building into an ominous cloud.

"Let me in," a voice commanded, barely drifting to my ears on an imaginary wind. My eyes snapped open. The voice was indistinct but somehow familiar.

Unable to get a clear read on my vision, I finished showering and turned off the water. Stepping out, I grabbed my robe and rushed into the drying chamber Tempest and I had created together. It served for drying herbs of all kinds, but was mostly a place that helped keep us toasty, healthy, and dry. Pulling the opaque glass door open, I tiptoed into the enclosure and sighed as a warm blast of air shot up from multiple holes located in the floor, warming me instantly. Living in an underground castle could be cold and required some creative magic when it came to our everyday conveniences, and being allowed to use our gifts so freely here was just one more thing I loved about this place.

Tightening the tie of my robe, I walked to the built-in bench and lay down as the warm air continued to circulate around me. I closed my eyes to concentrate on the voice and its message.

"Let me in."

The air thickened as the temperature continued to rise. I cast a protection spell and grounded myself through the stones beneath me, falling deeper into my meditation. The next fifteen minutes were a blur as I tried to pinpoint the source of the voice, following the whisper as it rode the currents along the back of my mind. Just out of reach, the voice eluded me, remaining on the periphery of my thoughts. Frustrated, I pulled myself from the meditation and sat up.

"If you want me to 'let you in', then why are you running from me?" I said out loud, immediately regretting the words.

"Who are you talking to?" Tempest's voice rang out from the other side of the door.

"No one. Never mind. I'll be out in a sec."

I took a deep breath, the stones beneath me suddenly cold despite the warm air surrounding me. *What are you doing?* I scolded myself. Being careless—that's what. Words held power, and I'd practically invited something potentially malevolent to communicate with me without knowing anything about it. I shook my head and left the drying room, completely disappointed with myself.

"I thought you were going back to sleep?" I slid up next to Tempest as she washed her face in one of the stone basins along the main wall.

"I was but knew you'd want to dive into researching that room, so here I am." She shook her head, tossing her wild, bed-head topknot from side-to-side. "Bright-eyed and bushy-tailed, and ready to help however I can."

I laughed, her cheese-ball grin immediately brightening my mood. Tempest was never bright-eyed or bushy-tailed in the mornings, so I quickly let her off the hook. "It's okay. Honestly. Go back to bed, and I'll find you once I know more. I'm going to get dressed and head back over to Eirhal to see if I can sense anything without any of the Regents breathing down my neck."

"Are you sure? I can come with you," Tempest offered with a yawn.

"Thanks, but I'm sure." I smiled and left her in the bathroom, rushing to our room to get dressed. My jeans slid on easily, as did my black moon-phase T-shirt. But after pulling on a black and gray flannel and lacing up my combat boots, I still felt like something was missing. I walked to my nightstand and grabbed my amethyst pendant and slid it around my neck before heading out the door. I wanted to make sure I was gone before Tempest got back. After everything that happened recently, she'd been having nightmares and needed all the rest she could get.

Pulling my mop of hair into a low pony-tail, I made my way down the spiral staircase, frowning as I crossed the empty great room—everyone was still off enjoying their break, the lucky jerks.

Cool air hit me as I stepped out of our tower doors and into the openness of the campus. I loved the early morning feel of the cave, the dappled light flickering down through the mountain-top, but was bummed I wasn't waking up at Micah's instead. Tempest and I had big plans for the long weekend—breakfast at Coffee Haven, a visit to Callie's Consignments for some new clothes, and a stop by Into the Mystic New Age Books and Gifts to check out their latest tarot and oracle cards . . . *Oh well.* I shook my head and jogged over the bridge to Eirhal, entering the medical arts building with a jerk of the handle and a firm purpose in mind. I was going to figure this out and prove, once again, that just because my name was Putnam, it didn't mean I had anything to do with the bad shit going down.

CHAPTER 6

The main hall in Eirhal was empty, eerily so, but the voices of a few professors and doctors kept most of my wild thoughts at bay. At the end of the corridor, I turned toward the labs, quickly making my way to the cursed room at the end. The glamour was still in place, making it look completely normal, but I was surprised it hadn't been blocked off by the Sky Boys or something more. I stepped forward, searching for the edge of the spell. An invisible bubble pushed against me a foot or so outside the door, and while I hadn't heard the exact words the Regent used to reveal the room, I quickly chanted a version of my own.

"Remove the magic blocking me. Goddess allow me to clearly see. Show me what I need to know, so through this challenge I learn and grow."

I jumped back.

A green, putrid-smelling cloud filled the room, while the floor and walls were completely black.

And it was spreading.

Climbing like a vine up a trellis, charred veins spilled past the doorframe, creeping into the hallway and up to the ceiling. I minded my steps, tiptoeing closer to see if I could still make out the bodies within. I could barely see the first two who lay farthest into the room, but the third, fourth, and now a fifth, sixth, and seventh were there, all barely breathing. *Dammit!* What were they doing down here? I thought pretty much everyone had already left on break. I squinted, trying to make out the newly fallen students, but only recognized two of them. Infiniti Clausman and Joe Greg. *Oh, no!* This damn thing had only started a day ago and had already claimed seven people so far. *Think, Natalie, think!*

"Let me in." The words from my vision flitted to my ears as an angry plume of the toxic smoke surged straight for me.

I jumped back, quickly recasting the glamour, then hauled ass down the corridor and straight out of the building. *Holy shit!* I gasped for breath, sucking in massive gulps of cold air.

"Making any headway, Miss Putnam?" The ice in Gabriel Doyle's voice sent another round of chills down my spine.

I stood up straight, squared my shoulders, and lifted my eyes to meet his. "Not exactly."

"Then I suggest you get back to it and reverse whatever you did to cause this." He nodded toward Eirhal and turned away with a smirk. "You need to rectify this situation immediately."

What the hell? Why did he care how fast I figured this out? It wasn't like he had anything to do with it. *Hmmm . . .* or maybe he did.

My brain started spinning. What if all the crap that had been happening lately did have to do with the Board? I jogged across the path from Eirhal and quickly crossed back over the bridge to Hel, eyeing the large golden Valkyrie statue that stood protectively atop our tower. I had to think this through, and maybe . . . just maybe, our winged-warrior would provide some guidance. What would the Regents have to gain by messing with the new students? We'd all been invited here, so why would they want to make things worse for us now? Or maybe it wasn't the entire Board. Maybe it was just Gabriel Doyle himself. Perhaps he was killing off students to increase his nest numbers. Maybe that's why he offered to back the school in the first place. *Damn!* It was the perfect set-up to skulk around and hand select the recruits he'd want to turn.

Taking the steps two at a time, I climbed the corkscrew staircase to the second floor and headed straight for my room.

"Hey, that was quick!" Still in her pajamas, Tempest lifted her head out of the magazine she had sprawled across her bed, propping her chin in the palm of her hand. "Did you learn anything new?"

"No. Not really, but I have an idea that I may need help investigating."

Tempest pushed herself the rest of the way up and hopped off the bed. "Sure thing. How can I help?"

"I need you to make a list of all the people who've been put in harm's way recently, and if a Regent had any involvement or contact with those specific students."

"Ookkaay . . ." Tempest raised a brow.

I sighed and walked to our mini-fridge, grabbing a bottle of water and cracking the lid. "Just go with me on this, Temp."

I leaned back and took a swig.

"Well, during my ordeal—once I pulled my head out—I talked to Micah of course, but other than that, off the top of my head, I know Vanna visited Gabriel's nest when she was researching the Gjenganger, but that's it. I'll have to go digging for the others."

"Great. That'll be a big help. Thanks."

I downed the rest of my water and climbed into my favorite window seat. I didn't know much about most of the Regents, but I'd sure as hell be paying more attention to them now. So far, if I was right, Mr. Doyle was involved with two of us—Vanna and me—and I had a sneaking suspicion his name would continue to pop up. I looked out over the entire campus from my open window and was now less worried about a cursed classroom and more concerned about the bigger picture.

*T*empest and I hadn't gotten far in our research since yesterday, seeing as everyone we needed to question was still off-campus for Samhain break. We already knew Vanna's story, obviously, and it wasn't like I could just stroll into the Administrative Offices and accuse Mr. Doyle outright. I needed to figure out how to get this info, because from the lessons I'd learned growing up, if you knew the root of the problem, you could weed it out a hell of a lot faster.

"Hey, I'm going to run down to Howe's Herbal Shoppe for a few ingredients. I want to try something before I go back to Eirhal again." I stuffed some cash in my back pocket and headed for the door.

"Okay. I'll be here." Tempest grinned and rolled her eyes, giving a little wave around the room. I knew she didn't mean to, but the small show of her frustration made me feel like complete shit. We were stuck inside doing research over break because of me.

I left our tower and crossed the bridge and campus with my head down. Pulling open the double doors to Halstein Hall, I walked through the archway and wondered if Howe's Herbal Shoppe would even be open during break. My boots thumped on the white marble floor as I crossed the open area of the Student

Union, making a beeline for the herbal shop which was located to the far left, right before you got to the dining hall entrance. Lucky for me, the little bell on the satellite shop dinged as I opened the door and pushed my way inside.

"Hey, Natalie. I'm surprised to see you here on break. What brings you in?"

I lifted my head and took in Scarlet's too sweet face and forced a smile onto my own in response.

"Hey, Scarlet." I hadn't thought about her, or Bale for that matter, since the parade. "I just need to grab a few things," I stated flatly.

Picking up a small hand-basket, I made my way to the apothecary that took up the entire back wall. Scouring the bottles and bags of fresh herbs, I quickly snagged some yarrow to boost my courage, some camphor to aid my divination, some vetivert to hopefully break the hex on that damn classroom, some angelica to help focus my visions, and of course some more sage to cleanse and protect. You could never have enough sage.

I walked to the counter and set my basket down. "This should do it, thanks."

Scarlet looked down at the ingredients and back up to me. "Does this mean you have something to do with what's going on?"

"What do you mean?" I shrugged nervously, pulling down the cuff of my left sleeve.

Scarlet lifted each item from my basket with care, placing them into a small paper bag. "When I came into work this morning, I saw another hourglass hovering in the quad," she placed the last bottle in the bag and handed it to me across the counter, "and these herbs are pretty telling." She laughed. "Here you go. Good luck with your spell."

"How much do I owe you?" I reached for the cash in my back pocket.

"It's on me." Scarlet smiled.

"Wow, really? You don't have to do that."

"It's no problem. Besides, I'll feel better knowing I helped solve whatever issue you're facing." She waved me off, returning to the inventory of candles she was counting behind the counter.

I walked to the exit, my mouth hanging agape at her unsolicited generosity. Stumbling through a lame attempt to express my gratitude, I stammered, "Wow . . . again. Um . . . thank you. I, ah . . . really appreciate it."

"Of course. Don't worry about it. You can owe me one." Scarlet winked just as the door closed in my face.

Well, shit. Now, it looked like I owed the witch whose boyfriend I wished I could steal. *Lucky me! Great start to the day so far, Nat.* I shook my head and took a deep breath, mentally cleansing my aura before returning to my room. I walked across campus, purposely focusing on the sound of the river flowing below in the chasm. A soft breeze whistled around the carved buildings, and I tried to gain a little perspective into Scarlet's and my exchange. It was one thing to owe someone a favor, but to owe a witch, particularly one with the last name Howe, was something that raised the hair on the back of my neck. Problem was . . . I didn't know why. Sure, our family histories were strangely intertwined, but that was so long ago it shouldn't factor into a friendship—if you could call it that—between Scarlet and me now. But I couldn't deny it; something about owing Scarlet set my teeth on edge. Funny thing was, I knew better than most how unfair it was to judge someone solely by their last name.

I took another deep, grounding breath, hoping to dislodge these depressing thoughts, and refocused on the task at hand. I needed to cast my revealing spell as soon as I could. I wanted to see if I could get a glimpse of the connections between the students and Mr. Doyle before bringing anything up to test my theory. And I didn't have time to wait until everyone returned from break. Again, I wasn't sure why, but understanding the bigger picture here seemed like an important piece to the puzzle, and I was never one to question my instincts—another lesson driven into me by my mom.

Refocused, I pulled open the red double doors of Hel and sprinted to the top of the stairs then jogged down the hall toward my dorm. I was ready to get things underway. I yanked opened the door to my room and froze, my eyes going wide. *What is with all the distractions today?*

"Hey, Vanna, what are you doing here?" I eyed Tempest over the hellhound's shoulder.

Tempest practically jumped in front of Vanna to explain. "She was just released from the infirmary, and when I heard her coming back to her room across the hall, I figured I'd invite her in and ask her about what we talked about," Tempest rambled out in a rush.

Vanna huffed. "You guys were there. You know what went down." She plopped down onto our leather couch, crossing a leg over her knee. "What else do you want to know?

"Sorry, yeah, I asked Tempest to help me with a little research. I was wondering if you had any contact with anyone on the Board of Regents lately, but you're right, we already know you went to town and talked to Mr. Doyle, so we're good here." I squinted at Tempest, wondering why she'd really brought Vanna here.

"Yeah, true. I guess you're right. We know all we need to about that . . ." Tempest paused awkwardly. "But what about Professor Hot Pants? Where do things stand with him?" She cocked her head and grinned, revealing her true motive.

I smiled and stood back, watching as Vanna rose smoothly from the couch and slowly adjusted her sunglasses, blowing a smoke-ring of hellfire in Tempest's direction—a subtle, yet friendly warning, no doubt.

"Look, I'm grateful for your help with the Gjenganger, but I'm not sure I'm ready to swap boyfriend stories just yet. Thanks for the invite, though." She strode to the door, turning back with a quick flick of her chin in our direction. "Your room's taken on a real goth vibe. I didn't notice the skulls before. I approve." With a slam of the door, our neighboring hellhound was gone.

"What the hell are you thinking?" I practically yelled at Tempest.

She laughed as if needling a hellhound was no big deal. "What? She owes us one. I figured now is as good a time as any to get the dirt on those two."

"Yeah, well, I don't think accosting a freshly-healed hot-head is a good way to rebuild your friendship." I rolled my eyes at my loveable roomie and proceeded to empty the contents of my shopping trip out onto my bed.

"Oooh, what'd ya get?" Tempest picked up Mystic who'd been hiding under her bed, and moved to get a closer glimpse of my stock.

"Just a few things for a revelation spell. I think it'll be faster than trying to talk to everyone."

"Cool. I'm in. Let me grab the candles."

Tempest proceeded to lay out a pentacle, marking the sacred space for our casting, while I grabbed the mortar and pestle and ground out my chosen ingredients. The smell of the herbs releasing their scent helped me focus and relax, even through the sharp bite of the camphor and yarrow. I tossed in a pinch of lavender to soften the fragrance and boost the spell—another trick my mom had taught me. It worked wonders, especially when you added a pinch or two to the bottom of your holders when doing candle magic. My mind drifted as I finished up muddling the herbs, the sound of them crunching beneath my pestle a welcome and familiar song. Once done, I tore up strips of paper and wrote down all the students who'd been put in danger's path recently—as many as I could remember, anyway. Next, I wrote down the names of all the Board of Regents members I could think of. My money was on Mr. Doyle, but it's possible it was even bigger than him. Who knew?

Placing the scraps in the middle of the circle, I sprinkled my ground-up concoction on top of them and grabbed Tempest's hands.

"Okay, all set. Let's do this." I closed my eyes and began my chant.

*"Goddess I ask, allow me to see. Show me exactly what needs be.
Reveal the link from student to adult, showing the Regent responsible
for our lot."*

I cracked an eye, peeking to see if anything was happening. Nothing yet.

I repeated my chant.

"Goddess I ask, allow me to see. Show me exactly what needs be. Reveal the link from student to adult, showing the Regent responsible for our lot."

Again, nothing. I opened my eyes all the way and squeezed Tempest's hands. "Say it with me this time."

She nodded and re-closed her eyes.

Together we called out for a third time,

"Goddess I ask, allow me to see. Show me exactly what needs be. Reveal the link from student to adult, showing the Regent responsible for our lot."

A light breeze blew through our open window, and I knew we'd done it. I opened my eyes and smiled at the pieces of paper floating in the air in front of us. The herbs twisted and twirled around the pieces, making tiny ropes that wove the scraps together until they were fused into one ragged-edge note.

I thanked the Goddess and watched as the paper floated back down to the ground, landing in my outstretched hands.

"What the hell?" I frowned.

Tempest scooted closer and leaned in. "What's wrong? What does it say?"

I lifted the piece of parchment for her to read.

"Nice try, Putnam. Now how about you really get to work? Stop looking outside for answers and focus within. – GD," she read aloud. Tempest looked up and questioned, "GD?"

"Fucking Gabriel Doyle," I deadpanned, tossing the worthless paper to the floor.

CHAPTER 8

"How the hell can a vampire block a witch's spell?" Tempest waved her hand, extinguishing the candles as she moved to clean up the floor.

"I don't know. I think I heard Vanna say he has a genie in his employ or something. Maybe he gets a magical boost from her?" I shrugged. "Who knows? Regardless, I'm back to square one. He's covering his tracks really well."

Tempest flopped down onto her bed, looking almost as frustrated as I felt. It was one thing not to get answers to our questions, but it was another to have our spell completely blocked. It wasn't a good feeling for any witch, no matter how closely involved they were or not.

"What do you want to do now?" Tempest asked.

"I don't know. I guess I need to go back to the classroom and see if I can get a better read on what's actually infecting the space."

"Do you want me to go with you this time?" Tempest rolled onto her side and ran her hand down Mystic's fur, earning a purr from our shared familiar.

"No, but . . . I could use Mystic for this one."

"What do you mean?" Tempest sat up, cuddling the kitty to her chest.

"Don't worry. I won't let her out of my sight. I just want to see if she can pick up on anything I'm not. Actually, on second thought, why don't you come with me? You can hold Mystic, and I can interpret anything she finds."

Tempest frowned and nuzzled her nose into Mystic's fur, their recent adventure clearly etched on her face. "Our baby's gotta work today. Are you up for this, cutie?"

Mystic blinked her mis-matched eyes and snuggled into Tempest's embrace, writhing and purring to show her excitement and willingness to help.

"Okay, just make sure you do exactly what I say when we get there." I grabbed my normal sachet of protection herbs and crystals and slipped it into my pocket.

"Will do, boss. Lead the way." Tempest shimmied off the bed, lifting Mystic in one hand, and saluting me with the other.

We left the room and descended the staircase again. I was sick to death of all the running I'd been doing lately. My bitterness over missing Samhain break was close to reaching an all new high. But I had to push on. Once we made the trek back across to Eirhal, I led Tempest and Mystic down the main corridor and straight to the lab, holding out my arm to stop them once we got close.

"Wait here. I need to remove the glamour to see how far it's spread."

"Spread?" Tempest eyeballed me.

"Yeah, hold on." I moved forward slowly, feeling for the edge of the glamour when the magic hit me just a couple of steps in. *Damn.* It was getting worse.

"Remove the magic blocking me. Goddess allow me to clearly see. Show me what I need to know, so I may face this challenge and grow."

"Oh my Goddess!" Tempest cried out. A yowl tore from Mystic as she squirmed in Tempest's arms.

The entire end of the hallway was covered in black sludge, and the toxic smoke had completely engulfed the lab and was now spilling out the door.

I turned back to Tempest and held out my arms. "Give me Mystic."

Tempest shuffled backward, holding tight to our familiar the best she could. "I don't know, Nat. That looks bad, and she's freaking out."

"I know! Which is why I need to see what she's picking up."

Tempest soothed Mystic with a few more pets and whispers, then handed her to me.

"It's okay, baby. I won't let anything happen to you," I promised our kitty as I secured her in my arms. Edging forward slowly, I reached the infection and cast my spell.

"Goddess Bast, I call on thee, use Mystic to help me see. Pierce the veil, and show us now, what I, a servant, should do and how."

Mystic fell quiet in my arms as both of her eyes turned white.

CHAPTER 9

"Natalie, wake up!" Tempest's panicked voice rang in my ears as she shook my shoulders.

"What happened?" I groaned and sat up, quickly realizing we were still in the lab hallway.

"You passed out as soon as Mystic jumped out of your arms."

Oh no! I scrambled up, searching the hall for our brave little kitty. Black sludge now covered parts of the ceiling and was creeping its way toward the room next door.

"She's fine. I have her." Mystic's mis-matched eyes blinked at me from the crook of Tempest's arm.

"Oh, thank the Goddess."

"Did you get anything from her?" Tempest asked, giving Mystic's sweet head a scratch.

I turned back to the growing threat in front of us and nodded. "Yeah. I think I did. Let me put the glamour back in place so we can get out of here."

I muttered a spell, adding in some extra protection, in case what I'd just learned turned out to be true.

"Okay, come on. Let's go." I led Tempest and our shared familiar out of the building, contemplating how I could ditch them the entire time. I slowed my pace as we crossed the quad, looking to the sky when inspiration struck. "Hey, you go ahead. I'll meet you back in the room. I need to stop by Howe's again for some more supplies."

Tempest side-eyed me, probably questioning my willingness to visit Howe's twice in one day, but relented and headed home with Mystic still tucked in her arms.

Turning toward Halstein Hall, I paused, deciding I'd rather be alone to contemplate my vision than face Scarlet again with no real reason in mind. Padding back across the quad, I meandered over the main bridge and took a right onto the stone path that led to the underground lake. I was born as a hereditary witch, sharing my family's powers—and their crappy legacy. But as I grew older, I found myself becoming more of a solitary witch, and solitude was certainly what I needed now.

Following the gentle slope, I rounded the final bend and sighed in relief—I had the beach all to myself. I walked to the edge of the lake, flopped down, and removed my boots. The cool sand under my hands and feet immediately soothed my nerves. I squished my toes further into the soft ground and closed my eyes. Things may be jacked at the moment, but I was so grateful to be here—at the Academy. Places like this were around every corner, and their sheer wonder kept me grounded and focused—something I'd definitely need to be, after what I just saw.

I pulled the vision into my mind's eye again: a dark force beating against the school's magic, trying to get in. I had no idea how or why, but now knew what was happening to the classrooms was a side effect of this creature's continued attempts to gain access. Question was—how the heck was I supposed to stop it? Concentrating, I watched as a plume of inky magic slammed itself against the wards.

"*Let me in,*" the voice echoed in my head again.

I sat up and instinctively drew a protection rune in the sand. Slamming my hand against it, my magic flared out in a blast, sending waves across the underground lake and up the stone walls of our school. It wouldn't hold for long, but it would at least give me a little time to figure out my next step.

I brushed off the sand before pulling on my boots then walked back up the stone path. I paused at the Valkyrie statues standing guard on either side of the main bridge. They were massive, and intimidating, and I could use some of their strength right now. Both wore winged helmets and gripped their long swords proudly. I stepped forward, placing my hand on the nearest statue's leg, and felt an instant jolt of confidence and strength.

I could do this. It was my turn to save our school, and I wasn't about to let anyone down.

Jogging over the bridge, I crossed the quad and headed to Howe's Herbal Shoppe again. The bell rang as I entered, but the shop appeared to be empty.

"Back so soon," Scarlet's voice startled me, drifting from a shadowy corner in the back.

I turned to ask for the ingredient I was looking for and came face-to-face with Bale. Stepping from their shared shadow, he glided by me with only a nod of his chin.

My jaw ticked as I looked back to Scarlet. Everyone thought she was such a goodie-two-shoes, but I think I just busted that theory wide open.

"Sorry to interrupt," I snapped.

"You didn't. Bale just brought me lunch and was headed back out." She pointed to a turkey sandwich and chips sitting on the workbench behind her.

"Sure," I whispered under my breath.

"Was there something I could help you with?" Scarlet asked between bites.

I was pissed I had to ask for her help—seeing her with Bale was never an easy pill to swallow—but I had to, in order to get what I needed. I didn't have a choice. "Yes, actually, there is. Can you get me some Asafoetida?

Shock lit Scarlet's eyes. "Are you sure that's something you want to mess with?"

"I wouldn't be asking it if wasn't important." I shuffled uncomfortably, hoping she didn't think this was something I used on the regular. I couldn't tell her about the classroom issue. From

Mr. Doyle's earlier encouragement, I needed to take care of this as fast and as quietly as possible. So I'd just have to deal with whatever crappy judgments came with my request.

Scarlet moved behind the main counter and lifted a large leather-bound book from behind it. She flipped page after page, finally stopping to inspect a section in the middle of page three hundred and twenty-three. "I think my grandmother may have some at the main shop in town. I can have it here for you tomorrow night, if that's okay." Scarlet met my eyes with worry and hesitation.

"Yes, please. That'll be fine. And thanks again." I dropped my head and left the store. Feeling as though I'd just lived up to the Putnam name.

CHAPTER 10

*B*ack in my room, Tempest and Mystic were nowhere to be found. I'd usually worry, or look for a note, but knew they probably both read me earlier and sensed my need to be alone.

Gathering my tools, I began to grind the base to what would become the powder I'd use to stop this thing from penetrating the school. Once I got the Asafoetida, I'd be all set. The herb was often called Devil's Incense, and was used to hex someone to leave you alone. While traditionally it was used in black magic, I was planning on using it to combat some instead. Thanks to Mystic's help, I could see it clearer now. The black inky sludge and toxic green smoke definitely had a clear signature of darkness to it. I needed to keep my plan under wraps, though, so I didn't get labeled a black witch. Living down something like that here seemed like an impossible task, given my family track record. *No. I'll just keep my head down and get through this without anyone being the wiser.* I loved my life here. I'd been accepted, not only by Tempest and Vanna, but by others whom I'd slowly been getting to know, and losing any of that was absolutely my biggest fear.

I blew a sealing breath over my concoction and pushed the mortar to the side before picking up my pendulum. The energy from the rose quartz bead pulsed between my fingers. It was familiar and welcoming. Dangling the amethyst point over my crystal grid, I took in a grounding, deep breath and asked my question. "Will my plan to stop this entity work?"

The chain waivered in my hand, swinging slightly forward—the beginning of my yes. But I gasped and stared as the stone changed direction, suddenly swinging wildly to the left and right. The answer was no. *Shit!* What was I missing?

I decided to sleep on it, knowing my final ingredient wouldn't be here until tomorrow night anyway. Hopefully, the Goddess would give me more insight while I dreamt, and I'd wake with a new plan in mind. *Hopefully.*

I changed my clothes, sliding back into my favorite PJs, and crawled into bed. My gray, tarot-inspired comforter weighed me down, bringing with it a welcome sense of security. My lids fluttered as I drifted off to sleep, the dim light of our chandelier flickering like candlelight warming my face.

Clouds roiled, building to a dangerous degree over the entire town of Havenwood Falls. Lightning streaked across the night sky, illuminating the crowd of supes gathered in the park below.

"Stand your ground," Saundra Beaumont shouted. The others tensed, waiting for the threat to show itself or make a move. Spells flew into the ominous storm bank as the Court tried to fend off the obvious attack.

"Putnam, this is all your fault, so get your ass in here and start contributing instead of sitting on the sidelines," some asshole mage named Roman yelled out for all to hear.

All my fault? How could that be?

Raised voices continued to shout orders, and the last thing I remembered was the cloud turning a toxic green before I heard, *"Let me in."*

"No!" I screamed, sitting up.

Tempest rushed to my side. "Natalie, you're okay. It was just a dream. You're safe in bed."

Panting, my chest heaved as I struggled to catch my breath. I'd just been shown what would happen if I didn't get this infected classroom under control, and fast. The last time I'd checked my hourglass in the quad, the sands were falling normally, but for some reason, I had a feeling things were about to speed up. *Fuck me!*

"Are you okay?" Tempest copped a squat on the edge of my bed, calling for Mystic to join us. Our half-black, half-ginger kitty jumped up and immediately curled into my side.

"Yeah, I'm okay. It's just that this thing taking over the classrooms is turning out to be a bigger threat than I originally thought." I crinkled a finger under Mystic's chin, giving her a quick scratch. "I'm not really sure what to do," I admitted.

Tempest ran her hand down Mystic's side. "Nat. You're the most powerful witch I know. If you just open yourself up a little more, I'm sure you can figure this out."

She smiled and carried our kitty back to her own bed, crawling beneath the covers like that was all that needed to be said.

Maybe it was.

Maybe I needed to stop being so scared to open myself up to whatever this dark magic was.

Rolling over, I lay there with my eyes open, staring out the arched window and thought about all the times Mom had tried to ease my plight as a little girl. *"Walk with your head high, Natalie. Because despite what these naysayers think, you have nothing to be ashamed of. The Putnam name is a strong one, with deep roots, and inherent magic. They could only dream to be as powerful and lucky as you."*

Lucky? I thought to myself. I definitely hadn't considered myself lucky then, and was not sure that I could even now. Not with knowing what was coming was somehow all my fault.

"Ugh!" I threw off my blankets and grabbed my robe. "Hey, I'm going to go take a soak in the baths. I'll be back after a while."

Tempest waved me off, already snuggled back under her duvet with only her topknot showing from beneath the covers.

Entering our bathroom at night was a completely different experience than during the day. Though light was generally limited at all times under the mountain, at night the torches and candelabras hanging from the stone walls shimmered with an even more ethereal glow. Lit and tended to by the gnomes of the castle, they cast a soft pinkish-red tone, setting the perfect mood within our Hel Tower spa, as we liked to call it. I veered left, opposite of the showers this time, and followed the pathway down into the lower room. The pools here were reminiscent of Roman baths from days gone by and were a consistent one hundred and two degrees, since they were fed by the underground thermal pools. When I first checked out our tower, I searched for pipes that carried the hot water up to the dorm room floors but never found any. Like so many other things here on campus, it was just another mystery the gnomes solved behind the scenes.

Easing into the middle pool, I laid my head back into the carved-out cradle and closed my eyes. The warm water didn't bubble like a hot tub, but the minerals and aether flowing within instantly eased my sore muscles. I needed this.

I let my legs float up and down, bobbing in the ripples they made while again trying to focus on my latest vision. I knew what I needed to do now, but I wasn't sure I could actually bring myself to do it. I was scared, plain and simple.

Edging past the fear, I allowed the plume of smoke into my mind's eye. It swelled closer and closer as I recalled its feel and shape. Opening myself up to the vision, I allowed the entity to reach me. The last thing I remembered was it being full of black magic that pulled at my soul.

CHAPTER 11

"Natalie!" Tempest's scream pierced my ears. Cold air washed over me, and my body convulsed as she and Vanna lifted me out of the bath.

"What the hell happened here?" Vanna's warm hands were a welcome relief, sending steam rising from my frigid skin.

They wrapped me in a towel and led me to the nearest bench cut into the stone wall. I looked back to the now black water and shivered. It had frozen around the edges.

"I recall getting in and focusing on my most recent vision, but after that, everything went blank." I closed my eyes and took a deep breath. "I seriously don't know what happened."

Tempest pulled me close, rubbing her hands up and down my arms. "After you left, I fell back asleep for a bit, but when you weren't there when I woke up again, I knew something was wrong."

"You look like shit, and whatever is going on with that water can't be good, so let's get the hell out of here." Vanna never minced words and if she felt something was off too, I wasn't about to argue.

We left the bathroom and rushed to our room. Vanna helped Tempest get me into bed, then left us alone. The layers of blankets felt good, but didn't really help to elevate my chill. It was bone deep.

"Do you want to talk about it?" Tempest's voice remained soft, though I knew she wanted to press me for answers.

"I don't mind talking about it. I just don't have anything to say. I can't remember what happened."

Tempest sat crossed-legged on my bed and gathered Mystic to her chest. "That's not good, Nat. Is there anything I can do?"

"I'm not sure." I sighed and pulled the blankets up to my nose as tears started to well. Mystic jumped from her arms, and nudged her way under my chin. Her fur tickled, but it was the calming energy she was radiating that did the trick. A single tear escaped me, and I released a cleansing breath.

"You're such a good familiar, Mystic." I buried my face into her ginger side as I ran my hand down her opposite black one.

A phantom hand ran down the back of my head, stroking my hair.

I jerked, sending Mystic running. "Holy shit, what was that?"

Tempest jumped from my bed. "What? What's happening?"

"Something just touched my head!" I mimicked the motion.

Tempest grabbed the salt from our shared altar. "Something like what? A ghost?"

I concentrated to get a read on the room. "No. No, I don't think so. It was more like a phantom memory, I think. Not a real presence."

"Okay, good. That's good … but weird. Seriously, what the hell's going on here?"

I met my roommate's eyes and lied, unwilling to share my fears. "I truly don't know."

"Well, I'm gonna smudge the room anyway, if you don't mind."

I shook my head and snuggled back under the covers, feeling like an absolute jerk. "You know I don't mind. And thank you."

The earthy scent of sage filled the room as Tempest chanted her cleansing spell. I closed my eyes with the hope of drifting off to sleep soon. Maybe tomorrow would bring another perspective of how I was supposed to handle this. Now more than ever, I was especially eager for the Asafoetida to arrive. I had a bad feeling, and if I didn't combat this rising darkness and fast, things were going to get much, much worse.

By five p.m. the next day, I'd visited the toxic lab twice, noting the sludge had spread even farther down the hall, completely enveloping the lab next door. I was now standing outside Howe's Herbal Shoppe, waiting for Scarlet's return. The door to the shop was locked, and I wondered why she didn't have anyone else helping her here at the satellite location on campus. *I don't think Bale counts as help.* I chuckled to myself.

"Natalie?" Scarlet's voice called out from over my shoulder.

"Hi. Yes. Sorry, I've been waiting for you. Did you get it?"

She nodded, dropping her eyes to the door as she fumbled with her keys. "Come inside."

I followed her to the counter where she retrieved the illicit herb. "Thank you so much. How much do I owe you?"

"Actually, I spoke with my grandmother, and instead of receiving payment, we'd like to ask for your help."

"Sure. What can I do?" I offered, somewhat surprised by the request.

"We'd like you to work for us here—in the store on campus."

My mouth hung agape. Did she somehow just read my mind, or had I read hers? "Really? Work here at the Herbal Shoppe?"

"Yes. We think you'd be a great fit since you already know your stuff." She smiled. "Plus, like today, I had to shut down the store while I ran to town, and that's just bad business. You'd really be helping us out."

I looked around the quaint store and realized how much it reminded me of the backroom Mom kept stocked at home. Besides the impressive apothecary here, the crystals and candles were of the highest quality, and the books and hedge witch recipes they contained were truly spot-on for any practicing witch. I realized, despite our strange "frenemy" status, I really did feel comfortable here. And the more I thought about it, I was the only one who'd seemed reluctant to become friends with a Howe witch, not the other way around.

"I accept." I smiled wide. "When would you like me to start?"

"How about Friday of next week? Everyone will be back on campus soon enough, and after break we'll probably get hit hard with homework, so if that sounds good to you, just head down here after your last class on Friday."

"That's sounds great! I'll see you around four then." I picked up the paper bag Scarlet had deposited my herb in and smiled wide. "Thanks again, Scarlet. And please, pass my gratitude onto your grandmother as well."

The bell rang as I left the shop, and I couldn't believe it—I'd just gotten a job working for the Howe witches . . . who would have ever thought?

"Tempest," I called out, "you'll never guess what just happened?"

The room was silent. When my bestie didn't answer, I set my bag on the bed and looked for a note, but there was nothing here. I closed my eyes and grounded myself through the stone beneath my feet and reached out with my mind's eye. I saw Tempest sitting on Clifftop with some dude I couldn't quite make out; I had no doubt it was Eryx, though. *You go, girl!* I'd hoped things would smooth out between those two.

I turned back to the bed and grabbed the Asafoetida from the bag, dumping the contents directly into my pestle. Adding in lavender to boost its effectiveness, I ground the two together and left it at that. I needed this to be strong to do the job I wanted it to do.

Stuffing my duffle, I tossed in the ingredients, a few extra candles, and some salt to the items I'd already packed within. Then I scribbled a quick note to Tempest to let her know I'd be at the lab and left it on her bed. Hel Tower was quiet as I made my way down the spiral staircase and across the great room. A few students had returned early from break and were milling about the campus here and there, but thankfully, there weren't a lot just yet. I needed to get this done and over with before the crowd returned. Especially since I was sure someone would be looking for poor Fin and Joe soon, if they weren't already. I couldn't imagine having to lie to Taylor or explain I was somehow responsible for her friends being knocked out and swallowed up by some dark toxic cloud trying to penetrate our school. Yeah . . . that would not go over well.

Rushing into Eirhal, I slowed my roll when I saw Brielle and Elliana—two chicks from Modi Tower—coming down the hall. I didn't know them well enough to stop and chat, but had seen Elliana more often since she was in my Ethics class.

"Hello," I offered as I passed them by, but neither responded. They both seemed too preoccupied with their whisper-shouting to pay any attention to me. I thought I heard the word "darkness" on the tail end of their conversation, and picked up my pace again.

At the end of the corridor, I turned left and came to an immediate stop. *Shit!* The bubble of magic from the glamour's edge smacked me straight in the face. I muttered the spell to dissolve it and gasped. The entire corridor was now engulfed in the green cloud and layered in black sludge. I could no longer see the entrance to the lab where the bodies still lay inside.

This was it. I could feel it—I had to get this under control or things were going to end very badly.

I uncrossed my duffle from my body, lifting if off my shoulder. The plume of 'ick' swelled, as if it knew what I was about to do. Magic started to build, tickling my skin as I slowly set out my candles in the form of a pentagram. With a snap of my fingers, they flared to life.

"Guardians of the watchtowers of the south, grant me your flame, so that I may stay safe while your power remains."

A tendril of black sludge surged forward, stopping a few feet ahead of me.

Next, I pulled out my portable cauldron, added a small amount of water to it from my thermos, and tossed in a pinch of salt.

"Guardians of the watchtowers of the west and north, grant me your protection as earth joins water in a sacred union."

Black smoke roiled through the green cloud, making it even more ominous—if that was possible.

Finally, I pulled out my trusty sage and lit the end, blowing on the embers until they burned bright red.

"Guardians of the watchtowers of the east, grant me your cleansing breath, and allow my magic to penetrate and repel this evil threat."

I sucked in a deep breath then blew the smudging smoke directly toward the cloud as I tossed a handful of the Asafoetida herbal mix into it at the same time.

I slammed my hands over my ears as an earthshattering scream reverberated off the walls. Flecks of fire sparked and spread throughout the plume, eating away at the growing threat. In a rush, the toxic green cloud and vein-like sludge retreated back down the hall, revealing smooth tile and clean walls. *Thank the Goddess!*

I followed it down the corridor until I reached the infected room at the end. *Oh, no!*

The number of bodies inside had doubled, and now . . . they were completely engulfed in sludge.

I crept forward, one tiny step at a time so as not to risk falling prey to its reach as well. I didn't bother scanning the faces of the newly fallen. It was traumatic enough seeing more bodies sprawled out and their chests barely rising—I knew I wouldn't be able to stay focused if I actually identified one of my friends lying there. Tempest's face flashed into my mind's eye.

"No!" I screamed out loud, shaking my head—I couldn't let myself go there.

Listening closely, I heard a rumble from within the room. My heart leapt into my throat. Perhaps I'd done it, and everyone was starting to come around.

Think again, Putnam.

The rumble continued to build, shaking the entire room as another cloud burst from the vents, filling the space with its roiling green fog that barreled straight for me.

With no time to utter a single protective word, I threw up my arms and braced for impact.

It never came.

I nervously cracked open one lid, then the other. The smoke had stopped inches from my face, swirling and twisting into itself as if it was trying to peer directly into my soul.

Panic gripped me as the voice sounded inside my head. *"You're mine. Let me in."*

"Like hell I am!"

Magic swelled deep within me. Magic like I'd never felt before. Faces flashed into my mind: Tempest's, Vanna's, Fin's, Joe's, Bale's, and even Scarlet's . . . faces of all the friends I was fighting to protect. Unfamiliar words flew out of my mouth, spinning and twisting of their own accord, battling against the invading cloud as if my magic was streaming from an external source. The toxic plume retreated, disappearing back into the vents, but unfortunately, the black sludge remained. Oozing from the mouths of the fallen victims, it bubbled and burped, causing the bodies to convulse—all but one.

The chest of the fallen Regent was motionless.

I lowered my shields and begrudgingly called out to Gabriel Doyle. I had no idea how I was supposed to explain that one of his colleagues had just died because I hadn't been fast enough or strong enough to fix this, but I had to let him know.

"You rang?" His clipped tone fell silent as he peered inside the lab. "Natalie, what did you do?"

My head snapped up to meet his gaze. "What do you mean? I stopped the toxic mess from spreading. The cloud has disappeared."

He looked back and forth between me and the bodies. "Then explain why one of our assistants is lying dead inside the lab, and your eyes are now completely black?"

"What are you talking about?" I rubbed my eyes, terrified I'd somehow gotten the black sludge in them or on my face. Mr. Doyle's intense stare made me want to squirm, but I stood tall with my mental blocks in place. I explained all I'd done, and how, again, I had nothing to do with what was happening to the lab, especially not to the dead man inside. Finally convinced, he let me go.

I raced straight back to Hel and up to my room. Fumbling past the end of my bed, I walked up to the crescent moon mirror hanging on the wall and peered inside. My eyes were brown and looked exactly like they always had. *What the hell?* Why was he messing with me? I wondered again if my previous theory about him being behind all this was really true. I had no way to prove it, but even if I did, he was a genie-boosted vampire skulking about in a position of authority. Who would believe me? Nobody, that's who.

The door to our room flew open, and Tempest strolled in, smiling wide. I glanced to her bed at the note I'd left earlier and realized I wasn't in the mood to talk about where I'd gone or what had happened. I snapped my fingers, disintegrating the paper into thin air before she had a chance to see it.

"Hey, you're back. Where've you been?" I didn't want to admit to spying on her either—I scratched my arm, probably a new itch from all the secrets I was starting to keep.

"Just hanging out up on Clifftop."

"With . . ." I prodded teasingly.

Tempest laughed. "With Eryx."

"How'd that go?" I grinned and climbed into my hanging chair.

"Good. Things aren't as awkward as they used to be."

"That's good. I'm happy for you, Temp." I pulled my knees up to my chest and closed my eyes, letting the sway of the chair relax me.

"Hey, are you okay?"

I let the chair rock back and forth a couple more times before I answered.

"Yeah. I guess. I'm struggling to figure out what's affecting the lab, and what it has to do with me." I opened my eyes, revealing the tears shining within—so much for not wanting to talk about it. "It's getting bad, and I don't know what to do next."

"Nat, what happened?" Tempest ran forward, pulling me from the chair and into a hug.

"Someone important has died, and they think it's all my fault."

"Oh my Goddess, who died? And who is *they*?" She stepped back, a severe scowl on her face like she was ready to kick whoever's ass was necessary.

"An assistant to the Board of Regents, and Mr. Doyle saw the body. He accused me of being responsible, and even though I told him I wasn't and he let me go, I'm not sure he truly believed me." I sucked in a sniffly breath and collapsed onto my bed. "I'm sure he's already informed the Board of what happened, and with the sands in the hourglass almost gone, I'm probably gonna get kicked out of the Academy." I buried my face in the pillow and let go. Full on sobs racked my body as all the pent-up stress and anger flowed out of me. How the hell was I supposed to solve this? I had no real idea what that thing was, or why it wanted into our school so badly.

I felt Tempest climb into bed next to me, her hand gently rubbing my back. "Nat, what can I do?"

I turned to face her, my make-up probably a hot mess, but I didn't care. "I don't know. I tried the most potent concoction I could think of, and it did a good job . . . at first, but if I don't figure something else out, I'm afraid it will start to spread again."

"Do you think Mystic could help this time? You said her vision helped you see more clearly before."

I shook my head. "I don't think so. It's getting stronger, and now with one person dead, I won't risk it. I can't let anyone else get hurt." I buried my face again. "Fin and Joe are in there," I mumbled into the pillow, "and I don't know how to save them."

Tempest fell silent and let me cry it out. I wasn't usually an emotional person, but the idea of leaving the Sun & Moon Academy was more than I could bear.

I forced my swollen eyes to open—my make-up a caked, hardened mess—and found Tempest staring at me from across the room.

"Hey, you fell asleep, and I didn't want to wake you."

"What time is it?" I sat up.

"Six . . . in the morning."

My mouth dropped open. "Monday morning? As in, students are back and classes are starting?"

"I'm afraid so."

I jumped out of bed and grabbed my bag, stuffing more candles, handfuls of herbs and crystals, and my very own book of shadows into it. "Our first class is supposed to start in two hours, and it's in the toxic lab, Temp! Why didn't you wake me?"

Tempest lowered her head, and her shoulders slumped forward. "A vision told me not to."

I froze, shocked by her words, then spun to face her. "What? A vision from who?"

"Mystic."

I jerked back, then quickly scanned the room for our shared familiar and found her hiding under Tempest's bed.

"Mystic . . . baby, why would you do that?" I bent down and scratched the black fluffy rug in an attempt to call her to me, but it didn't work. She remained where she was, forcing me to my hands and knees. She meowed and purred as I scratched behind her ears, tipping her sweet head into my hand, but when I went to pick her up, she squirmed out of my grasp and scooted completely out of reach.

"Dammit, I don't have time for this." I stood up and snagged my bag from my bed. "Temp, if you get any more visions, *please* let me know immediately. I'm down to the wire on this, and it's not looking good."

Tempest nodded, solemnly, and I wondered what else Mystic had shown her that she was keeping from me.

Once again, I flew down the spiral staircase and out the front door of Hel. Racing over the bridge and into the quad, I scanned the entrance to Halstein Hall. It was the first place to stir in the morning, offering glorious caffeinated concoctions and yummy baked goods, as well as last minute trips to the library. Luckily, there were only a few students milling around the stairs so far.

Running as fast as I could, I made my way through the double doors of Eirhal, and booked it to the end of the corridor where I found Dr. Underwood staring blankly down at the labs.

"Natalie. Good morning. Seems we have a bit of a problem here."

My shoulders sank. "Yes, sir. I'm aware, and as you may have noticed the hourglass hovering in the quad, it's my responsibility to figure it out. I'm sorry I didn't get it taken care of before break was over."

Dr. Underwood simply nodded and laid a hand on my shoulder. "I'll cancel class immediately. Good luck, Natalie. I have complete faith in you. And remember, not all things can be healed with magic." He turned away, and I immediately received his messages—the one regarding our classes sounding in my head: "*Attention all students. This morning's Field Medicine class, as well as all others taking place in the labs today, have been cancelled. You'll receive another update tomorrow. Enjoy your day."* —and the other subtle one he'd just provided as a reminder of our previous lesson. *"Not all things can be healed with magic."*

I stepped forward, reaching out again for the energy of the glamour and was pleased it was still only surrounding the one room where all this had started. I whispered the revealing spell and took a deep breath, thinking back to the lesson Dr. Underwood had hinted at.

"Some things are beyond the reach of healing magic . . . not much, but some." Dr. Underwood winked. "In most of those circumstances, you'll find there's a connection between the victim and the healer. Whether it's a lover that's fallen who can't be resurrected by his loved one, or a sibling that can't be saved by their brother or sister." He shook his head. "You'd think it would be the opposite, that a family connection would heighten the strength of your healing, but instead, it affects the one thing that limits us mentally—our hearts. In those circumstances, we're just too close to think straight, whether it's the pain of losing a person you love, or the opposite . . . the scars we carry from a toxic or tainted relationship; our hearts block the magic, which can be difficult to overcome. It's in these circumstances that we have to look inside ourselves and truly allow the connections to come to the surface, whether they're good or bad. It's the only way you'll stand a chance of healing the victim—and yourself."

I took a deep breath and let his words sink in. *Family connection . . . loved one . . . toxic relationship.*

My eyes snapped open. *Mother!*

CHAPTER 14

Herbs flew into the air as I rustled through my bag. Curling my fingers around my Book of Shadows, I hauled it out and spread it open on the tile floor before me. I took a deep breath and lit my smudge stick, chanting the same spell I'd frequently used at home to combat Mom's negative vibes.

"In the name of the Goddess I cleanse this space. Remove all negative energy that lingers here, so that only good may enter."

I thought back to the warning my recruiter gave me, even before I accepted her invitation to the Sun & Moon Academy: *"Your mother cannot be trusted . . ."*

I hadn't reached out to my mom even once after arriving here, knowing her memories had been altered. The recruiter's spell should have left her believing I was away at college and with the feeling all was well, despite not having the actual details. Obviously, my decision to distance myself from her had been my first mistake.

"Okay, Mom, if this is really you, show yourself so we can have this out." I closed my eyes and allowed myself to open up to our shared Putnam magic. Smoke billowed from the vents, mixing with the toxic green tint that I now openly reached for.

"Finally, you let me in," Mom's voice sounded in my head, clear as day.

"Why are you doing this? These people are my friends."

"Why have you been hiding from me? You've cut yourself off from our magic, and I needed you to see that denying who you are will only make you weak."

"Are you kidding me right now? You killing people is your way of teaching me to be strong? You're crazy! And now I know it's true—you can't be trusted. You've tried to hide it all these years, but you've never changed. You're still part of the evil Putnam legacy that I want nothing to do with!"

"Well, too bad, kiddo, because it's Putnam blood that runs through your veins, and if you can't find a way to accept that, I'm definitely going to find you and blow through wherever you're hiding."

I gasped, picturing the dream I'd had of the malicious cloud surging over Havenwood Falls, ready to devour it all.

"I will find you," Mother continued. *"You're mine."*

"Enough!" I closed my eyes, again hearing Dr. Underwood's words ringing in my ears. *"Not all things can be healed with magic."*

I was scared to death, but forced myself to peer into the depths of my soul; into the depths of where my family connection resided.

"Goddess, please, hear my plea. Disconnect my mother from me. Through our magic, she seeks to harm; give me the strength to combat her charm."

Dark energy surged deep within me, filling every pore of my body. The wave brought with it image after image of Putnam witches and their chosen path. Split like a wishbone, each leg—good or evil—sprouted from a center source, and I immediately knew what I had to do.

Within my vision, I took hold of the evil leg—the one my mother's magic clung to—and pulled as hard as I could. Snapping it cleanly from the main bone, I held it in my hand and listened as my mother screamed.

Punch after punch of dark magic flowed into me, churning my insides as I held onto the severed bone. I fought to gain control of my fear, praying the Goddess wouldn't let me go bad. I allowed the magic to settle within me but kept my eyes closed, terrified of what I'd see when I opened them.

I'd just been given the power to forge a new future for the Putnam witches that would come after me; a clean slate for those who shared my name. No longer would we be condemned and misjudged based on a lost legacy. I alone, however, now held the source of our magic—good and bad melded together within me to draw upon as needed.

Grunts and moans sounded in front of me, and I finally opened my eyes. Everyone who'd fallen prey to my mother's spell had awoken and begun to stir. All but one. I took a deep breath and called out to Mr. Doyle again, this time not fearing his reprimand or reprisal.

"I see you did it. Well done. I'll take care of the assistant's body." Again, his cool tone left me curious if he had anything to do with the overall threats to the school. But now, as I let the full power of my family's magic flow through my veins, I simply didn't care. There was nothing he could throw at me that I couldn't handle.

I watched as he strode inside the lab, gathered the man's body, and quickly disappeared. The other students woke on wobbly legs, most of them shaking their heads as they walked out of the classroom as if they'd just slept off a serious bender after another epic party atop of Hel Tower. Well, all but Fin.

Terror shone in her eyes as she looked around the room for Joe. I took a step forward to comfort her, but before I could offer an explanation, they blew past me, Fin crying into her hands.

Shit. That didn't look good.

Turning back to the lab, I stepped inside. All of my mother's magic had completely receded. I could no longer feel her in the classroom—or in my heart.

It was over.

I made the trek back across the quad at a much slower pace. I looked up at the sky and smiled, taking in the fact that my hourglass had disappeared, and thankfully—for at least one damn second—another hadn't taken its place. Students were scurrying to their first classes of the day since returning from break, as I made my way to inform Dr. Underwood his classes in the Eirhal labs could resume whenever he wanted. That is until Mr. Doyle appeared directly in front of me.

"Ms. Putnam, would you please accompany me to the Administrative Offices? We'd like you to explain exactly what happened, and how you were able to overcome it?"

"Do I have to?" I almost covered my mouth as the words spilled from my lips. Especially when his cold, blue eyes pierced mine and the muscles in his jaw flexed. I don't think he was used to be questioned like that.

"Yes. You have to. Now, please come with me," he insisted.

I followed the leader of the Lilith Nest through the double doors of Halstein Hall and up to the Administrative Offices. I had no idea how I was going to explain that what happened was, after all, completely my fault. That my family's dark magic had threatened the entire school and killed one of their own. I bit my bottom lip as he led me through the main office and into a conference room where five other Board of Regents members sat around a long, oak table. The walls were dark, covered in leather I think, which gave the room an ominous, nerve-racking feel.

"Have a seat," Mr. Doyle instructed, shutting the door behind me.

"Ms. Putnam, can you please tell us what you learned about the threat on the Healing Arts lab, and how you overcame it?" Elsmed, the oldest Regent, asked.

My chest tightened, and the vein in my neck throbbed as my pulse quickened. I wondered if they questioned everyone who had something to do with the hourglasses like this. It didn't matter. I swallowed hard. Telling them my evil mother was responsible and that I was now full of dark magic surely wouldn't benefit me in any way. So I cast the same spell I'd used to block out Mr. Doyle before . . . and lied.

"After meditating and seeking a vision of what infected the classroom, I simply used my knowledge of herbs and spells to combat the threat. It took a few days to accumulate and prepare everything, but in the end, I was able to overcome it with my magic and a special concoction I made."

They looked back and forth between each other, and I quickly regretted my decision. I squirmed in my chair, waiting for them to kick me out on the spot. Saundra Beaumont, my Ethics teacher—and the only other Regent I actually recognized—spoke up.

"Natalie, we know in coming here, you made the choice to leave your family behind. Literally and figuratively. However, as you soon may learn, denying that part of yourself may have an unforeseen side effect." She smoothed her jacket and shifted in her chair. "My suggestion would be to find a way to come to terms with your family's past, and figure out how it's going to shape you into the person you were meant to be. Until you can do that, your future here at the Academy will remain . . . tenuous. You are excused from my class today, but I expect to see you back and refreshed by Wednesday." Saundra smiled kindly.

I sat dumbfounded for a split second, until I was excused from the room. I stumbled out of the office and back down to the Student Union, more confused than ever. They shouldn't have been able to read my mind, and if they truly didn't have a hand in all that had happened lately, how in the world could they know what was going on with me? *Ouch!* I looked down at my wrist, and my heart sank. My school tattoo sizzled on my wrist. It was still there—in the shape of an hourglass, even though the large one in the quad had disappeared.

Apparently, I hadn't learned my lesson quite yet.

With my schedule now open for most of the day, I climbed the stairs to my dorm and fell face-first back into bed. My next class wasn't until three p.m.—Basic Combat and Defense with Professor Shimizu up on Clifftop. I wasn't prepared for it, physically or mentally. I needed sleep before I could concentrate on fighting, or on the ethical dilemma I was now facing.

I shouldn't have lied to the Board, but when it came to my family's past and the person I wanted to be in the future, I made my choice. What else did I need to learn about their wrongdoings? I wasn't them. I was my own person and had always walked the path of a white witch growing up, even when everyone around me treated me like crap. I never fell prey to the darkness carried by so many of my ancestors. I contemplated what in the hell I was supposed to do next as my wrist continued to burn, but I was too drained to figure it out right now.

Tossing and turning, I fought my way through a fitful sleep, only to wake to Mystic licking my nose just two hours later.

"What is it, baby?" I sat up, pushing her into my lap and ran a hand down my face.

"Natalie?"

Goosebumps broke out over my skin as a cool breeze blew over me. I turned my head and found my mom sitting on the edge of Tempest's bed.

I jumped and scooted away, pulling Mystic and the blankets with me. "How did you get in here?"

"I'll always be a part of you, Natalie." Her sad eyes were encased in dark circles, and her hair was thinner than I remembered.

"I know that, Mom. But I had to do it. I couldn't let you hurt anyone else at my school. This place and the people here are important to me."

"And I'm not?" she questioned with less emotion than I expected.

"Of course you are. But I'm not like you, Mom. I never was."

I sat Mystic to the side, despite her yowls, and pushed out from under the covers. I crossed to Tempest's bed, ready to offer Mom whatever small measure of comfort I could give her. Sitting beside her, I reached up to place my arm around her shoulders.

"Holy shit!" My arm drifted straight through her ghostly form.

I sat up in bed, terrified from the dream I'd just had. Mystic was there, protectively curled around my feet at the end of my bed, but thankfully my mother's ghost was not.

This was bad. I had to go home and check on her—now.

Throwing on a flannel over my jeans and sweatshirt, I laced up my boots and raced to the Administrative Offices again. Approaching the woman behind the desk in the reception area, I asked to speak to Professor Beaumont immediately.

"Which one?" the woman asked.

"Excuse me?"

"Which Professor Beaumont? We currently have two teaching here, you know." Her tone was full of snark.

"Natalie, dear, what is it?" Saundra Beaumont appeared from around the corner and ushered me back into the same conference room we sat in before, the receptionist's question ignored and forgotten.

"I need to be excused to go home and check on my mom. Please. I think it's a matter of life and death."

Professor Beaumont maintained a serious scowl as she contemplated my request. I wasn't sure if she was silently communicating with the rest of the Board, or just sizing me up as I stood there. Finally, she nodded and said, "Okay. You've been granted a leave of absence for the rest of the week. But Natalie, if you do not report back to me by three p.m. on Friday, your admittance to the Academy will be immediately revoked."

"I understand. Thank you." I gave her a clipped nod and ran straight out of Halstein Hall.

Back in my room, I threw some clothes into a bag, wrote a note to Tempest, kissed Mystic on her perfect little head, then raced out the door. By the time I made it across the quad, over the bridge, and to the portal vestibule, I realized I had no idea how I was actually going to get from Havenwood Falls all the way back to Salem, Massachusetts.

"Oh well, nothing like flying by the seat of your pants." I glanced down at my school tattoo, which was still in the shape of an hourglass, and hoped for the best. Stepping through the center arch, I tumbled out the other side and straight into a large, solid . . . *warm* wall.

"Micah?" I looked up from his massive chest to meet the angel's perfect eyes.

"Hello, Natalie. I've been informed you require transportation."

"Oh thank the Goddess. Yes. Well, thank . . . you!" I grinned, shrugging awkwardly. "I need to return to my home in Salem, Massachusetts."

"I know the place." He smiled and opened his arms.

Moments later, I stood in front of my ancestral home. I took a deep breath and swallowed past the fear creeping up my throat. I was scared to death of what I might find inside.

"Would you like me to go with you?" Micah offered.

"No. I need to do this alone." I took a step forward and stopped. "Then again, do you have one of those nifty angel stones I could use to call you for help if I need it?"

Micah's smile could light up the darkest day. He chuckled and handed me a piece of pure, heavenly crystal. It was smaller than the one Tempest carried, and I'm pretty sure I'd have to give mine back when this was all over, but still . . . I was so very grateful. "Thank you so much. And can you please let Tempest know where I am, and that I'll be back on Friday? I had to leave before I could speak with her."

"I will. Call if you need me." He winked then disappeared.

Turning back to the house, I was flooded with a wave of emotion. I never thought I'd have the chance to leave here, let alone find a place where I truly fit in, but that's what the Academy was—the place I truly belonged. I sucked in another breath and walked up the steps. The door was unlocked, as it usually was, but the moment I stepped inside, everything changed.

The polished wooden floors were now cracked and gray with age, the drywall had crumbled away in chunks from most of the walls, and even the furniture had taken on a long-forgotten quality even though I'd only been gone for a few months. I had a feeling, though, this had more to do with my recent spell than my absence from home.

"Mom?" I called out, creeping from room to room. The deafening silence that settled over the house terrified me, and I prayed I hadn't killed my own mother when I broke off her vein of magic.

"Natalie?" A whisper sounded from the storage room off the kitchen.

"Mom!" I raced past the island and the sink filled with dishes to find her slouched in the old rocking chair, staring out the small window that overlooked our garden. Her eyes were dull as they shifted back and forth over the brown, dead stems that littered the ground. I bent down and took her hand. "Mom, I'm so sorry." Tears flowed down my cheeks when she smiled, her skin pulling tight over her rapidly-aged face. "Can you tell me why this happened? I only meant to stop your spell—to block you from the school and the dark magic you were using."

She struggled to speak, but with a touch of her hand, I learned everything I needed to know. She'd been using the family's dark magic to extend her life and restore her youth more and more in recent years. Apparently, that's what 'book club' was all about. After she and her friends got a taste for it, the more they abused the magic: lotteries had been won, lovers had been found, and darkness had its opening to creep in. She never meant to let it go this far. She had worked hard in her youth to walk the path of a white witch, but Putnam roots ran deep, and denying the power of the twisted magic that was a part of our family gene pool could prove difficult for us all.

I shivered, knowing I'd have to fight even harder than most to keep all the magic I now possessed contained. I laid my head in my dying mother's lap. *Goddess, what have I done?*

"Mom, I love you much, despite our differences. Is there any way you can forgive me?"

With another light touch of her hand, her words drifted through my mind. *"My darling daughter, I forgive you . . . and I'm so proud of you."*

I continued to hold my mother, crying throughout the early evening hours and stayed with her until she passed. After arranging her body on a pyre in the garden, I snapped my fingers, setting her body and soul alight. "Be free, Mom. May your soul forever soar with the Goddess."

CHAPTER 17

Dust particles sparkled in the early morning sun as I finished cleaning every nook and cranny of my childhood home. *My home.* It was a strange feeling to know this house now belonged solely to me. The paperwork regarding Mother's death, the deed, and any other 'official' documents had all happened magically earlier in the week—as it had for all of our family throughout the years. I'd repaired all the damage the day after mother's passing, and spent the past few days organizing, meditating, and doing a little self-healing before having to head back to school. But now, it was time.

I tucked the leather brief containing the papers into my school bag, and finished wiping down the butcher's block countertop and worn wooden table in the kitchen. Moving into the storeroom, I smiled and placed Mom's favorite blanket on the back of the rocker, and shut the cabinet doors on the small apothecary cabinet.

"Protected now, and forever be, encase this home in your energy. Sealed from those that would do it harm, I can leave for now, confident in this charm."

A bubble of protection formed around my home, and I

thanked the Goddess as I walked outside and locked the back door.

The four days I'd spent here alone—cleaning, grieving, and discovering more about my family magic—had been the best and worst days of my life. I missed my mother and regretted the actions I'd been forced to take in order to save my school, but for the first time ever, I was no longer afraid of who I was or the magic contained within me. Yes, the Putnam name and the magic I carried had a dark side to it, but that didn't mean I couldn't be a good person and use it to my advantage. I'd scoured through Mom's old grimoires and found others who'd learned to do the same. Light and dark in perfect balance. That was going to be me.

Pulling the angelic stone from my pocket, I called out to Micah.

"All set?" His deep voice sounded from behind me.

I turned around and squared my shoulders. "All set."

One hug and a blink later, I was back in the Falls Campus chamber room. "Thank you, Micah. I truly appreciate the help." I held out the stone in my hand, offering its return.

The angel smiled down at me. "Keep it. If Tempest ever needs me and is unable to call, I trust you'll only use it to keep her safe."

"Of course." I re-pocketed the stone, waved goodbye, and stepped through the portal.

The vestibule was empty, but the hum of commotion from the main campus up ahead reverberated all around me. School was back in full swing and oddly enough, I couldn't wait to return to my classes. But first, I needed to report to Professor Beaumont.

I walked over the bridge and started across campus, waving to Elliana and Brielle who were huddled together on one of the stone benches, still whispering intently to one another. Looking up, I noticed no other hourglass had taken the place of my own—thank the Goddess. As I climbed the stairs to Halstein Hall, I caught sight of a raven perched in one of the alcoves high up the stone tower. Its eyes followed me all the way up to the double doors, at which point, I quickly yanked the handle and stepped inside.

The open area was packed with students, some of whom I recognized and others I didn't. I made a mental note to do a better job reaching out to more of them once things were back to normal.

The Administrative Offices were relatively quiet. The receptionist nodded in my direction and without a word, pushed a button and called for Professor *Saundra* Beaumont.

"Natalie. I'm glad you made it back. Please come with me." She led me back into the same conference room where we'd previously met.

I took a seat, in a different chair than before, and let her begin the questioning I knew would follow.

"Were you able to settle your family issue?"

"Yes, ma'am."

"And is there anything you'd like to share with me?"

I smiled and sighed, knowing there was no way to avoid this. My psychic powers had blossomed at home, so I returned here knowing exactly what I'd done wrong. My spell to block Mr. Doyle's ability had no effect on a few other species that made up the Board here the day I was questioned. Especially not a true witch like Saundra Beaumont, or the mind-reading fae, Elsmed.

"As I assume you know, the threat on the school I was tasked to combat came from within my own family. Unfortunately, the legacy of the Putnams has always been tainted by dark magic, and it was that soul-deep source I had to pull from in order to save our school." I shook my head. "I'm sorry I lied to you and the other Regents, but I didn't think admitting to my use of dark magic would earn me any points here at the Academy."

Professor Beaumont remained still, not saying a word. I shifted in my chair, crossing my ankles and folding my hands in my lap and continued.

"Upon visiting my home, I found my mother on the verge of death, sent to its edge by my actions here." I picked at my nails and swallowed past the lump in my throat. "It was difficult to let her go, but I came to understand the magic that now resides within me is a gift, one I plan to use for good, despite what anyone thinks." I lifted my chin, meeting her solemn stare. "I hope you can forgive me for misleading you, or for not solving this task exactly how the Board hoped I would. But I will no longer fear or be ashamed of being a Putnam. I am in control, light and dark balanced. It's simply who I am." I shrugged.

Professor Beaumont's smile sparked a nervous energy inside me. I wasn't sure if my Independence Day-style speech was what she was expecting, but the words flowed from a place deep within me. I felt lighter after saying them—stronger than I ever had before.

She shifted slightly. "You know, many years ago, I made a terrible mistake in trying to suppress what I believed to be an uncontrollable darkness in my granddaughter, Adelaide. I'm sure you know her?"

I nodded. Everyone knew Addie Beaumont.

"I feared the Beaumont name would be forever tainted by what ran through her blood. But the consequences of trying to eliminate it became near catastrophic. I should have known better. We can't deny our true natures. That only makes things worse. I believe you. Like Addie, you will be able to maintain a balance, allowing you to draw on *all* that you are, making you more powerful than you could otherwise be." She smiled warmly. "Take a look at your wrist, Natalie." She nodded to my left arm resting in my lap.

I pulled back my flannel sleeve and gasped.

"Is it back to normal?"

"It is!"

"I thought it might be. Despite your earlier . . . theory," she winked, "none of the Regents know what's going on with all of the extra trials being put before some of you. And after attempted interference from a couple of Regents, we've learned we can't stop them without serious repercussions. I, myself, was portalled into the middle of the forest on the far side of Mount Mae, stripped of my magic, cell phone, everything. It took two days to hike my way out and another day for my magic to return. Fortunately, nothing serious happened in town during that time, but what if it had?"

I clapped my hand over my mouth, trying to imagine the polished professional woman, her silver hair always perfectly coifed in a twist on the back of her head and never seen wearing anything but a business suit, stumbling into town after two days in the woods.

"One thing I've noticed, though," she continued, "is these challenges each contain a valuable lesson, and I suspect you've learned the exact one you needed to. No assumptions, no judgments, only peace. Balance of power can come from facing your demons, and that seems to be exactly what you've done. Be proud of who you are, Natalie. Embrace the magic you've inherited, and your family's legacy will never be forgotten."

I didn't care if it was appropriate or not—I stood and hugged my professor with tears in my eyes. "Thank you. I'll see you in class on Monday."

I secured my bag and ran downstairs, checking my phone for the time.

Texting out a quick message to Tempest, I let her know I was back and headed to Howe's Herbal Shoppe, since today was the day I was also supposed to start working there part-time. I pushed the send button then opened the door, the shop's bell announcing my arrival.

Scarlet popped up from behind the counter and smiled. "Hey, Natalie! I'm glad you made it. I hadn't seen you around campus for a few days, so I wasn't sure if you'd show or not."

"I'm here!" I smiled, not ready to offer any further explanation. "What can I help you with first?"

"If you'd like to sort the new crystals that came in, that'd be great."

I made my way behind the counter, depositing my things in the cubby Scarlet had indicated, then sank my hands into the large box filled with tons of small hemp bags containing the shop's latest order.

Amethyst, citrine, black tourmaline, and jet—the energy from each stone flowed into my receiving hand.

"Just check off each bag on the inventory sheet as you sort

them. Then, once they're all checked in, you can cleanse them and place them in their designated bins over there." Scarlet pointed to the organized crystal section of the shop.

"Will do." I smiled, extremely excited I'd decided to take this on. I didn't necessarily need the money—I came with my own—but the energy here and the balance it provided me was worth more than any paycheck. I continued to riffle through the box, checking in the inventory bag after bag, when the bell rang and shifted my attention. Bale Grayson walked in, and for the first time, I didn't feel a pit form in my stomach. I knew I'd run into him here, and while I still thought he looked like sex-on-a-stick, I now understood he wasn't for me.

Scarlet smiled and dipped her head as he handed her the dinner he'd brought. She looked up, meeting my eyes from under her lashes and grinned. I suddenly understood their relationship was slow-burning and something they didn't openly display, and for some reason, that made me feel better. Instead of angsty teenagers, they seemed more like an old married couple, or even something more—soul mates.

I turned back to the crystals buzzing between my fingers and let the two have their privacy. The feel of the smooth obsidian wand I pulled from the box next reminded me of my own crystal tower up in my room. I smiled and closed my eyes, letting its protective energy settle my soul. This was it—the perfect reminder—I was truly where I belonged.

My eyes snapped open as the store began to shake. Scarlet, Bale, and I looked back and forth between one another as a loud gong reverberated through the entire campus. The two of them immediately looked to their wrists, both sighing in relief. We left the shop together and made our way out into the quad, joining the rest of the student body gathered and looking just as confused as the three of us.

The gong had barely stopped ringing, but for some unknown reason, no hourglass appeared. Whispers floated through the crowd . . .

"What does it mean?"

"This is bad."

"Oh no, not again."

I scanned the faces surrounding me, looking for anyone who showed signs of distress.

To my right, a few clusters of kids over, Infiniti Clausman raised her head with tears shining in her eyes.

Oh no, not Fin! Hadn't she been through enough?

CHASING TIME

ROSE GARCIA

CHAPTER 1

$\mathcal{I}$nfiniti shifted in her seat in the back of her Intro to Inter-Dimensional Travel and Exploration class, trying not to think about the unfinished hourglass tattoo on the inside of her left wrist. It had appeared in place of her school tattoo after Natalie Putnam solved the mystery of the classrooms a week ago. Or, to be exact, it had halfway appeared.

It'd been two weeks since she'd gone looking for Dr. Underwood and ended up in the Healing Arts lab, surrounded by bodies and a strange fog. Terror set in, and she had tried to run but couldn't move, engulfed by the cloud and a thick black sludge traveling up her legs. She didn't remember anything after that until she woke up to Natalie clearing the room of the curse. Infiniti spent the rest of that week in a cloud of her own, dazed and confused, but was slowly recovering . . . until the all-too-familiar and terrorizing gong shook the campus a few days later and her tattoo with the regular image of the school crest overlaid with her Jory Tower emblem had started giving way to the hourglass, but then stopped. Even stranger, an hourglass from the artifacts room had never appeared in the courtyard. It was as if there was a glitch in the system, and Infiniti had no idea what that meant. In fact, nobody did. All she knew was that she was scared as hell at whatever dangers might be coming her way. So the longer she could avoid being officially tagged, the better. Maybe whatever supernatural forces were behind all the chaos didn't really want to pick her. Maybe it was waiting for someone else to choose.

If only.

Pulled back to the reality of Dr. Fraser's class, she inched up the sleeve of her black sweater to sneak a peek at the tattoo. The image was still the same. She pressed her fingertips against her skin, tapping the messed up design. So far seven guardians had been challenged, and seven had been triumphant. Now it was her turn. Or at least, it was going to be her turn at some point when and if the dumb thing finished. If she was really chosen, she couldn't help but think she'd ruin the streak. She was new to the whole supernatural way of life and had no idea what she was doing. Plus, her grades in just about every class sucked. She was a mere struggling student, and not anywhere close to a supernatural guardian.

She wished her mom were alive. She needed to talk to her more than ever.

Forcing herself to think of something else, she lowered her sleeve and started drawing leaves along the side of her paper. Big ones and little ones, all caught in a breeze as they searched for an end to their fall. She felt like those leaves—lost, drifting about aimlessly, looking for a place to land. No matter how hard she tried to fit in at SMA, she didn't feel like she belonged. And then her favorite red scarf popped into mind. She had wanted to wear it today but couldn't find it. She did a mental scan of her room, wondering where it could have gone.

"Miss Clausman, am I boring you?"

Infiniti dropped her pencil, and it started rolling off her desk. She stopped it with a smack, then smiled sheepishly as she eyed Dr. Fraser who was standing in front of her. He stared down at her with an intensity that was equal parts smoldering and frightening. She sat upright.

"No, Dr. Fraser. Not at all. I was just, uh . . . thinking about the inter-dimensional thing you were talking about." She smiled and forced herself not to laugh. She had a bad habit of laughing when she was nervous. "It's sooo . . ."—she cleared her throat —"fascinating."

The tall, red-haired, kilted Scottish professor leaned in a little. He narrowed his blue eyes at her, then glanced at her artwork for a long second. Normally she wouldn't mind the unshaven, sexy professor getting close, but this was not one of those normal situations. She was busted.

"How kind of you to be so interested in my inter-dimensional . . . thing," he finally said in his mild Scottish accent, letting her off the hook and not mentioning her doodling.

A smattering of laughter broke out among the class, and Infiniti's cheeks flushed. *How embarrassing.*

Dr. Fraser made his way back to the front of the class, continuing with his lecture. Taylor Augustine, her roomie and best friend, whispered from beside her.

"Fin, you okay?"

Infiniti nodded, then rolled her eyes. Taylor muffled a laugh, then pointed at the whiteboard Dr. Fraser had started drawing on.

"Pay attention," she mouthed.

Following her roomie's directive, Infiniti brought her gaze to the front of the room, but not before meeting the bitchy glare of Cat Vega.

"Really?" Infiniti whispered to herself, doing her best to ignore the copper-skinned, long-legged, dark-haired Transhuman vixen who seemed to have taken an interest in her boyfriend, Joe. She lived in Heimdall, the same tower as Joe. She was also in the same major he was, Special Forces with an emphasis on Advanced Combat. Just about everywhere Joe was, Cat was there too— laughing, flirting, shaking her hips, showing off her cleavage, always trying to get close to him. Taylor kept telling Infiniti that Joe didn't even notice Cat. And maybe he didn't, but Infiniti still didn't like it. Not one bit. Cat needed to stay away from her wolf shifter. She wished Cat wasn't in Heimdall. In fact, she wished Cat wasn't at SMA at all.

"Okay, then," Dr. Fraser said from the front of the room,

cutting off Infiniti's thoughts. "That's enough for today. And class, I realize everyone is excited about Thanksgiving break next week, but don't forget to sign up for your individual skills test this Friday. Everyone must be able to display purposeful mastery of time manipulation before leaving campus. The test will be tailored to everyone's specific talents and abilities. As the syllabus states, this is a major part of your final grade."

The room filled with chatter as everyone filed out of class. And once again, the all-too-familiar sinking feeling of academic inadequacy settled in Infiniti's gut.

Purposeful mastery of time manipulation? In one week? Ugh.

She had been able to freeze a few small things—a spinning wheel, a clock, even water being poured out of a glass. But only for a few seconds. She was pretty sure that didn't qualify as mastery of anything.

"You can do it, Fin," Taylor encouraged. "I know it."

Infiniti slipped her arms in the straps of her backpack and sighed. "I hope so. I can't take a bad grade right now."

Rooming with Taylor had turned out to be a huge blessing. Taylor was fun and laid back, and they had instantly hit it off. She was part witch and Itako with the super cool ability to talk to people in the spirit world. Taylor had been tagged in an earlier challenge—what the students had started calling the chaos that followed every gong—that involved possessed students and had overcome that pretty well. She had even come out of it with a boyfriend, Clay Washburn. He was a witch from Maine with the ability to manipulate air.

She and Taylor signed up for their test times and were almost out of the classroom, when Dr. Fraser had other ideas.

"Miss Clausman."

Infiniti stopped by the doorway. Her stomach dropped. She turned around slowly.

"Yes, professor?"

"Please stay behind."

"Oh. Okay." Her shoulders tightened. She was pretty sure he wanted to talk to her about spacing out in class. Especially since it wasn't the first time he'd caught her mind somewhere else during his lecture.

"See you later," Taylor said with wide eyes.

"Yeah, later," Infiniti replied, with even wider eyes.

Infiniti scooted back into class and took a seat closest to the professor's desk. It was covered with piles of papers. He shuffled his things around and stuffed a small stack into his brown satchel.

"Please come with me to my office."

Office? She eyed the cluttered desk. Examining the setup, she thought the room had served double duty as his office and his classroom. To hear he had an actual office somewhere was unexpected. Even though she'd been there three months now, she wondered when she'd get used to the supernatural college. She scanned the room for a doorway other than the exit, but didn't see one. And as far as she knew, there were no offices on the floor.

"Is it, like, up in the air somewhere?" she asked with a smile, trying to make light of the situation.

He cocked an eyebrow. "I guess you will have to see, young lady."

He swished his arm in a circular motion, the movement revealing a swirling mist of purple and green. It reminded Infiniti of the portal she had used to enter the campus on her first day. She wanted to ask Dr. Fraser a million questions about the opening, but didn't. She didn't want to look dumb.

"Right this way," Dr. Fraser said, stepping aside so Infiniti could go first.

She knew allowing her to go before him was the gentlemanly thing to do, but stepping into that supernatural swirl first terrified her. Did he have to be so proper? She shuffled her feet forward, then took quick steps through the warm mist. The air shifted from open and airy to cool and earthy as she found herself in a small, dark windowless room. Shelves filled with books lined every inch of the wall space. In the middle was a desk piled with various stacks of papers, much like the desk from the classroom. And then Infiniti did a double take. Was it the same desk? Like, the actual desk from his classroom? Did it somehow magically follow them?

He motioned to a dark leather chair. "Have a seat, please."

Infiniti sat on the edge of the seat, keeping her backpack on. Dr. Fraser set his satchel on the ground, then retrieved a paper from the top of one of the stacks. He handed it over.

She held it close, and the words ACADEMIC PROBATION came into focus.

Fear struck her. Her hands lost their grip on the paper, and it slipped from her fingers. Dr. Fraser snatched it up before it hit the ground. Instead of handing it back to her, he placed it where he had found it.

Dr. Fraser crossed his muscular arms. "I have yet to submit this to your academic advisor because I wanted to show it to you first."

"I'm on probation?" Probation usually led to expulsion. Infiniti's mind reeled at the thought of being kicked out of school and leaving Joe. Where would she go? Lyra Beaumont, Addie's mom, had been nice enough to take her in for the short-term, but leaving campus and going to live with her wasn't a real solution.

"Not yet. But close."

"Close?"

"Yes, close. You have a chance to raise your grade with your skills demonstration at the end of the week, and I think you can do it."

Infiniti gulped. "You do?"

"I do indeed. Do you?"

Infiniti blinked. *Did she?*

Dr. Fraser furrowed his brows. "Do you believe in yourself?"

She wasn't sure, but in that moment she knew she didn't want to leave the school. Even with the potential of a horrific challenge hanging over her head, she wanted to stay.

"Yes. I, uh, do. And I think I can do it."

"I think so is not good enough." He went to his bookshelf. His fingers walked across the spines until he pulled out a small antique-looking brown book. He handed it to her.

"*Mastering the Art of Time Manipulation*," she read out loud.

He folded his arms. "You are here because you demonstrated

the right to be a part of this group. Now you need to master your abilities and prove you belong."

Infiniti lost her words. *Prove she belonged?* She considered his directive until it sunk in, and she realized he was right. She had earned her place at SMA, and now she needed to keep it. She hoped she could.

"Thank you, Dr. Fraser. I promise to work really hard."

"I expect nothing less from you."

Infiniti started getting up when Dr. Fraser held out his hand. "One more thing."

She hovered over the chair a few seconds before easing back down. She held her breath, scared at what else he was going to say, when she noticed the professor's eyes softening. He rubbed his scruffy, chiseled face.

"Miss Clausman, I am aware of the difficulties you've overcome of late. The ones involving your run-in with reaper Shade StormIron, your altercation with Death, and the unfortunate loss of your mother. My sincere condolences."

She'd seen Shade around campus. Even though he had said she was off his radar and that he was around SMA on school business, she didn't exactly believe him. He had tried to claim her life twice. The first time was when her car crashed outside Havenwood Falls, and the second time was when her house caught on fire. Images of her charred and waterlogged home sprang to mind. If not for Joe, she would've died in that house too. She willed the sorrow away because she didn't want to cry. Not here.

"Thank you," she said in a low voice.

"You know who Dr. Burn is, I presume?"

"Dr. Burn?" Infiniti thought she knew every professor on campus, but didn't recognize the name.

"Apologies, Miss Clausman. Dr. Burn prefers to go by Dr. Lavinia, which is her first name. Dr. Lavinia Burn."

"Oh, Dr. Lavinia, the school counselor. Yes, I've heard of her. I've seen her Crisis Intervention flyers around campus." And then realization struck her. "Are you saying I should go see her? Like, I *need* to see her?"

"Yes, and yes." He took yet another sheet of paper from his desk. "Here's her office information. I have it on good authority she's free this afternoon if you want to stop by. She's always willing to lend an ear to students who may need one."

Infiniti took the paper, feeling so small she wanted to disappear. She needed academic help and now mental help. A horrific supernatural challenge possibly loomed in her future. And Cat wanted Joe. *Great.*

CHAPTER 2

$\mathcal{D}$r. Fraser reactivated the portal, and Infiniti returned alone to the empty classroom. With her confidence deflated and feeling like total crap, she decided she needed a pick-me-up. And Joe was the perfect person for the job. He had Basic Weaponry at Ansgar I at the same time as her class with Dr. Fraser. And just about every day after class, he'd go to Clifftop for a workout. The mere idea of him made her feel better, and she couldn't wait to see him. Plus, there was also the bonus of him being shirtless and sweaty.

She was halfway down the stone hallway when she slowed her pace. Where were the stairs? She usually didn't have to walk that far before coming up on the exit out of Asketill Hall, and there was no one around for her to ask. Had she gotten turned around somehow? She eyed the cave walls and stone floors, then picked up her pace. She started to feel like a character in a horror film locked in a spooky castle with no way out.

"Don't be silly," she muttered out loud. "I'm not trapped. This isn't even spooky."

Even though she tried to reassure herself, her heart pounded. Her hands grew sweaty. Tingly fear crept over her entire body.

Finally, she came upon the stairs. She raced down the steps as fast as she could, desperate to get out in the open.

She didn't care for the creepy medieval vibe of the campus. Even with the magical lighting illuminating the common areas and the buildings, everything seemed so bleak and dreary. But then again, the campus *was* inside a mountain. She looked up at the enormous skylight overhead. Yep, the sun and the sky were still up there. Way up there. Seeing the brightness so far away made her miss the hot and sunny Houston weather, the large oak trees of her neighborhood, and the lake across the street from her house. Suddenly, she didn't just want to see Joe; she also needed a healthy dose of the outdoors of Clifftop.

She walked across campus with her arms folded across her chest. Even though she didn't want to think about her troubles, she couldn't help herself. Would the chaos ever stop? She felt a throbbing at her wrist and slowed her pace. She'd been scratching at her tattoo and hadn't even noticed. She dropped her hand and pulled up her sleeve. Blood streaked her skin.

"Oh, shit," she said. She thought of the paper Dr. Fraser had given her with Dr. Lavinia's office information. Maybe she was more messed up than she thought. Maybe she did need to see the doc.

Walking on autopilot and maneuvering through the shadowy campus, Infiniti soon found herself across the sky bridge, past Steivar and Ansgar I, and almost to the opening to Clifftop. With each step closer to the trees, the air smelled fresher, the light from above shone brighter. She didn't even mind that her thighs were on fire. The closer she got to the outdoors, the better she felt. And when she made it to the top and was surrounded by the magnificent beauty of nature, she drew in the deepest breath. She needed to come out here more often.

She scanned the snow-covered trees and saw a few wolves dashing about, but none of them were her white wolf. Overhead, Dingane, or D, the magnificent black and white feathered Impundulu lightning bird, zipped through the skies. A game of soccer was taking place in the distance, and she knew for sure Joe would be one of the players. If he wasn't with her or in class, he was out here getting physical. When Infiniti spotted the blond hair and perfectly sculpted chest of her man, her heart fluttered.

She tossed her backpack near a tree and started heading his way when someone else sprang into view—Cat Vega. She wore a tight black sweat-suit that clung to her body like a second skin and had her hair pulled up in a high ponytail. She must've come to Clifftop right after Dr. Fraser's class. With a huff, Infiniti quickened her pace. Her breath puffed out in little bursts of vapor as she got closer to the players. As if catching her scent, Joe perked up, and his gaze landed squarely on hers. He started raising his hand when Cat bumped into him, and together they tumbled to the ground.

Infiniti paused her step.

"Oh, hell no," she muttered under her breath. She marched onward. Who the hell did Cat think she was?

Joe got up with a laugh. He helped Cat to her feet and then started jogging over to Infiniti. He slipped his arms around her waist.

"Hey, babe," he said, pressing his warm and soft lips to hers.

She kissed him back, barely, then pulled away. "What was that?"

"What was what?"

She put her hand on her hip and stuck out her foot. "You and Cat? Rolling around on the ground?"

He let out a deep laugh. "Babe, she fell on me, and that was it. There was no rolling."

He tried to kiss her again, but she turned her head. "You know she's after you."

"Pfft, no she's not. Besides, if she is, then the joke's on her. You're the only one for me. You know that. Hell, everyone knows that."

She knew Joe had no interest in anyone else but her, and that he was oblivious to Cat and her flirty ways. But Cat's advances were getting to her.

"I know," she admitted, giving in to him. She tugged him

closer and kissed him, slipping her tongue in his mouth not only because she wanted to, but also because she wanted Cat to see.

He hugged her tightly.

"There's my girl," he whispered against her mouth, kissing her back with intensity.

"Get a room!" someone yelled.

Infiniti separated from Joe but kept her hands on his firm chest. She stared up into his gorgeous and perfect face. *Get a room?* They'd done a lot, but hadn't gone all the way. Sometimes she thought she was ready, but then other times she thought she should wait.

"Come on," he said, kissing her forehead. "Let's get out of here." He waved at the players. "I'm out!"

Infiniti caught Cat looking at them. She inwardly did a victory dance as she wrapped her arm around Joe's waist and Joe wrapped his arm around her neck.

"So what brings you out here?" he asked. "Everything okay?"

She shrugged, suddenly not wanting to tell Joe about what Dr. Fraser had said about her grades and seeing Dr. Lavinia. She didn't want him to worry. After everything that had been happening on campus, his protective instincts for her had kicked into overdrive. She didn't need to lay any more troubles on him.

"Yeah, everything's fine. I was just missing you, that's all."

He smiled down at her. "You were?"

"Yeah." She smiled back. "I always miss you when we're apart."

"And I always miss you."

He led her to a line of bushes where shirts and jackets and bundles of clothes were hanging. Since shifters and other supes weren't bothered by the cold weather, the bushes served as the official holding area for unwanted and unneeded clothing. Joe grabbed his hoodie, shook it out, and slipped it on. He took her hands, and a serious expression came over him.

"Are you sure there's not something else? Maybe your tattoo?"

She hid her internal gulp. He knew her so well. And in that moment, she wanted more than anything to be her old self. Ever since her mom died, she'd been so scared and fearful. And the craziness at SMA was only making things worse. She resolved to see Dr. Lavinia and handle her shit on her own. She'd schedule an appointment right after Thanksgiving.

She straightened her back and flashed her best confidant smile. "My tattoo is the same. Besides, can't a girl want to see her boyfriend just to see him?"

He laughed. "I guess so."

With their backpacks on, and Infiniti getting chilly without a coat, she nestled into Joe where it was always warm. They made their way back down to campus, across the sky bridge, and headed toward Halstein Hall. Almost to the double doors, Dr. Lavinia's name popped into Infiniti's head, repeating over and over and over. She slowed her step.

"What is it?" Joe asked, fresh concern in his green eyes.

Her mouth fell open for a minute. She didn't even realize she had stopped. "I, uh . . ." Her mind scrambled as she searched for an excuse to give Joe while Dr. Lavinia's name blasted between her ears. "I forgot I have a study group thing."

"Oh. When?"

She let out one of those nervous laughs. "Right now, in Halstein Hall."

He kept his stare on her for a second. She could tell he wanted to say something, but he stopped himself.

"All right." He rubbed the back of his neck, something he always did when he didn't know how to act or what to say. "Well, I'll head over to Heimdall for a quick shower then. Want to meet after for dinner?"

"Yeah," she said. They started walking again, falling into the flow of others making their way to Halstein. "We can meet for dinner."

Once inside, they stopped in front of the fountain with the Valkyrie statue in its center. Infiniti dropped Joe's hand. She eyed the stairs and started in their direction. "I'll text you?"

"Yeah, okay."

Seeing Joe looking a little sad and helpless made her feel bad, but Dr. Lavinia's name was so loud in her head, she could barely think. She needed to see her and fast. She trotted up the stairs. When she thought she was out of Joe's sight, she slowed down and sifted through her backpack for the flyer Dr. Fraser had given her. Pulling it out she saw that Dr. Lavinia's office was on the third floor.

Great. Another climb.

Infiniti wasn't sure if she'd ever get used to all the stairs, but at least it was only three flights. With Dr. Lavinia's name still bouncing around in her head, she picked up her pace. She kept plugging upward, issuing a few "heys" and "what ups" to the friends she passed by. Finally she made it to the landing for the third floor.

Catching her breath, she peered to the right and then to the left. Unsure about the direction of Dr. Lavinia's office, she chose the right because it looked a little brighter than the left. And then she realized the doc's name in her head had silenced.

"Infiniti?"

Infiniti yelped, slamming her hands over her chest.

A chuckle sounded from behind her. "I'm so sorry," the voice said again. "My office is over here, on this side."

Infiniti turned and saw a petite woman with curly, shoulder-length brown hair and oversized dark-rimmed glasses. She didn't look at all like a scholarly psychiatrist. Instead, she resembled a favorite aunt. One with the ability to prepare a scrumptious dinner complete with a killer chocolate cake.

"Dr. Lavinia?"

"Yes, that's me. Dr. Lavinia Burn. I'm the school counselor, and a witch in case you were wondering. I prefer to be called Dr. Lavinia as you already know, since that's what you just called me. And you're Infiniti Clausman, a Transhuman with the new ability to freeze time. And your friends call you Fin. I see you got my message?"

Infiniti repositioned her backpack and walked over. "The message in my head? Yes, I got it. Loud and clear."

Dr. Lavinia wrinkled her nose. "Was it too loud?"

"Um, a little."

"Oops, sorry." Dr. Lavinia ushered Infiniti into her office. "Since you're new to your powers and all, I amplified my reach. Guess I overdid it."

"That's okay," Infiniti said.

Dr. Lavinia's office was a small and simple room with a desk, a credenza behind it, and two brown leather recliners in front. The smell of gingerbread permeated the room, and trinkets covered just about every empty space. Infiniti spotted a unicorn figurine, a Rubik's cube, glass jars of candy, and a pineapple plushy, just to name a few. A replica sorting hat from Harry Potter took up most of the credenza. Next to that was an eight-by-ten picture of the doc in full Hufflepuff garb. Infiniti smiled inwardly. She was a Hufflepuff, too. Stenciled over the credenza in big purple lettering sprawled the phrase *Always Believe in Yourself.*

Infiniti paused. Dr. Fraser had asked her that very question, if she believed in herself.

"Please, sit," Dr. Lavinia said.

Infiniti set her backpack down and sank down into one of the recliners. It moved from side to side, causing her to slam her feet on the ground.

"They swivel." Dr. Lavinia smiled, sitting behind her desk. "Just don't move too much and you'll be fine."

Infiniti found her balance. "Oh, okay. Neat."

A black and white cat jumped on the desk. Dr. Lavinia scooped up the pet and set it on her lap. "This is Gizmo." She stroked the cat. "He's a sugar booger."

Infiniti thought of her neighbor Jan and Jan's cat Tinker. She wondered how they were. The last time she had seen Jan was before she and Joe had left Houston. That was back in early August. Jan had said she'd be coming to Havenwood Falls to see her, but when? An overwhelming feeling of homesickness grabbed her from the inside, and a sharp pain permeated her heart.

"Well," Dr. Lavinia said. "Do you know why I summoned you here?"

Infiniti thought she knew, but wasn't completely sure. "I think I kinda know."

Dr. Lavinia folded her hands together on her desk. "Well, what do you think you kinda know?"

"Well, I, uh . . ." Infiniti had no idea where to start when her eyes blurred over. And then, everything spilled out—her tears, her pain, and her story.

She told Dr. Lavinia everything. How the reaper Shade StormIron had been after her and how freaked out she was every time she saw him on campus. How Death had taken her mom and had almost taken her, too. How Joe and the Transhuman Fleet had saved her. How she feared Death would always be coming for her. How scared she was to be at SMA. How her tattoo had started to change, but then stopped. How she feared getting kicked out of school, and if she did, she had nowhere to go. She even mentioned Cat and how she was trying to steal Joe.

Dr. Lavinia got up and went over to Infiniti. She placed her hand on Infiniti's shoulder.

"There, there, dear."

A warm and peaceful feeling came over Infiniti, seeping through her body from her head all the way to her toes. Her tears slowed down and then stopped. The heaviness in her heart lifted. Infiniti placed her hand on top of Dr. Lavinia's.

"Wow," she muttered. "Thank you."

"You are most welcome." Dr. Lavinia patted Infiniti's shoulder a few times, handed her a tissue box, and then sat back down.

Infiniti tugged out a few tissues and patted her eyes. "That was a lot. I'm so sorry."

"Never be sorry for your feelings. Ever. Okay? A feeling is the spirit's way of communicating what you have inside of you, what you know, what you need to know, and what you've experienced. Sometimes even what you need to get rid of. Every feeling is important. The good ones and even the not-so-good ones."

Infiniti nodded. The explanation made perfect sense to her, but she had no idea how to process everything inside of her. She moved her hands in front of her heart in a circular motion.

"Okay, so what do I do with all this heaviness?"

Dr. Lavinia took the pineapple plushy from her desk and

tossed it to Infiniti. It wasn't a plushy at all, but one of those soft squishy stress thingies. Infiniti molded her hands around it.

"Well, I'd like to meet with you once a week so I can help you. Our first order of business will be death. The big baddie himself, and the process of leaving this life for the next. I sense great fear of these things inside of you. I can help you overcome these fears."

Death . . . the person and the event. She'd love nothing more than to not be afraid of either.

"And my grades? And my so-called powers that I can't really control? And my tattoo and possible impending challenge?"

Dr. Lavinia picked up one of her candy jars. "Fear is a magnet. It causes great turmoil in many different ways." She drew in a deep breath, then let it out with a whoosh. "I believe conquering your fear of death will help every facet of your life. Let's call it the source."

Infiniti found herself gripping the stress pineapple so hard she thought it might rip. She loosened her hold and set it back on Dr. Lavinia's desk. The doc smiled, then handed Infiniti the candy jar.

"I give these out at the end of our time together."

The candies were wrapped in colorful paper and twisted on each end. She picked a red one. It reminded Infiniti of hot Cheetos, which she loved. "Thank you. So when do I come back?"

Dr. Lavinia tapped her chin. "Today is Monday, and everyone leaves campus Friday for Thanksgiving, so my calendar is a little full. How about I text you Thursday morning and see if I can work you in?"

"Okay, that sounds great. Thank you so much, Dr. Lavinia."

Dr. Lavinia put Gizmo on the floor, reached for the pineapple, and handed it back to Infiniti. "In the meantime, go ahead and take this with you." She gestured at the purple message behind her. "And don't forget to believe in yourself."

Out in the hall, Infiniti stuffed the pineapple in her backpack, unwrapped her treat, and popped it in her mouth. The hard candy tasted like cinnamon with a hint of tanginess. The flavor was not at all like hot Cheetos, but it was still yummy. She thought of her stash of hot Cheetos in her room. Her supply was all gone. She had sworn she had a ton in her bin. She thought maybe the guys in Jory had helped themselves, which was fine. She made a mental note to get more as she headed downstairs with a fresh spring in her step.

She was almost down to the first floor of Halstein when a soft rumble sounded. She slowed her pace. She strained her ears.

What was that?

"Hey, Fin." It was Vanessa Shaw, the tall, slender hellhound shifter that lived in Hel Tower. Wearing her usual sunglasses so she didn't accidentally kill someone with her stare, she was coming around Infiniti, heading downstairs with a box in her arms.

"Hey, Vanessa. Did you hear that really weird sound?"

Before Vanessa could answer, a boom shook the building as if a thunderclap had exploded overhead. The stone beneath Infiniti's feet vibrated. Chunks of rock careened from overhead, and a rippling fissure tore through the stairs.

"Vanessa!"

The hellhound shifter's box flew out of her hands as she scrambled to back away from the crack. Metal instruments clanked all over the place. The split expanded with a bang, forming a massive crater in the middle of the stairs. Vanessa fell to her back and started sliding into the dark opening.

Infiniti dropped to her stomach. She stretched out her arm. "Grab my hand!"

Vanessa reached for Infiniti, and Infiniti lunged, clutching her by the wrist.

"I got you," Infiniti grunted.

Hollering broke out from all over the place as Infiniti struggled to keep her hold. Vanessa's sunglasses were barely in place, and Infiniti averted her eyes, keeping her stare on Vanessa's dangling legs.

"Don't let go, Fin."

"I won't," Infiniti puffed out.

Stretched to her limit with her arms burning, Infiniti slipped forward.

"Shit," she muttered. She tried to somehow brace her body

against what little was left of the stairs, but there was no way. They were goners.

"I'm so sorry, Vanessa," she muttered, when suddenly a strong hand grabbed her ankle. Infiniti couldn't see who it was, but slowly she was pulled up with Vanessa in tow.

Back on the landing of the second floor, Infiniti and Vanessa grabbed on to each other.

"You girls okay?" It was Caleb Hayes. The tall and lean muscular bear shifter kept them close as he eyed the opening in the stairwell.

"Holy shit, I'm not dead," Vanessa panted. "I mean, thanks."

Infiniti sank down to the ground, her body shaking so badly she could hardly stand. "I thought we were both dead."

People down below started bustling about, calling for help, saying someone was injured. Others from the floors above joined Infiniti, Vanessa, and Caleb to see what was going on.

"Don't get too close," Caleb warned, his arms blocking the gawkers who were trying to peer into the hole.

"Hey," Vanessa said, eyeing Infiniti. "Do you think this was your challenge?"

"You were tagged?" Caleb asked Infiniti with a raised brow.

Most everyone knew about her half-inked tattoo, but it seemed as though Caleb didn't. She and Vanessa climbed to their feet.

"I'm sort of tagged," she admitted to Caleb.

Vanessa pushed her long light blond hair out of her face and pointed at Infiniti's wrist. "Check your tat."

Infiniti lifted her sleeve. Her heart fell when she saw the ink was the same—half school crest and half hourglass. She pulled her sleeve back down. "No. This wasn't my challenge."

"Well, this sure as shit is linked to something," Vanessa added, studying the abyss. "And I'd be willing to bet it's part of whatever is going on with your tat. You need to be ready, Fin."

Dread crept up Infiniti's spine. Vanessa was right. This definitely wasn't in the realm of regular happenings, as if anything was regular at SMA. Something told her this was the start of something terrible.

CHAPTER 3

Joe walked to Heimdall Tower with nothing but worry on his mind. He couldn't make sense of Infiniti's sudden change outside Halstein Hall. She was fine, and then she wasn't. She had even made up a bogus study group excuse. He knew she was trying to work things out on her own, but he wished she'd let him in on whatever she was going through.

His tennis shoes pounded against the stone floor of Heimdall as he walked across the main floor great room to the stairs in the back of the tower. He took them two-by-two up to the sixth floor. He jerked open his door and found that Kase wasn't there, which was good. He didn't feel like talking. He dropped his stuff on the floor and paced the room for a few minutes, clenching and unclenching his fists. Then he let out a huge breath. Finally calm enough, he started getting his stuff together for a shower when he realized his toiletry bag was missing. He rifled through his closet, pissed at having lost another item. It seemed he'd been misplacing shit all week. Coming up empty-handed, he took Kase's stuff and headed down the hall to the bathroom. He knew his best friend wouldn't mind.

At first, it was strange getting used to the co-ed bathroom, but after a while Joe realized it wasn't that bad. The showers, tubs, and toilets had their own private doors with locks. The only truly shared area was the large space in the middle with sinks, a mirror that ran the length of the room, and long stone benches for seating. And with everyone's varying schedules, the bathroom was never crowded.

He went into the first shower stall, stripped down, and stood under the hot stream. Water ran down his body as he kept thinking how Infiniti was always in some sort of danger. He pressed his palms against the wet stone. Why did she have to go through so much? If only there was something he could do to trade places with her, but he knew there was no way.

A knock sounded at his shower door, interrupting his thoughts. He glanced at the lock, realizing he hadn't latched it.

"I'm in here."

The door swung open, and there was Cat, naked. "Hey Joe." Her brown eyes scanned his body, lingering on his midsection. "I left my body wash in my room. Can I borrow yours?"

Son of a bitch. Infiniti was right. The way her eyes deepened with lust told him she definitely wanted to be more than friends.

He handed her the bottle of body wash. "Not cool, Cat."

She flashed him an innocent look and raised her shoulders. "What?"

"You don't even live on this floor."

"The showers on my floor didn't have hot water, so I thought I'd come up here."

"Yeah, right."

She plucked the bottle from his hands. "Gracias." She turned around, then paused so he could get a good look. "I'll return it later."

She strolled away, and Joe shut the door behind her. "Keep it."

He finished his shower in a hurry and started drying off, figuring he needed to straight up tell Cat he wasn't interested. Pulling on a fresh change of clothes, dreading confronting her, a tingle struck him. A hard shiver raced across his spine.

Something was wrong with Infiniti.

He laced up his tennis shoes and tore out of the bathroom,

racing out of Heimdall and booking it for Halstein Hall. When he neared, he saw a sizeable crowd gathered outside the double doors of the hall. Joe muscled his way through the throng. When he got up to the front he saw Dr. Fraser manning the entrance. The professor spotted Joe and waved him forward.

"Dr. Fraser, what's happening? Where's Infiniti?"

The professor placed his hand on Joe's shoulder. "She's inside, and she's okay. As for what's happening, we're not sure. Addie and others are inside making an assessment."

The professor stepped to the side and let Joe pass. When he entered the building, he saw a body covered with a sheet. Blood splattered all over the floor. He recognized the sleeve of a dining hall uniform. He scanned the faces of the students and staff that were standing around as he searched for his mate.

"Infiniti!" he called out.

"She's upstairs," Addie said, coming up quickly. "Clay is up there, too. He's bringing everyone downstairs one at a time."

"Bringing everyone downstairs? With his wind power?" He rubbed the back of his neck. "Why?"

Addie motioned toward the stairs. "You'll have to see for yourself."

From Joe's vantage point, nothing appeared out of the ordinary, but when he got closer, he saw what Addie meant. Chunks of stone and clumps of debris piled around the base of the stairs. And up above, where the stairs should have been, stretched a gaping hole of darkness.

"What the hell," he muttered.

"Joe!"

It was Infiniti. Clay was holding her by the waist, using his powers to lower her to the first floor. When they touched down, Clay released Infiniti and shot back up to the top floors. Infiniti rushed into Joe and buried her face into his chest.

Neither one said anything for a minute as they held onto each other.

"What happened?" he finally asked.

She pulled back and looked up at him with terrified eyes. "The stairs opened up, and Vanessa and I almost fell in."

Joe looked from her to the emptiness. "The stairs opened up?"

"Yeah, there was like an earthquake or something. Everything was shaking. And then the stairs just—" she gestured with her hands—"cracked open and disappeared."

Elsmed Fairchild from the Court and Board of Regents showed up with a small entourage and started interviewing everyone. Several hours later, Joe and Infiniti were dismissed.

Back in Joe's room, and with Kase deciding to stay at Elle's for the night, Joe took off his shirt and jeans and pulled on a pair of sweatpants. Infiniti changed into a pair of pajamas she kept in his room. They crawled into bed, and he held her to him. He didn't say anything, letting her process her emotions.

"I thought I was going to die," she finally said. "Like, for real this time."

He kissed her forehead and gave her a squeeze. "I'm so glad you didn't."

She lifted herself up on her elbows. "Why does this crap always happen to me?"

He stared into her big brown eyes, tracing her ivory skin with his fingertips. "I don't know."

She let her head flop down on his bare chest. "I'm really sick of it."

"I am too."

She stretched her head and kissed his neck. And then, inch by inch, she worked her mouth up to his lips. His body burned with desire as their tongues explored each other's mouths. She straddled him, grinding into him, moaning with desire as they kissed long and deep, their hands exploring each other's bodies. He wanted to do so much more to her, wanted to experience every inch of her, but he wasn't sure if she was ready. And so he took his cues from her, matching each stroke and movement while his body exploded with desire and longing for his mate.

"This is getting dangerous," she said after a while, pulling away and staring down at him.

Her cheeks flushed with desire, and he wanted nothing more than to be with her in that moment. He pulled her long wavy hair away from her face, thinking she was the most beautiful woman he'd ever seen. He brushed his fingers over her lips, then ran them down her neck, his hardness bulging under her.

"You have me, Infiniti. All of me. Whatever you want. Whenever you're ready. I'm yours."

She kept her gaze on his. For a minute there, he thought she was about to say she was ready to be with him completely, but she didn't.

"I love you, Joseph Greg."

He smiled. "I love you, Infiniti Clausman."

She lowered herself, snuggled into him, and fell asleep. And while she slept, Joe focused on her safety, vowing to stay by her side no matter what. If and when her tattoo activated, he'd do whatever he could to help her. Including risk his own life.

A somber vibe filled the air the next day. Everyone buzzed about the disappearing stairs and how Infiniti and Vanessa had almost died. And when the body of the dead dining hall worker was picked up by the Havenwood Falls morgue, the mood turned so thick, Infiniti could hardly function. She was on edge, terrified about what other catastrophe might occur, spending her time trying to forget about her unchanged tattoo, but also so preoccupied with it, she couldn't think of anything else. And when Wednesday rolled around with her tattoo unchanged and no other disasters on campus, she wanted to explode.

Back in her room after an uneventful day of class, Infiniti flopped face first on her bed. Taylor wasn't home, and she knew Joe was still in class. She rolled over on her back and stared at her ceiling. Taylor had worked her magic so that the top of their room looked like the Milky Way, complete with a giant glowing full moon embedded in different shades of purple and blue. She brought her half-inked tattoo up to her face and scrutinized it. No sands moving, no burning sensation, no nothing. Then she thought of the assignment for Dr. Fraser's skills test in just two days. Could she do it? Could she really display mastery of time manipulation?

With a groan, she rolled over and sat up, grabbing the book Dr. Fraser had given her from her nightstand. She opened it when a knock sounded on her door.

"Come in!"

Tyr peeked his head in. His long dark hair was pulled back and his ice blue eyes danced with excitement. "Hey, party tonight at Hel Tower! Tempest and Natalie finally perfected their brew, and they've made a shit ton!"

Tempest and Natalie had been working on different drink recipes for months. She had tasted some early versions that were disgusting. "They did? How?"

"I heard Charleigh helped. Tell everyone, okay?"

"Yeah, sure."

Tyr left, and Infiniti grabbed her phone. She hadn't been to a party in a long time and could definitely use one. Especially before Dr. Fraser's test and before her challenge presented itself. Blowing off a little steam never hurt. In fact, it could only help.

"Party tonight then study tomorrow and hopefully see Dr. Lavinia tomorrow too," she muttered to herself, thinking it sounded like the perfect plan. She texted Joe.

ME: Out of class yet?

JOE: Yep, just now. Did you hear about the party at Hel tonight

ME: Yes, and I so need to go

JOE: Everything ok?

She hesitated a few seconds. She still hadn't told Joe about her conversation with Dr. Fraser or that she had seen Dr. Lavinia. She'd tell him later. Plus, she really needed a little social drinking therapy without her worries or his hanging over her head.

ME: Yeah, just need some fun tonight

JOE: And your big test on Friday?

ME: I can study tomorrow

There was a long pause. Infiniti bit her bottom lip, wondering if Joe knew what was up.

JOE: Ok. I'm gonna workout, I'll come get you around 9

ME: Sounds good

She spent the rest of the afternoon flipping through the book Dr. Fraser had given her and trying her best to not stare at her tattoo. At around eight, she started getting ready. Rummaging through her cluttered and crammed closet, she decided on ripped dark jeans and a snug low-cut purple t-shirt that showed off the little cleavage she did have. She completed the outfit with a full face of makeup. She hadn't worn makeup in a while and wanted to go all out.

A knock sounded on the door.

"Come in," she said.

Joe entered, and his eyes roamed her body while he licked his lips. "Wow, babe, you look amazing."

She blushed and put her hand on her hip. "You think so?"

"Oh, I know so." He issued a low growl, came at her, and pulled her closer to him. "I think we should stay here instead." He nibbled her neck, keeping one hand on her lower back and the other behind her neck. "Forget the party."

She let out a moan and ran her fingers through his short blond hair. She was definitely tempted by his offer, but she also wanted to go out. So she offered a compromise.

"How about we go to the party, then ditch early and come back here?"

He continued sprinkling her with kisses, then covered her mouth with his. He kissed her long and slow before stopping. "You drive me crazy you know."

"I know," she answered, taking his hand and pulling him out of the room.

They made their way to Hel Tower, joining groups of others headed the same way. Everyone buzzed with excitement about the new brew and about going home for Thanksgiving break after class on Friday. Infiniti should've been excited too, but she wasn't. The reality of possibly failing out of school clutched her tight, along with the dread of facing her hourglass challenge. Not to mention she missed her mom something awful, what with all the talk of Thanksgiving. Yep, she most definitely needed a drink. Lots of drinks.

When they stepped onto the rooftop, they also stepped through the magical barrier containing the din. Suddenly, they were surrounded by DJ Dragonclaw's booming music. Kase and Elle came up to Infiniti and Joe right away.

"Hey, guys!" Kase said. They were each holding a copper mug filled to the brim with clear liquid.

"Ooh," Infiniti said, eyeing the drinks. "Is that the new brew?"

As if on cue, Tempest and Natalie showed up with a tray of copper mugs. They wore proud expressions on their faces.

"Here it is," Tempest announced.

"We call it Forever-Ever Clear Beer." Natalie laughed.

Joe took a mug and handed it to Infiniti, then got one for himself. He raised an eyebrow.

"Forever-Ever Clear Beer?" he asked the witches. "What does that mean?"

"It means the mugs magically fill up when you're finished," Tempest answered.

"So it lasts forever," Natalie tacked on with pride.

"Wow, really?" Infiniti asked. She brought the mug to her lips and took a sip. The liquid was cold and smooth with a taste that reminded her of a mix between a light beer and a mojito. "This is delicious!"

"Why, thank you very much," Natalie said with a small curtsy. "Charleigh was the secret weapon behind the concoction."

Charleigh must've heard her name because she gave a loud whoop from nearby.

Tempest and Natalie bumped heads as they laughed, and Infiniti wondered how many drinks they'd had. She was also really glad to see Natalie acting like her old self after losing her mom so recently. If anyone understood that level of pain, it was Infiniti.

The pair took off with their tray, leaving Joe and Infiniti with Kase and Elle.

"How about we toast?" Infiniti suggested. She held out her mug, and so did the others. In that moment, she just wanted to be a normal girl, having a great time at an awesome party. She didn't want to think about time manipulation or hourglasses or not fitting in or missing her mom or deadly challenges. She just wanted to get drunk. She held her glass high. "To a badass party!"

"Badass!" they all said, then drank.

"Hey!" Joe exclaimed. "Let's see how the refill magic works!" He chugged the rest of his drink, and so did Kase. They held out their mugs. Everyone watched as a fresh supply rose up from the bottom of the cup and stopped at the brim. Joe laughed. "Pretty convenient!"

"Right?" Kase added, clapping Joe on the back.

A group of guys from Heimdall Tower came over. Smiling wide with their own mugs, they circled Joe and Kase with excitement, going on and on about wanting a rematch at darts.

Kase eyed Elle and Infiniti. "You ladies mind if we show these boys a thing or two about darts?"

Joe and Kase had never lost a dart match, and they were always challenged whenever there was a party.

Elle shrugged at Infiniti. "I guess that'll be fine."

"Sure," Infiniti chimed in. "Just don't take forever."

Joe leaned in and kissed her on the lips. "I won't."

Taylor joined Infiniti and Elle, and the three of them watched the guys join another group of guys at the far end of the rooftop where rows of dartboards were suspended in midair.

"Why is it that every time we all get together at a party, the boys end up together and the girls end up together. Huh?" Taylor asked with a huff.

"Where's Clay?" Infiniti asked.

"Over there," Taylor pointed.

Infiniti saw Clay with the other witch dudes playing pool.

"Well." Infiniti shrugged. "I say we have a good time and not worry about it."

She clinked mugs with Taylor and Elle, finished her drink, then let it fill up again, marveling at the awesomeness of all things magical. She thought of their first party on top of the tower. The music was so loud, vibrations caused pieces of rock to crumble from the tower itself. They had all been reprimanded by the Board of Regents. After that, the witches of Hel Tower quickly learned to place a silencing spell on the tower anytime they got together. As far as the Board knew, that was their last party.

With music blaring and drinks flowing, Infiniti and her friends started dancing. After a while, their small group turned into a large group, and soon the minutes turned into hours. The rooftop blurred with motion. Forever-Ever Clear Beer splashed everywhere. Couples started bumping and grinding. Infiniti saw Roxy dancing with Tyr and Vid. Tyr was behind Roxy, grinding on her while he kissed Vidar who was standing in front of her. The trio swayed together in perfect motion, their bodies so close it was hard to tell where one ended and the other began.

With an ample supply of drinks in her and all her inhibitions dissolved, a rush of desire swept over Infiniti. She needed Joe. She craned her neck, looking for him, and found him in the same spot with the same people, laughing and playing darts. His shirt clung to his body in the most perfect way, showcasing his muscular physique. His tight jeans hugged his firm butt. She was definitely ready for some alone time with her man. But first, she needed to go to the bathroom.

She squeezed through the throng, zigzagging her way to the stairwell, then rounded the corner to the bathrooms. But instead of the bathrooms, she nearly walked into a wall.

"What the?" she asked herself, thinking she had had way too much to drink.

Sidetracking her steps a little, she finally found the bathroom. When she finished, she started making her way back to where Joe was when Cat Vega came into view. Red leather pants, a tight low cut black leather shirt, her perfect hair cascading down her back. And what Infiniti saw cut her to her core.

She slipped her arms around Joe from behind, and Joe turned and kissed Cat.

Infiniti stumbled back. She dropped her mug. Heat rushed her cheeks. It felt as if her heart had been jabbed with a dagger. She dashed back to the restroom. She gripped the sink with both hands and stared at the mirror. The image of Joe and Cat kissing seared her brain, and it was all she could see.

"Oh my god," she whispered to herself.

Nadine DeBeaux, an Amazon hybrid, and Tess Richards, a tiger shifter, came out of two stalls in the back.

"Oh my god, what?" Nadine asked Infiniti. She leaned toward the mirror, working her fingers through her long red hair and bouncing up her curls.

So many emotions raced through Infiniti's head—hurt, betrayal, but most of all an overwhelming need to disappear and leave SMA forever. She didn't belong at the school. She knew that now.

"Oh my god, I'm not, uh, feeling well," Infiniti said, issuing the first excuse she could think of. She tugged at a paper towel, got it wet, then started dabbing her forehead. "I-I-I think I have a fever."

"A fever?" Tess asked, her brow raised over her thick black-rimmed glasses. "Are you sure you're not just wasted? You look kinda wasted."

"I-I-I'm kinda drunk, but mostly sick." She hiccupped, then issued a series of fake coughs. "I've been fighting a cold. I should probably go. If anyone asks for me, tell them I went home."

"Okay, sure." Tess shrugged, smoothing out the wrinkles of her black dress.

With her heart in her throat, Infiniti tore out of there. How she thought she could ever fit in at a supernatural college was beyond her. And to think a super-hot wolf shifter like Joe would really want a human with barely any abilities was ludicrous.

"I'm so stupid," she murmured.

She cut across campus, hurried up the stairs to her room, and started throwing her things into a duffle bag while tears poured down her face. With as much stuff shoved into the bag as possible, she sat on her bed and started strategizing.

"Okay," she said to herself, grabbing a blanket and wiping her face while she formulated her exit strategy. "I'll go through the portal and head to Lyra's. I'll tell her I want to go home. That SMA wasn't for me." She eyed the tattoo on her wrist. The dumb thing hadn't changed at all. She scrubbed it with her tear-laden blanket, as if that would really do anything. "If I'm leaving, I bet this'll go away. Then someone else can be tagged."

With her plan in place, she sat at her desk. She got a paper and pen and started writing a note to Taylor.

Taylor,

I've left SMA. This place just isn't for me. Tell Joe not to come after me. Thank you for being such a great friend and roommate.

Fin

She folded the note in half and placed it on Taylor's pillow. She pulled on her favorite oversized gray hoodie then started for her backpack, but couldn't find it. She always put it by her bed, but it wasn't there. She performed a frantic search of the room.

"Forget it," she said with a grunt, thinking she didn't need it anyway.

She slung her duffle bag over her shoulder, took one last look at her room, and spotted the silver and gold Christmas ornament keychain she had given her mom years ago. It was the only thing she had of her mom's. She palmed it, placed it in her bag, and then left.

She made her way through the cold night, avoiding the lighted pathways, and headed for the portal—the entry place in and out of SMA. Once inside the vestibule, she eyed the twelve-foot statue of the Valkyrie. For some reason, she felt like she needed to issue some sort of explanation for her departure. After the big presentation for her acceptance, it was the least she could do to the winged mascot.

"Um, Warrior Woman." She cleared her throat, her head feeling woozy from all the alcohol. "I'm sorry, but I'm leaving now. For good." She eyed the massive sword gripped in the Valkyrie's hand. "Oh, and take my tattoo away, okay? And give it to someone else who knows what the hell they're doing." Her near-death experiences at the school flashed before her eyes. "And by the way, I don't appreciate all the crap I've been through," she huffed. "None of it was cool." She thought of saying something else, but couldn't find the right words. "So, um, bye."

Turning away from the Valkyrie, she eyed the swirly mist of the portal behind the great falls. She took a deep breath, and stepped through. She found herself in the chamber room of the main Falls Campus and rushed out of there in a hurry.

Out in the wide open space with the actual sky overhead, she thought she'd feel better away from SMA, but didn't. She stared at the brilliant stars, wondering if she had made the biggest mistake of her life, when the inside of her wrist started tingling. She rolled up her sleeve. The hourglass tattoo was fully inked and glowing. The sands of the top chamber were tricking down to the bottom.

She hiccupped, and then gasped.

"Oh, shit."

CHAPTER 5

*J*oe could spend every waking moment with Infiniti. Every day, all day, for eternity, but he forced himself to play things cool and take their relationship at her pace. So when she turned down his suggestion to skip the party and spend time together, he wasn't surprised. And when she said she needed social therapy, he understood. She definitely needed to blow off some steam.

He begrudgingly stopped kissing her neck, holding on to the promise of spending some alone time with her after the party, and together they took off for Hel Tower. Hand in hand, they strode across campus and were soon on the rooftop. Music thumped, and drinks were pouring. Or, with the magical mugs Charleigh, Tempest, and Natalie had spelled, drinks were filling. And when his friends swooped in and pulled him away to play darts, he went, thinking Infiniti could use some girlfriend time.

"You two don't have to be glued together, you know," Kase teased.

Joe gave his best friend a push. "Dude, whatever! You and Elle are just as bad."

Kase laughed so hard he almost spat out his drink. "Not even!"

Loosened up from the drink and the fun, Joe let his guard

down as he played darts. But he still kept an eye on Infiniti while she danced with her friends. He'd do anything for her. And after losing her twice already, he didn't take anything for granted.

"Joe, dude, she's fine!" Kase urged after a while.

Joe didn't even realize how tense he was until he unclenched his jaw. "You're right." He watched Infiniti dancing and laughing a few seconds more before turning away from her and facing his best friend. "She is."

"Of course she is." Kase pointed at the dartboard. "Now throw the dart! Our reputations are on the line here!"

"Yeah!" someone called out over the music. "Throw it!"

Holding his drink in one hand, Joe used his other hand to aim his dart at the board that magically disappeared and then reappeared in different spots. He narrowed his focus on the bullseye, forcing himself to remain steady even though the Forever-Ever Clear Beer had started dulling his precision.

"Whoever spelled this board is evil." Joe chuckled, his hand moving in small circles as he tried to predict where the board would materialize next. When it came into view, he flicked the dart, and it thudded smack dab in the middle.

Slender arms laced around his waist, pulling him around, and a pair of lips landed on his. He returned Infiniti's kiss for two seconds, but then realized the lips weren't Infiniti's. He pulled back and saw Cat Vega in front of him. A gasp of ooooh's echoed all around him.

"Cat, what the hell?" He grasped her arms and moved her away from him. He scanned the area quickly, hoping Infiniti hadn't seen. Luckily, she wasn't around.

"What?" she asked innocently, batting her long eyelashes. "It was a good throw, and I was congratulating you. Nada más."

"Not cool," Joe said.

"At all," Kase added.

She put her hand on her hip.

"Whatevs," she said in her thick Spanish accent before sauntering off.

"Dude, she has it bad for you," Kase said.

Joe shook his head. "I know." He looked one more time for Infiniti just to be sure she hadn't seen the exchange. With her nowhere in sight, he brought his attention back to his friends. "Come on. Let's play."

After a few more games of darts and a lot more rounds of drinks, Joe was ready to leave. He hoped Infiniti was, too. He said quick goodbyes to his friends, then went in search of her. His first stop was the crowded dance floor, but she wasn't there. He circled the perimeter of the rooftop, still nothing.

He was wondering where she could've gone, when Death sprang to mind. His heart pounded with fear. They had faced-off with that deadly monster over the summer and had barely survived. A heightened fear that he had come back for Infiniti gripped him. After all, she'd had more than her fair share of near death experiences on campus. Plus, Shade seemed to always be around. He told himself he was overreacting, yet picked up his pace anyway. He spotted Taylor and rushed over to her.

"Hey, have you seen Infiniti?"

She set her drink aside. "She went back to the room."

"The room?"

"Yeah, I'm sorry. I thought you knew. Nadine and Tess saw her in the bathroom earlier. She told them she had a fever, and then she left."

Joe was stunned. She had a fever? And left without telling him? That wasn't like her at all. The alcohol in his system started burning off as his metabolism kicked into high gear.

"When?"

Taylor shrugged a little. "I guess about an hour ago?"

Joe's mind raced as he calculated the timing in his mind. An hour ago . . . Cat had kissed him about an hour ago.

"Great," Joe mumbled under his breath.

"Everything okay?' Taylor asked, catching on that something was up.

Joe ran his fingers through his hair. "I don't know. But I'm gonna find out. Thanks, Taylor."

Joe took off, feeling sick to his stomach at the thought of

Infiniti seeing him kiss Cat. He'd never hurt her, not ever, and he hoped she'd gotten sick like Taylor had said. But he knew better. She had seen him with Cat.

He crossed campus quickly. He dashed up the stairs of the Jory Tower. He flung open Infiniti's door and found the room empty.

"Shit," he muttered. He scanned the room quickly and spotted a note on Taylor's pillow. He snatched it up. And when he read it, his heart sank.

"Joe, what's going on?" Taylor and her boyfriend Clay entered the room. "When I saw that look on your face, I got worried, so we followed you over here."

Joe handed Taylor the note. He paced the room while she and Clay read the message.

"She left?" Clay asked.

Taylor's mouth hung open. "As in, *left* left? Through the portal? And doesn't want you to come after her?" Her brows stitched together as she looked from Clay to Joe. "Why?"

Joe kept moving about the room, ready to explode. "Cat Vega, that's why."

Taylor folded the note. "Cat Vega?"

"She kissed me tonight. I pushed her away, but Infiniti must've seen and took off."

"Oh no," Taylor muttered. "Poor Fin."

Everything inside of Joe screamed with guilt. "I'm going after her."

"And I'm coming with you," Taylor tacked on without hesitation. "She's my best friend."

"Yeah, man," Clay said. "Let us help you."

Joe appreciated their offer, but no way could he get them involved. It was his mess, and he needed to fix it alone. Besides, he wasn't sure what state of mind she'd be in, and the last thing he wanted to do was fight in front of Taylor and Clay.

Joe shook his head. "I'm going alone. It's better that way. And don't tell anyone that she took off or that I went after her, okay?"

Taylor bit her bottom lip, her face telling Joe how worried she was about her roommate. "Yeah, okay. But if you don't come back by morning, we're coming after you."

Clay put his arm around Taylor. "Damn straight."

"Fair enough," Joe conceded.

Taylor handed over the folded note. "Be careful, Joe."

He shoved the paper in his pocket. "I will, thanks."

Bounding down the stairs, a million ways to apologize to Infiniti cluttered his brain. But the overriding emotion coursing through his veins was worry for her safety. Infiniti had a knack for getting in trouble, and trying to make her way out of a supernatural campus alone after a night of drinking seemed like a recipe for disaster.

CHAPTER 6

Fear and anxiety crept over Infiniti as she watched the tiny grains of her tattoo stacking together on the bottom chamber. She dropped her duffle bag and sank to the snowy ground. Her throat clogged with tears. Her eyes watered over. She didn't want to cry, but couldn't help herself. She had ditched school, her tattoo didn't disappear like she had hoped it would when she stepped through the portal, and most importantly of all, Joe had kissed Cat Vega. She had never felt so alone and wished her mom were still alive. She needed her now more than ever.

She buried her face in her hands and let the tears flow, her heart hurting so badly she thought she might die.

"Hey, Tiny," a voice called out.

She lowered her hands and saw Fleet in front of her. She hadn't seen the Transhuman since her admission tests to SMA. She got up and rushed into him, burying her face into his chest.

"Oh, Fleet," she sobbed. "Everything is all messed up."

He patted her back for several long seconds. "What do you mean?"

Her shoulders shook as she mumbled incoherent things against Fleet's tear-soaked shirt.

"Slow it down, Tiny. Take a deep breath, okay?"

Her breathing quivered as she struggled to take in steady gulps of air. She pulled away from him so she could speak.

"I'm supposed to be able to freeze time, but I can never do it right. And Professor Fraser said I needed to do well on his test this Friday or I'd be put on academic probation. And the classes are so hard for me, and I know I'm going to fail. And then . . . and then . . ." Her voice trailed off as she thought of Cat's lips on Joe's. "He kissed her," she squeaked out. "And . . . she's beautiful and sexy . . . and so I left because I don't belong at that school."

Fleet did a double take. "He as in Joe? He did what?"

"He kissed her! And so I left!" She pulled up her sleeve and showed him her tattoo. "And I thought this stupid tag would transfer to someone else when I stepped through that stupid portal, but it didn't! And now there's some stupid challenge I have to complete or the whole stupid campus might go to shit!"

She wiped here face with the sleeves of her hoodie. She gazed up at the bright half-moon. There was so much sadness inside of her, she could barely breathe.

"And it's almost Thanksgiving, and I don't even have a family to go home to."

A hush seemed to fall down around Infiniti as unbearable pain worked its way through her. The wind stilled. The roar of the nearby waterfall seemed to mute for a bit. It was as if all of nature could feel her pain and quieted in a sign of solidarity.

"Listen, Tiny. Family for you may have changed, but you know you have a home with Lyra as long as you want. There are good people in Havenwood Falls, and I have a feeling they'll always be there for you. As for Joe, I spent a lot of time with him in Houston when he was looking for you. You're the only one for him. So I don't know what you saw, but I bet there's a good explanation."

She wanted to believe Fleet more than anything, but she couldn't deny what she had seen.

"I don't know, Fleet," she whispered.

"Yes, you do." He let that sink in for a bit before he went on.

"And school can suck, I get it. And I don't know anything about this tattoo challenge business, but I'm thinking you can handle it. I mean, the school labeled you a Transhuman."

When the school officially admitted her as a student and labeled her a Transhuman, she hadn't really thought about what it meant. She was just thrilled to be a part of something so new and exciting, and to be with Joe. Maybe that was why she was struggling so much. She had no idea who she was anymore.

"I guess, if I knew what that meant."

"Well then, let me give you the condensed version. A Transhuman can control the energy in and around them. It's a power that comes from utilizing the full capacity of our brains. We can do a lot of pretty incredible things with energy, and some of us have specialized abilities. My specialty is tracking and transporting; my brother Farrell's specialty is healing. Yours must be time manipulation. And it must be something that was awakened in you from all the time-jumping you've done. It's pretty fucking kick-ass, if you ask me."

She let the explanation sink in for a minute. "Wow," she muttered. "I never really thought about all that. So how do I control it? Or make it work?"

Fleet put his hands on her shoulders. "You have to figure that part out."

Her mouth fell open. "What do you mean, I have to figure it out? What kind of advice is that?"

Fleet smiled. "It's the kind that's gonna make you fight." He stepped back. "You're a fighter, Tiny. Tough and scrappy. I've seen you in action." He pointed at the building Infiniti had come from. "Now go back to that fucking school and show them what you're fucking made of."

She turned and looked at the structure. Her mind filled with the image of the three arched mirrors that transformed into portals when activated. She brought her gaze back to Fleet, but he was gone. She stared at the empty spot where he'd been standing.

"I really hate it when you do that," she muttered.

Any alcohol that had been in her system from the Forever-Ever Clear Beer had completely worn off. The cold air had started to chill her to the bone. She wrapped her arms around herself and shivered. Fleet was right. She had to go back—for her friends and most of all for herself. Her mother didn't raise a quitter. And then she thought of her neighbor Jan and how she said easy peasy for things that were anything but easy.

"This is one of those easy peasy things," she muttered out loud. "I can do easy peasy. Or at least, I can try really hard."

And then the image of Joe with Cat sprang to mind. She shuddered, but she also knew Fleet was right. There had to be an explanation for Joe kissing Cat. There just had to be.

She glanced at the nearby trees that held onto thick clumps of snow. Patches of snow dotted the stone ground. She eyed her duffle bag, ready to pick it up and head back, when she saw Joe emerge from the building. He raced over to her.

"Infiniti!"

His face took on an expression of relief, but all Infiniti could do was see him with Cat. Anger worked through her, and before she could stop herself she slapped him with every ounce of strength she had.

He covered his face with his hand and stared at her in disbelief.

"Wow." He lost his words for a minute. "I deserved that. I know. But please hear me out."

Infiniti cradled her throbbing hand with her other one while hot tears stung her eyes. "How could you do that to me? *How?*"

He approached her with caution. "Babe, I promise you. Cat came up from behind me and kissed me. As soon as I realized it was her, I pushed her away." He inched closer. "Please believe me. I would never, ever do anything to hurt you. Not in a million years. I belong to you." He clutched his hand over his heart. "Forever until the day I die I will belong to you. You know that, Infiniti."

Infiniti looked up at his beautiful face, his hazel green eyes brimming with emotion. She knew he was telling the truth, and her heart burst with so much love for him, it filled her completely.

He belonged to her, and she belonged to him. She knew that. She felt that. And she should've known better.

"Oh, Joseph," she whispered.

He cupped her face with his strong hands and brought his mouth to hers. He brushed his lips over hers ever so lightly and whispered, "Infiniti, I am yours. Forever."

She loved the way he called her Infiniti when everyone else called her Fin. And she especially loved the way he made her feel inside. Tingles raced up and down her body while she breathed in his breath. Parting her lips, her senses were drowned in every connection they made. They kissed with love and passion and longing. Over and over they explored each other's mouths, neither one of them wanting to break from the other. After a while, their kisses slowed down, but they stayed in a tight embrace.

She had never had a serious boyfriend before, had never done anything but kiss, but in that moment she knew she wanted to give herself to Joe completely. He would be her first and her last. All she needed was the right time. And standing by the portal to campus with the sands of her hourglass tattoo running, the timing couldn't have been worse. And then she remembered she hadn't yet told him about her tattoo.

"Oh my God, Joe. My hourglass activated."

He pulled up her sleeve and saw the fully inked hourglass and the running sand. He flashed a worried glance at her. "Damn, the sands are running fast."

She focused on the spilling grains, noticing their high speed. "Shit, you're right."

Puffs of vapor escaped Joe's lips as he processed their situation. "We need to go back, like right now."

She thought of all the crap that had already happened on campus. Spirits invading the school, vampire attacks, killer beasts, a water monster in the lake, and that wasn't even the half of it. Her mind raced as she imagined worse things than that.

He squeezed her hand. "You ready for this?"

She wasn't ready at all, not by a long shot, but she had to go.

She needed to prove her place, no matter how scared she was. And they needed to hurry. Time was not on their side.

She swallowed. "Absolutely not."

"Me neither."

He picked up her bag and together they made their way back to the portal. Staring at the swirly mist, Infiniti wondered what fresh hell awaited her on the other side.

She was about to find out.

CHAPTER 7

Hand in hand with Infiniti, Joe stepped through the portal. They were met by a small group standing around the Valkyrie statue. The murmuring in the vaulted chamber hushed when the crowd saw the pair. Joe figured they'd found out about Infiniti's tattoo.

"You guys know?" Joe asked

Kase stepped forward. "Elle and I saw the activated hourglass in the courtyard after we left the party. Since no one else claimed it, we figured Fin's tattoo must've fully etched on her skin, so we went to her room right away."

"And I had to tell them where you went," Taylor added. "I'm sorry, Joe. But we were all so worried."

"It's okay," Joe said. "I would've done the same thing."

Taylor moved closer to her roommate. "You all right?"

Infiniti hugged Taylor. "Yeah. I'm just a little freaked out now that my challenge has started."

"Good, now don't ever leave again," Taylor admonished. "Okay?"

"I won't." She smiled.

Joe scanned the crowd. His pack-mates—Kase, Willa, Maria

627

and Ana—were there. Others from Jory Tower were there, too—Vid, Tyr, Roxy, Caleb, Clay, and D.

Joe rubbed the back of his neck while he gathered his thoughts. "Has anything happened yet? Any sign of the threat?"

"No, nothing," Kase answered. "Just the hourglass showing up and tipping in the courtyard."

"Well, nothing that we know of," Willa offered. "But there is a sizeable group forming in the courtyard."

Calming himself, Joe faced Infiniti. This was her challenge, and she needed to take the lead. Whatever she decided, he'd support her to the death.

"What do you want to do?"

The space between her eyes wrinkled. He could tell she was calculating her first move.

"We got your back, Fin," Taylor encouraged.

"Hell yeah, we do," Clay added.

She nodded while a look of appreciation and gratitude spread across her face. She drew in a deep breath. "We should gather by the hourglass in the courtyard. I need to compare it to my tattoo. Then we need to send out groups to try and identify whatever danger has been set on the campus. We need to figure out what we're up against, and we need to hurry." She lifted her sleeve. "The sands are running fast."

Roxy and Taylor stepped forward and eyed the tattoo. Roxy sucked in her breath. "That's not good. Mine was never that fast."

"Mine wasn't either," Taylor added.

"Exactly," Infiniti added. "And since everything having to do with me is a little out of the norm, we can't exactly handle my challenge like the others. So instead of waiting for something to happen, I think we need to seek it out."

Light murmuring filled the space. A few "this is our house" and "we got this" chants sprinkled throughout the small crowd. Everyone seemed pumped. And maybe it had to do with the unlimited supply of drinks everyone had just been chugging.

Joe clapped his hands. "All right then! Let's do this!"

Everyone filed out of the chamber. Joe stayed extra close to Infiniti and took her hand. "Good idea."

She squeezed back. "Thanks."

Joe kept a keen eye on the space all around them, as if a demon or some other deadly being might attack as they walked across campus, which was totally within the realm of possibility. They'd seen a lot of crazy shit already.

Stone pillars with bowls of fire on top lit the path from the portal along the river and across the bridge to the courtyard. They worked their way to the center of the quad where the hourglasses usually appeared once activated.

"There," Joe pointed. "I see something."

The object came into view as they got closer, and Infiniti halted in place. She gasped, tightening her hand around Joe's and holding him in a death grip. "It can't be."

Joe eyed Infiniti. He knew that sometimes the hourglass and how it was displayed reflected the challenger. But staring at the setup, he thought it looked ordinary. The all-glass hourglass that was about a foot tall sat on top of a simple wooden table.

"What is it?" Joe asked, wondering what was so special about the piece of furniture.

Infiniti dropped his hand. She slowly walked over to the table. When she neared, she knelt to the ground. Joe motioned for everyone to stay back as he went to her and joined her on her knees. She was staring at the table in disbelief, her face set in an expression of pained surprise. He watched her gently touch the wood grain with her fingertips.

"This table is from my house," she whispered.

Joe's mind took him back to that moment when he had time traveled and appeared in front of Infiniti's house. The two-story structure had been blazing with flames. He remembered dashing inside and finding Infiniti passed out. He had scooped her up from the ground and brought her out. Infiniti had lost so much in that fire—her mom, her belongings, things she'd had her entire life.

He put his arm around her. "Infiniti, I'm so sorry."

A lone tear trickled down the side of her face. She wiped it away, then faced him. "So much has been taken from me, Joe. So much."

"I know."

With her hands still on the table, he watched as she slowly formed two fists. "I'm not losing anything else. I can't." She rose to her feet, working her jaw as a look of determination spread across her face. "I'm going to kick this challenge's ass."

"Absolutely, you are."

He was relieved to hear her fighting spirit return, but alarmed that the hourglass was already half-empty. As if mirroring his thoughts, she pulled up her sleeve and compared it to the hourglass.

"Oh no," she muttered.

"I know. Whatever is going to happen is going to happen soon, if it hasn't already."

She lowered her sleeve, scanning the dimly lit courtyard. "Can you and your pack make a perimeter check? Do you think Willa will go for it?"

Joe hesitated. He hated the idea of shifting and leaving Infiniti's side, but he knew she was right. They needed to find the danger, and he and his pack were best suited to make a sweep of the campus. And since Willa was the alpha, everything needed to go through her. But he knew she'd be all over it.

"Yeah, she'll do it. You just need to ask."

Joe and Infiniti walked back to the group, and Infiniti started explaining her plan. "We need to find the threat. Willa, can you and Joe and the pack do a sweep of the campus?"

Willa stepped forward with her hands on her hips. "Of course."

"I can shift into my lightning bird and scan from above," D offered.

"Great," Infiniti said. "Thank you, D."

Joe nodded at D, grateful to have his help. With Willa and the pack on the ground and D in the air, Joe thought they'd find the threat pretty quickly.

"Let's head out," Willa ordered, signaling the pack with a tick of her chin as they started walking away from Infiniti and the others. D broke away, too.

Joe looked over his shoulder at his one true love. Her long brown hair framed her perfect face. She was petite and delicate, but in that moment she stood tall and strong. His heart swelled with pride at her bravery and determination.

He, Kase, Willa, Maria, and Ana moved out of the lighted pathway and into the darkness. The cool air against Joe's face invigorated him. The energy building inside of him raced through his veins. He couldn't wait to shift.

"What's the plan?" Joe asked Willa.

"We'll split the campus in half. You and Kase take the east side from Ansgar II all the way to Clifftop. Maria, Ana, and I will take the west, starting with the beach. We'll meet you at Clifftop."

Joe thought of their professors. They usually stayed out of the way because whenever they tried to help, it backfired. He thought it best to remind the others. "And avoid the faculty building."

"Of course," Willa said, breaking away with Maria and Ana. "Avoid the profs."

Joe was grateful to have his pack with him, especially Kase, his best friend. They'd been through a lot together, and being with him now gave him a sense of comfort and confidence.

"You ready?" Joe asked him.

"Yep."

"Then let's go."

They broke into a run. Joe's heartbeat drummed within his ears. His muscles strained and flexed. He growled, feeling exhilarated and deadly as he let the animal inside him break free. Teeth baring and claws out, fur rippled up and down his body as he dropped to all fours in a flash. With Kase also shifted, the two wolves bounded their way across campus. His sharp eyes examined every inch of space around him. His ears picked up the smallest sounds. He spotted D overhead, soaring and swooping as he surveyed from above.

So far, nothing appeared out of the ordinary, and that scared the hell out of Joe. What were they up against?

Joe huffed, slowing down his pace, and Kase followed suit. They crisscrossed the entire east side of the campus, roaming around every stalagmite and structure in their path. Still, they found nothing. After a while, he and Kase met Willa, Maria, and Ana at Clifftop. They gathered around, signaling to each other with their barking and huffing that nothing had been spotted. Joe thought they should report back to the others. Willa must've had the same idea because she jerked her muzzle to the right and then to the left, letting the others know to flank out as they returned back.

In a straight line, and still on high alert, they spaced out so they could cover more ground and trotted back to where they had left Infiniti and the others. The hazy glow from overhead told Joe that day was breaking. He thought that was good. It'd be a lot easier to spot dangers in the day than at night.

They were almost to the courtyard when shouting rang out. Joe howled, racing back to Infiniti with lightning speed. And when the hollering sounded again, the pack redirected course. The din was coming from Jory Tower—Infiniti's tower.

Joe's heart lodged in his throat. Fear prickled his skin. He ran with furious panic.

Infiniti, please be okay.

Infiniti and the others had been waiting by the hourglass, nervous and on edge about the challenge that had started but hadn't yet shown itself.

"When is it gonna happen?" Infiniti asked Taylor, moving around in circles and rubbing her hands together, grateful to have her best friend with her. "And what more should I do? I feel like I should be doing something."

"I think the smartest thing right now is to wait for intel."

"I guess," Infiniti blew out.

Taylor gave Infiniti a soft elbow poke. "Be cool, but look behind you."

Trying to be subtle, Infiniti glanced over her shoulder and saw Cat huddled with vamps Molly Shaw and Marcia Lawson. The trio was super powerful and super bitchy. Infiniti wondered if they had seen Cat kissing Joe at the party. They probably had. But did they know that Infiniti had seen? When Cat kissed Joe she was facing the opposite direction, so there was no way she could've seen Infiniti coming out of the bathroom. Not that it really mattered. Cat knew Joe was her boyfriend.

Infiniti turned back around. "I can't think about her right now."

"You're right," Taylor conceded. "We'll get through this and *then* we'll kick her ass."

Infiniti and Taylor were probably the most petite girls on campus, and the image of them getting into a fight with long-legged Cat was kinda funny. They'd seen her physicality in combat training, and she was tough as nails. Them, not so much. They started laughing at the absurdity of them fighting with Cat when a piercing scream cut through the night. Everyone faced the direction of the sound.

Infiniti and Taylor looked at each other. "Jory!"

Everyone started running to Jory Tower. And when they got there, Infiniti couldn't believe her eyes. The top floor of Jory was disappearing, as if someone had a giant magical eraser and had started rubbing it out of existence.

Infiniti slapped her hands over her mouth.

"Oh my God," she said between her fingers.

People were running out of the tower, some of them barely clothed. More shouting rang out as confusion and mayhem took over.

Infiniti found her voice and started yelling, "Get out! Everyone needs to get out!"

Joe and his pack exploded onto the scene, barking and howling, agitated and on edge about the phenomenon.

Infiniti needed someone to use their powers to go in and make sure everyone came out. She spun around. "Someone needs to go in there!"

"On it!" Tyr said, summoning his god power and disappearing into the building in a burst of light.

"Me too," Vid, the Valkyrie hybrid called out. He ripped his shirt off and let his massive wings unfold from his back, taking flight in a whoosh.

Infiniti reached down for Joe's neck and buried her fingers in his thick fur. She pressed her legs against his body, getting as close to him as possible.

"I don't know what to do," she whispered, watching helplessly as the tower slowly disappeared from the top.

Tyr reappeared with someone in his arms, disappeared, and then reappeared with someone else. Vid was flying back and forth with people, too. There was so much commotion and chaos that it took Infiniti a while to notice D overhead, circling low, squawking with fervor.

"He's saying the other towers are disappearing!" Cat yelled.

Infiniti whipped around to face the Transhuman. She had no idea what she could or couldn't do, but right then she figured Cat was right because D was going berserk.

Cat grabbed Infiniti's arm. "Let me help, por favor."

She didn't want to trust Cat, but Infiniti didn't have time to argue. It was an all-hands-on-deck situation. "Fine. Whatever you can do."

Cat nodded, signaled to Molly and Marcia, and the three blurred away as they took off at lightning speed. D spread his enormous wings and flew after them. And then Tyr and Vid were suddenly in front of her, huffing from exertion.

"We got everyone out that we could find," Vid said.

Infiniti's heart stopped. A blast of icy fear raced down her back. "Everyone that you could find?" She glanced down at Joe then back at Tyr and Vid. "What does that mean?"

"The top floor is completely gone, and we don't know if anyone was up there," Tyr answered, looking visibly shaken.

Infiniti clutched the fabric of her sweatshirt at her neck and gathered it into a ball. People were dying? No, no, no . . . that wasn't supposed to happen. It couldn't be happening.

Cat, Molly, and Marcia zipped back to the group in a blur. They slowed to a halt.

"The other towers are disappearing," Cat rushed out. "Todos. And everyone is doing what we're doing. Trying to get people out. Brielle and Elliana are flying people out like Tyr and Vid were doing, but they need help."

"Oh my god," Infiniti whispered, in full panic mode. She lifted up her sleeve, and examined the hourglass. The bottom was now two-thirds full, and Infiniti had no idea what to do.

Taylor and Elle clutched each other, groups huddled nearby,

and everyone watched as Jory continued fading away. The scene reminded Infiniti of the movie *The Titanic*, the part where the people in the boats were watching with horror as the ship sank into the ocean. She felt like those people, terrified and helpless. There wasn't a happy ending for that ship. Maybe there wouldn't be a happy ending for SMA either.

Infiniti noticed Rhian close by, standing apart from the others. She was a student that Infiniti would see from time to time around SMA but didn't have any classes with. Her braided hair and dreadlocks were piled high on her head. Thick eyeliner encased her big, blue eyes. She tilted her head, in an almost disapproving way, as if wondering if Infiniti could do anything to overcome her challenge.

Feeling a little pissed, but mostly thinking Rhian was right, Infiniti turned away from the girl. A nudge moved her hand, and she looked down at Joe. He pressed his snout against her and pushed again, this time harder, his green eyes telling her that he believed in her.

"Okay," she said out loud, trying to work the problem and not freak out. "My thing is freezing time. Or, at least it's supposed to be. So that means I need to actually do it. Freeze time." She wrung her hands together while she processed. "I need to freeze whatever is happening to the towers so I can save everyone. And I need to do it right now."

Joe stomped his paws and huffed, giving his approval.

She squeezed the top of his neck, then walked closer to Jory. She turned and faced the crowd.

"Okay, everyone, I'm going to freeze what's happening to the tower, and then we can figure out what to do next. You should all probably get back a little."

"You got this, Fin," Taylor called out as she backed up.

Willa let out a bark, and the packed moved back. Except for Joe. He stayed by Infiniti's side.

"Okay," she said out loud. "Let's do this thing."

Infiniti turned back around to face the vanishing tower. The rooftop and now the top two floors were gone. Only eight remained. She needed to act fast.

She closed her eyes, thinking of everything she had learned in Dr. Fraser's class. She focused on her center. She slowed her breathing. She extended her arms, holding her hands palms facing out. She envisioned the tower freezing in time.

"Stop," she commanded, repeating the directive over and over in head.

She held her position. She clenched her teeth. She focused with laser determination on each floor of Jory, and then she envisioned the entire campus. Convinced she'd done enough, and filled with the hope that she'd been able to stop Jory and the other towers from disappearing, she opened her eyes. But the tower was still vanishing. Her stomach dropped. She started to face her friends to see if they had any ideas when a whirring sounded overhead.

She gazed up and saw a flurry of black and white feathers careening her way. D was plummeting to the ground as he spun out of control. Infiniti darted out of the way as the six-foot magnificent lightning bird thudded against the ground. The tip of his magnificent wing clipped her legs, and she crashed down on her knees.

She stayed still for a few seconds, catching her breath, then crawled over to D.

"D," she said, hovering her hands over his sprawled out form because she was afraid to touch him. "D, are you okay?" His eyes were open and unflinching. "Taylor! Help!"

She didn't respond.

"Joe!"

Still nothing.

In a panic, she whipped around to face her friends. They were motionless. All of them. And that's when she realized she had frozen everything *but* the tower.

*I*nfiniti's body shook. Fear gripped her. If she hadn't cried so much earlier, she'd probably be bawling. Instead, stunned disbelief overtook her. She rose to her feet and shuffled over to Joe. He was looking up, eyes wide, ears in the radar position. He had heard something, probably D falling. Staring at his motionless form and the still bodies around her, all she wanted to do was fix them. But how? She wrapped her arms around Joe's neck and hugged him.

"Oh, Joe. What did I do?"

"You froze them."

Infiniti raised her head. She recognized the thick Spanish accent right away and saw Cat winding her way through the bodies, examining them as she passed by. She even snapped her fingers in front of some of the faces.

"Estan congelados," she said.

Infiniti watched her nemesis move closer. How was it possible that the one person she wanted to be frozen was the only one who wasn't? Talk about bad luck.

"Yeah," Infiniti said, figuring Cat was saying in Spanish what she had just said in English. "I can see that they're frozen. So your statement of the obvious is not helping."

Cat raised an eyebrow, but continued working her way over to Infiniti. "I get that you hate me. I don't blame you. But can we put that aside and solve this problem? I'd like to not die."

She'd like to not die? Infiniti's blood boiled. The nerve of her only being worried about herself. She got up in Cat's face. "Listen, Cat. You are a bitch, okay? A fucking bitch, so back off unless you can help because I want us *all* to not die."

Infiniti shrunk back a little, surprised at her courage because she usually avoided confrontation. But then a touch of regret settled in. She drew in a deep breath, feeling bad about what she'd said. Even if Cat had kissed Joe, it wasn't in her nature to be a bitch to a bitch.

"Please, Cat. Leave me alone unless you can help."

She turned away from Cat. Thinking about her tattoo, she pulled up her sleeve. The sands were running even faster now. She examined Jory. Another floor had vanished. That left seven remaining. She was pretty sure that when it totally disappeared, it would be game over. She couldn't let that happen, but what could she do?

Cat circled around and stood in front of Infiniti. She had her hands on her hips. "I propose a truce while we figure this out."

As much as Infiniti hated to admit it, Cat was right. They needed to work together, and a truce sounded like a good solution. She could go back to hating Cat later.

"Fine, truce."

The pair stood side by side, both of them examining Jory.

"I wonder what's happening to the other towers," Infiniti whispered. Even though they were outside, it was too dark to see Muninn or Modi.

"Want me to go check again?"

Infiniti was pretty sure the same thing that was happening to Jory was happening to the other towers, so investigating wouldn't solve anything. "No. We should stay here. If we can fix Jory, we can fix the others."

"Claro," Cat said.

"Claro?" Infiniti asked.

"Sí, claro. That means clearly."

"Oh," Infiniti said. She had learned a lot of Spanish hanging with her best friend Trent and his mom and grandmother back in Houston, but had never heard that word. She wondered how they were for a few seconds but quickly forced herself to focus. She didn't have time for sadness. She went back to examining the structure when the simplest of ideas came to her.

"I've got it. I just need to reverse what I did." She motioned with her hands in a big circle. "Like a redo."

"A redo?"

"Yeah, a do-over."

Cat rubbed her chin. "Do you even know what you did?"

Of course she didn't know what she did, so she focused on the literal. "Well, I was thinking of the building and repeating the word *stop* in my head. So I'll do the same thing, but think of the word *start.*" She thought the plan sounded good enough, but needed reassurance. "Right? You think that's good?"

"Sure." Cat nodded, but added a small shrug as if she really wasn't sure. "I say we try. Why not?"

Infiniti looked at Joe's white wolf, desperate to revive him and others.

"Okay," Infiniti said. "Here goes nothing."

A cold breeze swept over Infiniti, sending shivers up and down her body. She looked up at the massive skylight over the campus. The thick darkness had started giving way to daylight, revealing the incredible stalactites hanging down from above. Some of them on the outer edges of the campus were so enormous they touched the stalagmites protruding from the cave ground. When she had first walked onto campus, she had been so awestruck by the magnificence, she almost cried. The grandeur and beauty of nature was more than magical to her; it was heavenly. But now, standing with frozen bodies all around her while the towers on campus disappeared, she was terrified.

"Come on, chica," Cat urged.

"Sorry," Infiniti whispered.

Swallowing her worries and doubts, she raised her arms and

held out her palms. She closed her eyes. *Please let this work*, she thought, then said out loud, "Start."

She put all her focus on the word start, repeating it over and over in her head while she thought of her friends unfreezing.

"¡Dios mio, ya!"

Infiniti snapped her eyes open. She dropped her arms. Looking out at her friends, she saw that half of them were missing.

"Holy shit, what happened?"

"They vanished," Cat said in a quivering voice. She clutched Infiniti's arm, and the two of them stood together, dumbstruck. And when D's glorious bird disappeared into thin air, they both yelled.

"I-I-I didn't mean for them to start disappearing," Infiniti said, her throat so tight she could hardly get the words out.

Cat made the sign of the cross and started mumbling words in Spanish Infiniti couldn't make out. But she didn't need to hear them to know that her nemesis was praying. Infiniti believed in prayer, too, but she wasn't ready to concede anything, and prayer to her felt like an action of finality.

Infiniti went to Joe, who hadn't disappeared yet. She knelt beside him and put her arms around his neck, pressing her face next to his.

"I need you," she whispered. "So badly."

Snuggling against his fur, she thought that if he could, he'd tell her to keep trying and to not give up. That there was still time. The tower hadn't completely vanished. There were still students who hadn't yet disappeared. She just needed to figure out what to do.

"I need to stop everything and bring everyone and everything back," she whispered to him. "Like chasing time. I need to somehow go back to the beginning of all this." She paused while an idea sprang to mind. "The beginning," she muttered. She hurried over to Cat. "The beginning of all this!"

"The beginning?" Cat stitched her brows. "What do you mean?"

The words spilled out of Infiniti fast while her mouth tried to keep up with her brain. "Dr. Fraser gave me a book to help me pass his skills test. I was flipping through it, and I remember reading something about going back to the beginning."

Cat perked up. "Where is it?"

Infiniti gulped. "In my room."

The girls held hands. They faced Jory. Cat squeezed Infiniti's fingers. "What floor is your room?"

The once grand stone structure stood tall and amazing. Now it looked like a scene out of a supernatural horror story, the erasing of the floors almost reaching Infiniti's.

"I'm on the second floor, the floor just above the Commons. The last remaining floor of rooms."

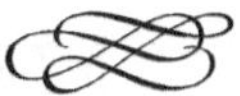

The horror of going into the spelled tower gripped Infiniti. Her courage had almost completely drained. But this was it. She needed to do something or die, and she believed that book could help.

"I'll go get it," Cat offered. "I can be in and out in a few seconds. Muy rapido. Just tell me where it is."

Infiniti's mind raced as she thought of her cluttered and disorganized half of the room. She pressed her fingers against her lips. "Oh, shit. Where *did* I put it?" Her mind picked apart everything she'd done after Dr. Fraser gave her the book "Maybe my desk? Or my bed?"

"Okay." Cat nodded. "I'll be right back."

Before she could pull away, Infiniti stopped her. "No, no, no. I have to do it. Only Jory residents can gain access from this level. Plus, my side of the room is a disaster."

Cat considered her request. "We go together, then. Juntas."

More friends were disappearing as the tower kept erasing. There was no time to argue. "Okay, fine."

Infiniti took one last look at Joe, then ran with Cat toward the hidden entry to Jory. She placed her palm flat on the stone and said, "Angrdroba." The doorway parted and a deep vibrational hum filled her ears. The girls dashed over clumps of debris as they made their way to the inner stairwell that led to the commons. Cutting across the open room, Infiniti spotted the oversized stone clock in the center of the room. The hands had stopped moving and were frozen like her friends.

"Faster," Cat urged.

Pushing herself forward, Infiniti grunted while she forced herself to pick up the pace, pumping her arms with fierce determination. Luckily, they only had to race up one flight of stairs to get to her room. They rounded the corner with speed and practically tumbled into her room.

"Search my desk for a small brown book," Infiniti rushed out.

Cat started sifting through her desk while Infiniti picked apart her bed and closet.

"Here!" Cat announced, holding the book out to Infiniti. "This is it, right?"

Infiniti took it as if it were the Holy Grail itself. "Yes, this is it."

She was about to open it up when Cat interrupted her. "Hold on, Fin. Necesito confesarte halgo."

"Huh?"

"I need to confess to you something."

Infiniti gulped. People confessed things when they thought they were dying. She did not want Cat to think they were dying. She held up her hands to stop Cat. "No, no, no. Don't you do that."

"I saw you go into the bathroom, Fin. At the party. And I kissed Joe at the exact moment you walked out so you could see."

Infiniti lowered the book. "You wanted me to see? Why?"

Cat's eyes watered over. "Because I wanted you to break up with him, so I could have a chance at being with him. I've never had a guy love me, or want to protect me, or want to die for me. I've always been alone." Her bottom lip quivered. "You don't know the pain of being alone and for such a long time." A tear trailed down her cheek, and she wiped it away fast. "I kissed Joe because I didn't want to be alone anymore. And before we die I need you to know and I need you to forgive me. Lo siento mucho. Can you please forgive me?"

A wave of sympathy washed over Infiniti. She was ready to hate Cat forever, but now she felt sorry for her. "Of course I forgive you. And you're not alone. You've got a whole family here at SMA, if you'll just let us in."

They hugged tightly, as if they were old friends meeting after a long absence.

Infiniti released Cat. "Now let's get to work, okay? Because we are not dying."

Infiniti opened the book. She started scanning the table of contents. "Cat, come closer so you can help me look."

Cat didn't answer. Infiniti looked at her, but she was gone.

Infiniti's stomach dropped. Her hands shook. She peered up and saw her ceiling disappearing, the moon and stars mural Taylor had magically created fading away in patches. She forced her attention back to the table of contents.

"Come on," she pleaded out loud, scanning the chapter titles. "Where's the part about reversing time and going back to the beginning!" But the titles were super long and confusing, and she felt like she was chasing the impossible. She hollered and chucked the book against the wall. She slumped down to the ground.

"I'm done," she whispered.

Her gaze swept her room as she examined everything that would soon disappear when she spotted the squishy pineapple Dr. Lavinia had given her. She started to lunge for it when she noticed something else. The clock next to her bed was working.

"Everything is frozen and disappearing, but the one thing that's still working is my clock?" She studied the moving second hand. "Right before I stepped through the portal I said I wanted to disappear. But I didn't. Then my challenge activated and the towers froze and then my friends started disappearing." She sprang to her feet. "It's me! I don't need to focus on the towers or my friends. I need to focus on me! I need to stop chasing time and instead call upon what's inside of me!"

She lowered herself back down to the ground and forced

herself to focus on the clock while ignoring her vanishing room and the vibrations that shook her body through to the core. She closed her eyes. She thought of Joe and how much he filled her heart and soul. She thought of how much she cared for Taylor and the rest of her friends. Even Cat. She thought of her Houston friends, her neighbor Jan, and lastly she thought about her mom. She missed her so much. Focusing on all the love, she imagined a frozen clock, the same size as the one by her bed. But it wasn't a regular device, it was magical and it represented herself. And she needed to fix it.

She blew out.

She calmed her nerves.

She envisioned herself touching the minute hand and the hour hand, repairing everything that was broken.

"Go back to working," she whispered. "Go back to the way everything was."

The vibrations stopped. A thick stillness filled Infiniti's ears. Was she dead? She pried open her eyes, afraid to see what had happened, and discovered her room looking totally normal. Solid walls surrounded her, and the dust and debris that had fallen from above had vanished.

"You did it!" Cat said, dropping to her knees and hugging Infiniti.

Infiniti hugged her back, slowly at first, then gripped her tighter. "Oh my god, Cat. You're back."

They stayed like that for a long moment before pulling apart. They shared a look of understanding, a moment of peace, and an unspoken promise that no matter what happened, they'd always be there for each other.

Joe came running into the room in wolf form and skidded to a stop. He blinked, looking from Infiniti to Cat.

"I see your man is here," Cat said to Infiniti. She got up and dusted off her leather pants. She straightened her back and flipped her hair over her shoulder. "See you later," she said, leaving the room.

Infiniti couldn't help but smile as Cat put on her old persona.

But she had seen the real her. She knew who she really was. And she'd never forget it.

Joe moved in, and Infiniti crouched down next to him. He pressed his head against Infiniti's, snuggling into her as he rested his chin on her shoulder. She wrapped her arms around him and held on for dear life.

"Oh, Joe," she whispered.

Kase came in the room, also in wolf form. Behind him were Taylor and Caleb. They gathered around Infiniti while a slew of other students crowded the doorway. Murmuring filled the room while everyone started chattering.

"What happened?" Taylor asked. "How did you stop it?

Infiniti released Joe. She wanted to tell her friends what had happened, but also didn't know how to explain what had happened. "Well, I changed my focus. And it worked."

"Break it up, break it up," Addie said, squeezing her way through the small crowd. She entered Infiniti's room dressed in ripped jeans, a white shirt, and a black leather jacket. Her hair was pulled up in a loose bun. She eyed Infiniti from over her dark-rimmed glasses. She wore a serious stare on her face that slowly gave way to a proud smile.

"Congratulations, Infiniti. You did it."

Infiniti rose to her feet, but kept her hand on Joe. "Thank you, Addie."

Everyone started clapping and cheering. Addie shushed the crowd. "All right, all right. Everyone, back to your normal routines. It's Thursday morning, and there's still plenty of time for everyone to make it to their classes. Remember, Thanksgiving break begins tomorrow after the last class. You can celebrate this victory later."

She crossed her arms, then followed the last student out, leaving Infiniti and Joe alone.

Infiniti needed Joe's arms around her. Craved his lips on hers. She locked the door so he could change into the clothes he kept stashed there, but stayed facing away. She'd never seen him naked.

She heard the familiar grinding of muscles and low growling as

Joe shifted back, then heard him open the dresser and slip on his jeans.

"Come here," he said, tugging at her fingers and pulling her around. His pants were unbuckled. His chest was bare. She placed her hands on his hard abs.

"I thought it was all over," she said.

"Me too." He slipped his hands around her waist. "I'm so glad it's not. I really wanted more time with you."

He kissed her with so much love and passion, she thought she'd melt in his arms. Their kissing grew deeper when someone knocked. Joe pressed his lips against hers and whispered, "Don't answer."

"Fin?"

It was Taylor. Joe groaned under his breath, then stepped away from Infiniti while he buckled his pants.

"Uh, give me a sec," Infiniti said.

Joe slipped his shirt on, and she opened the door.

"Hey," Taylor said, looking a little sheepish for interrupting them. "Sorry to bother you. Wanted to let you guys know that everyone is gathering for a huge breakfast. Apparently we're all starving after the party and near-death after party." She laughed.

"You want to go?" Infiniti asked Joe.

Joe hooked his finger around Infiniti's belt loop. "Up to you."

"Well, are you hungry?" she asked Joe.

"I could eat."

She was definitely up for a meal. Plus, after everything they'd been through, she wanted to see everyone. Make sure with her own eyes that everyone was really okay.

"Let's go. It'll be good to see everyone. Plus, I'm a little bit starving."

"Sounds good," Joe said with a smile. "But I'll need to go to my room and get some shoes." He wiggled his toes. "So I'll see you ladies there."

Joe took off to Heimdall Tower, and Infiniti and Taylor made their way to Halstein Hall and the dining room. And when Infiniti walked in, everyone started cheering. Blood rushed to her cheeks, and her eyes blurred over. She had been through so much in such a little time with all the people at SMA, and she loved them all. Even the ones she didn't like that much. They were a family, and they belonged together. She motioned for everyone to stop, and then she and Taylor sat with their usual friends from Jory Tower. And when Joe showed up, he joined her, and together they had the most amazingly scrumptious breakfast.

The day was filled with everyone doing their best in their classes, but mostly swapping stories about the party, about the towers and the students disappearing, and about how scared everyone was. There was even talk of having a "we survived" party on top of Hel again, but by the end of the day everyone was way too tired.

Later that night, lying in her bed, Infiniti thought of every terrible detail of what she had gone through, still amazed that they had made it.

"You want to talk about it?" Taylor asked in a low voice.

Infiniti shifted in her bed. "How could you tell?"

"Your thoughts are so loud, I can almost hear them."

Infiniti sighed. "You should hear them in my head."

"Tell me," Taylor said. She sat up in her bed, folded her legs, and wrapped her arms around them.

Infiniti let out a huge sigh. "Well, I really thought we were all gonna die. I mean, really and truly." She paused for a few seconds as her mind replayed that moment in her room when Cat disappeared. "I kept thinking about how much I love Joe and how I want to be with him forever."

"Wow," Taylor whispered.

"And then I was thinking that my mom had never met him, and it totally bummed me out. And all the pain from losing her just hit me something fierce."

Taylor sat up. "Oh my God, Fin, I can like totally help you with that."

Infiniti sat up too. "What?"

"I can communicate with spirits, and I can help you communicate with your mom."

Infiniti's heart jumped. "I can talk to her?"

Taylor flung off her covers. "Yep. Do you want to?"

Infiniti was on her feet. "I want!"

"Okay, let me set it up."

Taylor started rummaging through the things on her desk, pulling out her white candles. She set them around the room, struck a match, and lit each one. The darkness quickly gave way to dancing white light.

"Do you have something of your moms?"

Infiniti only had one thing from her mother—the silver and gold Christmas ornament keychain she had given her mom one year for Christmas. Fleet had salvaged it from their house and had given it to Infiniti the night of her SMA trials.

"I've got the perfect thing." She still hadn't unpacked her duffle bag from when she had left school. Diving into the bag, she fished out the keychain and handed it to Taylor.

"Perfect, but you keep it and hold it tight. Okay?"

"Yeah, okay."

"I will call your mom and bring her over from the other side. Once her spirit is in the room with us, I will lend my energy to her, which will allow her to be slightly visible. So you'll be able to see her, but you can't hear."

"So how will I talk to her?'

Taylor sat down on the ground and crossed her legs. "I'll be the messenger." She patted the plush rug that covered the stone ground between their beds. "Come sit in front of me."

Excitement and fear took hold of Infiniti, and she thought of all the times she'd played the Ouija board with her friends. She was scared then, and she was just as scared now. She sat in front of Taylor, crossing her legs like her roommate. Even though they were on the rug, the cold air seeped through from the stone floor, and she shivered.

"What do I do?" Infiniti asked in a whisper.

Taylor closed her eyes. "Focus on your mom. Picture her as if she were here. I'll do the rest."

Infiniti clutched the keychain, thinking of her mom—short

curly hair, big brown eyes, small nose, petite in size. She had the funniest sense of humor and a deep laugh for a small woman. If Taylor could really bring her mom over, she had so much to tell her.

Taylor's breathing hitched. She seemed to hold it for a while, and then blew out a slow steady breath.

"Got her," she said in a low voice.

Infiniti's gaze darted around the room when a shadowy figure appeared beside her. It was her mom, her eyes wide with surprise.

"Mom," Infiniti choked out while her eyes filled with tears.

Her mouth moved, but Infiniti couldn't hear her.

"My girl. My beautiful, sweet girl," Taylor said.

"Oh, Mom," Infiniti said, getting to her feet and standing close to the ghostly image. "I wish I could hug you."

She reached out to Infiniti, and her misty hand passed through Infiniti's body like a cool breeze. "I wish, too, my baby. More than anything."

Infiniti wiped the tears that covered her face. "I'm in college now. It's called Halvard, and it's in a mountain in a supernatural town. Apparently, I've got some powers."

"I know. I've been watching. And I'm so proud of you."

Taylor changed her tone of voice. Her eyes flinched as she struggled from her efforts. "Fin, I can't hold her much longer."

Infiniti's heart sped up. A twinge of panic struck her, forcing her to hurry with her words. "I met an amazing guy, Mom. His name is Joseph Greg, and I'm crazy in love. He's the one, and I'm pretty sure I'm going to marry him."

Infiniti's mom moved her hands and held them to her heart.

"He sounds wonderful. As long as he makes you happy, then I'm happy."

Her image started breaking up. Her translucent form wavered in and out of view. Infiniti reached out. "Mom! I love you!"

Her mom extended her shimmery arms, as if trying to take Infiniti's hands.

"I love you, too, my girl. So much. Now get on with your life. Do amazing things. And don't worry about me. I'll see you again."

The image faded away until any trace of her mom's spirit was gone. Infiniti sunk down to the floor. Her heart filled with seeing her mom, but also broken all over again at her loss.

Taylor reached out and took Infiniti's hands. "I felt the love and happiness, Fin. So when she said that she's okay and for you to move on, she meant it."

Infiniti nodded, then lunged forward and embraced her best friend.

<hr>

When Infiniti awoke the next day, she was ready to do as her mom had said. She was ready to move on—with her school, with her friends, and with her one true love, Joe. She was ready to do amazing things. But the top two things on her list for the day were seeing Dr. Fraser for her skills test and then Dr. Lavinia before she left for the break.

She had read the book Dr. Fraser let her borrow. She rewrote her notes from class two times. She had even talked to Harlow, Taylor's sister, for tips on freezing time. She was terrified and nervous, but had put in the hard work. So no matter what happened, she'd be okay with the results.

Making her way to Asketill Hall, Infiniti kept her pace light and her breathing steady. And when she got to Dr. Fraser's room, she took a seat in the front and waited for the Scottish professor to show up.

"Ah, Miss Clausman," Dr. Fraser said, breezing into the room wearing his multi-colored brown kilt with his satchel slung over his shoulder.

"Hey, Dr. Fraser."

He set his bag down. Instead of firing off instructions for the test like he usually did, he scooted his desk chair closer to her and sat down. He rubbed his stubbled face while studying her with his dreamy green eyes. She would have blushed, except she was so nervous about her test.

"I heard about your hourglass challenge, young lady."

Infiniti gulped. "Oh, yeah." And then, unsure of what else to say, she laughed and added, "Pretty neat, huh?"

"Pretty neat, indeed." He leaned forward. "I also think freezing your friends, then making them disappear, and then bringing them back and restoring the towers earns you a pretty neat A plus."

His words danced around her head for a minute before they sank in. "Um, what?"

He smiled wide. "You have earned an A plus on the skills test. Congratulations." He got up, reached for his bag, and slung it over his shoulder. "Enjoy your Thanksgiving Break."

Her heart jumped with joy as she sat there in a daze for a few seconds. "I will. You too!"

Her next stop was Dr. Lavinia's. When she got to Halstein Hall and the double doors, she stopped. She thought of the disappearing stairs. They reminded her of the towers. And then she thought of all the other stuff that had disappeared over the last two weeks when her tattoo was in hourglass limbo—her red scarf, her Cheetos, the entrance to the bathroom at the top of Hel, her backpack. Even Taylor and Joe had mentioned not being able to find things. She was pretty sure others had been missing things as well.

"Unbelievable," she muttered out loud, realizing it all had to have been linked. She wondered what other signs her challenge had been throwing at her that she had missed. She entered Halstein, rounded the corner and headed for the stairs, finding them as good as new. Magic definitely had its benefits.

"Hello, dear," Dr. Lavinia said, coming up from behind her.

"Hey, Dr. Lavinia. I was heading your way."

"And I was heading to meet you." She laughed. "Good timing!"

Once inside Dr. Lavinia's office, Infiniti took a seat in the swivel chair, and Dr. Lavinia sat behind her desk. Gizmo sprung up on the desk and tiptoed her way into Dr. Lavinia's lap.

"You've had quite an eventful few days, Fin," the doc said while stroking her pet.

"You have no idea." Relaxing in her seat, Infiniti started recounting everything that had happened. And when she got to the part about believing in herself, she eyed the painted phrase over the credenza.

Dr. Lavinia looked over her shoulder at the saying. And when she brought her attention back to Infiniti, she smiled. "You believed in yourself."

Feeling better than she had in months, she said, "I did." She reached down and took the pineapple squishy out of her backpack and set it on Dr. Lavinia's desk. "This really helped too."

Dr. Lavinia eyed the yellow fruit. "I'm so glad to hear."

For a second there, Infiniti thought of asking if she could keep it, but changed her mind. "I've brought it back so that it can help someone else."

Dr. Lavinia nodded. "Good idea."

Infiniti and Dr. Lavinia talked for about an hour more. Her fears, though not completely gone, had greatly lifted. And when Infiniti left Halstein and headed back to Jory, she was ready for anything, including an amazing Thanksgiving break with Lyra and Joe and his family.

Back in her room, Infiniti started packing her stuff. Taylor had already left campus, so she was alone as she sifted through her things, waiting for Joe. He showed up not much later and wrapped her up in a bear hug.

"You ready for a break?"

She rested her chin on his chest and looked up at him. "I am so ready."

He brought his lips to hers and kissed her softly. "Let's go then."

Hand in hand they strolled to the portal out of campus. Joe's excitement about going home magnified with each step as he shared his family's traditions for Thanksgiving, describing the Croatian delicacies his mom always made for the season. Since her mom's death, any talk of family or holidays struck sorrow in her. But this time, Infiniti's reaction was different. Her mom was okay, she was with an amazing guy, and her future was bright.

She knew it. She believed it.

After the most amazing Thanksgiving break, Infiniti returned to school refreshed and with a new outlook. She didn't feel like an outsider to the supernatural world anymore. She belonged, really and truly belonged. And for the first time in a long time she wasn't afraid anymore. Hanging out with Joe and spending time with her friends, she was beginning to feel like a normal girl with normal problems . . . like preparing for finals in a week.

With her books sprawled out on her bed, she leaned her head back on the pillow, her eyes so tired she could barely keep them open. The peaceful crackling from the fireplace almost lulled her to sleep.

Taylor let out a sigh from across the room. "I say we go to bed and start up again in the morning."

"Good idea," Infiniti mumbled, curling up on her side.

She snuggled into her pillow while her body drifted to sleep, but suddenly she awoke screaming bloody murder. Taylor was also screaming. Shouting filled the tower and hollering could be heard in the distance.

Infiniti and Taylor shot out of their beds, clutching on to each other in the middle of the room.

"What the hell?" Infiniti asked.

"I-I-I don't know."

The girls approached their window with caution and peered out. Infiniti wondered if it was possible for the entire campus to have a nightmare at the same time. She was about to ask Taylor when a piercing gong rang out. The walls and floor shook with a jolt. The girls backed away from the opening and stared at each other.

"Oh, shit," they said.

TEST OF TIME

KRISTIE COOK

The energy hummed a beautiful melody—dark and haunting like the force itself, yet exquisite and mesmerizing, calling to me like a lover's serenade. I could almost hear my name woven into the play of notes. *Brielle Sophia*, it seemed to sing, a ballad skating over my skin, trying to reach my soul.

The seductive song of the Darkness.

It came through the tall, arched window of our room, where I sat on the sill under a pile of blankets with a book in my lap. Standing, I undid the latch keeping the panes together and opened them wide. The tune became almost tangible, wrapping itself around me like one of the blankets I'd just shed. Curling my socked feet over the edge of the ledge, I looked down to the bottom of the cavern ten stories below.

Then following the melody, I stepped off.

I did a swan dive toward the ground, enjoying the tickle of the freefall in my belly. As I approached the bridge between Modi Tower and the courtyard, I snapped my wings open and arched up, chasing the sweet sound toward Hel.

But then came the screams.

The wails of terror and cries of pain tore a rent through the lovely tune, and I snapped out of the near dreamlike state. They came from the top of Hel Tower, where I knew my sister and Charleigh were partying with many others. More came from directly below me in the quad.

I dropped to the courtyard, taking in the scene of students surrounded by black mists—spirits of the darkest kind trying to take possession. Even as I watched on, many succeeded. The looks in their eyes changed and fangs dropped just before they went on the attack, going after whoever caught their interest first.

Grounding myself, I pulled on the protective magic given to me by the local Luna Coven and exhaled a long breath, surrounding myself with a lighter energy, keeping that blackest of black forces away. I would not give into it.

And then I saw her.

My twin, Elliana, floated down from the direction of Hel Tower, several of those black mists swirling around her. Her wings —purple and black like mine, like our mom's—were spread out behind her, guiding her slowly down, her dark curls lifting from her shoulders. When she landed, she looked at me with a wicked gleam in her brown eyes and a smirk curling her lips. She did a spin on one foot, as though dancing with the Darkness. She stopped, facing me again, threw her head back, and laughed.

Then twisting and twirling her hands in the air, she began directing the black mists away from her—and toward other students to possess them.

I had no idea how to stop her. Thank God Taylor Augustine did.

The one thing I knew for sure:

If we'd had any doubts before, there were none now.

The Darkness had found us again.

CHAPTER 1

I shut the book I'd been studying a little harder than necessary, sending a plume of dust into the air. Blowing it away from my face, I shoved my hands into my hair with frustration. It fell in dark curtains around me as I circled my thumbs over my temples while staring at the pile of books and notes before me. None of them contained the answers I sought, and with the semester quickly coming to a close, I was running out of time.

My phone's alarm suddenly sounded, inciting a bunch of indignant noises from around me. Not all from students. In this library, many of the books themselves made clear their annoyance about the break in silence. I quickly grabbed the device, glancing at the screen as I shut the sound off.

Shit. Shit, shit, shit.

How could it be dinnertime already? I had barely studied for my upcoming finals, too focused on the side project I'd been researching, losing hours of precious study time. Now I was going to be late, and Charleigh and Elliana were probably waiting on me for our standard Wednesday night dinner date. Since they were usually the ones late, they couldn't be mad at me if I was for once, but I just couldn't stand the thought of it myself. It wasn't in me.

I quickly gathered the books and dropped them on the librarian's circular desk, then pulled my notes together before rushing out of there. Shuffling the papers and trying to stuff them into my bag as I went, I hurried down the steps, rounded the corner toward the doorway that connected the library to Halstein Hall, and ran smack dab into a large, hard body. Papers flew everywhere.

"Sorry," I muttered as I bent down to gather them again.

"Brielle Knight," the deep voice murmured, dropping to my level.

I sighed, while my traitor heart did a little flip. I knew that voice, as much as I hated to admit it. My gaze lifted and collided with gorgeous hazel eyes, a light bluish-green around the outside and yellow encircling the pupils. Then it fell to the perfectly full cupid's bow lips that were curving into a small grin. My stomach dropped at the sight and even the piece of stone in my chest warmed, but I ignored the buzz humming through my body and focused on picking up the papers.

"Aithan Lanrete," I replied as we both stood. I held out my hand for the pages he'd collected. "Thank you."

"My pleasure." He smiled again, more widely this time, as he stood up to his full height, which I estimated to be around six foot four, considering he was at least a foot taller than me. He was built like a god—which made sense, since he was a demigod—with broad shoulders, muscular limbs, and an ass nobody could help but admire. Even Elliana, who didn't like boys. And every time Charleigh did, I was inexplicably annoyed with her. Giving the papers to me, he ran his other hand through the mop of coppery curls on his head. "But if you want to make it up to me—"

My phone dinged again. "Uh, sorry, maybe another time. Gotta run."

I had no idea what he expected and didn't really care. Or so I told myself. Aithan Lanrete was Trouble with a capital T. He lived in our tower, Modi, and I had three classes with him. Almost four months into the year—and five since meeting him, if the trials counted—I didn't really *know* him, know him, but I was well aware of his reputation. Apparently the only classes he did manage to go to on a regular basis were the ones we shared. Otherwise, he was known to blow off responsibilities, choosing to play his guitar in the Modi commons room or hang out on Clifftop instead.

Without a backward glance, I hurried off to find my twin and our cousin. She wasn't really our cousin by blood, but we'd grown up with her since we were all babies, so she was basically family. That's how we'd been raised, though—little of our family was by blood, but much of it was by choice. We were all very protective of each other, but everyone was extra protective of Elli and me. We were considered royalty at home.

This was not our home, though. Not this town, this state, this country, or even this world. We had crossed dimensions through a gate created by our brother, and into an alternate universe. Our parents left us here, believing it was a safe place to hide us from the factions on our world that wanted to use our powers or kill us because of them. Mom also hoped this was a safe place from the Darkness that pursued us.

Elli and I had opened a dimensional gate, too. To a world of Darkness, completely taken over by evil. We'd never been there, but we'd felt the energy oozing out, calling for my sister and me. We hadn't meant to open that gate, to connect to a place so dark it might have been a level of Hell—we were only six years old at the time and neither of us knew how we even did it. But we did it, and apparently, nobody could get it to close and stay that way, that world's Darkness leaking into our own, wanting to devour it. And use Elliana and me to do so.

So when we came here, our parents made a deal with the Court of the Sun and the Moon that allowed us to stay within their wards and attend SMA at the Halvard Campus—as long as that Darkness didn't threaten their beloved town or school.

Unfortunately, things weren't going as planned in that regard.

Thus, why I'd spent the last two hours researching energy cleansing instead of studying for my upcoming Cultural Relations final. I had an idea sparked by Dr. Jameson, our Energies professor, early in the semester that I'd been working on ever since. It would not only help Elli and me while we were here, but could be a huge boon to our world when we went back, allowing us to return technology to civilization. Something our world hadn't really seen since before we were born, when the supernaturals came out to humanity and destroyed the world—and billions of people—with nuclear and black magic bombs. Ever since, the residual black magic interfered with any kind of technology our people tried to redevelop. I had Phase One of my idea—energy transference and containment—nearly perfected. Phase Two—actually purifying the Darkness out of the energy—was proving to be more difficult. I'd been secretly testing on my own, but to no avail yet.

In the meantime, ever since the fiasco with the spirits nearly three months ago, Charleigh had been infusing the faerie stones in my and Elli's chests with Amadis power—the power of light, love, and goodness—to keep the Darkness at bay. The Amadis served as the angels' army on our world, made up of various kinds of supernatural creatures. My mom was the matriarch and leader of the Earth's Angels, who were charged with rebuilding earth after the War of Armageddon. That had been started by our grandfather, former leader of the Daemoni—the demons' army on earth. Now they were led by our brother.

Actually, now we weren't sure what was going on, because Mom had possibly started another world war right before we left. For all we knew, they were all dead. That thought made my breath catch, and I pressed my hand over the piece of faerie stone implanted in my chest, over my heart. It was a chip broken off the one embedded in our mom's chest, which looked like a ruby but wasn't, and was connected to our dad. They'd hoped the stones in Elli and me would somehow keep us all connected, even across dimensions, but if so, we'd seen no evidence of it. But even if I didn't feel physically connected to them, just feeling the warmth of the stone in my flesh was a reminder of the love we all shared.

That's what we hoped Charleigh's magic reinforced every time she infused her power into the stones. She'd probably be furious if she knew what I'd been doing. But I was on a mission, and had to believe it would all work out.

"There you are!" Elli called as she and Charleigh rounded the fountain with the Valkyrie statue that sat at the entrance of Halstein Hall. "We thought we were late again, but we must not be if you're just getting here, too."

Elli and I may have been identical, but I couldn't fathom how people mixed us up. I kept an easily maintained look—my wavy dark hair either hanging plainly down my back or pulled up in a ponytail, and my fashion statement just as simple, usually a hoodie or sweater, jeans, and my favorite combat boots. That only changed when Elli and Charleigh insisted on it.

Elli, on the other hand, was her own fashion statement. She liked her long hair curly and her mahogany brown eyes emphasized with black winged eyeliner and long, thick lashes. Although we lived under a mountain in cold temperatures that even sometimes had me shivering, despite our being impervious to air temps, she cherished high style. Even when she wore jeans, she was a sight to behold in a lacy tank top and three-inch spike heeled boots. She caught all the guys' eyes, which Charleigh and I found hilarious considering they weren't Elli's type. Elli was a little annoyed about it, but really couldn't care less. She dressed for herself. High fashion wasn't exactly something that we had in our post-apocalyptic world back home, so she was having fun with it while she could.

Charleigh, too. Her bright orange hair—the color of Cheetos we'd learned since being here—was styled beautifully, curling over her narrow shoulders. Her eyes, a strange brown that was almost as orange as her hair, were accentuated with eyeliner and mascara, too, and her cheekbones were brought out by what they called contouring. I barely paid attention to the makeup lingo, letting them do their thing with me only when they insisted and I was in the mood for something different. I always had other things on my mind.

"Can we go to Blaze's for dinner?" Charleigh asked as she readjusted the bag on her shoulder. "Vanna didn't stop talking about chili cheese fries earlier, and now I have a severe craving."

"Yum! Sounds good to me," I said. "Elli?"

I looked over at my twin, who was gazing at Destiny Nelson standing in line for the dining hall with her redheaded girlfriend, Linnie, and Rhian Delaney, another resident of Muninn Tower. Talk about someone with their own sense of style—Rhian wore her beautiful blond hair in braids and dreadlocks that were almost always piled on her head, and was either dressed like a boho hippy or in black jeans and a leather jacket, like a biker chick. Today she displayed the boho hippy look, wearing a maxi dress with Doc Martens and a scarf around her head.

Waves of jealousy floated from my sister to me. I didn't know if she was jealous of Linnie—Elli and Des had almost hooked up early in the semester—or just the fact that Destiny and Linnie had found each other. Elli had finally found someone back home, but that had ended disastrously. I thought it was one reason Elli seemed more open to the Darkness.

I'd never experienced heartbreak myself. Heartbreak required loving someone first, and I'd never had that. Not beyond family anyway.

"Elliana," Charleigh said.

"What?" Elli snapped, turning back to us.

Charleigh threw her hands up, as though in surrender. "Dude! Don't yell at me, you hangry bitch. Are you good with Blaze's?"

Elli's eyes suddenly lit up. "Sounds great!"

She strode off toward the Student Union, where Blaze's Burgers was. Charleigh and I exchanged a look, but then Charleigh shrugged.

"The promise of yummy, greasy, fat-covered carbs can change my mood in a heartbeat, too," she said before following my sister.

I supposed she had a point. We didn't have junk food at home, so we tended to over-indulge here. Thankfully, Elli and I couldn't get fat (bonus of having angel blood). Charleigh's metabolism was ridiculously fast, but she still had to pay attention to carbs for the first time ever—we were just glad to eat whatever was available at home.

Elli seemed off all evening. She shared her queso dip with us, when she'd normally bite our hand off if we even tried to dip a fry in it. But she had no interest in sharing my peppermint mocha that I grabbed from Coffee Haven on the way out, which she usually ended up drinking more than half of. She didn't even want to hang out in the commons room back at Modi after dinner. Definitely not her normal social butterfly self.

So we went up to the extra-large room the three of us shared at the top of Modi to study. Charleigh, a witch, conjured firewood from the pile at the bottom of our tower and made it appear in our hearth, and I threw a fireball from my palm at it, lighting it up. With a snap of our fingers, the dozens of candles around our room ignited.

Our beds were nestled in arched alcoves carved into the stone walls of our room, leaving a bit of space in the center for a small seating area—a loveseat and a round chair with a low table in the middle. When we wanted, we could turn them to face the only flat wall in our room, where we magically projected television shows and movies. Around the perimeter, in between the alcoves, were our wardrobes and desks.

Charleigh had decorated the arched ceilings and walls of the alcoves with tapestries. Mine were white with twinkle lights behind them, lighting up my area. Charleigh preferred black, white, and gray, with moons and other witchy motifs. Elli's were designed with mandalas and paisley prints in various shades of blues and purples. I kept a purple blanket on my bed. Our mom loved purple—and our wings were purple and black, like hers—so the color helped us feel closer to her.

My favorite feature of our room, though, was the window. About three feet wide, it rose to an arch six feet high, and there was a perfect little window seat. I loved sitting there with a mug of coffee or hot chocolate and gazing out over the campus. From this high, we could see down over the courtyard and bridge over the river all the way to the lake.

After changing into a SMA hoodie and yoga pants, I crawled under the blankets of my bed, my laptop and books spread out before me. Sasha, our lykora, curled up at the end of my bed. She was an angelic being that in her natural state looked like an oversized white wolf with wings and tiger stripes. She was fiercely loyal to her masters—Elli and me—with a killer protective instinct, and she could grow to whatever size she needed to protect us. But most of the time, like right now, she looked like a little white puppy, about the size of a toy poodle, and we claimed she was Charleigh's familiar, allowing us to have her here.

I fell asleep thinking of Aithan Lanrete, of all things, and awoke screaming from a nightmare.

Elliana and Charleigh were also sitting up in their beds, screaming as they looked around the room with wild eyes. Shouts and cries came from elsewhere in the tower, and my keen hearing picked up more from other towers in the distance. It was as if the whole campus woke up from a nightmare at the exact same time.

Just when silence returned, the ominous gong rang throughout campus, shaking our walls and floor. As soon as it stopped, I was out again.

The smell of baby powder filled my senses as a wet tongue dragged across my cheek. Sasha nuzzled her nose into my neck, which meant it was six a.m. She was my natural alarm clock.

Ugh. How did morning come so quickly? I felt as though I'd slept like the dead, but at the same time, like I hadn't slept at all. Begrudgingly, I rolled over, dropped my feet to the ground, and grabbed a blanket to wrap around me without opening my eyes. Barely cracking them now, I stood and tried to tiptoe across the dark room for the door, but my body felt sluggish and uncooperative. Shuffling my feet, I managed to make it without waking the others.

When I returned after showering, Charleigh's eyes were open, though she still lay in bed, staring at the overhead tapestry, but my sister's bed was empty and she was nowhere to be seen. I'd just come from the bathroom, so I knew she wasn't in there. She and Charleigh were not morning people. It wasn't like her to be up and gone already.

"Where's Elli?" I asked.

"No idea. She was gone when I woke up," Charleigh said,

rolling over onto her side. "Yuck. I feel like I've been drugged. Or spelled."

"Same." The shower had done little to wake me up. I rubbed the back of my neck, shifting the towel on my head. A flash of an image jumped in my mind. "Did something strange happen last night?"

"Um . . . you mean everyone waking up screaming and then the gong?"

"Oh, right, that." I rubbed at my wrist, then dropped onto my bed and fought the urge to lie back down, curl up, and stay there the rest of the day.

"I wonder what shitshow is about to go down now," Charleigh muttered as she forced herself out of bed.

"We can hope the gong has nothing to do with all the bad stuff that's happened. It could just be a coincidence."

Charleigh threw me a dark look. She was usually the optimistic one. "I believe that about as much as I'd believe Dr. Fraser doesn't free-ball under his kilt."

I smirked. That had been an on-going question, at least among the females, for those in his classes. More than one put themselves in awkward positions to catch a glimpse, and Marina Del Mar actually did, accidentally-on-purpose. She claimed there was nothing under there except the gloriousness we'd all expect.

Glancing around the room, I still felt like something was . . . off. "But was there something else? Like in here?"

"Besides the fact that Elli was up and gone before both of us?" Charleigh padded over to her dresser, grabbed a few things, and headed for the door.

"Yeah, that's definitely weird."

Charleigh shrugged. "Maybe she went to get us coffee."

"And I believe that like I believe Dr. Fraser will give us all As on our final."

She laughed as she left the room. I loved my twin more than anyone in any world, but Charleigh and I both knew Elliana did not get up early and sneak out to surprise us with coffee. That wasn't exactly an Elliana thing to do. And neither was going easy on us a Dr. Fraser thing to do.

Unwrapping the towel from my head, I forced myself up again to get ready for the day. All three of us had Combat Training & Defense at eight, and then I had Intro to Energies right after, which I was anxious for. Later in the afternoon was Intro to Inter-Dimensional Exploration & Time Travel with Dr. Sam Fraser. In between, I'd be stopping by the R&D lab to check on my Phase One experiment.

As I bent over to pull my pants on, something on the stone floor caught my eye. It looked like a drop of dried blood. When I moved to inspect it closer, I noticed another one beyond it, though smeared. And then another and another. A path trailed across the room directly to Elli's bed, although it appeared as though somebody had half-heartedly tried to clean it up. I yanked the covers back on my sister's bed to find traces of more blood on her sheets, up by her pillows. So likely not having anything to do with shark week, as Charleigh and Elli had come to call that particular time of the month.

I wondered what else could have possibly happened, though. First of all, it wasn't an easy feat to hurt us enough to draw blood. We were considered *hybrid* angels because our DNA also included that of fae, Weres (they called them shifters here), mages, demons, and vampires. If our skin could actually be penetrated, it usually healed up before any blood spilt. This much blood meant a serious injury—or something repetitive to keep the wound open. And if that were the case, my lovely but sometimes melodramatic sister surely would have woken both Charleigh and me up.

I could only hope that gong had nothing to do with her and that I'd see her in class, perfectly fine. She'd probably tell me all about some crazy mishap.

But as I turned to go back to getting ready, a glint on the shelf next to her bed caught my eye—a small chip of red stone, the color of a ruby. I sucked in a breath. "Oh, shit, Elliana. What have you done?"

CHAPTER 3

*W*hile Charleigh grabbed coffee at Coffee Haven, I searched the Student Union for my sister, but caught no sight of her. I could only hope she'd be in class. As we trudged up to Clifftop, I couldn't bring myself to tell Charleigh what Elliana had apparently done—cut out her faerie stone. I wanted to talk to Elli first and figure out why she would have done such a thing. And hopefully put it back before Charleigh ever noticed.

I didn't know what Charleigh would do, but she'd sworn a vow to protect us first and foremost, and something like this would likely throw her into protector mode rather than cousin or BFF. I felt the need to protect my twin from our protector, even if it was only a tongue-lashing or severe disappointment. Because Elli would take that personally from our best friend, rather than from someone looking out for our very lives.

Then once the stone chip was back in my sister's chest and Charleigh's magic did its thing again, I could refocus on my side project and solve this problem completely.

But first, classes.

The bridge from Halstein to Clifftop was long and narrow, and on an incline. Just getting to class was a workout for many. The light grew the closer we came to the opening, especially once we passed Steivar and Ansgar I. I blinked as we walked outside, my eyes adjusting to the brightness of a cloudless winter day. More snow had fallen overnight, blanketing the evergreens surrounding the top of the cliff, as well as Clifftop itself. The sun never directly hit this north side of the mountain, so the last snowfall had never melted. Sometimes they magically cleared the snow if it was too deep, but Professor Shimizu thought it was good for us to practice in all conditions, as the real world would be, so usually we dealt with whatever Mother Nature threw at us.

Elli was already out here, standing out in the clearing, dressed identically to me in a black hoodie, black leggings, combat boots, and a black beanie hat. She looked fine, physically, even when class began with advanced sparring. Judging by the way she tore into D, though, she certainly wasn't emotionally or mentally fine. Good thing he was an Impundulu and could take it.

I tried to focus on my own partner, Cole Silver, an Unseelie fae, but my attention kept drifting to my twin. Our connection felt unusually weak, but I could still feel her anger. Hell, probably everyone out here could feel it.

When she conjured a mini-tornado of ice and snow and shot it at D, Professor Shimizu said something in Japanese that sounded a lot like a string of profanity.

"Brielle," he called, waving me over to where he stood in only a black shirt, black hakama, and barefooted. I'd never seen the man wear shoes, even in several inches of snow. His long black hair was pulled up in a topknot today. He was nice looking, but a little too pretty for my taste.

I looked at Cole, who shrugged before tossing his shaggy dark hair out of his light green eyes and lifting a brow. Returning his shrug, I jogged over to the instructor.

"I do not know what's wrong with your sister," Professor Shimizu said, speaking slowly and with a heavy accent, "but this"—he gestured at her—"is after an hour of aikido forms with me before class this morning. She have no mushin. Too much mind." He swirled his hands around his head to emphasize his point.

Our parents taught us aikido since we were young. Our dad had been a master before the war. I understood. A good fighter needed a clear mind, and Elliana obviously did not have a clear mind.

"She need fudoshin. Let it go, clear it out. You partner with her before she kill someone." He gave a small bow. "Be careful, Brielle. Her ki is very strong, but also dark."

Exactly what I was afraid of.

As I strode toward Elli and D, her eyes darkened when she noticed me. Then she gave me a smirk right before swinging around and roundhouse kicking the lightning bird in the jaw.

"Son of a bitch, Elli!" he swore, backing away as he held his hand to his face.

"I'll take care of her," I said apologetically as I took his place on the field, facing my sister.

"Awesome." Elli's smirk became a wicked grin as she snapped her wings out. Great. She really was in a mood.

"So it's going to be like that?" I said as my own appeared.

Our wings were big and dark, with feathers that were purple on the edges and gradated to black at the barbs. They could be soft as silk or harden as though made from titanium with razor-sharp edges, making them excellent shields as well as weapons. We could even release feathers, shooting them like darts, as Elli did now.

I spread my wings out wide, catching the impact before her feather-darts overshot and hit another student.

"What's wrong with you?" I asked as we both lifted into the air.

"Me?" she shrieked. "Why is there always something wrong with *me*, Brielle? Maybe you need to take a look at yourself for once!"

She flew at me, and our combat *practice* felt entirely too real. Too personal. Why was she so mad at me?

Professor Shimizu eventually sent poor D back into the air to break us up.

"Class ended five minutes ago," he said when he finally managed to take us both back to the ground.

Great. Now I only had twenty-five minutes until my next class, all the way in Eirhal. That meant no time to go back to the room and change.

"That was fun, wasn't it?" Elliana asked, striding up next to me as I re-entered the cavern that was our campus. Charleigh had apparently already left, probably fed up with both of us.

I glanced sideways at Elli. Her whole demeanor had flipped like a switch.

"Mood swings much?" I mumbled.

"I'm sorry, Brie. I guess I just needed to work some steam off. Last night—"

I stopped on the bridge, grabbing her arm. It was so narrow here that if she jerked back, she'd fall. Good thing we could fly.

"What about last night?" I demanded. "How could you do such a thing? Why?"

Her eyes rounded and widened. "Why the hell wouldn't I? What were you even thinking?"

I blinked, confused for a moment because she was turning it around on me. "I'm thinking that cutting your stone out was the stupidest thing you've ever done in a long list of reckless behavior."

Now she blinked, looking like I'd slapped her. Then she threw her hands up in the air. "You know what? I was just trying to help you. Yeah, I've fucked up a few times, but this one's all on you, sister. *You* were the one trying to cut out your stone. I only tried to stop you."

I reared back. "What are you talking about? I'd never! That doesn't even make sense. Are you sure you're okay?" A thought occurred to me, and I gasped. "It's you, isn't it? The gong last night . . ."

I grabbed her wrist and lifted it up, pushing back her sleeve. Her school crest tattoo looked normal enough. Every other time the gong sounded, someone's tattoo changed to an hourglass, and something terrible happened afterward. Whoever had the hourglass inevitably ended up being the one to resolve the problems and take down the monsters—first Roxy, then Nadine, Taylor, Linnie, Vanna, Tempest, Natalie, and Infiniti. I'd heard Natalie's conspiracy theory that someone was behind it all, but nobody could figure out who, not even the Board of Regents. I thought my sister was next, but apparently not.

"As I said, it's not always me," Elli snarled as she gripped my wrist and turned it over, shoving my own sleeve back.

Then she snapped her wings out and flew back to campus, leaving me to stare at the hourglass that had replaced the school crest on my wrist.

"Fuck," I groaned. As if I needed anything else on my plate. I had a mission that I needed to accomplish. I didn't need to be chasing after rabid monsters. A raven flew overhead, cawing as if in agreement.

I could have flashed back to our room so I could change, but I didn't want to risk running into Elli there. So instead of getting where I needed to be in a blink of the eye, I walked, not in the mood to fly. I needed the time to clear my head before Energies class anyway. I had no mushin. And I certainly needed it.

CHAPTER 4

"Nice moves back there."

The deep timber skated across the back of my neck and down my spine in a not unpleasant way. I hated how my body reacted to just his voice. I mean, it was an amazing voice—I'd heard him singing enough to know. Not just because he'd belt out seemingly random lyrics in class or the dining hall, but he put on one-man shows a couple of times in the Modi commons room. He was definitely talented. But I hated that I even knew that. I seriously had no time for these thoughts. Especially now.

I continued walking toward the back of Halstein on my way to Eirhal. Of course, Aithan caught up and walked with me. We did have class together.

"I don't think I've ever seen a sight like the two of you fighting," he continued when I didn't answer.

"There are a lot of remarkable fighters here. It's a school for an elite army, you know." I didn't intend for it to come out so snippy, but my subconscious knew it was best to keep him and anyone else at arm's length. Besides, I'd already had a really shitty morning and wasn't in the mood to do nice talk.

"No argument there. There's just something different about you and your sister. You've been training for years, haven't you?"

677

I glanced sideways at him. Big mistake. He was peering at me with those light hazel eyes through copper curls that had fallen in his face. My mind blanked out for a moment. Forcing my gaze forward, I found my brain again.

"Yeah, you could say that," I replied. We'd been training since we were three years old. We'd been fighting demons and others since we were thirteen. We had a little experience, yes. But we didn't exactly advertise that we were from a post-apocalyptic world. That would negate the whole "hiding" thing, if the wrong person were to discover our brother's gate and come here looking for us.

We reached the back of Halstein Hall, and Aithan opened the door before I could even reach for it. My dad often did that for my mom, and when we asked about why she couldn't open her own door, Mom explained that opening a door, pulling out a seat, helping someone in any way was not meant to be demeaning or patronizing. She said it was a show of consideration, regardless of who was doing it for whom, and when such a thing as common courtesy was often lacking in the world, we should appreciate it when it was offered. So I thanked Aithan as I walked past him.

"My pleasure," he murmured. "So are you going to tell me why you and Elli were all riled up? That was not practice."

"Why were you even out there?" I averted the question. "Don't you have class?"

He shook his curls. "Nope. Not that early in the morning."

"But you can be out there watching us that early?"

"There's a difference between having to function intelligently in class at a ridiculous hour and drinking your coffee while appreciating a beautiful view." He paused, and I felt his gaze on me. "Of the mountains, of course," he quickly tacked on.

I nodded, not understanding why he felt the need to add that last bit. "I guess I can't blame you there. The view really is breathtaking, especially with all the snow."

Aithan chuckled next to me, the sound making my heart do a little flip.

We made our way through the maze of Halstein's passages in silence that continued to grow more and more awkward.

"Are you ready for finals?" I finally blurted.

At the same time, he asked, "Are you going to tell me what that was all about?"

"No," we both answered at the same time.

Thankfully we reached Eirhal. I needed to make a stop before class, though.

"See you in class," I said, before turning for the door to the ladies room.

But at the same time, he shifted out of another student's way, causing us to collide and my body to tilt right into his arms. Again. My whole body lit up at the contact, but I froze at the same time, not knowing what to do.

Balancing me back on my feet, Aithan moved his hands to my shoulders and turned us so we were both facing the way we each needed to go. Before releasing me, he leaned in and murmured in my ear, "The next time I catch you, angel, I might not let go."

He walked off before I could respond, my mind blanked out once again. Blinking and questioning myself—was he really flirting with me?—I rushed into the restroom. The sight in the mirror brought me back to earth, though. My knit hat sat askew on my head, my hair was a wind-blown mess, and a bluish-green bruise still healed on my cheek after the fight with my sister that had indeed been more than a practice spar. The reminder brought reality crashing back in.

Drawing on my fae blood, I did enough glamour to clean myself up, but didn't care much beyond that, even if I was still in workout clothes.

Since it was the last class before finals, Professor Jameson spent the next ninety minutes reviewing the major points of everything we'd learned this semester. I was hoping she'd go into more detail about our last reading assignment on energy uses and intents, but apparently that was not for this introductory class. I tried to catch her after class, but she had to go and said to email her or check the library. As if I hadn't already spent hours perusing over the books.

"Try *The Importance of Intentions in Energy Management*," she suggested as she rushed out the door.

Making a mental note of the title—it didn't sound familiar, so I didn't think that had been one I'd already "tried"—I decided to head back to the room, clean up, and change before lunch. I could stop by the R&D lab before or after my afternoon class, since they were both in Asketill.

The new hourglass glowed in the quad, and many voices whispered about who was "tagged" this time. My high tolerance for pain had made it easy to keep my secret—unless Elli gave it away. I didn't think she would, but she was unpredictable lately.

I was both relieved and disappointed she wasn't in the room when I got back. We rarely fought, and I hated it when we did. It felt like half of myself was cut off. But I still couldn't believe what she'd accused me of. Why would she lie so blatantly? Make up such ridiculous accusations? Was she projecting her own issues onto me? Or just trying to wriggle her way out of admitting she'd done something wrong by blaming me, as though we were five again?

But more importantly, why would she feel the need to remove her stone in the first place?

As I sat on my bed, staring at my sister's empty one, I had the sinking feeling that I already knew deep down. Elli had always been a little less fearful of the Darkness than I was. A little more welcoming of it. Sometimes she even seemed to embrace it, and removing her stone would open her to it. This wouldn't be the first time she'd done something stupid because of it. Last time, years ago, our parents and their advisors had our powers suppressed because it could have been so devastating. If Charleigh knew now . . .

No, she couldn't know. It was time to take Phase One out of beta and put it to good use. If I got caught . . . well, the consequences would be bad. I'd probably get expelled. But I needed to protect my sister. And myself. And the whole school from both of us.

Hopefully that would also take care of this hourglass on my wrist. Maybe if the Board of Regents saw that I was preventing another tragedy on campus, they'd be less likely to kick me out for what I was about to do.

CHAPTER 5

About twenty minutes before my next class, I hurried to the Research & Development Lab in Asketill Hall. Students in certain classes were allowed to use the lab for class projects, and while my project wasn't exactly for class, nobody seemed to even notice any time I went in. It wasn't like these particular labs were used much yet—they were probably for the higher-level classes, which we didn't have, being SMA's first year.

The room was dark, but I could see fine with my superior eyesight. Bar-height square tables created two rows, and I walked down the middle to the cabinet in the back of the room. When Professor Jameson had brought us in here for an energies demonstration earlier in the semester, she'd mentioned that the cabinet was a magical safe, spelled so that anything inside couldn't escape. I'd added my own spell to the vial I kept there so nobody else could remove it but me. The last thing I—or this campus—needed was for the wrong person to get nosy about what was in the vial and open it.

Glancing over my shoulder to ensure I was alone, I opened the cabinet and plucked my vial off the shelf, holding it up between my thumb and forefinger. I studied the charcoal gray mist-like substance swirling inside. It hadn't grown, which was good, and it hadn't decreased either, which was even better. That meant my seal had stayed tight. Phase One of my project had two primary objectives: ensure I could control and direct the dark energy into the vessel and that my spell kept it properly sealed. After all, we didn't need this stuff leaking out into the world. I'd only siphoned off a little bit from myself as a test, so this amount couldn't do too much harm, but my plan was much, much bigger.

Satisfied that I'd mastered the spell, I closed the cabinet and—

"Whatcha doing there, angel?"

My heart stopped, and I spun around, closing my fist around the vial. "Aithan! Where the hell did you come from?"

He shrugged. "Going to class, just like you."

"That's not what I mean."

"From my mother?" He winked.

"You're impossible," I huffed, and I tried to move around him to leave, but he was blocking the aisle.

"Yeah, she says that, too. My mom, I mean. I just like to keep you on your toes." His gaze dropped, sliding down my body before coming back up. I shifted to sneak past him, but he moved, too. "So what is Brielle Knight doing, sneaking around in the R&D lab?"

"None of your damn business." Now I shoved him out of the way to pass him, but he wrapped his hand around my wrist. As I spun and glared at him, I wished I could shoot daggers from my eyes. I made my voice low and my words slow and clear. "Remove your hand from me. Now."

He let go right away, holding his hands up in surrender. He looked toward the cabinet, and I moved on, toward the door.

"I know what you're doing, angel," he said from behind me. There was no way he could know, so I kept walking, ignoring him. At first. "You know it's a bad idea. You don't want that shit getting out. Or the Board of Regents finding out."

I stopped in my tracks, my back ramrod straight, my jaw tightening. "What? Are your going to tell your daddy?"

According to rumor, his dad was a big benefactor of the school, particularly the technology aspect. He owned a major multinational conglomerate and often went yachting with the likes of Bill Gates. I only knew this because of rumor—and because most of the devices Dad bought for us when we first came to this world were made by Aithan's dad's company.

He laughed from behind me. "Hell no. I don't really care what his position is with this school. But I do care about what happens with the shit in that vial in your hand."

"I don't know what you're talking about." I moved again, reaching out for the doorknob, but he was suddenly standing in front of me. My breath caught, his scent filling me on the inhale. I had to take a few seconds before I could lift my gaze up to his face. Our eyes locked for a drawn out moment, then his flicked down to my fist and back up.

"The vial of dark energy in your hand?"

I opened my mouth to deny it, but then figured, why bother. He obviously knew something.

"What? Are you spying on me? Should I turn you in for stalking?"

His so very full lips curved up into a smile. "You don't want to do that."

"And why not? It's apparently true."

He leaned forward and whispered in my ear, his breath warm on my skin. "You need me."

"I don't think so."

"I know so."

"And what makes you think that?" I stepped back, needing to put space between us because I was filled with a sudden urge to lean up and find out what those full lips of his felt like on mine. I crossed my arms over my chest.

He tilted his head, studying me through the copper curl that fell in his eyes. "Because if you don't let me help you, then I'll have to stop you. What you're doing . . . if it all goes to hell, don't you think this school has seen enough bad times already? And if something happened to you . . ."

He trailed off. Part of me wished he'd finish that sentence, but the smarter part knew it didn't matter. I couldn't care. "And what exactly do you think I'm doing?"

"Well, you've been transferring very, *very* dark energy from yourself into that vial in your fist. And I have a pretty strong feeling—and my hunches are always right—that you're about to take it to the next level."

I blinked. How the hell could he know?

"You ask Professor Jameson a *lot* of questions about energy transference," Aithan explained without my asking aloud. "Also, I can see the history of any object, including that cabinet. Just putting two and two together here."

"Wait. You can see the history of any object?" I repeated, a bit dumbfounded.

He shrugged. "I'm a descendent of Aion, the god of unbound time and space. Time has a completely different meaning for my family than it does for humanity."

My brows scrunched together. "You can manipulate time like Infiniti?"

"No. My powers aren't about controlling what is referred to as time. They're more about seeing and experiencing all of time at once. It's hard to explain, and I haven't come into them all yet anyway. But if I choose to look, I can see the history of objects as though it's all happening right now, before my eyes."

"Wow," I breathed. I had so many questions for him. I was so intrigued. But no. I didn't have time, and I really did not need to be encouraging him. "So what does that have to do with what you think I'm doing, and how do you think you can help me?"

"Not what I think. What I know. You plan to use this same concept on your sister, don't you?" He smiled when my mouth fell open. "I watch. I see things. Especially when it comes to you. I've noticed the dynamics between you two. I pay attention to the questions you ask in the classes we share. And based on what I've observed, I know you just want to help your sister get out of whatever funk had her all riled up this morning."

I didn't know what to say, so I blurted the first thing that came to mind. "You seem to pay way too much attention to me, creep."

He laughed, but then his voice dropped. "It's my favorite thing to do, angel."

His words sent chills over my skin, in a good way.

"You intrigue me," he added, holding my gaze with his. My throat went dry, and my tongue darted out over my lips. His eyes dropped to my mouth and stayed there as he spoke. "And I don't know yet exactly how I can help, but I'm sure there's some way. I want to."

"Why?" I managed to whisper.

His gaze lifted again. "Because you can't do everything by yourself, angel. You don't *have* to. Besides, it's in my best interest to keep you alive and well."

"Why?" I repeated.

He smirked. "You'll find out later."

I tried to think of a witty comeback, but didn't have a chance because my phone dinged with my personal five-minute warning. "Yeah, well, right now, I think we better get to class."

"Of course. Don't want to piss off Dr. Fraser." He finally stepped to the side, allowing me to pass.

As I sat in class, listening to Dr. Fraser and watching him intently—hey, he was nice to look at—I realized I might have had a type. After all, both Aithan and our professor had the copper curls and light eyes, but Dr. Fraser's were blue. They had terrific builds, although the professor always wore a kilt, so I couldn't know for certain if his ass was as nice as Aithan's. Honestly, I wasn't sure if anyone's was—if that were even possible.

Ugh! *Stop it, Brie. Focus.* Maybe my not quite perfect grade in this class was less about Dr. Fraser's strictness and more about my drifting attention. Which just wasn't my normal. What was wrong with me?

CHAPTER 6

Hoping to avoid Aithan, I ducked out of class as soon as Dr. Fraser dismissed us. Elli's attitude hadn't changed, and Charleigh seemed mad at both of us. I just wanted everything to get back on track. First, I needed to make a trip to town. While Howe's Herbal Shoppe's satellite store in the Student Union provided some supplies for witches, I just wasn't sure I wanted to trust any old vial or jar. The bit of dark energy I pulled from myself had just been a test, and I really didn't know how much I'd have to extract from Elli or how much it would expand when I did—or how powerful it would be. I couldn't take any chances.

I headed straight for the portal before any of them stopped me or asked questions.

Havenwood Falls was a winter wonderland and looked as though it belonged in a snow globe. The trek from the Falls Campus to the town square wasn't far, and with so much beauty and charm, it went by fast. Old Victorians lined the residential street with bungalows, cottages, and log cabins scattered between them, and all were decorated for the holidays.

It wasn't even five o'clock yet, but with the cloudy day and the sun mostly behind Miles Mountain already, dusk was falling.

Almost every house was lit up with twinkle lights, and once I reached the town square, I saw that it was no different. I thought the town was decked out when we were here for Thanksgiving break last week, but now it looked like Santa's elves had partied too hard and vomited Christmas everywhere. A huge Christmas tree stood in the northwest corner of Town Square Park, opposite the gazebo, which itself glittered with white lights. Oversized ornaments hung in the trees, and the old-fashioned style streetlights were dressed in greenery and red ribbons. Every store's window beckoned with beautiful displays. Our holidays at home had always been special, but I'd never experienced anything like this. I understood a lot better why our parents and aunts and uncles missed the Before time so much.

I went to Hey, Nice Glass! first, hoping they'd have some kind of vessel that would serve my needs. I could sense the magic inside and thought maybe it was infused into the glass. After all, they claimed to blow the glass right on sight. As I was contemplating an intriguing red piece, a large figure came up behind me and his familiar scent filled me.

"That won't do," Aithan said quietly. "Nothing in here will."

"Do you have a better idea?" I demanded, not bothering to ask if he'd been following me. He obviously was.

"As a matter of fact, I do," he said smugly. "Come with me."

He took my hand and led me out of the shop. An electric tingle ran through my fingers where they touched his skin, not unpleasant, but also quite distracting. I pulled my hand free as we crossed Main Street toward the large Victorian manor on the corner, Whisper Falls Inn. Then we made an immediate right and crossed Eleventh Street, staying in the town square. We passed by a pawn shop and a place called Madame Tahini's, then came to Callie's Consignments—Elli's, Charleigh's, and my favorite shop in town. Well, besides Coffee Haven. Oh, and Shelf Indulgence, at least for me.

A bell chimed when we opened the door and entered the store's warmth. I followed Aithan, weaving around racks and shelves of vintage and eclectic clothing to the stairs. The second floor contained some amazing and unique pieces of furniture and home décor. Aithan led me to a shelf of vases and decorative jars beautifully displayed.

"That one right there," he said, pointing to the one that had already caught my eye because it was purple with black hieroglyphics painted on it. The glass was just translucent enough to see the bottle behind it, which meant I'd be able to keep an eye on the dark energy I planned to trap inside.

"It looks kind of . . . delicate, though," I said.

"Looks can be deceiving, angel. You of all people should know that. This one has the power of Thoth infused in it."

"Thoth?"

"The Egyptian god. A thousand years or so ago, he had many djinn and made vessels to contain them. This one belonged to one of his elite guard, who used it to trap wayward djinn. And if it's strong enough to contain a djinn, with your added magic, it'll be strong enough for what you need."

"And how do you know—oh, yeah." I picked up the vase. It was heavier than it looked, and it even had a stopper in its mouth that proved to have a tight seal. Aithan was right—a powerful magic vibrated through it. "Okay, I guess this is it. And now you've helped me, so thank you. You're off the hook."

He chuckled as he followed me downstairs and to the cash register. A tall woman with dark hair and dark olive skin stood behind the counter.

"Interesting piece you chose there," she said as she lifted the bottle to look at the price tag tied to its neck. "Christmas present?"

I hadn't exactly thought of it as a present until she mentioned it, but I liked the idea. I was giving Elliana a gift by doing this. And possibly more than just her. "Um, yeah, for my sister."

"Callie sent that over just last week."

"You're not Callie?"

She shook her head and smiled. "Nikita. Callie's in Egypt right now, with Ronan, her husband. She sends her finds back to stock for the store, but this one . . . this one is special, I think." She eyed me for a long moment, and thinking I understood her meaning, I nodded. She returned the nod, then shrugged. "I would have never guessed this one for you, but Callie always says people have a way of finding what they need here. Or, as her great-grandmother Calla Lily liked to say, things have a way of finding the people they need. I'm sure it's perfect for your sister."

Once it was wrapped and bagged, Aithan opened the door and held it for me.

"So, uh, are you hungry?" he asked, shoving his hands in his jean pockets as we stood out on the sidewalk, snow falling around us. "Napoli's has amazing pizza. And their garlic rolls are killer."

My mouth watered, but I looked down at the bag in my hand. I didn't think my stomach could handle food right now. I was suddenly nervous about what I planned to do. The sooner I got it done, the better. "I think I better get back to campus."

"Okay. Rest in Pizza is good, too."

We headed back down residential streets toward campus, and I couldn't help but stop and wonder at the homes alight with twinkle lights and fat bulbs, their colors reflecting on the snow. The scent of woodsmoke trailed from the chimneys and filled me with a feeling of warmth and comfort. Christmas music floated faintly on the air, and I could see shadows of people moving around in their homes, preparing for dinner and whatever evening activities they had planned. I imagined families gathered around the table or on the sofa for game or movie night, or couples snuggled up in front of blazing fires. All images that were conjured from books and movies, definitely not from experience, though I longed for it with a nostalgia that didn't belong to me.

"What's it like where you're from?" Aithan asked, and I was immediately pulled out of the moment.

"Not like this," I said quietly.

He chuckled. "I don't think anything is like this. This town is surreal."

"Your hometown isn't like this?"

"Seattle? No, not at all. You've never been?"

I shook my head. Seattle didn't even exist on our world

anymore, although I'd heard a little about how it had once been. Uncle Owen said it had a great music scene at one time.

"The best part of it is the music, I think," he said. So it was similar to how ours had once been. Since coming here last spring, we'd learned that a lot of places were like how our world had been in the Before time, at least, based on stories our parents and others told. It was interesting how the two realities could be so similar yet so very, very different. I often felt like an alien in this place.

"You're good," I said, then added, "at singing and playing. Do you write music, too?"

"I sure do." He voice alit with passion as he spoke about his music. "I'm currently working on something unexpected." He paused, as though considering his words, then added, "About an angel who is just as unexpected."

We'd reached the Falls Campus while talking and now were in the courtyard with the fountain, where it had all begun in August. We both stopped, facing each other. His eyes pierced into me, as though searching to ensure I understood whom he was talking about. He'd written a song about me. Why? He didn't even know me. We'd spoken more in the last two days than we had in the previous four months. Yet . . . I couldn't deny there was some kind of connection.

I broke the eye contact, looking down at my black boots in the white snow. Unfortunately, I just couldn't afford a relationship with anyone. I had enough problems as it was. Gripping the handles of my bag as though it were a lifesaver in the sea of conflicting emotions I felt, I forced myself to look up at him again. He still stared at me intensely, making my heart pound.

"Why are you suddenly so interested in me?" I blurted, kicking myself before I even said the last word.

"You're kidding, right?"

Oh, God. Why did I even say that? My gaze dropped again.

"Oh . . . uh . . . so you're not interested. I'm sorry. I thought —" I stammered, wishing I could dive into the fountain and never come back up. Except it was just a fountain and not very deep.

Aithan stepped closer to me, his finger sliding under my chin and lifting so I had to look at him again. "Brielle Knight, I've been interested since the day I saw you in combat during the trials."

"Are you sure that wasn't Elliana? She really showed what we can do that day."

"I didn't miss her—but it was you and your focused intensity that caught my interest and hasn't let go since. You just finally noticed me."

My brows furrowed. Was that true? A few things clicked into place—like how he never missed the classes we had together, despite his reputation for skipping others, and how he was often out on Clifftop during our combat class when he had no reason to be. Charleigh had noticed and teased me about it a few times, but I hadn't thought her serious. He was right. I hadn't really been paying attention. Although . . .

"Not exactly," I said.

His head tilted. He was standing so close, I could feel the heat pouring off his body. "Not exactly what?"

"I haven't *just* noticed you." I bit my lip, my face heating. "I noticed you that day, too. Well, your ass."

He laughed. The sound was enthralling. "My ass?"

I shrugged, fighting a smile. "It's quite noticeable."

"Are you saying I have a big ass?"

"What? No!" Now I laughed.

"Then what are you saying, angel?" He moved even closer, leaning over so his breath trailed heat over my ear and neck. "I want to hear you say it."

I swallowed, my throat suddenly dry and my tongue thick. My heart pounded so hard, I was sure he could hear it. It was all too much—I could barely breathe. I had to break the tension before these feelings consumed me.

"I noticed that *you're* a big ass," I said, grinning up at him.

He leaned back, looking down at me, his lips pulling into a smirk. "Is that what you really think?"

I nodded. "Yep. An arrogant one."

"Not arrogant. Just confident." I lifted a brow, and he shrugged, that smirk still plastered on his face. "So confident that

I'm going to tell you to leave now and don't look back if you don't want this." He gestured between us. "Go on. Go to the portals, back to campus, and I'll never bother you again."

My brain yelled at me to go, but my heart refused and my feet wouldn't move. I just stood there, holding the handles of my bag in both hands as I stared up into his beautiful eyes. Our gazes held, the sound of the fountain trickling right next to us and the falls in the near distance muffling my racing heart. Fat flakes dotted his copper curls and fell into my eyes. His smirk stretched into a full smile.

"That's what I thought," he murmured as his arm snaked around my waist and pulled me into his warm, hard body. He leaned down as I pressed up on my toes, and our lips brushed, feather light, once, twice, three times. My whole body warmed, sensations running through it like I'd never felt before. We hadn't even really kissed yet!

I couldn't do this. That little bit of touch set such a fire within me that I knew anything more would become uncontrollable. And I just couldn't have that distraction right now. I leaned away from him. He smiled down on me.

"I know," he said, trailing his thumb over my cheek. "Not now. But soon, angel. We *will* do this."

"Do what?" I half-teased.

His eyes narrowed, and he growled. "We'll be doing a lot. Trust me."

"So now what?" Aithan asked once we were back in Modi.

We crossed the walkway over the great room below and stopped in front of the spiral stairwell that circled its way upward all the way to the top floor.

I held up the bag containing the vessel. "Now I go work my magic and pray like hell it works."

"Well, if it worked half as well as it worked on me, everything will be fine."

I looked up at him, his light eyes piercing me as our gazes locked.

"I hope we get that sometime," I whispered.

He lifted his hand and brushed his knuckles over my cheek. "Me, too, angel. Me, too."

CHAPTER 7

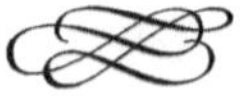

"Where the hell have you been?" Charleigh demanded when I entered our room.

Crap. I hadn't thought of a story yet.

"In the library?" I hated that it sounded more like a question.

"We looked for you there." She crossed her arms over her chest, her nearly orange eyes studying me closely. Her gaze fell to the bag in my hand, and she looked back up with a brow raised.

I sighed. "Okay, fine. I went to town." I looked around, making sure Elli wasn't there. "Had to get a Christmas present."

"Oh! For me? Or Elli? Show me what you got!"

Thinking quickly, I blurted, "It's kind of for both of you. And no, you can't see. You'll just have to wait."

Her eyes narrowed. "Wait. You went to town alone? You know—"

I rolled my eyes. "I'm pretty sure there's no place safer than Havenwood Falls. If anyone happened to come through our gate, the Court would immediately know, and they'd warn us."

"And if it happened to be when I had no idea where the hell you were? You shouldn't be leaving campus alone, Brie."

I pulled my phone out of my pocket.

"You could have reached me." Glancing at the screen, I saw

that she'd indeed tried. "Sorry." I sighed again. "So here's the deal, but don't tell anyone, not even Elli. There's nothing to it." I paused, then added, "For now, anyway."

"Spill it, feathers."

I really didn't want to because she'd make a big deal out of it, but I needed to distract her from the bag in my hand and where I'd been. "I was with Aithan."

Her entire face lit up, her eyes widening and her mouth dropping open. "You mean ass-of-the-gods Aithan?"

I couldn't help my smile as I thought of that ass, but the heat rushed to my face when my thoughts moved to his lips so close to mine, to the words he'd said.

"Holy shit! You better tell all, Brielle Sophia Knight!" She shook her finger at me.

"Tell what?" Elli asked, stepping through the doorway.

"Nothing," I said.

"Oh, yeah, I'm sure it's nothing," she muttered as she crossed the room to her bed. "At least, once I came into the room. You and Charleigh were having quite the gossip fest, though, weren't you?"

"Elli, it was nothing like that. I did a little Christmas shopping in town with Aithan Lanrete, but it was seriously nothing. Charleigh's blowing it way out of proportion. There really is nothing to tell."

"Whatever," she said under her breath as she crawled into her bed. "Not like I really care what my twin, who's my best friend in the whole world and practically my other half, is up to."

"Elli—"

"I'm not feeling well, so I'd appreciate it if you just let me sleep. Go have your sharefest with Charleigh downstairs." She rolled over, giving her back to us.

Charleigh rolled her eyes and turned on her heel for the door.

"Are you coming?" she asked.

"No, I'll stay up here and study. Finals have me a little freaked out," I said with a weak smile.

"Yeah, so freaked out you just had to get away for a romp in the snow with Aithan Lanrete?" she teased. She flipped her hair over her shoulder. "You'll tell me all about it soon enough, but I'll let you keep that little secret for now. I'm off for a study date myself, now that I know you two are okay."

"With who?" I demanded, turning the tables on her.

She smirked. "For me to know . . ."

Knowing she didn't need to finish the sentence, she sauntered out.

"Elli?" I said once Charleigh left. My sister ignored me. I tried a couple more times and even shook her leg, but apparently she really was tired and had fallen asleep. Weird.

Worried that things were growing even worse than I thought, I set about preparing everything for the spells. Mine and Elli's magic was different than Charleigh's or anybody else's, for that matter, but we used some of the same concepts and reagents. I gathered black tourmaline for protection and a crystal quartz to boost it, and dressed candles with lavender and frankincense oils, arranging everything in a box that I put in my wardrobe until later.

Then I sat in the window and watched the campus below, snow falling through the skylight onto the quad. Some of the students threw snowballs at each other, and I could hear their laughter from here. I tried to draw on their joy to boost my power, but found it more difficult than it should have been. The Darkness was definitely growing and strengthening around us.

Not knowing when Charleigh would return and knowing her response to what I was doing wouldn't go well, I tried to study, waiting until she was back and both she and Elli were deep asleep before pulling out the box and going to work. I put up a block around Charleigh's bed so she wouldn't sense the magic, then arranged the items around the open side of Elli's bed. I sat on a pillow in front of it all, rested my hands on my knees, and breathed deeply, bringing myself to center. I probably looked like I was meditating, and if Elli awoke, hopefully she'd think that's all I was doing.

However, I sent out my intent and lifted my left hand, turning my palm toward the lump in the bed that was my sister. Inhaling, I felt outward for her essence—her life energy. Finding the thread of

Darkness in it wasn't difficult. It was thick and alluring, drawing me to it as much as I was pulling it toward me. Latching onto it, I pulled it from her, extracting the dark energy and directing it into the open vessel in the arrangement before me. The candle flames flared for a moment before settling as the energy streamed into the purple vase.

My plan was working beautifully. Elliana's demeanor flipped like a switch again, but after two nights of siphoning the Darkness out of her, she remained stable. In fact, she'd become almost annoyingly bubbly.

"I can't believe Christmas is almost here! It won't be the same, but in some ways, it'll be so much better. Have you seen what the town looks like? And think of the gifts we can give each other! Nothing like what we did at home. Do you think Mom and Dad will be able to come?" She reminded me of our aunt Blossom, Charleigh's mom, the way she babbled Saturday morning while sitting on the loveseat in our room, flipping through a leather-bound book that I didn't recognize as a textbook.

"I wouldn't get my hopes up," I muttered from my bed, trying to focus on my studies.

Finals started in two days. Although my grades were pretty much top-notch, I didn't take anything for granted, especially not in Dr. Fraser's class. Because of course he hadn't given us that pass Charleigh and I had joked about. None of the teachers seemed to care that we'd all been through hell this semester, either, threatening the most difficult exams were still ahead of us.

All of the whispers and buzz about the hourglass didn't help my concentration. By the time Infiniti had been tagged a couple of weeks ago, everyone had pretty much figured out what the hourglass and the gong meant—trouble was coming. So instead of waiting for more people to die or get hurt, they went in search of it. Everyone had known it'd been Infiniti's challenge, though, and they'd all wanted to help her.

Elli had apparently kept my secret, and I didn't want anyone to know, because I was protecting her secret, too. And I had it under control. The tattoo hadn't disappeared yet, but I was sure that once I trapped all of the Darkness and it couldn't harm anyone, we'd be in the clear. Just another night or two, and we'd be good.

I would have felt even better if the dark energy wasn't only trapped but also cleansed, but Phase Two would have to wait. I needed to get through finals first.

"You don't need to be such a Negative Nancy," Elliana said, closing the book with a clap.

I sighed, rubbing my temples. "I'm not being negative. Just realistic. Our parents are possibly fighting a war. And even if they aren't, coming through the gate at Christmas, of all times, would be like yelling at our enemies, 'Hey! We're going to see the girls for Christmas! Want to come?' They told us when they left us not to expect anything."

My own words made me sad, and a heaviness grew in my chest. The ache of missing our parents and the rest of our family never went away, but just talking about them and the holidays made it feel so much worse.

"Yeah, you're right. I just miss them fiercely." Shrugging it off, Elli stood and dropped the book she'd been reading on my bed as she walked by. "I guess you ordered this from the library? Want a coffee? I think I'm going to make a run to Coffee Haven."

"How'd you get this?" I asked, reading the title. It was the book Dr. Jameson had recommended. I'd put in an order for it yesterday.

"Dillys brought it after her shift at the library last night. She might have thought I was you. Interesting reading there." She checked herself in the mirror before turning to look at me. "Did you want a coffee? You know what, I'll get you a peppermint mocha. I know you can't say no to that."

My brows knitted together as I watched her saunter out of the room. I hadn't realized just how much she had changed since everything had happened at home and her heart had been broken until now, when she seemed so much more like the Elliana I'd always known and loved. In fact, she was probably even better now, because her powers weren't suppressed to make her be this way. Maybe I really was on to something.

My gaze bounced from the textbook I needed to read to the tome I *wanted* to read as my mind warred with my heart.

"I just need a little break," I finally murmured, grabbing *The Importance of Intentions in Energy Management*.

The book wasn't the kind of escape reading I looked forward to after the end of the semester, but Elli had been right—it was definitely interesting. Where our text had barely touched on it, this one dove in deeper about how the intentions we gave the energy we produced affected its behavior, especially when used in magic and manifestation. When I got to the part about how like attracts like, I put the book down. We *had* discussed that more thoroughly in class—how an energy will draw in other energies like itself, growing and becoming more powerful.

Counting that as a review of materials for Energies class, I shut the book and considered what to study next, but then Elliana finally walked in.

"Here's your latte." She handed me the cup.

Taking it, I frowned. "It's cold."

"Oh, yeah, sorry about that. I got caught up. There's a bunch of people in the Student Union, but it's a designated study area, so it's super quiet and really weird. They're giving away free snacks and stuff—oh, and these coffees—and I swear, everyone's stress-eating, and unless they're lucky like us, they'll end up the size of Haldor Hall. So that's all you can hear—munch, munch, munch, crinkle, crinkle, munch, slurp, with an occasional page turning."

"Okay, that's nice," I mumbled before taking a sip of my lukewarm coffee and trying to push down the anger that was building in my gut. I had no right to be angry. I hadn't even asked for the coffee—she was actually doing it as a nice gesture for me. But the anger was still there, growing. "So what? Did you feel the need to stop and listen to it all?"

She laughed, ignoring my snippy tone. "Oh hell no. I ran into Charleigh and Dillys and a couple others downstairs. We're putting together a Release the Stress Party tonight. Charleigh and I went to get ingredients to make up a big batch of Pegasus Potion, and she's tweaking the spell she helped Tempest and Natalie with for the bottomless drinks."

"Like that was such a good idea last time." I rolled my eyes. "Don't you have studying to do?"

"Psh. I studied this morning and have all day tomorrow and then whatever I can throughout the week." She waved her hand in the air dismissively. "And I know I can't concentrate tonight anyway. Not when others are downstairs having a great time. You should take a break and come. There will be pizzaaaaa," she sang, tauntingly.

I waved her off, but a few hours later, I realized trying to study in my room was pointless. Their "little" party could be heard all the way up in our room, seven floors apart. At least, with my keen hearing. Gathering my books, I was about to leave for the library or Student Union or *somewhere* when my stomach growled.

"I guess I could stop in for a slice of pizza," I said to myself as I went down the stairs.

The pizza came with a drink. And then another and another, considering my mug kept refilling.

"Your drink packs a punch," I yelled at Charleigh over the music.

She laughed, her eyes looking more orange than ever. "You're just a lightweight!"

"But I'm not supposed to be able to get drunk." My cells regenerated too quickly, part of that whole angel hybrid thing.

"Elliana complained about the same thing, tired of barely getting a buzz before the whole effect wore off. So I did some magic, and voila! But don't worry—you won't get drunk-drunk.

Angel trumps witch every time." She pretended to scowl, but then shrugged and laughed as she flitted away to socialize. As powerful and talented as she was, the uniqueness that was my sister and me continued to stump Charleigh on a regular basis.

More content with observing the fun than being right in the middle of it all, I dropped onto an oversized, cushy seat by the window, my gaze traveling over the teal and silver décor of the room, including the big painting of a giant white horse with beautiful wings hanging on the enormous hearth. We'd voted for Pegasus to be our mascot, but for the life of me, I couldn't remember why at the moment.

I knew I'd regret it tomorrow, but I just couldn't make myself leave.

Especially when Aithan Lanrete plopped down in my chair with me.

"I'm surprised to see you here," he said, moving my legs to drape over his lap so I'd be turned more toward him.

I shrugged and grinned lazily. "Just needed a break."

His gaze seemed to scrutinize me. Maybe because he heard my words slur.

"I think your break might be lasting the rest of the night," he teased.

Liquid courage urging me on, I leaned forward, closer to him. "I think you might be right. Especially now—"

My words were cut off when some guy not even from our tower practically yelled, his words slurring worse than mine as he swayed on his feet, "All I know is that whoever's tagged this time is a fucking selfish coward. They need to man up so we can all take care of it. If I fail finals because of that fucking hourglass, I'll be killing the mofo who let it happen."

"Ugh. What a buzzkill," I murmured while dread sank like a pit in my stomach. Part of me wanted to tell him he was an idiot and everything would be fine, but then I would out myself and possibly have a whole great room full of accusations. Grabbing Aithan's hand, I stood. "Let's go someplace else. Somewhere a little more quiet." Looking at him through my lashes, I gave a shy smile. "More private?"

Catching my drift, he rose, a slow smile stretching on his face. He led me out of the great room and into the stairwell. My stomach twisted as I thought about going to his room, but we exited the spiral stairs only two rotations up, on the third floor of the commons area. Up here was a balcony that looked down at the party, but there were also rooms off of it for smaller gatherings. Aithan led me into an empty one. Private, yet not *too* private. I had a feeling he did that for me.

These smaller rooms up here magically changed décor and function, depending on who was in it and their purpose. Right now, this one was like a small cave, decorated with poufs and tons of pillows of all sizes on the floor. Aithan dropped down onto an oversized pillow and patted next to him. Instead, I knelt down onto his lap.

"Brielle—" he started.

"We promised each other *sometime*. Why can't sometime be now?" Before he could answer, I leaned forward and crushed my lips to his.

CHAPTER 9

$\mathcal{I}$ expected him to taste like the pineapple and coconut flavor of the Pegasus Potion, but I should have known better. His flavor was stouter, more pungent, what I figured whiskey might taste like, though I wouldn't know since I'd never had it. His full lips were just as luscious as they looked, firm yet giving, soft yet demanding. He was obviously more experienced at this than I, his tongue leading the way for my own. My stomach had that same sensation it did when flying, when I let myself freefall toward the ground. As the kiss progressed and deepened, my whole body heated, my breasts tightening and my thighs clenching. Sliding my hands into his hair, I rocked forward on the hardness growing beneath me, both of us moaning from the friction.

"Brielle," he whispered between kisses.

"Mmm . . ." I answered, shifting again on his lap.

"Fuck," he murmured, sucking my lip between his before letting it go as he pulled back. "You're gonna fucking kill me. I can't do this."

I frowned. "Why not?"

"Because you've had entirely too much to drink."

"I'm fine." I leaned in as I pulled his head toward me.

"I won't do this," he said more firmly, wrapping his fingers around my wrists and releasing my hold on him. "I want to. Fuck if I want to. But I won't."

His fingers skated over my skin as he held my wrists between us. When they touched my tattoo, his body stiffened, his head cocking.

"It's you," he declared.

Shit. How did he know? Others had said their tattoos burned, but mine never really did, so I hadn't so much as flinched.

I did what I had to. I shook my head in a lie.

"You can't lie to me about this, angel." He lifted my left hand and turned it over, pushing my sleeve back to expose the hourglass. "It's *time* magic. I feel it."

I sighed and began to crawl off his lap, the never-lasting buzz already gone, but his hands clamped on my hips, holding me still.

"Why didn't you tell me?" he asked.

"There was no need. I have it all under control."

He lifted a brow. "Are you sure?"

"Positive."

"Then why is it still there?"

I pursed my lips and shrugged. "It won't be for long. I promise."

Feeling suddenly irritated, I pushed his hands off of me and climbed off his lap. "I need to go. Please don't . . . "

I couldn't bring myself to ask him to lie for me, but that was exactly what I needed him to do.

"Your secret is safe with me," he started, and I let out a breath of relief. "Until it's not safe for others."

I nodded. It was the best I could hope for. But I wasn't worried. Perhaps some liquid courage remained, but I was sure I had everything under control.

"Thanks," I whispered as I strode for the doorway.

"You don't have to do this alone, angel," Aithan called after me.

I looked over my shoulder. "Yeah, Aithan, this one I do."

Not for me, but for my sister. I'd already involved him too much. Besides, there really wasn't anything he could do. Phase One was almost done—the Darkness in my sister had already lifted significantly. Just a little more extraction, and she'd no longer be a danger and the hourglass would surely disappear. And as long as the energy remained trapped in the vessel, everything would be okay.

"Why didn't you tell me?" Charleigh demanded as soon I walked through our door. She was in front of me in a flash, lifting my hand and turning it over just as Aithan had done not ten minutes earlier. She eyed the tattoo, which now seemed to be giving off a bit of a glow. "Son of a bitch, Brielle!"

I jerked my hand out of her grasp, scowling. "How the hell does everyone know all of a sudden?"

"*Everyone* knows?" she shrieked.

I lifted a shoulder in a half shrug. "Apparently. First Aithan. Now you."

"Elli told me."

I looked around for the tattle-teller, but she was nowhere to be seen.

"She did it for your own good. I can't believe you kept this a secret from me. *Me.* I know I'm not Elliana, but fuck, Brie, I'm pretty damn close. And I swore a vow to your mother!"

Guilt shot through me as I recalled the moment she'd become our sworn protector. "I'm sorry, but I didn't want you getting all crazy about it. I already know what it is, and I have it under control."

She crossed her arms over her chest, jutted out a hip, and raised a brow. In case I didn't understand, she tapped her foot, too.

I shook my head. "I'm not going to tell you. I won't put you or anyone else at risk. Like I said, I have it under control."

"Yeah, well, there's a growing number of students who are pretty pissed off that nothing's being done about it yet. They're going to force it out if you don't come clean. Hell, for all you know, Aithan's already told them."

"He wouldn't do that." I had to believe that. I felt something between us—he cared about me. I didn't know why, but he did. I trusted that he wouldn't expose my secret, unless, like he said, he had to. I wouldn't let it come to that, though.

Charleigh stared at me, shaking her head, her eyes full of hurt. "I can't believe you trusted him over me."

My jaw slackened. "That's not—I didn't. He's a time god or whatever. He just knew."

"Yeah, whatever." She obviously didn't believe me, and I didn't have a desire to try to convince her. She spun around, her orange hair flying, and headed for her dresser, so I went over to my bed and plopped down to untie my boot laces. "All I know is if that hourglass is still there tomorrow, you're going to have a mob to deal with, on top of whatever your real challenge is. And you need to have this back where it belongs first."

She turned back around and strode toward me, holding a small red stone between her thumb and forefinger. Oh, shit. She knew.

"That's not mine. It's Elli's."

"So you've *both* been keeping secrets from me," Charleigh huffed, but I could hear more hurt in her voice.

"I'm sorry." I dropped my head into my hands. This was becoming such a big mess. I had the urge to tell her everything, but then I thought of Elliana. Charleigh may have been our best friend, but Elli and I had a connection on a whole different level. More than a sister thing, it was a twin thing.

On the other hand, she'd ratted me out, telling Charleigh about the hourglass. I should have been hurt, but it manifested into a sudden anger.

I looked up at Charleigh and spilled. "Elli's getting worse. The Darkness . . . we've both been feeling it, but it's hitting her harder, just like it always has. I think it's because of what happened at home . . . before we came here. She tries to hide it, but I'm worried about her, Charleigh. I was only trying to protect her, though. I've been trying to help her, and it seems to be working."

She nodded, but her eyes narrowed. "I've noticed a difference, for the better. In Elli, anyway."

My brows pulled together. "What does that mean?"

"I've also noticed a difference in you. You two have practically switched places, especially in the last two days. If I couldn't tell you apart, I would have been royally confused."

"I'm fine, though."

Her brow lifted once more, and she held up the stone again. "This explains the change in you, at least."

I shook my head. "I told you. That's Elli's."

"I've put enough magic into this thing to know whose chest it belongs in. You really can't tell yours is gone?"

I pressed my fingers to my chest and felt around.

"Holy shit," I gasped. How had I not noticed? "Elli . . . she cut it out of me? But why?"

Charleigh's eyes grew wide. "No. She wouldn't have done that. Would she?"

I told her about what I'd woken up to the other morning, and how Elli had accused me of cutting it out myself.

"Well, I don't know what the fuck happened," Charleigh said. "Both stories sound all kinds of messed up. The three of us need to have a serious discussion, because I can't do my job when you two are lying and sneaking around my back. For now, though, we need to put this back. Can I?"

Nodding, I pulled my shirt off so I sat there in only my bra and my pants. Charleigh pressed the stone chip against my skin, right over my heart, closed her eyes, and murmured the spell under her breath. A warm tingling spread through me as the chip sunk into my flesh and reseated itself. Now that it was back, I really didn't know how I hadn't missed it. I felt more like me again. Charleigh had been right—I'd also been off—but I hadn't noticed until now. I sighed with relief. A surge of light energy shot through me as Charleigh gave it an extra boost of her power.

"There," she said, then she looked me direct in the eyes, holding my gaze. "You have until tomorrow, Brie. Then we all need to come clean with each other and with everyone else, so we can get help in figuring your challenge out. But at least whatever happens, you're protected again."

Nodding, I changed for bed, then lay there waiting for Charleigh to fall asleep and my sister to come home so I could do another round of extraction. I'd have to up the power and draw out as much as I possibly could tonight—hopefully enough to resolve everything before tomorrow came and Charleigh followed through on her threat. Elli might feel weak tomorrow, but that was better than the alternative.

Pressing my hand to my chest, I drifted off, confused but grateful to have the protective stone back in place.

When I awoke the next day, I sat up to find blood all over my hands and a gaping wound in my chest.

CHAPTER 10

The room was dim, and a glance out the window showed an especially gloomy day outside. Hardly any light came through the skylight, making shadows as thick as they were at night. An uncanny darkness seemed to blanket the campus.

Elliana and Charleigh were both gone. Charleigh's blankets were in a pile at the end of her bed, but Elli's didn't even look like it'd been slept in.

I hurried to the bathroom, hoping nobody was in there to question what happened to me. It was completely empty. I cleaned up my hands and chest. The wound had already closed, but the faerie stone chip was definitely missing. I noticed now. *Shit.*

I kicked myself for falling asleep too early and not following through on my plan. I needed to find Elliana and confide what I'd been doing, then hopefully convince her to allow me to finish the process.

Back in my room, I quickly dressed. Strange noises came from the campus, many sounding like shouts and screams.

"Brielle Sophia."

My head snapped up. My name came as that familiar sweet siren call.

"Let's play, Brielle."

Stepping up into the window seat, I opened the panes and followed the call outside, unable to resist the soft, welcoming current that flowed in and around me. A scream stopped me from diving off, pulling me out of the near trance-like state. Across the quad, Infiniti Clausman was yelling at Joe Greg, but more surprising was Joe yelling back. It was so out of character for them both. When she shouted at him that she never loved him and her feelings had all been a lie, I knew something was wrong.

Then Tempest and Natalie ran into the courtyard, involved in their own fight. Spells flew from one to the other, and each deflected hit slammed into another student or blasted into benches and a Valkyrie statue.

Clay Washburn ran across the quad, straight through their line of fire, his hair and eyes wild, screaming about how it was all too much. "I can't take it anymore! Fuck finals! Fuck this school!"

Sobs and shouts came from inside Modi, and I took off down the stairs. As I passed each floor on the way down, I heard what sounded like nightmare-type screams. The great room was so dark, any light from the fireplace and sconces muted, only the sound of crying indicating anybody was in there.

"I can't do this anymore," somebody whimpered from a corner.

"I'm done. It's over," cried another from a different location.

Their despair was tangible, filling every cell of my body until I felt so heavy I couldn't move. I forced myself to trudge outside, for fresh air or . . . something.

Outside was barely much better, though, the air thick and pressing, making it hard to breathe. More people were fighting in the quad, shifters in their beastly forms attacking each other. Sobs and screams came from various residential towers.

"What the hell is going on?" Aithan asked, suddenly appearing beside me.

"I don't know," I whispered as my gaze fell on the large hourglass in the quad. I looked at the one on my wrist. The dim glow I'd noticed last night was brighter now, and the sands were falling faster than ever. A thought occurred to me. "Oh, *fuck*."

I felt the Dark energy as soon as I woke, but didn't want to believe it true. How could I deny it, though? Especially when she'd done it again—Elli had cut out my stone, obviously not wanting me to be protected. Why was she so persistent about it? Was it the need for me to join her in her love of the Darkness? No. It had to have been the Darkness itself, wanting us both. She'd probably removed her own faerie stone, but more carefully so we wouldn't know and all fingers would point to me.

Elli was worse than I thought. She must have been faking the whole turn-around, knowing what I was doing and patronizing me because she loved it so.

I didn't have time to run up the stairs, even with my inhuman speed. My wings spread open, and I launched myself upward, flying to our window. I blasted the panes open and rushed to my wardrobe. The box with the vessel was gone. Turning frantically, panic exploding from within, I scanned our dorm room.

There it was.

"No!" I lunged at the fireplace, picking up the pieces of broken purple glass scattered over the hearth. "Oh hell no! This can't be happening!"

But I'd already known it had. I'd felt it.

"Oops. That doesn't look good. Outside either."

I spun around to find my sister smirking at me, a disturbing glint in her eyes.

"How could you do this, Elliana?" I shouted. "Do you know what's going on out there?"

"Oh, you mean all the fighting? Or is it all the students on the sky bridges about to commit mass suicide?" Her voice lilted, teasing. I couldn't tell if she was serious.

I flew out the window. The Darkness had grown over the last few minutes, filling every space available and extinguishing almost all of the light. I could taste its tantalizing sweetness on my lips and smell it in the air. The black force hummed through my body in an undeniably pleasant way. I couldn't succumb to it, though.

The fighting continued from all over campus. But not everyone was fighting each other. Vanna battled a large, sentient book that morphed into a nearly invisible beast and bit her before returning to its book form—only to attack her again. The Gjenganger she'd supposedly eliminated weeks ago.

Tempest had stopped fighting with Natalie, her focus now on a big, hellish-looking creature with mismatched eyes attacking other students. Natalie had her own problems with some kind of black goo pouring out of Halstein Hall, a green smoke burping from it as it devoured everyone in its path. Bodies dropped, whether dead or unconscious, I didn't know.

I spun, taking in more. Down by the lake, the Amazon girl, Nadine, fought with a beast that appeared to be part woman and part dragon. *Impossible.* She'd already defeated that thing once. At least, according to the rumor mill.

Roxy, Vidar, and Tyr faced off with a man-scorpion on the bridge, its stinger slamming into the stone, narrowly missing the girl just as she shifted into a cougar.

Various students fought spiders the size of houses and snakes that could swallow a bus for a meal. Rats, bugs, even ghostly images—all the typical fears people held, no matter how badass they were. The Darkness only thrived off of it all, growing and terrorizing.

But the worst of it . . . oh, God, no. The worst of it were the dozens of students lining the edges of various sky bridges, black mists enshrouding them. Despair poured off them, feeding the mists, as they sobbed about being failures.

"See what you've done?" Elliana asked from my side as we hovered over the highest bridge—the one that led out to Clifftop.

"Me?" I spun at her. "This is *your* doing, sister! Why must you love it so?"

One of the students stepped off, screaming as she dropped toward the cavern floor a hundred feet below. My heart seemed to plummet with her.

"No!" I shouted. Many supes could survive the fall, but I didn't know if she was one of them. I soared after her, but the Darkness became so thick, not even my eyes could see through it.

"You can't save us all!" Elli yelled right before she slammed into me.

I smashed into a stalagmite, pieces of stone chipping off and falling. Having lost track of the student who jumped, I went after my sister instead. If I could help her and trap the Darkness again, maybe I could save them all.

I soared after her, finding her hovering over the quad. I knew when she sensed me—she swished her wing to the side, and several feathers flew at me, their tips sharp as darts and their edges like razors. I whipped my own wing out to take the hits, deflecting some, but several sharp pains jolted all the way into my shoulders and spine when others pierced my shield.

"Why are you doing this?" I screamed at her.

She soared at me, swinging herself around so her booted foot came at my head. I caught it, though, and twisted, flipping her over. Her fist slammed into my temple before I ever saw it coming. I shot my paralyzing power at her, holding her still, but she threw a stream of fire at me. I had to let her go so the stream would stop.

"Why won't you let me help you?" I asked.

"Why are you always blaming me?" she retorted. She conjured an icicle like a pick and threw it at me. "Why are you always trying to change me?"

Deflecting the icicle, I stopped in mid-air, gaping. "Not *you*, Elli! This." I lifted my arms up, gesturing at the mayhem across campus. Everyone was fighting something—including the Darkness itself, which had grown and was beginning to take an almost corporeal form. "I just want to stop this. Stop you from bringing this here."

She flew toward me, halting right in front of me, her face only inches from mine. "But you never once thought that it might be you, did you? For someone who hates it so much, you sure do like to invite it in. I'm only trying to open your eyes to the truth, sister —*you're* the one who needs to be stopped!"

"Trying to turn it on me again? Real nice, Elliana. Lying like this is a new low, even for you."

"Just do me a favor, Brielle." Her voice dropped, low and with an edge to it. "Take a moment and think about what you know of energy behavior. Then look around you. If you don't stop what you're doing, I'll have to stop you myself."

I blinked, not understanding. My gaze swung around, and it suddenly became clear—as clear as the Dark but pure energy surrounding me.

Me.

Not Elli.

"Oh no!" I gasped.

She was right. I'd done this. Like attracted like, and all I'd been thinking about since we came to this world was the Darkness. I'd made it my mission, giving it my full attention when I wasn't studying, ignoring all else, even friends, claiming there was no point to making new ones. I'd shut them out while letting it in. And now it surrounded me like a blanket, and I'd been relishing in its comfort without even realizing it. Had I really been the one to remove my own stone, *twice*? Had it deceived me so well? Of course it had. Evil loved lies and treachery—deceit was its most powerful weapon.

"Oh my god." I sunk downward, barely realizing when my feet hit the ground in the quad. "What have I done?"

I looked around at everyone fighting for their lives and the lives of others. Bodies lay on the ground, many crying with obvious injuries while others remained uncannily still.

"No." I shook my head, not wanting to believe what my eyes saw and my heart felt.

"*Yes, Brielle,*" it cooed at me. "*We did this together. Everything that happened this semester? That was all us. You invited me, welcomed me, brought me forth. And we did this.*"

I shook my head harder. "No."

"*You know it's true. They even saw you, you and your lovely sister, at the scenes of the crimes. Why is that, Brielle? You know deep down.*"

"No," I sobbed again, falling to my knees.

"*Oh, yes. Think about it. Think about every challenge your friends faced. The boy who hacked the system? The vampire seeking revenge for his sister? The gjenganger that only wanted to return to this physical world? Darkness filled them all. Your friends, too—Nadine, Taylor, Tempest, Natalie, and even sweet Infiniti—all have their Dark side, but you strengthened it. You brought me in. You fed me.*"

I scrubbed at my cheeks, finding them wet. My arms wrapped around my stomach, which clenched so tight, I felt like I might be sick.

Elliana dropped in front of me, her hands cupping my face as her eyes tried to catch mine. I couldn't bring myself to look at her, though. The guilt ripping through me hurt more than she could ever do, yet the Darkness seemed to only feed on that, growing exponentially larger.

Dark thoughts only fed more Dark thoughts. I'd given it energy by giving it all of my attention. And now it had taken all of my power, too. I couldn't do a damn thing about it.

How long would it take for the Darkness to consume us all? How long until it spread to Havenwood Falls? And beyond?

Would this world become like the Dark one Elli and I had opened the gate to? Would this Darkness find the gate from this world to ours? Would everything we'd done, everything our parents had fought for, be for naught?

My gaze slid over to Aithan fighting some kind of phantom-like beast. Our eyes locked for a moment, and something flickered in his, as though a realization hit him. Probably the realization that I was the monster who caused all of this. The evil force surrounding me grew again. Someone in the distance—or maybe nearby, I couldn't tell anymore—screamed with heart-wrenching despair. The Darkness grew larger.

Aithan turned and ran. I couldn't blame him.

He sprinted over to Infiniti and leaned in, as though whispering in her ear.

"Brielle," Elli said, but I couldn't tear my eyes from Aithan. Something deep in the pit of my gut—or maybe deeper—in my heart or soul—began to form, but the Darkness was pushing it out. "Brielle!" she screamed now. "Stay with me! We can fix this. Just don't lose yourself."

I shook my head—or maybe I'd never stopped shaking it, still trying to deny it all.

Fin grabbed Aithan's arm, and I recalled her fight with Joe. More sadness welled inside me, along with anger and . . . jealousy. The Darkness laughed and expanded, thick and black, a beast with dozens of tendrils that stretched across the campus, manifesting in various forms that terrorized students, trying to reach into their very souls and devour them.

Then everything came to a sudden halt.

Everyone froze right in the middle of battle, arms raised, legs poised, expressions full of fury and fear. Even the monstrous form the Darkness was taking seemed to be paralyzed.

But no, not everyone was frozen. Aithan suddenly appeared in front of me.

"Did you stop time?" I managed to ask.

"Can't do that, remember? But I gave Fin a big boost of power so she could." He placed his hands on my shoulders, turning me away from a frozen Elli and toward him. His palms replaced hers on my cheeks. I tried to jerk away. He should have been revolted by me. "Don't pull away this time."

"But—"

"No buts. Listen to me." He bent down to catch my gaze, pulling me into his. "I know you're blaming yourself for this, which is only making it worse. But you know how to fix this, angel. Feel it from Charleigh. From your sister." His hold on my face tightened as his voice dropped. "Feel it from me."

I looked over at Charleigh, whose frozen face was filled with alarm as she stared at me, her hands lifted with palms toward me, as though she'd been sending a spell my way. But what kind?

My gaze went to Elliana, and I saw it in her eyes. My heart broke into a hundred pieces. She didn't glare at me in anger or blame or even disappointment—all things I'd been feeling toward her. No, she gazed at me with love, and I realized what she'd been doing when she grasped my face.

Amadis power.

She and Charleigh had both been trying to push Amadis power at me. The power of light and goodness and love.

And then my parents' words echoed in my mind—words they ingrained in us. "Family until the end. Always." Whoever family included. And also, "Love conquers all, especially evil." Their love for each other had conquered so much.

I looked back at Aithan, who still held my face. I saw it in his eyes. Felt it in his skin on mine.

Swallowing the lump in my throat, I breathed deeply and nodded. "I know what to do."

CHAPTER 12

"*B*ut first, I need a boost," I added.

The Darkness had been powerful, but my intentions had been good, and that had to count for something. Like attracted like, and I needed to grow the good.

I launched myself at Aithan. Our mouths collided, and maybe because I wasn't buzzed now or maybe because I threw myself in the moment, but his lips were even more amazing than they'd been last night. His mouth took command of mine, and I gave him back everything he delivered, relishing in his taste and his scent and in the way he hummed as though in bliss. One of his hands continued to cradle my head as the other trailed down my back, pulling me even closer to him, melding us together. My hands pushed through his thick curls as my tongue explored his mouth.

The feeling he sent ignited within me, blossoming. Warmth. Lightness. Maybe even love. If not that, close enough. It fed me, boosted my power, gave me exactly what I needed. I drew it in, letting it course through my veins and flood every cell of my body, pushing out the Darkness. I felt the moment I was freed from its hold.

Reluctantly, I pulled away, breaking the kiss.

Aithan gazed down at me, his thumb brushing over my bottom lip as his tongue swept over his own as though savoring my lingering taste.

"Ready to kick some ass, angel?"

"Ready," I said with a sharp nod, the best solution already running through my mind and a plan formulating. "And we'll finish that later?"

"I fucking guarantee it."

I smiled. "For now, this is what we need to do. Who's still fighting and is our fastest?"

I explained the plan.

"Well, that would be me, love. I move through time."

I didn't know what that meant, and before I could ask, he appeared back at Fin's side and grabbed her hand, delivering the instructions. She looked over at me and nodded.

Preparing, I wrapped my arms around my sister. When Fin unfroze time, I whispered, "I'm so very sorry. I love you so much."

"Family until the end," she replied, and she fed me her power as she'd been trying to do before. I felt Charleigh's hit me, too, soaking it in before beckoning her over.

I grasped Elli's hand and faced the Dark monster looming several stories over us, taking the shape of another grotesque beast. Charleigh placed her hand on my shoulder just as an enormous winged wolf with tiger stripes landed in front of us. Elli lifted our joined hands to Sasha's neck, and our fingers sank into her fur. All three of them fed me their love, their loyalty, and their Amadis power as I lifted my free hand toward the monster, directing the energy to the beast.

Fin and Joe hurried over, holding hands. Fin grasped Elli's arm, allowing Elli to pull on her and Joe's energy. Linnie and Destiny rushed to Charleigh's side. Nadine and Clay were next, followed by Roxy, Vidar, and Tyr. Other couples and friends joined us, and then I felt Aithan behind me, his job done. When he wrapped his hand around my shoulder, I pulled.

And I felt it. The love. The friendship. The connections all these people had made over the last several months. It had been a difficult and painful semester, but they didn't let that bring them down. They let love conquer—love, friendship, light. I'd tried to shut them all out, but they'd all made their way in anyway, and I was grateful for that. We were family in our own way.

"Family until the end," I murmured. Then I shoved all this Lightness at the beast and yelled, "You will not hurt this family anymore! You are not welcome here, and I think no more of you!"

The black energy swirled overhead and yawned open a huge, toothy mouth as it dove toward us. I squeezed my eyes shut and thought only of Lightness and goodness, gathering my Amadis power—along with Elli's, Charleigh's, and Sasha's, fed by everyone else—into a big bubble surrounding all of us. Then with all my might, I pushed it outward, at the beast.

A loud *boom* shook the ground.

Followed by silence.

And a moment later by cheering.

When I opened my eyes, light poured through the skylight again. The energy under the mountain had transformed completely. A lightness we hadn't seen or felt since the beginning of the semester filled the air and stone and our very bodies.

The big hourglass crashed to the ground and shattered, its pieces becoming a mist that evaporated into the air.

More cheers rang out loudly.

"That was the last one!" Tyr yelled, followed by a fist pump into the air.

Questions flew at him, and he and Roxy confirmed there had been nine hourglasses in the artifact room when she'd accidentally tipped the first one over and everything had started.

"We went back to the artifact room to check. The Regents had it sealed off for months, thinking that might stop things, I guess, but with Dillys's help, we broke in last night," she said.

"There was only one left," Vidar continued, dropping an arm over her shoulders. "The rest must have broken when their replicas in the quad did. The last one looked exactly like the one that just shattered."

The cacophony became nearly unbearable as everyone

celebrated, congratulating each other on a battle well fought. Even the injured smiled through the pain. Charleigh, Elliana, and I threw our arms around each other, holding on tightly—until Aithan butt in, grabbing his own hug.

It was over. Really over.

"This isn't over," Saundra Beaumont announced. She stood at the top of the steps to Halstein Hall, addressing all of the student body that had gathered in the quad in a big party to celebrate our victory and the end of the semester. She and the other Regents had shut down the celebration, though.

I hadn't been a part of it, really. I couldn't bring myself to celebrate that we'd survived something that would have never happened if I hadn't brought it here in the first place. I tried to remain focused on the good and the light, but the guilt still gnawed at my gut.

Voices murmured throughout the crowd as we all stared up at her with some of the other Regents. Some complaining about wanting to continue the party. Others wondering what she meant —what else was going to happen.

"The hourglasses are indeed gone," she said to an eruption of more cheers. She raised her hands, and silence fell again. "The magic that had created the mayhem appears to have lifted."

More hoots and hollers.

"However," she continued, quieting them once more, "you still have finals starting in less than twenty-four hours. You might want to save the partying for Friday."

The whole crowd groaned as one, murmuring to each other as they began to disperse.

"Miss Knight," a cold voice said right behind me, his voice low, "you need to come with me. Your sister and Miss Wotsit, too."

I looked over my shoulder to find a man dressed in a suit, his dark hair impeccable, his blue eyes like ice as they glared at me.

Charleigh and Elliana turned around, their brows lifted with suspicion and concern. But Gabriel Doyle was not a man you said no to, especially considering the circumstances.

"I'll come, too," Aithan said, not releasing my hand as I turned from him.

"You were not asked," Mr. Doyle said pointedly.

"I'll be fine," I told him, offering a small smile that I hoped was reassuring.

His hazel eyes remained locked on me for a long moment before he finally nodded and gave my hand a squeeze before letting it go. "I'll be right out here."

We followed the Regent around the crowd and into Halstein Hall, then up to the Administrative Offices. He led us into a small conference room, which was furnished with a table and six chairs, all of them empty. Mr. Doyle closed the door behind us and gestured toward the chairs. All three of us remained standing, Elliana and Charleigh flanking me. Part of me hated that they were even here—they didn't deserve to be—but I knew they'd never leave my side. That's not what family did.

"Do you remember this past summer, during the admissions trials and tests," Mr. Doyle began, "that each one of you declared in an interview that you understood the conditions for your attending this school?"

I took a half step forward. "Mr. Doyle, this is all on me. It's completely my fault, and I should be the one punished. Elliana and Charleigh had nothing to do with it except—"

"Do you remember?" he demanded in a near snarl, cutting me off.

I stepped back, and Charleigh and Elliana each grasped one of my hands. We all nodded.

"We promised we wouldn't bring the dangers of our home world to this school," I said.

"And do you remember discussing the consequences if that were to happen, despite your best efforts?" he asked, his voice low now.

I bit my lip as we all nodded a second time. I opened my mouth to speak, but he cut me off again.

"I just want to make sure you remember," he said, then he abruptly strode out of the room, closing the door behind us. "Stay here until you're retrieved," he added from the other side.

"Fuck," Elliana breathed.

I turned to them, tears building in my throat. I could barely bring myself to look them in the eye, but I had to.

"I'm so sorry," I croaked. "I didn't want this . . ."

Words failed me. I didn't want this, but I'd been fully aware that what I'd done could have gotten me expelled. I never meant for Charleigh and Elliana to go down with me, though. It wasn't supposed to happen like this. I'd been arrogant and naïve in thinking I'd had it all under control.

And now what would happen? If they expelled us, we'd probably have to face the Court of the Sun and the Moon next, the deal our parents had made broken. We would lose the town's protection.

"If worse comes to worst, we leave the school and Havenwood Falls altogether and find someplace else to live on this world," Charleigh said as she dropped into one of the chairs and rested her arms on the table, then her chin on her arm. "It was fun while it lasted, and I love this place. I've even learned a few things about my abilities. But maybe this was a luxury that we were never meant to have. We'll be fine, whatever happens, as long as we have each other."

She sounded so mature and so strong, and I knew she was right. We *would* be fine. We were the Triple Threat.

"Family until the end," Elliana said, taking my hand and squeezing it.

I turned to her, gazing into her dark brown eyes. *I'm so sorry*, I shared with her through our twin connection.

"I know you meant no harm. Besides, I'm kind of glad I'm not the only fuck-up now." She smiled as she gave me a hip bump.

"This was a pretty bad one," I admitted, dropping my gaze to the floor. "Everything that happened this semester—it's all on me. I don't even want to think about when Mom and Dad . . ." I couldn't finish, their disappointment too much for me to imagine. "Those poor people . . . our friends and everything they went through . . ."

The dam burst, and she pulled me into a hug, holding me as I sobbed into her shoulder. We'd seen worse—war, famine, disease, and far more than our share of death. The people here, our fellow students, though, they didn't know our life. I never wanted them to know it, to have to experience it. Yet, I'd brought just a taste of it. How could I have been so careless? So oblivious?

We waited for what felt like hours, sitting, standing, pacing, lying on the floor, on the table.

"What is taking so long?" Elliana groaned at one point. "How much time does it take to expel us?"

More time passed. Elli's stomach growled. Charleigh had to pee. A while later, Elli did, too, and then so did I.

"Maybe they forgot about us," Charleigh said. "Or maybe we were supposed to be long gone by now. Did they even lock it?"

She strode over to the door to try it, but just as she reached for the knob, the door flew open.

"Ladies," Addie Beaumont said, "come with me."

We followed her down the hall into a larger conference room, where it appeared all of the Board of Regents had gathered. Some of whom were also on the Court. It was quite likely the final decision for our future would be made right here, in the next few minutes. We'd not only be expelled from SMA, but banished from Havenwood Falls.

The room was long and oval shaped, the opposite wall sloping with the curve of the cavern. Water trickled down the wall in a natural fountain at the far end, a constant reminder of how badly I needed to use the bathroom. But with the stares coming off of all the stoic faces, I wasn't about to ask for a break before we started all of this. I just wanted to get it done and over with so we could pack our stuff and move on, then figure out what we were going to do until we could go back home.

The three of us stood at the end of the conference table, waiting for someone to start. The silence—except for the water tinkling in the back—was unbearable, and I couldn't stand one more moment of it.

"I'm so sorry!" I blurted. "I know it was all my fault. Everything that happened over the semester—it's all on me. I brought that Dark energy, the exact thing you warned us about, to the campus, and it did horrible things, and I don't know what I can do or say, but please know that I'm so very sorry." I was babbling, but I couldn't stop because if I did, I'd break down into uncontrollable sobs again, in front of all these people.

Saundra Beaumont stood up from her seat halfway along the table and turned to us, forcing me to stop. "The Darkness deceives, does it not?"

I blinked, stared at her for a moment, then nodded. "My parents say deception is its greatest weapon."

"And yet you believed it when it blamed you for everything that happened?"

"Of course," I said easily, "because it was obviously tru—" I stopped. My gaze bounced around to all the eyes staring at me, and I felt a sense of expectation in the air. An anticipation, as though they waited for me to catch on. I looked back at Ms. Beaumont, tilting my head. "It's . . . not true?"

She shook her head, her hands clasping in front of her. "All semester the Board of Regents has been trying to figure out what's been going on here. We created a rigorous program and had no need to add extra trials, as some have suspected us of doing. Yet, it seems that the campus itself believed that some of you could be even better guardians, better warriors, better leaders, if you learned the right lesson. We've detected a kind of magic within the mountain itself that is quite like the magic in our town—the magic that seems to know when a person belongs in Havenwood Falls . . . or doesn't."

Elsmed Fairchild, another Regent who also sat on the Court, leaned forward and looked down his long flat nose at us. "You were merely one of the students chosen to learn such a lesson, along with others, it seems."

"But the Darkness—that came from us, from my sister and me," I insisted, though I should have kept my mouth shut. Charleigh hissed under her breath, and I knew if she could, she would have stomped on my foot. Yet, I continued. "It was *our* kind of Dark energy, not of this world."

"True enough," Ms. Beaumont replied, "but the magic had a way of turning that into a valuable lesson."

"Just as it knew what to do for the other students who were— as many have come to call it—tagged," Mr. Doyle added.

"But all those people who died—they lost their lives so a few of us could learn something extra?" I asked, bemused and angry at the unfairness of it.

"We don't fully understand how the magic works," Addie admitted. "We're testing samples and trying to figure it out."

"But what happened throughout the semester is exactly the point of this school," Mr. Fairchild said. "Terrible things happen in the real world, for both mundane humans and the supernatural. You are all here to learn to combat attacks of the supernatural kind while also protecting our own. You did just that. Unfortunately, as there is in any battle, as you three should especially know, there will be casualties. You students were able to keep them to a minimum. We couldn't have asked for more from you in this first semester."

I knew the truth in his words. We did know about casualties

and collateral damage probably more than most in this school. But that didn't mean I liked it.

Charleigh stepped forward. "So what exactly are you saying? Are we expelled or not?"

Everyone at the table looked around at each other, their gazes eventually landing on Saundra Beaumont. Her head declined as she seemed to stare at the floor for what felt like the longest moment ever before she finally lifted her gaze to us.

"No, you are not expelled," she said. "We wanted to make sure you understand that none of this is your fault. We don't want you to blame yourself or carry that guilt around, especially you, Brielle. We'll make sure the entire student body, faculty, and staff understand this, as well."

"But we hope that you did learn the lesson," Elsmed added.

I nodded fervently. Boy, did I ever. I didn't quite understand how it had all played out, how the magic worked when it came to the Darkness Elli and I carried. But I did know better than ever that Darkness led to more Darkness. Negative thoughts only fed it. I'd seen people at home spiral into deep depression because they could only see the bad stuff, becoming blinded to anything good to the point of hopelessness. It was so easy to fall into the abyss, especially in a world of turmoil and chaos.

But it was also possible to do the opposite—to spiral upward by appreciating the good, no matter how small, because focusing on the light, on the love made it easier to see more of it, bringing more joy and happiness that made the hard stuff more bearable. I'd seen that at home, too. I knew plenty of people who'd managed to hold on to hope and optimism, even with all the war, disasters, death, and black magic that was part of our everyday life.

The choice of which to focus on belonged to each of us. I would, from now on, always choose the Light.

When I walked back out onto the quad and saw Aithan standing there and opening his arms when he saw me, I made an addendum to that choice.

Love. I would always choose love.

"I don't know what was worse—all the challenges this semester or finals," Charleigh complained as the three of us exited Halstein Hall with coffees in hand after the last final of the semester.

"They definitely kicked my ass," Elli said, but then she did a little wiggle of her body. "But we have a month off to fill with skiing, snowboarding, and whatever else we feel like doing! Do you know Havenwood Falls has a Hot Cocoa & Cookie Crawl? We *have* to do it!"

"Yes!" Charleigh agreed. "I heard one place makes a bourbon hot cocoa. Oh, and we can't miss the Torchlight Parade on New Year's Eve!"

Elli nodded enthusiastically. "Christmas in Havenwood Falls will be amazing."

They were keeping up their end of the deal the three of us had made—a vow to focus on the good. It wasn't always easy, especially during the holiday season and knowing we probably wouldn't spend it with our parents and extended family. But at least we had each other and our new family here at SMA and Havenwood Falls. Some of the local students had invited us to join them for the holidays.

We were definitely looking forward to our time off. We deserved a break, after all, and it'd be nice to spend time above ground, if just for a few weeks. We'd practically grown up living in a bomb shelter, and when we'd first learned SMA was in a mountain, Elli had thrown a conniption fit worthy of a two-year-old. Life hadn't been so bad under here, though. At least, if you didn't count all the crazy stuff that happened.

"I know what Brielle will be doing with most of her time off," Charleigh teased as Aithan headed toward us.

Heat crept up my neck, but I couldn't help the smile as he approached and grabbed my hand while leaning over to drop a kiss on my forehead. I was going to fall for this arrogant demigod. Hell, who was I kidding? I'd already fallen for him. While I didn't know how long we'd be on this world—how long he and I would have together—I was keeping my vow to focus on the light and the love. I'd enjoy every minute I could.

"Ready to get the party started?" Charleigh asked rather loudly, referring to the afternoon bash in Modi Tower while everyone packed for the break.

Several people around us whooped, hollered, and shouted, "Hell, yeah!"

A raven flew out of the library doors like a bat out of hell, causing a couple of girls over there to squeal with surprise and others to laugh. But then a moment later, Cole Silver came running out, too, uncharacteristic panic on his face as he yelled.

"ZOMBIES!"

TIMELESS PART II

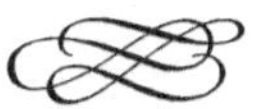

HAVENWOOD FALLS COLLECTIVE

CHAPTER 1

I could feel the sense of relief wash over campus when the last final exam came to an end. Right after, it was like everyone suddenly woke up from a weeklong semi-conscious stupor, talking excitedly about the upcoming break. After this hellacious fall semester, I wondered how many would choose not to return. This certainly was no ordinary school for the weak-minded or the weak-stomached. I was proud to be here, and honestly, I didn't really want to leave. On the other hand, a few weeks on the slopes of Mount Mae in Havenwood Falls sounded like fun. The perks of having no family obligations for the holidays.

When I walked into Muninn Tower, I felt like the volume had been at five all semester and now it was at twelve. Music blared from a few stories above. Molly Shaw and Marcia Lawson squealed cheerfully about something in the commons room as I passed through, making several of the guys burst into laughter. I'd become comfortable enough over the last few months that I didn't try to hide myself as I scooted by them, so they all waved and we wished each other a good break and happy holidays. Then I climbed the stairs to my room, smiling at all of the shouts from various doorways as students hunted for lost items, made plans to meet up over break, and said their farewells.

"Hey, Rhian," Linnie Andrews greeted as I passed her and Destiny on the way to my room. "Looking forward to the break?"

The belladonna had changed some from the first time I met her, no longer the shy girl with wander and excitement in her eyes. She'd matured quite a bit in the last few months. Killing somebody would do that to a person. I was just glad she'd found Destiny. They were the cutest couple.

"I guess so," I replied. "You?"

Linnie shrugged. "I'm going home to see my family for a few days, but then Destiny and I are coming back to town. Check out the sights." She shrugged again, her thin shoulder rising up enough to make her red strands of hair sway.

"What about you?" Destiny asked.

"Just hanging out in Havenwood Falls and hitting the slopes as often as possible."

"Maybe we'll see you around. Have fun!"

"You, too!"

As soon as I opened the door to my room and saw what greeted me on my bed, I groaned. I'd forgotten to grab the library book on my way out for my last exam. Shit. I just came from there, but I didn't dare not return it. The library was like a sentient being, and I wouldn't be surprised if it sent some bizarr-o creature to my room to retrieve the missing tome, doing who knew what kind of damage in the process. With a sigh, I dropped my bag, scooped up the heavy, leather-bound book, and turned to head back out.

I slipped into invisible mode for the trip back. Not that I was truly invisible, but I made it so nobody noticed me. I wasn't really up for any more chatter about holidays and family, and going ninja was my preferred state of being. So I skirted past everyone easily and into the dark tunnel that led to the library's basement.

The library was one of the best features of this fantastic campus. The smell of old paper and leather covers was inviting as always, but the dark voids and the freaky sounds that came from those voids were discomfiting. Anyone who thought going to the library couldn't be an adventure needed to visit ours at Halvard. I'd like to say I'd become used to it, having to pass through to get home to Muninn a few times a day for nearly four months, but I'd be lying. Because it seemed that some places in the library were never the same as the last time you were there, so you never really knew what to expect.

When I reached the center of the mezzanine level where the circulation desk was, I found nobody there. That wasn't unusual, but I wanted to make sure my book was checked back in. No library monsters would be visiting my room over break!

"Hello?" I called out. "I need to return this book."

Tittering came from the shadows behind me, but I sensed no human(ish) life there.

"Hey!" I yelled louder. "Anybody still here?"

I walked around the circular desk, peering into the dark shadows surrounding it and listening for a heartbeat or the sound of breathing. I was about to give up when I thought I heard someone—or something—whimper.

"Hello?" I said again. "Is someone there?"

The sound came once more, and then what sounded like "help." Following the sound, I weaved around desks and stacks of books, went down a corridor, and turned a corner, when my boot kicked something heavy.

"Oh, shit!" I gasped when I looked down.

A body lay in the doorway of a cavern. And just beyond it were more.

"Oh, no! No, no, no!" My blood began to hum as electric energy buzzed through it, seeking an outlet to reach the dead. For I was not only goddess of the moon and night, but also of death. At one time, that meant I had the power to return newly departed spirits to their bodies. My precious birds could sing the dead back to life, bringing joy to their loved ones. Oh, my beloved birds! Tears gathered at the corners of my eyes at their memory—and their loss. Hermod, a minor Asgardian deity, had taken them in his war on magic. He'd tried to eliminate me, believing that would eliminate all magic, but instead he only transformed my ability, making it dark and ugly. And wickedly powerful.

If I didn't keep control of that power, it had a way of unleashing itself and making the dead . . . well, not dead anymore. A form of necromancy, although that term was usually reserved for witches with that special ability. I was often mistaken as a necromancer, and I knew that kind of magic was forbidden in Havenwood Falls. This was the side of myself I hated. The side Addie, Taylor, and Vanna had sensed in the beginning. The side I'd done so well in suppressing.

Until now.

Panic warred with the power that was nearly intoxicating, and I began to back out of the space, trying to figure out what to do, but I couldn't think. *Mine. Make them mine.* I shook my head. *No! I will not!* I clenched my fists, trying to hold the force in. My eyes looked wildly at the corpses as my breaths came shallow in my lungs.

"Oh, fu-uck," I moaned when my gaze landed on a familiar face among the dead. Shirley, the basilisk who'd died right before Halloween—whose body had surely been returned to his family by now—lay with the others. Dead as a doornail. Then I recognized another as Cody Stevenson, the Sky Boy vampire Linnie had killed.

I stepped back inside the cavern, inspecting each face more closely without actually touching any of them. My power was coursing so strongly now, I couldn't trust myself with even a poke. Except . . . would it really be so bad if I brought them back to life? It was perfectly clear these bodies were those who'd been killed throughout the semester in the campus's sick way of teaching some of the students "bonus" lessons. Maybe, though, this had been a setup from the beginning. Maybe their families hadn't really been notified, and I just needed to bring them back to life. Maybe this was why I was here—to clean up the campus's magical mess and make sure everyone knew no harm was truly done. That everything was really okay and nobody should fear coming back next semester.

Really, Rhian? the voice of reason asked. *Do you honestly believe that?*

No. No, I did not.

My power was growing stronger and harder to control. My fingers rubbed against my palms as I hopped from foot to foot. I had the ability right here to fix everything, to make it all right again. To clear any guilty consciences, to prevent any families from learning their loved ones had died while at college, of all places.

You know you can't do this. You know it wouldn't really make anything right.

Well, that was only true if they were really dead. Maybe they were spelled to appear that way. I squatted down to take a closer look at Shirley's face. My hand tentatively reached out to check for breath and a pulse, but energy zapped between us.

"Oh no!" They were most definitely dead.

Of course they are! And you knew that. Otherwise your energy wouldn't be called to them, you idiot.

Gods, I *was* an idiot. Fuck. Fuck, fuck, fuck. I had to get out of here.

I sprang upward and rushed for the door, but my foot hit a lifeless arm, and I went sprawling forward. My hands landed and fell into Cody's rotting chest, my face coming within inches of his, the putrid smell of death that I'd managed to ignore until now filling my senses.

My power roared through my veins and out every pore of my body.

Cody twitched underneath me. Energy zapped from him to the corpse closest and then to the next and the next.

"No!" I shouted out loud. "This is not happening!"

As though in response, that gods-forsaken gong rang, bouncing off the walls of the small cavern, echoing in my head.

"It's supposed to be over!" I cried out. I hated that fucking sound more than anything I'd ever known in my long existence. It was the same pitch as the warning bells before Hermod came that day. The same sound his sword made when it had struck my armor —right after slicing through my birds. "Why are you doing this?"

When my own words stopped echoing, I realized everything had fallen quiet, and my power had retreated. I looked around. The corpses lay still. The process didn't finish. Everything was fine.

Holy fuck, was that a close one!

I needed to tell someone about these bodies. Did anyone know they were here? Or had that been my test—retaining control—to go along with the others? Had I passed?

Rushing out of the cavern and through the still empty mezzanine, I headed for the doors that led to Halstein Hall and administration, working out a plan of what I would tell them about the bodies. Nobody was there, either, not even the receptionist. Where was everyone? Had the faculty left before the students?

As I passed through the doorway, I saw movement out of the corner of my eye.

"Hello?" I called out, turning.

A Valkyrie statue stood in a decorative alcove at the front of the Administrative Offices. She was only two feet tall, smaller than most of the replicas scattered about the campus. I frowned—I swore this was the direction where the movement had come from, but there was only the statue and an expanse of stone wall.

Brows still furrowed, I turned away slowly, one eye still on the statue, but nothing moved. Of course it hadn't. I must have been imagining things.

"Anybody here?" I called one more time, but silence answered.

As I passed through the Student Union again, still in stealth mode, I noticed now what I'd been in too much of a hurry to before—everyone seemed perfectly normal. Actually, better than normal. Spirits remained high, many of the students joking around with each other, lots of laughter ringing on the air. Charleigh and the Knight twins chatted amicably with Natalie, Tempest, and Taylor, discussing their holiday plans as they all stood in line at Coffee Haven. Students passed by me groaning about how they still hadn't packed for the break, while others talked about an end-of-term bash in Modi Tower this afternoon.

Hadn't they heard the gong? I glanced out the arched doorways as I passed them by, but saw no hourglass hanging in the air over the quad. None had appeared on my wrist, either.

My chest loosened, and breathing became easier. *Okay, I managed to avert that crisis. Everything is fine. Let's just check on those bodies . . .* I didn't know why I felt the need to, but I did. And I found the small cavern empty. All the bodies were gone, all evidence removed, even the stench.

It must have all been a figment of my imagination—the bodies, the gong, all of it. An illusion created by this ridiculous library. I had a lot to discuss with my so-called friend and what I believed she'd created here, and this would be high on my list. I didn't find her joke funny in the least.

Although I was angry, relief still flooded me as I headed toward the stairwell for the basement and the passage to Muninn. The library made its usual strange sounds, especially on the higher levels that were lost to the shadows when I looked up. As I passed through the bookstacks, though, I realized some noises came from this level, just ahead. I crept closer, relying on my inhuman vision since I didn't have a flashlight or even a phone with me. What had happened to the orbs that usually lit up the end of the stacks?

Bracing myself and ready to call on my strength and speed, I rounded the corner . . . and nothing. I was still alone. Seemingly completely alone in the entire library. A chill traveled down my spine, but I continued, the door to the basement in sight.

But then movement passed at the end of the next row. A shadowy shape. That stopped. And turned. Right toward me. And it wasn't alone.

More shadowy forms were gathered behind it, shuffling forward as I backed up, a wheezing sound and moans coming with them. I didn't want to think about what I saw or heard, but deep down, I had a feeling I already knew. As they moved closer where I could see them better, my breath caught. *Oh, shit. Shit, shit, shit.* My fears were confirmed.

The dead hadn't stayed dead after all.

And they ran. The fuckers *ran* at me!

"Gah!" I yelled, spinning and running, but they were right on my heels. I could smell their rotting flesh, hear their raspy breaths. Something touched the back of my arm, and I screamed again. Sprinting forward, I glanced over my shoulder. A few yards separated me from the one in front. As I ran, I grabbed a random book off the shelf—a nice large and heavy one—spun and launched it at them like a flying bowling ball. It plowed into the first two, but to my horror, as soon as it hit them, they multiplied. As the bodies behind them stepped on the book, they replicated, too.

Panicked, I did the only thing I could think of—I transformed into my raven self and flew upward. They reached for me, but I flew higher. They followed my flight, knocking books off shelves as they rushed by, moaning and groaning when they couldn't catch me. I tried to think of what to do—how to un-revive them. But that had never been an issue before! I didn't even know if it was possible, especially now that they had clones.

While one eye watched the undead, ensuring they kept their attention on me, my other one scanned the bookshelves as I flew by, hoping to come across something that might have answers. I was very careful not to touch any, though. Randomly selecting that one to throw at them had obviously been a big mistake. You never knew what kind of magic the books in this library held.

But then someone came into the library from the basement door. A tall guy with dark hair—Cole Silver. He lived in Muninn Tower. I cawed loudly at him, trying to warn him, but he only gave me a cursory glance as he weaved through the stacks.

"Weirdo bird," he muttered.

It was just loud enough for the not-dead to hear. As one, like they were controlled by the same mindset or instinct or whatever, they all turned toward the sound. And followed.

Cole must have heard them, because he looked over his shoulder, and then did a double-take.

"Holy hell!" he squawked before he took off running for the front doors, the dead and their clones following. They were headed for the quad.

The very busy quad filled with students freed from classes and exams and deadly challenges. Or so they thought.

Shit. I had to warn them.

I soared overhead, yelling at the bodies, at Cole, at the girls just outside the front doors, but it only came out as obnoxious caws. I flew outside, startling the girls, and soared up to a ledge, my little heart pounding as I tried to think of what to do.

Cole burst through the doors and out onto the quad, yelling, "Zombies!"

Laughter and disbelief turned to questioning shouts that quickly became fear-filled screams as the students processed the deadly horrors spilling out of the library. One by one came the undead, looking every bit like they did on TV—clouded eyes, rotting flesh, straw-like hair with patches missing. Cody's chest gaped open where I'd fallen through it. The sweet-and-sour stink of death surrounded them like a cloud. What had been eight or ten bodies were now dozens, moaning and groaning, their unseeing eyes seemingly set on the crowd that had begun to gather together in the center of the quad.

Murmurs and shouts of what to do came from the tightening group. Someone shot a spell at the zombies, but it did nothing. More ideas flew amongst them as I watched, trying to think of an idea myself. If I tried to undo what I'd done—if that were even possible—my powers connecting me to the dead would not only be revealed, but I'd be kicked out of SMA in a heartbeat. Addie's warning from months ago was still fresh in my mind.

As I debated internally and the students discussed their options out loud, that fucking gong rang out. Truly this time. Screams and worried shouts confirmed everyone heard it. As soon as it fell silent, the ground began to tremor and the sound of crunching stone filled the caverns. The group stilled completely, then slowly turned as one, staring with mortification.

The Valkyrie statues had come to life.

Somehow animated, the many stone statues around campus began to move, stepping off their pedestals and platforms. Several students took off, trying to make an escape. Some sprinted down the bridge, only to be cut off by the two Valkyries at the far end. Others used their abilities to soar across the river, landing near the portals, but the largest statue of them all stood outside her vestibule now, blocking the way.

Moving far faster than big blocks of stone should, more Valkyries came running out of Halstein Hall and the other buildings, including the small one I'd seen up by the Administrative Offices minutes ago. I'd been right—she had moved! The statues, including the two on the bridge, closed in, herding the group of students until they were trapped between the moving statues and the zombies.

A thought occurred to me then, and everything became clear. My old friend had given me a mission while I was here. It was why she'd told me about the school in the first place. She wanted eyes and ears on the ground. It had seemed simple enough, but I hadn't felt good about it from the beginning. When the hourglasses started to drop and everything went to hell, I knew I was right to be suspicious. When the Board of Regents gave their official announcement to the student body after the last one that they believed these to have been special challenges provided by the magic of the campus itself, I knew they weren't wrong. Every person tagged with the hourglass tattoo had been on my list to observe—they'd been purposely chosen. And the magic came from the campus, but someone had put it there. She'd been behind it all. I was absolutely sure of it.

I had no doubt she was behind this, too. She'd used me to start it—one last lesson for the students to learn. And I supposed I was meant to observe, as always, and report back to her what I witnessed—how well they handled the obstacles, who stepped forward as a leader, who fought hard, and who ran and hid.

Except I'd never been directly involved before now. I didn't know if I could stand back and simply watch this time. It didn't feel right. Even though I'd been warned of consequences if I interfered or revealed anything, including my true self. Hopping around the ledge, I debated my options. Which consequences would be worse? Hers? The Board of Regents' and Court of the Sun and the Moon's? Or more potential deaths?

"Stay together!" Natalie Putnam yelled below. She threw out her arms, whispering a chant that produced a protective barrier— the boundary wavering in the air, barely visible.

Grabbing Tempest's hand, she nodded confidently, already in-tune with her sister witch. Together they'd proven to be a formidable duo, but were they enough?

"Stay inside the bubble," Natalie shouted.

Everyone shuffled together, back-to-back, watching the zombies closing in on one side of the circle and the statues on the other.

The first zombie tested Natalie's barrier, groaning as its skin boiled and bubbled. The second one, already free of its flesh, stuck its skeletal arm through and grabbed the hoodie of the nearest student.

"Look out!" a shout came from the other side of the circle at the same time.

The Valkyries had lowered their battle helmets and raised their massive swords. The first swing nearly took off the heads of some of the taller students.

"Run," Natalie screamed. Her protective bubble had been compromised on both sides, and there was no time for her to reinforce it without a coordinated effort between all the witches first.

The crowd broke, scattering like rats in search of higher ground in a flood, the zombies chasing them. Consequences be damned. I couldn't let them fight when I was the one who started this. I flew down into the shadows, shifted into my human form, and ran out into the mayhem.

A few yards away from me, emerging from the path that led from the beach, Fin and Joe came racing onto the scene. Joe slowed his pace and assessed the situation. Fin's mouth fell open as she looked from the massive Valkyrie statues to the flesh-hungry zombies.

"Statues and zombies," Joe said in disbelief.

Sensing new targets, some of the zombies turned their attention to Fin and Joe, rushing for the couple. Two of the Valkyries also turned toward them, raising their swords.

"Shit," Joe murmured, pulling Infiniti as they backed up.

The wolves weren't having it, though. The Kasun pack, led by Willa, sprang into action, charging in a flurry of claws and snarls in and out of the path of the zombies, trying to knock them into each other. Joe dropped Fin's hand. He glanced at his mate, then fell onto all fours in a flash of white fur, and joined his pack.

At the edge of the courtyard, near the drop-off to the chasm below, Natalie and Tempest faced the two larger Valkyries that had guarded the bridge all semester. Natalie whispered something to Tempest then hugged her tightly. Her eyes turned black right before she took off, running straight at the statues. Flying between steel and stone, she slid between one of their legs, slapping at its calf as she glided by. Casting another protection to encircle just herself, Natalie jumped up, veering out of the Valkyrie's reach as it tumbled to its knees.

Black smoke seeped from Natalie's mouth as she took off

running toward the other one. Behind her, swords, spells, fangs, and all measure of magical defenses flew as the rest of the students fought both zombies and statues. Natalie reached the second large Valkyrie, this time snagging a piece of its arm as it raised its sword high above its head, readying for another strike. It went down on top of the first.

A group of zombies swarmed toward Natalie, and she dropped into a crouch. She channeled every single lesson from our Basic Combat and Defense class, her kicks and punches landing with a deadly precision, followed by a blast of her magic. She moved as though in a choreographed dance: pivot, strike, drop, jump. Charleigh fought beside her, moving to the same rhythm, and a line of witches gathered around them, including Taylor, Tempest, Marina, Dillys, Bryony, and even little Fiona, shooting their own spells. The zombies were dropping like flies. The Knight twins soared through the air, using the razor-sharp edges of their wings to decapitate several zombies.

Except . . . to everyone's horror, each time one went down, two more would pop up in its place. They were *still* replicating. What kind of magic had that book contained?

No matter how many spells they flung, the zombies kept clambering back up. Decayed and rotted, some of them fell apart from their own exertion. I suddenly regretted not finishing the job of bringing them fully back to life. If I'd completed the task, at least they would have been truly revived, and they'd be easier to kill. Instead, Natalie, Tempest, Taylor, and the others—even Charleigh, who was experienced in fighting zombies—were being worn down. How much longer before their magic depleted?

I jumped in and fought, using my speed and goddess strength, but reining in all of my powers. It didn't seem to matter, though. Every time I came within a few inches of a zombie, my power zapped between us. Each time I punched or kicked one, I fed them more energy. They were becoming stronger. Faster. Snarling and biting with a new ferociousness. Shit! I was making it worse, not better!

I slipped into unseen mode and ran for the other side, just as someone screamed in that direction. The wounded Valkyries had recovered, joining their comrades on a fresh attack.

More students poured out of the towers and into the quad, entering the fray as the Valkyries started moving again. They came running in, fierce expressions hiding any fear they might have felt. Among them were students from Muninn and Heimdall, who must have heard the gong and the fight.

My blood ran cold at the sight of Marcia Lawson with her teeth bared. She was as beautiful in fight as she was fixing her lip gloss. Linnie, Molly, Destiny, Tank, and others rushed the zombies and dodged the Valkyries.

The Valkyries were pissed. Grimacing with anger, they swung their swords low to the ground, swishing back and forth, their stone gazes sweeping the air, as though with purpose. They seemed to be looking for something specific.

Wolves ducked and dodged in a blur as they went on the attack, when one of the pack, squeezing between a statue and a zombie, made a misstep. At the same time, a Valkyrie lunged, and the tip of her blade clipped the hind leg of the wolf. It let out a whine as it crashed to the ground and thudded to its side.

"Destiny, watch out," Linnie shrilled, pushing her girlfriend aside as a great statue beat its fist way too close for comfort. I ran over and helped her back to her feet. "Rhian! I didn't even see you!"

She didn't wait for a reply as she hurried over to help Destiny fight Cody, the Sky Boy—the undead version. One of Cody's victims, a woman who had worked in the infirmary, wrapped her surprisingly strong arms around Linnie. The bella struggled, and I watched in horror, afraid to come any closer to the zombie. Worried I'd only give it more strength—enough to kill her. Marcia flew at them, though, dislodging Linnie from the dead woman's hold. A few feet away, Destiny still fought Cody, but her friend Tank, who was built like his namesake, flung him away as if he weighed nothing at all.

"Molly!"

My head jerked at the sound of Marcia's cry. I missed what

happened, but blood flowed freely. I wasn't sure how the vampires were managing to stay sane out here. So much of it came from Molly. Her arm was tattered, the brown skin frayed to the bone.

"Somebody help her!" Marcia screamed.

I hurried over, jumping over a fallen body to reach her. Vampires could heal fast, but bellas were slower, especially those who hadn't reached full maturity yet. Linnie ripped off her sweatshirt and threw it at me. I wrapped it tightly around Molly's arm, pushing some of my healing power into her.

More zombies crowded around us, though, as if they could sense the weakness. The golden statue from the top of Hel moved our way, too, her sword raised. She swung it down just as I grabbed Molly and blurred us away. But not before I felt the wind of the blade as it swished past my head. The sound of the sword hitting the stone where I'd been only a moment ago had several people cringing. The Valkyrie spun around, searching for her prey. I felt her stony gaze land on me.

Ensuring Molly was safe, I made myself disappear. The Valkyrie groaned, as though in frustration, but she wasn't without a target for long.

Nadine DeBeaux took charge, squaring up against the Valkyrie. She ducked from the swing of a sword, narrowly missing her shoulder. She threw a fist into the statue's bared side, stone crumbling in her hand. Dusting her knuckles off on her pants, she watched the remaining stone fall to a pile at her feet. She stood there, mouth agape, as the pile of dust swirled around, taking form once more.

"You've got to be kidding me. What the hell is going on here?" She glanced around at her classmates battling against the undead. "Why aren't the Valkyries *helping* us? Aren't they supposed to be protecting the school?"

She was right. What had made the Valkyries attack the students? I mean, it was obviously the school's magic—*her* magic —but why? Simply because they were formidable opponents didn't set right with me. Not with what I knew about the Vanir deity whom I'd once called my friend. I hadn't figured out her reason for all of this yet, but she had a penchant for poetic justice. She wouldn't send the statues after the students for no reason. Would she?

Disappearing behind a stalagmite, I shifted into my raven form and flew back to my ledge that looked down on the whole courtyard. I seemed to only be making things worse down there, anyway, and I needed to watch from a different viewpoint. My gaze traveled over the melee, taking in the students fighting for their lives, blood staining the stone floor around them. I watched the zombies relentlessly attacking, falling, and getting up again, and the Valkyries looking enraged, but moving with a determined and purposeful focus. And then I knew. The realization sank like a stone in my gut.

Vidar suddenly dropped next to me on my ledge, pulling in his wings. "You know what they want, Rhian."

He was the first to have identified the raven as me. Being half Valkyrie himself, he sensed what the statues did. But since he was real, he was quite a bit smarter.

I swallowed and bobbed my head.

"Then you know how to stop this." He took off again, soaring over to Aithan Lanrete and Brielle Knight. I wondered if he told them. Whatever he said, a moment later, Aithan called to Infiniti, and they both ran for the front of Halstein.

Infiniti stood at the top of the steps in front of the doors, Aithan just behind her. He closed his eyes, and his face hardened with concentration. His hands curled into fists at his sides, the muscles of his arms bulging with tension. He was feeding Infiniti his power, as he'd done last week, but at a lot higher dose—I could feel it from here. Infiniti yelled as she raised her hands, her face set with determination. A white light sparked along her palms, and then they began to glow. All of the statues and zombies suddenly froze in place.

CHAPTER 3

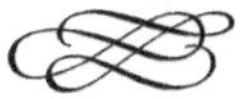

The students stopped in mid-motion, too, but they weren't frozen. Their chests heaved as they panted. Many looked around, stunned. Others, injured and exhausted, dropped to the ground or already lay there, trying to stifle moans and whimpers of pain. When they realized they had a moment to catch their breaths, those who could moved closer to the center, gathering in front of Halstein.

The wolf pack paced in front of the steps. Infiniti eyed them, muttering about not knowing how long she could hold the aggressors. One of the zombies twitched. The wolves lunged and barked at it.

"Hold them, Fin!" Natalie yelled.

Fin nodded while she bit her bottom lip.

"I'm right here," Cat said to Fin, moving in close. Only weeks ago they'd been enemies, but after Fin's challenge, they'd become fast friends.

Cat flipped her hair over her shoulder. "Those pendejos don't know who they're dealing with," she hissed. Her power oozed from her hands and gathered in her palm. Dressed in leather from head to toe and looking like a femme fatale, she took a wide stance, ready to strike anything not alive that moved.

"We need to figure out a game plan," Natalie said, running up the steps and facing the crowd.

"How did they even get here?" Nadine asked, gesturing toward the zombies. "And what's up with the statues? What do they want?"

"*WE WANT WHAT WAS TAKEN FROM US AND THE ONE WHO STOLE THEM.*"

The fierce female voice boomed across the cavern, making several people jump. Everyone looked around, trying to figure out where it came from. It seemed to come from everywhere and nowhere at the same time, much like the gong. But I knew.

Vidar knew, too. He stood at the edge of the crowd next to Roxy in her cougar form and turned to look up at me over his shoulder.

With another head bob, I stretched out my wings and floated to the ground. Landing in the center of the throng, I transformed back into my human form—blond braids and dreads piled high on my head, my thin frame in black jeans and a black hoodie. Whispers and gasps rang out among my fellow students. Revealing myself, I called out to the crowd as I made my way to the front.

"Thank you all for risking your lives and fighting for our school. But this is my fault, and the Valkyries want me." I turned around to find two hundred confused faces staring back at me.

"Why?" Linnie asked from the crowd, frowning.

I swallowed, gathering my courage. I seriously did not want to admit this, but I had to. They deserved to know the truth, especially with everything they'd been through. Bracing myself for their reaction, I explained.

"The Valkyries want the souls of these corpses so they can choose who they want to take to Valhalla, and they're upset that they were denied their opportunity."

"But they're only statues," Bryony called out.

"Statues who serve the true Valkyries," Vidar answered. "They are acting on my kin's behalf."

"So why did they go after us?" D asked. "They want our souls, too?"

I shook my head. "I realized they were not fighting us. They were after the undead. We only got in their way. They needed to remove any obstacles—including students—but their targets had always been the dead. Well . . . and me."

"What do you have to do with it?" Tempest asked, eyeing me.

Pressing my lips together, I inhaled a deep breath and blew it out. "They believe I stole the souls from them when I reanimated the corpses."

Several gasps and curses came from the crowd.

"You said you're not a necromancer," Taylor accused.

"I'm not. Not in the way you know. My power is different, and I . . . I lost control," I admitted. I took another deep breath. It was time they knew who I really was. I lowered my shield and shed what little remained of the extra magic Addie had given me, revealing my true self. My body grew from petite and wispy to tall, fit, and muscular and took on a golden glow as my armor slinked down my torso, arms, and legs.

"Oh my goddess," several people gasped at once, all of them witches.

"Rhiannon," others said more specifically. The mages all circled around me, and I let them draw on my energy, boosting their own.

"Our queen." Several fae dropped to a knee. I was surprised they remembered me at all. I hadn't been Queen of the Faeries in many eons, thousands of lifetimes ago. But they felt my essence, nonetheless.

"Many of you know me as a goddess of the moon, of the night, and of death," I said as the witches stilled, encircling me. "Unfortunately, my rein over death is different than it used to be. Now my power only creates monsters, like these." I gestured at the zombies. "I suppress it always—it's not something I'm proud of or ever use. But for some reason, the bodies of those who died this semester were piled in the library, and I literally stumbled into them. Doing so unleashed my power. I didn't mean to. I would have never done such a thing! But it happened, and now this is all my fault."

"Well, let's end them right now!" Vanna yelled, calling on her inner hellhound. Flames erupted in her palms. It was a good idea, but—

She threw a fireball at a zombie. The corpse lit up, but instead of burning, it broke free of Fin's hold. And with surprising speed, it took off—straight for Infiniti herself.

"Fin, look out!" Natalie shouted.

Taylor whisked her wand in the air, trying to project her power to the dead guy heading for her roommate, but she didn't have the strength. Elliana shot a stream of water, at least extinguishing the flames, but the zombie never stopped.

"Fin, he's coming!" Taylor yelled as she collapsed to her knees, panting.

Sweat beads lined the top of Fin's forehead. She blew her breath out in bursts, as the zombie wearing a dining hall uniform slowed, but still hobbled toward the stairs. She unleashed a string of curses while desperately trying to keep her new powers activated, but she was losing strength. Even with Aithan's help, her powers weren't enough. Her face was strained and red, her arms shaky. Her knees wobbled. She wouldn't be able to hold them all much longer.

Joe charged at the undead worker and pounced, knocking the dude in the chest with his paws. The zombie crashed to the ground and thudded to his back, snarling and clawing at the white wolf. Other wolves dove in, ripping the corpse to shreds.

A frozen Valkyrie sprang back to life. Her blade swiped through the air, inches above Infiniti's body.

"Ay, no!" Cat yelled, diving in front of her. The blade missed them both. Cat scrambled over to Fin. "¿Estas bien?"

Fin nodded with a gulp, but her arms drooped in the air. She eyed the Valkyries and the zombies, all of them twitching, breaking through her weakening hold. Cat let her energy flow out of her palms as she touched Infiniti's shoulder. Her boost combined with Aithan's kept Infiniti on her feet, but just barely. Her poor body still looked on the verge of collapse.

Another zombie broke free—the Sky Boy, Cody. His handsome features were no more. What remained of his face resembled gray beef jerky. He didn't get far as Clay Washburn pinned him to the ground with a steady blast of wind that literally howled like a banshee.

"We need to round up the zombies so we can give the Valkyries what they want," I yelled over the gale, wishing we had longer to formulate a plan, but I couldn't risk Fin's health any longer. I nodded at her. "You can let go now."

Fin reluctantly lowered her hands. Aithan and Cat stepped back. Time released, and the battle began again.

This time, I was ready to fucking fight.

The crowd dispersed, several charging after the zombies again. But we needed a circle to surround the zombies. With our collective abilities, we'd be able to contain them long enough for the Valkyries to take care of business. Then it dawned on me. I was overthinking things. A circle was already in place—the witches had formed one when I revealed myself. I just had to lure the zombies in.

I directed Taylor, Clay, Charleigh, Tempest, and Natalie, all formidable witches in their own right, to fan out and create an opening. Timber grew plants right out of the ground, forming hedges that served as a barrier, creating a path of sorts. The spring green of the leaves were such a contrast to the gray stone that was so predominant inside the mountain. From above, D shot down bright white lightning and the Knight twins threw rows of icicles, all of them corralling the undead. They steered the zombies to walk between the hedges and right toward me in the center of the circle. I was the bait.

Calling on the power of the moon, my skin took on its glow, making me a beacon. They were drawn in, their cloudy eyes focused on my light—and on my power humming through my veins. In stilted, uneven steps, they slowly came. The stench of death grew stronger as they filled the circle until I had to hold my breath. One took a swipe at me, and almost succeeded.

"Not today, ya undead bastard," I said, and taking a step back, I transformed into my raven form. Seconds later, I joined D and the twins in the air and watched as the witches closed the circle.

Rather than the panicked survival mode of earlier, everyone worked together as one, effectively containing the zombies. Charleigh put up a shield, instructing the other witches on how to help strengthen it while Timber's vines wrapped around the corpses' legs. Makenna and some of the other fae used glamour and created an illusion that kept the undead moving in circles. The zombies were bound to the circle.

I dropped back down, shifting into my goddess form as I landed in front of the Valkyries. "You have what you want now."

"Not entirely," they said, the single voice coming from them, though their stone mouths didn't move. "But first you must choose. Destroy them or return their full lives?"

I pulled back, blinking up at them. They were asking *me*? After all this—ah. I smiled with understanding. This was my challenge. It had been all along. Though putting me and everyone else through this was unnecessary. I knew too well that the dead must stay dead. I hadn't needed to learn that lesson.

"Destroy them," I said easily enough.

"Good choice."

With that decision made, the zombie clones poofed into ash, leaving only the real ones.

"They can be destroyed now," the Valkyries said.

I started to move, but the Valkyries closed in, pinpointing me with the tips of their swords and their unforgiving glares, as they said, "You stole what was rightfully ours, and for that you must pay."

"She gave you what you wanted!" Taylor protested.

"She stole what was rightfully ours, and for that she must pay," they repeated. Then they lifted their gazes. "Or you all pay."

The students surrounding me took a step back. I couldn't blame them. I'd created this mess, and I did need to pay for it. But would they turn me over to the Valkyries to do who knew what to me? A strong bond had formed among the students as they'd fought side by side over and over this semester. But I didn't know if that bond included me. I hadn't fought with them. I'd only observed, as I'd been ordered to do. At least until today. They owed me nothing.

But I owed them everything.

They'd taken me in, making me feel at home for the first time in this lifetime. I may have only observed the battles, but I experienced everything else alongside them—classes and lessons, parties, friendships, a shared life—experiences I'd never had on this level. I didn't know if they considered me family or even a friend, but I did feel that way about them.

Squaring my shoulders, I stepped forward, into the points of the Valkyries' swords. "I pay. Only me."

"You stole what was rightfully ours, and for that you must pay." The largest Valkyrie lifted her sword. I inhaled a deep breath and nodded.

"Wait!" Natalie stepped forward. "With her essence uncloaked, I recognize Rhiannon as one of the many moon goddesses, and I for one, will stand by her side. She made a mistake, but she owned up to it and fought with us to fix it. What was rightfully yours is returned to you." She turned to me and whispered, "I have no idea if they can understand me, but figured it was worth a try." She winked and moved closer, standing bravely by my side.

Tempest stepped forward to join her sister witch. "I stand with Rhiannon, too."

Taylor and Clay, their hands clasped, came to stand beside Tempest. Charleigh and the Knights came to my other side. One by one the other students moved forward, forming a wall around me. Many were wounded, all were exhausted from the fight, but they stood prepared to protect me. Wolves, hellhounds, vampires, witches, fae, deities, angels, and more were all willing to put their lives on the line. For me.

An unfamiliar lump of emotion formed in my throat. A new kind of strength filled me.

"You will let them die for you?" the Valkyries asked me.

I jutted my chin out. "Absolutely not. They are my friends. And I will die for them."

At once, all of the Valkyries stood up straight at attention. I braced myself once again.

"Your lesson is learned," they said. The zombies suddenly became ash, and the Valkyries all turned, and with the sound of stone grinding and crunching, they walked back to take their normal places, becoming stone statues once again.

CHAPTER 4

$\mathcal{N}$atalie put her Field Medicine training to use and again raced to the rescue, laying her healing hands on the back of one of the injured students. A golden light radiated from the wound, healing him within seconds. Paisley Underwood and other healers joined Natalie, weaving their way through the injured, healing each one as quickly as they could. The damage sustained by the zombies was worse than that from the Valkyries, but fortunately, we lost no more lives on this day.

Once everyone was treated, the crowd seemed to breathe a collective sigh of relief. Then in a delayed reaction came the cheers. Students whooped and hollered and congratulated each other. A handful of students ran straight for the portals, escaping campus while they had the chance, but most prolonged their stays. Nobody outside this mountain could understand what we'd been through, so the need to hang around with those who did was understandable.

The celebration that had been planned in Modi Tower earlier moved out to the quad. Drinks flowed, each of the tower's signature beverages on offer, and music blasted. Charleigh and Dillys worked together to counter the echoes of the cavern and magically perfected the acoustics. The center of the quad became a dance floor.

I sat on the steps in front of Halstein Hall, back in my wispy young girl form with my hair pulled back in its massive ponytail, watching it all. So I was one of the first to see the Board of Regents striding across the bridge with purpose, Saundra Beaumont in their lead. After passing through the archway, they stopped at the edge of the quad, forming a line. The music fell silent, and the crowd hushed, turning toward the authorities in anxious anticipation as the Regents' gazes took it all in, before they zeroed in on me. *Shit. Here we go.*

"It wasn't Rhian's fault," Natalie declared pre-emptively.

Everyone's attention focused on her, and she seemed to shrink a little, her cheeks flushing. My heart swelled with appreciation and something more—a feeling of comradery. Of real friendship.

"We're not here to place blame," Saundra replied, and she gestured at the line of Regents. "In fact, I don't know what they want, but I want a Mountain Dew Me."

The cavern became awkwardly quiet, the sound of the river rushing all that could be heard in a long, drawn-out moment. Then Charleigh gave a *whoop* before everyone else burst into laughter. When they named the school's signature drink, they probably never expected Saundra Beaumont—member of the Board of Regents, seat holder on the Court of the Sun and the Moon, and high priestess of the Luna Coven—to not only ask for one, but to do it loudly in front of a hundred people. Tempest quickly brought her a mug, and she took a swig, before nodding her approval.

The music started up again, followed by the dancing, and the rest of the Regents put in their own drink orders. The celebration was back in full swing.

Only Addie Beaumont came my way, after grabbing her own cup of Hel's Fire while bringing me a mug of Purple Rain, Muninn's drink. Handing it to me, she sat down beside me.

"I can't believe I'm sitting next to a goddess of the moon," she said, surprising me. That wasn't at all what I expected her to say. "You're one of my favorites."

"I can't believe you're not pissed and banishing me," I admitted.

She laughed. "We don't know all that happened here—the campus locked us out—but we got the gist of it. You'd definitely be facing the Regents *and* the Court if this had happened six months ago." She took a swig of her drink. "But we all know this campus has a mind of its own. Correct me if I'm wrong, but I believe you were set up. You had a lesson of your own to learn. We all believe that, and so we can't blame you any more than we can blame any of the other students who were challenged this semester."

I nodded. "Thank you."

"Thank you for choosing right. We think you'll be an asset to this school and hope you'll stay. And not just because of who you are. Although . . . the Luna Coven wouldn't mind if you wanted to give us a boost of power every now and then." She gave me a sheepish grin.

"I'm pretty sure my time here isn't over," I said. "And I'll help in any way I can." To prove it, I let down my guard and shared a little of my energy with her.

The party carried on for a few more hours, until more and more students had to leave, their families expecting them home. Lots of hugs were exchanged, as well as phone numbers and email addresses so we could all keep in touch. While everyone was excited for the break, the bond connecting us all—including me—made it hard to say goodbyes. At least I knew I wouldn't be the only one returning and braving another semester at SMA.

What I told Addie was the goddess's honest truth—this goddess's, anyway. My time here wasn't over. I had more work to do, but not for the deity of Vanaheim anymore. In fact, I had a few things to say to her. Although there was still a slight chance I was wrong about her being behind everything, I knew in my gut I was right. And I didn't like one bit how she'd gone about her little "lessons."

On the other hand, I understood her goal—she wanted an elite supernatural army just as much as the Court did. In fact, probably more. After all, she and I had fought side by side more than once to protect various worlds from supernatural threats, and we hadn't always won. If we wanted to protect this world from the same dangers, we needed to be proactive this time. And I could get behind that.

So yes, I'd be returning next semester. I wanted to be a part of this—the future of this world. A guardianship made up of some of the strongest, brightest, loving, and most determined people I'd ever met in my existence. I was so proud to consider them friends and looked forward to calling them comrades.

Besides, I wasn't done experiencing life as a student, learning, growing, making friends . . . maybe even finding love. Life at SMA was full of danger and mayhem, but also of hope and opportunity. I couldn't wait for next semester to start.

EPILOGUE

*O*ur break was already halfway over, but I'd made the most of it so far. I'd skied and snowboarded pretty much every day, visited the beautiful Havenwood Falls Library, ice skated at the park, went to the Hot Cocoa & Cookie Crawl, celebrated Yule with the Luna Coven and Christmas with the Knight twins and Charleigh, watched lots of cheesy Hallmark movies, read for fun, and consumed a ton of Coffee Haven lattes and blueberry scones with Tempest and Natalie.

Whisper Falls Inn had been booked, so Brielle, Elliana, Charleigh, and I rented a vacation condo near the ski resort. When I learned of all the things they'd never experienced because it no longer existed on their world, I promised them I'd take them places over Spring Break and summer. At this time of year, though, there was no better place to be than Havenwood Falls.

It was nice to be out of the mountain for a while, but to be honest, I couldn't wait to go back.

We were about to head out to do some shopping when I received a text from Addie Beaumont:

Please meet me at Falls Campus in thirty minutes

"You go on," I told the girls, frowning. "I'll meet up with you later."

They didn't ask questions. I liked that about them. They knew too well that some secrets needed to remain that way. In fact, they'd only recently opened up to me about where they were from and why they were here. Addie's text wasn't exactly something to keep secret, but it was so out of the blue and therefore a bit worrisome. I didn't want to bother them with it.

Her head covered in a beanie hat and wearing a thick black parka, Addie stood out by the fountain when I arrived and led me inside to the chamber that contained the portals to campus.

"Sorry to bother you, especially on New Year's Eve," she said, "but something's come up."

She left it at that, gesturing for me to go through the portal. The campus was unusually dark and quiet, feeling even creepier than usual as we crossed it. Addie led the way to the Administrative Offices, and I gave the stink-eye to each Valkyrie statue as we passed, suppressing the urge to give them the finger.

We entered a large, oval-shaped conference room where much of the Board of Regents were gathered. They got straight to the point.

"I believe we have a friend in common," Elsmed Fairchild, the ancient fae, said as I sat in the only available chair—the one at the head of the table. That wasn't awkward or anything. He gazed at me with his ice-blue eyes, and I immediately put up my shields against this mind-reader. "Kialah Torsten?"

Oh. Fuck. He had my full attention.

So they knew. But how much?

I nodded. "I'm not sure I'd call her a friend, though."

"She's always been friendly to us. It was Kialah who led us to discover this campus."

Ha. Of course, she had—led them to the campus, that was. My suspicions had been right all along. But always been friendly to them? They might have a different perspective if they knew what I did. I wasn't sure yet, though, if I should tell them. I kept my defenses against the old fae up, even as he narrowed his eyes, knowing I was blocking him out.

"How do you know her?" Saundra Beaumont asked, tilting her

head with its always present silver French twist. "Have you spoken to her recently?"

I swallowed. Shit. I didn't know how much to say. Kialah said there would be consequences if I revealed too much. I'd take them, but I didn't want the board or the school or the town to suffer.

"I've known her for eons," I admitted. "But no, I haven't spoken to her recently." That wasn't a total lie. It'd been nearly a year since she'd contacted me about the mission. She said she'd reach out to me, but I hadn't heard from her since. "What's going on?"

"Kialah is an interesting one," Elsmed said. He pushed a small wooden box to the center of the table. It looked a lot like the ones we'd been given to announce our acceptance to SMA, although it lacked the disc on top carved into a sun and moon. "Over a century ago, she left me this puzzle box, explaining I'd know when the time was right to bring it to the falls. When I did last year, it opened up, and to make a long story short, we discovered the Halvard site." He pushed another box, almost a duplicate of the first, to the center of the table. "None of us have heard from her since that day in 1897, but on the Winter Solstice, this one was delivered to me."

I leaned forward. Kialah had been in contact with him? What was she up to now?

Elsmed got up from his seat, walked over to the far wall where water trickled down the side, and swiped his long fingers through the small stream. He came back and sprinkled water on the second wooden box, the aether in it shimmering. The pieces of the box started to shift, opening up, and the image of the little Valkyrie rose in a shower of purple sparks. Like with our acceptance message, she carved purple fire into the air, the flames forming words:

> *The destroyer of magic*
> *Comes our way*
> *Bringing death and destruction*
> *And a world of decay*

"Hermod," I breathed, my heart stopping for a moment. More words continued rising.

But my friends,
*   Do not fret*
*   Within the rock guardian*
*   Our hope is kept*

Entombed in stone
*   Difficult to find*
*   Is the weapon of the gods*
*   Broken in nine*

Together with their staff
*   The nine become ten*
*   And hope for our world*
*   Will be restored again*

May the lady of the moon
*   The ruler of night*
*   The protector of magic*
*   Bring you her light*

"We believe you're the one referred to in that last bit," Saundra said. "So can you enlighten us to what this means?"

"You said Hermod. What or who is that?" Addie asked.

Dread had blossomed in my gut while reading the fiery poem, growing so that my chest tightened and breathing became a bit difficult. A lump had formed in my throat, and I gulped to push it down.

"Hermod is an Aesir deity. A minor one, but still powerful. He's a holdover from the Aesir-Vanir War. He hates all magic and does everything he can to destroy it. He's the one who changed my power over death, inadvertently making it worse."

"He's coming here?" Saundra asked, her brow lifting into her hairline.

"Kialah would know," I said quietly. "We fought him together in the past, trying to protect different worlds. It was how I got caught up in their Asgardian feud."

"What does the rest of the message mean?" Gabriel Doyle asked.

I studied the words as they hung in the air, then let out a small, humorless chuckle. "It means we're in for another interesting semester, if I know Kialah at all."

Elsmed nodded as he looked around at the others. "That's what I told you. Kialah will help us."

"There's a weapon hidden in the campus?" Addie asked, clarifying the meaning of the poem.

"That's what it sounds like. A very powerful one," I said. "And very dangerous in the wrong hands. Which is why it was broken into pieces and hidden away. But it *is* our only hope against Hermod."

"Then we will find all of the pieces," Saundra declared.

I grimaced, but nodded. "It won't be easy, though. Kialah obviously knows the magic of the campus—some of it, perhaps all of it, is hers. That same magic protects the pieces. Be prepared for more trials. This past semester was only the beginning."

"Should we close the school?" Gabriel asked, his tone sounding like he wasn't too keen on that idea.

Discussion broke out with strong opinions on both sides. As much as I hated the idea, closing the school would probably save some lives of the students. But at what cost? If the pieces weren't found and the weapon assembled, all magic in this world could be destroyed. Meaning all supernaturals would cease to exist.

"I think that would backfire," I said, quieting everyone. "Kialah has a reason for everything she does. She knew exactly what she was doing giving the campus to you and now warning you."

"Well, based on what we've seen, our students can handle it," Addie said. "It will only make them better warriors."

"Hopefully this box means we'll hear more from Kialah, too, if she has more information," Elsmed said. "She's a good ally to have on our side."

His belief in her was strong, and I knew then I couldn't tell them everything I knew about Kialah. Based on her message, they needed to believe that she was indeed a good ally and search for the weapon on her request. Knowing her full story would have them abandoning the search and the campus, shutting it down. Our world couldn't afford that.

No, I couldn't risk them knowing that Kialah Torsten was only one face and one name they knew of the Vanir deity. They'd quite recently known her by another face and another name—someone they'd gone to war with.

Well, they didn't know the name she used now. Only the title she'd given herself:

The Collector.

ABOUT THE AUTHORS

Victoria Escobar—Multi-genre author of the Of Legacies series, Peerless, Unpretty, Songbird, and many more. www.facebook.com/V.Escobar.Writes/

Justine Winter—Bestselling author of the Nature's Destiny series, Wanted series, *Wicked Sunshine*, and Havenwood Falls. justinewinter.wordpress.com

E.J. Fechenda—Bestselling author of *The Beautiful People*, book one of the New Mafia Trilogy, the Ghost Stories Trilogy, and Havenwood Falls. www.facebook.com/EJFechendaAuthor

Amy Richie—Bestselling author of the Blood Vine Series, When Leslie Cries Trilogy, The Girl from Ortec Trilogy, Speak No Evil Trilogy, the Immortal Love Series, the Aella Duology, and Havenwood Falls. authoramyrichie.com

Belinda Boring—Bestselling author of tThe Mystic Wolves Series, Damaged Souls Series, *Loving Liberty*, *Broken Promises*, *Enchanted Hearts*, and Havenwood Falls. belindaboringauthor.com

Victoria Flynn—Award-winning author of the Voodoo Revival series, Rescue Squad Shifters series, *Ravaged* (A Voodoo Revival Universe Novel), *Warrior's Kiss: Mountain Mermaids* (Sapphire Lake), and Havenwood Falls. victoriaflynn.com

Tish Thawer—Award-winning, bestselling author of the Witches of Blackbrook Series, the Women of Purgatory Series, the Rose Trilogy, *Handler*, the Ovialell series, the TS901 Chronicles (co-author), and Havenwood Falls. TishThawer.com

Rose Garcia—Award-winning, best-selling author of The Final Life Series and Havenwood Falls. RoseGarciaBooks.com

Kristie Cook—Award-winning, bestselling author of the Soul Savers Series, the Book of Phoenix trilogy, and creator, author, editor, and publisher of the Havenwood Falls universe. KristieCook.com

ACKNOWLEDGMENTS

"It was a labor of love"—nothing could be more truly said about this book. The authors put so much sweat, probably some blood, and gobs of tears into this project that sometimes made us feel like we were in our own hourglass challenge, trying to wrangle a beast. After many sleepless nights, coffee-fueled days, and chocolate and wine keeping us motivated, we managed to subdue the monster into something we think is really fucking special. In the process, we became pretty tight-knit, supporting each other like family does. So huge appreciation goes to each other. We did it, ladies!

Of course, we must thank our families, too. You don't get to spend as much time as we have on this book without sacrifice, and unfortunately, that often means family time. Thank you to the husbands, boyfriends, significant others, kids, and other family who put up with more fast food and pizza than they probably should have—and a very stressed out and exhausted loved one. We couldn't do this without your support! We couldn't do this life without you, period.

Many thanks to our cover designer, the ever so talented Regina Wamba. To all of the other Havenwood Falls authors who helped create the magical universe of our new school. To our editors and beta readers, including Seven Jane, Jessica Ramirez, and Crystal Gray. To Inkslinger PR for helping us reach new booklovers.

Last but not least, so much love and appreciation goes to our readers, supporters, and the Havenwood Falls Book Club. Your enthusiasm for this world and for this book means so much to us! Sometimes, it's all that keeps us going. Thank you so much for loving this town and its people as much as we do. We hope you've enjoyed *Sun & Moon Academy Book One: Fall Semester*. We can't wait for what comes next!